THE REMNANT TRILOGY | BOOK 1

NOAH

MAN OF DESTINY

TIM CHAFFEY &
K. MARIE ADAMS

Thank You

Writing a novel requires a tremendous commitment of time and energy from many people other than the authors. We realize this project could never have been completed without the assistance of so many wonderful individuals. We would like to offer a sincere "Thank you" to the following people.

Tim Dudley and the team at Master Books, thank you for choosing to publish a work of fiction and for being so easy to work with.

Reagen Reed, thanks for working with us to clean up our mistakes and improve our writing in every area. Your expertise is always appreciated.

Casey, thanks for the many hours of story and plot discussion, and for working on the initial edits so that Reagen will think we are better writers than we really are.

Ben, thanks for using your tremendous talents to produce the cover art and giving people the first glimpse of Noah in his world, as we have imagined it.

Janice, thanks for the prayers and encouragement. Tony, thank you for giving us some great ideas. Steve, thanks for your help in editing the nonfiction material.

Most importantly, Tim and K. Marie thank our Creator and Savior, Jesus Christ. Thank you for dying in our place and conquering death so that we can be forgiven of our sins and dwell with you eternally. May this work be used to point people to your matchless love and grace.

First printing: August 2016
Third printing: August 2020

Master Books®, P.O. Box 726, Green Forest, AR 72638

Master Books® is a division of the New Leaf Publishing Group, Inc.

ISBN: 978-0-89051-972-1
Library of Congress Number: 2016913246

Cover design by K. Marie Adams; cover illustrations by Ben Iocco

Unless otherwise noted, Scripture quotations are from the New King James Version (NKJV) of the Bible, copyright © 1982 by Thomas Nelson, Inc. Used by permission. All rights reserved.

Please consider requesting that a copy of this volume be purchased by your local library system.

Printed in the United States of America

Please visit our website for other great titles:
www.masterbooks.com

For information regarding author interviews,
please contact the publicity department at (870) 438-5288.

Master
Books®

A Division of New Leaf Publishing Group
www.masterbooks.com

CONTENTS

Dear Reader,

Most people recognize Noah as the man who built the Ark, but have you ever wondered what he was really like? How did he have the necessary skills to accomplish such an overwhelming task? Who were Noah's parents? When and how did he meet his wife? Was she a godly woman?

The Bible tells us he was a righteous man, but was he a faithful believer from a young age? Were there plenty of righteous people in his life as he grew up or was the world already filled with violence and depravity?

And while we're on the subject, how did Noah age? During this time, many people lived more than 900 years. Such a concept is difficult for us to imagine, but what might it have been like to live so long? Did people back then age at a slower rate so that at 600 years old, Noah could pass for someone who's only 60 today?

More than a fourth of all of human history passed by the time the Flood devastated the earth, yet this period is compressed into just six chapters of Genesis. So we are left to wonder about how many things might have been. In some cases, the Bible gives little clues on which we can build our speculations, but we must be careful to always distinguish between Scripture and our own ideas. For example, many Christians believe the Bible teaches that Noah was mocked while he built the Ark, but even though this idea is often repeated, you will never find this anywhere in the Bible. While it is certainly believable that a righteous man would be scoffed at by a wicked society, the Bible just does not tell us this about Noah. So even though it makes sense, we must realize that idea is merely speculation instead of Scripture.

As strange as it may seem, one of our main goals in writing this novel was to help readers distinguish between fiction and biblical fact. Yes, you read that correctly. We want to use fiction to teach how to discern between fiction and biblical, historical account. To help in this goal, we will include a non-fiction section at the end of the book that includes answers to multiple questions that may arise as you read, as well as some surprises for readers who have visited or plan to visit the Ark Encounter theme park in Kentucky. But we are getting ahead of ourselves. First, you need to meet young Noah. So join us as we respectfully imagine what life for the man who built the Ark might have been like.

— Tim Chaffey and K. Marie Adams

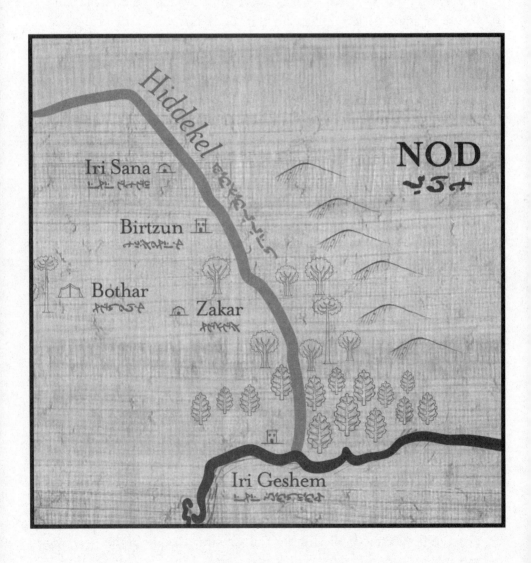

CHAPTER 1

Iri Sana — Noah's 38th year

Wood shavings dropped to the floor like the curls of a child's first haircut as Noah repositioned the chair seat he was carving. He examined each edge, then pushed his blade along the perimeter, carving away a wafer-thin slice. Tilting his head, he examined the result, then, satisfied, exchanged the carving blade for a polishing stone and began the long process of smoothing the wood.

Having done this numerous times before, Noah allowed his mind to wander as his right fingers felt the scratchy grain of the wood and his left hand guided the polishing stone in confident, careful strokes.

He had been only 30 when his father, Lamech, declared his intention to build a new, larger shelter for their family's expanding herds. With a grimace, Noah remembered the effort he had exerted to persuade his father to include the woodshop. Only after many revisions to the building drawings — wherein father and son went back and forth — and after much reassurance that Noah's woodcarving projects would not get in the way of his helping on the farm, had this room become a reality.

Noah looked around the small space. It was well worth the many heated discussions. Here, in the place with barely enough room for him to stretch out on the floor, there was sufficient area for him to work and ample space to dream. His few tools hung neatly along one wall, their shadows dancing in the flickering light from his lamp. They weren't much, but they were enough. Each tool, each completed project, gave him a small measure of hope that he would not always have to work in the fields with his father. Still, Noah's restlessness increased as his Rovay approached, the ceremony in which the community officially recognized him as a man.

This warm season was his least favorite. The longer days meant the stolen time before sunup afforded Noah his only opportunity to work on something he really enjoyed. Not that he hated his farm duties. In fact, he liked working the ground. It was hard work, but there was gratification in planting seeds, tending the shoots, and watching them grow to produce a harvest. But none of these labors brought the same degree of satisfaction as selecting the proper piece of wood and revealing, chip by chip, portions of the form until the final product took shape.

Noah set the stone down and ran his palm across the seat. He grinned, thinking of what could ensue if a guest happened to sit on this chair without all the splinters removed. Pleased with his work, he turned and stared out the open window. A gentle breeze cooled his sticky skin and carried the scent of springal blossoms, a welcome relief from the barn's customary pungency. An almost-whole moon bathed the earth with its soft light, and a faint glow on the horizon indicated that the sun would be up soon.

Another long day in the fields. It was up to him and Jerah to prepare the orb plant field today. A stab of rebellious energy pierced him at the thought of the tedious work stretching before him. He resolved anew to speak with his father, only to deflate moments later at the thought of his father's look of disappointment. Noah shook his head, muttering to himself as he returned the stone to its place on the shelf. "He just won't understand."

Noah gazed at the quickly fading stars. Following the example he had witnessed countless times from his grandfather and father, he offered a quick prayer. *God, thank You for providing in abundance everything I need. Help me to remain faithful to You in all things today. May my work —*

A shout from inside the house shattered the silence. Noah's head jerked up. Why would his brother be creating so much noise this early in the morning? He strode to the doorway of the barn just in time to see the silhouette of a man crash out of the door of their house and into the dusky terrain. Moments later, Jerah ran out the door and yelled again.

"Stop!"

The shadowy figure ran across the yard in Noah's direction as Jerah gave chase. Alert, heart pounding, Noah tightened the knee-length cloth wound around his waist before he sprinted away from the barn. The stranger spotted him and turned left toward the row of springal trees Noah's mother had planted on the north side of the house. Knowing that only 20 of the short, bush-like trees were in that row, Noah altered his course and dashed down the other side of the trees, hoping that Jerah would pick up on his strategy and flank the fleeing man.

The row of trees between them made judging the man's speed in the faint light difficult, but hearing sounds of brush cracking under feet nearby, Noah guessed they were nearly even in their pace. He sped toward the last tree, hoping to tackle the man as they came into the open. As Noah attempted to plant his left foot to cut in front of the stranger's path, he slipped in the dew-covered grass and slid to the ground. The intruder jumped over him, but Noah shot his arm out in a desperate attempt to thwart his escape. He barely missed as the man twisted to avoid Noah's grasp.

While the man's maneuver prevented his capture, he landed awkwardly and stumbled. He splayed in the long grass and skimmed across the moist ground ahead and to Noah's right. Both men scrambled to gain their footing as Jerah approached.

"Stop!"

The invader ignored Jerah's command and ran into the malid orchard, which was about one hundred paces from the house.

"Come on, Noah," Jerah said as he sprinted past. "Try to keep up."

Needing no further taunts, Noah bolted into the trees. *There's no way my little brother is going to outrun me.* Ducking under branches as he ran, Noah struggled to keep the stranger in his sights, thankful it wasn't later in the year, when he would need to dodge the large fruit that would dangle from the limbs. He strained to hear the man's footsteps, but his own breathing and his brother's yelling blocked out any other sounds.

Knowing the wide river at the edge of the orchard would likely force the man to head right in a few moments, Noah cut across the second-to-last row of trees, aiming to put himself directly in the path of the trespasser. If Jerah continued his pursuit directly from the rear, the fleeing man would be trapped between the stream and the two brothers.

Slowing his pace slightly, Noah broke free of the orchard just in time to see the darkly clad man veer right to avoid the river, exactly as he had guessed. The stranger took several steps in Noah's direction before spotting him. He was only 20 cubits away when he stopped. He glanced first at Noah and then at Jerah, who emerged from the orchard and closed in.

Now that his eyes were well-adjusted to the dusky morning light, Noah saw a loaf of bread in the man's hand. "Who are you?"

The burglar looked at the brothers, dropped the bread, and then raced toward the river.

Noah shook his head before continuing his pursuit. Jerah, who had not slowed, tackled the man, sending them both toppling down the waist-high riverbank into the mushy silt of the river's edge below. Undeterred, the thief punched Jerah's cheek and then kicked himself free.

As the morning sky turned from pink into a lighter, brighter hue, Noah caught his first good look at the man. Dark, unkempt hair draped over his forehead. He possessed a muscular, but wiry, build. Noah clenched his fist. *Who is this man who thinks he can steal from us?*

Upon clearing the last several patches of tall orchard grass, Noah jumped down the embankment and used the drop as well as his anger to fuel his force as he slammed into the man. They fell into the cool, shallow water with a splash.

Keeping a grip on the stranger was more difficult than Noah had imagined. Quickly sizing up his opponent, Noah concluded the man was a little shorter and lighter, but he was solid and quick. Noah would have to use his height to his advantage if he wanted to maintain control. He gripped the man's shoulder and pressed his weight down to keep the challenger off balance in the soft, muddy river bottom, which squished and shifted constantly beneath their feet. Before Noah could react, the thief grabbed him around the neck with his left arm, and with his right, he delivered a sharp elbow into Noah's ribs, knocking the wind out of him.

As Noah staggered back, he saw Jerah attempt another jump on the man. However, this time, the man dodged the attack, causing the momentum of Jerah's body to slip right over him and drop in the deeper portion of the river. Anxious not to lose the intruder, Noah fought for air, but nothing seemed to enter his lungs. With great effort, he lunged toward the man and clipped his foot just as he exited the water. Any air left in Noah's lungs whooshed out as he landed flat on his stomach.

Gasping, Noah expected to hear sounds of the man scrambling away, but he only heard a splat as the thief landed in the nearby muck. Noah wanted to get to his feet, but the breathless sensation in his midsection caused him to contort in pain instead.

Jerah trudged through the water's edge and bent over to give his brother a hand up. "Ouch. That can't feel good."

"Go." Noah whispered, each word taking great effort. "Get him."

"There's no need. Look."

Fully sitting up now, Noah took in a deep breath and turned. He spotted the motionless man lying face up on the shore only a few steps away. "What happened?"

"You tripped him, and he got knocked out by that big rock. I don't think he's going anywhere for a while."

"Make sure he's still breathing."

Jerah walked over to the still figure and knelt down. "He's breathing." He checked the man for further injuries. "He's a little torn up, and already he's got a pretty good knot on his head. But nothing looks broken."

"Are you both alright?"

Noah looked up to see his father standing on top of the bank, wheezing from the sprint. "We're fine. That's more than I can say for him."

Lamech studied his two sons and then the man who had broken into his house. "Looks like you did a good job. Tie him up, and let's get him back to the house. We'll have to keep an eye on him."

Noah untied his belt and handed it to Jerah. "Here, use this." He wound his knee-length tunic around his body a little tighter and tucked the end of the cloth into the fold at his waist.

Lamech stepped down next to his sons as Jerah took the pliable leather strap and bound the man's hands together with a series of tight knots. "Tell me what happened," Lamech said. He reached out his hand to help steady Noah, who slowly climbed to his feet.

"I woke up early and heard some noise coming from the main room," Jerah said. "I assumed it was just Noah heading out to the woodshop, but decided to check because it seemed too late for Noah to be starting out. When I came around the corner, I saw him" — he gestured with his thumb to the prone man — "in our house. He was grabbing some food." He glanced at Noah before adding, "It's a good thing Noah was already out in the barn. I wouldn't have caught him alone."

Lamech frowned, though whether because of the invasion of his home or because of Noah's activities in the barn, Noah couldn't tell. Not caring to discover the source of his father's displeasure at the moment, he turned away and began climbing up the embankment. He paused at the top to pick up a soggy loaf of bread lying in the tall grasses. As he held it up to show his father and brother, it began to separate and slop into pieces down his raised arm. Quickly dropping the rest of it, Noah shrugged, "I doubt he'll want this anymore."

Jerah's quick grin lit up his face. "He won't miss it."

Lamech put a hand on Jerah's shoulder. "Come on, let's get him back to the house."

CHAPTER 2

Noah emerged from his room wearing a clean work robe. He strode from the side hallway into the main living area, where he watched as his mother, Nina, pulled two rounds of bread from the back of the brick oven.

They had lived in this home for only 20 years now. Noah remembered watching as his parents planned for the expansion soon after his sister, Misha, had been born. On more than one occasion, he had peeked through a break in the curtains that sectioned off Jerah's and his bed pallets to see his parents sitting at the low table, heads bent, as his mother sketched in the dim light from nearby oil lamps. His father would point at a few places on the sketch and comment. Their soft voices carried no discernable words, just excitement.

Noah and Jerah, as young as they were, had helped build the expanded timber-frame house. The back half of the large, single room was separated into two equal-sized bedrooms. Two other sleeping quarters were added, along with a hallway connecting all four rooms. The hallway turned at a right angle, opening into the large room at the front of the house, which contained the kitchen and dining area, and was the hub of family activity. Growing up, Noah liked that his room was the closest to the kitchen. That meant fewer steps to get to the food.

"Noah."

Noah jolted at his mother's voice.

"Can you get some honey on the table?" she asked. "Firstfeast is almost ready."

"Of course." Noah passed by the low table where the family ate their meals, noting that it was already filled with food. The clay oven on his right held a prominent position, dividing the table area from where the main room extended back in an "L" shape — the place they now kept their food stores. Noah moved to the right of the oven where he had installed the wooden cabinetry he built for his mother a few years ago. He inhaled the fresh aroma. *Mmm. There's nothing like the smell of fresh-baked bread.*

Noah opened the cabinet closest to him and reached on the topmost shelf, fumbling around the containers of dried figs and preserves until he found the honey. Stomach grumbling, he retrieved a crock filled with golden goodness. Had he been a bit younger, he might have given in to the urge to sample the contents.

The door opened. Lamech entered and hugged his slender wife. "Looks delicious, Nina."

Brushing back a strand of wavy hair that never would stay out of her face, she leaned in, gave him a quick kiss, and pointed to the table. "The fruits, nuts, and herbs are out, and the rest will be ready soon."

"Here's the milk. I'll go wash up."

Noah took the warm, fresh milk from his father and placed it and the crock of honey on the table. He walked over to the far side of the main room, where they kept all their dried goods stored in large earthenware pots and woven baskets. Jerah and Misha looked up at him from where they kept watch over the unconscious intruder, who lay on a low cot usually reserved for visitors. Noah had constructed the wooden frame of the bed, and Misha's talented fingers had tightly looped many cords around it in a diamond pattern, weaving and knotting them to provide a firm base.

Jerah stood at the head of the cot, one leg casually crossed over the other, and leaned his arm on the wall. Misha sat on a stool close to the injured man and checked a bandage on his arm.

Sunlight beamed through the large, open window next to Jerah, giving Noah an opportunity to get a good look at the prostrate man. He looked younger than Noah had guessed — perhaps just a few years older than Noah. Dark, curly hair spilled over a bandage covering the wound on his head, and a short scraggly beard gave the impression that he hadn't groomed himself much in recent days. Noah saw scratches and other marks on his limbs from the tussle early that morning. Peering closer, he noticed other scabs and scars, indicating deeper wounds that had mostly healed.

Noah glanced at Jerah. "How is he?"

"He's groaned a few times, but other than that, he seems to be resting well."

"And you?"

Jerah smiled and touched the bruise that swelled on his cheek. He winced but kept his grin. "This? This is nothing. I'll be fine."

Misha nudged Jerah with her bony elbow and looked up at him. "The girls at the market are going to think you look tough now."

Jerah laughed, stuck out his chest, and placed his hands on his waist, elbows out.

"Well, except those skinny arms will betray him," Noah said pinching his brother's biceps.

Jerah turned red as Noah and Misha laughed. "Hey, you would've never caught him by yourself."

Noah nodded. "That's true. You were pretty brave this morning. You should've seen him, Misha."

"Yeah, I jumped on him twice."

"And got thrown off twice." Noah smiled, turning up just one side of his mouth. "I'm the one who took him down."

"You just got lucky that he hit his head when you tripped him. Otherwise, as slow as you are, he would have been long gone."

Before Noah could fire his next comeback, Misha pointed. "Look."

Noah looked down at the bound man and called out to his father, "He's waking up."

The stranger briefly opened his eyes and then squinted hard. He tried again, looking toward Misha and blinking several times.

Lamech strode into the room and stood next to Noah. "How is he?"

Noah shrugged.

The young man attempted to see where the voice had come from, but flinched and quickly rested his head back down. He tried to move his hands, but the binding held fast. "Where am I? Why am I tied up?" His speech slurred a little. "Who are you?"

"Why don't you tell us first who you are?" Lamech placed a hand on Misha's head. "Let your mother know that we'll be there soon."

Shoulders slumped, Misha walked out of the room.

"Who are you?" Lamech resumed his questioning as he sat down on Misha's stool.

Rolling his head slowly, the stranger looked up at Noah and then at Lamech. "My name is Aterre." He opened his mouth to speak, but then stopped and closed his eyes. "Are you the ones I fought with?"

Noah nodded. "I'm Noah." He motioned to his brother, who was still standing by the window. "And that's Jerah."

Aterre shifted slowly and placed his bound hands unsteadily on the edge of the cot. Using them as a prop, he carefully scooted himself into a more upright position and leaned his back against the wall. With clenched jaw, he squinted into the sunlight, trying to see Jerah better, then he turned guarded eyes back to Lamech as the older man continued.

"I'm their father, Lamech. What were you doing in my house?"

"I was trying to find something to eat."

Noah noticed Aterre had a different accent. He pronounced some vowel sounds much more quickly than Noah had ever heard. *If I'd been able to travel, maybe I'd know where he was from.*

"And you thought to steal it from us?"

"I was hungry. It's how I've been able to survive these last several whole moons." He shifted again in obvious discomfort. Noah couldn't tell if it was because Aterre was uncomfortable over getting caught or if his injuries caused the distress.

"What about before that?" Noah asked.

Aterre shook his head. "I was never a thief, but lately I've had to." He paused and closed his eyes, his whole demeanor hardening. "All because they came."

Noah and his father exchanged glances.

"Who came?" Lamech leaned closer.

Aterre sat there stiffly.

"Young man." Lamech's voice firmed in a way Noah knew all too well. "I'm asking because I'm trying to decide whether I should turn you over to the town protectors. So unless you want to be punished by them, you need to start talking. Who came?"

"Men. They attacked my village one night. It happened so fast. I heard screams and saw bodies strewn everywhere." Aterre's eyes fixed on nothing, and they were filled with hatred. "My mother and sisters are

18

gone. They would've killed me if I hadn't grabbed the knife I keep under my pallet and swung it at the face of the man who grabbed me. Judging by the amount of blood I felt, I think I cut him pretty bad. He screamed and let go of me." He slumped, his voice falling to a whisper. "I fled and kept on running until I was sure no one was following me."

Lamech gently placed his hand on Aterre's shoulder. "Do you know who the men were?"

Aterre shook his head, wincing at the sudden movement, and then shrugged off Lamech's hand. "No. There were just too many. They came so suddenly."

"Were they from around here?" Noah asked.

"I doubt it." Aterre sighed and looked at the wooden poles that comprised the main frame of the peaked thatched ceiling. "I've been on the run for nearly six whole moons, so I'm not sure if I know precisely where 'here' is. We lived in the land of Havilah, on the southwestern side of the Blue Sea. With no family left and no clue who attacked us, I just wanted to get far away from that place. I thought I'd take my chances and go to the land of Eden. I knew no one would even try to find me there."

Noah knew rumors about the land of Eden, which was located far away to the northwest, following the Hiddekel River up through the land of Asshur. Still he was curious to know what Aterre had heard. "Why there?"

Aterre raised his eyebrows. "You don't know?"

"Tell me." Noah knelt down to be at his eye level.

"There are tales that the land was cursed in ancient times and is haunted by the spirits of everyone who has died attempting to enter it. They say that anyone who goes there will either die or lose their mind."

Noah raised his eyebrows. "And you aren't afraid to go there?"

"My mother always taught us not to believe the legends. She said spirits of people couldn't harm anyone — that when we die, we just go to the ground and stay there. I guess I trust her more than the stories."

"We have our stories about Eden here too." Jerah leaned in.

"What stories?" Aterre tried to scoot closer but his jaw clenched and he quickly abandoned the attempt.

Jerah sat at the foot of the bed. "My great grandfather was named Enoch. He spent a lot of time in the land of Nod warning people that the Creator would judge the wicked."

"Of course, they mocked him," Noah said. "Father says the people there are pretty evil."

"One time he decided to go to the land of Eden with my father's uncle, Berit." Jerah lowered his voice. "But Enoch never came back."

"What happened to him?"

Lamech held his hand out to stop his second son from continuing. "My uncle says that he was walking behind my grandfather. He looked to the side for a second, and when he turned back he only saw a flash of light and my grandfather was gone."

"Really?"

Lamech nodded. "My uncle thinks he crossed the border to Eden and was turned into a spirit."

"Is that where the rumors come from?" Aterre looked more awake now.

"Maybe, but I don't think that's what happened. My grandfather walked closely with the Creator."

"What do you mean? They took walks together?"

Lamech shook his head and smiled. "No, that's our way of saying he faithfully followed the Creator's ways. So, my family and I believe that the Creator took him because he was so faithful."

"Why would He do that?" Aterre asked.

"Maybe to spare him from all the wickedness in this world."

Aterre raised an eyebrow. "By killing him?"

"He didn't die. He was taken so that he didn't need to face death. Now, he lives with the Creator."

Aterre let out a deep breath.

Lamech studied the young man for a long moment. "Do you have any idea what happened to your mother and sisters?"

Sadness swept over Aterre's face. "If they're still alive, my guess is that they're slaves."

"Slaves?" Lamech asked. "That's happening in Havilah too? My grandfather said that some places in Nod took people as slaves, but I didn't know anyone else would do something like that."

"I'd heard rumors about it," Aterre said, "but I never imagined it would happen to my family."

"I'm sorry about what you've been through." Lamech paused, looking critically at Aterre. "How would you feel about staying with us?"

Aterre looked up with widened eyes. He appeared as stunned as Noah felt. "With you? But I just robbed you and fought your sons. Why would you be so kind to me?"

"The Creator expects us to be kind to others, particularly to those in need." Lamech shifted in his seat. "If what you told us is true, then it seems to me that you need to be part of a family again." Lamech motioned to Aterre's hands. "Noah, Jerah, untie him."

"Yes, sir." Noah worked to untie the leather belt that had secured Aterre's hands together while Jerah undid the one at his feet. Misha entered the room again and stood next to their father.

Aterre stretched out his hands and gingerly flexed his arms. "Thank you."

"You're welcome. You know, there are other ways of getting food around here." Lamech motioned to Noah and Jerah. "I'm sure the boys wouldn't mind having some more help in the fields."

"The fields?" Aterre's eyes lit up ever so slightly. "You're a farmer? I'd love to help." Aterre attempted to sit up straight but quickly changed his mind. "I guess my head is still spinning."

Lamech lightly patted Aterre's shoulder. "Just take your time. I'll have Misha bring you a plate."

Misha jumped to her feet and smiled at Aterre. "You talk funny."

Aterre grinned. "I might say the same about you."

She laughed and hurried into the kitchen.

Lamech stood up. "Here's my proposal. Take some time to heal up, and then as long as you're willing to work on the farm, you're welcome to stay with us. Noah can teach you what you need to know."

Aterre looked at him steadily. "I don't know what to say."

"Don't thank me just yet," Lamech said. He smiled and put an arm around Noah and pulled him close. "You haven't had to work with my son yet."

Chapter 3

Noah set the stone blade of the hoe on the ground and leaned against the staff as he scanned his surroundings. A light breeze carried small, fluffy white clouds across the great blue expanse. The sun neared its high point of the day, but the air remained mild and comfortable. The beautiful weather would soon give way to the hottest days of the year, so he wanted to enjoy this while it lasted.

Thanks to Aterre's hard work over the past several weeks, they had not only planted grain in the two fields still fallow when he arrived, but they had cleared, plowed, and planted a brushy area Lamech had long been desiring to convert to useable land.

Noah looked at the small, healthy orb plant shoots at his sandaled feet and then up in the direction of the house. Although it was blocked from view by the barn, thinking of the house brought to mind the mid-meal preparations going on inside. Noah's stomach grumbled. The table was always so full of good things this season that sometimes Noah pictured the carved wooden joints he had labored over giving way to the weight of the food. Midmeal provided the family a chance to gather together while they rested and let the hottest part of the day transition into the sun's descent. It gave Noah the energy he needed to finish working late into the evening.

Nestled between the Hiddekel River at its back and the barn in front, the house was the heart of the growing farm. The malid orchard and smaller river that emptied into the Hiddekel, where Noah had chased and tackled Aterre, lay to the right. Rising high above the north side of their house was Sacrifice Hill, as his father called it. At its crest, their family made regular offerings to the Most High: fruit, grain, and occasionally the best of the flock. While the hill hosted the most solemn occasions, it also was the location of some of the finest playtimes for Noah and his siblings.

Taking in the view, Noah visualized himself and his brother as boys, chasing each other down the slope. Sometimes they would race, seeing who could roll down the large mound fastest. The two boys competed at everything, and being the older brother, Noah usually came out ahead, but Jerah was never far behind.

Noah also thought back to the countless times he'd climbed that hill just to be with himself and his dreams. He remembered the boyhood ritual he'd observed whenever he got his chores finished early. He would climb Sacrifice Hill and watch for the small cargo boats on the river, carving replicas and longing to be on one. They rarely passed by, but Noah's mind raced with the potential for adventure that each one carried. Where did they come from and how far up or down the river would they travel? Perhaps they would encounter bandits and would have to prove their strength. What would it be like to visit other lands and see other peoples?

Alas, for now he was confined to the vicinity of Iri Sana, a town just up the Hiddekel. His father called it a small town, but it was the largest Noah had ever seen. Home to a few hundred people, it boasted a large farmers' market and a handful of specialty shops along its main road. What he wouldn't give to see the world, but that would have to wait for at least another year — until he turned 40. He sighed. *If Father lets me.*

Immediately ahead, the pale green stalks of gold and brown pebble fruit were already knee high, and in a whole moon would tower above him. To the south, fields of long grass would grow tall before being harvested about three times a year. Beyond that, several cattle and other livestock grazed on the rolling hills that stretched to the forest.

Something smacked Noah in the back of the head.

He spun and barely blocked a second clod of dirt before it reached its intended target. Brushing off his hands, Aterre laughed. He had recovered from his wounds in a few days and had joined Noah and Jerah in the farm work for the past several weeks. Though he tired easily at first, Aterre was a quick study and easy to get along with, despite their less-than-ideal meeting.

"Are you going to work or just daydream?"

"I've been working all morning, just like you. But I think it's almost time to head in for midmeal."

"I was thinking the same thing." Aterre put down his hoe. As he adjusted the upper portion of his robe, Noah noticed, not for the first time, a dark image on his back before it disappeared once more beneath the fabric covering.

"What is that?"

Aterre looked confused. "What's what?"

Noah closed the distance between them. "That mark on your back. I've never seen anything like it. It looked like a tree."

Aterre exposed his back again so Noah could see the inked image more clearly. The tree symbol began at the base of Aterre's shoulder blade. The trunk curved as it followed the shallow lines made by that bone. Leaf representations spread out gently to the right, and made a bolder statement as they crossed the rounded boundary made by his spine. "It is the mark of Sepha. Back in Havilah, the young men who join Sepha receive this symbol on their backs."

Noah furrowed his brow. "I've heard of Sepha before, but only in a negative way. My father says they distort the teachings of the Creator."

Aterre tucked the cloth into the fold at his waist. "With all due respect to your father, I don't see how that's possible. Sepha just teaches us how to calm our minds and focus our thoughts. My order also taught us some defensive and attacking moves. That doesn't go against the Creator's ways, does it?"

"Not that I know of," Noah said. "But that explains how you were able to take on Jerah and me at the same time."

"That might've had something to do with it." Aterre flashed a sly grin. "Although you farm boys are pretty tough."

As the two headed off toward the house, Noah wondered why his father would have spoken negatively about the group if they were not truly bad. "So Sepha doesn't have any kind of moral or spiritual teachings at all?"

"Well, we're taught to protect our families and our fellow members. We're told that if we focus properly and clear our minds of any distractions, then we can discover true wisdom."

Noah arched an eyebrow. "True wisdom? From inside yourself?"

Aterre shrugged. "I don't know. It never really made sense to me. I ignored a lot of those things and just concentrated on the personal combat skills. I thought they might come in handy someday." He paused. "Turns out when I needed those skills most, I was too late to save anyone but myself."

Noah was silent for a while. "From what you've shared, it sounds like you did well to get out of there alive."

"I guess. Anyway, that's what I know of Sepha."

"Well, the idea of wisdom from within is probably why my father disagrees with it. I think he'd say that true wisdom can only come from the Most High."

"But what if the two beliefs aren't really incompatible? What if when we block out distractions and calm our minds, it's the Creator who shows us true wisdom?"

Noah scratched the back of his head. "That's a good question. I don't think that's how it works though. We should talk to my father about it sometime."

A pair of young bovars skipped about their sturdy wooden pen as the young men approached. When grown, these animals brought a supply of milk to the family or helped with the plowing, but this pair had a different purpose. They were being kept safe and fed in this pen so that Lamech could one day sacrifice them to the Most High.

As Noah rounded the barn corner and headed toward the house, a small, gray, long-eared bounder stared at them as it nibbled on tall green sprouts growing close to the barn. Both young men walked to the well to wash up. Noah rotated the windlass he'd crafted, quickly drawing up a pail of the refreshing, underground spring-fed water.

"These blisters are finally getting better." Aterre held out his palms to receive the clean splash Noah offered.

"That's good," Noah said, rubbing his own hands together to get them clean. "Maybe now you'll finally stop whining about them."

Aterre playfully shoved Noah and the two laughed.

"You and your family talk about the Creator a lot," Aterre said when they had sobered. "How do you know what He's like, or that He's even real?"

Noah hesitated before speaking. It was true that his family often spoke of the Creator. His existence had never been something Noah questioned. But Aterre's words were not cynical or confrontational. He

25

seemed to have a genuine interest in finding an answer. Noah decided to respond with a question of his own. "You don't think He exists?"

Aterre shook his head. "No, I didn't mean that. I don't have any problem with the idea that an all-powerful Creator made us. That makes a lot of sense. But you and your family talk about Him as though He's right here, as if He cares deeply about you and this world. How do you know that He's really like that?"

"What else would He be like?" Noah asked.

"Well, the way He's talked about in Havilah, it's as if. . . ." Aterre ran his fingers through his hair. "It's as if He were distant, unconcerned. It's almost like we made up this concept of God so that we'd have someone to blame when things went wrong or someone to call out to when we need help." Aterre looked straight at Noah. "So when I see your family having such complete trust, not only in God's existence, but in His goodness, it makes me wonder how you can be so confident about it."

Noah shrugged. "I've always believed in Him." Noah motioned to the expanse of the farm. "Growing up where I have, with these people around me, I've always taken those things for granted. Everywhere I look I see the Creator's handiwork — the animals, the plants, the stars, and mankind. I've never bothered to ask how anyone knows the Creator exists because I just *know* that He does."

"So are you saying that it's just a feeling you have? You feel like God's real?"

"No, it's more than that." Noah looked up as he searched for the right words. "It's a deep conviction of my soul. Somehow, deep down, I just know. That probably sounds a little weird, although not as weird as finding true wisdom within yourself." Noah laughed.

"Fair enough." Aterre took a small cloth out and dipped it into the water before wiping sweat from his forehead. "I'm not trying to be obnoxious, but with all I've been through, I don't see how I can believe the same way you do. Do you know any way to show me that your view is true?"

"If my great grandfather were still around, I'm sure he could tell you. The Creator spoke with him." Noah stared off into the distance. "I wish I could hear directly from the Most High."

Aterre gave a nervous laugh. "No, thanks. That would scare me too much."

"Why?"

"Think about it. If the old stories are true — that the Creator banished the first two people because they ate a certain fruit, then I don't even want to think about what He'd do to me."

Finished with his washing, Noah smiled as he returned the bucket to its place. "You sure have a way of seeing things from a different perspective than I do. The way my father tells it is that they did the one thing God told them not to do. It was their fault. They rebelled against Him and brought death and the Curse into this world. Then He banished them so they wouldn't eat from the tree of life and live forever."

"Doesn't that seem harsh to you?"

"I guess it depends on how you look at it. It seems merciful to me."

Aterre's eyes widened as he cocked his head. "Merciful?"

"Yeah, can you imagine how miserable it would be to live forever in the world they broke? We work hard for our food. People commit all sorts of atrocities. If you could never die, then there wouldn't be any hope of being free from pain. It would eventually become an awful existence. And imagine how much worse the wicked would become with no fear of death."

"Hmm, I never thought of it like that."

As they neared the door of the house, Misha peeped her head out. "Noah, Mother wants you to bring some water in." With both hands, she thrust out a large clay container.

"Alright. Thanks, Meesh." Noah grinned at Aterre as they retraced their steps. He stepped back over to the waist-high, circular rock wall and once again lowered a bucket down the middle of the pit.

Aterre leaned against the well. "So how do you know your great grandfather told the truth about hearing from the Creator?"

Noah filled the jar as he spoke. "I trust him. I wasn't there to hear the Creator speak to him, but according to everyone who knew him, he was a very honest and upright man. So I don't believe he would lie about the most important issues."

"I guess when you have people you trust, it helps. Your family is becoming that to me." He grinned at Noah and slapped him on the back. "Well, except for you." Aterre grabbed onto one of the attached braided leather handles. "This place and your mother's baking — maybe I really did reach Eden after all."

CHAPTER 4

Iri Sana — Noah's 39th year

Noah reached over the side of the wooden cart to stabilize the baskets and clay pots that jostled against each other. The large wagon was filled with a variety of produce grown on the farm to be sold or exchanged at the weekly market in Iri Sana.

His father placed a steadying hand on the front corner of the cart. "Whoa. Easy, Meru," Lamech said as he used his other hand to tug lightly on the reins to slow the lunker through the rough terrain. The large, gawky beast stood a head taller than Noah at its shoulders and stretched about six cubits from the tip of the proboscis above its mouth to the end of its unimpressive tail. The short brown and white fur around its torso rippled above muscles as the creature towed the fully loaded wagon with ease.

Noah glanced up to the top of the hill and spotted more deep ruts cut into the path. "That rainstorm really tore up the trail."

Lamech nodded. "It sure did."

The early morning air carried the fresh, sweet aroma that lingered after it rained. His father said the smell came from oils produced by the plants, which, when mixed with rainwater, gave the earth a pleasant scent. He was probably right. This particular stretch of the trail smelled the best and it boasted the most vegetation. Massive trees lined both sides of the route. Early in the year, before they budded, these trees would be tapped to extract their sap, which Noah's mother would convert into syrup or sugar.

Long strands of gray fibers and green ivy draped themselves across random branches. Low-lying ferns and a colorful assortment of weeds, grasses, and flowers threatened to overtake the trail heading north from Lamech's farm to Iri Sana's main thoroughfare.

"Aterre and I will fill in the ruts before next week."

"Good." Lamech glanced back at Noah. "You two work well together. He's already like one of the family."

"Yeah." In a little over a year, Aterre had helped Lamech's farm thrive. The barn had been expanded again. They prepared and planted three new fields, which meant they painstakingly removed dozens of stumps. Noah thought about how sore his shoulders had been from the time spent hacking at roots so the stumps could be pulled away. Of course, a hard day's work in the heat was often capped off by a refreshing swim with Aterre and Jerah in the Hiddekel. Noah smiled. Those swims usually turned into some sort of crazy contest between the three of them.

"I'm proud of you boys," Lamech said. "You've really done some great work."

"Thanks." Aterre had made life on the farm more enjoyable, but his stories and descriptions of other parts of the world made Noah's heart grow even more restless. He had to see it for himself. He swallowed hard. *Creator, please give me the right words, and help my father understand.*

They crested the hill. In harvest season, after the leaves fell from the trees, parts of Iri Sana could be seen, but the lushness of the forest prevented any such view at this time. The path leading down appeared to be in better shape. Lamech eased the rein and Meru resumed her lumbering gait. It would not be long before they joined the main road.

"Father, with my 40th birthday coming up next whole moon, there's something I need to talk to you about."

Lamech took a deep breath and let it out slowly. His face showed a hint of sadness. "What is it?"

Noah looked down and kicked at the packed dirt inside one of the ruts, leveling the rough ground. The silence stretched. Finally, he looked up and held his father's gaze. "I know you prefer it when we get straight to the point, so here goes. I'd like to become a carpenter's apprentice."

Lamech pursed his lips and nodded. "I feared this day would come. You have a knack for woodworking, and it's easy to see how much you like it. But, Son, what's so wrong with farming?"

"Nothing." Noah shrugged. "I don't mind working the fields, but carpentry is different. There's a certain. . . ." He paused, eyes on the canopy above, searching for the right word. "A certain *satisfaction* I gain whenever I get a chance to build something. I just love doing it."

"I know you do, and you do great work. Why don't you continue working the farm? I could cut back some of your responsibilities to give you more time to build things."

"Maybe Jerah would have to pull his weight then." Noah chuckled, and his father rolled his eyes. "In all seriousness, I'm not looking for a lighter workload."

"But haven't things been better since Aterre arrived?"

"Oh, no doubt about it. The three of us have a great time." Noah stared at the trail. *How can I help him understand?* "I believe that the Creator has given me this passion for a reason. Maybe I'm supposed to pursue something different than you did. And I've learned all I can on my own. I want to study with a master."

"Have you sought the Creator about this matter?" Lamech asked.

"Yes. Almost every night I pray for guidance."

"And has He responded?"

Noah held up his hands. "I'm not sure. He hasn't spoken aloud to me, but it seems that the more I pray about it the more certain I become that this is what I want to pursue."

Looking down the road, Lamech scratched Meru's shoulder. They walked in silence until they reached the bottom of the hill. A hint of shame nagged at Noah for disappointing his father. However, Noah realized, there was a blend of some relief at finally broaching the topic. He straightened his shoulders.

Lamech halted the beast and turned to face his son. "Do you know what my prayer was when you were born? And why I named you Noah?"

Noah nodded and watched as his father's eyes welled up.

"Of course you do, I've told you before that I prayed you'd be the one to bring us rest from the Curse on the ground that our greatfather brought about when he sinned." Lamech reached down and picked up a fist-sized rock from the path and then whipped it into the undergrowth to their left. "How can you do that if you aren't a farmer?"

Noah let the question hang for a few moments. "What if that's your plan but not the Creator's? And how can I possibly bring rest to ground that the Almighty has cursed?"

Lamech hung his head and shook it. "I don't know. Maybe it's just the wishful thinking of a proud father." He looked Noah straight in the eyes. "I'm still proud to be your father, always." He coaxed the lunker forward again.

"And I'm grateful to be your son." Knowing his father's dissatisfaction, Noah remained silent for many steps. Yet he'd finally brought up the subject, and he wanted an answer. "Father, I know this is hard for you. Will you give me your blessing to become a carpenter's apprentice?"

"Where will you go? Who do you know that would be willing to train you?"

Noah held his palms up. "I don't know. I'd really like to see the world, but if there is someone nearby, then I'd settle for that."

"What about Darge? I'm sure he'd train you."

"I thought about that, and I'd love working with him. But Darge only does fine carving. He doesn't build large items like I want to."

The lush vegetation on the trail thinned and the road to Iri Sana came into view. A short, white-haired man, plodding next to a small cart towed by a spotted brown pack animal, crossed the intersection.

"Looks like Nuca and his load of roasted beans is going to beat us into market today." Lamech cracked a smile. "He must've had two helpings of his famous brew this morning."

Noah laughed and sensed that his father was happy for the subject to change. "Yeah, he moves pretty well for someone in his 800s. We'd better not forget to buy a pot of beans from him, or you'll be sleeping in the barn 'til next week."

Lamech snorted. "Your mother certainly takes her morning brew seriously. Don't let me forget."

The storm had carved another large groove just before the intersection. Lamech carefully guided Meru around the short, but now difficult turn. With her considerable strength and size, Meru had little trouble negotiating it. The problem Lamech faced was slowing the beast down enough to keep the goods safe in the wagon behind. Once again, Noah steadied the cart to the best of his ability until they reached the smooth, well-traveled road. Nuca and his cherished beans were now even farther ahead. Far behind them, Noah spotted two more farmers toting their produce to the market.

The damp coolness from all the shade and vegetation on the path had given way to a warmer, drier air. The sun stood about a fourth of the way to its peak and bathed the earth in a soft morning light. Multiple fields with crops at varying stages of growth stretched to their left, while to their right, the grass and weed-covered uneven ground gradually descended to the river.

Iri Sana stood directly in front of them. Initially established on the banks of the lazy Hiddekel a century earlier as an outpost for adventurers, the town gradually grew into the economic hub of the entire farming region. Quiet and slow every other day of the week, the town bustled with activity on the sixth day as nearly every farmer within walking distance gathered to buy, sell, or trade.

More than a dozen shops lined either side of the main street, each offering unique goods or services. At the end of the row, the road veered right and led down to the dock. The first building ahead to their left was Noah's favorite store — Darge's Crafts. The quaint wooden building outdated the town itself and was originally just Darge's home before he transformed the front room into a shop, selling various wood-carved toys, puzzles, and trinkets. He had farmed many of the nearby fields until, a decade before Noah was born, a falling tree crushed his right leg, which had to be amputated below the knee. Armed with an odd sense of humor and a kind spirit, Darge carved a variety of peg legs designed to look like animals from the region — he even used wood from the tree that injured him to make several of the artificial legs. At first, he made them to ward off the bitterness of losing a limb, but he soon found children flocking to his front door every market day to see what animal his leg sported that week and to hear the corresponding tale he would tell. He began carving other items, everything from toys and puzzles for the children to bowls and utensils for their parents.

Years ago, Noah had been one of those children. One day, the peg was in the shape of a fish, complete with detailed scales and fins, and Noah couldn't keep his eyes off it. His hands itched to try to imitate Darge's craft. He begged his father to buy him a set of woodcarving knives — a decision Lamech probably questioned several times and

32

especially regretted after this morning's conversation. After some brief instructions from Darge, Noah honed his craft and before long could whittle anything he set his mind to.

As Meru lumbered near Darge's door, Noah reached into the wagon and withdrew a wooden limb he had carved to look like a fish, similar to the one he remembered from so long ago. He'd made it as a gift for the man whose imaginative carvings had made such an impact on him. Noah held the fish up for his father to see. "You think he'll like this?"

"I'm sure he'll love it." Lamech winked. "As long as he isn't envious of your work."

Noah chuckled and slid the fish into his bag. "I don't think there's much chance of that. He's far better than I am."

"If you say so. It's hard for me to tell the difference. I just don't have an eye for that sort of thing."

"Maybe, but you can grow a crop of beans in a weed-infested field." Noah climbed the short steps to Darge's front door. "I'll meet you at the market after I'm done here."

"Very well, Son."

Noah opened the door and stepped in. A wave of memories blasted him as the familiar wooden scents struck his nostrils. How many times had he explored this small shop looking for a new contraption to occupy his free time? How many times had he listened to Darge weave tales of adventure to the children who came to see his leg? A smile tugged at his lips as the fond memories flooded his mind.

"Ah, young Noah. Morning peace." Darge stood up behind his counter and smiled. On a shelf farther back rested two dozen pegs that the children enjoyed the most. "Did you come to see my newest leg?"

Noah's smile widened, and he stepped across the room, skirting wooden toys set in piles around the floor. "Morning peace, Darge." The two men exchanged a firm hand-to-forearm grip before Noah reached into the sack slung around his shoulder. "It's great to see you. I'd be happy to see your latest work, but first I wanted to give you something."

"What's this?" The middle-aged man cracked a broad smile as he took the gift. "You made me a fish peg?"

It pleased Noah to see the man's delight. "Not just any fish peg. I tried to make it like yours from so many years ago — the one you wore the day my father bought my first set of carving knives from you."

"Your craftsmanship is remarkable." Darge held the gift up close to his face and turned it slowly, inspecting the quality. "Well, let's see if it fits." He bent over and replaced his current prosthesis with the wooden fish, locking it into place. He gently placed his weight on it and then took a couple of steps. "It's perfect. Thank you for this."

Noah nodded. His eyes moved from Darge's face to the previous peg now resting on the counter. "And is this your latest?"

"It is." Darge handed it to Noah. "What do you think?"

Now it was Noah's turn to marvel. It was clearly a bird with its wings spread out — the two wingtips corresponding to the two ends of the peg. The feathers had been exquisitely cut into the wood. A sharp hooked beak and a pair of perfectly formed clawed feet jutted out from the middle. "It's magnificent."

"Do you recognize it?"

"Yes, it looks like a soaring taroc. Spectacular." With no small effort, Noah pulled his gaze away from the bird and caught Darge's eyes. "What tale will you spin today to go with this?" Noah gently returned the masterpiece to its designer's hands.

Darge grinned. "I've been dreaming up a good one. The children will love it. You should stick around for old times' sake."

"I'd love to, but I need to help my father in the —" Noah's eyes focused on an intricately designed box on the counter. "What's this?"

"I wondered how long it would take before you noticed my latest invention." Darge picked up the miniature chest and handed it to Noah. "It's a puzzle safe."

Noah flashed a quizzical look. "A puzzle safe?"

"See all of these small cubes on the top? Each of these can twist and move around. When they are arranged in just the right sequence, the box will open."

About 30 little blocks were nested in the cover. Noah moved some of them and twisted others. "Fascinating. What's it for?"

"You can put valuables in there or anything that you'd want to keep from the prying eyes of your brother or sister." Darge flashed a half grin. "Just put them in the puzzle safe, spin a few blocks, and they'll never get into it without breaking the entire thing. But it's pretty sturdy. What do you think?"

"It's amazing, but I can't open it."

"That's because you don't know the arrangement." Darge reached out and placed the box on the table. "I used slightly different colors for the blocks so that they would create a picture when it's finished." He quickly spun parts and slid them into place. The pieces soon formed a recognizable shape, which filled out more and more as Darge worked.

"It looks like a long-eared bounder," Noah said.

Darge slid the final piece into place. "Because that's what it is. Watch this." He flipped a latch on the front of the box to the side and lifted the lid. About a span in length and width, the well-oiled interior drew out the deep colors in the grain.

Noah let out a quiet whistle. "Is it for sale?"

Darge nodded. "One silver pikka, but for you Noah, I'd sell it for three copper pikkas."

Noah's pulse quickened in excitement. "Only three pikkas? I'll take it." He unfastened the leather strip around his neck and counted the small flat piks and round pikkas of copper and silver that were strung on it. After some quick calculating, Noah slipped off a silver ball and handed it to Darge. "I don't mind paying full price for something like this. Besides, the Creator has truly blessed our farm this year. I can afford it."

The shopkeeper dropped the silver pikka into a drawer beneath his counter. "Thank you, Noah, and may He continue to bless you and your family."

"Thank you, and may He do the same for your family." Noah turned to leave. "Farewell, Darge."

"Farewell, Noah. Don't be a stranger."

Noah slipped the unique box into his bag and left the store. After his eyes adjusted to the morning's brightness, he hurried down the street, passing several shops and a handful of farmers with their carts or wagons in tow. He turned right at the end of the street and made his way down the hill. The famers' market was just getting started. Wagons, booths, and tables of every type of fruit, vegetable, herb, and nut Noah had ever known were on display. He spotted Meru among the animal stalls to his left so he knew his father had arrived. The Hiddekel flowed softly behind the market. One small dock extended about 30 paces into the water. Beyond the river lay rolling hills covered with forest as far as the eye could see.

Noah wove his way around multiple tables and greeted each vendor he passed. He recognized all of them, but some were mere acquaintances.

He found his father busily organizing their wagon for a day of trading and sales. "Sorry I'm late."

Lamech looked up from his work. "Actually, you're right on time. Help me with these."

One by one, Noah and his father unlatched each side wall of the wagon and allowed them to hang beneath the flatbed. They slid their wares to the edge, and using a low table Noah had built, they elevated the fruits and vegetables in the middle of the bed so that every item could be easily viewed.

"So what did Darge think of his gift?" Lamech asked.

"He really liked it."

"Noah." A deep voice resonated behind him.

Noah knew that voice. He spun quickly to greet one of his father's friends. "Master Toman, it's great to see you."

The broad-shouldered, barrel-chested man stood a handbreadth higher than Noah. His wavy jet-black hair and deep brown eyes complemented his dark complexion. If any man was as strong as Meru, this was he. Toman nodded. "And it's good to see you, young Noah, son of Lamech. Your father tells me that you want to be a carpenter's apprentice."

Noah glanced back at Lamech, who turned away and acted as if he weren't paying attention, but not before Noah saw the gleam in his father's eyes. Noah fought back a smile and faced Toman again. "Yes, sir."

"Well, as I told your father, my brother is a carpenter and lives a one-day journey from here. I don't know if he's looking for an apprentice or would even want one, but I'd be happy to send word to him to find out. That is, if you're interested."

Noah instantly pictured himself as an apprentice who quickly made a name for himself because of his work. It took a moment for his mind to come back and configure a response. "Yes, please find out for me."

The man nodded again. "Your father tells me that your Rovay celebration is next whole moon. Hard to believe you're that old already."

"Yes." Noah stood tall. "I'll officially be a man."

"I'll try to get word from my brother before that." Toman held out his arm.

Noah cringed internally and braced himself for the vice that would soon crush his forearm as he extended his hand. He squeezed Toman's arm tight, but his fingers didn't seem to make a dent in the man's muscle-bound forearm. At the same time, Noah imagined his own hand going numb from the man's mighty grip. Finally, Toman released the vice and Noah felt the blood flowing back to his hand.

"I will see you soon," Toman said.

"I'm looking forward to it. Thank you!"

Noah turned and walked over to his father, who was arranging some of their first crop of leafy vegetables. When he was sure Toman was no longer looking, Noah stretched out his fingers and arm, hoping to loosen the muscles up again. "Father." He waited for the man to look up. When he did, Noah gave him a tight hug. "Thank you." After releasing him, Noah looked him in the eye, and cracked a smile. "I'll finish setting up. Why don't you visit Nuca, so we get some of those beans before we both forget."

CHAPTER 5

Noah darted across the yard, slowing just enough for Misha to stay right on his tail without catching him. Playfully, he taunted her as he zigged and zagged just out of her reach. "C'mon Meesh. You almost caught me."

More than two dozen young people cheered her on, waiting for her to tag him so another game could start. "Go, Misha!" "Get him!" "He's an old man now!"

Noah dashed behind a syringut tree. Misha stopped, waiting to see which side he would come out. She giggled as he faked one way and then the next. Noah surveyed his options as the others slowly closed in, making his escape more difficult. He sprinted to the right and easily avoided his sister. He looked back to see how near she was. As he spun back, he caught Jerah out of the corner of his eye.

"Watch out." Jerah pushed Noah to the side and laughed.

Noah lost his balance and tumbled to the ground. He got on his hands and knees, but before he could scramble to his feet, Misha jumped on his back and screamed in triumph.

Noah stood up as easily as if his sister weighed nothing at all. She let go and he turned to hug her. "You got me." He grinned at Jerah. "I'm not sure if it was fair, but you got me."

Misha jumped away. "Let's play again."

"Just one more," Noah said as he brushed some grass and dirt off his robe. "Who wants to start?" Since Noah had been the last one caught, he won the right to pick who would start the next game. He looked at his brother and tapped a finger on his chin, faking a tough decision, but then turned and pointed at his cousin, Dunal, who was about the same age as Jerah. "You start."

The youths scattered to avoid Dunal, who had started counting.

Aterre came around the corner of the house. "Noah!"

"Is it time?" Noah asked.

"That's what your father sent me to tell you."

"Okay, I'll be right there." Noah caught Dunal's attention. "You're in charge now."

"Alright," Dunal said. "I'm looking forward to your big night."

Noah nodded and followed Aterre. His friends and close relatives had gathered to celebrate his Rovay today. By this evening, he would be considered a man. Every part of the day was designed to celebrate this rite of passage. In the morning, he played games with all those under 40. Now he would meet with his father and some other godly men. They would pray with him and for him as he prepared his mind and heart for the evening events. Then he would bathe and put on his father's cere-monial clothes to offer, for the very first time, sacrifices on behalf of his family. When it was complete, neighbors and friends would join them for a great feast in his honor, and they would celebrate late into the night. Noah glanced back at his younger relatives, feeling the symbolism of leaving them behind. *I'm no longer a child.*

"You look nervous." Aterre nudged him with his shoulder.

"Because I am." Noah cracked his knuckles. "This is important for my family and for me. My grandfather says that we've practiced this for many generations."

"So you'll offer the sacrifices tonight, and then what?"

"Then once I get married, it'll be my responsibility to offer them for my family each year."

Aterre stopped and motioned to the crowd of young people running around the yard. "You have your eye on any particular young lady?"

Noah laughed. "Honestly, I haven't given it much thought yet." It was fairly common for a man to marry a close relative, and Jerah occa-sionally teased him about their cousin, Pivi. Although she had grown quite lovely, Noah had never had more than friendly feelings for her. He knew that the teasing was really due to Jerah's own interest. He scanned the grounds — sure enough, Jerah seemed more interested in flirting with Pivi than the game. He looked back at Aterre. "I'm more nervous about what Toman might say tonight."

"And if his brother wants an apprentice, you're just going to leave me here?"

Noah shrugged his shoulders and laughed. "Maybe. At least you like farming. Besides, this way you and Jerah could fight over who gets to marry Pivi."

Aterre pushed him and then sprinted for the house with Noah close behind.

* * * * *

The fire crackled and an overpowering aroma of burning flesh assaulted Noah's nostrils as he raised his arms. "Almighty Creator, please look with favor on this sacrifice and continue to bless Your servants."

A thick gray cloud enveloped him as he opened his eyes, causing them to burn and tear up. The smoke blocked any view of the house or barn at the bottom of the hill and obscured the early evening sun. Pulling part of his robe over his nose, Noah bent low and picked up the blood-soaked knife he had just used to kill the fatling. He had watched his father perform the sacrifice annually. The grain was offered first, and Noah had little trouble putting the firstfruits of their harvest on the fire. But the blood sacrifice was always painful. Even when his father did the actual killing, Noah's heart ached as he watched their best young bovar squirm and kick during its final breaths.

He had just learned how much harder it was to slit the animal's throat and hold onto it while its life flowed out. Blinking back tears, he glanced at the burning sacrifice, haunted by the stare of betrayal the young bovar had fixed on him in its final moments, horrified anew at the cost of sin.

As the fire burned lower, Noah stood and wiped the knife and his bloody hands on his apron. Head low, he stepped away from the flames and joined his family, who knelt around the earthen altar. Lamech placed a hand on Noah's shoulder and said a prayer of thanksgiving for the Creator's provision in spite of the Curse on the ground.

The annual sacrifice came to a close after several other men prayed. Noah rose and looked again at the offering. The fatling was nearly burned up and the fire smoldered. As they descended the hill to prepare for the feast, several family members congratulated Noah on a job well done.

His ceremonial duties complete for the day, Noah focused on the crowd gathering near the house. One man in particular stood out, or rather, above the others. Noah fought the urge to run toward Toman, but he could not resist picking up his pace. The large man spotted Noah and made his way through the crowd to him.

"Master Toman, thank you for coming."

"Congratulations, Noah. You have grown into an honorable young man." Toman held out his hand for his customary painful greeting.

Noah held up his blood-stained arm. "My apologies, sir. I haven't yet had an opportunity to wash up."

Toman pulled back his hand, unaware of Noah's relief. "I well remember my first sacrifice."

Noah nodded and a solemn feeling came over him as he reflected on his first sacrifice. "Indeed." An awkward silence hung for a moment as Noah tried to figure out how to shift the conversation. He decided a direct approach would be best. "Master Toman, have you received word from your brother about an apprenticeship?"

The smile vanished from Toman's lips. "I'm sorry to be the bearer of bad news on your big day. I wish it could be better. My brother said that he just took on a young charge earlier this year, and as long as it works out, he won't need another one for nearly four years."

Noah unsuccessfully fought against showing disappointment. "I understand. I appreciate you asking him."

"I'll be sure to let you know if the situation changes." Toman put an encouraging hand on Noah's shoulder. "I know you have your heart set on this. Trust the Creator. If He wants you to learn carpentry, then He will guide you to that when the time is right."

The corner of Noah's lip curled up in a half-smile. "Thank you, Master Toman." Noah believed his tall friend was correct. The Creator would make His will known when the time was right. But that did not make it easy for his restless heart to wait. Still, a feast in his honor was about to begin, and he wasn't ready for it. "I'd better wash up." Toman nodded and turned to greet others.

Noah entered the house, determined to hold his head high this night, even though his hopes had been dashed. On his way to his room, he dodged several women, who were scuttling about in final preparations for the feast.

He entered his room and went to the bucket of water. Scrubbing the bloodstains off his hands and arms took longer than he anticipated, and despite his best efforts, thin semicircles of dried blood lined his fingernails. Eager to get back to the celebration, he put on the brand new robe his mother had woven specially for this evening. Deep blue strips stitched onto the light brown fabric gave this outfit a more distinguished look than his ordinary work clothes. Noah closed his eyes, took in a deep breath, and then let it out. *Creator, thank You for bringing so many loved ones here today. Help me to see past my disappointment so that I may see Your goodness. Help me to trust You in all things.*

Noah avoided several women again as he moved through the kitchen. A hundred scents filled the air as trays and dishes were filled and delivered to their destination outside. Amid the cacophony, Noah heard his mother's voice. He turned just in time for her to smother him with a hug.

"I'm so proud of you," Nina said, tears suddenly appearing in her deep brown eyes. "You did wonderfully today."

Noah looked into her dark eyes. They always gave the impression that she knew exactly what he was thinking. "It was a great honor."

She let go of him. "And it's an honor for your father and me to watch you become the man you are." She smoothed a loose part of his garment and fussed with the way it draped over his shoulder. "Do you like your new robe?"

"I love it."

She kissed his cheek. "Now, get out there and enjoy your celebration."

Noah stopped Pivi's mother as she attempted to step past them with a woven tray of cakes. "I'll take those for you." He grabbed the tray and headed for the door.

"You'd better not eat all of them," she said.

He flashed a mischievous smile. "I'll be sure to save one."

Noah walked outside, and after thanking half a dozen well-wishers, he found an open spot for the desserts he carried on one of the four large rectangular tables that stood waist high. Setting the cakes down, he licked a finger that had "accidentally" scraped against one of the treats. Most of the guests found seats around the dozen rounded, low-lying tables in the yard. The more elevated platforms, including the one on which the recently delivered cakes sat, were laden with the largest array of food Noah had ever seen at his home. It was as if the farmers' market from Iri Sana moved to his house for the night. The women had outdone themselves. The smells of spices enticed him to inspect closer. He saw many of his favorite sauces, ready to be placed on grains or scooped up with pieces of bread. There were savory stews, generops, and stuffed peppers. Gourals were cut in half and steamed, then lavishly sprinkled with a variety of herbs; their yellow interiors looked like cheery suns. All this made his stomach growl.

He had been to Rovay celebrations before, but never paid close attention to the details. He had always been too busy playing with his friends. But now it was his turn to be at the center of what many considered to be the most important celebration in a person's life. He took his seat at the head table and scanned the crowd, which had doubled in size since the sacrifice.

Jerah had a small cluster around him, and he clearly enjoyed being the center of attention, especially since Pivi was part of the group. She and Misha laughed at something his brother said. Toman reclined on a cushion nearby, looking like a small mountain next to his diminutive wife. Aunts, uncles, cousins, and longtime family friends chatted, laughed, and reminisced. Noah paused to treasure the moment, but then furrowed his brow. *Where is Aterre? And Father?*

The flurry of activity near the door of the house slowed as the last of the trays and bowls were carried out. His mother motioned for Jerah and Misha to join her at the place of honor. The other women soon took their seats as well. *There they are.*

Noah's father, grandfather, and Aterre came around the side of the house and made their way to the head table. "Where have you been?" Noah asked as Aterre sat in the chair to his left.

Aterre raised his eyebrows and shrugged.

Noah tried to read his friend's expression. *What is he hiding? Is it good news or is he in on some sort of mischief?* Noah decided it was most likely the latter and determined to stay alert during the rest of the evening to make sure he wouldn't be caught unaware.

Lamech stood behind Noah and spread his arms out wide, waiting for the crowd to quiet down. "Dear friends and family. Thank you for honoring our home with your presence here tonight." He put his hands on Noah's shoulders. "As you know, my oldest son became a man today, and you honor him tonight as well."

"A fine son you've raised," someone said from the back.

"A fine son, indeed," Toman said. "The Creator has blessed you."

Others nodded or shouted in agreement.

Lamech held his arms out again. "Yes, the Creator has blessed Nina and me richly with such fine friends and family."

Noah nudged Jerah with his sandaled foot to get his attention and leaned in close. "Well, maybe not you."

Jerah shook his head and smiled. For once, he seemed to struggle with finding a comeback.

Lamech continued to speak. "Forty years ago, the Creator entrusted us with our first son." He looked at Noah. "At that time, I never could've imagined how much my love for you would grow over the years, and how proud I would be as a father, watching you grow into the man you've become." He wiped a tear from his eye. "Seeing you offer the sacrifice today, knowing that you love and trust the Creator and want to follow His ways, is the greatest joy of my life." He paused as Noah stood to embrace him.

"Thank you."

Lamech's tears flowed freely. He nodded to Methuselah, who took that as his cue to stand.

"One hundred and eighty-two years ago, I stood up at a party like this one to bless one of my sons," Methuselah said gesturing in Lamech's direction. "I know you're all looking forward to eating, so I'll keep this short. Lamech, you've followed the Creator's ways and, along with Nina, have faithfully begun to raise your beautiful children. I pray that God will bless you with many more." He approached where Noah stood with his father. "Lamech, you'll remember this. At that celebration, my father Enoch asked you to publicly commit yourself to follow the Creator."

Lamech nodded. "I remember."

Methuselah smiled. "And you've kept that promise. Now, if you don't mind, I'd like to ask my grandson to do the same."

Noah put an arm around his father and grandfather.

"Noah, son of my son, before all those gathered here tonight, do you vow to serve the Creator with all of the days He gives you?"

Noah took a deep breath and nodded. "I do."

Methuselah placed a hand on his shoulder. "And if God grants you a wife and children, do you promise to lead them in following the Creator's ways?"

"I do."

"As you know, my father, your great grandfather, spoke boldly against the growing wickedness in this world. Enoch was the godliest man I've ever known, and I see the same sort of spirit in you, Noah. Do you pledge to stand against evil and to stand for the truth no matter what it might cost you?"

Noah took another deep breath and affected the most serious tone he could muster. "I promise to stand against evil and to stand for the truth, even if it costs me my life."

"May the Creator give you the strength and courage to honor these vows." Methuselah hugged him tightly.

The crowd stood and applauded. Noah noted that the first star had made its appearance amid the backdrop of the still blue sky, and he bowed his head in silent prayer.

Lamech once again held his arms out. "Before we eat, I just have one more announcement. Please, everyone, have a seat."

Aterre tapped Noah's shoulder and grinned, a knowing look in his eyes. Confusion spread across Noah's face. *What are they planning?*

"Hearing my son commit to following me in serving the Creator makes me the proudest man on earth." Lamech fought to keep his composure. "He does not wish to follow in my footsteps as a farmer. Instead, he feels called to become a carpenter's apprentice."

Expressions of surprise and confusion registered on faces in the crowd. Toman nodded. This wasn't news to him.

"I trust the Most High is guiding him in this decision," Lamech said. "And as much as I'd like to keep him nearby, I've learned that my father's cousin is a carpenter and I'm giving my blessing for my son to become one as well."

Everyone present clapped, but Noah only sat up straight, his eyes wide.

"Let the celebration continue for my son, a carpenter."

As the crowd's focus dispersed, Noah leaned in to the circle formed by his father, grandfather, brother, and friend. "A carpenter?"

Methuselah unbound a leather strap wound around his forearm. "Of a sort. My cousin Ara is a shipbuilder in Iri Geshem. He builds the

45

boats you see on the river once in a while. If you're interested" — he waved the leather strap — "I'll give you my armband as a pledge for Ara that you come with my blessing. I'm sure he'll have a place for you."

Noah could hardly contain his excitement. "Of course I'm interested." He paused. "Iri Geshem? Isn't that all the way at the end of the river on the Great Sea?"

"Yes, it will take you about two whole moons to travel there," Methuselah said. The thin lines around his eyes deepened in a shrewd look. "Are you still interested?"

Noah thought of all the time he'd spent watching for the boats that occasionally passed by. He'd often wondered where they came from, where they went. His heart pulsed with excitement of the discoveries such a journey would bring. So soon after being crushed, his dreams were becoming a reality.

Aterre's kick brought Noah back. "Yes. Yes, I'm interested. It sounds amazing. And you're really letting me go, Father?"

"On two conditions. First, you keep the vows that you just made. And second . . ." Lamech hesitated. "Take Aterre with you."

"But what about the farm?"

"Jerah's still here, and if this is truly of the Creator, then we'll have enough hands to do the work that's here. I'd rather know that you have a companion for this distant adventure of yours. And it would be good for Aterre."

Noah looked at Aterre. He was beaming and nodding his head. *So that's what they were planning.* Noah hugged his father as hard as he could. "Thank you, Father. I'm happy to accept."

"Good," Lamech said. "Now let's eat."

CHAPTER 6

Land of Havilah — Noah's 40th year

Naamah sat in the corner, rocking back and forth. She idly twisted a thin lock of her silky, rich black hair between her fingers. She blinked dully, not wanting to think, not wanting to care.

"What's wrong?" Tubal-Cain knelt in front of her.

To block him from view, Naamah lowered her head, letting her hair become a barrier.

"You know, sitting here moping isn't going to help things. Let's go for a walk. We've got time."

"No."

"Talk to me," he said, his voice gentle.

Peeking through the curtain of hair, she could see that he hadn't moved. Knowing his concern made her feel just a little better. "No."

His knees straightened and she heard him stride over to the window of her spacious bedroom. The dreary, gray sky matched her mood perfectly. "Come on, Amah. Being sullen won't help anything. What's ever been so bad that we haven't been able to get through it together?"

Silence. Too mad, she would not give in by speaking to him.

"This isn't my fault and you know that."

Not one word, she commanded herself, tightening her full lips.

"You know you'll feel better just talking it out. So talk."

With head still bowed, Naamah caught a smile just in time before it crept up the corners of her mouth. She liked this. He was worried about her. That felt good. And there was something else too, but she couldn't quite place it. Influence. That is what it must be. She had some effect in another person's life. Lifting her head slowly, she looked at her tall, handsome brother and sighed. "I just feel helpless. And so worthless, you know?"

"How do you feel worthless?" he asked and sat down on one of the many large cushions scattered around her room.

"It's been different ever since *she* came here." Naamah spat out her words. "We were a family and a happy one. Sure, Da wasn't always involved, but it was good. When we'd go to the little retreat home, we had such fun times." Naamah got up and began to pace. "But then Da had to bring her home. What? Wasn't Mam enough for him? He had to have another wife? And what did Mam do about it? Nothing. She just let things happen and accepted it all. Da practically ignores Mam because he's so enamored with *her*. And Mam just lets him. She sits around and does nothing about it."

Naamah stopped and stood directly in front of her brother. "I can't do it. I don't want to." Knowing she wasn't finished, she lowered herself onto her soft, opulent bed. The words kept pouring out. "Do you know what it's like when I'm around town now? People look at me strangely. They know our family is different, and they look at me as if I'm different, as if I'm tainted somehow. And now with Da becoming more involved in the city council, that just makes it worse."

"I agree that Adah feels like an intrusion on our family, but it wasn't her choice either. Da brought her here after one of his trips." Tubal-Cain's care for her was evident in his eyes. "Plus, it's not like this happened yesterday."

Naamah ignored the reason in his comment and pointed to the middle of her chest. "The hurt's been here ever since she arrived. I guess today makes it feel like someone's taken the pain, sharpened the edges, and jabbed it into a fresh part of my heart." Naamah's quivering voice grew louder as she spoke. Angrily she wiped away tears that appeared in spite of her wishing them not to. "Don't you realize what this means? She's having a baby. It's not just Mam that's being replaced. Now we're being replaced too."

"Come on, it's just a baby. You like babies. You can cuddle and help care for the little one, and we can both teach him what it means to be part of our family."

"You'll see. It's not 'just a baby.' Things will only get worse around here."

"No, Amah. Things don't have to be that way. It'll depend on what you make of it. No matter the circumstances, you can always choose to have the right attitude; and that makes all the difference."

Naamah plopped one of the many pillows that fluffed about her bed into her lap and gently fingered the rich purple fabric. "So you're saying that if I change my perspective all this will go away? You know that's impossible, right? Even if that woman and her newborn were banished from Havil, things would still be different."

Tubal-Cain sighed. "I'm not saying the situation would change. I'm saying how you view it would change." He walked over to her and gently placed a hand on her cheek. "Why don't you try it? What's the worst that could happen?"

She glanced up at him, sadness in her eyes. "It doesn't work."

"So you'd be right where you are now."

"Yeah, I guess."

"With one difference." He grinned at her.

"What's that?"

"You wouldn't have this pillow because I'm taking it." He snatched the pillow from her lap and hit her soundly with it on the side of her head.

"Ow! Hey!" She threw her arms up in protection. "You're too old to do that."

"Oh, am I?" He laughed as he continued to swing it at her.

"Yes," she mumbled through a mouthful of one of his pillow attacks. She sat up straight. "And at 30, I'm too old too."

"You won't be 30 for another eight whole moons and you know it. Trying to make yourself sound like you're not still a child. Ha. I know better."

"Well big brother, do you know enough to avoid this?" She snatched up a sturdy pillow in each hand and returned blows, one to his head and another to his waist. She giggled. "Direct hit."

"Children, stop. Your father has summoned us to the birthing room."

Naamah looked up. Her mother, Zillah, had entered the room. The dour look on her face showed she wasn't any more pleased about the situation than Naamah. She crossed her arms and huffed. Clearly, her agenda

49

did not include patience at this time. Tubal-Cain and Naamah dropped their makeshift weapons and quietly followed her out of the room.

As Naamah walked behind her mother and brother down the narrow hallways and up several couplets of stairs, the painful feelings rushed back. She dragged her feet as her chest tightened and her breathing grew heavy. She didn't care that she lagged behind. All too soon, they reached the birthing room and Zillah opened the thick, ornately carved wooden door. The three stepped inside and stayed in the back of the room. Naamah placed her hands behind her back so that they touched the wall; she liked the comfort it brought to know that she was as far away as possible.

Naamah hated how each aspect of the room showed her father's preference for his new wife, Adah. While her own room was by no means small, this room dwarfed it, making hers look like a closet in comparison. She saw the vaulted ceiling, as well as two columns that formed three openings to a balcony overlooking the city. Sunlight flooded into the room. Hanging metal orbs caught the light from the balcony and reflected it around the room. A raised platform supported the bed and colorful curtains dropped from the ceiling surrounding it. Naamah was grateful for the obscured view. Not ready to pay attention to the occupant or the reason why they were all there, Naamah focused on the dais, which was large enough to support a bed three times the size of her own. Yet it still seemed like a small portion of the room.

Everything about this room showed care, prestige, comfort, even pride. *So this is what Father's been building in all these renovations.* She knew that the size of their original home had almost tripled, but she had always stayed away from Adah's extensive quarters.

The sounds of painful effort from the woman in labor rang out. Suddenly a new cry broke through. It was the squeal of a healthy baby. Naamah looked over at her own mother, who blankly stared at her slippered feet. Though her eyes did not hold their old spark, she was still stunning. Her body still sported the curves that had originally held captive the attention of a young warrior — the same warrior who now had shoved her aside for his new conquest.

At that moment, her father yanked apart the curtains and lifted the baby. "A son!" Naamah heard the exultation in his voice and saw his pride as he held the tiny bundle high above his head. He proceeded to the balcony and announced the arrival of yet one more of his progeny to whomever happened to be passing by.

Naamah looked at Tubal-Cain, her eyebrows raised. He shrugged but did not look as at ease as earlier. Several more people hurried into the room. Adah struggled and writhed in pain. Concern spread across the faces of those attending her. Naamah nibbled her little finger. *Maybe she'll die and we can go back to the way things were.* She shook her head. *Come on, Naamah. How could you think that? That's not fair.*

Fighting to rein in her thoughts, Naamah focused on the turmoil at the bedside. Adah groaned weakly several times, and one of the attendants rushed to summon the father and his new son back to the bedside. He leaned close, whispering something to his wife. She sat up and gripped the sheets tightly.

"There's another one!" a midwife shouted to no one in particular. After a few agonizing moments, another cry broke the air.

A nursemaid examined the newest addition. "A second son!"

Naamah's father exchanged the first twin for the second and held him up. He looked at Adah. "Two boys! You are indeed worthy to be my wife." He turned to face his older children. To Naamah it seemed as if he were on the stage and they were merely shadows whose only value came from his attention. "Zillah, Tubal-Cain, Naamah, come see my two sons."

Slowly, Naamah separated from the wall and followed her mother and brother. The painful grip that had been squeezing her heart ever since Adah's arrival intensified and dug in its fingernails. Her breath caught in her throat as she tried to keep her composure. Feeling a hand on her shoulder, she looked into the caring face of her brother and exhaled, the pain just a little less because it was shared.

CHAPTER 7

Iri Sana — Noah's 40th year

I'll miss you too." Noah bent low and wrapped his arms tightly around his sister.

"I don't want you to go," Misha said.

"I know, but this is something I have to do." He kissed her cheek, let go of her, and turned to his brother.

"It's about time you leave." Jerah smiled and hugged him.

"I love you too." Noah laughed. "Take care of our sister."

"You know I will."

Noah pulled back, put his hands on Jerah's shoulders, and looked him in the eyes. "I'll miss you broth —" He choked up and then swallowed the lump in his throat. "Honor the Creator."

While Aterre said his farewell to his stand-in parents, Noah took in the familiar surroundings one more time. The early morning sun was mostly hidden behind light gray clouds that released a soft drizzle. The gentle current of the Hiddekel lapped the side of the boat, which was partially beached on the shore at the edge of their property. Taht, their trusty pack animal, stood unsteadily on the deck, apparently unsure what to make of the lightly swaying surface. She was secured in a small pen next to their bags. Red and pale green malids sparsely populated the trees in the orchard. Sacrifice Hill rose to their right, its top obscured by fog.

When Aterre turned his attention to Jerah, Noah stepped to his mother and held her fast.

"I can't believe how quickly the time has gone." She kissed his cheek. "Be safe, Son."

"I will. I love you, Mother." He kissed the top of her head and freed his grip. "I'll miss you."

"I love you too."

Lamech embraced Noah. "Never forsake the Creator's ways. He will guide your steps as you walk with Him."

"I won't forget." Noah wiped his face to remove some of the light rain as well as his tears. "I love you, Father. Thank you for everything."

"I love you, Son." Lamech released Noah and his eyes welled up. "Remember, if things don't work out. . . ."

"We'll be on the first boat back home." Noah backed away and looked at his family against the backdrop of the only home he had ever known. He inhaled deeply and then exhaled. "I can't believe this is really happening. I'll miss you all so much. May the Creator keep you safe and well."

Each family member said their farewell. Noah wanted this moment to extend longer — at least part of him did — but he also wasn't sure how much more of it he could take.

"You ready then?" Aterre asked, as if reading Noah's thoughts.

Noah wiped his eyes again and nodded. "Let's go."

He couldn't believe how the days had passed by so swiftly. At the onset of the agreement with his father to wait until after the harvest, the delay felt long. But now that time seemed to have vanished like a night fog on a sunny morning. Noah was satisfied with what they had accomplished. The majority of the produce from the garden had been gathered for Misha and Nina to preserve for the land's rest season. The grains and grasses had also been harvested and properly stored. During the last few weeks, Noah and Aterre trained two young hired hands on the inner workings of the farm. They caught on quickly during the harvest, leaving Noah confident that his father would be able to maintain productivity in the next year.

As Noah and Aterre walked up the small incline onto the boat, Noah looked the vessel over. It stretched no more than 20 cubits from bow to stern, yet was the biggest boat he had ever boarded because it was the only boat he had ever been on. His father had made arrangements and paid for this trip during a previous visit to Iri Sana, and Noah had eagerly met the crew when they loaded their cargo moments earlier.

Deks, the leader of the ship's three-man crew, gripped Noah's forearm. "Allow me to officially welcome you aboard my boat."

"I'm glad to be here. Let us know if you need any help along the way."

"I'm sure we'll find plenty for you to do." Deks pointed to the ramp. "You can start by giving me a hand with this."

"I got it." Aterre bent down and grabbed one side of the wooden incline while Deks picked up the other side. They stowed it along the inside edge of the boat.

Noah slipped the bag off his shoulder and set it next to the rest of their gear, which was packed under a hide to keep it from getting soaked. Looking to occupy himself with something other than the sorrowful thoughts of missing his family, he scratched the back of Taht's neck, just beneath her short black mane, comforted by the familiarity she brought. "How you doing, girl?"

One of the crew shoved the boat away from the shore and jumped in, splashing the deck and soaking the hem of his garment in the process as the small craft drifted backward. The other crew member spun the boat until it faced downstream by stabbing a long, sturdy pole into the water.

Noah's family stood near the shore. His mother waved while wiping a tear with her other hand. His father appeared stoic, but Noah knew the man agonized over his departure. Jerah waved both hands above his head while sporting a crooked smile.

Misha ran next to the river, her long dress flapping against her heels. "It's not too late to stay, Noah!"

Noah forced a smile and couldn't stop a couple of tears from appearing. "I love you, Meesh!"

Aterre moved close to Noah. "So do I, little sister!"

She continued along the Hiddekel's edge, struggling to stay even with the boat yet not giving up. She passed the orchard and slowed when she neared the bank of the stream that emptied into the river, where a little over a year ago, her brothers had fought with Aterre. Misha stopped at the stream as if finally acknowledging that she had to let go.

A flood of emotions rushed through Noah. He ached for Misha and wondered if he was making the right decision. He had known it would be difficult to leave, but he hadn't realized it would hurt so much. And he hadn't considered how much it would affect his little sister. She was only half his age, and there was so much of her childhood that he would miss. For a brief moment, he considered jumping out of the boat and swimming to her, but the thrill of adventure and conviction that he was following the Creator's will overrode his emotions.

Noah's family became smaller and smaller as the boat drifted farther away. Jerah had reached Misha and put an arm around her. She clutched him tightly. His father remained where the boat had launched, holding his wife close.

The river carried the vessel around a bend, blocking Noah's view of his loved ones. He closed his eyes and turned around. *O Most High, please watch over them and keep them safe. Please help Jerah and Misha to follow Your ways.* Noah took a deep breath and let it out before opening his eyes. The sun peeked out from behind the clouds before quickly retreating, and a light breeze blew across his face.

"That was harder than I expected," Aterre said, breaking the silence.

Noah forced a half smile, appreciating Aterre's frankness. "Much harder." He scanned both sides of the river and felt a surge of energy course through his body. "But look. We're really doing it."

"Yep, you finally get to see the world."

"And what do you want?" Noah looked at his friend, suddenly realizing that Aterre might have goals and dreams of his own.

"I'm not totally sure. I know I eventually want to find a place to call my own."

"You could have done that by staying with my family."

"True. But being a part of your family has made me long to know what really happened to mine. I assumed they were killed like the others in my village, but I don't know that for sure. If they are still alive, I need to find out somehow. I don't know how to begin, but I do know that Iri Sana is too small and too far away to get word of them. Who knows? Maybe someone we encounter on this journey will be able to help. Plus, we're going to a seaport. I'll have a better chance of running into someone who knows something of those raiders and their prisoners there."

"I'll do what I can to help." Noah clapped Aterre on the back. "Well, future, here we come." He bent down and ran a finger along the ship's deck. "I can't believe that I'll actually get to build these." He grinned up at Aterre and increased his volume in confidence and excitement. "I'm going to be a shipbuilder."

"You say you're going to build boats?"

Noah turned to see the ship's captain lumbering toward them, his uneven gait slow and purposeful. "Yes, sir."

Deks pushed back a lock of black hair that had stuck to the side of his wind-hardened face. "Then you must be heading all the way to Iri Geshem to work for Ara."

"You know Ara?"

"Met him one time, when I bought this rig." He scratched the dark stubble on his chin. "That would've been about 20 years ago. Nice fellow, that Ara. You know him?"

"Not yet. He's my grandfather's cousin. I'm planning to become an apprentice."

"Well, I hope you have the talent." Deks stamped his foot on the deck. "Ara's craftsmanship is without equal." He turned to his assistant on Noah's right. "Valur, if all goes well, our next boat might be built by our passenger here."

Valur looked at Noah. The muscles on his sun-darkened forearms rippled as he gripped the long pole he used to keep the boat from gliding too close to the shore. His dark hair was loosely tied up behind his head. "Is that a fact? Well, youngster, make it a good one, and if you can figure out how to make these things larger, we'd make a lot more profit on each of these trips."

"I'll drink to that," the other assistant said.

"You'd drink to anything, Recharu," Valur said.

The portly man's belly jiggled as he chuckled. "That I would. But I'd drink double to a larger boat because I could afford it."

"Only if you did double the work," Deks said. "In your case, that wouldn't be too hard since double of nothing is still nothing. I'm surprised you haven't asked for a break already."

Recharu waved him off. "I was just getting ready to ask our guests if one of them would like to fill in for me so I can take care of the sail."

"I would." Noah hustled over to the heavyset man. "Show me what to do."

"The river opens up in a bit, and we'll steer with the rudder then. But for now, take this." Recharu handed Noah the long rod. "Just keep pushing down into the water to make sure it's deep enough for the boat. This thing has a draft of about three cubits."

"That means that it sinks three cubits into the water?" Noah asked.

"That's right. If you see us drifting toward the shore, push us back toward the middle."

Noah steadied himself and plunged the pole into the water. He drove it at least eight cubits deep, without finding the bottom. He brought it back up and waited until Valur put his pole into the water to repeat the action.

Recharu and Deks untied the small sail attached to the mast. They quickly hoisted it and fastened it in place, angling it to catch the wind. The boat lurched forward.

"I'll steer, Boss," Recharu said. He walked to the front of the ship and grabbed the navigating mechanism, which was essentially a waist-high rod connected to a post that ran below deck.

"How does that control the steering?" Aterre asked.

"Have a seat," Deks said. "Noah, you can put that down and join us."

Noah found a spot near Aterre as Valur went into the small cabin near the rear of the boat.

Deks pointed to where Recharu manned his post. "That shaft is connected to another rod down below through a series of gears, and that one runs to the back and connects to the rudder."

"Rudder?" Noah asked.

"It's a fairly small piece of wood at the rear that steers the entire ship. So when Recharu moves the shaft, it turns the rudder, allowing us to steer wherever we want to go."

"I would never have thought of that," Aterre said.

"Like I said, Ara is the best," Deks said.

"This may seem like a silly question." Noah scratched the back of his neck. "Obviously, the current and sail propel us downriver, but how do you make it back against the current? I've watched your boat go up and down the river over the years, but I was never sure how that worked."

"That's not a silly question. We use the sail, which usually means moving in a zigzag across the river to continue catching the wind properly. It takes longer; what takes three days going downriver becomes nearly twice as long to return, and that's only if we have some wind. If it's a calm day, we don't go very far."

Soon the morning fog lifted and the light rain stopped, revealing the tops of the trees on either side of the river. With no sign of civilization, the land's ruggedness heightened Noah's sense of adventure. He leaned forward, wrapping his arms around his knees. "You said earlier that you've only met Ara one time."

"That's right," Deks said.

"Why don't you sail all the way to Iri Geshem? I'm sure the people there would want some of the products from around here."

"I'm sure they would." Deks leaned against Noah's small pile of belongings. "It just wouldn't be worth the trouble to take the boat that far. Not far beyond Birtzun, the river gets pretty rough, and I don't want to risk wrecking my source of income."

"So you just travel between Birtzun and Iri Sana?" Aterre asked.

Deks nodded. "Mostly. There are a few small stops along the way that we occasionally make."

"It's a three-day journey to Birtzun, right?"

"That's right."

Aterre rubbed his eyes and yawned. "So what's Birtzun like?"

"In the daytime, it's a lot like Iri Sana, but a little bigger." Deks flashed a mischievous smile. "But when it gets dark, well, let's just say that good boys like you wouldn't want to be part of the night life. It can be a pretty rough place, especially around the taverns."

Recharu looked back at them. "I love the taverns. You just have to keep your head down and guard your money."

Noah raised an eyebrow. "What time will we arrive?"

Deks laughed. "No need to worry, young Noah. We should get there in the middle of the day. You'll have plenty of time to pick up provisions at their market, and then take the southern road that leads toward Iri Geshem."

CHAPTER 8

Birtzun — Noah's 40th year

"Thank you for taking us this far. We appreciate your help, and I really enjoyed learning about the boat." Noah deposited three silver pikkas into Deks's hand and waved to Recharu and Valur, who busied themselves unloading cargo to sell at Birtzun's market.

Valur grunted as he struggled to stabilize his awkward load. "Farewell." Recharu set down the tall crate he was carrying and waved. "Remember, Noah. Bigger boats."

Noah laughed. "I'll see what I can do."

Deks held out his empty hand and met Noah's eyes squarely as the two men gripped forearms. "Buy what you need and then head out of town on the south road. You'd do well to be a good ways out of town when it gets dark. And guard your belongings."

Noah nodded, unconcerned. As Deks had promised, they had arrived with plenty of time left before the sun went down. "I hope to see you again someday."

"Likewise. Farewell."

Noah and Aterre walked beside Taht toward one of the fruit stands. The beast pulled a small two-wheeled cart, laden with their belongings, up the gentle slope. The market was about the same size as the one at Iri Sana, but the tightly spaced structures that made up the surrounding town were larger and more established. The buildings occupied either side of the wide street like eager animals lined up in the barn, ready to

59

greet whomever passed by. Colors abounded. Dozens of small flags hung in rows, connecting one rooftop to another. At least six shops proudly displayed their wares of brightly dyed garments. A few buildings boasted vibrant awnings, under which were round crates displaying produce of varied type and quality.

A dizzying array of sounds filled this marketplace. People clustered in groups, laughing and talking. Loud bartering punctuated the pervasive hum of voices as merchants argued the value of their wares with savvy customers. A calic barked as it chased behind a small child. Noah looked in the direction of a sudden bleat and saw rows of animals tethered at one end of the long street, each waiting for its master to return.

"Deks said the next river town is about a two-week journey and that we'd be able to take a boat from there to Iri Geshem," Aterre said, leaning closer to be heard. "So let's be sure to buy items that won't spoil in that time."

"Less fruit and more grain. I like that." Noah stepped along quickly, his energy fueled by the bustle around them.

A shadow from one of the taller buildings fell across them, and Noah glanced up. Upper windows were curtained closed, while a few customers in the dim interior of the ground level sipped their beverages with sullen focus. Just the feel of the place seemed dirty. He guessed this was one of the taverns Deks had warned them of and looked at it with curiosity. *What would make men choose to spend their time in such a place?*

Deks's other warnings came back to him, and he placed a hand on the edge of the cart and peered inside. "Let's also keep an eye on the wagon at all times."

Aterre looked back at the place they had just passed. "I agree."

They stopped at two fruit stands to purchase a few fresh items before searching out a grain merchant on the next street over. Before long, Noah and Aterre had purchased their provisions and made their way toward the southern edge of town.

The buildings here were smaller and farther apart, though there were still quite a few people hurrying about their business in the street. Noah led Taht around a woman leading three young children — the eldest looked no more than 20 — then had to yank the animal to a halt to avoid an old man who stepped right in front of him, one shaky hand extended. "Excuse me, boys. Might you have time to help out an old man?"

60

Touched by the wavery voice, Noah looked the man over. He was probably in his seventh century. His back was slightly hunched, and he shifted on his feet as if trying to regain as much of his former height as possible. His face was speckled with tiny darker brown spots, like spice sprinkled over flatbread.

"I'm sorry to trouble you lads, but my cart broke down on my way from the market, and I was wondering if you might be able to help me." Although narrowed by the steady sloping of aging eyelids and wrinkles, his deep eyes held concern as he shifted his gaze between Noah and Aterre.

They silently sought each other's council, and Aterre gave a slight bob. "Of course we will help. How far away is it?"

The man pointed a shaky finger back over his shoulder. Next to one of the more established buildings on the road Noah and Aterre had just traversed, Noah could see a cart tipped forward and listing to one side. Several crates had fallen and lay beside it in the grass. A grey-coated nuzzler stood beside the upset load, looking dejected. As the three headed to the cart, the old man pushed his hat farther back on his head. "It's kind of you boys to go out of your way to help a stranger."

Aterre scanned the man's face. "We don't mind at all. You asked the right people. Noah here is great with carpentry. He should have you on your way in no time."

"And Aterre is good at volunteering other's services."

The man grinned. "Well, I'm Ebal. Here, let me tie up your animal next to mine while you get started."

Noah dropped on all fours and examined the bottom of the small wooden wagon. "Looks like this support is badly splintered. It's going to need something to hold it together." Noah stood and scanned his surroundings. "Aterre, stay with our things." Noah fumbled around in their cart before finding a small axe. "I'll be back soon."

Noah jogged toward a large grove of trees several hundred cubits beyond the edge of town. Noting that the sun's power had already begun its waning, he quickly searched the ground for a fallen branch that could make a suitable repair. Before long, he spotted a large piece that, with some minor fashioning, would probably work.

Rushing back to the wagons, he held it against the broken wood, eyeballing the new piece and figuring out how to shape it. Noah glanced at the old man. "This shouldn't take too long." Noah quickly cut the wood to the appropriate length and chipped away a few rough edges to approximate the form of the original piece before it broke. "Aterre, can you come help me attach this?"

"Of course."

When Aterre joined him, Noah slipped under the cart while Aterre supported its weight from the outside. After some time of steady work, punctuated by Aterre's grunts and Noah's occasional instructions, the cart stood evenly once again.

Standing back, Noah admired their work. "That should get you home at least."

"Home? That would get me across the earth and back if I so chose. I'm indebted to you both."

Noah dismissed that comment with a wave of his hand. "It felt good to be able to construct something again. I have to admit I enjoyed it."

"Evenfeast." Ebal inserted the word suddenly.

"What?" asked Aterre.

"Let me buy it for you. See that place across the street with the lamps inside? They have the best meals in town. I'm a regular when my stomach can handle it. Go in there and tell them to fix you up a plate and to place it on my account. Show 'em this." He handed over his carved armband as a token. "I'll be inside in a moment and will join you both."

Aterre slowly accepted the offered talisman and led the way across the street. He ducked through the doorway and Noah quickly followed.

"Hello, travelers. What can I get for you?" A tall woman sidled over to them and ran a finger down Aterre's arm, her eyes flirtatiously following the line her finger traced before returning to his face.

Aterre's look never changed, and Noah couldn't decide if he was amused or unaffected by her forward manner. He cut in. "We're here as Ebal's guest" — he pointed to the armband that dangled from Aterre's grasp — "and we'd like something to eat. Please."

"Right this way." She led them toward the center of the room to one of a dozen or so tables in the establishment. As they followed her, Noah noticed that about half of them were full with what looked like contented townspeople. "Have a seat. I'll bring out your meals in a moment."

Waiting until she was a little farther away, Noah leaned across the table and spoke in low tones. "It's impossible to see our cart from here." He glanced at the window. "I know that it's still fairly light, but Deks's warning makes me nervous."

"I thought of that. Anyone could just walk by and take something."

Noah stood quickly. "I'll check on Ebal and make sure our things are safe."

"Good idea."

Noah hurried to the door. Taht stood at the hitching post, but the contents of their wagon were not as they had left them. "Aterre!" Noah motioned to him, and he quickly scrambled over. "Look."

They bolted out the door and ran to the cart. Everything had been ransacked. Clothing and other items were strewn all over not just the back, but the ground as well. A barrel of malids had been shoved roughly aside. Several of the round fruit had rolled around the floor of the cart, coming to rest against whatever pile of clothing or food stopped their progress.

"That happened so fast!" Noah slammed a fist against the side board, causing Taht to flinch. "Sorry, girl." He turned to Aterre, who had started to put things back in their places.

"Some of our food is gone. And your axe. It looks like they made off with my extra tunic." Aterre narrowed his eyes. "Deks wasn't kidding. We were only in there for a few moments. I don't see how someone had the time."

"Unless that someone had been able to look at our things while I was fixing his cart," Noah said slowly.

"Ebal? But he's — no, you're right. Why else would he be gone? At least he only got a few things."

Noah jerked his head as a thought hit him, and he frantically searched around for the puzzle safe Darge had made. It lay askew under an overturned basket. Noah snatched it up and with fast-moving thumbs, he flipped the pieces to their right places in order to open the lid. His stomach clenched. "Gone. All of our money is gone. I just have the small amount I always carry." He shook his head. "I don't understand. Only you and I know how to open this."

Aterre grinned and slapped him on the back. "I have our money. I pulled it from the box when you went to get the wood to fix his cart. I didn't suspect Ebal, but just thought it would be best to be safe."

Noah exhaled, too relieved to be annoyed by his friend's highhand-edness. "That was good thinking."

Unhitching Taht, Aterre took the lead rope. "What do you say we get out of here?"

Noah walked beside him. "I'm thinking evenfeast on the go is sounding pretty good."

CHAPTER 9

They followed the dusty trail as it passed over low rolling hills. A handful of trees on the side of the road provided intermittent shade from the late afternoon sun. At first, pastures and fields filled the countryside marked by an occasional dwelling. Noah recognized all of the crops but two.

Eventually, the road forked, just as Deks had told them it would, and they stayed on the trail closest to the river, which soon narrowed to a single lane as it descended into a forest. The evergreen trees grew tall and straight, and their sharp, resinous scent filled the air. A variety of birds flitted through the treetops. Noah only caught a glimpse of them as they darted from perch to perch.

"We'd better let Taht get a drink here," Noah said as they approached a small stream that meandered through a shallow channel.

"I need one too," Aterre said. "This dry air is making me thirsty."

Noah let the animal drink as long as she wanted. He bent down, scooped some water with both hands, and after an initial taste, he gulped it down. "Oh, that's so good."

Aterre leaned his face to the stream and sucked up a mouthful.

"Did Taht teach you to drink like that?"

Aterre grinned. "You should try it."

As he bent in for more, Noah pushed Aterre's head into the creek and chuckled as his friend came up sputtering and gasping.

Aterre coughed several times, trying to clear his throat. When he finally caught his breath, he threw a handful of water at Noah, who lunged to one side, scooping up another round and hurling it at Aterre. Having now received two barrages in the face, Aterre launched a full out attack. By the time Noah called for truce, they were both half-drenched and laughing.

Noah leaned back to catch his breath. "How much farther do you want to walk tonight?"

"Let's try to find a place to camp before dark." Aterre wiped his face with his robe. He looked around. "I wonder how much longer we'll be in this forest. It'll grow dark sooner in here."

"Well, let's press on and see if we can find the end before nightfall." After filling their leather containers, Noah stood and guided Taht slowly across the stream while Aterre braced the cart. "Easy, girl. Nice and steady."

On the other side of the brook, the damp ground rose sharply. Noah looped Taht's lead rope in the harness and joined Aterre in pushing the wagon from the back, guiding it away from the mushiest portions of bank. Upon reaching the top, Noah stood up straight and studied the trail ahead. "No end in sight yet."

"That's what I was thinking." Aterre sighed. "Well, we may as well keep going."

They continued through the still forest, each taking brief rests in the wagon from time to time. As the light became fainter, the noises picked up. The squawks, chirps, and sporadic cries led the men into a game of guessing what sort of animal made each sound.

The woodland eventually thinned. Noah spotted two large birds soaring above the canopy. He watched as they flew straight ahead and then dropped. "Look." He pointed up. "It's either a clearing, or we've made it to the end of the forest."

"I think we've finally made it," Aterre said. "Just in time. Let's go."

"C'mon Taht," Noah said as he stroked the creature's neck. "Just a little farther tonight."

With renewed energy, they made their way to the edge of the forest. A flock circled in the sky ahead, and Noah heard screeches coming from the far side of a small hill.

"I've never seen so many tarocs in one place. What's going on?" Aterre asked, concern etched across his face.

"I'm not sure. Something huge must've died. Let's check it out." He ordered his obedient animal to stop and tied her to a mature tree before following Aterre to investigate.

The squawking increased as Noah and Aterre crept up the hill on their hands and knees. When they reached the top, Noah pushed some long grass out of his way.

"I've never —" Aterre broke off, shaking his head.

It took a few moments for Noah to realize what he was looking at. More than two dozen tarocs clambered over a huge carcass splayed out in the field. Countless flies buzzed about, adding to the cacophony. The creature's long neck was ripped open about halfway between its body and its seemingly undersized head. The tail, which Noah estimated to be at least 20 cubits long, stretched to the bottom of the hill, where the clearing gave way to more forest.

Aterre stood on his knees to get a better look. "I've never been so close to such a large creature before."

Noah let out a low whistle. "My father called them earth shakers because the ground seemed to move whenever the larger ones walked. I used to see them occasionally come to the river's edge for a drink when I was younger, but I don't know if any were that big. What do you suppose happened to this one?"

"Tarocs don't kill large animals; they only eat them after they're dead. I think it was attacked by something pretty large." He pointed to the exposed rib cage. "Look at how those bones are broken. There's no way birds did that."

"Right." Noah looked up and saw a few more tarocs join the circle above them. "We shouldn't linger."

"While you get Taht, I want to get a closer look."

"You want to get closer to that smelly thing?"

Aterre shrugged. "Guess my curiosity is stronger than the stench . . . at least for now."

Noah turned and hurried down the hill, the cries of the boisterous birds filling his ears, and the carnage lying on the other side of the ridge fresh in his mind. He had seen seared muscles and the inner workings of animals lying loose on the outside of the livestock they had sacrificed. But somehow on this grand scale, in this setting, it unnerved him. He shook his head, trying to clear the uneasiness of what he felt. *Violent.* The word suddenly came to him. *That's the difference between the deaths I've seen and this.* Even though he had not witnessed the final moments of this towering creature, everything about the scene said violence: from the splintered branches and saplings surrounding the clearing, to the prodigious amount of dried blood under the neck, to the large missing hunks of flesh where the thighs joined the hips, to the contorted way the body lay now.

Noah reached Taht, untied her, and then slowly led her up the hill, giving wide berth to the feeding frenzy to his left. Even with the distance, Taht's feet danced nervously as they passed, and she tugged at the rope, eyes rolling. He could not have taken her closer to the mountain of a carcass even if he wanted to. Ahead and to his right, he noticed more broken branches and a pathway of small broken trees leading into where the clearing became woods again.

Aterre rushed over, brandishing something sharp over his head. "Look at this. I found it lying close to the carcass."

Noah took the dagger-shaped object and turned it over in his hands. It was nearly a span in length. He pointed at some blood and a small chunk of flesh at its thicker end. "Is this a tooth?"

Aterre nodded excitedly. "I think so. But I don't want to find out what it's from. Let's get out of here."

"I agree." Noah urged Taht to pick up the pace but suddenly stopped after a few steps. "Look at that. Those branches are split at least ten cubits up. Whatever broke them was pretty tall."

"You aren't kidding." Aterre pointed to his feet.

Noah did a double-take. Aterre was standing inside a shallow depression in the ground that was unmistakably a giant footprint, about a cubit and a span in length. Three long toes pointed toward the trail of the broken branches. Fear gripped Noah. "That's a footprint."

"Exactly. It went that way, and I don't want to be here if it comes back."

"Me neither. Thankfully our trail is straight ahead and not that way." Noah motioned to the broken branches. "C'mon Taht."

Noah handed Aterre the tooth and then drove his beast forward at a quickened pace. Entering the forest again, they found themselves in much darker surroundings. The light of the setting sun was evident in the distance, but did little to help them see much as the shadows of the forest merged with the deepness of the evening. As they pressed on, the noise of the tarocs grew quieter while the typical forest sounds increased. He felt more secure with the familiar sounds.

Aterre held up the tooth again. "Can you believe the size of this thing?"

"I can't imagine. You could make a knife out of that."

"That's a great. . . ."

A blood-curdling roar cut him off, and in an instant the forest grew silent, with the exception of a slight echo, which alone had the courage to mimic the terrifying sound. Noah stared wide-eyed at Aterre as they both instinctively grabbed tighter onto Taht to keep her from scampering. Unexpectedly, dozens of flying creatures bolted from their perches in the trees. The clatter of shaking branches above bombarded his ears. Noah hitched a thumb over his right shoulder. "It came from that direction, but it sounded far away."

"I don't care how far away it is, it's not far enough. Move."

Another roar filled the air, and then a new sound registered in Noah's mind. *Footsteps.* Massive footsteps. And their rumbles were getting louder. Noah kept his voice low. "It's coming back."

Taht let out several nervous snorts, and hitched her back legs like she was getting ready to flee. Noah spoke to her soothingly as he tightened his grip on her rope.

Aterre rubbed her neck behind the tall bony protrusions at the top of her head as they hurried away from the approaching danger. "C'mon girl, steady now." He paused briefly and looked back down the trail. "I think it's heading for the dead earth shaker."

Noah glanced back, but couldn't see the clearing anymore. Tarocs flew overhead, and to Noah it sounded like they were screeching in anger at having their meal interrupted. "Let's just make sure it can't hear or smell us."

They continued walking in silence. After a short climb that put a small ridge between them and the dead earth shaker, a sense of relief rushed over Noah. Behind them, branches snapped and thudded on the forest floor and footsteps pounded before all went silent. Noah stopped Taht and held up a hand to stop Aterre. "Did you see it?"

Aterre shook his head and spoke softly. "No, but that's a good thing. It would probably haunt my sleep forever."

Noah forced a half-smile. "I know what you mean."

They walked in silence and when it became too dark to see, Aterre lit a small lantern and moved in front of Taht to guide the way. They arrived at another small stream, and Taht continued drinking long after they filled their water containers.

Aterre returned to the cart and grabbed the lantern again. "We should go just a little farther, get off the trail, and set up camp for the night."

"What's wrong with staying here?" Noah asked.

"Well, it's on the path, so it'd be easy for anyone passing by in the night to rob us."

Noah shook his head. "That's right. We aren't in Iri Sana anymore."

"Exactly. And we don't want to be too close to the water in case any predators come for a drink."

"Good idea. Let's find a place soon though. I'm exhausted."

"Enough adventure for one day?"

"Definitely." Noah stored his drink and led their animal away from the brook. "Can you imagine what this world would've been like if our Greatfather Adam hadn't sinned?"

"What do you mean?" Aterre asked.

"Originally, all of the animals ate only vegetation like we do. Those tarocs wouldn't have been scavenging on the earth shaker, and it never would've been killed in the first place."

Aterre held the lantern up and looked side to side. "And we wouldn't have had to flee from the owner of this." He pulled out the massive tooth and stared at it next to the light. "What should we call it?"

"What? The one with those kind of teeth?"

"Yeah. How about razor mouth?

Noah laughed. "Well, we haven't technically seen it yet. So let's go with what we heard. How about thunder step?"

"Or rumble throat? Tree smasher? Dagger tooth?"

"I like dagger tooth," Noah said.

"So do you really believe that?" Aterre slowly rotated the tooth next to the lantern, and the light revealed the jagged sides.

Noah's face registered confusion.

"That originally the animals only ate plants."

"Oh, yeah I believe that. It's what my grandfather said." Noah scratched his head. "Plus, it's hard to believe that the Creator would make a world where one creature needs to kill another."

"Then why'd He make them with teeth like this? This monster seems to be designed to kill and eat flesh."

70

Noah shrugged. "I'm not sure. Maybe those teeth are useful for eating fruit with thick shells, like melons, or maybe He changed the beasts when He cursed the ground."

"I have a different theory," Aterre paused thoughtfully. "I think that these beasts are gradually becoming more vicious. My mother told me many years ago that tarocs used to eat fruit. She said her grandmother remembers a time when they had one as a pet, and it only ate plants. Then one day they saw a carcass in the field, and several of the birds were eating the dead animal. That's the first time she'd ever seen anything like that."

"Interesting."

Aterre held the lantern to their left and took a few steps in that direction. "This might work. Let's head over here to see if we can find a good place to make our camp."

CHAPTER 10

Thankful for the change of scenery and climate, Noah breathed in the moist air and gazed at the vast array of vegetation around him as he and Aterre entered a dense tropical forest. They had spent the last week fighting through tall grasses and muddy trails of a wildly beautiful prairie after leaving the forest where they had encountered the dead earth shaker. On their third day traveling in the open plains, a heavy rainstorm drenched them and inhibited their travel.

While this new habitat offered a measure of relief from the elements, it was not more conducive to a faster pace. As the cart slowed to a stop, Noah jumped off to assist Aterre in removing yet another overgrowth in the path. While he hacked at the obstruction, he noticed the animals were different here too. Instead of an abundance of small, furry creatures skittering across the branches, green and brown-scaled reptiles sidled over the ground and in the trees. He ran his fingers along a leaf that was as long as his arm. "Have you ever seen anything like this?"

Aterre nodded. "We have trees like this where I'm from. And I also saw some while I was on the run."

"Did you take this trail during your journey?"

"So far none of it looks familiar. I tried to stay off the roads as much as possible and away from the river. I think I was probably farther west than we are."

Noah took a drink. "I can't believe you traveled all this way on your own. I would've been bored out of my mind. Except for that family on their way to Birtzun, we haven't seen anyone."

Aterre slowly turned the large tooth in his hand. Noah had wrapped its root in leather, and Aterre spent each evening honing one edge to create a dagger. "I hope they heeded our warnings about that creature." He paused before continuing. "Sometimes I can't believe I fled so far either. I guess I was so terrified at first and then so heartsore that I didn't realize how far I'd gone and how many weeks had passed."

Noah cuffed him on the shoulder as they started moving again. "I'm glad you're here. I may be sore and tired, but this trip's been amazing so far. I've always wondered what the world looked like beyond Iri Sana."

"Just wait until you look upon the Great Sea."

"What's it like?"

"I don't know really know how to explain it. Crystal blue water as far as the eye can see, and when the sun rises above it in the early morning. . . ." Aterre shook his head. "It's beautiful."

"I can't wait."

"And the sea creatures." His eyes lit up with excitement. "You won't believe this. Some of the great fish are even bigger than the earth shakers. Much bigger. And then there are the supergliders."

Noah cocked his head sideways. "Supergliders?"

"Yeah, they are sort of like giant birds without any feathers. I'll bet their wingspans can be over 15 cubits."

"You're teasing me, aren't you?"

"No, I'm serious. I told you that you wouldn't believe me."

Noah stared at a bizarrely scaled creature, with eyes protruding from the side of its head. It clutched a branch a few cubits away. Suddenly, its colors changed to match the background and Noah nearly lost sight of it. "No way," he said to himself.

"Really, I'm being serious," Aterre said.

Noah laughed. "No, it isn't that. Would you believe me if I told you that I've seen an animal that changes colors?"

"What? Now you're making up stories to try to outdo mine?"

Noah pulled Taht to a stop. "Think so? Look at this." He pointed to the odd creature still resting on the limb.

The cubit-long reptile slowly stretched one of its front legs forward and regripped the branch. One eye remained still while the other moved around, looking forward, up, and then down.

"That is the strangest thing I've ever seen," Aterre said.

"The Creator's artistry never ceases to amaze me. Keep watching."

Several moments later, the green near its belly turned orange and then purple.

Aterre laughed. "Crazy."

"Isn't it? I guess maybe I'll believe you about those supergliders and great fish."

The reptile focused its eyes ahead, opened its mouth, and sluggishly stuck out a strange-looking tongue. Without warning, the tongue shot forward and snatched a bug off a leaf more than a span away. Instantly, the bug was in the creature's mouth.

Noah and Aterre looked at each other in disbelief. Aterre put his hand on the top of his head. "That's incredible."

"It really is, but I guess it's not just the large animals that are changing their diets." Noah pulled lightly on Taht's rein. "Let's go girl."

* * * * *

Throughout the rest of the day, they continued on the trail, clearing some occasional vegetation, and marveling at many colorful birds and exotic creatures they had never seen before. As the sky grew darker, they arrived at a large clearing. About a dozen modest wood-and-reed homes formed a circle in the middle. Next to each of these buildings was a small garden. A taller and much larger wooden barn stood on the far side of the village. Several children laughed while they chased each other in a dirt field spotted with grass.

"Hello, travelers."

Startled by the voice, Noah turned and saw a middle-aged man strolling toward them. "Peace to you, sir." He looked different than anyone Noah had encountered before. His skin was light, and his thinning hair reminded Noah of the sand along the Hiddekel. *And what color are his eyes? Gray? Blue?* A knee-length garment hung about his waist, but his torso was bare — at least of clothing. His skin sported a variety of intricate designs and images.

"Ah, if you are men of peace, then I welcome you to Zakar." The man placed his fingers on his forehead and bowed slightly in greeting. As he straightened, his uniquely colored eyes met Noah's in a way that seemed to measure his character. "My name is Varelk." He motioned toward the huts. "I'm one of the elders in our village."

Aterre returned the bow. "Greetings, Varelk. It's good to meet you. My name's Aterre. Indeed, we mean you no harm."

Noah also greeted the man. "And I'm Noah, son of Lamech of Iri Sana."

Varelk's gaze drifted up as if he were thinking deeply. He shook his head. "Iri Sana? That's not familiar to me, but from your bearing, I would guess it's north of here."

"Yes, sir," Noah said. "We've been on foot for the past week, and before that was a three-day journey by boat."

"No wonder I've never heard of it. You've come a long way." He put his hand on Noah's shoulder. "Would you care to lodge here for the night? We'll have a small celebration to welcome you."

"We appreciate that, but don't go out of your way," Aterre said. "We don't require anything special."

Varelk laughed. "Nonsense, my boy. Around here, we look for excuses to celebrate. Come."

Noah and Aterre met at least two dozen citizens as they gathered around a pile of wood that was set up for a bonfire on the outskirts of the village. The people all shared Varelk's light-colored features, and the men bore similar markings on their arms and shoulders.

A young boy, who Noah estimated to be a little younger than Misha, stared at Aterre's knife, his blue eyes wide. He slowly reached out to touch the long tooth that hung from Aterre's belt.

Aterre spun and put a hand up. "Whoa. Careful, child."

The boy yanked his arm back and turned to run away.

"Wait. What's your name?"

As he tilted his head down, the child's curly, light-brown hair dropped over his eyes. "Elam."

"Hmm, I've never met an Elam before." Aterre pulled the knife from his belt and held it out to the boy. "You wanted to see this?"

Elam nodded and wrapped his fingers around the handle. He held it up and inspected both sides of the large tooth. "Grandfather, look!"

Varelk stepped to Elam's side. He carefully took the knife, examined it, and looked at Aterre. "Where did you get this?"

"Near a dead earth shaker." Aterre motioned to Noah. "We never saw the creature that it came from. We heard it roar, but fled before it came back."

"Yeah, we saw some three-toed footprints that were about one-and-a-half cubits long," Noah said. "Do you know what it was?"

Varelk grinned and tousled Elam's hair with his free hand. "My young friends, if I'm not mistaken, this is the tooth of a grendec."

"A grendec." Aterre took the knife as Varelk handed it back to him. "We just called it a dagger tooth."

The older man snorted. "That's a fitting name, indeed. Grendecs are terrifying. They stand more than ten cubits high and are about as long as our barn." Varelk motioned toward the large building with his head. "They have a mouth full of those daggers, but I've never heard of one of them attacking a person before. So you probably would've been safe if it saw you."

"That's a relief," Aterre said. "Can you imagine having to face one?"

Noah shivered and shook his head. "It makes me wonder why the Creator would make something so fearsome."

Varelk gave a knowing smile. "I used to wonder the same thing. I concluded that He made creatures like that to humble us when we realize how powerful He is."

Just then, an elderly man moved near the center of the gathering and raised his hands. "Your attention, please!" His long white beard bounced up and down as he spoke. When the crowd quieted, he said, "We are delighted to celebrate tonight in honor of our two guests, Noah and Aterre. I am Mehul, and I welcome you on behalf of the Zakari." As Varelk had done, Mehul placed fingers on his forehead and gave a slight bow. Then he turned to face the other side of the circle. "Let us thank the Creator for His blessings."

With the exception of Mehul, the Zakari dropped to their knees. Noah and Aterre glanced at each other and knelt.

"O mighty Creator," Mehul said. "We thank You for giving us life and a home. And we thank You for our two guests tonight. Please grant them safe passage to Iri Geshem. We ask for Your blessing on this evening. Teach us Your ways."

Immediately the Zakari repeated in unison, "Teach us Your ways." Then they stretched forward, putting their forearms and the right side of their faces on the ground.

Aterre looked at Noah, his eyes full of confusion. Noah shrugged and made a quick gesture by tilting his head, urging Aterre to follow their example. While unsure why the Zakari struck such a pose, he didn't want to offend. Noah held the side of his face to the ground for several awkward moments before closing his eyes and offering a silent prayer. *Creator, thank You for protecting us and providing for us on our journey. And thank You for the hospitality of the Zakari. Please bless them for their generosity.*

"Thank You, Creator," Mehul said. The Zakari repeated his words.

Noah opened his eyes and realized the prayer had ended when he saw people getting to their feet. He tapped Aterre's shoulder and stood.

Varelk stepped in front of them and motioned to a large board, laden with food, being carried by two young men into the circle. They set it on two sizable tree stumps that reached a little higher than their waists. "Please. Our guests eat first."

Noah and Aterre each filled a dish with fare from the makeshift table. Noah recognized most of the food options, and decided to select samples of those he had not seen before. Once everyone had filled their bowls, the board was moved away. Meanwhile, a plump man eagerly grabbed a torch and lit the pile of wood.

Seated on one of the many logs placed around the fire, Noah enjoyed his meal while he and Aterre talked with Varelk and other people of the village. As the evening wore on, mothers took their children back to their homes. Out of the corner of his eye, Noah saw Elam slowly get off his perch on top of a high stump as if not wanting to leave so soon. His mother waited patiently for him before leading the way to their hut. She, along with many other women, soon rejoined the festivities.

A steady beat caught Noah's attention. He spied a tall, thin man tapping a small drum. A woman, whom Noah guessed was the man's wife, set down her dish and picked up an instrument formed from a plant stem. She placed her fingers across some holes on the top of the reed, and blew into one end, producing a high-pitched, yet melodic sound. Soon another woman picked up a ringed object with several thin metal pieces inserted into it. She rattled it and clapped it against her hand in rhythm with the drum beat. The three musicians marched around the fire, prompting others to join with them.

Varelk rose and smiled. "Do you boys like to dance?" He hurried into the moving line that had formed behind the musicians.

"Count me in." Aterre jumped up and followed Varelk. "Come on, Noah."

Noah held up his hands. "Let me watch first."

Mehul approached. "Mind if I join you?"

Noah gestured to Aterre's recently vacated spot. "Please do."

The village elder gingerly took a seat. He looked at the celebrants dancing and yelling around the fire and laughed. "I'm a little too old for that."

Noah smiled. "Thank you for your hospitality. I'm delighted to know that your people worship the Creator."

"Indeed we do. That's one of the reasons we live so far into the jungle."

"What do you mean?"

"My older brother, Varelk's father, founded this village when I was a child. He said that the people of our city were no longer concerned about following the Creator, so he led a small group to this place so that their children could be raised to know the ways of the Most High."

Noah shook his head. "People turning away from the Creator — that's becoming more common." He stared at the fire and allowed the leaping flames to carry his thoughts from one idea to the next before settling on his next question. "Where did your people come from?"

Mehul pointed across the clearing. "A city called Bothar. It's a three-day journey west through the forest. I've heard things have only gotten worse since we left. Some of our young families have moved back there. I fear they've rejected the Creator and are following Sepha."

Noah spotted Aterre dancing around the fire and breathed a sigh of relief that his garment was still wound around his torso, covering the tattoo. Noah faced Mehul. "Why 'fear'? My father spoke ill of it, but . . . a friend told me that the group just teaches discipline and self-defense."

The older man arched an eyebrow. "They do much more than that. They're now in charge of Bothar. The leaders completely control their followers, who pledge to obey any command without question. They steal from travelers and murder men who oppose them. And I even hear rumors that they practice the dark arts."

"The dark arts?"

Mehul leaned back and sighed. "The dark arts refer to people trying to gain supernatural power and understanding by communicating with the dead or with spiritual entities."

"My father said the group was evil, but I don't think he had any idea they believed such things."

"Indeed they are wicked, but enough about Sepha. We're here to celebrate what the Creator has given us." He swept his arm out to the people happily weaving amongst each other, keeping time to the music. "What do you think of Zakar?"

"Your people have truly blessed us, and we're happy to have met you."

Mehul gave a slight nod. "Likewise."

Noah scratched the back of his neck and stared at his dusty feet. "Do you mind if I ask you a question about your people?"

"Not at all. Please, ask."

Noah lifted his eyes and held the man's gaze. "When your people prayed, why did they. . . ." An orange light far behind Mehul caught Noah's attention. His mind raced as his mouth fought to form the word. "Fire!" He pointed past the man to the village barn.

Mehul turned back and jumped to his feet. "Fire!"

The music suddenly stopped and everyone stared momentarily at the conflagration before springing into action. Noah and Mehul rushed to the barn. The thatched roof blazed orange, but the main part of the structure had not yet been engulfed in flames. Men and women scurried into the barn and then back out with arms full of food and supplies, many of them coughing from the smoke.

Noah wrapped the end of his garment around his face and darted in. Shelves of foodstuffs were stacked against the far wall, and large baskets of berries and vegetables sat on the floor. Noah spotted a wide board leaning against the left wall. He grabbed the arm of the nearest man. "Help me with this."

Noah moved quickly to the wooden panel. "Grab the other end." They picked it up and carried it to an open spot on the floor. Noah quickly lowered his end. "Here, fill this up!"

Within moments piles of food were loaded. Noah snagged the attention of two other men for their assistance. The four men hefted the platform and carried it a safe distance away from the burning structure.

"Dump it and let's make one more trip," one of the men said.

They hustled back to the room, which was now hotter, brighter, and smokier. Noah felt as if his hair would soon be singed. Thanks to the hasty work of the townsfolk, the barn only had a fraction of what it held before the fire. The men swiftly loaded up their table again. As they headed for the door, a large flaming beam fell from the ceiling and crashed to the ground right behind Noah. They rushed out of the inferno and into safety.

Noah fought for fresh air and collapsed, causing the food to crash to the ground beside him. Between his coughs, he heard many others doing the same. His lungs burned. When he finally caught his breath, he saw many of the Zakari watching helplessly as the barn succumbed to the fire. The center of the roof fell first, followed by the two end walls that collapsed inward.

"Is everyone unharmed?"

Noah turned and saw Mehul moving hurriedly among his people, checking on their condition. Some of the men fanned out around the building, stamping out any embers that managed to escape.

Aterre walked over to Noah. "Are you hurt?"

"No, I'm alright. What about you?"

The flickering light reflected in Aterre's eyes. "I'm fine."

Noah looked around the crowd. "It doesn't look like anyone's seriously injured."

A scream pierced the air. The door of a nearby house flew open, and a woman bolted through it. "Where's Elam?" She ran toward Varelk and another man, whom Noah thought might be Varelk's son, Elam's father. "I can't find Elam." Trying and failing to catch her breath before speaking again, she gasped out the rest of her words. "He was in bed . . . now he's not there!"

"Our son is missing?" the other man asked.

Varelk placed his hand on her shoulder, while Elam's father hurried toward their hut. "We'll find him. He probably woke up with all the noise and is out here somewhere."

Elam's mother cupped her hands to her mouth and yelled her son's name, echoed by her husband. Varelk moved off in another direction, also calling for the boy.

Suddenly, a cry rang out from the other side of the village. A petite woman ran toward the field where the children had been playing earlier in the evening. "Kani! Where are you? Kani!" A man hurried to her and joined in shouting her daughter's name.

Mehul clapped his hands and directed the villagers to make sure their children were accounted for.

Noah and Aterre ran around the edge of the clearing, calling out for Elam and Kani, while the distressed parents hastened to their homes.

Before long, the people gathered near the bonfire where their dancing had heralded peace just a short time ago. As Noah moved toward the crowd, several parents frantically waved their arms and shouted, while others knelt, weeping.

Mehul tried to calm them, but to no avail. "We won't stop until we find the four missing children."

Elam's father pointed at a couple of men. "You two, take some torches and check the east road. Look for any signs that they might have gone that way." He turned to the man who had been shouting Kani's name. "Liun, come with me. We'll check the northern trail. They couldn't have gone far."

As the four men raced off, fear and confusion gripped Noah. *Where can they be?*

"Do you think they're just hiding as a joke?" a short man with a bushy beard asked.

With tears streaming down her cheeks, a woman stepped forward, "Were they in the barn?"

"No," Mehul said. "It was nearly empty when it collapsed, and everyone made it out."

"Maybe they accidentally started the fire," the crying woman said, "then ran because they were afraid."

Another woman shook her head. "But they were all in bed, right? I put Kani there myself. She's never snuck out before."

"What if they were kidnapped?" the short man asked.

Aterre clenched his fists. "Then we go rescue them."

The conversation became impossible to follow as the frightened men and women shouted over one another. Noah turned and looked toward the north road. A man and woman near the edge of the clearing shouted out the names.

"Please. Please, try to calm down," Mehul said, his arms held up, slowly quieting the group. "I don't like to assume the worst, but I think we must consider kidnapping. Maybe the barn fire was a diversion."

"No!" Kani's mother threw her hands over her ears and shook her head, as if the words could somehow be unheard. She sobbed and dropped to her knees.

"Listen," Mehul said. "We aren't doing them any good standing around here. Go back and check your homes again, search every place you can think of." He motioned to Varelk and another man. "Grab some torches and let's search the edge of the forest."

"What should we do?" Noah asked.

"Do you have any tracking skills?" Varelk asked.

Noah dropped his gaze and shook his head.

"Then plead with the Creator that the children might be found."

Aterre hit Noah's shoulder. "I'm going with them."

The crowd quickly dispersed. Kani's mother slowly stood and returned to her home, calling her child's name as she went.

Noah stared into the night sky. "O Most High, please keep the children safe. If they are lost or hiding, help the Zakari to find them soon. If they're kidnapped. . . ." He felt his face redden with anger, and he gritted his teeth. "If they were taken, then please help us rescue them, and may the kidnappers receive justice."

Chapter 11

Something squeezed Noah's shoulder. He paused as his mind clumsily drifted from dreamland to reality. Someone was shaking him.

"Noah, wake up."

He blinked a few times, trying to get his eyes to adjust, but darkness filled the room. Aterre's voice eventually registered.

"They're getting ready to leave."

"Who's leaving?" A short, fitful night of sleep fogged his thinking. Noah felt like he was clawing at many vague concepts, trying to land on what was solid. Thus far, a losing battle.

"The Zakari. The men are heading out to track down the missing children. You said you wanted to go with them."

Noah sat up, the memories from the late evening finally rushing back. He stood quickly and shook his legs in an effort to wake his tired body for what lay ahead. "Of course." With the grogginess slowly fading, he girded his waist and wrapped the remainder of the robe over his shoulder. Then he slipped on his footwear and followed Aterre out of the guest hut. The day was dawning, but the stars held their nighttime posts like trustworthy sentinels posted across the sky, except in the east, which was painted with faint swaths of pink and red.

Stopping Aterre, Noah leaned close so as not to be overheard. "I forgot to tell you last night. Don't let them see your tattoo. They have a very negative view of Sepha."

"How do you know that?"

"Mehul talked to me about it. Be careful."

83

"I will. Thanks."

They jogged toward a small group at the west side of the clearing. The cool morning air filled Noah's lungs and invigorated him. As they neared those who had gathered in the stillness of the morning, Noah counted eight men and four women. The men were armed with thick, cubit-long blades with short handles. Two of them carried bows and each sported a quiver of arrows.

One of the men held a torch aloft, and with his other hand he pointed toward the edge of the trees. "This is where they passed into the forest."

"Are you sure?" Varelk asked.

"Yes, Father, the footprints lead up to here, and look at the broken blades of grass and that snapped twig."

Noah recognized him in the faint light as Elam's father. *Korel? Vorel? What was his name?*

Varelk turned. "Ah, Noah and Aterre. Thank you for joining us. Please know that you're not obligated to help us."

"We want to. No child deserves —" Aterre broke off. Tilting his head back, he took a deep breath and clenched his fists. "No child should ever be taken from their parents."

"We're glad to help." Noah stepped beside Aterre.

"And we're grateful for your assistance," Varelk nodded and looked to his son. "Parel, we'll follow you."

Parel. That's it.

"Father, I don't think it's a good idea for these men to join us." Parel angled his blade in Noah's direction.

Varelk crossed his arms. "We can use all the help we can get."

Parel glared at Noah and then Aterre. "How do we know that they weren't part of a plan to kidnap our little ones? What if they came as a diversion, knowing that we'd take them in and celebrate their visit? Then somebody else set the barn ablaze to keep us busy?"

Unable to believe what he was hearing, Noah opened his mouth to defend himself, but closed it when he realized that from Parel's perspective, the scenario made sense.

"Then why would they risk their lives running into a burning barn?" Varelk asked.

Parel held his torch higher and looked Aterre in the eyes as he spoke. "Maybe to make the deception even more believable."

Varelk stepped between the two men. "But why stay?" His voice was gentle. "Couldn't they have run off during the fire or while we slept?"

"I don't know." Parel's scowl turned to Noah. "Maybe so they could lead us off the trail today."

Noah refused to look away, thinking that a failure to hold his stare would seem like an admission of guilt. "May I speak?"

The man nodded.

"I understand why you don't trust us. If I were in your position, I'd probably think the same thing." Noah paused, searching for the right words. "We're willing to do everything we can to rescue the children, even if" — he glanced at Aterre — "even if that means staying behind. But if you want our help, be assured that we'll follow your lead."

"I'll take responsibility for them," Varelk said.

After a long moment, Parel sighed and nodded. "Very well." He met his father's eyes. "But I still don't trust them. They stay to the middle of the group and no one goes off alone with them."

"Agreed. Now, let's get going before we lose more time." The older man turned to the four women. "Pray for us."

Parel waved his torch in a circle over his head. "Let's go."

Noah fell into line behind Aterre as the company marched into the forest. After about 20 cubits, Aterre dropped back and walked beside his friend. "I can't stop wondering about what happened to my mother and sisters. What if they weren't actually killed like I initially assumed?" Aterre looked up and spoke softly, as if to himself. "If they were only kidnapped. . . ."

"Then we'll see what we can do to find them," Noah said. "Just like we're doing here."

Aterre snapped out of his contemplation. "Right."

Progress came slowly at first as Parel and another man regularly paused to look for signs of recent activity, a task made more difficult by the semi-darkness. Using their long blades, the men hacked their way through a few places where the forest was densest. As the sun rose higher in the sky, their tracking duties became easier.

The farther from the village they traveled, the more convinced Noah became that the children had not wandered off. When Varelk pointed out a man's footprint in the soft terrain next to two smaller prints, it only confirmed Noah's fears. Shortly before midday, they stopped when Parel discovered a shredded piece of cloth and a carved wooden hair rod not quite as long as his hand. He held them up. "Anyone recognize these?"

The muscles in Liun's cheeks bulged as he clenched his jaw. "Those are Kani's. The carved butterfly on the end is her favorite." He took the item as tears welled in his eyes. "She had two of these."

"You've got a smart girl," Varelk said. "She's leaving us a trail to follow."

Parel faced Liun. "We'll find them."

"Indeed we will, but first let's take a short break." Varelk sat on a fallen tree. His cheeks sagged in a face grown haggard overnight. "We'll need to eat to keep our energy up."

Erno, the thin drummer from the night before, slipped his pack from his shoulder and handed a small bag of food to each person. Erno's son had also been snatched in the raid. The man had said very little during the morning, but his countenance spoke volumes in its look of pure determination.

Noah found a spot on the log near Varelk. Very little was said while they hurriedly ate their meal. The combination of hunger and fear set the pace and subdued their tongues. No one smiled, and no one laughed.

During the temporary reprieve, Noah took a chance to look at his surroundings. Here were the same kind of large-leafed trees from the day before. Insects skittered across the giant foliage at various speeds. A green and yellow buzzbird zipped in and out among the white blossoms of a broad bush. Noah marveled at the tiny creature as it darted to a blossom, hovered, and then darted to another flower. Songbirds sang to each other in the canopy above. A faint cry from an animal echoed in the distance, but he couldn't discern the source.

Aterre stood and shoved the last of his rations in his mouth. He motioned for Noah to follow. "Come with me."

Noah swallowed his last bite as he trailed Aterre to an open area several paces away from the group.

"Where are you two going?" Parel asked.

"Just to the other side of these trees," Aterre said.

Varelk motioned for his son to sit back down. "I can see them from where I am. They're fine."

"What?" Noah asked when his friend stopped in the small clearing.

"I've been thinking that we may have to fight the kidnappers to free those children."

"And?"

Aterre cocked his head. "And you're a farmer. You've never been trained to defend yourself."

"I knocked you out." Noah gave him a half smile.

Aterre rolled his eyes. "You got lucky. But this could be a life or death situation." He spread his feet a little more than shoulder-width apart, left leg in front, and bent his knees slightly. "Take a defensive stance, like this. And put your hands up." Aterre raised his fists to the level of his chin, the left slightly ahead of the right.

Noah mimicked his friend's stance.

"Good." He pulled his knife from the side of his belt. "Now, if I was going to stab at you, how would you get out of the way?"

"Run." Noah chuckled. Aterre was not amused, so Noah got serious. "I guess it depends on how you attacked."

"Here."

Noah took the tooth dagger that Aterre handed him.

"Now stab straight at my chest."

"Are you sure?" Noah asked.

"Yeah, just go about three-quarter speed, and I'll show you what to do."

"Okay, here goes." Noah lunged forward.

In an instant, Aterre twisted sideways and grabbed Noah's arm. Planting his left hand under Noah's elbow, Aterre put downward pressure on Noah's forearm with his free hand.

"Ouch!" Noah dropped the knife.

Aterre released his grip.

"You could've broken my arm."

Aterre grinned and nodded. "I know." He picked up the blade. "Now you try."

Noah assumed the stance. "Go ahead."

As Aterre lunged at about half speed, Noah shifted to the side and grabbed his friend's arm. He locked Aterre's elbow and pushed down on his wrist.

"Not bad for a start. You're a quick study."

Noah let go of him. "Thanks."

"Let me show you what to do if he slashes at you from the side."

Parel ducked under a branch and stepped into view. "Are you boys ready?"

"Sure." After picking up the knife, Noah handed it back to Aterre. "Let's go."

Continuing due west into the early afternoon, the group came across a narrow road running north and south. The forest had thinned, and the air warmed with more sunlight breaking through the canopy. Parel and Liun studied the scene for a few moments.

"There are footprints heading north," Liun said.

Parel walked a few steps in that direction, bent down, and picked up the matching hair stick. He handed it to Liun. "Looks like your daughter left us another clue."

"Follow Liun." Parel motioned for the group to pass him and then fell into step next to his father, just behind Noah and Aterre.

"What is it, Son?" Varelk asked.

"Is this the way to Bothar?"

Varelk hesitated a beat before answering. "It is if we turn west after a while."

When Parel spoke again, something in his voice sent a chill through Noah. "If the rumors are true, that would mean. . . ."

The older man cut him off. "Don't even think about that. We'll get to them first. Let's pick up the pace."

Parel said nothing more but jogged back to the front of the pack.

Varelk caught up to Noah and Aterre. "Can I ask you a question, Aterre?"

"What is it?"

"Those fighting stances you were teaching Noah — where did you learn them?"

Aterre glanced at Noah and then stared at the ground. "I, um, I learned them a long time ago."

Varelk gave a small chuckle. It sounded forced to Noah's ears. "You aren't old enough for a long time ago." After an awkward silence, he spoke again. "Tell me, where did you learn them?"

Slowing down, the three men allowed the rest of the group to move out of listening range, and Aterre spoke softly. "I grew up in Havilah, where I was part of a group called Sepha. They taught us how to defend ourselves. But I left the group after . . . many seasons ago."

"But you bear their mark?"

"You know about them?" Aterre asked.

"More than I'd like to. They've become a very sinister group in Bothar."

"Do you think they had something to do with the children?" Noah asked.

"I hope not, but I strongly suspect them." Varelk rubbed his chin. "Do all followers of Sepha know how to fight like you?"

"That was part of the training — at least where I'm from."

"I was afraid of that. Our men aren't trained to fight. We're a peaceful people. Much of the reason we left Bothar was to get away from the evil and violence there."

"What rumors was Parel talking about?" Noah asked.

Some deep emotion crossed Varelk's face, and Noah felt again the chill of dread. "Some of the people of Bothar — those who follow Sepha — practice the dark arts." He swallowed. "We've heard rumors that they've recently started sacrificing children in the name of Sepha."

Noah's stomach clenched. "How could. . . ." He lowered his voice. "How could anyone do something so evil?"

"This world's growing darker all the time. When I was a boy, such an abomination would've been unthinkable, but in Bothar. . . ." He shook his head.

Noah looked at his friend. He'd worked beside Aterre for more than a year, journeyed with him, played and laughed and eaten with him. Yet it was hard to keep the accusation from his voice when he asked, "Aterre, do you know anything about this?"

Aterre scowled. "No. Never something so twisted and sickening. Like I told you before, I only knew about certain disciplines within Sepha." He pulled his shoulder wrap to the side, exposing part of the tattoo for Varelk. "If it's connected to such evil as you've said, then I can no longer be proud of this."

The older man stared at the mark. "Why did you leave?"

Aterre looked away and kicked at a twig lying on the trail.

"Sir." Noah's heart filled with compassion for his friend. "His family was attacked in the night, much like the children of your village. He was the only one to escape."

Varelk pursed his lips as concern spread over his face. He turned back to Aterre. "I'm sorry about your family. I hope you understand the reason I had to ask."

Aterre met the older man's gaze with a long, intense stare. Finally, he nodded. "Thank you. I'm sorry about your family too. We're going to get them back."

"A word of advice: don't let my son see that mark. If he doesn't trust you now, imagine how he'd behave if he knew."

Aterre nodded again. "I won't."

Hiking north, the party reached a fork in the road. The sun was low in the sky, causing a small signpost at a fork in the path to cast a long shadow. The marker indicated that the trail ahead and to the right led to a place unknown to Noah, and the route to the left went to Bothar. Parel and Liun examined the paths closely for a few moments, and then, unsurprisingly, headed left.

CHAPTER 12

As daylight faltered, Noah and Aterre followed the Zakari on the wide path's ascent through the woods. Parel and Liun exchanged a series of whispered conversations, and Noah sensed they were gaining ground.

Parel held up a hand and gathered everyone close. Keeping his voice down, he asked, "See that light up ahead? It looks like a campfire, and I'd be surprised if it isn't the kidnappers."

Noah squinted and barely identified a small orange flicker through the trees in the distance. *How'd they spot that?*

"We need to get off this trail, but don't make a sound," Liun said, and they all followed his lead. He gestured to Parel. "We'll sneak up there and check it out. The rest of you wait here for us." In an instant, they were gone.

Varelk herded the remaining search party members a little farther off the road. "Try to rest a little, but stay low and be on alert."

Noah's feet and legs ached from the long march. He plopped down and leaned back on his elbows, closing his eyes. *Creator, please protect the children and help us rescue them without a fight.*

"Noah, tell me about your relatives and where you grew up," Varelk said. "It'll help me keep my mind off all this."

Noah sat up. Talking about his family made him long for home. Nearly two weeks had passed since he said farewell. He shared about growing up on the farm, and that he often wondered how Jerah and Misha were doing.

Varelk stood and stretched. "I can see you're a godly young man, Noah. I'm certain my son has misjudged you."

Noah shook his head. "I don't blame him, but I will do whatever I can to earn his trust." He rubbed one forearm vigorously and then the next to warm up. "Besides what we saw yesterday, what is life like in Zakar?"

As Varelk talked about his town, Parel and Liun returned. The eight other men crowded around them, leaning in to catch every bit of their report.

"It's definitely the kidnappers," Liun said.

"Did you see our children?" Erno asked.

Parel nodded. "Yes, they appear to be unharmed but are tied up near one of the tents."

"How many kidnappers?" Varelk asked.

"We counted four, but it's possible that there were more in the tents or standing watch."

"Only four?" Erno clenched his fists. "We can overpower them."

Varelk held up a hand. "Not so fast, Erno. You know the followers of Sepha are fighters. We have no such training. We need to be careful."

"So what's the plan?" Liun asked.

After a short pause, one of the other men spoke. "Wait until they fall asleep, then sneak in and untie the children."

Liun shook his head. "Maybe, but if they keep watch, getting close enough without being seen will be almost impossible."

"What if we *want* them to see us? Or at least a couple of us?" Erno asked after a long pause.

"Why would we want that?" Liun scoffed, but Noah was intrigued.

"For a diversion while everyone else circles their camp."

"That won't work," Parel said.

"Why not?" Erno asked. "It worked on us. The barn burned down, and we didn't suspect any other trouble until it was too late."

Parel lifted both of his hands and touched his chest with his fingertips. "Look at us. They'll know we're Zakari."

Erno gestured toward Noah and Aterre. "Not if *they're* the diversion."

"No." Parel folded his arms over his tattooed chest and scowled.

Liun looked at Parel. "Why not? It's a good plan."

"What about it, Aterre? Noah?" Varelk asked. "Are you willing?"

Noah opened his mouth but stopped when Parel cut him off.

"Father. No. We can't trust them."

Varelk looked at his son. "Yes, we can. They aren't like the men of Bothar, and I don't believe for a moment that they're part of the abduction."

"You want to place our hope on the shoulders of two men we just met yesterday?" Parel's voice rose, and he stopped himself with obvious effort before continuing in a quieter tone, "Is that really a risk you want to take with your grandson's life?"

"I don't want to do any of this, but I believe the Creator sent them to us at the right time so that we can rescue all our children." Varelk spread his arms, palms open. "Do you have a better plan?"

Parel stared off into the treetops for a long moment before relenting. "No."

Varelk motioned to Aterre. "You don't have to do this."

Aterre nodded at Noah. "Yes, we do. We said that we'd do anything to help, so tell us what to do."

"Erno, what's your plan?" Varelk asked.

The tall man cleared his throat. "Noah and Aterre will act like travelers from the north who are heading to Bothar and need directions. So they will need to approach the campsite from the road. I think Aterre should do most of the talking since he sounds different than the rest of us."

"Forgive me for interrupting," Noah said. "But won't it seem odd if we see the children tied up and don't say anything about them?"

"Not necessarily," Varelk said. "If our suspicions are correct, they were kidnapped to be sacrificed in Bothar. Since you two will pretend to be heading there, you can ask if that's why they have them."

"Right," Erno said. "While the two of you distract the men, we'll spread out around the campsite, still hiding in the trees. Parel and Liun, you'll move behind the kidnappers, so that Aterre can see your sign when we're in position."

"What's the sign?" Parel asked.

"We'll each carry torches, but keep them dim and shielded. For the signal, get them blazing." Erno turned back to Aterre. "That's when you and Noah will position yourselves between the kidnappers and the children. Then the rest of us will show our torches. In fact, we should all light two of them. Since we'll be spread out, it'll look like there are at least 16 people surrounding the camp."

"And then what?" Liun said.

"Then Parel will call to them from the woods and tell them they're surrounded. If they walk away from the children without harming them, we'll let them go. And just to let them know that we're serious," — he lifted his bow — "I'll fire a warning shot into the ground near their feet."

Parel jerked his head toward Aterre and Noah. "And if they betray us, fire an arrow into them."

Frustrated by Parel's lack of trust, Noah sighed.

Erno put his arm in front of Parel as if to stop him from attacking Noah on the spot. "If everything goes according to plan, we can rescue our little ones without a fight."

"And if it doesn't?" Parel asked.

"Then we improvise." Erno motioned to Aterre. "You may have to put those skills you were teaching Noah to good use."

Aterre nodded. "If it comes to that."

"Let's pray that it doesn't," Varelk said. "In fact, if no one has anything else to add, we should pray and then move quickly."

The Zakari men lowered themselves to the ground in the same awkward pose as the previous evening. Noah and Aterre knelt, but this time neither copied the Zakari. Varelk offered a brief, but deeply heartfelt prayer, pleading for the safety of the children, protection for Noah and Aterre, and for a peaceful resolution. Following the customary silence at the close of the prayer, the men stood.

Torches were prepared and distributed. Varelk approached Noah and Aterre. "Please be careful. May the Most High be with you."

Parel placed a hand on Noah's shoulder. "I hope I'm wrong about you. And if I am, you'll have my respect and sincere apologies."

"Thank you," Noah said.

An agonized scream rang out in the distance and Parel stiffened. "That was Elam. We have to go now!"

Aterre and Noah hastened back to the trail and headed for the kidnapper's campsite. The stars sparkled in the early evening sky, and a crescent moon hung overhead. A light wind wafted through the night, evaporating the beads of sweat on Noah's face. On both sides of the path, insects chirped and buzzed, all but drowning out the sounds of their feet hitting ground and the pounding of Noah's heart. The peace surrounding them belied the gravity of their mission. *God, please guide our actions and protect those children.*

"Nervous?" Aterre asked.

"Of course. I've never been involved in something so dangerous. You?"

Aterre shrugged. "Definitely. But you can't show it or they may get suspicious. Just keep praying and follow my lead."

Moments later, they turned off the trail and trekked up a slight climb through the small patch of woods leading to the fire. For the first time, they clearly saw the situation. A moderately sized tent stood on the far side of a small bonfire. Three men sat on the ground around the blaze, while a fourth man stood nearby and jabbed a rod into the embers. The children were tied together to the left of the tent. They huddled closer together than their bonds required. With bowed heads, either in utter fear or defeat, a few sobs broke free. Elam rocked back and forth with his bound hands pressed against his upper left arm.

Aterre stopped behind a large tree several cubits before the clearing. "Are we sticking with the plan?"

"Yeah. It looks just how Parel described."

"Okay. Then act natural. If possible, don't let the children get a good look at you. They may give us away." Aterre smiled. "Loosen up. Don't be afraid to step on a twig or two. We aren't trying to surprise them."

Noah took a deep breath and slowly let it out. "Let's go."

Aterre led as they stepped out into the open. They continued forward until one of the men spotted them. "Evening peace, men," Aterre said.

The man stood and stepped around the fire. "Who are you?" His voice was gruff and threatening. While not a large man, his tenor indicated no lack of confidence. His dark, scruffy beard hid his mouth.

"My name is Aterre, and this is my friend, Noah." He turned his right foot outward and folded his hands together against his stomach in a peculiar manner that Noah had not seen before. Aterre's left hand enclosed two fingers of his right hand while his thumb stretched upward.

The man's face and stance relaxed as he copied the unique position. "And what's your business here, Aterre?"

Noah tried to make sense of his friend's action. *Is this some kind of secret Sepha greeting?* Although he desperately wanted to make sure the huddled Zakari were all right, he forced himself to keep his eyes on the man.

"No business, sir. We're on our way to Bothar for the first time and saw your fire. We decided to see if you might be headed that way too."

"Indeed, we are."

Aterre relaxed his stance, let his hands drop to his sides, and turned to Noah. He spoke loud enough to be heard by all the men. "I told you we were on the right path."

The kidnapper who had been poking something into the fire suddenly joined them. He was about a span taller and at least that much broader at the shoulders than the first man. Even with just the light from the fire, there was an unexplainable air of ruthlessness about him that made Noah want to protect the children even more. "You say you're making your first trip to Bothar?"

"Yes sir," Aterre said. "Is it much farther?"

"About two more days traveling by foot," Ruthless said. "Aterre, I've never heard that name before, and your speech is strange. Where are you from?"

Aterre motioned toward the fire. "May we join you for a bit and warm ourselves?"

"Have a seat," Scruffy Beard said.

Noah and Aterre found spots on the ground across from the four men.

"I'm from the land of Havilah, far away to the south." Aterre laughed. "And from my perspective, it's everyone around here who talks a little funny."

Ruthless relaxed only slightly and motioned toward Noah. "And what about your friend? Does he speak?"

"When necessary." Noah elbowed Aterre and attempted to keep his voice from shaking. "Now this one — he'll strike up a conversation with anyone."

Still seated, the man farthest to the left set a dish on the ground, and his soup sloshed over its brim. "You must be traveling to Bothar for the big Sepha festival. How long have you been part of the brotherhood?"

"I joined years ago in Havilah, and when I heard about Bothar and the festival, I knew I'd have to visit someday." Aterre tipped his head in the direction of the children. "Is that why you have them?"

Smiling, Ruthless pointed to his captives. "Them? Yeah, they're perfect for the sacrifice." At his words, a chill slithered its way down Noah's back.

Elam still rocked back and forth. A red and white burn covered the boy's upper arm. Noah's gaze drifted to the fire and he spotted the metal instrument used to destroy flesh. A large wooden handle encased the top, while glowing red hot at the bottom end of the rod was a tree-shaped piece of metal. *Was Elam just marked for sacrifice?* Noah swallowed his revulsion. He had to focus, had to be on the lookout for Parel's sign.

"So will all of them be sacrificed? Are there any more?" Aterre asked. The calm in his voice unnerved Noah.

"We have to mark the rest first, and then I guess it depends on the other group that traveled south, and how many. . . ." Ruthless's eyes drifted upward as he seemed to search for a word. A sinister smile spread on his face. "How many *recruits* they found."

"Did you buy these ones?" Aterre asked.

"Nah," Soup Spiller said. "We raided a little village last night." He playfully pushed the silent man next to him. "Sterk used to live there, so they were easy pickings."

Noah's eyes darted toward the surly fourth, then he looked away, afraid the man would read his emotions in his gaze. *How could he betray his own people, some of whom are probably his close relations?* A glimmer of light flickered in the woods behind the abductors. *Finally.*

Sterk jolted upright and pointed past Noah. "Do you see that?"

Noah knew what to expect, but jerked his head back to play the part.

"Over there!" Soup Spiller pointed to his right.

Aterre jumped to his feet. "And back there!"

"Don't move! You're surrounded!" Parel's voice carried throughout the campsite.

Ruthless picked up a knife and turned in the direction of Parel. "What do you want?"

"We want our children back. Now put the knife down."

"Over my dead body," the large captor yelled back.

Parel's laugh chilled Noah. "We can arrange that."

An arrow zipped past Noah and landed just short of Scruffy Beard.

"That's your only warning," Parel said. "I promise, the next one won't miss."

Aterre stood and put his arms up. "Wait! We aren't with them." He backed toward the children. "We're just passing through."

Noah slowly edged toward the young captives as well.

"Halt! All of you get on the ground!"

The abductors exchanged glances and slowly bent down. Ruthless mumbled something under his breath, but Noah could not make it out.

"On the ground!"

The kidnappers finally knelt.

"Now I want the man closest to the children to untie them."

Because Parel had singled Noah out, he stood and pointed at himself. "Me?"

"Yes, do it now."

Noah hurried over to the children, who stared wide-eyed at him. Tears streaked down Elam's face. Noah held a finger to his lips, urging the children to remain silent. "Your fathers are here. Run to that torch over there." Noah pointed in the direction of the road. He untied the two girls first, and then Erno's son. As he began to work on the knot that bound Elam, one of the kidnappers spat and growled.

"That one's already been marked. He has to die!" The man stood faster than Noah thought possible and bolted toward him in a rage.

Aterre sprang into action, but could not reach Noah in time. Bracing himself for the onslaught, Noah knew he only needed to buy enough time for Aterre to get there to assist him. Ruthless never slowed, lunging at Noah with a knife. Noah sidestepped to dodge the attack, but the blade caught his garment, cutting a long gash in the cloth. As the knife caught on the fabric, the man lost his grip on it. The force of the snag slowed him and yanked Noah into his aggressor, sending them both tumbling.

Noah scrambled to his knees, spotted the knife, and dove for it. The large man pounced on him just as Noah reached for the handle. Unable to grasp the weapon, Noah pushed it out of reach and rolled under the man's weight. Before Noah could react any further, a powerful fist landed a blow to his cheek. Noah blinked as a starburst flashed across his vision, but a sudden surge of energy coursed through his body. He planted one foot into the man's stomach, grabbed his shoulders, and then flipped him back over his head. Ruthless hit the ground with a thud.

Noah cringed in pain as Aterre leapt on the man and held his dagger-tooth knife to his throat. "Move and you die."

Clambering to his feet, Noah spotted movement out of the corner of his eye from the direction of the fire.

Scruffy Beard screamed and dropped to the ground several paces in front of Noah, an arrow sticking out of his leg. The other two men remained by the fire.

"Get the boy," Aterre said, still holding their assailant at bay.

Noah scrambled over to Elam and finished untying him, being careful to avoid his wounded arm. He helped the lad to his feet and pointed him toward the road. Then, picking up some of the rough rope, he moved back toward Aterre. They quickly bound the pinned man's hands and feet.

With arrow nocked and pointed toward the men at the fire, Erno stepped into the clearing. "If any of you makes a move, you'll go down like your friend."

Scruffy Beard still writhed on the ground. Blood gushed from his thigh as he grimaced in pain. Liun ran to the injured man and bound his hands while he screamed and cursed. Four more Zakari men emerged from the woods, drew their weapons, and circled the two men near the fire.

"I have all the children." Noah recognized the voice from the woods as belonging to Varelk.

Parel soon joined them. He marched straight to the two men at the fire and pointed to the one on the right. "Tie him up." He took a long look at Sterk. "How could you do this to your family? You'd sacrifice your own nephew for Sepha?"

Sterk's eyes filled with rage. "You're a fool, Parel! You have no idea what we're capable of." He spat in Parel's face.

Parel wiped away the spittle with the back of his hand. Then he raised his blade and thrust it toward Sterk, stopping the point just short of the man's chest. "You won't be capable of anything if we kill you."

"You don't have the guts." Hatred filled Sterk's words. "I don't know what my sister ever saw in you."

Parel's eyes glistened in the firelight. Without taking his stern gaze off Sterk, he simply said, "Bind him."

"Now what do you want to do with them?" Erno asked.

"I think we should treat them as they treated our children," Parel said.

Liun's jaw dropped. With eyebrows raised, he leaned forward and said, "You want to kill them?"

Parel shook his head and pulled the rod out of the fire. Holding it up, he looked closely at the glowing design on the end. "I think we should mark them."

"No!" Terror edged Sterk's voice. "You can't!"

Parel gave a knowing smile. "And why can't we?"

Sterk snarled and looked away.

"We could never go home," Soup Spiller said. "We'd be marked for sacrifice."

"Exactly." Parel pointed to two Zakari and then motioned to Sterk. "Gag him and hold him fast."

Liun drew Parel aside, his eyes questioning. "Are you sure?"

Noah wanted to object, but he saw the logic in Parel's decision. Freed kidnappers would return to Bothar and gather reinforcements to launch another attack. The Zakari were not a violent people, so executing the abductors was not an option, nor would it do to tie them up indefinitely so that they starved.

Oddly, Parel glanced at Noah before he replied. "It's the only way."

Sterk struggled to free himself, but the guards and ropes held him fast. Noah looked away, but he couldn't avoid the sounds. Sterk's whimpering, the sizzle of skin. The screams.

"Now you can never go back to Bothar or to Sepha," Parel said. "As much as I hate what you've become. . . ." He paused as if having second thoughts. "As much as I hate this life you now stand for, if you choose differently, for my wife's sake, I'd open my door to you — even though you mutilated my son."

Erno extracted the arrow from the wounded man's leg and treated it with some sort of powder he took from a pouch on his belt. Parel and the other Zakari quickly gagged and branded the remaining kidnappers, and this time Noah watched. Not the branding, but the Zakari, who winced and turned away each time, showing they did not relish their task. Then Parel ordered that the kidnappers be tied together.

He stood before the seared and seething men, holding up Ruthless's knife. "I'll leave this at the edge of the clearing. Once you figure out how to maneuver over there, you can cut yourselves free." Parel turned to leave, but stopped and looked straight at Sterk. "Know this. If you ever seek to hurt my family or community again, I will kill you."

CHAPTER 13

Varelk embraced Elam, but when Parel and the other men made it to the road, the boy ran to his father. Parel knelt down and squeezed his son like he would never let go. As Noah watched the reunions, his weariness faded into pure joy. Liun openly wept as he picked up his daughter and kissed her repeatedly. Holding a torch in one hand, Noah nudged Aterre with his other arm. "Makes it all seem worth it, doesn't it?"

"Absolutely." Aterre started when he looked at Noah. "Your face looks pretty sore."

Remembering the blow, Noah touched his cheekbone and winced. "I guess it does hurt. I was so focused on everything in the moment that I hadn't really noticed."

"Now you're just trying to act tough." Aterre pushed him and laughed. "You did great back there."

"You were pretty convincing yourself. You almost had me believing you were one of them. I half expected Parel to shoot us." Noah tilted his cheek toward his friend. "How bad is it?"

Aterre took a closer look in the flickering light from the torch. "Well, be prepared for girls to scream when they look at you."

Noah held his chin high, chest puffed out. "As if that's even possible."

"I'm kidding. They'll be too busy running away." Aterre smirked. "Seriously though, it'll be black and blue in the morning, but you'll be alright." He started to leave, but his attention locked onto the front of Noah's garment. "Might need to take a look at that though."

Noah's gaze followed Aterre's. A blooming line of blood marred his robe, tracing a long tear in the fabric. He lifted the cloth away from his chest to find the source. "I guess he must've cut me after all. It doesn't look very deep." Pouring some water over the gash, he flinched before tearing a piece of fabric from the end of his wrap and pressing it against the wound. "That's better."

"Noah, use a little bit of this on your wound. It will help stop the bleeding and keep it from festering." Erno handed him the pouch from his belt.

Noah withdrew a pinch of the powder and rubbed it into the cut, biting his lip at the sting. "Is that enough?"

"Should be. Check it in the morning when we have enough light."

"I will."

Parel walked Elam over to Noah and Aterre and then bowed before them. "I owe both of you an apology." He glanced down at Elam, placing a hand on the boy's head, and tears filled his eyes. "You saved my son's life. I'll never be able to repay you." He embraced Noah. "I'm sorry I misjudged you."

Noah flushed with satisfaction. He let the words sink in, warming his soul. At once, his father's voice rang in his head: *All we have comes from the Creator, Noah. Never forget that.* Feeling humbled, Noah mirrored Parel's bow. "I'm happy the children are safe and that the Creator gave us success."

Parel then embraced Aterre and apologized.

Noah bent down and looked into Elam's eyes. "How are you feeling?"

"My arm hurts, but I'm happy you came." He threw his good arm around Noah's neck. "Thank you, Noah."

"You're most welcome, Elam." Noah chuckled.

"I hate to cut this short," Varelk said, "but we'd better get far away from here tonight. I don't think those men will find the knife in the dark, so they probably won't be free until morning. But to be on the safe side, let's put some distance between us."

"Do you think they'll come after us, Grandfather?" Elam asked.

Varelk shook his head. "I doubt it. There are only four of them, and one won't be walking well for a while. But you never know what people might do when they're angry, so I don't want to take any chances. Parel, lead the way home."

Energized by their success, the Zakari walked as the darkness of night deepened into its stillest time. Noah estimated the deepest dark had long passed when they stopped at the small clearing they had used as a resting place earlier. With the exception of Elam, the other children had fallen asleep in their fathers' arms sometime during the long hike.

"Let's set up camp here," Varelk said. "Some of us can go no farther without sleep."

"We need two people to take the first watch," Liun said.

Noah's legs and face were sore, but his mind still raced. "I'd be happy to."

"And I'll join you," Parel said.

Varelk clapped his hands. "Good. It's settled. Let's get some rest. Elam, you can sleep next to me."

"I want to stay with my father and Noah."

"I'll bring him back here when he falls asleep." Parel put an arm around his son, and they led Noah a short distance down the trail they had just walked. Parel sat on a log and pulled Elam close beside. He patted a spot, inviting Noah to sit next to him.

Noah stared up at the litany of stars shining through the sparse canopy above, though the swelling around his left eye and his tiredness blurred the lights to some extent. He stretched and yawned before taking the seat. Feeling part of his skin catch oddly, Noah looked down and saw congealed blood on his midsection. Carefully he pulled the torn cloth from the laceration.

Elam yawned and snuggled into his father's side.

"Are you well? That's a bit of a gash you have there."

Noah suppressed a smile at Parel's concern for his well-being. "I didn't even notice it until after the rescue." He gingerly prodded the wound, feeling the blood stick ever so slightly to his two fingertips.

Parel shook his head. "Good thing it wasn't worse." He bent his head to look Noah in the eye. "And what about your face? Looks like he got you pretty good."

"Yeah, that was a strong man. I hope I never see him again."

"Same here." Parel sighed. "I hope never to see any of them again. Although I half wish Sterk would feel remorse and come home."

Surprised, Noah's jaw dropped a little and he winced. "What happened? Why did he leave Zakar?"

"I'm not really sure. He's my wife's older brother. My father-in-law used to travel a lot when Sterk was young, and he occasionally took his son along. I guess Sterk was seduced by what he saw of the world. Their father has never forgiven himself." Parel looked down and shook his head. "I've never seen such hatred in a man before. The way Sterk and those men acted tonight — they were more like beasts than men."

"I thought the same thing." Noah shuddered. "I'd like to think he can change."

"So do I." Parel rubbed his eyes.

Elam shifted to get comfortable and leaned against Noah.

Parel grinned. "I think he trusts you. And now, so does his father. It means a lot."

Noah returned the smile and draped a loose part of his robe over the boy.

After a long silence, Parel asked, "Do you agree with my decision to mark them?"

Noah nodded. "It's harsh, but given the circumstances, I can't think of a better solution. I'm glad you didn't execute them, even though they planned to sacrifice your son. But I'm also glad you didn't just set them free to strengthen their numbers and seek revenge against your people. You showed great wisdom in your judgment. Do you think they might still try to do something?"

Parel shrugged. "I wouldn't be surprised. We'll have to post a guard every night, especially if two strangers show up as a diversion." Parel chuckled softly so as not to wake the boy, and winked.

"You definitely can't trust people like that." Noah grinned but quickly turned serious. "What about his arm? If Sepha followers ever see that mark. . . ."

Parel shook his head. "I'm not sure. We can cover it for now. But I'll consult the elders. I don't want to do it, but . . ." He lowered his voice. "We may have to burn another design to mask that cursed one."

Noah cringed and glanced at the child resting comfortably against him. "Poor little boy."

"Listen, Noah, I'm truly sorry for misjudging you. You risked your life to help strangers, and you and Aterre gave me my son back. If you ever need anything, anything at all, please let me know."

Noah nodded. "There's one thing you could do."

"Name it."

"Could you give us directions to Iri Geshem from Zakar?"

Parel smiled. "I can certainly do that. There's a trail from the village that goes directly east to the Hiddekel, just over half a day's journey. On the third day of every week there's a boat that heads downriver. You could sail the rest of the way and be there in two weeks."

Noah yawned again but this time abandoned the stretch. "Two weeks? That's great. I thought we'd be walking for at least a whole moon."

"You're welcome to stay with my people until the boat leaves. We'd throw a great celebration to honor you and Aterre."

"I'll check with Aterre, but I'm sure we'd be happy to stay a few more days, especially knowing there will be good food. Plus, we could help rebuild the barn."

Casting a sly smile at Noah, Parel nodded. "Yes, my father always taught us to leave a place in better condition than when we found it. When you first visited, we had a barn, so we should probably have one when you leave."

CHAPTER 14

Taht nickered and shook her neck as Noah stroked her mane. With a slight catch in his throat, he turned and faced the dozens of Zakari who had formed a semi-circle to say their farewells. The cool morning air gave him a quick shiver.

Five activity-filled days had flown by. Extravagant in their joy, the Zakari had thrown a huge celebration on the night of the rescuers' triumphant return. In the following days, Noah and Aterre helped the villagers rebuild much of their barn — only the roof needed to be finished.

Mehul stepped forward, touched his forehead, and bowed slightly. "We're sad to see you leave so soon. You're always welcome here."

Varelk pulled Noah into a strong embrace. "May the Creator bless your journey." He had only just let go when Elam ran forward and wrapped his skinny arms around Noah's waist. "I'll miss you." The thick dressing around his upper arm hid the gruesome wound that looked nothing like the original mark. At his son's insistence, Parel had made the heart-wrenching decision to obscure the vile symbol by burning a large circle the size of a fist over it. Chewing bark from a wispy tree helped Elam cope with the pain.

Noah bent low. Carefully avoiding the bandaged area, he squeezed the boy who had followed him around for much of the last week. "I'll miss you too. You've got a lot of inner strength. Use it to serve the Most High."

Aterre mussed Elam's hair in farewell.

Pulling out a coiled object, Parel placed it in Noah's hand. "To show our gratitude."

Noah saw the distinct spheres of piks and pikkas laced on a cord and twisted into a loop. He shook his head and extended his palm. "No, this isn't necessary."

Parel held his arms out. "It's a gift for you and Aterre from all of us." Parel looked at his son, who now clung to Aterre. "It's the least we could do."

While his heart was ready to get back to the adventure that awaited them, Noah was sad to leave the Zakari, who had become like family in the short time they'd been together. He said nothing more, only embraced Parel again and held up a hand to the gathered villagers before turning away.

Their farewells said, Noah and Aterre set out at a brisk pace. The road to the tiny river town was far better maintained than the one that had brought them into Zakar. Wide enough for two pack animals pulling a wagon, the road accommodated the Zakari's supply runs to Novanam, which, according to Parel, consisted of nothing more than a few dwellings on the Hiddekel.

Noah secured the gift into one of their bags in the cart before rejoining Aterre next to Taht. He patted the animal's neck. "Just a short walk and then you get to ride on a boat again."

"I'm sure she'll love that," Aterre said.

Noah chuckled. "It took me a whole day to get my — what was the term Deks used? Sea legs? Maybe she'll get hers on this trip."

As he shifted his focus to the journey ahead, energy rushed through Noah's body, and he whistled a playful tune that matched the bounce in his steps. He felt ready to take on the world.

Throughout the early hours, scores of colorful birds and small reptiles made appearances along the way. But as the morning's coolness dissipated, a thick humidity blanketed the trail, bringing with it swarms of pesky insects to vex Noah's head and neck. By the time the sun had reached its zenith, his springy stride had flattened into a trudge. Noah found his mind wandering to home, thinking longingly of the cool breezes that played through the malid orchard, keeping heat and bugs alike at bay.

He perked up briefly when, at one point, a massive furry creature that was nearly twice Noah's height loped across the trail. Watching it walk on its hind legs and the knuckles of his front limbs, he almost

108

laughed in spite of his discomfort. Taht stopped and tensed up, but the brown and white creature paid them no heed. It lumbered into the forest, snapping branches and twigs in its wake.

The excitement of the odd sighting faded quickly. Wiping his forehead clear of sweat with one hand and swatting another pest away with the other, Noah winced as the wound on his chest throbbed. He drew aside part of his garment to inspect it. The salve from the Zakari seemed to have sped the healing, but it didn't end the occasional ache or the persistent itch every time something rubbed across it. Focused on the injury, Noah stepped in a small rut and his ankle twisted, sending a sharp pain up his leg. "Ouch!"

"You alright?" Aterre asked.

Noah limped the next few steps as the soreness subsided a little. "I'll be fine." Truth be told, gone was the happy-go-lucky attitude of the morning. Instead, irritation mounted as discomfort and annoyance crowded his senses with relentless pursuit. He swatted at another insect. "Get off me!"

Aterre chuckled. "Settle down."

"These bugs are so annoying." Noah shook his head and wiped both arms in succession.

"Just ignore them."

"That's easier said than done. They aren't going after you." Noah tapped the side of the cart. "Let me ride for a while."

Aterre looked up from where he sat squeezed among their belongings. "We just switched spots a little while ago."

"My foot hurts."

"And you don't think my feet hurt? We've been on the go for weeks."

Noah scowled at him. "But I've been walking while you keep riding."

Aterre laughed. "What's gotten into you? I've walked just as much."

"You wish." Noah drew his garment back to reveal his wound. "I'm the one that risked my life to save those children."

"What's your problem?" Aterre pierced Noah with a gaze and jumped out onto the trail with his fists clenched. "I was right there, fighting with you."

Noah crossed his arms. "You mostly just let that mouth of yours run." Noah knew he wasn't making sense, but that just fueled his anger, his need to win.

"That's ridiculous. But if you need it, take the back of the cart." Aterre pointed and emphasized his words to leave no doubt that he thought Noah was being childish.

Noah tugged on Taht's lead rope. No way was he going to look weak. "Forget it. I'm good. Let's just get to Novanam so we don't miss the boat to Iri Geshem."

Time seemed to drag on Noah's thoughts, which eventually drifted back to his family. Loneliness filled him. What he would give to see them again. Like a cool breeze brushing against his skin, his father's final charge nudged at his mind, dampening the heat of his ire. *Don't forget your promise to follow the Creator.*

He looked back at Aterre, who walked in silence behind the cart. Noah shook his head. *My actions aren't honoring the Most High.*

Noah stopped the cart. "Aterre."

His friend ignored him and kept walking.

Noah put his hand on Aterre's shoulder. "I'm sorry about that back there. I don't know what came over me."

"And what? I'm just supposed to forget about the things you said?"

"I don't expect you to forget them, but I do ask that you forgive me."

Aterre stared at the ground for a few moments. "I guess I do owe your family one. Don't worry about it." Aterre smirked. "You're just lucky I didn't beat you up."

Noah shook his head but smiled. "I appreciate that."

CHAPTER 15

Iri Gesham — Noah's 40th year

I've never seen anything like it." Noah stood on his toes at the bow of the boat and leaned as far out as he could over the water. Reflected early-afternoon sunlight danced across the rippling surface that stretched to the horizon. Squinting, he looked past the water directly beneath him, beyond the riverside buildings of Iri Geshem on either side of the Hiddekel, and into the glistening expanse of sea before them. "It's spectacular."

Aterre put an arm around Noah's shoulder. "I knew you'd like it. Here we are at last."

After their adventure with the Zakari, the past two weeks on the Hiddekel had been tame to the point of boredom. Now, as they finally reached their destination, Noah yearned to get off the boat.

He pulled his gaze away from the Great Sea and focused on the ivory-colored buildings immediately ahead to their right. Numerous one-story structures lined the river. "Are those made out of stone?" he asked Farna, the vessel's captain.

"No, they're mud-brick," he said as he joined them at the bow. "They usually have wooden frames with the bricks placed around them."

"Look how many there are. This is so much bigger than Iri Sana."

Ahead, a dock built parallel to the river stretched along the shore. Farna's men slowly guided the boat alongside the wharf, while their captain tossed the mooring to a man on the shore, who quickly secured the line to one of the several tall posts jutting out from the water and evenly dividing the dock. A handful of men joined Farna's crew in unloading the ship.

Noah strode to Taht and stroked her mane, feeling her muscles slightly relax at his reassuring touch. "You made it, girl." He double-checked the cart to be sure their belongings were fastened inside and then hitched it to her.

"Noah, Aterre." Farna waved them over to him. He was a firm and demanding man when needed, yet fair and approachable. Noah admired the way he carried himself, and how he earned the respect of those around him.

Slowly and steadily, Noah guided Taht across the ship's deck.

Farna reached into a pouch and handed each man three copper pikkas. "You've earned some of your payment back through all of your help."

Noah smiled. "Thank you, sir. We appreciate all that you've taught us."

"You and Aterre are always welcome on my boat. Just don't bring that animal with you again." Farna chuckled.

Noah snorted. "I wouldn't dream of it." He pointed to the lane that led away from the dock and divided two rows of houses. "So we take this road until Sarie's Bakery and then turn left, and that'll take us all the way to Ara's shipyard?"

Farna nodded. "It will. Really, as long as you head to the coast, you'll find Ara. Since he's the one who builds all the boats, you can't miss it."

"Peace to you," Aterre said.

"I hope to see you at Ara's sometime," Noah said.

"Until next time then." Farna raised a hand, his attention already on the unloading process going on near the stern.

Noah carefully led Taht onto the dock and had to restrain her as she tried to hurry to the shore. "Easy. We'll be there soon enough." As soon as they stepped onto dry ground, she stamped her feet several times before snorting and shaking her head. She was finally at ease.

With all their belongings in tow, Noah and Aterre strode into town. Passersby greeted them with a nod or a smile. A group of young children played in the space between two of the buildings. An older woman stood on the roof of a one-story home, hanging clothes on a line tied to posts. A stone staircase ascended the side of the house.

"Farna wasn't kidding about this place," Aterre said. "They really are friendly. Not at all like Birtzun."

"I love it already. Look at all this." Noah gestured to one side and then the other. "At all this life."

Aterre shrugged. "I would've been happy to stay at the farm."

A stunning young woman, perhaps a bit older than they were, turned the corner. She smiled at them before ducking into a nearby house.

Aterre grinned at Noah. "On second thought, I could get used to this place."

Noah rolled his eyes and shook his head. As he tried to think of a clever response, the unmistakable scent of fresh-baked bread floated into his nostrils. He breathed it in deeply. "That must be the bakery." Ahead and to their left stood a two-story building. Faint smoke floated away from a nearby rooftop. A wooden sign over the door announced that it was indeed Sarie's Bakery.

They turned left before the shop, and from the top of the hill spied Ara's shipyard. At the end of the road, up against the shore of the inlet, the wooden frame of a boat rose a little higher than the mud-brick building not too far from it.

Noah tugged Taht's lead as he quickened his own pace. "Come on."

Aterre matched his stride. "Have you thought about what you're going to say?"

"To Ara?" Noah shrugged. "I haven't rehearsed anything. I figured it'd be better to just be natural."

"That's probably best." Aterre pushed him playfully. "Don't mess it up."

The closer they came to the shipyard, the larger the dwellings were, at least on the right side of the road. Spaced far apart, the two-story homes stood in yards adorned with a variety of trees and bushes. The district to the left was filled with small older homes; some wood and others mud-brick.

After crossing a wide dirt road, they stood at the gated entrance to the shipyard. Working on the boat frame, three men set a beam into place and fastened it with hammers and pegs, while another man cut a log with a saw. A hint of the sweet scent of sawdust amid the salty aroma from the water beyond, amplified Noah's senses. He took a deep breath and looked uncertainly at Aterre. "Time to find out if the journey was worth it."

"And if it doesn't work out," Aterre said, "remember, we helped save some lives."

"And had some adventures."

Once inside the gate, Aterre shut it behind them and Noah secured Taht's rein to a post near the building. "Think the wagon will be safe here?"

Aterre shrugged. "Farna said we shouldn't have to worry about thieves. The people still follow the Creator here."

Noah ascended the two small stone steps and stood before the front door. He knocked and waited.

"Can I help you?"

Turning in the direction of the gruff voice, Noah saw one of the men who had just been swinging a hammer striding toward them. He appeared to be in his third century, and black curls peeked out from under a snug covering on his head. Dark eyes complemented his sun-browned complexion, and his muscular build would probably intimidate most people.

"Yes, sir." Noah stepped down to the ground. "We're looking for Ara. Have we reached the correct place?"

The man's broad smile belied his husky voice. "Indeed you have." He stopped before them and bowed slightly. "I'm Ara. And you are?"

Noah gestured to his friend. "This is Aterre, and I'm Noah. We've come all the way from Iri Sana to meet you."

Ara bit his lip and furrowed his brow. "Iri Sana? That's beyond the rapids, right?"

Noah nodded. "Yes, sir."

He laughed. "Please, call me Ara. You say you came all this way to meet me? Do you seek to buy a boat?"

"Not exactly." Noah untied the band from his upper arm and handed it to Ara. "My grandfather is your cousin Methuselah."

Ara's eyes lit with recognition. He stepped past Noah and opened the door. "Please, come inside." He nodded toward Taht and the cart. "Your things will be safe there."

Noah and Aterre followed Ara into the building. Wooden furniture and shelves filled with trinkets, instruments, and tools nearly obscured the walls. A breeze carried the scents of the yard in through the small window in the front, which also afforded Noah a view of the back end of their wagon.

Ara moved behind a counter and withdrew a tall stool. "Here." He handed it to Aterre and then retrieved one for Noah before sitting down. He looked across the counter at them. "So you're Methuselah's grandson? How is my cousin? I haven't seen him in about half a century. He visited here not long after his father, my Uncle Enoch —" He looked away and tapped his front teeth with his fingernail a few times. "After his disappearance."

Noah could see the man was uncomfortable talking about what happened to Enoch, so he determined not to mention it. "My grandfather's doing well. He has 12 children and lives about a day's journey from us. My father, Lamech, is his third-born son."

"Well, I'm glad to hear that." Ara sat up straight and examined the armband as he slowly twirled it in his hand. "So how can I help you?"

Noah glanced back once more at their cart and swallowed the lump in his throat. "My father raised me to be a farmer, and even though I didn't mind it, the only work I truly enjoyed was found in my woodshop. I love building things, but there weren't any carpenters in our area that needed an apprentice. So my grandfather recommended that I travel here to work for you." Noah pointed to the band. "He sent that along as his pledge to you that he believes I can do the job."

Ara set the armband down and held Noah's gaze. "You wish to be my apprentice?"

"It would be an honor, sir."

Someone passed in front of the window, and Ara looked toward the door. "Excuse me for a moment." He bent down and pulled out a tightly wound scroll with a string tied around it. He walked around the counter, and as he crossed the room, the door opened.

Noah turned to see who had entered, but Ara's frame blocked his view.

"Hey, Emz." Ara handed the scroll to the person. "Please take this to Zain before heading home today."

"Of course, Baba."

At the sound of a female's voice, Noah craned his neck to see this "Emz." As she hugged Ara, her hands, forearms, and dark ponytail came into view, but nothing more.

115

He let go of her. "I'll see you tonight."

"Sounds good." The door opened again. "I love you, Baba."

"Love you too, Emz." As the door shut behind him, Ara returned to his place behind the counter. "That's my daughter, Emzara." He playfully hit himself on the forehead. "I'm sorry. I should've introduced her. That's alright. I think there will be time for that. Do you have plans for evenfeast tonight?"

"No, sir." Aterre said.

Noah shook his head.

"Great. I'd like you both to join us for the meal. We'll eat shortly before sundown." Ara pointed to his left. "Just follow this main road along the shore until it turns right to go up the hill and back into town. Instead of going up the hill, stay straight on a wide path that leads right to my house. Oh, and if you don't have a place to stay, you're more than welcome to stay with me."

"That's very kind of you. We'd be happy to join you," Noah said.

"Yes, thank you."

"Did you just get into town?" Ara asked.

"We did. We rode on two of your boats," Noah said. "Farna said many nice things about you."

"Farna?" Ara leaned back and put his hands behind his head. "He's quite the character. I trust the boat was nice and sturdy."

"It was," Noah said.

"Farna. We go way back." He chuckled and then stood up. "Noah, about that apprenticeship. I trust my cousin when he says you are qualified, but I already have an apprentice."

Noah's heart sank, and he struggled to hide his disappointment.

"But let me see what I can work out." Ara pointed toward the ship under construction. "We have enough men working on this project already, but if another order comes in soon, I could definitely use your help."

Noah nodded slowly. "I understand. I guess I should pray that you get another order soon."

Ara's gravelly laugh lightened Noah's mood a bit. "I need to get back to work. You should go explore Iri Geshem a little. I think you'll like it here."

"Thank you, sir," Aterre said. "I'm sorry to keep you from your work, but can I ask you one quick question?"

"By all means."

"Do you know any farmers looking for help?"

Ara pursed his lips and his gaze drifted upward. After a few moments, he said, "As a matter of fact, I think I do. Follow me."

They walked outside and Ara pointed back in the direction of the Hiddekel. "There are plenty of farms on the other side of the river. Go to the end of this road, and you'll find a man who'll ferry you across for a copper pik. Ask him for directions to Cada's farm. Cada is a good friend of mine, so tell him I sent you. I'm sure he'll find some work for you."

Aterre bowed. "Thank you."

Noah bowed slightly as well. "I look forward to seeing you tonight."

"Likewise," Ara said. "Give greetings to Cada for me too."

Aterre nodded. "We will."

Noah reached for Taht's tether.

"You can leave everything here if you'd like," Ara said. "We'll keep an eye on it. Besides, I'm not sure if the ferryman would be willing to take your animal."

"I hadn't thought of that. Thanks again." Noah scratched Taht's neck while Ara returned to the boat frame. "We'll be back in a little while, girl." He reached under one of the packs, withdrew the monetary gift from the Zakari, and tied the bag of piks and pikkas inside his robe.

"You ready then?" Aterre asked.

"I suppose. Hopefully, one of us will get to do what we love."

CHAPTER 16

Emzara fingered the cloth carefully, enjoying the feel of the soft folds as they rippled through her hands. She pondered the possibilities of what to embroider along the trim. *Unless* — her eyes sparked with a new idea. *No one says I have to follow the edge. I have this whole cloth as my canvas. What if* — A knock sounded below, breaking through her planning.

Setting the fabric on the low table in her room before rising from the floor where she had been sitting, she pushed past the heavy curtains blocking the doorway and pattered down the wooden steps to the main entrance below.

"Greetings, Bakur. What brings you here from the shop?"

"Good. You're home." Bakur was just as stoic while speaking as he had been while she welcomed him. "Your father sends word: Plan on guests for evenfeast."

"Oh wonderful! Who will it be?"

Bakur blinked. "Two relatives. From upriver."

"Hmm, upriver. I wonder how far, perhaps a long ways. Will they be staying longer with us?"

Bakur nodded.

"Then I'll get their rooms ready while Adira and Nmir prepare the meal. Thank you."

He raised his hand in farewell before traveling on the pathway back through the rows of trees that would usher him onto the road to the shipyard.

"Adira! Nmir!" She called the two servants — though perhaps *servant* was the wrong word. Nmir, her mother's old nurse and hers, had been part of the family for so long she practically was family. And Adira, well she was Emzara's closest friend.

The two women appeared in the doorway to the kitchen, Adira young and pretty; Nmir old and wrinkled. Vigor pulsed through Emzara at the challenge and excitement of not knowing if they'd finish before Father came home with the houseguests. "We've got company coming tonight."

* * * * *

Early in the evening, Emzara surveyed herself in the polished copper disk that hung in her room, large enough to reflect not only her face, but most of her torso as well. She checked to make sure none of her frenzied tasks from that afternoon would be evident in her appearance. She twisted and pushed one loose chunky curl back into its rightful place in the tiered bun she usually wore. Satisfied with the results, she replaced her coarse outer work garment with a finer threaded fabric, folding the pleats carefully before rolling down the top edge so that it was tightly situated just under her arms. Gathering what was left of the long cloth, she placed it over one shoulder and allowed it to flow down her back.

Adding two bangles to the four already adorning her wrist, she adjusted them and then held out her arm, pleased at the effect. She glanced critically at her reflection one last time, trying to still the nervous fluttering in her midsection.

You're a fraud. Her inner voice accused her. *You're play-acting hostess. They'll see it in the food or in a detail you've overlooked. There will be an awkward pause in the conversation and you won't get it flowing again, and it'll be your fault.* Her fingers trembled as she twined delicate earrings around her ears.

Without warning, Emzara's mind skipped back to a memory of childhood. Her father had come from the shipyard to find her in tears.

"What's wrong, Emz?" Concern showed in his face as he bent over her.

"Does Nmir love me, Baba?" Emzara barely choked the words out between her sobs.

119

"Why, of course she does." He picked her up and just held her close. "Tell me what happened."

Calmed in her father's embrace, Emzara said, "I was making a house out of the table. I had used some cloths for walls and I invited her to play with me. And she told me that it would be better for me to learn how to keep a real house than to waste my time on silliness. Then she took down the cloths, folded them, and put them away." She looked up at her father, watching him, waiting for him to make things in her world good again.

"My dear, Nmir is a woman who loves very few people, but those whom she loves, she loves with a very big heart. You're one of those special people."

"But my playhouse! She ruined it. How does that make me special?"

"She would prepare you for life, my love. She would see you grow to be a strong and capable young woman." He brushed a lock of hair from her face. "I understand why you hurt. But some people don't show how much they love a person by tenderness. Nmir is one of those people. You can see her love for you in how she takes care of you and teaches you. Look in her eyes. Trust me, you'll see love there when you least expect it."

She took a deep breath to focus her thoughts, and relaxed her brow. *Nmir has trained me well and loves me; I can do this.* She straightened her shoulders and marched downstairs. *Why so nervous? These guests are probably making one last pilgrimage to see family before they die. They probably won't even be able to see the food, much less taste it.* She skipped down the remaining steps and headed into the kitchen.

"Alright, Nmir, what's left to be done?"

"You just leave it to me. We don't need more bodies in here anyways."

"We have ample space. Tell me what I can do."

"It's almost done." Nmir turned, her exasperation palpable, but when she saw Emzara, her expression softened. Only briefly — the next moment she had moved away to check the contents of the oven — but Emzara thought again of her father's words, and her confidence rose.

"Good, I'm just in time to help then," Emzara said. "Let me lift the heavy things and you can take a break."

"Are you calling me old?"

Emzara grinned before taking the earthenware platter that the trusty housemaid held out to her.

Nmir was just as much a habit of the home as Emzara and her father were. She had been the nursemaid for Emzara's mother and had traveled with her when she married Ara and moved to Iri Geshem. Nmir had loved her first charge, and when Emzara entered the world shortly before her mother exited, Nmir extended her affections to her mistress's baby as well.

"Hold on. I'll take that." Adira relieved Emzara of the platter, interrupting her thoughts.

"How are things on your end of the preparation?"

"Just fine. After helping Nmir, I tidied some areas, made the cushions fluffier, things of that sort. But if you're going to do so much of the cleaning, why do you pay me to hang around?" Adira set the tray on the table.

"Ha. As if I could get along without you." Emzara followed her back into the kitchen. "You're the one who keeps me sane. Now that I spend half my time at the shipyard, someone has to be here for Nmir to boss around." She bent down and kissed the old woman.

"Humph." Nmir shook her head.

"So tell me, do you know anything about these visitors? Any handsome young men in the bunch?"

"I doubt it. Just a couple of relatives from upriver. Father must know them. I'm not sure how long they're staying."

"Bakur didn't chat about all the details?" Adira asked in mock surprise.

Emzara laughed. "Not so much."

"Well, you have to tell me everything. That's part of my contract as your friend."

"Oh, I will. You'll hear every detail about their aches and pains and how hard their journey was. You'll get all the stories. If I have to listen to them, so do you."

"Deal. I. . . ."

"Emzara." Ara's voice came from the front of the house. "Come and meet our guests."

"Here we go."

"Well you look lovely and you'll do fine," Adira said. "Whether they're 50 or 500, they'll be enthralled."

"Stop." Emzara made a face and pushed her grinning friend away. Turning to the doorway, she smoothed her clothing and went to join her father.

"Noah, Aterre, I'd like you to meet my daughter, Emzara."

Emzara stopped when she saw the men, and she fought to hide her surprise. A slight smile crept across her lips. *This just got a lot more interesting. Adira's going to like this.*

She stepped forward, extending her neck to touch cheeks with each man in the customary greeting among family. "It's nice to meet you both."

The taller man, Noah, smiled and glanced at her father before his deep brown eyes focused on her. "It's a pleasure to meet you too."

A confusing whirl of thoughts swept over Emzara, and she barely had the presence of mind to look away. "Um. . . . Please come to the table. You're both welcome in our home." Emzara glimpsed Noah once more as she spun around before leading them past the entryway to the well-lit banqueting room beyond. *Don't trip, Em.* She focused on her steps and took a deep breath. *What am I supposed to say next?* With a graceful gesture, she indicated the cushions around the table. "Please make yourselves comfortable." She leaned to kiss her father and then stepped into the kitchen.

"They're here. Let's get the warm dishes out." She leaned over a large clay container, which warmed over a firepot, and sampled the contents. She added several pinches of spice and stirred.

"So what were they like?" Adira asked.

Emzara shrugged. "Can you take the beverages out?" When her friend left with the tray of drinks, Emzara chuckled to herself, anticipating Adira's reaction.

Nmir, having already gone out with the bread, re-entered the kitchen and let out a low whistle. "Just a couple relatives from upriver, hmm? More like two handsome young men."

"Hmm?" Emzara focused on her preparations, feigning disinterest. "What did you say?"

The older woman put her hands on her hips. "I know you heard me. I said they were two handsome men from upriver."

Emzara faced her and raised her eyebrows. "Oh, I guess I didn't notice."

Nmir stared at her until Emzara could no longer suppress a laugh. "Well, I. . . ."

Adira burst through the door and rushed to Emzara's side. "Why didn't you warn me they were good looking?"

Emzara raised her palms in mock innocence. "What? And ruin the surprise?"

Nmir reached for the soup. Keeping her voice down, she nudged Emzara and flashed Adira a rare smile. "Looks like one for each of you girls."

Adira giggled. "I like the sound of that." She took Emzara's hand. "Let me guess. You like the taller one."

Emzara rolled her eyes and shook her head, but a flush crept up her neck. "How could I? I don't even know him." Though she downplayed the moment, Emzara found herself hurrying to see the men again. Using a thick cloth to place two dishes on woven-grass serving plates, Emzara finished gathering the last items and followed Nmir to the table.

"Ah, there she is." Ara gestured for his daughter to sit.

As Ara stood to pray, Emzara pushed aside thoughts about the food, the presentation, and performing her role. *Help me, Most High.*

When the prayer ended, she opened her eyes and found Noah looking at her. She blinked and he glanced away. Taking a deep breath, she passed each dish first to their guests and then to her father as the men continued their previous conversation.

"That was one of the most awe-inspiring moments of my life, being so close to a dagger-tooth," Noah said.

Ara leaned back. "I've never seen one of those beasts myself, but I've heard some of the boatmen talk about them."

"Look at this, sir." Aterre's impressive upper arm muscles became more defined as he set a knife made from what looked like a giant tooth on the table.

Ara's eyes grew wide. "You should thank the Creator that this was all you came away with in that encounter."

"We definitely did and do." Noah said. "I think that's the first time I've been truly scared."

Adira entered the room carrying a pitcher to refill their drinks. She bent low and filled the guests' cups first.

Ara looked at Emzara. "They'll be staying with us until they can find a place of their own. Aterre will be working on Cada's farm."

"For Cada?" She looked at Aterre. "That's wonderful. He'll probably send you home with fresh food every day."

Filling Emzara's cup, Adira said in a voice meant for her ears only, "It's time for me to go home. Tell me everything."

Emzara nodded and had to suppress a smile when Adira winked.

"Noah came all the way from beyond the rapids to work for me," her father said. "Apparently, he's pretty good at construction."

"Oh." She smiled at Noah, but her smile quickly faded, and she furrowed her brow. "Do we have a spot for him at the yard?"

"Not at the moment, but we might tomorrow. A potential customer stopped in today. I have to go into town to meet with him tomorrow morning. If he gives us his business, we'd have a few more ships to build, and we'd certainly need him then. Just in case, can you show Noah around in the morning? Introduce him to the men and give him a feel for the place?"

Emzara nodded.

Noah wiped his mouth with the small cloth set beside his plate. "I'm looking forward to the tour."

"My daughter is quite the wonder. I couldn't do without her. She was the only one that kept me going when her mother died. She's always helped our housemaid, and in the last few years, she's helped me with the administrative duties at work." Ara leaned back. "Emzara will be able to answer just about any question you have — maybe even better than I could."

"I believe it. This meal is a wonder." Aterre indicated his nearly empty plate.

Emzara bowed her head in acknowledgement of the compliment.

"Yeah," Noah agreed. "You don't know what I've had to suffer these last few weeks trying to work down whatever Aterre's scrounged up for us whenever it was his turn to cook. This is truly a treat."

"Sure, I wasn't the one who decided to try that new vegetable from that marketplace," Aterre said. "We boiled it overnight, but it never changed consistency."

"Guess I should've found out a little more about it." Noah laughed easily at his own expense, and Emzara found herself thinking it was a pleasant sound.

"Well, we're glad to welcome you. Emz has made up a room for each of you, and I'd be honored if you both considered this your home until you get your bearings and settle in."

"Thank you," Aterre said.

"If you would like to follow my father to the comfort of our sitting room, I'll fetch the leaf-brew."

Noah raised a brow. "What's leaf brew?"

"You haven't had leaf brew?" Ara asked as he rose from the table. "Then you're in for a treat. Thank you, Emz. Boys, let's continue our conversation out here."

As Emzara cleared the table, she heard Noah ask her father about his opinions on animals like the dagger tooth being given such frightening teeth if they were created to be vegetarian. She moved into the kitchen and grabbed the kettle from above the fire. Intrigued by the topic, she tried to eavesdrop as she poured the scalding hot water through the silver sieve attached to the kettle's mouth but couldn't make out her father's response.

She set the four drinks on a tray, stepped into the sitting room, and served the small rounded bowls, filled with a translucent, honey-colored liquid.

The men each took a sip of the steaming contents. Noah looked up. "This is delicious."

"Agreed." Aterre took a second sip. "What do you make it with?"

Emzara sat beside her father. "Well, I grow certain plants in the garden and dry their leaves. For others, Adira and I go outside of the city to the forest and gather. I blend them to get different flavors."

"Have you ever made a drink with roasted beans?" Noah set his empty cup aside.

"No."

"Well, it's a good thing we still have a bunch left in our cart. I'll make some for you."

"Beans? To drink?" Emzara looked at him and wondered if he was serious or if he was teasing her.

"Hey, at least beans are edible. Who eats leaves?" He cracked a small smile.

Emzara raised an eyebrow. "Doesn't everyone? How else does one make a salad?" As his smile faded, she wondered if she had said too much.

"She has a point, Noah." Ara laughed loudly and hugged her.

"Emzara, you should ask Noah what we planted in one of his father's fields last year for the family to eat." Aterre chuckled, clearly enjoying the opportunity to embarrass Noah a little.

125

Gaining confidence through the fact that Noah seemed to enjoy the light-hearted barbs, Emzara pressed on. "What was it, Noah?"

"We planted several crops. How am I supposed to know which one he's talking about?"

Aterre crossed his arms. "You know."

Emzara set her drink down and grinned. "Yeah, you know."

Noah shot a look at Aterre before sighing and sagging his shoulders in mock humiliation. He smiled at her, "Well, you see, uh, um . . . it was orb plants."

She gave him a knowing smile. "And what are orb plants?"

His face reddened before he said, "Essentially round bundles of leaves that we eat."

Emzara laughed along with everyone else.

As the evening waned, Ara got up slowly. "Boys, Emzara and I have rooms upstairs. Your two rooms are off this hallway over here." He looked at his daughter. "Emz, please take care of these bowls since Nmir went home. I'll help them unload their cart. Then we can all get some rest."

Chapter 17

Slowly the wick of the oil lamp caught fire and brightened the dim interior of the kitchen. Noah had extra energy this morning as he anticipated how his mission might go over. He looked around in wonder, surprised by the spaciousness. *Mother wouldn't know what to do with herself in here. This might take me longer than I thought.* Finding the oven wood pile in a dedicated bin to the left of the large clay oven, he snatched a couple of the smaller pieces and poked them into the still-glowing embers at the base of the yawning opening. Over that he littered several woodchips, which he found in a small crock. Bit by bit the embers sparked, and little flames appeared, before the fire awoke to full force — just as gradually and groggily as a person might.

Attempting to get all the necessary things in order before the others came down, Noah crushed a handful of Nuca's beans in a mortar and dumped the grounds into a fine cloth. He pulled the corners of the fabric together, tied them off, and set the pouch into an empty kettle. He found a pot positioned above the flame and, after filling it with water, replaced it so the contents could heat to a boil. Then he located four drinking vessels and placed them on the table.

With nothing left to do but wait, Noah leaned against a counter. *Creator, thank You for a safe and successful journey and please grant me guidance through the day.* Noah wondered if the other thing on his mind would be worthy to bring before the Most High. Before he could ponder that, he noticed the water was ready and poured it over the sack of beans waiting in the kettle. When he was satisfied that the contents had

127

successfully diffused, Noah pulled the kettle from the heat and removed the spent grounds. He was searching for a place to dump them when Emzara entered the kitchen. He stilled. The room, which had been spacious only moments ago, seemed to shrink. He simply blinked at her, and felt his body temperature rise. Her wondrously large eyes looked at him in mild surprise.

"Oh, you're up early."

"Yes. Old habits die hard. We were always up early on the farm." *She's lovely in the morning, too.* Noah held up the cloth, the bottom firmly rounded from the contours of its contents. "Plus, I have this."

"Smells amazing." Emzara leaned closer and breathed in slowly before exhaling.

Noah concentrated on not dropping the bag and resisted the urge to lower his head so he could again inhale the spicy-sweet blend of her scent that had mystified and delighted him yesterday when she greeted him at the door.

"Wait until you taste it."

"This is the bean brew you talked about last night?" Emzara twisted a small curl on the side of her temple.

"It is, and I'll pour some for you soon."

"Well, you've certainly done a good job of making yourself at home. Although, we might not want to tell Nmir that there was a man in her kitchen." Emzara's eyes twinkled in fun. "She won't know whether to scold first or to rush and make sure all is still in order. Then again, that might be kind of entertaining to watch." She looked up at Noah and smiled.

"Nmir?"

"Oh, that's right. You probably saw very little of her last night since she went home to her own little place right up the road. Her official position is cook, but she's so much more than that. She fusses on the outside, but on the inside she's as soft as can be."

"If she helped with last night's meal, then she's an excellent cook."

"That she is. By the way, thank you for getting the fire going." While Emzara continued talking, she gathered the needed items for preparing firstfeast, and Noah admired the graceful, yet confident way she moved.

He drained the brew into the cups and then stirred some honey into her drink. "I'm almost done with this. Is there anything I can do to help you?"

"Well, the warmed kerbs are not quite ready to go on the table — they have to boil for a bit. Just to warn you, we usually eat a light first-feast around here, so there's not much else that needs to be done. I guess you can help by putting the dishes on the table." She glanced up at him as she spoke. "They're tucked away in this cabinet over here." Reaching above her head, she grabbed four shallow bowls and handed them over her head to Noah.

He took the dishes, and with hands still aloft, tried to step past her toward the dining area. Instead of reaching open space, he found Emzara had moved in the same direction. They bumped into each other. Trying to save the dishes and his balance, his arms lowered around her waist, hands still clasping the bowls.

Emzara dropped her gaze, and Noah detected a deepening in color at the edges of her cheeks.

"Whew, that was close." He smiled shyly as he eased away from her, trying his best to save the situation. "I'm glad these didn't break. Nmir won't have a reason to yell at me yet."

"Yeah, you're safe still." She smoothed her hands down her garment and then tucked an invisible piece of hair behind her ear.

"I'll get these on the table, and then you can try your drink." Noah made sure to give her plenty of room before hastening into the feasting room with the bowls. Upon returning to the kitchen, he handed Emzara a low rounded cup. "Try it. Tell me what you think." He watched closely while she took a sip.

"It's strong. I can see why you drink it in the morning." She took another sip. "I like it."

"I put a little honey in yours to sweeten it. I drink mine without, but my mother won't touch it unless there's something to reduce the bitterness."

"So yours is plain?" Emzara pointed at the cup near him.

"Yes."

"May I try it?"

"Of course." Noah offered his cup to her, glad she wanted to see how strong he preferred it.

"Whew." She shook her head and smiled. "That's something else. It might take a while to get used to." She handed the brew back to him. "Thank you."

Noah took the cup and deftly turned it so that he would drink from the same spot her lips had touched.

* * * * *

"Bakur, this is Noah." Emzara waved at a man who looked to be a few centuries old.

The scrawny, bare-chested man nodded but continued to push a hand plane in unbroken rhythm over a long, thin piece of wood Noah guessed would become part of the ship's hull.

"He'll be staying with us for a while." Emzara looked up at Noah. "How are we related again?"

"Your father is my grandfather's cousin."

Another man walked around the bow of the boat. Broad-shouldered, with a chiseled upper body and an unreadable expression, the man stepped toward Noah. "So, Noah, you're staying with Emzara?"

"I'm staying in Ara's home, yes." Noah shrugged. "For now at least."

"I'm Pennik. Ara's apprentice." He put a hand on Noah's shoulder and squeezed harder than necessary. "Welcome."

So this is Ara's apprentice. Noah ignored the man's attempt to intimidate him, if that's what it was. "Glad to be here."

Pennik looked past Noah and smiled broadly. "Morning peace, Emzara. You look beautiful, as always."

Bakur cleared his throat, and Emzara glanced at Noah with a sheepish smile. "Thank you, Pennik. Morning peace to you."

Suddenly Noah found himself irritated by Pennik. He moved toward Bakur. "Can you explain what you're working on here?"

"Strip of the hull." He gestured at the skeleton boat above him. "Today we start enclosing the frame. You here to give us a hand?"

"I'd love to." Noah clenched and released his fist as if by doing so, he could get to work faster.

"You can't have him." Emzara laughed. "He's here for a tour of the yard. I still have to introduce him to Fen and Tssed."

"Whatever you say, Boss." Bakur winked at Emzara and leaned toward Noah. "Make sure you stay on her good side."

Oh, I'd like nothing better. The surprising thought came out of nowhere, and Noah turned away to hide his sudden confusion. "Uh, thanks

130

for the advice, Bakur. Nice meeting you. As soon as the boss gives the word" — Noah tipped his head at Emzara and she gave an approving nod — "I'll be ready to assist you."

Emzara set off again, looking over her shoulder at him as she picked up her pace. "Most of the construction goes on outside. We'd like to build shelters at some point, but for now, we have just two buildings. The smaller one is where Baba holds his meetings. I think you were in there yesterday. And this is the main building." She pointed to the modest-sized, two-story building made with the same mud brick as most other buildings in the city. "This is where I keep the ledgers on the days I'm here. Most of the tools and expensive supplies are kept in here."

"You aren't concerned about thieves?"

"Not in Iri Geshem. I've never heard of anything being stolen here."

She ducked into the doorway and Noah stayed close behind, looking around at the interior. On his left, broken only by a window, rows of various tools hung neatly on the wall. Some Noah recognized and he flushed with pleasure at the thought of working with them again. On the opposite side of the room stood various crates he assumed held the supplies. The morning's coolness still filled the air in this place.

"What's that?" Noah asked upon seeing a round wooden lid-like object in the corner.

"Oh, Fen made it. Kind of crazy, but it's an indoor well. Not only is it easier to get water during the day, but the men keep their midmeals here to keep them cooler." She picked up the lid, and Noah saw a small shelf jutting out not too far from the opening.

"And up those steps?"

"That's where I work. There's really nothing up there but a table and my accounts."

Curious to learn all he could about this young woman who had suddenly captured his thoughts, Noah asked, "Can I see?"

"Of course." Despite her shrug, she looked somewhat pleased and led him up the stairs. "Here it is. See? Nothing much."

As Noah's head cleared the threshold of the upper room floor, he saw tidily arranged and stacked pieces of wood, no more than a finger thick and all roughly the same size. "So tell me what I'm seeing."

She went over to one of the piles and lightly rested her hand on the edge. "These are made from the leftover pieces of wood. I keep records on them about our customers, the details of their order, and when we promised to deliver. I also keep track of all the supplies that come through and where we get them from. We cut down most of our wood. Baba owns a forest on the other side of the river. But we're also able to get other types of lumber from all over as traders come in with their wares."

"This looks like a strange customer. Did you draw this too?" Noah picked up one of the wood tablets and held it up for her to see.

"Oh, that. Yes, well," Emzara extended her arm to grab it from him, and for the second time, he saw the color in her face deepen. *This could be fun.* He held it out of her reach.

"I don't think I've seen someone with that long of a neck. Plus, that's a lot of hair coming out of his ears. And what are these horns in the center of his head?" Peering closer at the drawing allowed her the opportunity to snatch it out of his hands.

"This is a keluk." She looked at him with what seemed to be a hint of a challenge.

"I know what a keluk is. Those pesky animals kept getting into our malid orchard."

"You've seen them before?"

"Many times."

"Then I envy you. I wish I could see one. They don't live around here, but I've seen them on objects that some traders have brought and heard merchants talk about them. They're my favorites."

He nodded toward the portrait. "It's pretty accurate for never having seen one."

"I like drawing animals." She paused. "And anything else, really."

"Well, if that one is any indication, you're pretty good at it." Noah said.

"Thank you."

"So that's what you do when you're working then, huh?"

She feigned offense. "Yes, that's why Baba hired me, so I could spend all day drawing."

Noah smirked.

"I drew this during some free time." She hesitated as if not sure what to say next. "Well, should we go down and finish the tour?"

"Lead the way."

Emzara headed downstairs. "Do you have any questions about anything so far?"

"Seems straightforward enough. Why did you start working here?"

"I wanted to spend more time with my father." She paused and leaned her attractive figure against the frame of the open door. Tilting back her head, she closed her eyes briefly, welcoming the warming rays of the sun. Unable to look away, Noah couldn't decide what he liked better, the effect of her long lashes resting down or the playfulness in her eyes when they were open wide.

"As you know, my mother died right after I was born. Even though I was under Nmir's care, I spent much of my childhood here. I loved spending time with Baba and watching the bustling activities. I wanted to be near him, so I strived to be as helpful as possible. The energy here is invigorating: the hard work, the deadlines, the focus, and the people that come through. I love it all. The other men treat me like I'm one of their own daughters." She made a face. "Well, except for Pennik."

"They don't. . . ." His words stuck and he cleared his throat. Brushing at a speck in his eye, Noah suddenly felt out of sorts. "They don't mind taking orders from someone so young?"

"I don't really have any authority, but they treat me as if I do. I just do what I can to keep things on track." She crossed her arms. "Besides, I'm not that young. I'm 34, which can't be much younger than you."

"I turned 40 earlier this year. That was the day my father told me about this place. I'd been longing for some time to become a carpenter's apprentice, but it seemed like I was destined to work on the farm for my whole life. Then my father surprised me by telling me about a relative of ours who builds the boats that run the river." He ran his finger along one of the tools on the wall, trying desperately to keep from staring at her. "Did your father train you to do your job or did you figure it out along the way?"

"As I got older, Baba started teaching me little things about the business, and then a few years ago I started this system of keeping records. I split my time between working here and managing our home with the help of Nmir and Adira. It keeps me busy but I like what I do."

Noah joined her as she pushed away from the doorpost. "Speaking of what I do, I should probably turn you loose so I can get started on my duties." She walked toward the open shipyard and threw a grin back his

133

way. "If you're able to get work here, do you think you'll catch on, or will Baba have to find someone else?"

He hurried to move alongside her. "Oh, I catch on pretty quickly. You won't get rid of me so easily."

"I guess we may find out soon enough."

With palms sweating and heart racing, he tried to respond, but something held his tongue. *What's wrong with me? I've never felt like this.* He stole a couple of glances at Emzara as they walked and it hit him. He was smitten. *So this is what it feels like.*

Chapter 18

"Hand me that piece of rope in the corner." Noah grunted as he used one arm to hold onto the roof's beam and dropped his free hand into the ceiling space of his and Aterre's future abode.

Aterre retrieved the requested item. "Here."

"Got it." Noah pulled himself up and double-checked the positions of the two beams that met at the apex of the roof to his left. "Does this look straight from down there?"

"Yeah, it's good."

"Okay." Noah carefully lashed the timbers together around a crossbar at the peak. Finding its way through the trees, a light breeze brought a welcomed coolness to an otherwise warm evening. The rhythmic lapping of waves on the shore joined with the irregular squawks of sea birds soaring over the large bay, creating a melody all its own. "Now I need the hammer." While he waited, Noah dug two pegs out of the pouch slung at his side and was ready when Aterre handed the tool up. *Bam, bam, BAM.* The sound echoed through the milknut trees. With the next peg in place, he squeezed the handle tight and drove the hammer violently against its mark. No longer focused on the peg, all he sensed was the impact each strike created.

"I said it's good!"

After three more blows, Noah lowered his throbbing arm. He grumbled as he tossed the mallet aside. Using the newly stabilized timber, he swung over the side and dropped to the floor.

Aterre gave him a clay drinking vessel filled with water and stared at him.

Sitting with his back against the mud brick wall, Noah savored the cool surface against his warm flesh. He took a long drink and then closed his eyes while massaging his tight neck muscles with his free hand.

"What's going on?"

"I'm so frustrated."

"With the building?"

"No, this is fine. But it's been two whole moons since we came here and I've got nothing to show for it. If only that order at the shipyard had gone through." Noah set the vessel down, and water sloshed over the edge.

"At least you still have a job and Ara allowed us to build a home here."

Noah scanned the small room, about 12 cubits square, just large enough for a kitchen and dining area and a place to sleep. Two more rooms would soon be built beyond the opposite wall. "Yeah, but I'm stuck farming again. I'm just not cut out for it."

Aterre slumped down beside him.

Noah wiped his forehead with the back of his arm. "It's great for you. You love what you're doing. But I was so close to fulfilling a lifelong dream, only to find it's still out of reach."

"But you only met Zara two whole moons ago." Aterre chuckled.

Noah glowered. "What are you talking about?"

"You're talking about your dream, so I figured this was about her."

"My dream of being a carpenter. Besides, what's the use of talking about her?" Noah let his head bump against the wall and blew out a breath. "I'm pretty sure she's interested in Pennik."

"I don't think you have to worry about him. But enough about that since you clearly weren't thinking about her." Aterre's sarcasm could not be missed. "I was wondering though. . . ." Aterre paused, becoming serious. "You told your father before we left home that you believed the Creator was guiding you down this path. Do you still believe that?"

Surprised, Noah sat up straight. Aterre had not discussed the Creator in weeks. "Of course I do. Why else would I have come all this way? Why would I stay?"

"If you truly believe that, why do you complain?"

"Because, I —" Noah cut short his instinctive reaction to defend himself as he realized the inconsistency between his actions and beliefs. He shook his head slowly. "You're right. Sometimes I wish He'd just tell me what I'm supposed to do."

Aterre nodded.

"But you're right. Just because this is taking longer than I expected, it doesn't mean God has changed the plan. I'll be a carpenter someday."

Aterre snorted. "I didn't say all that."

"No, but you said enough." Noah stood and dusted off the back of his garment before helping Aterre to his feet. "And I really needed to hear it. I'll try to remember it the next time I get angry about all this."

"You mean tomorrow morning."

One edge of Noah's mouth curled up. "Give it a couple of days at least. What about you? Have your thoughts about the Most High changed since the last time we talked about Him?"

Aterre pressed his lips together and shrugged. "Somewhat."

"Meaning?"

"I told you before that I wasn't sure if He existed, although I was open to the idea. But now, I'm pretty sure He does."

"Well, that's good. What changed your mind?"

"I'm not sure if I can pinpoint one specific thing. I know one of the reasons is your family — even after what I did, they took me in and loved me. And I saw the same thing with the Zakari and again here with the way Ara accepted us. If this is how people who serve the Creator act, then I figure there must be something to their beliefs, and to the Creator Himself." Aterre tilted his head back, apparently thinking about what to say next. "After our journey, the world makes more sense when I think of it being made by an all-powerful God. I hadn't really bothered to consider how everything came about, so I never took time to think much about the world around us. With all the amazing creatures and plants we saw, it just makes sense that God made everything. But . . ." Aterre paused and shook his head. "Never mind."

"But what?" Noah held up a palm.

Aterre's face turned sullen and he stared at the stone floor. "My family. I don't understand why the Creator would allow them to be killed or taken. I guess it'd be easy to trust Him when everything is going great, but when you've seen the evil things I've seen. . . ." He swallowed. "It's just hard."

Noah folded his arms. "I can see why that might make it harder to believe. But I don't agree that the evil in the world should be blamed on the Creator. My father said that the world was perfect until the Great Deceiver showed up."

"That's just it." Aterre leaned his shoulder against the wall. "Why would the Creator make anything bad in the first place?"

Perplexed, Noah shook his head. "I'm not sure. What if the Deceiver was originally good, like the rest of creation, and then chose to rebel, like Greatfather Adam did?"

"Hmm, if that's true," Aterre said as if speaking to himself, "then everything the Creator made would have been good originally, even people and the serpent. And the horrible things in this world could be traced back to their rebellious choices, right?"

"That's what my father taught me."

Aterre opened his mouth, but stopped before speaking. Instead, he bent down and picked up a long beam. "Let's finish a few more tonight. I'd like to move in while I'm still in my first century."

Noah wanted to continue the discussion, but he knew Aterre liked to think things through at his own pace. Resolving to broach the topic in the near future, Noah jumped up, seized one of the recently placed rafters, and pulled himself above it. "Let's do it." After steadying himself on the roof, he reached down to take the next piece from Aterre. "So why'd you say that about Pennik?"

Aterre chuckled. "I knew you'd bring things back around to Zara."

Noah settled the wood in place. "I didn't say anything about her."

"Then why'd you ask about Pennik?"

Noah shrugged. "I was just curious what you meant."

"Because you wanted to talk about Zara again."

"Is there something else you'd like to discuss?"

Aterre handed him some rope. "Not really. I'd just like to finish our home."

Noah bent low and tied the wood to the crossbeam and to a peg built into the outer wall. Standing and stretching his back, he spotted Ara walking toward them. "Evening peace."

"Evening peace, Noah." He pointed toward the door. "Is Aterre in there?"

Aterre stepped outside and greeted Ara with a nod. "I'm here. Noah's making me do all the heavy lifting."

Noah rolled his eyes. He sat on the edge of the roof, allowing his legs to dangle, and then dropped to the ground. "How are things at the shipyard?"

Ara inspected the roof, running his finger along the ends of the timbers. "They've been better."

"Is something wrong?" Noah asked.

Ara shrugged. "I guess that depends on you."

"I don't understand."

Ara looked at the roof again. "My cousin was right. You do fine work. And that's good, because, as of today, I'm in need of an apprentice."

Noah wondered if his imagination was playing tricks on him. He shot a look at Aterre. "What about Pennik?"

"That's why it was a rough day. He quit on me without any warning."

"Did he say why?"

Ara's mouth quirked in a smile, and he looked Noah in the eye. "No, but I think I can guess the reason."

"So Pennik's gone?" Noah asked, trying to hold his excitement in.

Ara nodded. "So if you're still interested in being —"

"Yes!" Noah's response came out louder than he planned. "Sorry — yes, I'd love to work for you."

"Good," Ara said. "And I appreciate the enthusiasm."

Aterre laughed. "You *sure* you don't want to continue farming at Cada's with me?"

Noah slapped Aterre's back hard enough to make him "oof," and grinned. "Not a chance."

Ara peeked inside the unfinished house, peered closely at the joints between doorposts and lintel, then turned back to the young men. "Why don't you two get cleaned up and join us for evenfeast? Whatever Nmir's making, it smells wonderful. We can discuss the terms of your apprenticeship after the meal."

CHAPTER 19

"There and back." Aterre pointed to a small ship anchored in the bay several hundred cubits down the coast.

"Do you need a head start?" Noah asked, knowing full well Aterre was faster than he was.

Aterre laughed. "Just say when."

Noah bent his knees and dipped beneath the water to acclimate himself to its coolness. He emerged from the sea and pushed his hair back. Licking the saltiness from his lips, he took a deep breath. "Ready? On three. One."

Noah plunged forward and glided under the water for a long stretch. Breaking the surface, he kicked hard and quickly settled into a steady pace. *One, two, three. Breathe. One, two, three. Breathe.* Every so often, he pulled extra hard on a stroke to lift his head up and check his trajectory. Knowing the lead from his early start would not last, he focused on keeping a rhythm.

As he reached the boat and turned for the home stretch, he spotted Aterre from the corner of his eye. Determined to hang on to his body-length lead, Noah felt a surge of energy and increased his tempo. He came up for a breath and sensed Aterre straight across from him. Kicking furiously and drawing every ounce of strength from his arms, Noah strove to keep up. But it was no use. Aterre grabbed the lead, and Noah's strength flagged.

Struggling to settle back into an easy rhythm, Noah rolled onto his back and tried to catch his breath as slow and deliberate strokes carried him back to the starting point. A splash from Aterre let him know he had made it, and he allowed his legs to sink until his feet hit the bottom.

Breathing hard, Aterre said, "I'm still faster."

"Not by much. I'm gaining on you."

"Only because you had a head start and I wasn't trying very hard." Aterre grinned.

Noah stepped closer. "Well, if you're so fast, then why can't you dodge this?" He lunged forward and locked his arm around Aterre's waist. Planting his feet, Noah lifted his friend above the water and then slammed him under it.

When Aterre pushed to break free, Noah released him and quickly stood again, wary of retaliation. When none came, he wiped his eyes and raised his arms in triumph.

Noah spun at the sound of familiar laughter from the shore, where Emzara and Adira sat giggling. He kept one arm raised in a greeting to them, but Aterre slammed into him and drove him under. The surprise attack caused him to swallow a bit of seawater, so as he staggered to his feet, Noah coughed and gasped for air.

"Now we're even," Aterre said.

"Yes, we are. Truce?"

Aterre nodded and then flashed a sly grin. "For now."

Noah waved at Emzara, but she and Adira were talking to each other. He looked back at Aterre. "She must be here to watch the sunset."

"So when are you going tell her how you feel about her?"

"I don't know." Noah crossed his arms, pleased that their intense race had caused his muscles to look larger and more defined, at least temporarily. "It's tricky since I work for her father. What if she doesn't like me that way? Could I still work for him? And even if I could, how awkward would it be?" Noah looked back at her and sighed. "I'd love to be the one she watched sunsets with."

Aterre laughed. "You're so blind. Why do you think Pennik disliked you so much? Everyone else can see that she's interested. She flirts with you all the time."

"And what if you're wrong?"

"Well, there's only one way to find out. Ask her." Aterre started for the shore. "Come on."

"Wait, you mean right now?"

Aterre looked back and shook his head. "Coward."

Trudging through the water toward the beach, their speed increased as the water shallowed. Noah checked to make sure his garment was tied tightly about his waist. The girls stood and sauntered toward them as the men reached their robes on the shore. Picking up his outer wrap, Noah quickly dressed himself.

"Evening peace," Adira said.

Noah smiled at her and then at Emzara. "Evening peace. How long have you been here?"

Emzara grinned. "Long enough to know who the faster swimmer is."

"And that would be me." Aterre used both hands to point at himself. "Were you two here to watch the sunset or to see him lose?" Aterre gestured to Noah with a nod of his head.

Emzara pursed her lips and held up a bundle of squared black objects, each about a span in length. "Actually, we went to town to pick up some new drawing sticks for my artwork and then decided to enjoy a walk on the shore."

"Yeah, it's the first time that we've had a chance to — ever since you moved here," Adira said. "But since you moved into your own place last week, we finish our chores earlier. Plus, the days are getting longer."

"Do you like your new home?" Emzara asked.

Noah brushed some sand off his robe. "It's coming together." In just three whole moons, they had constructed their small home, but there was still much to be done. "But I confess I miss the meals."

"That's not all you miss." Aterre's words were almost mumbled, and Noah hoped they weren't clear enough for Emzara to hear. Aterre looked at him and the left side of his mouth curled up.

Oh no. Please don't.

Aterre's grin spread across his face. "Zara, you know, Noah was just telling me that he wishes you'd watch the sunsets with him instead."

Fear gripped Noah, and he barely withstood the urge to pummel Aterre, who now beamed with his arms crossed. Sheepishly, Noah looked away as Adira laughed. He struggled to find the right words to extricate himself, but he only said, "I didn't say that."

"So," Adira said, "you're saying you don't want Zara to watch them with you?"

Noah felt his face warm even more. He couldn't deny it without lying, and if he answered truthfully, she would certainly know his feelings. He was stuck. His gaze dropped to the ground, and then he spotted his way out. Aterre had not finished wrapping his robe and part of it lay on the ground near his feet. Noah stepped on the end of the cloth and shoved him. When his robe caught, Aterre lost his balance and tumbled backward into the shallow water, landing on his backside with a splash.

Adira squealed in delight and then laughed along with Emzara. Satisfied that the last question was abandoned for now, Noah walked to Aterre and held out a hand to help him up.

"I deserved that." Aterre smiled and took Noah's hand. "Nicely done."

Noah nodded. "You know?" He spoke loud enough for the girls to hear. "This reminds me of how we met."

"You met in the water?" Adira asked.

Noah wanted to embarrass Aterre some more, but he remembered his promise that he wouldn't tell others about Aterre's past, particularly his shady activities while on the run. "Something like that. It's a long story for another time."

Emzara pointed to Aterre as he rewrapped his garment, though he stopped when he realized that much of it was wet. "What's that mark on your back?"

Aterre sighed. "Another long story for another time."

"Sounds like you have a lot of stories," Adira said.

"Too many, but they're in the past." Aterre walked toward the trail that led to their house. "Looks like I need another robe."

Seizing the opportunity to avoid the potentially awkward questioning again, Noah hurried behind Aterre. He looked back briefly at Emzara. "I'll see you tomorrow."

"If you're lucky," she said.

Noah bit his lip to stop a smile from escaping. "Evening peace."

The trail wound through a patch of milknut trees and led all the way to Ara's house, but they turned off the path to go to their new home, just a few hundred cubits from the beach.

Noah followed Aterre through the door and closed it hard. He hurried to his room as Aterre strode to his. Noah changed out of his wet undergarment. With a clean and dry robe on, he rejoined Aterre, who had already changed clothes, in the tiny dining area that had yet to be furnished. Noah walked to the wall and slumped to the floor. He buried his head in his hands. "I can't believe you did that."

Aterre laughed. "Did what? Tried to help you out?"

"Help me out?" Noah held his hands out and glared at him. "You made me look like a fool in front of her."

"Calm down. You should thank me."

"Thank you?" Noah raised his voice. "If you ruined my opportunity with Emzara, I'll —"

"I didn't ruin anything. Stop overreacting." Aterre sat next to him and spoke softly. "Didn't you see her reaction?"

Noah shook his head. "I was too afraid to look."

"You really love her, don't you?"

Rolling his eyes, Noah asked, "Whatever gave you that idea?"

"Um, maybe it's the fact that when she's around you suddenly freeze up, stutter, and act like a little boy."

"It's that bad?"

"Worse than Jerah with Pivi." Aterre chuckled. "No, not that bad, but you do change. You just need to be yourself around her."

"I try, but can't help it. She makes me so nervous."

"That's because you're trying too hard, but you don't need to. She already likes you."

Noah ran his fingers through his hair. "Why do you keep saying that? And since when are you an expert on women?"

"I didn't know there was such a thing." Aterre stood and gazed out the window. "When you were too scared to look at her, she was smiling wider than I'd ever seen before. And that's saying a lot, because she always smiles when you're around."

"Probably because she thinks I'm a fool."

Aterre shrugged. "Could be, but I doubt it." He lowered his voice. "Speaking of Zara."

"What about her?"

Aterre put his finger to his lips and shushed him. Then he gestured to the front of the house.

After a long pause, three soft knocks patted the door. "Noah?"

"Just a moment." Noah jumped up.

Aterre grabbed his arm and stopped him. "Take a deep breath. Act natural."

He closed his eyes and inhaled slowly and let it out. *Don't make a fool of yourself, Noah.* Taking another deep breath, he opened the door. Emzara stood with her arms in front of her carrying a small covered basket. Her outfit perfectly complemented her lithe figure. The bottom of her robe ended just above her ankles, which were wound about by the leather straps of her sandals. Her hair, no longer pulled back and tied behind her head as it had been at the beach, draped over her shoulders. A stray lock hung down the left side of her face. Standing in the doorway in the fading daylight, she had never looked so breathtaking. "Emzara. I didn't expect to see you again tonight."

Holding up the basket, she smiled and her eyes sparkled. "You said you missed our cooking, so I brought you some leftovers from tonight."

"I'll take that." Aterre stepped between them and grabbed the basket. "Thanks, Zara."

"You're welcome. Just be sure to share it with Noah."

"I won't," Aterre said over his shoulder.

"He probably won't." Noah wracked his brain for something worthwhile to say during the long pause that followed. Emzara looked expectantly at him, adding to his mounting frustration. *Just say something. Tell her she looks nice.* "You —"

"Adira already left for home. Did you want to watch the sunset with me? There's still time."

Noah fought to control his excitement; he did not want to overreact. "Sure, I'd be happy to." His heart racing, he stepped outside and closed the door.

Emzara led him up a small hill between the shipyard and the beach. "It looks better up here," she said. "The edge of the harbor doesn't block the view."

"Is this where you'd normally watch it?"

"Most of the time. Although, I think it'd be better on Superglider Cliff." She pointed to the edge of the coastline. "That's what we call it."

"Have you seen a superglider up close?"

"Not yet, but I'd love to. I want to draw one for my collection."

"You're a very talented artist. Other than technical drawings, I can't draw anything. But the Creator gave me the ability to make things out of wood."

"That's what my father says." Emzara pushed aside a low branch and allowed him to pass by. "He said that you do a great job. Do you like working for him?"

"I do. It's hard work, but when you love what you're doing, it's not really toilsome."

"That's what I think about art. I love watching the animals and drawing them. It takes time, but it's so rewarding." She pointed to the grassy outcrop ahead. "That's it."

After allowing her to pick out her spot, Noah sat about a cubit away. He stretched his legs in front of him and leaned back on his hands, approximating her pose. The bay extended to the south, opening into the Great Sea. To the southwest, the sun hung just above the horizon, and immediately to its left, Superglider Cliff climbed above the edge of the water. The boat that he and Aterre had raced to lay in the water ahead of them.

"It's perfect." Noah said.

A slight breeze blew her hair across her face. She closed her eyes and breathed in. "It sure is."

Noah watched her. It seemed impossible, yet she grew more beautiful each time he saw her.

With her eyes still closed, she asked, "So did you say that earlier?"

"Say what?" Noah asked, hoping she was not referring to Aterre's embarrassing revelation.

She turned, fixed her gaze on him, and her lips curved slightly. "That you wished I would watch the sunset with you instead."

Her dark eyes drew him in and he couldn't pull away. Not that he wanted to. A spark of courage flashed inside of him. *Maybe Aterre's right. Maybe she really is interested in me.* "Those weren't my exact words." The spark grew into a flame that filled his body, and in his mind, he crossed the point of no return. He would never get a better chance. He held her gaze. "I think I said that I'd love to be the one you watched sunsets with."

Her lips spread into a wide smile and her eyes danced. "I was hoping you'd say that." She moved her left hand and placed it on top of his.

Every fiber of his being sprang to life, and his whole body tingled at her touch. He turned his hand over and allowed her fingers to cross between his. Feeling as though he would burst from emotion if he continued looking at her, he turned his attention to the setting sun along with the bands of orange and pink that stretched across the southwestern sky.

Moments later, Emzara scooted closer and leaned her head against his shoulder.

For a while, neither of them spoke. Words were not needed for the moment.

When the sun was almost gone, Emzara tilted her head up at him. "You're right. It is perfect here."

Noah glanced down and their eyes met briefly. "It is now."

"Sadly, I need to get home before it gets too dark or my father will be upset."

"I understand." He stood and helped Emzara to her feet.

Hand in hand, they walked down the hill and too soon they were back at the trail between Ara's house and the beach. Noah walked her most of the way back to her home.

"Would you like to do this again tomorrow night?" he asked.

"Definitely." Nodding, she pulled away slowly. "I'll see you at work in the morning."

"I can't wait."

She smiled and then turned, humming a tune as she went to the front door.

Noah walked back to his home with a lively bounce to his step. He forced himself to stop smiling and then went inside. He spotted Aterre at the counter scraping the last bit of salad out of Emzara's bowl.

He held up the empty dish. "I'm really sorry. I ate everything. It was too good."

Feigning anger, Noah crossed the floor and stood before Aterre, glaring at him. When he could no longer suppress his joy, he reached out and hugged Aterre tight. "Thank you!"

Aterre laughed and pushed himself free. "I guess that stupid grin on your face means I was right."

"For the first time, I'm glad you were right and I was wrong." Noah turned and put his hands on his head. "This is the best night ever."

CHAPTER 20

A whole day together." Emzara shifted her hand within Noah's warm grasp and leaned slightly against him, enjoying the feel of his strong presence. "I'm so excited."

Noah regarded her and a thrill coursed through him. He squeezed her fingers gently. "I've been looking forward to spending this much time with you."

She grinned. "Me too." She hung on to those words, making both of them a few syllables long. "So what's the adventure for today?" She pointed at the full satchel that hung from Noah's shoulder.

"Well —" Noah paused.

"Tell me." Her eyes begged him as she rocked on her toes.

"I thought that since we have the time we should finally check out Superglider Cliff instead of just talking about it." He held up the leather bag. "This is in case we get hungry."

"Oh, how fun! We've never crossed the river for an outing before. Do you know the way?"

"Aterre's been there before. He said it's not far from Cada's farm. I think we can find it. We have to go through your father's land, and then past all the fruit trees."

Emzara swung their joined hands and skipped a little in her excitement.

"Did you hear what happened to Fen at work two days ago?" Noah asked as they left the grassy knolls beyond the river and entered a lush tropical forest.

"No. Tell me."

"After midmeal, Bakur sneaked away and retied Fen's nuzzler in a hidden spot. And since Fen lives far away from the shipyard he certainly didn't want to walk home."

"Yeah. What happened?" Her eyes sparkled in merriment at the joke.

"After work, of course he couldn't find her. He went to the market-place, thinking his wife had taken the animal to load up supplies, but he came back just before dark, concerned that neither his wife nor the nuzzler were at the market."

"Just before dark? What were you still doing at the shipyard?"

"Bakur and I were finishing up the stern."

"You're really getting the hang of things, aren't you?" she asked.

"I love it. Time seems to whisk by whenever I'm working." He looked at her as he had so often, and Emzara instinctively knew he was telling her she was beautiful. "And whenever I'm with you."

A warm feeling spread over her and she spoke softly. "These moments go by too fast, but when I'm with you, there's no other place I'd rather be."

They were silent for a while, connecting with each other in spirit. As they picked their way through the uneven terrain, sounds of exotic birds and occasional flashes of brightly colored feathers added to their enjoyment. Soon the ground veered upward as they approached the rear of the cliffs.

"Ready for a bit of a climb?" Noah asked.

"Absolutely. Mind telling me the rest of what happened to Fen?" Following his lead, she started up the steep incline of the hillside.

"Oh, so he traveled all the way home, ready to give his wife a piece of his mind, only to discover that she didn't have the nuzzler either. When he arrived at the shipyard yesterday, his animal was right where he usually ties her."

Emzara laughed in delight.

"Fen eventually saw the humor in it, and Bakur was thrilled — for him, anyway. He even cracked a smile. However, I know that Fen is planning a way to pay him back. Bakur's going to have to watch out."

She laughed again, picturing the exchange between the two men that were like family to her. "Good thing they never did something like that to Pennik. He had an even longer travel each day than Fen does. And not nearly as good a sense of humor."

Noah tilted his head and gave her a questioning look. "Whatever happened to him? Don't get me wrong, I'm glad he's gone."

She sighed. "He always assumed that I was interested in him. And I guess I was a little at first, but it didn't take long to see that he thought too highly of himself. Once you came along, I think he felt threatened."

"By me?" Noah smirked. "He could have crushed me."

"I'm not so sure about that." Emzara squeezed his upper arm. "He could tell that I was interested in someone else. In fact, I think everyone knew, except for you."

Noah kissed her hand. "Well, I know now. So what happened with Pennik?"

"He heard me talking to Baba about you one morning, so he came to my office around midmeal. He told me flat out that I needed to stop talking about you because I was supposed to be with him."

"I'm glad you didn't agree."

Emzara threw her hair back. "Me too. I told him that I wouldn't marry him, and he stormed away. That was the last time I saw him."

Noah paused before speaking. "So I should thank you for my apprenticeship then?"

"I can't really take credit. I was annoyed with Pennik at the time, but it wasn't my intention to hurt him. And I didn't expect him to quit."

Noah smiled to himself. His frustrating start in Iri Geshem had been well worth the trouble. "Be careful of that step there." Noah pointed to a rocky area. She gathered up the hem of her dress and readjusted it, giving her knees freedom to make the climb up the hill. Noah reached his arm out to help her navigate and she grabbed it with her free hand, letting him pull her up. He pulled her close, steadying her, and she fell easily into his embrace. "Maybe we don't need to go any farther." His words were only partly in jest.

"No way. I'm enjoying this adventure. No complaints from me." After a pause she softened her tone, "Although, I'm quite fond of being in your arms right here."

He tightened his hold before letting go. "I think I can force myself to release you just long enough to make it to the top."

She smiled, marveling that someone could come to mean so much to her in so short a time. Every time she saw him, her heart danced in pure joy, and she imagined that her existence before his arrival was simply that.

Existence. With Noah near, she felt more alive than ever before, and did not want to know life without him again.

She had been nervous to invite him to watch the sunset with her for the first time, hoping that Aterre was not playing a cruel joke. But on the whole walk home from the beach that evening, she'd contemplated all the little moments between them, replaying each to get a better understanding of what they meant. What did it mean when he rapped a pattern on the doorway every time he had to pass by the building she worked in? Was that his way of flirting with her, or was he simply saying hello? And what about the time he offered to help her pull a splinter from her small hand and held it in his? Or the time when his foot tapped against hers and he didn't move it away during the rest of midmeal? Was he even aware that that had happened?

After thinking things through, she decided that maybe they added up to more than just random occurrences. Asking him to watch a sunset wouldn't be too much — if he said no, or if things didn't go well, it wouldn't make life around him awkward for too long. She could shrug it off and walk away as if she was used to randomly inviting people to watch sunsets with her. Emzara smiled to herself in the afternoon sunlight, glad she had taken that small, uncertain step.

Since then, seldom did a day go by where they did not have some time together, even if it was only a quick conversation at the shipyard. The more they talked, the more she pieced together an understanding of him. And the more this happened, the more she valued him. Notwithstanding his dark, handsome features, or his strong physique, she found herself also attracted to his way of thinking, to his sureness in decisions, and to the pride he always took in his work. She liked the strength he displayed while building, but more importantly the strength of his faith in the Creator. With him around, she felt both at peace as well as strangely astir. Somehow, in his presence as she was today, she just felt complete.

"Here we are." Noah shouldered the satchel before helping her up the last step.

She looked at the expanse of grassy plain, broken only by a smattering of large rocks here and there. To their left in the distance, one of the cliffs jutted high overhead, and from it gushed a sparkling waterfall that crashed into a large pool. Another cascade fell to the sea from the opposite side of the pond. "It's breathtaking up here."

151

"Yes, you are." The edge of Noah's lips twitched upward.

Her cheeks warmed, and she pulled his hand toward her lips and kissed it. "I said this place is breathtaking."

"I wasn't disagreeing with you."

"Come on, let's get a closer look." She tugged at his hand, and together they ran to the pool. "Look, a rainbow!"

Noah gave her a knowing smile. "We've seen several of them together, haven't we?"

Emzara leaned her head on his shoulder and nodded, her cheek rubbing against the gathered fabric of his garment. "I like watching sunsets with you on clear days." She wrapped her arm around him. "And on the days when it's cloudy or rainy. Although I questioned your sanity a little bit the first time you invited me to see the sunset when it was pouring."

Noah laughed. "But we got both a sunset and a rainbow at the same time."

She remembered how pleasant the surprise was to them both when the dismal clouds suddenly burst apart to reveal a crimson sun along with the most brilliantly colored arc tracing its way across the sky. "Best ever. Although this is already a close second and we just got here." She settled on one of the large, smooth boulders that created the edge of the natural pool and reached up to Noah. "I'd like to draw this while we wait to see the supergliders. May I have the scroll I gave you and a drawing stick?"

Noah fumbled around the sack for a bit before handing her the two objects. He sat down next to her and inched a little closer, then scooted back, only to readjust and settle to where his knee was just a hair's distance from hers. He sighed a little. "So I had a good talk with your father last night after we closed up shop."

"Is that why he was so late to evenfeast?" She looked at him, but his gaze was on the water. He drummed his left hand fingers on the rocky surface. "What did you two discuss?"

"He told me that he's been very pleased with my work, and also my, uh, well, he said he's happy with my integrity too."

"He's told me how much he values you."

"I'm glad. I really enjoy the work. And your father is a great teacher."

"He says you're quick to pick things up and already work like you've been there for years."

152

"With all I've learned, sometimes it feels like I have been. But we didn't focus on my past last night; we talked about my future." Noah paused. "He told me that if I'm interested, within a few years he'd begin turning some of the management of the business over to me. But before that time, he'd continue to mentor and groom me."

Emzara laid down her artwork to clasp her hands together in excitement. She leaned toward him earnestly. "What did you say?"

"I told him that there's no place I'd rather be, but that I had one condition."

Suddenly feeling nervous, she glanced away. "So you might leave?"

"Well, we worked it out that I'll continue as his apprentice until he makes me his right hand man, and possibly someday, the future owner." Noah suddenly turned his gaze to her and she caught the faint hint of a smile on his lips. "But I have to work for more than five years before we can really talk more about any of that."

"Why five years? That's longer than the normal time for an apprenticeship."

"That's true, but it's the right amount of time for something else."

"What do you mean?" She shook her head, "I don't understand."

Abruptly, Noah shifted the conversation. "I have something for you here." He searched through the satchel, taking care that she couldn't see inside. "I made this." He held out a delicately carved figure of a keluk.

"My favorite." She accepted it eagerly and turned the animal over, fingering the expertly whittled ridges, when suddenly she became aware of a leather strap looped around the animal.

"What's this?" She glanced up at Noah.

"Look at it."

Slowly she unwound it from the carving and saw a little wooden disc attached in the center of the length of leather. She turned the front of the circle to face her and held it in her palm. A delicate outline of a rainbow rested on a small line of land. She blinked, not fully comprehending, when Noah gently took her hand in his and pointed to the token.

"I carved it. The land on the bottom here is from my father's symbol. But instead of having a stalk of grain coming out from it, I thought it might be nice if we had a rainbow." He clasped both of her hands in his. "Zara, you're my one condition. And you're the reason for the five years." His chest heaved and he spoke rapidly. "I care for you so much that I want you by me always. A thousand years if the Creator gives us that long." His hands trembled in hers. "I know you're not of age yet and won't be for another five years. But when that time comes — I talked to your father, but Em, I need to know if —" For the first time he paused the rush of his words and beheld her eyes. "If you want to be my wife."

"Noah," her eyes filled with tears. "I can't think of anything I'd rather be."

"So that's a yes?"

Emzara looked at him, emotions inside her swelling and feeling as if they would pound forth, just like the waterfall that surged into the pool beyond them. Angling in toward him, she rested her hand on his chest and tilted her head. "Yes."

He wrapped an arm around her and pulled her in closer. As he slowly leaned in, her heart pounded as both delight and contentment overwhelmed her.

"ARRWAK!"

The sudden piercing cry startled her, causing her to pull her lips away from his. They both jumped to their feet and looked around. Emzara's hand flew to her chest.

Noah laughed. "We have company."

Soaring above them, two supergliders nipped and squawked at each other. She had seen them flying over the bay several times, but they never ventured too close to the city. Now, up close, she staggered at the magnitude of these creatures. Whisper-thin leathery wings spread out at least five cubits to either side of their slender yet powerful bodies. The pointy beaks in front and long crests protruding from the back of their heads made them somewhat comical in appearance, but with their fierce temperaments, no one would dare tell them they looked funny.

As the pounding of her heart subsided, the humor in the moment made Emzara laugh. She watched as the two animals tumbled in the air. "Guess we did come to see them up close." She grinned and twined her fingers with his as she leaned into his body. "Think we'll ever squawk at each other like that?"

"With your spunk and my self-assurance?" He winked at her. "Perhaps."

"Noah, I —" Suddenly her heart was too full to give way to the words she wanted most to express.

"I know. Me too," he finished softly.

CHAPTER 21

Land of Havilah — Noah's 45th year

Naamah tucked her veil a little more over her face before leaving the relative safety of the tree trunk. The night was full of shadows and stars. Crossing the few paces between the edge of the forest and the clearing where the little house stood, she wished for just a few more clouds to aid in her concealment. She darted to the door and rapped lightly on the wood, huddling up against the cool mud exterior as if she might somehow be swallowed into the wall itself.

The door opened and an aged man stooped his head under the top of the frame and looked about. "Good sir. Could you help me?" Her voice was soft and held just as much of a plea as did her eyes.

"Come in. Tell me what you need," he said in slow, measured tones.

"I need your help."

"So you said." He held out a hand, pointing at the small fireplace across the single, cozily lit room. "Sit. Be warmed and at peace. And tell me what you seek."

She sat on the low, hard stool by the fire, twisting her hands in her lap before speaking, trying to figure out where to begin. "I need answers. I need to know what to do."

"Sounds like you have a story to tell. I'm here to listen. Tell me your troubles, child." His caring voice soothed her nerves and did more to comfort her than the friendly flames.

"My father is someone who's very important to the city I come from. His —"

"I know who you are, Princess of Havil, and I know who your father is." He settled into a high-backed wooden chair, its gnarled posts looking almost as if they had grown in their current position. Behind him, a glimmering figure caught her eye. A carving of the familiar Sepha tree rested on a shelf, but there was more. A golden serpent wrapped around the trunk and became entwined in some of the branches. "Don't worry, daughter of Lamech, your words will not leave this place."

How could he know me? I'm so far from home. Maybe he really can access the Creator's knowledge. Naamah loosened her covering and lowered it behind her head. "No need for pretenses then. I have your word? Our meeting is secret?"

He raised his hands and pressed them together beneath his chin and nodded. "Always."

She rubbed her arms to warm them. "Well, as I was about to say, my father's power grows each year. And each year, I'm wounded by it. I'm his only daughter and will be of age when I turn 35 next year, and yet I'm just a means to an end. In his eyes, my existence only matters because of what power he might gain through me." Her words tumbled out now as if compelled by the fears that had gripped her for so long.

"There have been about half a dozen suitors—warriors and important men—who have come, seeking his permission to take me as their wife. In most of them, I see only a hunger of temporary desire. In one of them, there lurked something monstrously sinister. Yet there was another." At the memory of him, her voice softened.

"He actually saw me for who I was and not just how I could advance his station in life. He spent just as much time with me as he did trying to win my father's favor. And yet, he, like the others was rejected. My father called me to him and said with contempt that one such as he wasn't worthy of my beauty. But I could see the greed. I could see that my father hoped for one still greater to align with.

"I'm frightened. I don't want to be mercilessly handed over to someone who cares only for himself. And yet, I long to be married. To have someone good. Someone I can love and adore. Someone I can give myself to and not fear. And that's why I've come. I've heard you can see what's ahead. Please tell me. If I go back to my father's house, what will become of me?"

The man leaned closer and looked at her, yet Naamah sensed that he was not so much seeing her, as seeing past her. He blinked rapidly, almost as if that action would bring his being back to the body that loomed before her. "Child, there's mystery surrounding you. And greatness. But I lack clarity. To learn what may be, I need some of your blood. Once blood and ground meet, only then will the voice of He who formed the ground truly cry out."

Naamah bit her lip. She had not expected this. She pulled away.

"Relax, it'll just be a tiny cut on your finger. You'll barely feel it."

She looked at her hand. *The minor pain will be nothing compared to the pain of not knowing.* She weighed her options carefully then timidly extended her hand. The seer gently held her finger steady and with his other hand, removed a small sharp blade from atop the mantle. She watched in mingled horror and fascination as he sliced a small groove in her tallest finger and then squeezed several large drops of blood, which landed decisively on the hard-packed dirt floor.

He breathed deeply, his eyelids slowly sinking. The silence seemed endless until his eyes rolled back, leaving only narrow slits of white.

"A storm brews in the north with thick, dark clouds, vexing your father. But a ray of sunshine pierces through it, lighting up your face." As he spoke, his voice rang out in confident tones. His eyes popped open — clear and intently focused.

A tingle traveled down Naamah's spine. *What did he mean? Does the storm represent a person? An army? Or simply a storm? Did any of it have to do with getting a good husband? Hmm . . . the sea lies to the north, so there isn't anyone in that direction, is there?* She stood and gathered her things, placing a strand of piks on the mantle as she did so. Puzzled as she was by his words, for the first time in a long time, she breathed freely. Absently wrapping her finger with a bandage the seer handed to her, she pondered this new feeling and realized what it was. Hope.

Chapter 22

Noah held his drink up toward Aterre, who lounged across from him in Ara's sitting room after evenfeast. "To your first harvest of Nuca's beans."

"Drink up." Aterre beckoned to them as if he were the master of a feast, joining Noah in being overdramatic.

Breathing in the aroma of the brew, Noah took a sip. The expected bitterness was largely absent, and in its place, a smooth and mellow taste enveloped his palate. He took another sip and it achieved the same result. "Outstanding."

"It's better than Nuca's." Emzara's face lit up. "It's not so strong."

Ara leaned back. "You're to be commended, Aterre. This is very good."

"How did you make it taste so different?" Noah asked.

Aterre shrugged. "I'm not sure. Maybe it's the soil here, or maybe I didn't roast them long enough. I was afraid to burn them so I didn't follow the directions perfectly."

"Well, whatever you did, this is delicious," Noah said.

Aterre set his cup down on the small table next to his chair. "Cada said that once we sell enough to cover his initial investment, he's going to split the profits with me evenly."

"Sounds like he made you a pretty good deal," Ara said before turning to face Noah. "Guess that's a good reminder to me that with patience, getting a better product is possible."

"I've been fiddling with it," Noah said. "I think I've narrowed down the problem, but I'm not any closer to a solution."

Emzara sighed. "If you two are going to talk shop, you might as well clue Aterre and me in."

"We're trying to figure out how to make bigger boats." Ara said. "We've been making the same two models for nearly 20 years, but sooner or later, someone's going to make something larger, and when they do, we'll be out of business."

"I know some of the riverboat owners would like to be able to transport more goods, but if you make them too big, will they be able to maneuver much?" Aterre asked.

"They might get stuck in the shallows," Ara said. "But we're not really talking about boats for the river."

"For the sea?" Aterre raised an eyebrow.

Emzara scooted up against Noah. "Why would you want something to cross the sea?"

Ara held up a hand. "Merchants and explorers want ships that can carry enough supplies and are strong enough to survive on the open sea. There are several cities along the coast that they could trade with. But our current boats can't handle the waves during a storm. That's why they hug the shoreline all the way, but doing so can add weeks to the trip, depending on how far one is going. So it's really not worth it."

"Is it even possible?" Aterre asked.

"Well, I'd like to find out," Ara said.

After grabbing a blanket from the open seat to her right, Emzara pulled her feet up on her chair and covered up. "What prevents you from doing it now, Baba?"

"Good question." Ara cracked his knuckles. "Do you remember when you were a little girl and one of my ships sank?"

Emzara shook her head.

"An adventurer bought a boat from me and planned on sailing all the way around the land to map it out. I warned him about taking it out in the big waves, but he didn't listen. A few weeks later, he returned to town and tried to ruin my business by telling everyone that my boats can't be trusted."

"What happened?" Aterre asked.

"He went east, trying to navigate all the way to the land of Nod, but he got too far from the shore. A storm came along and ripped the ship apart."

"He's lucky he didn't drown," Aterre rubbed his brow and blew out a breath.

"No question about that. He said he hung onto one of the boards throughout the night and swam to shore in the morning. He came back here determined to blame me for his stubbornness."

"Is he still around?" Emzara asked.

"No, he eventually left town." Ara smirked. "I think he decided to explore on land."

Aterre laughed. "Maybe he should've done that in the first place."

As Noah rubbed the back of her neck, Emzara asked her father, "You said the boat sank in the storm, but were you able to ascertain what went wrong?"

Ara shrugged. "Maybe. I tried to talk it through with the man, but he wasn't interested in working things out. Still, he said something that's stayed with me. He mentioned that the joints gave way first. Noah's agreed to help me figure out how to get past the added strain to the joints."

"What about using some sort of metal?" Emzara asked.

"I've thought of that." Ara scratched his head. "Copper isn't strong enough. It would bend too easily. Silver is too expensive and isn't strong enough either."

Aterre jolted upright. "I have an idea."

Holding up his cup, Noah said, "No, we aren't going to use your crop to make them."

"Ooh, there's a thought." Aterre smiled. "But in all seriousness, I think Emzara's right. Metal might be the answer."

"It hasn't been so far," Ara said.

"Maybe." Aterre pointed in the direction of town. "We may not have anything here that's strong enough, but in Havilah, where I grew up, they had figured out how to get another metal from rocks in the ground. They called it iron, and it's much stronger than copper."

"How much stronger?" Ara asked.

"I don't know for sure, but they make weapons out of it." Aterre looked away. "I can tell you this much, it doesn't bend like copper. It's very sturdy."

Ara stroked his beard with his thumb and index finger. "Hmm. That would require a trip to Havil, which poses a couple of problems."

"Like the time it takes to get there?" Aterre asked.

"That's one of them. We'll see at least two whole moons before completing the trip." Ara downed the last of his drink. "Although if the boats could survive the open sea, it'd be a lot faster."

"I'll go," Noah said.

Emzara squeezed his arm. "No. You can't leave for that long. We're getting married in less than a year."

Noah kissed the top of her head. "And that's why I must go. To secure the business for the future, so that I can provide for us and someday, our family."

Quiet and motionless, Emzara stared at her feet. Noah knew he would hate the separation as well, but at the same time, the thought of an adventure in Havil made his skin tingle.

"We're ahead of schedule right now, so I think I could spare you for that amount of time." Ara nodded toward Emzara, "That is, if my daughter will allow it."

"I understand it." She sighed and looked up. "But I don't have to like it."

"That's one of the problems," Noah said, eager to conquer any obstacle. "What's the other one?"

"This is a matter that needs to be brought to the town council," Ara said.

"Why?" Aterre asked.

"Because we don't have any official trade agreement with the land of Havilah, right Baba?"

"And I'm not sure our council will want to start one," Ara said.

Noah furrowed his brow. "Really?"

"There are rumors that the major city, Havil, has grown quite wicked. The elders don't want any of that influence here."

Emzara sat up and smiled. "Well, I guess you aren't going anywhere then."

Ara held up his palm. "Hold on. Noah and I will go to the next council meeting." He glanced up and used his fingers to count days. "I believe it'll be in eight days." He pointed to Noah. "If they're open to the idea, then you can go. They'd probably want to send a representative with you. And you'd need someone to help with the boat." He turned and looked at Aterre.

Aterre nodded. "I'd do it, but I'll have to check with Cada. The harvest is almost over, so he may let me once that is finished, as long as I'm back before the planting season."

"It's settled then. If the council approves, you two will leave for Havil to see if we can procure some iron."

Emzara grabbed Noah's hand with both of hers. "And what if I could persuade Noah not to go?" The tone of her voice made it clear she was only partly serious.

Ara laughed. "Then I could just order him to go. I am his boss, after all."

"You don't play fair." Emzara folded her arms across her chest, but the tiniest smile escaped her lips.

Noah's feelings were mixed too. Leaving Emzara for so long seemed unbearable, especially after they had seen each other nearly every day for the past five years. He placed a hand on her shoulder. "Before we make any decisions, we need to ask the Creator for clear directions in these matters." He looked over at Ara. "If the Most High wants me to go, then there's no use fighting it." He turned back to Emzara. "But if He wants me to stay, then I'll certainly not object."

Emzara kissed his hand that she still held tightly. "That is a plan I can't argue with."

Ara stood and held out his arms. "Then let us pray."

Chapter 23

Their long morning shadows kept stride ahead of them as Noah and Ara strolled through Iri Geshem's downtown. Two-story shops — many with residences on the top floor — lined the outside of the rectangular district. In the center of town, a small fountain featured a stone sculpture of a sea creature with a hole on the top of its head, which perpetually sprayed water a few cubits in all directions. Powered by an underground spring, the fountain produced the pleasant ambience of a light rainfall. The sunlight passing through the mist created a small color band. On the far end of the street, the recently completed three-story administrative building rose above the rest. Five stone steps led up to a large entryway highlighted by two wooden pillars stretching from the floor to the overhanging flat roof.

"Is this what Iri Sana looks like?" Ara asked.

Noah chuckled. "Not unless it's had some major renovations in the past five years. There's only a main street with about 20 small homes and shops. It looks much older than Iri Geshem."

"How far out of town is your family farm?"

"It's south, right on the Hiddekel, not too far."

"I see." Ara gestured to the large council building looming in front of them. "Zain told me the council was quite appreciative of your assistance with carving the pillars. They look very nice."

"Let's hope they'll remember that as they consider our request this morning." Noah draped the excess of his formal robe over his left arm.

163

They climbed the steps, and Ara stopped to examine Noah's handiwork on the wooden pillar to their left. Chiseled filigree designs wrapped around the town's name on the massive pole. "Emz described this to me, but it's better than I imagined. You definitely have a gift."

"She helped me figure out the design. She's quite an artist."

Ara nodded, still admiring the woodwork. "She's an exceptional young woman and deserves an equally amazing man." His eyes measured Noah, and then he shrugged and smiled. "But I guess you'll do."

Noah laughed then became serious. "I may not be her equal, but I love your daughter more than life itself."

"I know. So do I." Ara placed a hand on Noah's shoulder before stepping toward the entrance. "Come on, let's find out what the council thinks of our proposal."

Inside the new town hall, stairways along the left and right walls of the foyer wound to the second and third floors. The small, polished white and gray stones which comprised the flooring recreated the designs in the pillars. Ahead, a wide double-door led to the main hall. Ara opened it and allowed Noah to proceed into the back of the main room.

Four long benches lined either side of the space, and only one of them was occupied. An elderly man sat in the second row. *It's nice to live in a town blessed by the Creator where troubles are so rare.*

In the front, on a raised platform, five men sat behind a long curved desk. Noah recognized them all, but had only met three of the men, including Zain, who sat to the right of the center position. Zain had visited Ara's house and shipyard several times, and Noah appreciated his straightforward manner.

An old woman stood near a podium on the left, listening. Ara stopped short of the first row of benches and Noah stood behind him.

"Yes, you and your husband will still be able to access the well near the tanner's place when the improvements are made." Akel, the chairperson, who sat in the middle, held out an arm toward the woman. "In fact, it'll be even easier for you to get there. Did you have any other matters to raise today?"

"No. That's all. Thank you." The woman slowly turned, and using a walking stick, made her way back to her husband. She tapped his leg with her cane. "Let's go home, dear."

He stirred and then struggled to his feet. "What did they say about the well?"

Noah turned his attention to the matter at hand as Ara walked up to the podium and gripped the edges of its flat top. "Morning peace, honored councilmembers." Noah stepped to his side.

Akel smiled. "Welcome, Ara. It's good to see you."

"Likewise. I believe you know my apprentice, Noah."

"Indeed, he did great work on this building." Akel grunted as he shifted his seven-hundred-year-old body in his seat. He had been on the council for over two hundred years and, according to Ara, he had gladly stepped aside for the required amount of time every decade. His wisdom helped guide Iri Geshem in peace and prosperity. Most importantly, his insistence on following the Creator's ways had made the city safe, and every citizen was encouraged to worship the Most High. "And if I'm not mistaken, he's not far from becoming your son-in-law."

Noah couldn't hold back a smile at the thought of Emzara being his bride.

"That's true," Ara said.

"Well, what business do you have with us today?" Akel asked.

Ara paused and looked at each member. "We seek your permission to travel to the land of Havilah following the harvest."

Akel drew back and furrowed his brow. "Why would you need the council's approval to travel to Havilah? You're free to come and go as you please. Although, I didn't expect that you would want to travel so far."

"It's true, I don't intend to go. But my apprentice has offered to lead the trip."

"I see." Akel extended his arm with his palm up. "And that brings us back to my question. Why do you feel the need to ask for permission?"

Ara stood up straight. "We've recently learned that the people there have a technique to work with a metal much stronger than copper."

Akel raised his eyebrows. "Surely, that could be of great benefit to us in many ways. But what interest do you have in such an innovation?"

"I'd like to try building a larger ship. One that carries more cargo up and down the river, and if it works, one that could maybe even survive the open sea."

"You're aware of our desire not to open up trade with Havil?" the man on the far left asked. Having met him only once, Noah could not recall his name, but he was the only one on the council who lacked facial hair. "They do not honor the Creator."

"Yes. Hence my reason for coming today. I seek the council's wisdom on this matter." Ara pursed his lips. "Would it be a violation of the council's desire if we acquire this knowledge from these people?"

Several moments passed as the councilmembers spoke quietly, yet animatedly, amongst themselves. Akel listened. Zain pointed to himself and spoke more than the rest. Ashur, the youngest member, sat on the end next to Zain and said very little. Akel held out his palms when he talked and the others sat silently.

"Thank you for your patience with us," Akel finally said. "You've raised an interesting question. While we still don't desire an official alliance with Havil, your proposed endeavor doesn't violate our policy. Therefore, we'll not forbid your apprentice from making the trip. We do have one request we'd like you to observe, however."

"Of course," Ara said. "Name it."

Akel gestured to Zain, who cleared his throat. "I offer my assistance on this venture as a representative of Iri Geshem."

"I'm sure we'd be happy to oblige." Ara turned to Noah. "Isn't that right?"

"You'd be most welcome." Noah bit his lower lip and looked at the ceiling. Something was amiss, but he couldn't put his finger on it.

"You have some reservations?" Akel asked.

Noah hesitated briefly and the issue became clear. "Just one, sir. I have no problem with Zain coming with us. I'd enjoy his company. But if he joins us as an official representative of the city, would that not give the Havilites the impression that we seek to establish official ties with them?"

Akel lifted his head in understanding. "Ara, your apprentice has some wisdom beyond his years. Indeed, it could be seen that way."

"Then it's not worth the risk," the beardless man said.

"There's an easy solution." Akel looked at Zain. "You're a merchant, so you can go in that capacity. You'll be our eyes and ears, but the people of Havil don't need to know that you're an official representative of our city."

"If it pleases the council." Ashur glanced at the other men before he focused on Noah. "And if you'd permit it, I'd also like to make this journey." He pointed to himself. "I'm curious to know how inns and dining halls operate in other places to see if I can gain any insights about my own business. While I do have a private interest here, I may be able to acquire knowledge that can benefit our city. Of course, I'd also go as my own agent instead of an official representative."

Akel scratched the side of his head, where his thinning white hair was thickest. "And you'd submit to Zain's leadership?"

"Certainly."

"Do you have any qualms about this arrangement, Noah?" Akel asked.

After meeting Ashur a few times, Noah found him to be affable enough. "As long as these men are willing to help with the various tasks on the boat, then I welcome their company."

Akel fixed his gaze on Ara. "Are these arrangements acceptable to you?"

Ara studied Noah for a moment. "Yes sir. Your conditions are acceptable."

"Good, it's decided," Akel said. "After the harvest, Zain and Ashur will travel with Noah's crew to the land of Havilah to find out how they make stronger metals. Did you have any other business with the council this morning?"

"Actually, I have one more question about the previous matter." Ara spoke up. "If the people of the land require some form of payment in exchange for the knowledge we seek, would it be a violation of policy for Noah to offer fair compensation for their services?"

Akel glanced at his colleagues, but no one spoke and a few shook their heads. "As long as he uses your resources and makes it clear that he is acting on your behalf instead of the city's, then there will be no infringement."

Ara nodded. "That's all. Thank you for your time and guidance."

"Thank you, sirs," Noah said. "I'd ask that Zain and Ashur would visit the shipyard sometime soon so that we can finalize plans and prepare for the voyage."

"We'll certainly do that," Zain said.

"This concludes our matter today," Akel said. "May the Creator guide your path, Noah. Thank you for seeking our counsel on these matters, Ara."

167

Ara and Noah bowed slightly to the council, left the hall, and walked through the foyer before either of them spoke. Once outside, Noah said, "That went better than I anticipated."

"It did. Yet two things concern me."

"Two things?"

"Yes." Ara spoke softly. "Something about Ashur's request troubled me. I don't know what it is, but please keep a close eye on him. I don't wish to speak ill or imply something unbecoming of one of our town's leaders, but be on your guard."

"I will," Noah said. "What's the second one?"

Ara grinned. "I wonder if I'll still have an apprentice after you tell my daughter that you're really leaving for so long."

Noah smiled again at the thought of Emzara and chuckled. "Guess there's only one way to find out."

CHAPTER 24

The gentle, steady rocking of the boat nearly lulled Noah to sleep as he leaned against the side of the cabin. The sail just behind and above his head stretched tight in the strong, warm breeze. To his left, the coast lay in the distance beneath the late afternoon sun. To ensure their safety if a storm rose up, they remained within eyesight of the shoreline, yet not close enough to risk running aground.

Stretching far beyond his sight in the direction of Iri Geshem, the undulating water sparkled, but the scenery had long since lost its appeal in the tedium of the voyage.

Noah yearned to see Emzara again, to talk to her and hear her laugh, and to feel the warmth of her embrace. *Creator, please comfort Em during this time and keep her from harm. I give You praise for the safe travel afforded us so far and ask that You'd continue to watch over us and show us favor.*

Raucous laughter shook Noah from his contemplation. He turned to see the others laughing at Zain, who playfully tossed his game pieces into the middle of the group. Zain pointed at Aterre. "You got lucky this time."

Aterre smirked. "I think four games in a row is skill, not luck."

"I'll beat you one of these times, but not now." Zain shook his head. "That's enough for me."

"You're quitting?" Ashur asked.

"I don't need any more humiliation today."

Ashur held up both palms. "Come on. Just one more round."

Farna reached for the pieces to set up the next game and glanced at Ashur. "You just don't want us to gang up on you next."

169

Thankful for Ara's direction in hiring Farna to captain the voyage, Noah looked around at his crewmates. Farna's men were handling his usual river run in his absence, and Noah had come to appreciate the depth of the man's expertise in every aspect of sailing. Before setting out, Noah had been confident that he could captain the voyage himself, but after less than a day on board, he had discovered just how far in over his head he would have been. Humbled, he had set out to learn everything he could about sailing in open water, and Farna had readily accepted his role as teacher, even showing Noah how to use the stars to navigate.

With five people on board, the small ship felt nearly full, although they still had plenty of room below deck. Originally designed for a three-man crew and cargo, this particular model had undergone renovations before the voyage. Noah had expanded the small cabin to accommodate another double bunk, which had cut down on deck space, but simultaneously created more storage space above the sleeping quarters.

Zain joined Noah near the mast. "Still missing her?"

Noah nodded. "Sorry if I'm not much fun to be around."

"You're doing fine. I remember my first few solo trips after being married." He crossed his arms and leaned against the mast, a nostalgic smile creasing his face. "I was a wreck. I couldn't concentrate on my work because I missed Kmani so much. It got better as the decades passed. Now, although I love her more than ever and I still miss her, being away isn't as difficult as it used to be."

"I'm glad to hear it gets better." Noah sighed and stretched his arms above his head. Anxious to change the subject he asked, "Have you always lived in Iri Geshem?"

"We both grew up in a small town east of the city — about a four-day journey. After we married, I wanted to find a more strategic place for my little textile business. At the time, Iri Geshem was barely bigger than my hometown, but I knew it could become so much more. It's in a perfect location, right on the sea and at the mouth of a major river. So we packed up and moved there." He shrugged. "It was difficult for a while. I spent much of the daytime farming and made clothes at night, with Kmani's help, of course."

"Your business does very well now," Noah said.

"The Creator's been good to us." Zain rubbed his eyes. "Everything changed when Ara moved to town. Back then, his property was just a small farm. I still remember when I first heard about this newcomer building a boat by the sea. I wanted to meet him to see if he was crazy or if he could really do it. I knew if the rumors were true, we could buy and sell goods from all over the place. And there he was, this young man all by himself, building a craft about half this size."

Noah stomped his foot on the ship's deck. "Obviously, he wasn't crazy."

"No, he knew what he was doing. Emzara's mother, Biremza, invited me to stay for evenfeast, which I happily accepted." Zain pursed his lips and looked away. "You would've liked her. Emzara reminds me of her so much. She loved the Creator and was such a sweet woman. She became my wife's best friend and we spent a lot of time with them. It was such a tragedy to lose her."

"I wish I could have met her." Noah paused as the painful memory spread across Zain's face. Although he enjoyed hearing about Emzara's mother, he could see how difficult it was for Zain. "So did that first boat float?"

Zain raised his eyebrows. "It did. It tilted a little, but he compensated by putting more weight on the other side." He chuckled. "It wasn't much more than a rowboat, and it wasn't long before it started springing leaks. But he learned from his mistakes and soon drew up plans for a larger one that would actually carry cargo. By then, I believed in him, so I helped finance the business. Best investment I ever made."

"So that second model worked?"

"It floated perfectly, but it didn't have any means of propulsion. And it was too big to row, so it just sat on the shore for about a year." Zain tapped the bottom of the sail. "That's when he added a sail for propulsion and a rudder for steering. Before long he was making boats to run the river or the coast. Of course, they were still small and couldn't carry much."

Noah gestured to the deck under their feet. "When did he start making them this size?"

"If I remember correctly, it was shortly before Emzara was born." Zain pointed to the three men playing their game. "Farna was actually the first person to buy one."

"Really? No wonder Ara told me they go way back."

"Whoa!" Ashur suddenly jumped to his feet and pointed past the front of the boat. "Look at that."

The other men stood and Noah and Zain quickly joined them. Noah could not believe his eyes. Several hundred cubits ahead, an enormous splash of water shot high into the air, the only remaining visible marker of the thing that caused it.

"What was that?" Zain asked.

"A sea monster jumped out of the water." Ashur's eyes remained wide open. "Did anyone else see it?"

Noah shook his head "Just the splash."

Farna flashed a mischievous grin. "You boys better find something to hang on to right now."

No sooner had Noah grabbed the mast than the first wave slammed into the boat, causing boards to creak while the ship lurched sideways. Water sprayed over the port side, dousing him and the others. He tightened his grip and steadied himself for another surging blast. His short-lived wait ended as a second and then third wave crashed against the hull.

While Noah held on for dear life, Farna taunted the sea, laughing uproariously between shouts of, "Is that all you've got?" and "Send another one!"

As the surf returned to normal, Noah loosened his grip and looked at each of his shipmates, who all stared at Farna.

"You're crazy," Ashur said.

"You didn't think that was fun?" Farna asked.

Ashur shook his head side to side and then shrugged. "Well, maybe a little."

Noah quickly surveyed the rest of the ship. The top two crates above their sleeping quarters had shaken loose. After rapidly ascending the ladder on the right side of the cabin, Noah grabbed the nearest loose box at his head level and strained to slide it into position.

"Thanks, Noah," Farna said. "Be sure to tie them down tight. Aterre, lower the sail so that we don't drive right into that beast."

"Got it," Aterre said.

"There's another one!" Zain pointed ahead and to their left.

Noah traced the trajectory of Zain's finger. His eyes grew wide while his jaw dropped. A creature twice the length of their boat launched most of its massive body out of the water, then twisted in the air and crashed back into the surf. As it slammed into the sea, a gigantic spray shot up,

172

followed by the thunderous sound of the splash. Noah looked around to brace himself before the first wave hit, but nothing on top of the cabin offered any promise of safety.

Gripping the tie-down rope, he looked at the approaching swell. *I think I can reach the mast.* Just then the boat pitched forward and Noah staggered, his grip on the rope the only anchor keeping him from falling to the deck. The hull creaked and the whole ship reeled sideways. Everything seemed to slow as Noah spotted the source of the upheaval from the corner of his eye. His heart leapt into his throat when he realized one of the sea monsters was under the boat. He turned to renew his grip when another jolt shot the heavy box toward him. All of the air in his lungs instantly discharged as the crate hurtled into his chest, and he flew backward through the air. He tried desperately to reach for anything to stop his impending appointment with the deep, but his arms disobeyed his thoughts. Before hitting the water, intense pain from the crushing blow to his ribcage finally registered. He opened his mouth to yell, but no sound escaped.

Terror seized Noah as he plunged into the water. His arms still failed to respond, and the pain in his chest nearly caused him to pass out. Emzara's face raced through his mind, but imagination was instantly replaced by the reality of a long, scaly tail sweeping past him. Noah's kicks were too weak to propel him upward, and the fear of drowning or becoming a small meal for the sea monster gripped him. His mind flashed back to Emzara and then his family. *Creator, please —*

As his consciousness began to fade, he felt himself being yanked upward by a powerful arm wrapped across his chest. Light filtered through his eyelids as his head breached the surface. He begged for air, but his breaths were limited to short gasps.

"I got you, Noah. Stay with me."

Still fighting to inhale, Noah rolled his head back on the water and saw Zain's face next to his. The pain in his chest radiated through his body.

A nearby splash caught his attention, but his tension eased at the sight of Aterre's head and shoulders emerging from the sea. While Zain shifted to one side, Aterre grabbed Noah's other shoulder, and together the friends raised Noah's torso. Already the buoyancy kept him better afloat in his new position, "Just breathe, Noah. We've got you."

As they moved him toward the boat, Noah's gasps brought in a little more air. With the side of the hull looming overhead, Aterre and Zain lifted his arms up to where Farna and Ashur could grab them and lift him aboard. They pulled him onto the deck and he rolled to his stomach, coughing and pleading for his lungs to fill.

Several moments passed before he inhaled anywhere close to normal. Coughing yet again, Noah felt like he had swallowed the contents of the entire sea. Each breath came with a price as the agony emanating from his ribs nearly caused him to wretch. Slowly, he rolled to his back and all four of his friends stared down at him.

"Are you okay?" Zain asked.

Noah nodded weakly.

Ashur looked concerned. "Zain got to you just in time."

"Now you've got a story to tell the grandkids someday." Farna mussed Noah's hair and winked. "Welcome aboard. I think I'll give you the rest of the day off."

Noah thought about giving a short laugh, but his ribs reminded him it would be a bad idea. Tears filled his eyes. Not knowing if his voice would work again, Noah glanced at each of them and mouthed, "Thank you."

"Ashur, get that sail up," Farna said. "Let's get out of here as soon as we can. Zain, give me a hand with those boxes."

Aterre put his hand on Noah's arm. "I thought we'd lost you. Emzara would've killed me if I came back without you."

Hearing her name brought a smile to his face and he closed his eyes. *Thank You, Creator*. After several more breaths, Noah struggled to a sitting position with Aterre's help.

"Whenever you're ready, I'll help you to your bunk."

CHAPTER 25

Havil — Noah's 45th year

S o big." Noah put his hand on his head, wincing ever so slightly as the bruising in his chest from a week earlier reminded him to move slowly.

"The city or that building?" Aterre asked.

"Both. I've never seen anything like it."

Farna whistled. "It's grander than I imagined, and I've heard all kinds of stories."

The city of Havil spread before them as the boat sped toward the shore. Still at least a thousand cubits away, the enormity of the place dominated the view. Buildings stretched far down both sides of the coast, but all were dwarfed by a massive stone edifice resting on a hill behind the city.

"What is that place?" Noah asked.

Zain shook his head. "I'd guess it's some sort of administrative building, but it's at least five times the size of our new hall. What else could it be?"

Ashur squeezed his hands together. "Looks like we came to the right place to learn some business tips."

"Just remember, we are not officially representing Iri Geshem," Zain said. "In fact, do your best to avoid mentioning where we're from."

"Understood," Ashur said.

"I think we're going to create a scene." Farna swept his arm in front of him. "There aren't any larger boats out here at all. Just a few solo rigs."

"You would think a city of this size would have some," Zain said. "Maybe Ara is the only one who knows how to make boats like this."

Farna nodded. "We'll need to be extra careful. I'll stay with the ship while you all head into town. Aterre, grab one of the poles and make sure we aren't going to run aground too soon. Ashur, get ready to lower the sail at my word."

Zain picked up his bag and slung it over his shoulder. "Noah and I will seek out a metalworker. Ashur, you and Aterre check out some inns. Learn what you can, and we'll meet back at the boat before sundown."

"Got it," Ashur said.

Farna raised his arm and then swung it down sharply. "Now."

Ashur dropped the sail, and the boat coasted easily toward the shore. A small group of people gathered on a dock, pointing and staring in their direction. Tied to the side of the dock, a narrow vessel bobbed. The waves grew larger as they reached the shallows, and Noah heard them breaking and slapping against the hull.

Farna, manning the rudder, steered them closer to the pier. "Aterre, slow us down. Zain, ask them for permission to dock. If they let us, then you can get off there, and I'll take the boat out and anchor in deeper water for the day."

Aterre jabbed his pole into the water and strained to stop the craft. He pulled it out and thrust it back into the sea, holding them steady and turning them perpendicular to the dock roughly ten cubits away.

Zain stepped up to the bow and cleared his throat. "Peace to you. We are merchants and have come from far away. Is this the city of Havil?"

A young man in a green-hemmed robe stepped forward. "It is. Where are you from?"

"Far to the north," Zain said. "May four of us unload here?"

Confused, the man looked at his fellows and then shrugged. "What's your business here?"

"As I mentioned, we are merchants. We are interested in seeing what your city has to offer." Zain gestured to Noah. "He and I are interested in metalworking while these other two men would like to visit your eateries and an inn. May we dock?"

"I suppose. We don't have any laws against visitors — we've just never had them come from the sea before."

"Thank you, sir."

Aterre and Farna brought the boat up softly against the pier. Noah looped a rope around a post at the end of the dock, and then walked across the deck and gingerly picked up his pack. "Time for another adventure."

Aterre set his pole on the deck and grabbed his own bag. "You feeling well enough for this?"

"I think so. I'll just need to take it slowly."

Farna slapped Aterre on the back. "You boys be careful. I'll see you back here tonight."

Noah nodded. "We'll return by sunset."

Noah followed Aterre as he stepped down onto the dock. Zain and Ashur stood near the men of Havil, conversing in a friendly manner. Noah turned around and looked up at Farna. "Are you ready?"

"I'm always ready." He untied a rope on the mast.

As Farna hoisted the sail, Noah slipped the loop from the post and tossed it on the ship's deck. "See you later." Noah shifted his attention to the men on the wooden dock.

"Thank you for your help," Zain said to those gathered about him.

"You're welcome," one of the men said. "Enjoy our city."

"I'm sure we will," Ashur said.

Noah stepped past the group and joined Aterre. Havil, the greatest city of the south, lay before them. Two small boats, if it was fair to call them that, rested in the water beside them. "Where do we even start?"

Aterre shrugged. "Your guess is as good as mine."

Loud footsteps and creaky wood alerted Noah to Zain's and Ashur's approach. "Did you find out where we need to go?"

"They were most helpful." Zain pointed ahead and to their right. "Noah, you and I will find our metalworkers on the western side of town. And Aterre, you and Ashur will find eateries and inns all around town, especially in the market district just ahead. Learn what you can and meet back here. Be sure to get some provisions for our return trip." Zain took a step and then stopped and turned back. "Oh, and be careful. We don't know who we can trust around here."

They stepped off the dock onto a sandy beach littered with tiny broken seashells. An older couple strolled hand-in-hand and barefooted along the waterline, while a large group of boys chased each other around farther up the shore. Several young people played in the water while a handful of adults watched. Happy to be on dry ground once again, Noah inhaled deeply, but the stitch in his ribs cut it short.

As they crested the beach, Havil's enormity and busyness grew more evident. A wide street ran straight ahead into the city, fringed by an assortment of shops and vendors on either side. A smaller road ran to their left and right, but it was no less busy. People swarmed everywhere and paid little to no attention to the newcomers.

The familiar scent of roasted nuts captured Noah's attention. "Should we eat before splitting up?"

Ashur shook his head. "I'd rather wait until we visit one of the larger establishments, but you two can go ahead."

"Fair enough." Noah motioned toward the vendor selling the fragrant nuts. "Zain?"

"Sure, I could go for some. We'll see you tonight?"

Aterre stopped and gripped Noah's forearm. "Stay safe."

"And you do the same, my friend." He glanced at Ashur, who stood several paces away, and leaned close to Aterre's ear. "Ara wanted me to keep a close eye on him. Watch him and tell me if he does anything unbecoming a city official."

Aterre furrowed his brow. "Ara must have his reasons. I'll be on the lookout. I also plan to ask about a possible slave trade around here. Who knows? Maybe I'll get word about my family." He released Noah's arm. "Farewell."

"I pray your search will be successful."

Noah and Zain purchased some of the sweet-smelling food and enjoyed it as they moved through the town. Along the way, Noah spotted fruits and vegetables he had never seen before. The marketplace eventually gave way to a string of homes larger than Ara's sizeable estate. The doors of the residences boasted ornate designs fashioned out of an unfamiliar yellowish metal. Beyond the final home, rows of young skarep trees in full bloom lined both sides of the street leading to a massive stone wall rising more than 15 cubits high. Spreading far to their left and right, it seemed designed to protect whatever lay behind it, but the expansive opening before them gave the impression that protection was unnecessary.

"This must be what the men at the dock mentioned," Zain said. "We need to go right once we pass through the entrance."

Wide-eyed, Noah stared at his unique surroundings. "I've never seen anything like this."

"Nor have I." Zain looked at the stones high above their heads as they passed through the gap into a sprawling courtyard. "It's certainly impressive."

"That's an understatement. The metalwork on those homes and the stonework of this wall. . . ." Noah shook his head. "Simply incredible."

Zain smiled. "Yeah, but can they match your skill with wood?"

"Based on what I've seen here, I'm sure they can."

"Looks like they hold public gatherings here." Zain pointed to his left. "My guess is that the leaders sit up there."

A massive stone edifice rose to the height of the wall and leveled off at the top, creating a large platform highlighted by a pyramidal structure that rose even higher. Three wide, intricately carved stairways, one on each side and one in the middle, scaled the structure's façade.

"This place is unbelievable." Noah scanned the rest of the square. Opposite their position stood another, taller wall with a large double door placed at its base. Two men stood at attention, one on each side of the opening. "That must be the building we saw from the boat. I wonder how they —" Noah's words stuck in his throat as he spotted a large ska-rep tree in the middle of the expanse, with another guard stationed next to it. He nodded in the tree's direction. "Does that look familiar to you?"

Zain shook his head. "No, but it sure looks strange all by itself. You've seen it?"

Noah scrunched his forehead while staring at the lone tree. "I'm not sure. It seems so familiar, but obviously I've never been here before."

"Come on. Let's find ourselves a metalworker." Zain put an arm on Noah's shoulder and guided him to the right as he continued staring. "It's just a tree, Noah."

Noah broke off his gaze and looked ahead. "I know. I'm not sure why it grabbed my attention like that."

The courtyard stretched for hundreds of cubits in front of them, but was fairly nondescript other than the colossal walls on either side. Noah glanced back at the tree and another image instantly popped into his mind. *Aterre!* He bit his lip and breathed deeply as a wave of realization swept over him — *the Sepha mark on Aterre.* Was it merely a strange coincidence or did Sepha hold sway over the city of Havil too? Noah looked at the large ceremonial platform again and a chill shook him as he thought about the activities that might be held there.

"The metal shops are supposed to be just beyond this wall," Zain said.

"I'm glad we're almost there."

They walked through an opening on the western side of the square that matched the one they had entered moments ago. And just like the other entrance, this one featured skarep trees along the road. Noah's stomach tightened as he considered the evil these might symbolize. Still, he had not seen any hard evidence of Sepha's presence, so he forced himself to focus on the task at hand.

The street descended into a small marketplace, far different than the one near the beach. Instead of vendors peddling all sorts of food, the buildings featured a variety of silver, yellow, and black metals fastened to their wooden sides. Dark smoke billowed from the roofs of the shops, filling the air with an acrid odor.

"I think we've found it," Zain said.

Noah nodded. "Well, this is why we came all this way. I hope they can help us."

Zain gestured to the first building on the left, which was considerably larger than the rest. "Why don't we start with this one?"

Noah stepped forward and opened the door for Zain and then followed him into the shop. The pungent smell from outside intensified, as did the temperature. A high-pitched clanging echoed from the back of the shop at regular intervals.

"What can I help you with?"

As his eyes adjusted to the darkened room, Noah discerned the figure of a man several cubits away. He seemed to be nearly a span shorter than Noah but very strong.

"We're interested in talking to someone about a metal called iron," Zain said.

"Let me check if the boss has time." The muscular man turned and took a few steps. "Hey, Boss, there are a couple of men who want to talk to you."

"I'll be right there," said a man working next to a hot furnace. He struck a metal rod with a thick hammer a couple of times, turned the rod, and repeated the process before setting the mallet down. Next, he plunged the metal into some water, and as the water briefly sizzled, steam rose in the air. As the man strode toward them, he grabbed a cloth from a shelf and wiped the sweat from his face and brawny shoulders. He smiled broadly as he sized Noah and Zain up. "What can I do for you?"

Zain bowed slightly. "My name is Zain, and this is my friend Noah."

"I'm Tubal-Cain. It's good to meet you."

"It's good to meet you as well," Zain said. "I'll get right to the point. We've heard that the people of Havil have learned how to work with a metal called iron, and that it is much stronger than copper. Based on what I see in here, I assume the rumors are true."

"Yes, it's much stronger than copper."

Noah pointed to the spot where Tubal-Cain had been working. "Is that iron you were working with?"

"It sure is." Tubal-Cain wiped his face again and set the cloth on a nearby workbench. He picked up a metallic bar that was about a cubit long, a handbreadth wide, and less than a finger tall. "Here, look at this."

Noah grabbed the metal and ran his fingers along its surface. "It is heavy. You said it's stronger than copper?"

Tubal-Cain grinned. "Try to bend it."

Gripping each end of the bar, Noah exerted downward pressure on the ends while trying to force the middle to bow upward. He increased his force until his ribs reminded him of his recent brush with death. The metal would not budge.

"Use your knee," the assistant said.

Noah glanced at Tubal-Cain who gave him a go-ahead nod. Noah put the middle of the bar above his knee and grunted as he strained to push both sides down. The bar held fast. He gave up and nodded at Zain. "Much stronger."

Noah set the bar on the counter next to a small, shiny figurine. He touched the yellowish ornament. "May I ask what this is made from? I've never seen a metal that looks quite like this before today. It has an appealing quality to it."

"We call it gold. It's pretty common around here."

"Is it strong like iron?" Noah asked.

Tubal-Cain chuckled. "No, it's very soft. Sounds like you must not have it in your city. Speaking of that, where are you from?"

"We've traveled from the other side of the sea to find out more about iron," Zain said.

Tubal-Cain raised an eyebrow. "All that way for iron? What do you need it for? Weapons?"

Zain shook his head. "We've no need of weapons where we're from."

"Truly? I wish I could say the same about Havil — that's what a lot of our iron is for."

"Why?" Noah asked. "Do you have enemies?"

"No foreign enemies, but we arm our guards to keep the peace within the city. We've grown so quickly in the past decade that we've had to triple the number of troops." He shrugged and looked at his assistant. "Guess that's good job security for us."

The other metalworker nodded. "Indeed."

Noah stretched his fingers to relieve the minor cramping in his forearms. "So where do you find —" The door behind him swung open. Noah turned to see four armed guards file into the shop. Instinctively, he backed up and stood next to Tubal-Cain.

The guards wore the same uniform he had seen on the two standing by the massive door in the courtyard. Long light brown leather tunics with strategically placed pieces of shiny armor attached to them covered the troops from their thighs to their shoulders. One man stepped forward and removed his helmet. He stood tall and dropped his gaze. "Sorry for the intrusion, Master Tubal."

"No need to apologize, Kenter. What do you need?"

The man's eyes drifted from Noah to Zain before settling back on Tubal-Cain. "Four men arrived in our city asking where they could find the ironworkers."

"Have they done anything wrong?" Tubal-Cain asked.

The soldier shook his head. "No sir. The king would like to speak to them and welcome them to Havil."

Tubal-Cain crossed his arms. "And why would the king trouble himself with four men inquiring about metal?"

The man furrowed his brow. "Metal? No, it's not that. It's how they entered the city. The men came from the sea."

"How is that possible?"

"They arrived on a large boat. The king is curious about their vessel and wants to invite them for evenfeast."

Tubal-Cain turned to Zain. "Did you come on a large boat?"

Zain nodded, and Noah easily read the disquiet in his face. "Yes, sir."

"And the other two men?" Kenter asked.

"They are merchants," Zain said. "They stayed in the marketplace to visit some of your inns and to purchase supplies for our return trip."

The soldier gestured for Noah and Zain to follow him. "We'll take them to the king."

Tubal-Cain held up a hand. "Hold on, Kenter. We were in the middle of a good discussion. I'll take them myself. You can look for the other men if you'd like."

"As you wish, Master Tubal." Kenter turned and led his men out the door.

Curious, Noah gave the blacksmith an inquisitive look. "If you don't mind me asking, why do the king's guards take orders from you?"

Tubal-Cain smiled. "Oh, didn't I tell you? I'm the king's son."

Chapter 26

"I'm heading out for the day," Tubal-Cain said to his assistant. "Why don't you finish what you're working on and take the rest of the day off too?"

The burly man's face lit up. "Really? Thanks, Boss. I'll see you tomorrow."

Tubal-Cain nodded. "Greet your family for me." He opened the back door of the shop and gestured for Zain and Noah to move past him.

Noah shaded his eyes as he stepped into the sunlight. "Thank you for showing us the rest of your forge and for explaining where to look for iron and how to separate it from the rocks."

The king's son moved alongside them and guided them to a trail that led straight to the giant stone wall. "I'm glad I could help. It would be a shame for you to travel so far and not find answers." He stopped and looked up, rubbing his bare chin with his thumb. "You know, if my father would allow it, I would be willing to accompany you back to your city and train some people to work with iron."

Stunned by his offer, Noah noticed that Zain appeared to be equally surprised.

"Do you really mean that?" Zain asked.

"Of course. I've never been very far from here before. Just to a few small nearby towns and the mines."

Zain held up both palms. "And how much would it cost us?"

Tubal-Cain motioned to the enormous edifice rising before them. "Cost?" He chuckled. "My family owns all of this. I think I could manage to cover my own expenses. Well, I may need you to prepare some of my meals. I'm not much of a cook."

"Thank you for your very generous offer. We'll definitely consider it." Zain glanced at Noah, who nodded slowly.

"Fair enough." Tubal-Cain moved quickly toward the wall. "I'll take you to my chamber. You'll need to get cleaned up before meeting my father."

Noah and Zain followed him as he led them alongside the wall for about two hundred cubits. The wall doubled in height before they arrived at a small door. Tubal-Cain pulled a thin metal object from a pocket on the front of his robe, inserted it into a slot in the door, and turned it. He withdrew the object and opened the door.

Noah pointed to the item as Tubal-Cain slipped it back into his pocket. "What is that?"

"Oh, it's a key. Something we invented around here several years ago to lock and unlock doors."

Noah peeked inside the door. "I suppose I'll see plenty of new things this day."

Tubal-Cain grinned. "You probably will. Let's go inside and find out."

Zain and Noah entered the doorway, and Tubal-Cain stepped in behind them. He closed the door and turned a small knob above the handle. "Now it's locked again. Follow me."

He led them through a short hall and then up three flights of stone stairs. The stairway ended at a wide hallway. Tapestries and paintings lined the walls. Sunlight spilled in through openings on the roof and oil lamps burned to light otherwise dark areas.

"We just finished building this whole complex earlier this year. I requested that my room be built near Blacksmith Row. I'm the overseer for all the metalsmiths in town." He gave a goofy smile. "Now I can truly oversee them." He stopped and opened a door on the left. "Welcome to my room."

Noah stepped inside and his mouth fell open as he scanned the spacious room. A large bed rested against the middle of the far wall. Metal weapons hung from the walls along with paintings and technical drawings. In the middle of the stone floor lay a massive furry rug from an unfamiliar creature. "Incredible."

"You like it?" Tubal-Cain asked.

"It's very nice. Just a little bigger than mine." Noah laughed. "Actually, it's larger than my house." Noah studied one of the hanging weapons. "This is extraordinary work. Did you make this?"

Tubal-Cain nodded and reached into a large cabinet set against the near wall. He pulled out two luxurious robes and set them on the bed. "You may wear these tonight. I need to go find out when my father would like to meet with you." He pointed to a door past his bed. "There's a wash closet in there. Go ahead and get cleaned up, and I'll be back soon."

Zain and Noah looked at each other but neither moved.

"It's fine," Tubal-Cain said. "Make yourselves at home. I'll be right back." He closed the door behind him as he left.

"So." Zain kept his voice low. "What did you think about his offer to return with us?"

"I was just going to ask you that. I think he seems very genuine."

"I do too."

Noah glanced at the door. "How would the council react if they knew the king's son returned with us?"

"I'm not sure. I haven't really seen much to be concerned about yet. Our meeting with the king should be quite informative." Zain rubbed his eyes. "If our blacksmith is as honest as he seems, he may be willing to view this trip as if he is simply providing a service for us rather than establishing diplomatic ties. In that case, I would give you permission to accept his offer on behalf of Ara, as long as you understand this is not an official offer from Iri Geshem."

Noah nodded. "I'll think about it." Noah looked at his well-worn wrap. "We should probably wash up if we're to meet a king."

Zain tilted his head toward the washroom. "You go ahead."

"Can you believe this place?"

Shaking his head, Zain said, "I've never even imagined something like this. And our host is so friendly. I wonder if his father is the same."

"I do too." Noah grabbed one of the robes from the bed and strolled into the wash closet, which he soon found out was incorrectly named. The closet was larger than Noah's bedroom. A considerable basin full of water rested on a stand in one corner near the stool. *I've never seen one of those indoors before.* Along the far wall lay a lavish tub. An array of towels hung from a nearby rod. Noah dipped one of the smaller towels in the basin and wrung it out. He quickly undressed and cleaned himself thoroughly. When he finished, he put on a clean undergarment from his pack and placed his wrap in the bag before spreading the towel over the rim of the tub. He held up the ornate robe and examined it before putting it on. A shiny metal sheet on the wall reflected his image. He turned to the side and admired how the outfit appeared on him, although the robe had no belt, so he had to hold it to keep the front closed.

Knowing they may not have much time, Noah opened the door and moved back into the bedroom. "Your turn." He smiled. "Don't get lost in there."

When Zain closed the wash closet door, Noah moved toward the robe cabinet to find a belt. As he reached the animal rug, the door to the hallway opened and he froze.

"Tu, help me out." A young woman stepped into the room and stopped when she spotted Noah. Something about her reminded him of Emzara, and it wasn't just the fact that they were both beautiful. Her light green gown appeared to have been made from the same fine material he now wore. Hanging from the edge of her shoulders down to her ankles, it perfectly accentuated her attractive figure. She scanned from his head to his feet and smirked. "What are you doing here?" The words were more of a demand than a question.

Noah quickly closed his robe and tried not to blush at the awkwardness of the moment. "I'm sorry. I was looking for a belt."

"Where's Tubal-Cain?"

"He said he had to find out when the king wanted to meet with us and then he would be right back. And we're here because he said that we needed to get cleaned up before we could see his father."

"Wait." She pointed at him. "Are you one of the men from the boat that everyone is talking about?"

Noah nodded. "I see news travels fast around here."

"All day everyone has been buzzing about the sea people. That's what they're calling you." She crossed her arms and leaned against the wall. "Where are you from?"

"We're from a small town on the north side of the sea."

"You said 'we.' Is someone else here too?"

Noah gestured to the wash closet. "My friend Zain is getting ready."

She furrowed her brow and looked down as she pushed a lock of hair behind her ear. "Did you say you were from the north?"

Noah nodded. "Yeah, we left a few weeks ago and just arrived today."

She shook her head as if clearing her thoughts. "I'm sorry. I never introduced myself. My name is Naamah." She walked toward him.

"It's very nice to meet you, Naamah." He gave her an easygoing smile. "I'm Noah."

"Noah?" She pushed her lips to one side and gave a puzzled look. The young woman was playful like Emzara too. A tinge of green matching her dress gleamed from large, otherwise brown eyes, and her smooth brown skin dimpled in the middle of her cheek. "I don't ever remember hearing that name before. What does it mean? Wait, let me guess." She twisted a strand of hair around her finger. "Storm?"

Noah chuckled. "No, actually it's quite the opposite, although storm would be more intimidating. My name means rest."

She bit her lip, almost as if she were disappointed. Then she brightened and laughed. "I wasn't even close. Well, Noah, how about I help you find a belt, since my brother didn't leave one for you?"

"Thank you." Noah started for the robe cabinet again and then stopped suddenly. "Tubal-Cain is your brother? Then that would make you the king's daughter."

Naamah gave him a half-smile and nodded slowly.

"Forgive me. Is there a title I should use to address you?"

She snorted lightly and shook her head as she walked to the wardrobe. "How about Naamah?"

Noah breathed a sigh of relief. "That sounds good to me, Naamah."

She reached into the large cabinet and pulled out four stylish belts. She held them up in front of Noah to see which one would match his outfit. She handed him the last one she checked. "This one."

Noah quickly wrapped it around his waist and tightened it. "Thank you."

"Of course."

"What are these robes made out of?"

She raised an eyebrow. "They're silk. You don't have silk where you are from?"

"Not that I can recall."

She placed the other belts back in the wardrobe and then turned to face him. "I wonder if you would be so kind as to help me."

"Sure. What do you need?"

"I was going to ask my brother, but obviously he's not here. I'm trying to get ready for tonight too, but my necklace has a knot in it. Would you see if you can untangle it for me?" She turned her back to him and pulled her hair up, revealing that the neckline in the back of her gown plunged beneath her shoulder blades.

Noah took a step closer and caught a whiff of her appealing fragrance. Her raised arms were well-toned and the skin of her neck and upper back was perfectly smooth. Noah spotted the knot in the necklace and tried desperately to focus on it. Wishing he hadn't agreed to help her, he reached for the knot and carefully avoided touching her. He pulled it back slightly to give himself some slack. With his heart racing, Noah untangled the knot, and while holding a loose end in each hand, he quickly put his left hand over her shoulder and grabbed the end of the necklace with his right and pulled away.

She let her hair down and turned around. "Thanks."

Noah did a double take upon seeing the pendant in his open palm. The image of Aterre's mark flashed through his mind, followed by the memory of the tree in the courtyard. *Sepha!* Noah thrust his hand toward her but avoided making eye contact. "Here you go."

Naamah ran her fingernails across his palm as she snatched the necklace. "Now I can finish getting ready. You really helped me, and I'm glad you're here."

He nodded. "Thanks. It's been quite a trip."

"Well, I hope we can make it even better." She grinned and then turned away. "I'll see you tonight."

As Naamah headed for the door, Noah glanced once and caught her striking figure before averting his eyes. He had already seen more than he should have. He walked over to the bed and sat down on the softest surface he could remember. Noah closed his eyes and Naamah's smile popped into his thoughts. He opened his eyes and stared at the rug. Struggling to block the images of Naamah from his mind, he forced his thoughts back to Iri Geshem and Emzara. He finally relaxed when he could focus on her. *Em, how I wish you were here now.*

Zain opened the wash closet door at the same time as Tubal-Cain entered from the hall. "Is there a belt for this thing?" Zain asked.

Noah laughed to himself as Tubal-Cain hurried to his wardrobe and found the appropriate strap. He retrieved an outfit for himself as well.

"Looks like you both are ready." He walked to Zain and handed him the belt. "I'll wash up, and then we'll go see my father."

CHAPTER 27

The closed golden doors before him stood at least twice his height and were equally broad. Noah marveled at the fine detail displayed in the animals and people engraved on panels. He snorted when he saw his reflection distorted by one of the figures. Just then, the door to his right opened slightly and Tubal-Cain slipped through and closed it behind him.

"How can you even move these things?" Noah asked. "They must weigh as much as an earth shaker."

"They're not quite as bad as they look," Tubal-Cain said. "They are made of wood and overlaid with gold. That's one of the great things about this metal — it can be beaten so thin."

"Fascinating."

Tubal-Cain adjusted his robe. "Okay, they are ready for you. Just a couple of things to remember. First, don't speak unless my father asks you to. He's in a good mood today and eager to see you, so he'll probably be a bit relaxed in this regard. And second, a slight bow is considered a sign of respect here. You ready?"

Noah nodded and then followed his new friend through one of the massive doors. He quickly glanced around the room. Elaborate tapestries and gleaming weapons decorated the room's side walls. White stone pillars with oil lamps attached to their sides lined their walkway toward a small set of black stairs that climbed to the platform against the back wall. On the stage sat the king on a golden high-backed throne. He wore an exquisite robe bedecked with precious stones, and a golden crown speckled with jewels rested on his curly brown hair. Noah guessed the man was probably about his father's age. One woman with long black hair sat on a similar, but smaller chair to his left while another woman with shorter brown hair sat in an identical chair to his right. Both wore daintier versions of the king's crown. Two guards stood at attention on either side of the second step.

Tubal-Cain led them to within a few cubits of the first stair and stopped. "Greetings, Father." He looked to his left. "And Mother." Then he nodded to the other woman.

The king leaned forward. The soft light of the lamps revealed a scar running from close to his nose all the way back to his right ear. "Greetings, Son, how are the metalworkers today?"

"Busy as always, Father, but they are keeping up with demands. In fact, they are ahead of schedule."

"That's good to hear. But I didn't really invite you and your guests here to discuss smithery. Let me meet our guests."

Tubal-Cain stepped to the side. "Please, introduce yourselves."

Zain and Noah bowed slightly as Tubal-Cain had suggested. "Greetings, sir. Thank you for meeting with us. My name is Zain. I'm a merchant, and this is my friend, Noah."

"Zain and Noah, allow me to welcome you to the great city of Havil, the jewel of the sea. I am King Lamech."

Noah raised an eyebrow when the king mentioned his name. He realized that he should avoid drawing attention to himself so he tried to put on a straight face, but he was not fast enough.

"Did I say something you didn't like?" the king asked.

Noah felt all the eyes in the room turn on him. He shook his head. "No sir." His voice came out weakly, so he cleared his throat. "It's just that I had not heard your name until now, so I was surprised to learn that you have such a fine name — the same as my father's."

A small grin crept across the king's face. "Well, then I must agree. Your father has an excellent name." He nodded to the woman on his right. "This is my wife, Zillah." He gestured to the other woman. "This is my other wife, Adah."

Noah wanted to react but remained expressionless. He was a guest here and did not believe it was his place to tell the king that the Creator had established marriage at the beginning as a union between a man and

192

a woman. If the king flagrantly violated such a basic part of God's created order, what else might he be willing to do?

He pulled himself forward and sat up straight. "Are you a merchant as well?"

"No sir, but I do work with them regularly. I am a shipbuilder."

"Are you?" The king raised his head and smiled. "Then I have found my man. Did you build the boat that you came in on?"

Noah nodded. "I was part of the crew that did."

The king pointed up and to his left. "I have only seen it from the roof. It's too far away to for me to really know much about it, but I've heard reports. Is it true that you crossed the sea in the ship with five people?"

"We didn't really cross the sea." Noah drew a semi-circle in the air with his finger. "We had to stay pretty close to the shore."

"Why? If it floats, which it clearly does, why can't you go straight across?"

Noah nodded. "We could've done that if the water remained calm the whole time. But the joints aren't strong enough to survive in stormy seas. The boats are really made for running the river. That's the reason we made the trip to your city."

The king tilted his head slightly to the side. "What do you mean? Havil only has a few tiny boats. How can we help?"

"We heard that you had figured out how to use a metal much stronger than copper, and that it might be useful for making stronger joints. We decided to find out if the rumors were true." Noah glanced at Tubal-Cain. "That's how we met your son."

The king stroked his chin slowly as he eyed Noah and then Zain. "Son, you have spent time with these men. What is your impression of them?"

"I haven't known them for long, but I believe they are honest."

"Indeed." The king pointed at Noah. "How can I purchase a boat like the one you brought here?"

"Well, you could order one and we would build it in our shipyard. Or —" Noah looked at Zain who nodded in return. "You could send an ironworker with us to teach us how to use iron."

"A boat in exchange for a blacksmith?" The king pursed his lips and seemed to consider the offer.

Tubal-Cain glanced at Noah and his eyes brightened. "Father." He stepped forward. "I'd like to volunteer to travel with these men and teach them."

The king raised an eyebrow. "Who would supervise the smiths here?"

Tubal-Cain stood tall, exuding confidence. "Demek could do it. He's ready."

"And why would you want to go?"

"As you know, Father, I've never really traveled anywhere before, except for the mines and the nearby towns. I would like to see some more of this world." Tubal-Cain scratched the sizable muscle on his upper right arm. "Perhaps I could find other metals while there."

"Perhaps." The king turned to Noah. "How long would it take you to build me a ship like the one you have?"

Noah looked up as he counted on his fingers. "It takes about five whole moons to build the boat, plus up to one whole moon of travel each way."

"Seven total?"

"Eight, sir. There is another I must add to the total. I am getting married soon after we return."

The king grinned. "Congratulations, young Noah."

"Thank you, sir."

He extended an arm toward each wife and let out a short laugh. "As you can see, I like marriage. So in exchange for my son's services, you would deliver a boat like yours to these shores in eight whole moons?"

Noah glanced at each of the man's wives; neither seemed to find his joke funny. "Yes."

The king leaned back and looked at Tubal-Cain's mother. "Zillah, how many whole moons until the festival?"

The woman hesitated before speaking, apparently searching for the answer. "Just shy of eight."

The king pointed at Noah. "If you can guarantee delivery of my own ship like yours before the festival, then my son can go with you."

Tubal-Cain clasped his hands together. "Thank you, Father." He looked at Noah. "Will you have room for me and all my gear?"

"How much do you have?" Noah asked.

"Well, besides some personal items, I'll need to bring a load of iron pellets and a full complement of tools."

Noah shrugged. "We should have enough space."

"Great," Lamech said. "Return in time for the festival, and you will be our honored guests."

"That sounds like quite an honor, sir," Zain said. "Thank you."

"You're welcome." The king stood abruptly, allowing his decorative robe to fall onto his throne. He motioned toward a large open door on the side of the room opposite of where they entered. "Instead of spending all evening in here, I'd like for you to join us for evenfeast." The two guards and Lamech's wives followed the king down the stairs. He approached Noah and warmly clapped him on the shoulder. "Come."

Noah walked with the king. The man was a little shorter, but his broad shoulders, barrel chest, and thick arms made him quite intimidating.

"You never said where you were from," Lamech said.

Noah grinned. "That's because the king never asked. We are from a small city on the other side of the sea."

"I gathered as much. What's the name of your city? I wonder if I've been there."

"You've been on the other side of the sea?" Noah asked.

"Of course. I was born in the city of Enoch."

They walked into another spacious room. A long dining table stretched across the middle of the floor. Ten chairs lined each side, although only about half of the places were set with silver dishes and golden drinking vessels. Ornamental oil lamps hung above the table. A large purple curtain draped from the ceiling to the floor above a low platform in the middle of the far wall. As Noah marveled at the richness of the room, Lamech continued.

"My father was heir to the throne of the Nodite Empire, but his younger brother wanted the throne, so he framed my father for murder." The king stifled a cough. "We were exiled and decided to move far away from Nod. Sadly, my father became very sick and died along the way."

"I'm sorry," Noah said.

Lamech held up a hand as if to tell him it was in the past. "I moved to Havil and soon became involved with the town council. The city grew rapidly so we had to keep building. The council must have seen something in me. About five years ago, they decided to make me the sole ruler. It's hard to believe how much Havil has changed since we arrived. It's now the greatest city of the South."

"From what I've seen, it's a magnificent city."

The king gave him a sly smile. "Just wait until you see what else we have to offer."

A guard ushered Noah to a chair on the near side of the table. "Remain standing until the king is seated."

Noah watched as the king stood behind his chair on the far left until his wives reached their respective spots on either side of him. Lamech motioned for the women to sit, and then he followed suit. Noah sat to Tubal-Cain's right, and an empty spot remained to Tubal-Cain's left, between him and his mother, Zillah. A guard directed Zain to a chair across from Noah, with two open spaces between him and the king's other wife.

Lamech cleared his throat. "Noah and Zain, we would like to thank you for joining us for evenfeast. But before the meal is served, we have prepared a little entertainment."

A guard entered the room behind Noah. He hurried to the king's side and whispered something.

Lamech nodded. "Bring him in."

A second guard led Ashur into the room and directed him to sit near Zain.

Ashur, wearing a new outfit, bowed to the king before taking his seat. "Thank you for allowing me to join you for evenfeast, sir."

"We want to thank you for visiting our city. It's the least we can do as your hosts. I understand that you are a merchant as well."

"Yes, sir. I run an eatery and inn back home."

"And what did you think of Havil?"

"Marvelous. Spectacular." Ashur shook his head. "I don't know if I can find the right words."

Lamech chuckled. "I'm glad you enjoyed it. I understand your companion was not with you when my guards located you."

"Yes, that's right." Ashur gave him a half smile. "He left to take a load of supplies back to our boat. His loss. I'm sure he would've loved to be here."

"Well, maybe next time. Now for some entertainment." As the wife to his left turned around in her chair, the king turned and gave two loud claps.

Young twin boys dressed in elegant gold-trimmed robes stepped out from behind the curtain. The first carried a thin wooden rod, and strapped to the front of the other boy was a wide wooden tube with some sort of animal skin stretched across its top. They took their places along the wall on the edge of the platform.

Tubal-Cain leaned close to Noah. "My little brothers."

With his hands, the second boy beat rhythmically on his instrument. After a few moments of steady pounding, the other lad put one end of the wooden rod in his mouth and covered some of the holes in the top of the instrument with his fingers. As he blew into the rod's end, a high-pitched but soothing sound echoed through the room. The twins continued to play in perfect harmony. Noah had never heard such pleasant music, and it was even more impressive to hear it from children who could not have been more than six years old. Eventually, their tune ended and everyone at the table clapped.

The king extended an arm toward the boys. "My sons. Outstanding as always."

The boys nodded in acknowledgment and then started into a new and much faster song. The curtains parted slightly and four women moved through the opening, their dancing seamlessly synchronized with the music. Wearing different colored veils and dressed in fine matching silk gowns that revealed more than Noah believed to be appropriate, the women moved in ways that exuded sensuality. From left to right, they donned red, yellow, blue, and purple, respectively.

Not wanting to appear rude, Noah tried to make it seem as if he were paying attention. He looked past the women at nothing in particular.

Just then the music became softer, and a powerful and captivating voice rang out from behind the curtains, which slowly parted farther as the singer came forward. She moved effortlessly to the center of the platform, almost as if she were walking on air. Her soft brown skin complemented her light green silken gown and veil, which, like the outfits of the dancers, revealed too much of her flawless figure. Everything about this young woman seemed perfect. Incredibly, the loveliness of her voice surpassed her arresting beauty.

Temporarily lost in the enchantment of the moment, Noah became conscious of the fact that he had seen her outfit before. *Naamah.* He blinked when he realized he was gaping at her. Closing his mouth, Noah looked away and quickly checked to see if anyone else had seen his reaction, but they were entranced too. He chanced another glimpse at

Naamah, and her eyes met his. With considerable effort, he broke contact and willed himself to focus on the twin musicians instead. He smiled as he watched the young maestros, wondering how the boys could be so skilled at their age.

The song eventually came to an end, and Noah joined in the applause. The twins set their instruments down and sat between their mother and Zain. Two of the dancers moved around the table and sat to Noah's right, while the other two sat next to Ashur, who enthusiastically greeted them. Naamah strutted behind her father and sat between her mother and Tubal-Cain.

Servers quickly moved in and placed a variety of food in front of each person. Lamech's large plate included an array of fruits, and two fish. Noah shifted his eyes to his own plate, trying to hide his confusion and disgust at the meat before the king. *Eating animals? Does he follow any of the Creator's ways?* Relief swept over him as he realized the plate set before him contained only an assortment of spiced grains and colorful fruits and vegetables, some of which he recognized only from the marketplace that afternoon.

Lamech introduced the twins, Jubal and Jabal, to their guests. "And this beautiful young woman is my daughter, Naamah."

Naamah smiled congenially at Zain and Ashur as they acknowledged her. She turned to Noah, and her eyes glistened as she flashed a smile. "It's wonderful to see you again, Noah."

"Likewise," Noah said. "You're a fantastic singer."

"You've already met?" the king asked.

Naamah bit her lower lip and nodded rapidly. "Yes, Father. I went to Tu's room earlier, but I found Noah there instead. He told me that they came from across the sea."

"We've already heard much about it," Zillah said.

Tubal-Cain placed his hand on Naamah's shoulder. "Amah, you'll never guess what lies in my future."

She coughed. Noah thought he saw her shoot a glance at her father before focusing again on Tubal-Cain. "Hmm?"

"I'm going back with them to teach them how to use iron."

Her eyes shot wide open. "What?" She leaned forward and looked past him at Noah. "Then you're taking me too."

Tubal-Cain laughed. "Why would you want to go?"

"Because I've never traveled anywhere before."

"But I need you here," Lamech said. Noah turned away as the king shoved rectangular flakes of fish into his mouth. *It looks like woodchips.*

"For what, Father?"

"To plan the annual festival."

Naamah held her palms up. "But that's not for another seven whole moons. How long is he going to be gone?"

"They agreed to bring me a boat like theirs before the festival," Lamech said.

"It's not fair." Naamah crossed her arms and pouted.

Noah quietly let out a sigh of relief, then he wondered at himself and frowned. Naamah had done nothing to deserve his disapproval. *Maybe it's the Sepha pendant.* He looked across the table to see Ashur enjoying a lively discussion with the dancers.

"Can't someone else do the planning this year?" Naamah asked.

"You'll be 35 years old," the king said. "It'll be your first one as an adult, and you'll have so much to do. The whole city will be watching for you."

An adult at 35? Noah rubbed his forehead. *So many differences here.*

She leaned toward her father. "What if I came back early?"

"How would you do that?" Lamech asked.

"You could send a couple of guards with me, and we could walk or ride back."

Tubal-Cain snorted. "Do you know how far it is?"

She scowled at him. "I don't care. I want to go."

"I don't want to speak for their city," Tubal-Cain said, tapping a finger against his lips. "I don't know if it's possible, but maybe they can send her back on another ship and return with more of my supplies. I don't know how long it might take to locate some iron there, so I'd like to have as much as possible."

Lamech took a sip of his drink. "What do you think, Zillah?"

The woman studied her daughter. "I've learned by now that if she wants something bad enough, then it's best to stay out of her way. Tubal-Cain can look out for her until it's time for her to come home."

The king leaned back in his chair and shook his head. "Fine. You can go too, but I'm sending two of my best guards with you."

Naamah squealed in delight. "Yes. Thank you, Da."

Lamech smiled at his daughter and then shifted his gaze to Zain, but pointed at Ashur. "What's his name?"

Zain elbowed Ashur to draw his attention away from the dancers. "It's Ashur, sir."

Ashur spun quickly in his chair and faced the king. "Sir?"

"You said that you own an inn?" Lamech asked.

Ashur nodded. "I do."

"Is it a nice place?"

Ashur gestured to the spacious room. "It's not like this, but it's one of the finest places in the city. I'd be happy to host your son, daughter, and guards while they are in town, if that's what you were going to ask."

"That's precisely what I had in mind."

Noah searched for a way to prevent this plan from becoming final. "Sir, may I point out a difficulty with this idea?"

Naamah fixed her gaze on Noah as concern spread across her face.

"By all means," Lamech said.

Noah scratched the side of his head. "I don't mean to cause offense, but I don't think we have enough room on the ship to accommodate your daughter and two guards."

"I think we can make room for them," Zain said. "As long as Tubal-Cain's supplies don't fill up the entire cargo hold, we can set up some sleeping quarters below deck."

Noah furrowed his brow but conceded defeat. "I'm not sure, but we can try to rearrange things tomorrow to see if there will be room."

"That sounds fair to me," Lamech said. "Now let's eat."

CHAPTER 28

Naamah stepped around her brother's many crates full of tools and iron pellets, and left the small curtained-off area in the hull. Although she was not accustomed to such tight sleeping quarters, she was thankful for the privacy. Tiptoeing as quietly as possible to avoid waking her guards, she slipped up the steps to the main deck. She arched her neck, glad to be able to fully stand, and looked around. The deep hued sky, strewn with a myriad of stars, beckoned to her like an old friend while the moon hung low and large as if it longed to be near. Having dropped to the mild temperature she liked best, the evening air filled her lungs, and she succumbed to the dangerous invitation the wind gave as it softly whispered through her hair and the light folds of her dress. She smiled, knowing that the elements were on her side and would accentuate her beauty tonight. Looking over her left shoulder, she saw her brother and the farmer along with two others from Iri Geshem; all were engrossed in a game of sorts. She scoffed at the raucous noises they were making near the stern and headed toward the front of the ship.

Her foot caught on something and she stumbled forward, barely staying on her feet. "Oops." She put a hand up to her mouth. "I didn't see you there."

Noah, lying flat against the deck, lifted his head slightly off his arms. "Oh. Evening peace, Naamah. I meant no harm."

"Please, don't get up." She waved him back to his more comfortable position, her many bangles starting a cheerful chorus. "It was my fault. Mind if I sit?"

Noah shrugged before resting his head back against his crossed arms. "Not at all."

Naamah settled close to him, where she was sure to been seen and hardest to ignore. She laid a hand gracefully on her knee and dipped her shoulder ever so slightly toward him. "What are you doing here?"

"Watching the stars. This is the perfect evening for it."

"Mmm, I completely agree. It's absolutely enchanting out here." She gave him her most engaging smile.

"Indeed. But I'm also using them to track our movements. Right now, we're heading east."

"How can you tell?"

Noah pointed to his left just above the horizon. "See that bright star over there?"

"Yes."

"That one always leads north, so since it's to our left, then we're pointed east." Noah returned his hand behind his head.

His muscles bulged and shifted as he moved. *The physique of a warrior.* Not for the first time since meeting him, she recalled the words of the seer: *"A storm brews in the north, with thick, dark clouds, vexing your father. But a ray of sunshine pierces through it, lighting up your face."* The words had become like a litany, running through her mind again and again, shaping her thoughts and even her dreams. Now the question that had plagued her for weeks returned: *Could Noah be the storm as well as the sunshine? Maybe he doesn't have cause to harm my father yet, but I could give him plenty of reasons.*

Since their voyage began, she had searched for insights about him, but he seemed to go out of his way to avoid her. She was surprised he had not fled to the safety of the other men's company in the stern. Perhaps he was finally abandoning his reticence. Excitement rippled through her. The more she gleaned of his character, the more she was drawn to him, and not just as a means to further her ends.

Eager to extend this unexpected chance to be near him, she leaned in, letting her eyes widen in what she'd long ago realized was her most irresistible look. "What else do you learn from the stars?"

Noah quickly looked at the entirety of her and paused as he swallowed.

She hid a smile. *So he likes what he sees.* By shifting her long frame occasionally, she forced his eyes to keep peeking at her. He discussed names and how travelers used the stars' locations to keep their bearing. Stifling a yawn, Naamah blinked and tried to look interested. Suddenly, the ship hit a small swell, and she used the unexpected motion to her advantage. Feigning a loss of balance, she hitched forward and placed her hand firmly on Noah's chest as if to regain her equilibrium.

"Thank you." Allowing her thumb to lightly stroke him in the same spot, she let the curtain of her hair brush against his torso and peered at him through her lashes. "I'm glad you were there. I'm still learning how to steady myself on one of these."

Noah shifted away and sat upright. "You get used to it. The pitching and rocking become barely noticeable after a while."

Concealing her displeasure, she smiled demurely. "It's been several weeks and yet I'm still clumsy, while you manage so well."

"You don't seem clumsy to me."

She blinked slowly and tilted her head. "It's easy to feel at ease around you. Are you always this nice?"

"Ha. You should ask Aterre; he'd tell you the truth."

"Well you've been nothing but kind to me this whole time. I'm so glad I've come. I'm thrilled to see new places." Her fingers extended to their full length, as if they too could not contain their excitement. She almost brushed against Noah's hand with hers and he looked at the near contact before turning his attention back to her face.

"I know what you mean," he said. "I couldn't wait to see more of the world than the tiny corner where I grew up."

"And now, here you are."

"Yeah. I would've never thought I'd get to come this far in so short a time."

"You're a driven man, full of greatness. Noah, I —" She paused and looked down as if suddenly shy.

"What is it?"

She traced the edge of her garment and let the silence do its work.

"Tell me."

She smiled inwardly. "You and I are cut from the same cloth." Holding up her hem to make her point also revealed the skin just past her knee. She released slowly, letting the fabric flutter back — not quite into place. "We both long to know what's out there and to make something of ourselves. And" — she dropped her voice to a whisper, forcing him to lean closer to hear — "I confess, I also want to know you in a deeper way. I can see that you're not entirely indifferent to me."

"Naamah, I should —"

She softly put her finger on his lips. "Let me finish, please. Maybe it's out of place for so young a girl to speak this way, but I think we'd be good together as" — she gave him an alluring glance — "as husband and wife."

He gently placed her hand away from him. "I'm getting married once we return to Iri Geshem. I thought you knew."

She drew in a sharp breath. "No, I didn't." Silence took over once more as she pushed emotion aside and rapidly tried to find where her advantage lay. She chose to play the innocent victim. "You've been so attentive, I thought — I guess I thought you felt the same as I do. I thought you found me beautiful." She bent toward him. "Don't you think I'm beautiful?"

"Naam — uh, you certainly are. That's not it. It's just that —"

"You're promised to some girl," she interrupted. "I get that. But it's such a shame. You're ambitious and focused, and with your passion and my position, don't you see how far we could go? I have the money to finance your dreams. You'd have your ships and we'd sail the world, always searching for the next adventure. And we'd have each other; we'd have it all."

"Naamah, please listen. I did promise myself to Emzara, but it's not something I dread. I love her and long for her. I never meant for you to think that you and I had a future together." Noah stood, smoothed his wrap so it hung back down to his knees, and then offered to help her up. She could read concern in his eyes. "I don't know if you've thought much about him before, but Aterre is available."

Pretending not to see his hand, she stood and stepped back. Though her heart seethed with anger and hurt, she forced a little low laugh. "It's hard to notice the moon when it's always next to the sun. But thank you. I wish you — and her — all the best. Please, let's speak no more of my silly nonsense. Shall we see what the others are up to?"

Noah nodded, and she allowed him to pass by her before following him to the rear of the ship. The noisy game had ended, and only two figures remained, each using a large barrel as a makeshift stool. The illumination of a nearby oil lamp revealed the features of her brother. Quickly she hopped up next to him, leaning her head on his shoulder so he could not see her face.

"Amah. I thought you were asleep already."

Forcing her tone to be light, but still hiding her countenance, she spoke softly. "No. It was so beautiful out here, I just had to soak it in."

"Aterre." Tubal-Cain turned to the other man. "Let's catch these two up before you finish your story."

He paused and she sensed his hesitation. "I can leave if I'm not wanted here."

"She's fine."

Noah's words warmed her as he sat next to his friend.

"Your brother asked about my background. I told him I grew up very peaceably with my family in the western part of Havilah, and I was just to the part where all that changed."

For the second time that night, Naamah found her mind wandering. As bits and pieces of Aterre's story floated in and out of her conscious thought, she revisited the words of the oracle. *What good are they now?* Battling the emotions and willing the tears back, she bit her lip and forced herself to pay attention to the farmer's words.

"I thought I was done for. After a desperate attempt for freedom, I slashed into the darkness and felt his blood drip down my arm and heard my attacker yell. He released me to move his hands to where my blade had met his face." Aterre's shoulders shuddered as if the memory haunted him often.

Silence and uneasiness shrouded the group, but Aterre eventually filled in the blanks with quiet, but intensely spoken words. "My dreams often bring back that night and torment me with their vividness. I don't know what I'd do if I really saw him again."

"Have you come close to finding him?" Tubal-Cain asked.

"No. That was seven years ago, and I'm not even searching for him. I'd still like to know what happened to my family, though." He shot a glance at Noah and Noah gave a tiny shake of his head as some meaning passed between them.

Oblivious to the exchange, Tubal-Cain furrowed his brow. "But after everything that villain did to you?"

"I know." Aterre shrugged. "But, because of those events, I fled and ran straight into Noah and his family."

"Literally." The two men shared a small chuckle.

"And it's through them that I've come to have a greater understanding of the Creator." Aterre's voice cracked.

"It's been a long time in coming, I can tell you that." Noah shouldered his friend playfully. "This one is almost as hardheaded as I am. But after ever so many questions, he's pledged to learn and follow the ways of the Creator."

"Good has come out of my tragedy."

Naamah stared at him. How could he talk so? His mother and sisters dead or enslaved, and he sits here rambling about trusting God? Did their lives mean nothing to him? She jumped down from the barrel and moved to stand by the railing, looking out over the black and silver expanse of sea.

The men sat in silence for a long moment before Tubal-Cain cleared his throat. "That's quite a life you've lived already. I'm honored you'd share some of your pain with my little sister and me."

Naamah sneered at the water, then pasted on a smile and turned, brushing her hair out of her eyes. "Yes, thank you for including me, but it's time I headed downstairs. Evening peace to you three."

Later, while she lay in bed, her tears finally made their little paths down her cheeks and opened the door to the inner torrent. Aware of the tightness of the quarters and the thinness of her curtain wall, she sobbed into her pillow, her shoulders silently heaving. The pain of rejection gripped her chest, familiar and fresh all at once. The old scar, the one that appeared the day her father came back with a new wife, throbbed in dull counterpoint to the new wound. *I expect it of him, but not you, Noah.* She balled up her fists. *And how can you so easily dismiss me to the farmer? He's no better than my father. He found a new family too.*

She would never consider Aterre as a potential mate. Though she could never pinpoint why, he had repulsed her from their first meeting. And now — what she'd heard tonight only deepened her revulsion.

Something poked at the recesses of her memory, something about his story. Swallowing her tears, she replayed Aterre's words, but the connection eluded her. *Think.* She stared at the boards of the deck, which comprised her ceiling. *Noah probably worked on those. No, don't go there. Focus on Aterre's story. Why does it bother you?*

She sat straight up and clutched at the thin sheet covering her. *Her father's scar! Could it be?* Wildly, she pondered the ramifications. Seven years ago a new wife was not the only thing her father brought home. *The wound on his face.* And seven years ago, Aterre lost his mother and gave a scar to a raiding man. *Could Father be that man? Impossible. The timing is the same, but Father claimed his was a defensive wound. Of course, he would say that to keep the respect of the people.*

Just when she had convinced herself that these were crazy thoughts, born of her intense emotions from Noah's refusal, she straightened her shoulders and her eyes shot open. *His accent! Aterre's accent is the same as Adah's. My disgust of him is connected to her.*

Pondering the usefulness of this information, she lay back down, her mind spinning.

CHAPTER 29

Iri Geshem — Noah's 46th year

Sweat dripped from his cheek as Noah strained to bend a strip of wood for the hull of Lamech's ship. Just nine days remained before the wedding, and the week-long preparation rituals would soon commence. Looking forward to his two weeks away from work, Noah poured himself into his labors, trying to finish as much as possible before his departure. He held the wooden strip in place as Bakur lashed it to the stern with a temporary leather strap. Eager to use the iron binders, Noah remembered Tubal-Cain's admonition that they would need to be greased to prevent rusting. A hint of doubt touched his mind, but he pushed it away. No matter how much maintenance the new ships required, it would be worth it if they could sail the open sea.

The days had blurred together since their return from Havil, with Lamech's commission keeping everyone busy. Ara added another employee, allowing them to prepare the wood and completely frame the vessel in only two whole moons.

In addition to overseeing that project, Noah helped Tubal-Cain set up his forge — next to the shipyard, at Ara's request. After they constructed the new building, Tubal-Cain spent much of his time venturing to outlying regions around town, searching for a source of iron ore. He also showed Noah how to convert certain lumber to charcoal that would burn hot enough for ironworking. Before long, the blacksmith's shop opened for business.

During this construction, the long workdays left little time to spend with his beloved or their friends and guests from Havil. Thankfully, Naamah had put the awkward moment on the boat behind her, and she got along with the others well, even spending considerable time with Emzara and Adira. Earlier that day, they had all traipsed down to the shore to see her off as she departed for home with her guards on another Farna-led voyage.

"Steady. That should hold for now," Bakur said, bringing Noah's attention back.

"I'll get the next strip." Noah strode over to the stockpile and on the way picked up the container of water and drank deeply. The waves lapped the shore behind him, and a slight breeze carried only minor relief from the day's heat.

"Hey!"

Noah recognized Tubal-Cain's voice and spun to see the blacksmith jogging toward him with a larger than customary grin on his face. "Good news?"

Tubal-Cain closed the gap between them and stopped a few cubits away. "Great news, actually. We found deposits not far from Superglider Cliff. The hills there are full of iron ore."

"That is great news." Noah handed the water to his friend. "What's the next step?"

"It'll take a lot of work to mine and extract the ore, but I'm sure I can find a couple of apprentices that'll help."

"When I have the time, I'd love to learn how to do it," Noah said.

Tubal-Cain crossed his arms. "I'm sure you'd make a great black-smith, but your woodworking ability is unmatched."

"Thanks." Noah stretched his arms out and yawned. "Maybe after this ship is delivered to your father."

Tubal-Cain shook his head. "I was hoping you'd do that. I don't anticipate moving back there anytime soon."

Noah drew back. "You aren't going back?"

He shrugged. "Maybe someday. I am the king's oldest son after all. But for now, I'd rather live here. I love the smaller town feel, and the people are honest and much kinder."

"That's good news. We'd love to keep you around." Noah grinned and then added. "I guess it doesn't hurt that Adira's here too."

Tubal-Cain snorted but cast Noah a sheepish glance. "She might've factored into my decision, although she doesn't know that yet."

"I'm sure we can figure out a way to let her in on it. That seems to be Aterre's specialty, actually." Noah chuckled and then looked to the side and lowered his voice. "What'll your father say?"

"Well, that'll be the tough part. But if Demek's doing a good job back home, then I'm sure my father will let me stay here for a while, especially if he thinks it'll help his chances at opening up trade opportunities with Iri Geshem."

Noah raised an eyebrow. "Not likely. No offense, but I know the council here doesn't wish to establish —" He stopped as he noticed Tubal-Cain staring at the water behind Noah instead of listening. "What is it?" Noah turned around.

"A boat."

"Usually they unload at the docks on the river." Trying to get a good look at the craft being pushed into the shallows by crewmen on either side using pushpoles, Noah squinted against the light continually reflecting from the water. "There are quite a few people on there."

"Who are they?"

Noah opened his mouth to speak, but stopped when he caught his first clear view of the ship's occupants. His heart leapt and he shot an excited glance at Tubal-Cain. "It's my family! Come on." Sprinting across the beach, he spotted his sister waving her arms frantically as the boat softly ran aground. "Misha!"

"Noah!" Misha jumped up and down.

His parents beamed next to her as they watched Noah dash into the shallow water. His mother held the hand of a very young girl, and to her side stood Jerah and an attractive young woman.

As Noah reached them, Misha leapt off the deck into his arms. He squeezed her tightly, trying to make up for six years' worth of hugs. "I missed you so much." He kissed her cheek.

"I missed you too."

Noah set her down gently in the ankle-deep water. No longer the small girl he remembered, she was now a beautiful young woman. "Where did my little sister go?"

"All grown up." She hugged him around the waist. "Well, almost. Where's Aterre?"

"He's working on a farm right now. He'll be back tonight."

His father climbed out of the boat and turned to face him.

After gripping Lamech's forearm, Noah grabbed his father in a tight embrace, with Misha still latched onto his waist. When they separated, the two men reached up to help Nina out of the boat. "It's been so long. What're you doing here?"

Jerah bounded over the edge of the hull and splashed into the water. He helped the young woman disembark.

Noah raised an eyebrow at the size of Jerah's arms as he lowered the woman to the shore. Before he could comment, though, he recognized her. "Pivi?"

Jerah blushed. "Although you already know her, I'd like to introduce you to my wife."

Noah reached forward and embraced Jerah. "Congratulations, little brother, or not-so-little brother. Looks like all that constant flirting eventually paid off." He stepped back and smiled at Pivi. "And my condolences to you."

Jerah shook his head and laughed. "Same old Noah."

Noah shrugged and winked at Pivi. "When was the wedding?"

She blushed. "About six whole moons ago."

"I'm sorry I missed it. Congratulations to both of you."

"Mother, I need help." The little girl that had been holding his mother's hand stood above them, peering at the water with a determined frown creasing her forehead.

Noah stared at the youngster and then back to his parents. "Another sister?"

His father nodded. "Meet your newest sister, Elina."

"Elina." Noah reached his hands up to her. "Can I help you down?"

Her huge brown eyes locked in on his, but she stood fast.

"It's okay, baby," Nina said. "He's your oldest brother, Noah."

"Noah?" She carefully extended a hand toward him and leaned forward.

Noah swept her up in a joyous embrace and spun around. "A baby sister." Still holding her, he looked at his father. "I can't believe you're all here."

"You think Mother was going to miss your wedding?" Jerah said.

"My wedding?" Noah scrunched his brow. "How could you know?"

"We received a message many weeks ago," Nina said, smiling and taking little Elina from his arms. "We wanted to surprise you."

"Well, it worked." Noah hugged his mother. "I missed you."

She kissed his cheek and squeezed him tight. "It's so good to see you, Son."

Suddenly remembering his friend, Noah glanced up and saw Tubal-Cain standing on the shore watching. He released his mother. "Oh, I'd like you all to meet my good friend, Tubal-Cain. He's the best metalworker around."

As they greeted Tubal-Cain, Noah asked, "So who sent the message to you?"

"Your future father-in-law," Lamech said. "The letter mentioned that he wanted it to be a surprise."

"It sure is. The best surprise ever." He glanced toward the shipyard's taller building. "I'll be right back. Don't go anywhere." Noah sprinted toward Emzara's office. "Em!" Opening the door, he hurried into the darkened lower floor. Momentarily unable to see, he stopped a few steps into the space. "Em!"

"What's wrong?" Emzara padded down the stairs from her office.

"Nothing." He blinked hard and she came into focus. "Come here."

"What's all the yelling about?"

He blinked back tears of joy and grabbed both her hands as she joined him. "You have to come with me right now." He pulled her along as he ran outside. King Lamech's half-built boat stood between them and his family.

"What's the big rush?"

"You'll see in a moment."

"This had better be good. I was right in the middle of something important."

"Stop. Close your eyes. It's better than good." Noah readjusted his grip on her hand and walked backward in order to lead her carefully. "Your eyes closed?"

She bit her bottom lip and nodded.

Noah led her around the ship and toward his family who busied themselves unloading their belongings and chatting with Tubal-Cain. Jerah stood on the deck of the boat and passed a crate to Tubal-Cain on the shore.

"Keep them closed." He gently placed his left hand over her eyes. "We're almost there."

Misha ran toward them. "Noah."

"Who's that?" Emzara asked cocking her head.

Noah stood in front of her to block her view. "Open your eyes." He grinned and stepped aside. "I'd like you to meet my family."

Misha sprinted right into Emzara and wrapped her arms around her. Startled, Emzara held her and giggled.

"This is my sister, Misha. I think she likes you already." Noah put his hand on Misha's shoulder. "Meesh, this is Emzara."

She let go and rolled her eyes at Noah. "I figured that much. It's so great to meet you. Now I'll have two big sisters."

Emzara kissed her cheek. "And I'll finally have a little sister."

Noah pointed to his mother and Elina walking toward them. "Two little sisters."

"Two?"

Noah held his hands up and shrugged. "I was surprised too."

Misha grabbed Emzara's hand and pulled her. "Mother, this is Emzara."

Nina's smile grew even wider. She handed Elina to Misha and then stopped to look at Emzara. "I'm Noah's mother, Nina."

"It's wonderful to meet you, Nina."

Nina pulled her close and kissed her on the cheek. As she released Emzara, her eyes welled up and she looked at Noah. "Oh, Son, she's gorgeous." She grinned as she turned back to Emzara and spoke quietly to her.

Emzara's cheeks reddened but her smile broadened and she glanced at Noah.

Pivi joined the group, and as the women became better acquainted, Noah spotted Ara walking toward the ship. Noah hurried over and arrived in time to introduce him to his father and brother. "Father, I want you to meet my mentor. This is Ara."

Lamech gripped Ara's forearm. "It's great to meet you. Thank you for the invitation."

"I was hoping it'd reach you in time, and that you'd be able to come. You and your family are most welcome here. How is your father, my cousin?"

"Very well." Lamech hitched his thumb toward Noah. "I trust my son has been helpful."

A wry grin crossed Ara's lips. "He's not so bad."

Noah chuckled. "Well, your daughter's opinion is the one that counts." He turned around. "I'll help Jerah unload."

As he stepped back into the shallow water past Tubal-Cain, he overheard Ara. "He does great work. He's very talented and hard-working."

"This is the last one," Jerah said as he lifted a chest and handed it to Noah. "I was wondering if you were going to do some work here."

Noah grunted as he lowered the crate to his waist. "Who do you think built that boat you're standing on?"

"You made this?"

"Not by myself, but I did a lot of it."

"Impressive." Jerah jumped down into the water. "It's really great to see you again."

"Likewise." Noah carried the box to the shore and set it next to the others. "Where are we taking these?"

"My house, but just leave them there. I'll get a cart." Ara walked away toward his office.

Emzara, walking arm-in-arm with Misha, arrived at the pile of luggage with the other women.

Lamech stepped toward Emzara. "You must be my future daughter-in-law."

"And you must be Noah's father." Emzara hugged him. "It's a pleasure to meet you."

"And you as well," Lamech said. "I'm glad we could make the journey for your upcoming covenant."

"How were your travels? And with Elina, too?" Noah asked.

"Quite an adventure. And we met some friends of yours along the way."

"The Zakari?"

Lamech nodded. "We stayed with them for two nights. Great people. They spoke very highly of you and Aterre. They said you were heroes."

"Heroes?" Tubal-Cain cocked an eyebrow. "This sounds like a story I haven't heard."

Lamech explained. "When the boys passed through the remote village of the Zakari on their journey here, the place was attacked in the

214

night and four children were kidnapped. Noah and Aterre helped the Zakari men track down the assailants and rescue the children."

Feeling Emzara's arms wrap around his waist and squeeze him tight, Noah lowered his head, embarrassed. "You'd have done the same thing, Father."

"Perhaps. But young Elam said you risked your life to save him from some crazy man with a knife. He wondered if your cut healed up properly."

Emzara pulled away and looked into Noah's face. "You never mentioned that part."

Noah pulled his wrap up slightly and gestured to the horizontal scar above his stomach. "It's fine."

Lamech put his hand on Noah's shoulder. "I'm proud of you, Son."

Noah held his father's gaze. "Thank you."

"Oh." Lamech reached into a pocket in his wrap and pulled out a small cloth with Noah's name stitched into it. "Elam made this for you. Apparently, he's quite the seamster."

After examining the cloth, he smiled as he thought about his young friend. "How was his arm?"

"It's scarred," Lamech said. "But they said it looked so much better than before."

"That's good to hear."

"They also said our return trip will probably go much faster. The people of Novanam and one of the neighboring towns upriver were nearly finished clearing boulders out of the river and installing a system that will allow boats to sail that stretch."

"That's right," Nina said joining them and standing close to her husband. "Now it won't take as much time for you to come and visit."

"Wonderful. I'd love to show Em where I'm from."

"And then you can make good on your promise to show me a keluk," Emzara whispered.

Noah nodded, staring into her eyes and thinking of how much he enjoyed life with this woman by his side.

"Taht?" Jerah asked as Ara led an animal pulling a wagon up to the pile of luggage.

Noah nodded just as the creature raised her head in recognition of her name.

"You still have this old beast?" Jerah scratched Taht's neck. "It's good to see you again, girl."

As they loaded their belongings, Noah watched as Nina lifted Emzara's hand. "So, newest daughter, I want you to know that I'm here to be of any assistance I can."

Emzara nodded and brushed the corner of her eye. "That'd be wonderful. I'd love to have your help. Thank you." She hugged Nina tightly before both turned to help with the remaining few items.

The cart loaded, Noah came near to his wife-to-be and tried to put his arm around her, but Misha jumped between them and wrapped an arm around each of their waists. He shared a smile with Emzara over the young woman's head, and the three of them walked linked together toward Ara's house, the rest of the crowd following along behind them.

Chapter 30

I finally get to see you. Seems there's hardly been a chance all week." Emzara reached a hand up to Noah's face.

He rested his cheek against her palm. "There's been so much to do and so many people to see."

"You won't believe all the food that we've prepared. And to have your mother here, organizing it all — I can't express how much that's meant to me — how much she's meant to me. I wish they didn't have to leave so soon after the wedding."

"I do too. You know, my mother's quite taken with you."

"Having her around has been so good." Emzara blinked faster. "I —" She cleared her throat and tried again. "I didn't know all that I missed, but this week's given me a glimpse of what having a mother would've been like."

Noah kissed her hand. "You have all the qualities to be a great mother. And after tomorrow. . . ."

She blushed, but then looked back up at him.

Holding her tightly against his chest, he didn't speak for several moments as he took in the softness and eagerness of her gaze. Even the pounding of the waterfall in the background could not rival the intensity of his heartbeat. "Tomorrow."

"Yes."

Forcing himself to pull away from her, Noah gently touched the leather band on her upper arm and then gestured to the landscape around them, softly illuminated by the retreating sunlight. "Five years ago, at this spot, you agreed to be my wife."

A breeze from the cliff's edge danced around them and ruffled through the loose curls framing Emzara's face. "It's remained almost the same."

He scanned his surroundings, taking in not so much the details, but remembering that day, which somehow seemed ages in their past and yet, also felt strangely like only moments ago. He had been so nervous before kissing her for the first time.

"Although tonight, I don't see any pesky supergliders to bother us." Her eyes held the familiar spark of fun and invitation before closing as she pressed her lips to his.

Leaning back, she looked up at him. "No supergliders and now these stones that you've assembled. I can't believe you went to all that work this week."

"I know it's different, but I thought it'd be fitting."

"I love that you seek the Creator's favor for our marriage." She joined her hand to his.

Noah kissed her fingers. "You're one of a kind. Not many girls would want to spend the last night before their marriage sacrificing an animal. And that's just another reason that I love you and can't wait to marry you."

"Tomorrow is simply a day. What's more important than the ceremony is how we'll spend the rest of our lives living before the Most High."

Noah squeezed her palm. "You ready?"

"Yes."

They walked to the altar. Noah's arms still ached from lugging those stones out of the pool, and placing them just right. But the time spent with his father, Jerah, Aterre, Ara, and even Tubal-Cain had been worth it.

Kneeling, he caught the woolly bleater he had tied to a stake a few hours earlier. He quickly flipped it on its back and bound its four legs together before loosening the lead rope. Hating what came next, he paused and looked at Emzara, who shuddered and held her arms tightly around herself before nodding. His first sacrifice came to mind. Though thankful that the motions came easier, it still saddened Noah to watch the animal bleed out and to feel it go limp.

Walking over to the shallows where the water did not churn as much, he bent and washed the blood from his arms. Returning, he lit the high stack of branches and then stepped back to Emzara, receiving the dry cloth she held out to him. Rubbing himself dry, he dropped the cloth and spoke the words that came to him. "Creator of the heavens and earth, we thank You — for the life and mercy that You bestow. We are Yours. Guide us and lead us in Your ways as we walk in them together."

* * * * *

Noah stood alone in the center of a large circle created by the several concentric rings of standing guests, and waited nervously for the formal procedures to commence, officially uniting him with Emzara. The gray mid-morning fog, which gave a soft appearance to their surroundings, exposed at least four rows of people, with close friends and family in the central rings. Standing atop a large, low-lying grassy knoll just outside of town, he slowly turned, taking in the faces of those he loved. Aterre beamed proudly at his friend, and Noah gave him a nod. *I owe you.* Tubal-Cain stood to his left along with Zain and his wife, Kmani. Next Noah looked at his sister, Misha, and the lump in his throat grew. It had been so good to be around her this week and see the young woman she had become. Next to her, Jerah and Pivi smiled with the delighted, knowing expressions that usually accompanied those who recently experienced this ceremony for themselves.

He vaguely noted Nmir, Farna, Fen, and Bakur before he caught the look of approval from his father. Lamech stood alongside Ara on a small, slightly raised platform in the place of honor. Tradition dictated that Lamech initiate the ceremony, and Noah wished it would happen soon. He tried to look past the sea of faces to catch a glimpse of Emzara, but the fog made it impossible. Turning back to face his father, Noah saw him give a slight nod to someone beyond him before stooping at his feet and picking up a large clay jar. *Here we go.*

Solemnly, Lamech brought the vessel toward Noah and held it under his nose. Noah closed his eyes and breathed in the heavy scent of the incense.

Lamech spoke the customary words. "The Creator fashioned our Greatfather Adam out of the dust of the ground and breathed into his nostrils the breath of life. It's by that breath, each of us is alive and gathered today to celebrate this sacred rite."

Noah had heard this retelling of the first man every time the village had gathered to commemorate the union of a new husband and wife, but it suddenly hit Noah that these words were being spoken for him. He turned his attention back to his father's voice.

"Just as the Most High placed Adam in a deep sleep, so we symbolize that today." His father held up a thick cloth and placed it over his eyes.

As Lamech tightened it around his head, a knot grew in Noah's stomach and his knees trembled slightly. He opened his eyes but could only see a small slit of light, not even large enough to discern shapes or colors.

"The Most High said that it was not good for man to be alone. Noah, my son, it is not intended for you that you should be alone." His father placed a hand on his shoulder. "You need a helper." Lamech withdrew his hand and his words grew fainter, and Noah knew his father had returned to his place. His pulse quickened in anticipation, and again he tried in vain to peer beyond the cover. He sensed someone standing nearby and felt small hands working to unwind the cloth at his temples. A hint of Emzara's familiar spicy-sweet perfume reached his nostrils. He smiled and breathed it in deeply.

In soft, clear tones, Emzara said, "I can be a helper fit for you."

As the last strip fell from his face to the ground, Noah blinked and beheld the form of his beloved. His breath caught and he stood in stunned silence. Pulled back behind her head and held in place with two wooden pins he had given her the night before, Emzara's hair fanned out before dropping beneath her shoulders. The colorful wrap Kmani fashioned for her glistened as the scant sunlight reflected off the shimmering beads along the upper hem. Noah's eyes welled up as he regarded true beauty. Slowly, his mind prodded him to respond. Custom offered this opportunity for the man to accept or reject the woman standing before him. He always scoffed at the pause some men had taken, thinking that it would seem long indeed for the woman awaiting the response. Now, standing here, he finally understood the reason for the delay.

He licked his lips. "Here, at last, bone of my bones, and flesh of my flesh." The words leaped from deep inside of him. "You are truly the helper created for me. You are mine and I am yours."

At this juncture, Ara stepped forward with a sealed scroll in his hand. With tears in his eyes, he gave it to Emzara. "I've been saving this for your wedding day. Your mother would be so proud." He looked aside and swallowed. After a couple of deep breaths, he faced the guests. "As the father of this lovely woman, I get to pronounce my own blessing on the couple and initiate their vows."

Ara turned again and placed one hand on Noah's shoulder and the other on Emzara's. "Emz, before you were born, your mother and I prayed that one day you'd unite with someone who loved and served the Creator and loved you more than life itself." He deftly wiped away a tear. "You're everything we hoped you'd become and so much more. I love you more than my words could ever express."

Emzara sniffed. "I love you too, Baba."

Ara squeezed Noah's shoulder. "Noah, I've witnessed your devotion to the Most High, and I know you love my daughter. Will you vow before those assembled today to ever serve the Creator and to remain steadfast in your love for Emzara? And if the Creator blesses you with children, will you raise them to follow His ways?"

Holding Ara's gaze, Noah nodded slowly. "I promise each of those things before you and all those gathered here." He looked down into Emzara's eyes, their faces less than a handbreadth apart.

Ara stood next to his daughter and raised his hands high, "You are all witnesses to the forming of a new couple."

To complete the ceremony, Noah slowly unwound the length of leather cord around his waist and cinched it between himself and Emzara at rib level. He wrapped it around them, causing her to stand closer. As he pulled the cord, the space between them quickly disappeared. Her eyes shone brightly and she blushed. He never wanted to let her go.

She raised her mouth close to his ear. "Most couples wrap it pretty loose."

He winked. "Well, I guess we aren't most couples."

CHAPTER 31

Havil — Noah's 46th year

Naamah glanced in the reflecting plate hanging on the wall near her bed. She grabbed a small pot, and in confident strokes applied the dark contents to the contours of her eyes. Peering closer, she wished the metal disk showed more details. *Does my unhappiness really show as Mam intimated yesterday?* Unable to tell, she brushed on more of the dark liquid, hoping to hide whatever she failed to see. Just then, a knock sounded at her door.

"You may enter." She set down the items and turned to face the newcomers.

Two guards bowed and then stepped aside as one announced, "Your father, the king, wishes to speak with you."

Lamech entered and stood looking around as the guards backed out and shut the door.

You may be in control everywhere else in Havil, but this is my room. She donned a smile. "Da, this is unexpected. What brings you here?"

He remained silent as he continued to look about.

What? Just tell me what you don't like and get out. "Won't you please join me?" She walked over to the window and sat on the end of a long cushion that spanned the width of the opening. Her father followed her, and she was pleased when he sat on the other end.

"Naamah, I'm here to discuss the upcoming ceremony and your role in it."

222

"Yes, the dancers, I —"

"Where are you with those preparations?"

"There will be 13 of us total and —"

"You know this is a very big part of the celebration."

Frustrated at being cut off, Naamah clenched her teeth and let out a breath. "Yes, I —"

"I'm not sure that you do. This will be unlike any other festivity we've ever hosted at Havil. This will be the one that all future celebrations will hope to live up to. I have grand plans for it."

Realizing that her father just wanted to hear himself speak, she folded her hands in her lap and tried to look interested as he talked of his accomplishments. He droned on of how he not only made himself great, but also made the city of Havil rise to prominence.

"People look to us to lead the way, and that's what this ceremony will do. Up until now, Sepha's been an option for the masses, a way of living their life if they so choose." He pounded his fist on the wooden window ledge. "But these people are weak. They have no passion. They just go through the motions of life and if Sepha happens to fit in, then they shrug and allow its presence. But all that must change."

Naamah wondered why he focused on Sepha now since he rarely mentioned it. Sure, many of their guards had been through Sepha training to fight, and the famous tree stood in the square, but to him, it was nothing more than a means to an end. *Just like me.*

"The people have a strong leader." As he spoke, he stroked the front of his impeccable garb, which sported large feathers and gold bangles sewn in tight rows. Lamech smiled as if pleased, "Yes, a very strong leader, but they need a strong belief. And with that, they'll learn strong devotion." He turned his focus away from the city street below and looked at her. "I have something for you, my daughter. This will be part of that new beginning." He placed a necklace in her hand.

Her curiosity building, she looked down. Multiple strands of gold and silver beads the size of her smallest fingernail formed a large teardrop, which featured a large gold medallion at the point. Even though the pendant almost took up the whole of her palm, she imagined how nicely it would look, draped around her neck. The familiar crooked tree of Sepha was beautifully carved on it, but she noticed something else entwined up the trunk and into the branches.

"A serpent, Father?" *Like the seer's.*

"Yes. The ancients tell stories of long ago, when a serpent named Nachash, the wisest and most beautiful of all creatures, offered the knowledge of the gods to men."

"Yes, but —"

"And with Nachash added to the tree of Sepha, we'll have a new, improved religion to offer the people. They can have a better life and as we grow in knowledge, we will grow in power. The two elements are now fused."

Naamah snorted. "You really believe all that stuff about Nachash?"

Lamech arched an eyebrow. "It doesn't matter if I believe it. What matters is that the people believe it. That's why this ceremony is of such importance. We will enlighten the people and open their eyes to the way life could be." He pointed at her. "And you, my daughter, with your dancers, will lead the procession. It's a great honor I'm giving you. Make sure that you live up to it."

Feeling the familiar pressure rise to her throat, she got up and moved toward the small table beside her bed. Thankful to gain some distance from her father, she set the necklace on the low-lying carved wooden square. The ornate designs made her again think of Noah, and her failure to win him. *Don't think about him.*

As if reading her thoughts, her father continued. "Now, tell me about your time in Iri Geshem."

With her back toward him, Naamah rolled her eyes. Knowing that ignoring him was not an option, she slowly returned to her spot, sank back onto the cushion, and exhaled. "It's small compared to here."

"Good, good, I thought so."

"The people were welcoming. Tu really liked —"

"As they should have been to the offspring of a great man. But about the city itself. Was it as grand as Havil? Did it have large gates and walls?"

Naamah looked at him quizzically. "No. No gates or walls."

"And the city leader?"

"I don't know."

"Did he have a place like ours?"

Feeling neglected, as usual, Naamah glared at a spot on the floor and clenched a fist. "I don't know."

"Did you not see him? What of their feasts and marketplaces and weapons?"

She worked to control her response, "I spent most of my time with Tu. And he spent most of his time creating a forge. There wasn't much for me to do."

He looked pleased. "Ah, yes, for all your desire to explore, you realized that I've brought the best part of the world right here at your door."

This place will never be the best as long as you're around. If only Noah had chosen me instead of Emzara. She realized her arms were crossed tightly in front of her and loosened them. *Stop thinking about him.*

"Well then tell me about that young man, Noah. You must have at least seen him. How far along is he with my boat?"

That's right. He's coming back here. Naamah heard her father's voice, but her thoughts remained on Noah. *I don't ever want to see him again if I can't have him. No! I will have him. But how?*

The king placed a heavy hand on her shoulder. "Naamah? Is Noah going to deliver my ship on time?"

"I don't know and I don't care!" She swatted his hand away. "I don't want to talk about the ship or the people or anything else about Iri Geshem. Especially not Noah." She leapt to her feet and paced across the room. "Surely the guards you sent with me have given you all the information you wanted. Now leave me alone. I need to work on the songs I'm singing for the ceremony." Angry, she added as much bitterness to her voice as possible. "So they can be *perfect* for you."

Lamech stood. "Actually, I gave the singing for the ceremony to Navea."

"What?" Naamah stopped and put her hands on her hips. "How could you?"

"She's a lovely girl with a lovely voice."

"I know that. But just because she was one of my dancers when No—" She stopped before completing his name. Her temperature rose as she tightened her fists. "Ahh!"

Lamech cocked his head and watched her closely until she calmed. "This is my decision and it's been made. She will sing."

"But I wanted to."

He scratched his brow. "Yes, but you still get to dance."

"Before I left, I was going to do both. I'm a much better singer than she is."

"That was before. She came here while you were gone, I assume to spend time with you. And I realized that with you being away for so

225

long, she'd have more time to practice. She's been up here several times to perform for guests, and I must say, she's perfect."

Hurt, Naamah backed away. *I need it to be me.* "She's perfect? Or her voice is?"

"What?"

"You just gave her the part because of her looks."

Lamech folded his arms and gave her an incredulous look. "That's ridiculous."

"Oh really?" Her voice grew louder. "Then why ask her to come here so often? Was it really to practice or did she 'earn' the part some other way?"

Lamech's hand flew quickly and struck her face.

Stumbling, she caught herself on the bedpost. She raised her hand to her cheek and glared at him.

"No one speaks to me in that manner. Ever! I'm the king and whether you like it or not, you're my daughter, and you will do what I say." He glanced toward the door.

That hit a nerve. Was there some truth to it? She recklessly proceeded. "What are your plans for her? Make her your third wife?"

"Of course I'm not —"

She was on dangerous ground, yet his anger fueled her boldness. She pushed harder, using what little leverage she had. "What are you going to do with Navea's family? Are you going to raid her house too?"

"What?"

"Murder her parents and siblings just so you can take her?"

"What are you talking about?"

"Watch out. She has a brother."

"Naamah, what on earth is wrong with you?"

"When you go to kidnap her, watch out for her brother. He might just jump out of the shadows and slash you to add a matching scar to your face."

His eyes grew wide and he raised his hand toward her again. "Stop!"

She flinched and ducked. *I've finally gotten to him.*

"What's all this about?" He lowered his arm without striking.

She danced away from him and, drunk on her success, continued. "Oh, let's just say that I met the man who gave you that scar."

He shifted his weight to his rear foot. "I was attacked."

"That's not what he says." She practically sang the words in glee. "You went into their house at night and attacked them. You killed his

226

family, at least that's what he thinks. But I know that you spared his mother since you wanted her for your own. You would've killed him if he didn't get away. He tried to defend them." She pointed to his face and slowed her words to emphasize each one. "And that's how you got that scar. And that's how you got Adah." She folded her arms and smiled smugly. "And that's what I learned on my trip to Iri Geshem."

"Who told you all this?" His voice was cold. "What's his name?"

"I'm not telling. But now you know that I know the truth."

Stepping forward, he came a mere handbreadth away and glared at her. The muscles in his cheeks tightened as his jaw clenched.

A tingle traveled down her back as she caught the fury in his eyes. *I went too far. What price am I going to pay?*

Suddenly, his countenance changed. Lamech stepped back and broke out in laughter.

Confused, she stared. "What's so funny?" Her frustration grew as his amusement continued.

Slowing his laughter, he pointed directly at her face. "You are."

"What did I say?"

He shook his head. "Ah, my little tempest, you're just like me."

Shocked, Naamah drew back. "I'm nothing like you."

"I never realized it before. But like me, you crave power, and you'll do anything to get it. You manipulate people to get what you want." Lamech grinned. "Tell me I'm wrong."

Naamah opened her mouth, but nothing came out when she realized he was right.

Stunned by the revelation that she acted so much like the man she had grown to despise. Naamah sat on the edge of her bed, pouting, and crossed her arms tightly against her body.

"The reason you get so angry with me is because you're just like me."

She shook her head and looked up at him with pleading eyes. *It can't be.*

His smile flaunted his victory. "The difference is that I've mastered it, and you have so much to learn."

Naamah pulled her legs up and hugged her knees, absently tucking the end of her long garment under her feet. Blinking back tears, she tried to focus on the floor.

"You think that I took Adah as a second wife because I desired her, but you're wrong."

She furrowed her brow and sniffed. She had not cried since that night on the boat after Noah rejected her.

"I did it to demonstrate to the world that I'm above the old ways. The ancients claim that the so-called Creator established marriage to be for one man and one woman. Well, I make my own rules. I'm the lord of this land, and *no one* tells me what to do. No man, no woman, and no god sets my agenda."

Lost in her thoughts, she barely heard his boasts. *And Noah's married by now.* Several tears dripped from her cheeks, and she watched them land on the lap of her blue silken gown.

Slowly, he stepped to her bed and sat beside her. "Naamah, I have big plans for you. If you're willing to learn from me." He leaned in front of her to catch her gaze. "If you're willing to learn from and obey me, you'll have more power than you've ever imagined. And you can use it to get whatever you want."

His words echoed in her head. Her eyes flashed and she raised her head. "Whatever I want?"

He put his hand on her shoulder again.

Instinctively, she started to pull away, but then stopped. Perhaps this man she had scorned for so long actually held the solution. She looked at his hand and then raised her gaze to his face, a question in her eyes.

"*Whatever* you want."

Reading the implication in his gaze, she allowed one side of her mouth to curl up.

He squeezed her shoulder. "And that starts with leading the dancing *and* the singing at the ceremony." He rose and moved toward the door.

The conversation was over. Though he was the one walking out, she felt dismissed, and for a moment the old hurt reared. But instead of crumbling, Naamah wiped her eyes and drew herself taller. "What about Navea?"

Pausing, the king looked back, a small, knowing smile on his lips. An ugly smile. "You decide where she fits best." He turned again toward the door. "I need someone I can trust to lead our new religion. Prove your loyalty to me, and I'll make you the first high priestess of Nachash."

Chapter 32

Havil — Noah's 46th year

Those were amazing." Emzara brushed her fingertips together to remove the salty remains of roasted nuts. "I wish we had them back home."

"I do too." Taking Emzara's hand, Noah pointed with his free hand across Havil's busy marketplace. "Let's check out that one."

"A metal shop? Very well, but then I get to pick the next one."

"We've already been to three that you wanted." Noah pinched her side, then wrapped his arm around her waist and slowed to allow a group of young people to pass before them. "I should get to pick at least one place while we're here." He pulled back so he could glare at her with the full force of his mock indignation. "*And* don't forget, yesterday I took you to that farm with all the unique animals."

Unrepentant, Emzara slipped her arm around his waist and nestled her head against his shoulder. "And I loved every minute of it. I still can't get over that bird that copied all the noises it heard, even speech." She squeezed him tight. "Thank you for taking me on the trip this time."

Noah kissed the top of her head. "I don't ever want to be apart again."

As they approached the shop, he looked back toward the sea and spotted the two boats they arrived in tied to the dock. Unlike the first time around, Noah had enjoyed every minute of the voyage to Havil with his new bride. Once they landed, they had been met by a delegation from

Lamech, who welcomed the group and escorted them to two comfortable guesthouses. Everyone found something to do. Farna agreed to train a few of the king's select men in how to handle their new ship and immediately set about fulfilling that commitment. Zain spent time gathering details about the city's construction. Ashur and the other crew members frequented multiple establishments and markets, while Noah and Emzara simply took in the city together. Tonight, Noah, Emzara, Zain, and Farna would be guests of honor at Havil's annual festival.

Opening the door to the smith's market and then following Emzara inside, Noah expected an acrid odor to assault his nostrils but instead encountered a pleasant berry scent. As his eyes quickly adjusted to the well-lit interior, he scanned the room, surprised to see shelves laden with trinkets with no forge in sight.

"Welcome to the Gallery of Gifts and Gold." Standing next to a counter, the middle-aged woman wore a dark blue wrap, and her black hair draped evenly around her head, except where it was cut in a straight line just above her brows. Her eyes shifted from Noah to Emzara. "How may I help you?"

Emzara shrugged and hitched a thumb at Noah.

"Greetings. I'm looking for items made by Merka the goldsmith."

"Oh, nothing but the finest for your woman, right?"

Noah glanced at Emzara. "Well, she certainly deserves the best."

"Right this way, please." The woman stepped past the counter and moved to the wall along the left side of the store.

As they followed her down the aisle, Emzara glanced at the price of a pikka-sized golden pendant on a shelf. Her hand flew to her chest and she quietly gasped. She looked at Noah and shook her head.

The clerk stopped at the door along the back wall. "We keep Merka's items in a separate space for our wealthier customers." She barred the door with her arm. "Before allowing you into the showroom, I need you to prove you can afford one of the items inside."

Emzara leaned in close to her husband. "If they're more than that pendant, then there's no way we —"

Noah held up a finger, winking at her. He pulled out a tiny scroll from his pouch and handed it to the woman. "Here."

"What's this?" The clerk examined the scroll.

"You recognize the seal?" Noah asked.

The woman nodded. "I do."

"Go ahead and open it." Noah said. "I believe it's addressed to you."

The clerk looked askance at him and then broke the seal. She unraveled the tiny document and quickly read it. "And what's your name?"

"I'm Noah, and this is my wife, Emzara."

The woman smiled at Emzara and opened the door. "You're a lucky woman. The king's son says you may pick any item you wish."

Emzara's eyes grew wide. "Tubal-Cain did this?"

Noah kissed her forehead. "It's his wedding gift to us. He said you'd find the middle shelf particularly interesting." He nodded toward the opening. "Shall we?"

Holding an oil lamp, the clerk led them into the showroom. She reached up and lit a circular metal tray nearly one cubit in diameter. The flame spread around the ring, and the room filled with light.

Emzara's jaw dropped.

Three shelves lined the left, back, and right walls of the space. Resting on the top shelf, massive, intricately designed gold and silver plates, statuettes, and daggers sparkled in the firelight.

"Look at these!" Emzara pulled Noah to the left and pointed to the middle shelf. "Tubal-Cain was right."

Noah watched Emzara gaze in wonder at the wares before her. The amazement spreading across her face could never be matched by works of metal, no matter how spectacular. Finally, his curiosity got the best of him and he turned his attention to the shelf. Dozens of exquisitely crafted golden animals stood before him. Most were recognizable, but there were a few mysterious creatures he could not identify. He shook his head in astonishment at the quality of the work. "Fantastic."

Emzara squealed. "That one!"

Noah smiled when he spotted the item she pointed to. A golden keluk nearly a span in height stood behind several other flawless sculptures. "That's the one you want?"

She grabbed his arm with both hands and nodded. "Absolutely."

Noah turned to the clerk. "I believe she's made up her mind."

The clerk carefully removed the item from the shelf and handed it to Emzara. "Let me get a box to protect it."

As the woman searched for the proper container, Emzara asked, "How much does one of these cost?"

"It's best if you don't know." She held out a simple wooden box lined with soft scraps of cloth, carefully took the statue from Emzara, and gently placed it in the case. "It's also best if you don't let anyone around here see it. Keep it safe." When the figure had been secured, she motioned them toward the door.

Stepping back into the main area of the shop, Emzara grasped Noah's hand. "I don't need to see any other stores." She raised the box before him. "This has been more than enough. Let's just head back to our guest house."

CHAPTER 33

Only a short walk from the city square, the guesthouse he now shared with Emzara and Zain had been familiar — he recognized the gold-trimmed doors from his previous trip. Noah smiled as he lounged on a cushion in the meeting room of the large guest house. This was a far cry from the cramped quarters on ship.

Emzara slept against his chest. Absently massaging her head, Noah studied the wooden craftsmanship on the trim near the ceiling and the massive railing lining the staircase leading up to their room.

Zain returned from the kitchen with a drink in his hand. He lowered himself into a spot across the low table from Noah. "Looks like the shopping trip wore her out."

Noah yawned. "Me too. We thought it'd be good to get some rest before the ceremony."

"That's not a bad idea." Zain adjusted his wrap as he got comfortable against a cushion. "Noah," he said after a pause. "Do you have any concerns about this evening? I don't get the impression that this celebration will elevate the Creator."

A small knot in Noah's gut twitched and grew tighter. "I was thinking the same thing." Even though he was sure they were alone, he looked around before continuing. "I haven't heard them talk about it, but we know Sepha has influence around here. I told you before about their symbol on Naamah's necklace, and then there's that Sepha tree in the square."

"I thought about skipping the event," Zain admitted, "but I don't want to upset our host. The king's been very gracious, but, between the two of us —" He broke off, his gaze slipping out of focus as if his thoughts had taken him elsewhere. After a moment he gave a single emphatic nod. "We will go and observe. We'll need to be careful. Thankfully, we're leaving in a couple of days, and I can't think of any reason to come back here anytime soon."

Noah opened his mouth to speak, but a knock on the door interrupted his thoughts.

Zain stood quickly. "I'll get it." He strode to the front door and opened it. "Hello."

"Are you the special guests from Iri Geshem?" The man's firm and familiar voice carried through the expansive room.

"Yes, how can I help you?"

"We're looking for the shipbuilder — the man named Noah."

Noah perked up at the mention of his name, causing Emzara to stir.

"Is something wrong?" Zain asked.

"Is he here?"

Noah carefully wriggled away, unsuccessful in his attempt to not wake her. Sleep still clinging to her eyes, Emzara mumbled, "Where are you going?"

"Someone's at the door. I'll be right back."

Zain turned toward him. "Noah, these guards want to speak with you."

As Noah stood he saw Zain back away from the door. "Hey, be careful."

Four guards hastily entered the room and turned their attention to Noah. The leader stepped forward and pulled off his helmet, and Noah recognized him as Nivlac, one of the guards who had accompanied Naamah on her round trip to Iri Geshem. He pointed to Noah and turned to his fellows. "Seize him."

As the three soldiers advanced, Noah backed up but quickly ran out of space. "Nivlac, what's this all about?"

"Did you think you'd get away with it?" Nivlac asked.

"Noah, what's going on?" Emzara asked.

Noah glanced at his wife. "I don't know. There must be some mistake." He ran a hand over his head. "Get away with what?"

Nivlac remained silent until his men cornered Noah. The guard in the center drew his weapon and pointed it at Noah's chest, while the other two each grabbed one of his arms.

Emzara screamed. "What's happening?"

"Why are you doing this?" Noah asked.

Zain stepped in front of Nivlac. "I demand to know what this is all about."

Trying to free himself, Noah twisted and bucked, but the large men held him fast. "What have I done?"

As the guards pulled him toward the door, Nivlac looked straight at Emzara and raised his voice. "Noah, shipbuilder from Iri Geshem, you are guilty of assaulting our princess, Naamah."

"Naamah? Assault? What are you talking about?"

"There is but one punishment for attempting to lie with the princess."

"I never —" A guard struck Noah in the side of the head, causing him to stagger.

"No!" Emzara screamed. "Nivlac, you can't do this. It's not true!"

"Oh, but it is true, Emzara. I saw it with my own eyes on our voyage to your puny city."

"You lie." Enraged, Noah dove toward him but the guards restrained him just before he reached Nivlac. "Ask Naamah. She'll tell you the truth."

Nivlac jerked his head and one of the soldiers landed another blow to Noah's ear. "Don't worry, Emzara. He won't suffer — the execution will be swift. Get him out of here."

"No!" Emzara rushed Noah's assailant and jumped on his back, trying desperately to pull him away from her husband. The man grabbed her arm, bent forward, and flipped her over his head onto the hard floor. She landed flat on her back with a groan.

Zain shoved Nivlac to the side and then slammed into the man who had thrown Emzara, driving him against the door frame. Suddenly freed from one of his captors, Noah whirled in front of the soldier who held him, clutching the man's arm and pulling back with all his might. The force of his spin threw his adversary against Nivlac, and both men tumbled to the floor next to the stairs. Noah dodged a thrust from the guard who had drawn his weapon and now stood between Noah and his wife.

Emzara staggered to her knees. "Noah, run!"

235

With his back to the door, Noah spun and bolted outside. Sprinting toward the gate, he glanced over his shoulder and saw three men exit the house. His mind raced. *Not the city square — too many guards. Where can I go?* He hurried across the road and ducked between two skarep trees, pausing to draw a few deep breaths before turning right and dashing away from the center of town.

Behind him, shouts rang out, the guards calling out his movements as they gave chase. Noah only half listened, his mind flipping from one plan to another like a fish on dry land. After discarding half a dozen ideas, he decided to hide at the edge of town until nightfall and swim to the boat under cover of darkness. To that end, he turned away from the water and the luxurious homes bordering it, and soon found himself darting between smaller buildings and dodging trees. Before long he encountered a road teeming with crowds moving in both directions. Noah turned onto it and tried to lose the men trailing him among the masses of people.

His heart pounding and lungs burning, Noah glanced back to see two of his pursuers step into the road and turn in his direction. Rapidly surveying his options, Noah cut in front of an animal pulling a tall cart and walked ahead of it until an opportunity to sneak away presented itself. He did not need to wait long. From the opposite direction, a large beast reminiscent of Meru lugged a bulky wagon with several passengers aboard. Noah waited for it to pass and then immediately snuck behind it and bounded down a narrow alley between two buildings.

Rancid air filled his nostrils and he soon realized its source. Garbage and rotting food filled the huge containers lining the alley. Pulling his wrap across his face to block some of the odor, Noah squeezed between two of the receptacles and pressed himself tight against the wall. Struggling to catch his breath, he tried to figure out why Nivlac had falsely accused him. What could he possibly gain from such a lie?

Unable to settle on any explanation, his mind drifted back to Emzara and the soldier who had hurt her. Suddenly a horrifying thought struck him. *Emzara.* She'd attacked the guard. Could they arrest her for that? What if they tried to use her to get to him? Anger welled within him. *Creator, please protect her.*

"Mister, what are you doing?"

Noah searched for the source of the voice. Glancing up, he saw a young boy standing on a balcony above him on the other side of the alley. Noah raised his finger to his lips.

Confusion spread on the lad's face as he looked back and forth between Noah and the busy street. Then his expression changed and his eyes grew wide. Pointing at Noah, he turned to the street. "He's here! Right here!"

Noah shook his head rapidly and then peeked around the edge of the container. Two guards cautiously moved toward him. He took a deep breath and darted out of hiding, the soldiers yelling behind him as they followed. The alley quickly came to a dead end, and the walls around him were too high to climb. He spun to face his foes.

They drew their short swords and stepped a few cubits apart from each other, cutting off Noah's only hope of escape. "There's no way out," the soldier to his right said.

For one fleeting moment, Noah rashly thought to give his life trying to exact revenge. He studied their faces, hoping, but neither was the man who had thrown Emzara. He deflated. The guard was right. There was no escape.

"Put your hands above your head."

Noah slowly raised his hands and put them on his head as one guard placed the tip of his weapon under Noah's chin and the other circled behind him. Out of the corner of his eye, he spotted the man raising his arm. Suddenly, a sharp pain struck the back of his head and Noah fell forward before all went black.

* * * * *

Groggily, Noah opened his eyes. His head throbbed and he felt himself being dragged along by his arms, which were tied together at the wrists. Blinking hard, he scanned his surroundings and recognized the city square, but it was surprisingly empty, given the huge ceremony scheduled for that night. *Am I being taken to the palace?* Noah briefly closed his eyes in an attempt to focus and block out the pain. *At least I'd have a chance to explain myself and Naamah could set the record straight.*

Nivlac stepped into view. "Ah, you're awake. Good." His gaze flicked to someone beyond Noah's head. "Put him down right there."

"Where's Emzara?"

237

His captors pulled him a few cubits farther and then dumped him on the ground.

Nivlac grinned. "You should be worried about yourself. Not your pretty little wife. She'll be taken care of."

Noah's gut clenched. "Why are you doing this to us? You know I'm innocent of the charges."

"I know what I saw." Nivlac crossed his arms and nodded to one of his men. "Put him in position."

One of the men flipped Noah around and pulled him to his knees. "Stay right there."

From his new position, Noah could see the large ceremonial platform, where several dancers practiced a routine. As his eyes darted to his right, he jolted when he realized exactly where he was. The lone skarep tree, the symbol of Sepha, stood just a few cubits away. His gaze traced the trunk upward and then caught on something amiss among the branches. Coiled around one of the lower limbs, an unmistakable sculpture of a serpent wound its way from the branch around the back of the trunk, ending with its hideous face looking directly at him.

Noah shuddered as he realized the true root of Sepha's evil. It was the same source that tempted Greatmother Eve at the beginning of the rebellion.

Moving between Noah and the tree, Nivlac pulled out a large blade. "Hold him fast." He turned his body and gestured to the serpent. "How does it feel, knowing you'll be the first human sacrificed to the Great Serpent in Havil?"

Fear's tendrils started to worm their way into Noah's mind, but quickly dissipated as a peace came over him. Noah held Nivlac's gaze. "You worship the Great Deceiver. I serve the one true God, the Creator of heaven and earth."

Nivlac burst out in laughter. "You believe in ancient stories created by men of the past to control others through fear. But don't worry, you won't even feel this." Nivlac nodded and one of his men slid a box under Noah's upper chest while another looped a rope around his neck and pulled him forward across the crate.

Creator, I'm Yours. Please protect Emzara. Images of his wedding day flashed through Noah's mind. Seeing Emzara with his family behind her brought a smile to his face.

"O Great Serpent," Nivlac said. "We offer this man's blood to you as we seek your favor. May all of your enemies share his fate."

"Stop!" A woman's voice pierced the air. "Don't move!" The familiar voice came from the direction of the ceremonial platform and echoed off the cavernous walls of the square.

Noah twisted his head to see Nivlac standing near him with his blade held aloft, poised to strike. His heart rate skipped forward as the certainty of death came into question once more.

"Stop!"

Beyond his would-be executioner, a woman hurried toward them. *Could it be?*

Nivlac turned and instantly knelt. "Princess?"

Naamah.

The princess stormed forward and stopped just before the kneeling soldier. "What are you doing, Nivlac?"

"This man needs to be executed for a capital offense."

"And what has he done?" She looked past Nivlac and her eyes grew wide. "Noah?"

"Naamah." Noah's voice cracked. *Thank You, Creator.*

"Release him." She folded her arms as Nivlac slowly climbed to his feet. "Now!"

"Yes, Princess." With a gesture, Nivlac ordered his men to comply.

"And just what crime was he charged with?" Naamah asked.

Nivlac looked toward the ground and spoke softly. "For assaulting you, of course."

She drew back in surprise, and Noah's hope flared into confidence. "Assaulting me? Where did you hear such nonsense?"

"On the voyage to Iri Geshem." Nivlac glanced at Noah. "I saw the two of you alone on the ship one night, and then I heard you crying afterward. Anyone who hurts my king's daughter like that deserves to die."

Naamah put a hand under Noah's elbow and helped him stand. She touched the side of his face, her exquisite face twisting in sympathy as he winced. "Are you badly hurt?"

"Just bruised. Thank you for saving my life."

"I'm very sorry about this." She turned around, and her voice grew icy. "Nivlac, how dare you presume to execute someone without orders! You've disgraced yourself and our city. Go back to the palace and confine yourself to your quarters until I can speak to my father about what to do with you."

Nivlac hung his head. "I'm sorry, Princess. I was only concerned about your honor."

"Honor, maybe, but not truth." Naamah took a deep breath. "Did you do anything to his wife or companions?"

Nivlac shot a glance at Noah, who took a step forward, fists clenched. "What have you done with my wife?"

Ignoring Noah, Nivlac focused on the princess. "One of his friends got violent, so we have him locked up. I posted a guard outside their quarters to make sure the others didn't go anywhere until the ceremony. The woman is unharmed."

Noah closed his eyes and turned away. *Thank You, Creator.*

Behind him, he heard Naamah giving orders to one of the other guards. "Go immediately and release his wife and friends, including the one you incarcerated. Reassure them that Noah will be reunited with them soon and that this was all a terrible misunderstanding. They're free to go wherever they want in the city."

"Yes, Princess."

Noah collected himself in time to see the man turn and run toward the large opening to the north.

"And you." Naamah pointed to the remaining soldier. "Take Noah inside, get him cleaned up, and then let me know when he's ready for the ceremony. I have a wedding gift for him before he goes back."

The soldier nodded and offered Noah a small bow as he gestured for Noah to accompany him toward the large doors at the front of the palace.

Noah swallowed, relief warring with resentment in his heart. Focusing on the former, he looked at Naamah. "Thank you, Naamah. I owe you my life."

She winked at him. "Just remember that."

Chapter 34

Be calm. Emzara repeated the words again and again, but still the waves of panic rose and threatened to strangle her. She placed a trembling hand over her heart. "Most High, I won't make it. Guide me as You once walked with my father's relative, Enoch. I can't —" Tears flooded her deep brown eyes and overflowed down her cheeks. "I can't make it on my own." Attempting to wipe away the droplets, she realized it was in vain and sank to the floor, sobbing.

Farna! Renewed hope rushed over her. *Yes, I must find him. He's been here before. Maybe he can help me find Noah.* She stood and gasped at the pain from landing on the floor during Noah's arrest. When the spasm passed, she slid on her shoes and rushed to the front door. Stopping short, she backed up and peered out of the window, scarcely daring to breathe lest she be heard through the opening. A guard stood out front. *Now what?*

Walking past the two opulently decorated front rooms, she hastily pressed on until she reached the hallway adjacent to the kitchen. Her feet clapped against the ornate stonework of the floor. She had marveled at the designs upon arrival, but Emzara now wished for dirt surface so she could move more quietly. A large window at the end of the hallway provided light and fresh air to the kitchen. The aperture stretched from just above Emzara's knees to nearly touch the ceiling. Privacy curtains made of layered lengths of a delicate cream fabric obscured all but faint lines of what lay outside while still allowing in light.

Pulling back one layer, she barely made out the forms of the tall shrubs that lined the garden walk behind the house. She shifted another layer and more details emerged. *There's no guard back here.* Removing the third and final layer, she timidly stepped onto the ledge, glancing both directions before jumping down to the lush grasses below.

The lodging Farna shared with the rest of his crew lay next door. Danger awaited in the open space between the two buildings should the guard out front chance to look behind him. Reaching the corner of the house, she dropped to her knees and peered around the edge. *All clear for now.* Lowering herself even farther into the grass that reached mid-calf, she crawled forward slowly on her belly until she reached the back wall of the neighboring house. Shielded again, Emzara stood and quickly brushed her sore and scratched forearms.

She hurried to a much smaller window than the one she just exited. She jumped and attempted to hoist herself over the chest-high sill, but slipped and fell back to the ground. Determined, Emzara kicked off her shoes and took a few steps back. This time, her momentum gave her the needed boost to hook her right elbow over the edge and grip it with her left hand. Grunting and kicking her feet, she slowly inched her upper body onto the sill. Emzara allowed her legs to dangle as she rested and glanced around the room. Several large pots sat in the far right corner. Immediately below where she clung, a shallow table housed several herbs growing in little containers. *It's the kitchen. And no one's here.*

After a deep breath, Emzara slung one foot up. She heard footsteps coming from within and froze.

Farna appeared in the doorway. "Emzara? What are you doing?"

"Farna, you don't know how glad I am to see you."

The man rushed to help her through the window. Back on her feet, she readjusted the top of her wrap and tightened the fold. Between Farna's concerned look and the relief of seeing him, she felt the tears spring up once more. *Be strong, for Noah's sake.*

"What's going on? Why in all the wide river didn't you use the door?"

Gathering her composure, she shook her head and tried to speak, but her sentences came out forced and fast. "Nivlac and some guards came. They tried to take Noah, but he ran, and I don't know if he got away."

"What?" Farna gripped her upper arms and stared into her face as if he could read the history of the last hour in her eyes. "I don't understand."

Her frustration mounted. "I think they're going to kill him. They took Zain too, because he tried to stop them. They have guards out front now, and I need your help."

He started and released her. Moving quickly, he led her to the front of the house and peered out the window without showing himself to anyone who might be outside. He must have seen the guard because, when he returned to her, his face was grim. "Slow down. Start at the beginning."

She forced herself to take a deep breath, then recounted the main points of everything that had happened.

"Did they say why?"

It was the question she hadn't wanted to consider. She swallowed. "Naamah. Nivlac accused Noah of trying to . . . I can't even say it." She sniffed, trying not to acknowledge the tinge of doubt that had crept into her mind. "Wait, you were there. Did Noah ever . . . act inappropriately with Naamah on the boat?"

"What? No, not that I ever saw. He didn't spend much time with her at all. I even thought at one point that he seemed to be avoiding her." Farna shook his head. "Why would Nivlac say that?"

Encouraged a little by his words, Emzara turned her frustration on herself for allowing a doubt about Noah to find its way into her thoughts.

Farna took her arm and gently led her back toward the kitchen. "Do you know where they're going to take him if they catch him?"

"No. It — it all happened so fast."

"My first guess would be the palace. But if he escaped, he'll probably try to work his way back to the boat." He grunted. "None of this makes any sense. We just need to —"

Loud knocks on the front door caused them both to freeze. "Hide in the sitting room." Farna whispered, nudging her to his right.

Emzara rushed behind a large grouping of indoor plants.

Farna returned to the front and opened the left side of the gold-leafed double doors only a hand's width. "What can I do for you, sir?" His gravelly voice came out completely composed.

"We're looking for Lady Noah. She's not in her estate."

More guards. What have I gotten Farna into? Emzara shrank back and sank to the ground, clasping her legs tightly.

"Why are you looking for her?"

"We have important news for her."

Emzara's stomach tightened into a knot during the speaker's pause, the wait for his next words nearly unbearable. *O Most High, please don't let him be dead.*

"And?" Farna spoke with authority, like a man who was used to having people follow his orders.

"There was a mix-up with her husband and a couple of our guards, but it's all been straightened out. I was sent to find her and report that Noah is well and will be escorted to your specially reserved seats at the ceremony."

Emzara almost knocked over one of the taller plants in her hurry to get to the door. "My husband is fine?"

"Lady Noah." The lead guard's face remained placid, unaffected by her sudden appearance. "Yes. And the palace offers its apologies for the misunderstanding."

"He's alive?" Emzara gripped Farna's forearm for support.

"Yes, and he's being well taken care of."

"And Zain?" Farna asked.

"Your friend has been released and will also be escorted to the ceremony. Speaking of which." He snapped his fingers and one of the three guards behind him rushed forward, holding folded garments. "Garments for your group to wear at the festival. Again, the palace offers its sincerest apologies. To see that no harm comes to you, we'll wait here and personally escort you when you're ready."

He's alive. He's alive. Emzara grabbed the colorful gown from the top and headed for the other guest home, trying to ignore the unsettling sense that she was still under guard in a foreign land. Home had never seemed so far away.

CHAPTER 35

Walking between two guards along the hallway on the top floor of the palace, Noah pointed ahead. "Is Tubal-Cain's bedroom down there?"

"You've been up here before?" Garun, the other guard who had accompanied Naamah to Iri Geshem, furrowed his brow.

"Just once. I guess I have a pretty good sense of direction."

"Indeed." Garun turned toward a large entryway set into the right wall. He stepped toward a massive wooden door decorated with elaborate metalwork. He rapped sharply three times and waited. When no response came, he cracked open the entrance and called into the room. "Princess?"

So this is Naamah's room. Creator, thank You for sending her at the right time today.

Garun pushed the door open wide. "Follow me."

Like in Tubal-Cain's quarters, a large window flooded the expansive bedroom with light, only Naamah's view faced north, allowing her to see the city below and the sea beyond. Long strips of colorful cloths stretched across the ceiling, creating an interesting starburst pattern emanating from the center of the room. Expensive gowns hung on the near wall next to two expertly painted landscapes, and beneath them stood a low desk with a couple of scrolls and several pieces of jewelry. Covered in cushions and exotic fabrics, Naamah's large four-poster bed sat against the far wall next to a short latticework partition separating the corner from the rest of the room.

"Wait right here," Garun said as they reached the middle of the space. He nodded to the other guard who turned and left the room.

Noah stared out the window at the crystalline waters of the Great Sea. Floating through the room, a light breeze pressed portions of his silk robe against his chest. Thankful for the long bath in the servants' quarters to wash away the grime and stench from his earlier flight, Noah closed his eyes and breathed deeply. Even though they had just arrived two days ago and were to be honored at the ceremony that evening, Noah could barely wait to leave Havil for good.

Remembering Naamah's intervention in the scene beneath the Sepha tree, Noah shuddered as the image of the serpent jumped into his mind. Equally beautiful and grotesque, but all evil, the presence of the Deceiver meant that Havil had grown far more vile than he had imagined. *O Most High, I pray that the people of this city would turn from their perverse religion and serve You alone.*

"Noah. You're looking better."

Noah opened his eyes and turned in Naamah's direction. She stepped out from behind the latticework and moved purposefully toward him. The hem of her long black gown hovered just above her feet as she walked.

"I feel better. I know I said it earlier, but it's worth repeating." Noah bowed slightly. "Thank you for saving my life."

"It's nice to have people indebted to me." She tipped her chin at an angle and softened her gaze upon him. In this light, the green tints in her eyes gleamed strongly. She flicked her wrist in Garun's direction. "Wait outside."

"Yes, Princess." Garun pivoted and marched out.

"I'm just glad I happened to be in the courtyard at the time. We were rehearsing when I saw you."

"Will you be part of the ceremony tonight?" Noah asked.

"Part of it?" A full smile spread across her face. "Father put me in charge. Ten thousand people will pack into that square down there, and I'll be leading the singing and dancing."

"I'm sure you'll do an amazing job." Noah rubbed his wrist, massaging the soreness caused by the rope bindings. "You have an extraordinary singing voice."

"Thank you. It's a very important night for our people." She stood tall, raised her chin, and pulled her long dark hair behind her shoulders. "And for me."

246

Glimmering on her chest, a golden pendant bore the familiar shape of the Sepha tree, but it was markedly larger than her previous necklace and, on this one, tiny reddish jewels formed the unmistakable shape of a serpent. Noah tried to hide his disgust. "I can see why. Sounds like a lot of responsibility."

"It is. I've never performed before such a large audience." Naamah walked to the window and looked down. "It's filling up. See?"

Noah joined her and scanned the sprawling courtyard below. Droves of people spilled into the expanse through the huge northern and western gates. Several guards stood around the Sepha tree in the center. At the edge of the yard to their right, three stairways led up to the expansive stage for the ceremony. The middle of the platform housed a massive object, perhaps 15 cubits tall, shrouded by a large white cover. *I wonder what —*

Naamah pointed toward the base of the massive edifice. "Down there, that row of seats on the dais between the center and left stairways is where your group will be sitting." Her eyes sparkled as she smiled at him, and she gently brushed his shoulder as she turned and moved away from the window. "We know how to treat our guests of honor."

Noah snorted while searching the crowd for Emzara. "Other than that near fatal misunderstanding with your guards, I'd say that your family has hosted us graciously on both our trips."

"Your people were kind to me. You know, I really enjoyed my stay in Iri Geshem." She paused, and when she spoke again, she sounded a little closer. "It wasn't everything I hoped it would be, but what is?"

Noah shrugged. *Marriage to Emzara.* Staring at the sea, he spotted the two vessels against the dock. "Hey, I can see your new ship from here."

"Noah, about that conversation we had on the boat. I —"

Noah shook his head. "No need to apologize again. It was a misunderstanding." He smiled to himself. "And although I was flattered that you were interested in me, I'm glad we were able to put it behind us." Noah stepped back from the window and turned. "You know, the view from up here is awe —" As soon as he saw her, Noah averted his gaze, and stared at the floor to his left.

Naamah had removed her gown and stood fewer than ten cubits away, wearing only her far-too-revealing undergarments and that profane necklace. "I haven't put it behind us, Noah."

He sensed her moving closer and willed his eyes shut.

"In fact, I'd like to offer you a second chance." She moved around to his right as she spoke. "You were going to say the view up here is awesome. Open your eyes and tell me about the view now."

Stunned by her brazen indecency, Noah stood speechless. He wanted to run, but remembered the guard at her door.

Circling behind him, she ran a fingernail along his bare upper back causing him to flinch and turn his head to the right. "What's wrong, Noah? I know you find me attractive." She traced above his ear while speaking in almost a whisper. "I'm right here. Yours for the taking."

Noah clenched his teeth and took a deep breath. Suddenly, an urge to open his eyes rose from deep inside the recesses of his mind. He shook his head. *No! Creator, give me the strength, please.* He trembled. "I'm already married."

She chuckled softly. "Yes, I know. Emzara is lovely, and we got along so well. That's why I'm willing to be your second wife." Naamah slid the back of her hand along his cheek and then down the side of his neck. "I'll admit, I'm envious that she found you first, but just think, Noah, you could be married to two beautiful women."

"Naamah, please."

She stopped directly in front of him and forcefully pulled his chin to face her, yet he kept his eyes shut. "My father has two wives. Why shouldn't my husband?" She paused. "Look at me!"

Noah shook his head.

She put her finger on his lips and then ran it down his neck to his chest. Grabbing the back of his neck with her other hand, she pulled his head down.

Feeling warm breath on his face, he cracked open one eye ever so slightly and yanked his head back an instant before her kiss could land. "No."

Naamah laughed. "You're proving to be quite the challenge, Noah. That will only make our union that much sweeter."

"I will never be unfaithful to Emzara." Noah stood tall and exhaled. "And I will not sin against the Creator in this way."

A sharp pain struck his cheek, and he realized she had slapped him. "The Creator? You believe those ancient myths? Don't you know who you're talking to?"

Noah cocked his head.

"That's right. I am the high priestess of Nachash. Join me, Noah, and he will guide us into true wisdom and show us real power."

Pity joined Noah's range of emotions. *How can Naamah believe these things?* "I follow the Creator's ways, and I will not turn from them. And if you were truly wise, you'd do the same, instead of following the Great Deceiver."

Naamah's laughter told him she had moved farther away. "Yes, your quaint little village follows the Creator, and what's that done for you? Look at this great city, Noah. Why do you suppose we're so much greater than any other in the world? Because our god is the true source of wisdom. And tonight, the high priestess of Nachash will be revealed."

She stepped close to him and grabbed his hand, pulling it up to her cheek. "Do not deny me. Open your eyes."

Noah steeled himself during a long, awkward silence.

"I'm sorry for hitting you." Her words came out softly. "Seeing you again, here in my room — Noah, I need you."

Keeping his head up, Noah shook it slightly.

Naamah sighed. "Why do you have to be so stubborn? Just imagine all that we can be together. And it can start right now." She shifted her hold on his hand and pulled it toward her body.

Noah yanked his arm back. "Stop."

Her voice turned sullen. "After all I did for you today, this is the thanks I get? You owe me. You said it yourself. If it weren't for me, you'd be dead by now."

"And for that I am thankful, but —"

"Don't you realize I could order Nivlac to finish the job?"

This time the coldness in her tone made Noah shudder. He nodded. "I'd rather die than violate my vow to Emzara and my Creator."

"Aaah!" She slapped him again, her long fingernails scratching the left side of his face.

"Garun, get in here."

Immediately, the guard entered the room. "Yes, Princess?"

"Get him out of my sight and out of the palace."

A strong hand gripped Noah's arm. "Let's go."

* * * * *

Naamah stood still. Her chest rose and fell with her rhythmic, labored breathing. Closing behind Noah, the ornate door represented so much more than its ordinary function. Its bulk seemed insurmountable as it stood in the way of all her hopes for the future. Freely allowing Noah passage back to his life, it kept her trapped.

"Aaaah!" Her yell echoed through her chamber. She ran to the door and pounded it with the bottom of her fists, giving full vent to her anger, welcoming the throbbing pain from her blows. If only it could replace the pain in her heart. Finally tiring, she crumpled to the floor and leaned her back against the door. *How dare he refuse me!* She stared aimlessly at the rug. *He won't get away so easily. I can just have him brought to me after the ceremony.*

Fixing her attention on the black gown that lay crinkled in a small pile in the middle of the room, deep emotions welled within her. Hot tears emerged and descended her dark cheeks. *You're better than this. Don't cry over him.* She wiped back the moisture with her palms, then paused and stared at the site where the seer had pricked her hand. *I haven't lost only him. The oracle deceived me, gave me false hope. Now what? There's no storm from the north to destroy my father. It's all a lie.*

Large sobs racked her body, and she mourned the loss of everything that she had clung to. She gave way to the torrent of tears. Finally worn out, Naamah sat with her head bowed against her knees. Slowly opening her eyes and drying her face, she gazed at the pendant from her father. *Whatever I want? You couldn't even give me Noah. Why should I serve you?* Suddenly angry, she grabbed the chain, ripped it from her neck with a jerk, and hurled it across the room. *I hope you break.*

The adornment struck the narrow section of wall between the window and her bed. It ricocheted off the mud-brick and landed on the low table below. Naamah closed her eyes and leaned her head back, allowing it to hit the door with a soft thud. *How am I supposed to lead the ceremony like this?*

A bright light suddenly assailed her eyelids, causing her to squint hard. Shielding her eyes with a hand, she peeked out to see the brightness originating from the pendant.

Placing her palms on the floor, Naamah winced. "Ow." Gingerly, she got up and walked over to investigate. A small ray of early evening

250

sunlight shone through her window and reflected off the medallion. She picked it up and inspected it. "Hmm, not a scratch."

Shaking her head, Naamah let the jewelry slip from her hand and fall back to the table. The piece landed on the sheet of parchment she had placed there after returning from the seer's house.

A ray of sunlight pierces through it, lighting up your face. The words of the oracle jumped out at her.

She glanced out her window just as the sun disappeared behind a cloud low on the horizon. "Ray of sunlight, hmm." Scrunching her eyebrows, she pondered the familiar words again. "A storm." She picked up the document and held it in both hands. *My little tempest.* Her father's voice echoed in her head. *Why would he call me that? A tempest is. . . .* Her pulse raced as she turned her back to the window. She imagined her father's room on the opposite end of the palace's top floor. *He's on the south side, which would make my room —* She spun and looked out of the opening toward the sea. "The north!"

Holding the page aloft, she softly read aloud. "A storm brews in the north, with thick, dark clouds, vexing your father. But a ray of sunshine pierces through it, lighting up your face." She clasped her hands around the parchment. "It's me. I'm the storm. I'm the one who'll vex my father."

She gazed at her discarded gown and then back at the spot Noah had recently vacated. She snorted in derision. "All this time I thought you were the answer. I don't need you, N—" His name stuck in her throat. With a huff, she grabbed the necklace, retied it, and slipped it over her neck.

She clutched the pendant tightly in her hand and glanced back at the page. *I am the storm in the north.* Slowly she opened her palm and traced her finger along the jeweled serpent. A grin crept across her face. "And you are my light, Nachash." *Allowing her gaze to drift past the adornment, Naamah spotted the throngs of people below assembling for the ceremony.*

"All-wise Nachash, I will follow you. I will perform my best this evening. And I'll be yours." She closed her long lashes and tilted her head toward the ceiling. "Make me great — even more powerful than my father, and I'll devote my energy to you and show the people how to follow you." Opening her eyes, she scowled at the reserved seating near the base of the stage. "And about the one who rejected me . . ." Naamah smiled.

Turning back, she removed the jade dress for the ceremony from the hook where it hung in readiness. As she dressed, she smiled and shook her head at the symbolism. In one evening, her very being had been transformed as starkly as the change from her discarded black gown to the outfit she now donned. Her shattered soul now reshaped itself into her new purpose and new self. She stared at her reflection in the shiny silver plate on the wall. *Even though I might look the same, I hardly recognize myself.* She laughed. "How fitting that this night of all nights, I have truly come of age."

As she finished wrapping the fresh outfit around her torso, someone knocked on the door. Straightening the silk folds, she gathered herself. "What is it?"

The door cracked open slightly. "You have a visitor, Princess."

"If it's Noah, I don't want to see him."

"No, it isn't Noah. He says he's an old friend."

An old friend? "Bring him in."

The guard allowed a tall older man dressed in a dark robe to step past him. The man's right hand held a gnarled wooden staff topped by a golden serpent. "You sent for me, Princess of Havil?"

Having only seen the man in his darkened house, she failed to recognize him until he spoke. *The seer.* She nodded. "Your timing couldn't be more perfect."

CHAPTER 36

In spite of the unsettling afternoon, Emzara smiled as she neared the large north gate. The sun hung low in the sky, casting long shadows to her left. The balmy summer air warmed her skin, but not nearly as much as the news of Noah's safety warmed her soul. The burgeoning crowd scurried out of the way of the two guards escorting her and Farna.

Straight ahead, the lone tree in the courtyard stood defended by the king's protectors. Beyond that, the palace rose high into the air. She studied the giant façade. *I wonder if Noah is in there or already in his seat.*

"This way, please." The guard guided them to the left.

Emzara marveled at the dimensions of everything from the towering walls to the massive platform ahead and sprawling yard around her. An air of enticing mystery and celebration pervaded the atmosphere. As they passed groups of people, she noticed jewelry-clad women who had donned so many trinkets that their bare arms were almost covered in glittering objects. Feeling insignificant, she turned her attention to their guide. "How many people are you expecting tonight?"

The guard shrugged. "It'll be packed."

She raised her eyebrows and gestured to the entirety of the square. "This whole place will be full?"

"It should be. I suspect it won't be large enough to let everyone in."

Emzara looked around again, stunned at the thought of so many people in one place.

Several moments passed before they reached the reserved seating area. To her left, a grand stone staircase climbed up to the top of the massive stage above her. An equally impressive staircase to her right ran from the ground to the center of the stage.

"Right up here." The guard pointed and stood aside to let her pass.

Five short wooden steps led to a decorated platform which held about 20 seats, most already filled. As she reached the top, she quickly scanned the chairs for the familiar form of her husband. "Noah's not here."

"I'm sure he will be soon," the guard said. "In the meantime, I suggest you and your friend take your seats and enjoy the festivities. Help yourself to any of the food or beverages on the table."

Raising her eyebrows, she looked back at Farna. At his reassuring nod, she proceeded to a chair near the waist-high railing. The view from this angle was spectacular. Once she was comfortable, she shifted to observe the people below. "Now that I know he'll be here any moment, I might actually enjoy this." She grinned at Farna.

"Too much fuss for my taste."

As Emzara poured herself some water from the pitcher on the table, the scent of roasted nuts reached her nostrils. She quickly found the delicious items and grabbed a handful as she waited.

The crowd continued to swell. People began to pull out their own food items, and as they partook, laughter and conversation echoed. As time passed, she noticed several hand-sized jars being passed from group to group. Wisps of thin smoke curled up from the center of each. Every time a person accepted the jar, they inhaled deeply before handing it off. Curious, Emzara continued to watch as a rotund man maintained possession of one of the jars and continued to contentedly breathe its contents.

People to the far left began shifting quickly and Emzara peered in their direction to try to understand what was causing such excitement. A muscled man led a beautifully clothed girl to the outskirts of the crowd where a cluster of men stood against the wall. The men yelled to the strong man, and a few tried to touch the woman while she averted her face. Emzara turned away, sickened. *Those men are offering to buy the girl!*

She focused again on the portly man but saw that he no longer had one of the jars. He merely stared in front of him at his outstretched hand and made no comments when a few around him looked as if they were initiating conversation. *How strange. I wonder why he's acting that way?*

A few feet away from him two people cavorted and at one point almost tripped over the man; still he didn't budge. After the pair recovered their balance, their interactions became clear, and Emzara turned her head swiftly, feeling her cheeks warm. She focused on her lap for several moments and determined to restrict her people-watching to the more sedate people seated around her. Zain soon joined them, expression tight, but as the evening sky grew darker, there was still no sign of Noah. Twisting in her seat, Emzara looked every direction for him, doing her best not to recognize anything but the form of the man she knew so well.

A woman in front of her with long black hair turned and asked, "Are you alright, dear? You seem a bit restless."

Emzara knew the woman must have been quite important. In addition to sitting in the reserved seats, she wore an expensive-looking gown and a thin gold tiara rested on her head. "I'm sorry. I'm just waiting for my husband. I thought he'd be here by now."

"Oh, I see." She twisted and patted Emzara's knee. "I'm sure he'll be along soon. He wouldn't want to miss the ceremony."

A loud clang of metal reverberated through the yard. Emzara turned as two large doors at the base of the palace opened, allowing a number of dancing girls to sashay their way toward the center of the square. The leader wore a beautiful jade-colored gown, while the performers trailing her were bedecked in white. Dozens of servants walked beside them, bearing torches to illuminate the scene. Emzara had grown accustomed to the noise of the crowd by now, but suddenly the melodic tones of a musical instrument captivated her. Drums joined, and their sound swelled, drawing everyone's attention to the scantily clad figures weaving their way gracefully in and out of intricate formation.

"You know, I think I've changed my mind," Farna said. "I'm starting to like this place."

"Farna." Emzara playfully hit him on the shoulder.

"I wonder if one of them would want to travel with me." He pointed his large index finger toward the dancers.

Rolling her eyes, Emzara shook her head and struggled to hide her smile. As the dancers reached the tree, they whirled around it, bending low, before righting their torsos, arms outstretched to the heavens. Then suddenly everything paused in dramatic silence. Before long, the drums slowly picked up the pace and volume, causing Emzara's chest to pound with the beat. The dancers leapt into action and wove toward the focal point of the ceremony atop the main platform, each girl following the one directly before her. They slithered first to the right and then left while proceeding to the base of the stone stairs.

"They almost look like a serpent moving on the ground," Farna said.

"Yeah." Emzara watched the procession snake toward the front, and for the first time, she gained a clear view of the woman in the unique gown. *Naamah?* She glanced at Zain and pointed. "It's Naamah."

The serpentine formation climbed the central staircase to the top of the stage. Uncomfortable because of the way their movements accentuated their barely covered bodies, Emzara looked away.

Noah should be here soon. What's taking him so long? Her eyes searched the terrace when suddenly the drums stopped and clear strains of the most beautiful voice filled the air. All the dancers were gone, save one. Although she cared little for Naamah's dancing and attire, the princess's powerful voice captured Emzara's attention. A young boy drew close and accompanied her on an instrument Emzara had never seen before. *This part is beautiful. If only Noah were here to share it with. Most High, bring him soon.*

* * * * *

"I'm very impressed," Garun said. The middle-aged man hurried as he led Noah down the stairs that led to the side door not far from Tubal-Cain's forge.

Still deeply disturbed by Naamah's actions, Noah kept silent.

"We could hear almost everything. I can't imagine how hard it must've been to refuse her — again." He blew out a short whistle. "I admire your convictions."

"Thanks, Garun."

"Thank you for honoring the Creator. I prayed you would remain faithful."

They turned to head down the last flight of steps and one of the knots in Noah's gut loosened. "You follow the Creator?"

"Keep your voice down." Garun reached the landing and unlocked the door. "I'm one of the few around here who still do. But it's becoming more dangerous for us. I fear that things will only get worse after tonight."

"If Naamah's going to lead the people to worship the serpent —"

Garun held up a hand. "That's part of her plan, but I'm afraid she may have more in store for you." He looked around before speaking. "I don't know what more she and Nivlac have plotted, but your arrest this afternoon and the mock execution were just part of a scheme to drive you away from your wife and right to Naamah's waiting arms."

Noah frowned. "Is Emzara in danger?"

"She's safe, for now." He faced Noah squarely. "But you and your people should leave immediately. I wouldn't be surprised if she tries something directly after the ceremony."

"You mean we should walk out during the event?" Noah flexed his fingers to loosen his hands up. "Won't that draw too much attention? We'll be in the front."

Garun nodded. "Try to pick the right moment, though it would be better to create a scene than let the princess detain you again."

Noah grabbed Garun's shoulder. "You should come back to Iri Geshem with us."

"I've thought about it, but I believe my place is here for now." He held Noah's gaze. "If that changes, I know where to find you."

"I'll pray for your safety then."

"Thank you." He pushed the door open. "Let's go. Stay close to me." Grabbing Noah's arm with one hand, Garun drew his sword and held it aloft with the other. "Make way for the king's guard!"

The people near them stopped surging forward and created slight gaps. Garun repeated this multiple times, loud enough to alert those nearby, but not so loud as to create a scene. It took some time, but they finally reached the gate. Behind them tinges of orange streaked the lowest part of the horizon as the sun hid itself for the night. The swarm of people stretched farther back than Tubal-Cain's forge. *I don't think they'll all fit in here.*

Garun continued pulling Noah through the crowd as the last vestiges of sunset faded. Along with thousands of stars, the whole moon lit up the crystal clear sky and bathed the city in its cool glow. On the opposite end of the courtyard, the massive stage rose above the crowds. The swarm of humanity remained quiet, captivated by the song echoing through the expanse. One glance at the woman in green on the distant platform sent chills down Noah's spine. Naamah's magnificent voice, which once enthralled him, now only grated in his ears as thoughts of her brought disgust.

They picked their way through the sea of people toward the north wall, where the crowd thinned slightly. Naamah's song ended with a flurry of drumbeats accompanied by fire and smoke effects. Applause exploded from every direction.

Naamah held out both arms and waited for silence. "People of Havil, thank you for coming to the most important ceremony we've ever held. I am Naamah, Princess of Havil." Her strong voice reverberated against the walls surrounding the throng. "And as you'll learn soon enough, I've recently been given another title, but I'll allow my father to tell you about that."

"Did she get married?" a man next to Noah asked the woman at his side.

"I don't think so," the woman said.

Naamah turned slightly and gestured with both arms to her father on an elevated throne behind her. "I have the honor of introducing you to the most powerful man in the world. People of Havil, this is the reason you came here tonight — to hear from your ruler. Here he is, my father, King Lamech."

The massive assembly roared their approval, forcing Noah and Garun to stop momentarily. People soon chanted the king's name in unison until he stood and motioned for them to be silent.

Lamech stretched his arms out wide. "My people." His voice boomed across the space. "Welcome to our annual Sepha celebration. Tonight is a very special evening for many reasons." With his luxurious robe wrapped loosely around him, Lamech paced as he spoke. "You know that Sepha has been tremendous for our people. Under my rule, and through the disciplines taught by Sepha, we've achieved much in the past few years. Just look at this place." He swept an arm toward the palace to his left.

Cheering resumed along with chants of "Lamech" interspersed with shouts of "Sepha!"

"But I believe we can do more. We must do more." He stopped pacing. "Under my reign, Havil has quickly become the most powerful city on this side of the sea, but we have much to do if we're going to surpass the city of Enoch in the Nodite Empire."

Noah and Garun finally reached the north gate and pushed through the influx of people forcing their way into the congested square. Once they passed the cross traffic, they moved a little easier toward the reserved seating.

"To surpass Enoch, we need to learn all we can about this world. We must commit ourselves to seeking knowledge, wherever it can be found. To assist us in this endeavor, I'm implementing three important changes. First, tomorrow we begin construction on the House of Knowledge on the other side of this wall." Lamech directed an arm to the space behind him. "Our goal is to store all of the world's knowledge in this consecrated place and make it available to you, the citizens of Havil."

Applause broke out again as Noah finally reached the base of the stairway that led up to his spot.

"Thank you for the escort, Garun, and for everything else."

The guard nodded. "Be careful."

Noah gripped his new friend's forearm. "You as well. I hope to see you again." He glanced around. "Just not in this place."

Garun let a half grin form on his lips. "Farewell."

Noah turned and bounded up the wooden stairs. A sheer curtain fluttered in the light breeze, obscuring the guests from the view of those behind them. Noah stepped around the drape and located Farna a few seats away from the edge. Zain took up the chair next to him, and then following an open seat, Emzara. Slipping behind his friends, Noah slid into the empty spot and gently put his hand on her shoulder. "Em."

Emzara spun. "Noah." She threw her arms around him.

Wrapping her in a tight embrace, he closed his eyes and silently thanked the Creator for giving him the strength to resist Naamah. After kissing Emzara's forehead, he whispered in her ear. "We have to leave right now."

She drew back, looked in his eyes, and nodded.

Noah looked around, noting that one of the king's wives sat directly in front of Emzara. He then surveyed the stage.

The king now stood about four steps down the center staircase. "And our quest for knowledge will be greatly enhanced due to our honored guests from Iri Geshem." He pointed toward Noah. "Thanks to the ship they've made for us, we'll be able to travel farther and faster than before." He pressed his palms together and pointed them in Noah's direction with a slight nod. "Thank you."

After a brief ovation, the king continued. "The second change I am making has to do with my daughter, the lovely Naamah." He returned to the top of the platform, where she joined him.

Noah grabbed Emzara's hand and kept his voice down. "We have to go. It's not safe for us here and we have much to discuss. Come on."

"What's going on?" Zain asked.

"I'll tell you on the way. We need to leave the city. Tell Farna."

As Zain spoke quietly to Farna, Noah glanced back to the stage.

Lamech stood in front of the towering covered object. "In addition to being your princess, Naamah will also serve as the high priestess of our enhanced faith." He raised her arm as the citizenry shouted their praise and approval.

Noah looked past the father-daughter duo to the covered object that took up much of the stage. A shiver slinked down his back when he discerned the shape under the cloth. He cupped Zain's shoulder. "Right now."

Noah led his group off the platform and headed for the north gate, while keeping his ears tuned to the king's voice for any warning that their absence had been detected.

"The third change follows naturally from the second," Lamech said. "Sepha taught us great discipline. We learned how to fight and control our feelings. But if we're to achieve a deep understanding of this world, we need call upon the source of that knowledge."

Noah's stomach turned. The Great Deceiver was about to strike again.

"Many of us grew up with the story about the first man and woman being deceived by a serpent. Our ancestors used this story to create rules to control us — to keep us from doing what we wanted and to take away our freedoms. But our ancestors lied to us."

A nervous energy flowed through the crowd. Some of the onlookers they passed seemed confused, while others hung on every word in an attitude of eager anticipation.

"The Serpent wanted to help the first people acquire the knowledge of the gods. He told the truth, but the so-called Creator punished them for their desire to learn. As the years have passed, the one they call the Creator has become weaker and weaker, while the Serpent has grown in power and in knowledge. If we're going to become the greatest people in the world, then we need to serve the god who can lead us to those heights."

Noah turned and tapped Farna's shoulder when they reached the exit. "Head straight to the ship and get it ready to leave. We'll gather the belongings and the others and meet you there."

Farna nodded.

"People of Havil." Lamech's voice resounded more powerfully than before. "You have the distinct honor of being the first people to serve the giver of true knowledge. It is a great pleasure to introduce you to our new god, the Great Serpent."

Wild cheering erupted from all directions.

Noah, Emzara, and Zain stopped at the exit and turned back for a final look.

Naamah's dancers twirled around the cloaked object, while she and Lamech each picked up a rope connected to the covering.

Lamech held his arms upward. "People of Havil, feast your eyes on your god. I give you, Nachash!"

Lamech and Naamah pulled their ropes, and the huge cloth fell from the image. Coated in glimmering gold from its coiled base to its terrifying face, poised as if ready to strike, the towering statue of the Great Deceiver dominated the massive stage.

Naamah faced the multitude. "Bow down in reverence." She turned and fell on her knees before the image. Waves of people in the crowd followed her example.

Tears dripped from Emzara's eyes as she looked at Noah.

"I know." Noah grabbed her hand and pulled her through the open gate. "Come on. We must get onboard as soon as possible. We'll need the Creator's wisdom to stand against this abomination."

Enjoy a glimpse of Book 2 in the compelling Remnant Trilogy

CHAPTER 1

Naamah twirled, her bare feet tracing the same intricate steps to the dance that she performed earlier in the evening. Tap, tap, tap-tap-tap. In the final steps of the choreography, her toe gracefully patted against the sandstone flooring that lined the gardens on top of the palace. She dipped her left shoulder and glanced over it to where the seer lagged slightly behind, his lanky frame dark against the backlighting of the torches. Laughing, she ran back toward him and swirled around several potted kalum trees, enjoying the spicy aroma their flowers gave off.

"How did I do tonight?" she asked, looking up at him and hoping he approved.

"Very well, my child." The old man lightly patted her cheeks, as a father who was proud of his child would do.

"Did I?"

"Yes, your singing mesmerized the people. Hearing your talent in person was greater than I imagined."

"I'm so glad." Unable to keep still, she spun as they walked toward the waist-high parapet marking the edge of the expansive rooftop garden.

"You're a natural leader, and tonight you received some of the recognition you deserve."

Naamah glowed under his high praise and leaned against the low stone wall. "There were so many people. Look at all the lights below, even this late at night."

They both peered out at the city, which still bustled. Pockets of people moved about the streets below, laughing with their companions and calling out good-naturedly to other groups that passed by. The sheer number of lit windows indicated that the celebratory atmosphere moved beyond the streets. Music and drumbeats sounded out from a variety of places.

She flung her hands wide. "Isn't the city magnificent?"

"It's quite a sight. And you are its only princess."

"Yes, I am. Everyone got to watch me."

"And as priestess." He stroked the serpent image atop his staff. "Introducing them to Nachash was your greatest achievement tonight. Against the backdrop of your talents, the people saw the beauty in following him."

Naamah pressed her hands together and trembled with excitement. "I can't wait for next year's celebration. I'll dazzle them even more."

The seer gave a patient chuckle. "I have no doubts, but listen to me." He grabbed her hands. "Tonight was only a first step for you. With my guidance, you can achieve power you've never dreamed of. The success you now feel — and deserve — is only a glimpse of what is to come."

"More?"

He swept his arm out. "All that you see here — the might of your father's soldiers and the skill of your craftsmen." He shook his head slowly. "It's nothing compared to the power available through Nachash."

Intrigued, Naamah looked up and rubbed her chin, pondering the implications.

"The first time we met I saw greatness and giftedness in you. And power — that few can possess and even fewer will be able to resist."

Naamah leaned in closer. "Show me. Teach me everything."

A crooked smile spread across his lips. "Patience. It takes time. I'll guide you in the ways of Nachash, and as you learn, your power and wisdom will grow."

Hearing the rustle of leaves, Naamah stepped back as she glanced around. "Who's there? Speak."

Nivlac stepped forward from the foliage into the well-lit patio area, accompanied by Tsek, a mountain of a man. Nivlac bowed. "Princess, the king's captain has a message for you." Nivlac retreated to his post a short distance away.

Tsek bowed. "Evening peace, Princess. I'm here on behalf of the king. He wishes to inform you that he's pleased with your part in the festivities. Because of your efforts, the people learned how great of a leader they have. Now they have a god worthy of the leader who has done much to build this city into what it is. And you, Naamah, played a part in that."

Naamah stiffened as Tsek droned on. *It's just like Father to take what should've been a simple compliment and make it all about himself.* Discouraged, she looked up at Tsek's strong jaw line as she waited for him to finish. *Power? Can I really be as powerful as the seer promised? Could I turn Tsek's loyalty to me instead of my father? Imagine that. His own captain following me.* She grinned.

"I'm glad that you're pleased with your father's report of the evening's successes."

Pulled suddenly from her reverie, Naamah blinked quickly, attempting to speed up her brain's responses. "Of course. I'm happy as long as my father is happy."

Tsek bobbed his head. "Do you have anything you want me to take to the king in reply?"

She looked at the seer, who had taken a seat a short distance away, while she searched for the right phrase. Stepping close to Tsek, she brushed an imaginary speck from his broad, tanned shoulder, being sure to let her hand linger longer than necessary. She cast him an alluring look as she backed away. "Tell the king that my victory rests in his vast accomplishments."

Tsek searched her face before replying. "I shall relay that. And may I say that, personally, I thought you were the highlight of the evening."

She flashed him a broad smile. "You are most kind, Tsek. Thank you for bringing words from my father." She dismissed him with a small wave of her hand.

He bowed and looked back at her twice as he walked through the garden.

The seer rejoined Naamah, wearing a slight frown. "That was not the type of power I was alluding to."

With a flip of her head, she tossed her hair over her shoulder. "Oh, I care nothing for him, but it wouldn't hurt to have his complete loyalty." She turned around to look at the city again. "There is, however, someone that I'd like to bring to his knees before me. Do you think you could help with that?"

"Perhaps. Tell me what's on your mind."

"A man slighted me twice. He dismissed me once a while ago and again just today." She let tears gather at the corner of her eyes, playing the role skillfully and without hesitation.

"Would this be the man your guard mentioned this evening? Noah? The shipbuilder?"

She bit her lip and nodded.

"And just what do you want to do?" He gently touched her shoulder.

She wanted vengeance. *But how?* "I, I . . . never mind."

"Capture this man's wife so that he has to beg you for her life."

Once hidden in the recesses of her mind, her darkest thoughts became clear. And yet, the seer spoke them calmly and with even tones, as if he were simply discussing what would be served for the next meal.

Naamah's eyes widened. "How — how did you know?"

The seer looked steadily at her. "I've been trying to tell you that the power I can teach you is beyond anything you've imagined."

Still awed by his ability, she stared into the wrinkled face before her.

"If you're bent on making this man pay, then call your guards to go get his wife. But I must say, you're setting your ambition too low."

She shook her head, brushing off his disapproval. "Maybe I am. But if I put this behind me, then I can focus more fully on what you have to teach me." She raised her voice so that the sentry stationed on the terrace might hear her. "Nivlac!"

Her most dependable guard hurried across the roof and stood before her. "Yes, Princess."

"I have an urgent mission for you."

BEHIND THE FICTION

The first part of this non-fiction section, "Answering Questions Raised by the Novel," is designed to address certain questions that readers may think of during the story. Many of these issues will be apologetic in nature. That is, in this portion of the book, we will respond to numerous challenges raised by skeptics and critics. The goal is that these novels will also help you defend the truth of Scripture.

You may have noticed as you read the novel that several things didn't line up with what you may have expected. This was done on purpose to help break certain stereotypes about Noah and the pre-Flood world that many Christians assume are from the Bible, but aren't actually found there. We want you to see clearly what comes directly from the Bible and what comes from traditions people have developed over the years.

The second feature in this non-fiction portion is what we call "Borrowed from the Bible." Since the Bible only includes scant details about Noah's life and times, we must use artistic license to flesh out his story. We certainly do not wish to be seen as adding to Scripture and understand that these are works of fiction, with the exception of the few details that come straight from the Bible. Some places, we curbed the amount of artistic license taken by drawing from other biblical accounts instead. In "Borrowed from the Bible," we highlight certain events and customs in our story that will be somewhat familiar to those who know their Bibles.

The third special feature is entirely unique to this series. We had the incredible opportunity to work behind the scenes at the Ark Encounter for the past few years. Tim was involved in the planning of nearly every exhibit and was responsible for writing or overseeing all of the content while K. Marie took part in designing various aspects of several spaces on the Ark. We wanted to use our experience to bring this series to life in a creative manner. As such, many of the objects and animals described in the book are on display in the Ark Encounter, so visitors to the theme park can see part of what Noah witnesses in our story. The "Encounter This" section lets the reader know what these items are and where they can be found.

We hope you've enjoyed reading about what may have been, while learning to better discern between fact and fiction.

Answering Questions Raised by the Novel

Did the people before the Flood really live over 900 years?

The Bible tells us that Noah lived to be 950 years, and all of his male ancestors, with the exception of Enoch (365 years) and Noah's father, Lamech (777 years), lived over 900 years. Lifespans of this length are difficult for us to fathom, because people in our day do not exceed 120 years. But how is it possible for people to live so long?

Before listing the various theories to explain such longevity, the reader should be aware that the Bible is not the only ancient text that assigns great ages to the earliest people. The Sumerian King List, from one of the earliest post-Flood civilizations, describes a series of rulers before the global Flood who lived and reigned for many thousands of years. While this fictional list includes people living over 20,000 years and is not inspired by God like Genesis is, such an early document shows that people who lived soon after the Flood believed their pre-Flood predecessors lived extraordinarily long lifespans.

Various theories have been proposed to account for such long lifespans. Perhaps the most popular idea among Christians who accept the ages as accurate is that the pre-Flood world had some sort of vapor or water canopy around it that filtered out harmful radiation and allowed people to live for 900 years. There are numerous scientific problems with the canopy model, and it is not explicitly taught in the Bible but was just one possible interpretation of a passage. As a result, many creationists who once held it have now abandoned it.

Another proposal is that something happened genetically to reduce man's lifespan. In studying the Genesis genealogies, we see two drastic drops in lifespans. At the time of the Flood, life expectancy dropped from roughly 900 down to about 400, based on the small sampling of people mentioned. Then after three generations, the life expectancy dropped to around 200 years. This decrease is often associated with the rebellion at Babel. Then the lifespans slowly dropped over the next dozen or so generations to what we experience today. In support of the genetic argument, one can point to Lamech, Noah's father, who died five years prior to the Flood at the age of 777. Is this a hint that there was some genetic factor in Noah's line that would lead to reduced lifespans? Also, at the time of the Flood, humanity's genetic diversity was reduced to the information carried by eight people. This "population bottleneck" was somewhat repeated at Babel, as a large population was suddenly split into about 70 small groups that went their separate ways. Perhaps these two "bottleneck" events enabled a problem within Lamech's genes to become pronounced throughout all humanity. Of course, Noah still lived 950 years, so this may not be the best solution either.

The answer to why man does not live nearly a millennium anymore may be found right in the Bible's Flood account. Genesis 6:3 states, "And the LORD said, 'My Spirit shall not strive with man forever, for he is indeed flesh; yet his days shall be one hundred and twenty years'" (NKJV). While many Christians believe that the "one hundred and twenty years" refers to a countdown to the Flood, the text does not necessarily make that point, as the Flood is not mentioned for another 14 verses.

A cursory reading has given many people the impression that the "one hundred and twenty years" refers to a new limit on man's lifespan. But how could this be since Noah lived 950 years and his son, Shem, lived 600 years? Before dismissing the lifespan view based on this argument we should consider what the Bible reveals about lifespans from the time the announcement was made until the time it was written down by Moses. The following chart shows the lifespans of the people from Noah to Moses.

Name	Lifespan	Name	Lifespan
Noah	950	Terah	205
Shem	600	Abraham	175
Arphaxad	438	Isaac	180
Salah	433	Jacob	147
Eber	464	Levi	137
Peleg	239	Kohath	133
Reu	239	Amram	137
Serug	230	Moses	120
Nahor	148		

Man's life expectancy from that point in history steadily dropped from over 900 years to 120 years in the 16 generations from Noah to Moses. Lifespans continued to decrease after Moses. Joshua lived 110 years, and before long, it seems that few lived beyond 80 years.

It is quite interesting that the Bible records the ages of the people in the genealogy from Adam down to Moses. As soon as the lifespans decreased to 120 years, the Bible stopped recording how old a person was when they died. It is as if Moses showed the fulfillment of Genesis 6:3 by listing all the ages, but as soon as this passage was fulfilled, there was no longer a need to record the ages. Yes, Joshua lived to 110, but the ages of his immediate ancestors are not given, and there may be another reason why his age was specifically given. The Egyptians of that time believed the ideal age for a person was 110 years. As such, it is rather ironic when Jacob tells Pharaoh that his 130 years had been few compared to his ancestors. Moses outlived this "ideal age" and Joshua reached it.

Also, notice that in modern times we see a handful of people live beyond 110 years, but they do not reach 120. Much more could be said about this issue. Interested readers can learn more from my article, "Did Noah Spend 120 Years Building the Ark?" It is available at http://midwestapologetics.org/blog/?p=1445.

Does this mean that they matured at a slower rate?

When a person lived over 900 years, what would their maturation rate have been like? Certainly a 100-year-old person at that time did not look like a modern centenarian. Noah had children and built an Ark while in his 500s. Another potential clue related to the maturation rate can be found in Genesis: the youngest recorded age of a pre-Flood person having children is 65 (Mahalalel in Genesis 5:15 and Enoch in Genesis 5:21). Of course, they may have had other children prior to the sons mentioned in the Bible, but since Scripture is silent here, we have the opportunity to incorporate some artistic license on this point in the story.

Our novel depicts a person's development into adulthood as taking about twice as long as in our day. The early part of the story revolves around Noah's 40th birthday — when he would be considered a man and have the opportunity to set out on his own. From that point on, a person would age considerably slower, and once they reached about 250 years of age, you could divide their age by 10 to picture how they might look compared to people today. In other words, a 400-year-old man would look about the same age as a 40-year-old man today.

How many siblings did Noah have?

Our story begins with Noah having a brother, Jerah, and a sister, Misha, but these will not be his only siblings in the story. Genesis 5:30 states that after Noah was born his father Lamech lived another 595 years and had sons and daughters — at the very least, Noah had four siblings. The Bible does not specify how many brothers and sisters he had, and it does not name any of them.

We portray Noah as the oldest of Lamech's children, but the Bible is silent on this point as well. Some interpreters have assumed that each of the men listed in the lineage from Seth to Noah were the firstborn sons, but this is highly unlikely. We know Seth was not Adam's oldest child, so there is no reason to assume all the other men listed were the oldest either. Also, Genesis frequently focuses on someone other than the oldest son (e.g., Isaac rather than Ishmael, Jacob instead of Esau, and Joseph rather than Reuben). Noah may have had older siblings, but the Bible says nothing about them.

What does the Bible really teach about Enoch?

In the novel, Noah's great grandfather, Enoch, is a bit of a mysterious figure, and his sudden disappearance gave rise to multiple legends. The Bible sheds just a little light on him. Genesis 5:21–23 tells us that Enoch lived 65 years before his son, Methuselah, was born, and he had other sons and daughters over the next three hundred years. Then verse 24 states, "Enoch walked with God; and he was not, for God took him."

Scripture does not say much else about him, but Hebrews 11:5 clarifies what Genesis 5:24 means. "By faith Enoch was taken away so that he did not see death, 'and was not found, because God had taken him'; for before he was taken he had this testimony, that he pleased God." Enoch was a faithful man who walked with God. This does not mean that he took strolls with his Creator, but that he faithfully followed the Lord.

The final point that we learn about Enoch from the Bible is that he prophesied judgment against ungodly individuals. Jude 14–15 states, "Now Enoch, the seventh from Adam, prophesied about these men also, saying, 'Behold, the Lord comes with ten thousands of His saints, to execute judgment on all, to convict all who are ungodly among them of all their ungodly deeds which they have committed in an ungodly way, and of all the harsh things which ungodly sinners have spoken against Him.'" This is a quote from Enoch 1:9. The Book of Enoch was a popular writing in the first century A.D., but the fact that Jude quotes from it does not mean it should be included in Scripture. It simply means that Jude, whose writing was inspired by God, believed this particular verse was a genuine prophecy.

Much more could be said on this issue, but the important point for our purposes is that Enoch prophesied against wicked people. Approximately 70 years passed from the time God took Enoch until Noah's birth. Our story opens with many people still following the Creator, at least in the region in which Noah lived, but there are reports that certain places have become quite wicked. One of these places is the land of Nod and its primary city, Enoch, named after a different Enoch — Cain's son (Genesis 4:17). We envisioned this city as one of the places that Noah's great grandfather would have prophesied judgment upon the wicked.

What is the difference between land of Eden and Garden of Eden?

Genesis 2:8 states that "God planted a garden toward the east, in Eden" (NASB). The garden is where He put the first man, Adam, and where the Lord made Eve from Adam's rib. It was in this garden that God made two special trees: the tree of life and the tree of the knowledge of good and evil. And it was in this garden that Adam and Eve rebelled against God when they ate the forbidden fruit.

But the garden was just a part of the land of Eden. We do not know how large either one was. And we also do not know where they were located, only that the land was apparently in the east, although some Bible translations have the garden in the eastern part of the land. Many people have assumed that the Garden of Eden must have been in the Middle East, near the Tigris and Euphrates Rivers because these rivers are mentioned in Genesis 2:14 in connection with the garden. However, the description given in Genesis does not match the Middle East since it describes one river flowing out of Eden that divided into four rivers: the Pishon, the Gihon, the Hidekkel (Tigris), and the Euphrates. The modern Tigris and Euphrates Rivers are two separate rivers that come together before emptying into the Persian Gulf. We need to keep in mind that the global Flood described in Genesis destroyed Noah's world and completely reshaped earth's geography. And it would make sense for Noah's family to rename some of the places in the new world after the places they knew from before the Flood.

Was Noah the one to bring rest as Lamech thought?

Upon Noah's birth, his father Lamech uttered the following words: "And he called his name Noah, saying, 'This one will comfort us concerning our work and the toil of our hands, because of the ground which the LORD has cursed'" (Genesis 5:29). Lamech's longing for an end to the Curse on the ground formed the basis of our decision to have Noah grow up on a farm. This verse seems to indicate that Lamech had grown weary of working the ground. And since Noah would one day be required to provide for thousands of animals, it seemed natural to have him learn to grow crops and care for certain creatures at a young age.

Lamech apparently suspected or hoped Noah would be used by the Lord in a very special way, but was his utterance a prophecy, a blessing, or simply an ancient convention appearing frequently in Genesis?

Some commentators (Skinner, von Rad, Westermann, et al.) have suggested that this statement found fulfillment in Noah's discovery or advancement of viticulture (growing of grapes, particularly for wine). It is argued that Lamech's generation did not see an end to the Curse, but they were wiped out by the Flood. So the comfort from the Curse came through wine derived from the grapes. It's difficult to believe that Lamech's words would be fulfilled in such a seemingly trivial manner. Of course, these scholars do not truly view Lamech's words as being prophetic, and generally see them being attributed to Lamech after the fact.

Henry Morris viewed Lamech's words as a prophecy, although there are significant problems for this view. First, the text does not indicate that his words were prophetic, nor is Lamech ever cited as a prophet. Second, if it was a prophecy, how was it fulfilled? How did Noah provide comfort (or rest) from the work and toil of people's hands? All the remaining people in Noah's and Lamech's generations died in the Flood, except for those on the Ark. Obviously, the Curse was not lifted.

Two plausible fulfillments could be considered, but they do not seem to match the text. First, a massive amount of wickedness was washed away from the earth during Noah's lifetime, but so were all of Lamech's family members except for Noah and seven others. So how was the Flood a comfort to "us" from Lamech's point of view? Perhaps he was speaking of his family in general — Noah would bring relief/comfort/rest from the vast wickedness on the earth. With the restart after the Flood, certain effects of the Curse were lessened, yet the Curse on the ground remained, as did death and man's wickedness.

The other view is that Lamech's words pointed forward to the Messiah, Noah's distant descendant. Certainly, Jesus is the One who will do away with the Curse and bring comfort, but Lamech's words seem to imply something that would happen in Noah's lifetime — that Noah would bring about this comfort.

A third view is that Lamech just followed a typical naming convention seen frequently in Genesis and occasionally in other books of Scripture. These could have been prophetic in nature, although they are not necessarily so. For example, in Genesis 3:20, we see that "Adam called his wife's name Eve, because she was the mother of all living." Adam's naming of Eve did not require any special knowledge of the future from God, so it was not truly prophetic in that sense. He simply needed to know that they were the only two people on earth and that they were to populate the planet.

A child would often be named based on their appearance or actions at birth. For example, when Rebekah gave birth to Jacob and Esau, we read the following:

> So when her days were fulfilled for her to give birth, indeed there were twins in her womb. And the first came out red. He was like a hairy garment all over; so they called his name Esau. Afterward his brother came out, and his hand took hold of Esau's heel; so his name was called Jacob (Genesis 25:24–26).

Wordplays are involved in the naming of the boys. The word *Jacob* is related to the "heel," and *Esau* uses some of the same sounds for "hairy" (*se'ar*), and note that Esau's descendants would live at Mt. Seir.

At other times, children were named based on the emotions of one or both of the parents. With the birth of Isaac, whose name means "laughter," both parents had laughed upon hearing the announcement (Abraham in Genesis 17:17 and Sarah in Genesis 18:12). The naming of Jacob's sons provides a dozen examples of this (Genesis 29:31–30:24, 35:18).

Of course, God is fully capable of speaking the future through the lips of the godly and ungodly. So there are no theological problems with Lamech uttering a prophecy at Noah's birth, but the text does not specify that his words were meant to be a prophecy. Also, applying his words to the Flood would seem to stretch their meaning, perhaps further than can be allowed. Lamech and his immediate family (save Noah and his family) were not comforted from the ground God had cursed. The ground was (and is) still cursed following the Flood, so just how were his words fulfilled in Noah's life?

If Lamech's words must be understood as a prophecy, then it would seem that the words of each of the other parents in Genesis who used this naming convention should be understood as prophecy. However, if that is the case, then it seems that numerous false prophecies were uttered. The best solution seems to be viewing Lamech's words as a statement of what he hoped would take place rather than as an actual prophecy. Seeing Lamech's words as a typical naming convention would be in line with the practice that appears throughout Genesis in which parents often expressed what they hoped would occur as a result of the child's birth. In the text, there is an indication in his words that life was difficult and he sought relief from his toil. There is a bit of irony in his statement. The land would receive a reprieve from the violence of man for a time; however, the ground itself was destroyed with the Flood, and the Curse remained upon it.

When did carnivores become carnivorous and scavengers become scavengers? Also, how did attack/defense structures come about?

Genesis 1:29–30 explains that human beings were given green herbs for food. The same is true with "every beast of the earth," "every bird of the air," and "everything that creeps on the earth in which there is life." It is not until after the Flood that God gives man permission to eat meat (Genesis 9:3). But what about the animals? Did they begin to eat meat after the Flood or were they permitted to do so long before God destroyed the world?

The Bible is silent about when certain animals turned to carnivory or became scavengers. In rock layers deposited during the Flood, we occasionally find fossils with bite marks, and some fossils have been discovered with the remains of another animal in its belly region. So carnivory and scavenging seems to have occurred prior to the Flood, but when did it start?

One possible answer is that these activities began soon after Adam and Eve sinned. When He cursed the serpent, the Lord said, "Because you have done this, you are cursed more than all cattle, and more than every beast of the field; on your belly you shall go" (Genesis 3:14). The serpent may have undergone certain changes at this point, which may hint at other animals changing at this time as well. Adam's sin wrecked this world, so it makes sense that the animals were corrupted at this time too.

Another possibility is that the animals gradually became predators over the centuries from creation to the Flood. Just as mankind's wickedness seemed to gradually increase until it reached a climax at the time of the Flood, certain animals may have gradually started to eat meat and scavenge. This is how we portray them in our story because we thought it would be another way for Noah to vividly see the wickedness of sin. If he had grown up with carnivorous animals, then he may have thought of it as normal, but this activity is an intrusion in God's creation. Witnessing animals killing and eating other animals, and then seeing people eat animals shows Noah that the world is broken due to sin.

This raises a related issue. If these animals were initially designed to eat plants, then when and how did they acquire their various attack and defense structures? The Bible does not directly address this question, but at least three plausible answers have been proposed. First, since the serpent seems to have been altered in some way at the time of the Curse, it is possible that other animals were changed at that time. Second, the animals may have been created with these structures but originally used them for different purposes. Third, God may have created these animals with the genetic information for the attack and defense structures, but these were not displayed immediately, remaining latent until sometime after Adam's sin.

When did people start to eat meat?

As mentioned in the previous answer, man was originally instructed to eat vegetation (Genesis 1:29), and it was not until after the Flood that God gave mankind permission to eat animals (Genesis 9:3). However, the people before the Flood had grown exceedingly wicked. Consider the following verses to see how the Bible describes the people of that time:

> . . . the wickedness of man was great in the earth (Genesis 6:5)

> . . . every intent of the thoughts of his heart was only evil continually (Genesis 6:5)

> The earth also was corrupt before God, and the earth was filled with violence (Genesis 6:11)

> . . . it was corrupt; for all flesh had corrupted their way on the earth (Genesis 6:12)

> . . . the earth is filled with violence (Genesis 6:13)

It is not hard to imagine that many of these wicked people would have violated God's dietary instruction and were killing animals for food. In the story, we made sure that the righteous people, like Noah and some of his family members, did not eat meat. This detail also explains why Noah is disgusted by the fish served to the king. Up until this point in our story, he had not witnessed anyone violating this instruction.

Was Enosh's generation godly?

Genesis 4:26 states that when Seth's son Enosh was born, "men began to call on the name of the LORD." This verse seems rather straightforward in teaching that mankind began worshiping God around the time of the birth of Adam's grandson, Enosh. Based on Genesis 5:3–6, we learn that Enosh was born 235 years after Adam was created.

In our novel, we portrayed Enosh's generation as one that was largely faithful to the Lord. Given their 900-year lifespans, these people would have been the elders in many places in Noah's early years. This is most clearly seen in the city of Iri Geshem where a 700-year-old man named Akel leads the town council. Certain places lacking this godly influence became more evil as younger generations held sway.

Some Christians have claimed that Genesis 4:26 should be understood in the opposite way. That is, at the time of Enosh's birth, men began to turn away from the Lord. This is based largely on an ancient

Jewish work known as the Genesis Rabbah, which instead of having the verb "call on" uses the verb "pollute." So these people believe this verse teaches that men began to pollute the worship of the true God, probably through the worship of idols. In the Genesis Rabba, the "generation of Enosh" is a wicked one. However, the Hebrew text is accurately translated in all major English versions: the people of Enosh's generation began to call on the name of the Lord.

Was there one continent before the Flood?

Many creationists believe that earth initially had one large supercontinent. This conclusion is the result of an inference made from Genesis 1:9, in which God states, "Let the waters under the heavens be gathered together into one place, and let the dry land appear." If all the water was gathered into one place, then it seems as if the land would have been gathered in one place as well.

At the Creation Museum and Ark Encounter, this massive C-shaped continent is named Rodinia. Modern continents are made up of pieces of the original earth. These pieces, called cratons, can be put together like a jigsaw puzzle to give us a clue as to what the world may have looked like before the Flood. For more details about the original continent and how it was transformed into the seven continents we have on earth today, please see "Noah's Lost World" by Dr. Andrew Snelling, available at https://answersingenesis.org/geology/plate-tectonics/noahs-lost-world/.

Why are the animals described in the novel different than what we observe today?

You may have noticed that we avoided using modern names for the creatures and plants Noah encounters in our story. Let's look at the animals as examples to see our rationale behind this decision. First, and perhaps the most obvious reason, is that Noah would have certainly called them something different than what we do today. Even after accounting for language differences, people in different cultures often call animals by names that do not necessarily mean the same in another culture. For example, one people group may name an animal after the way it looks; another may name the same animal after the sound it makes, a third culture may name it after its behavior, and a fourth group may call it by its scientific classification.

Second, the animals would not have looked the same as they do today. The creatures Noah knew were the ancestors of our modern animals before those original kinds developed into the various species we recognize. For example, we are familiar with wolves, coyotes, jackals, dingoes, and regular dogs, but these varieties of the dog kind probably did not exist in Noah's day since they are descendants of the two dogs God sent to board the Ark.

The third reason we avoided using modern names for animals is that we wanted the pre-Flood world to have an otherworldly feel to it. Many of the animals were named based on appearance or their behavior. So the bounder on Noah's farm is part of the rabbit kind, and the supergliders spotted by Noah and Emzara are a type of pterodactyl, as shown on the cover.

How could Tubal-Cain and his siblings be about the same age as Noah if they were in the eighth generation and Noah in the tenth?

Three of the major characters in our story are members of Cain's line mentioned in Genesis 4. Lamech is in the seventh generation (Adam, Cain, Enoch, Irad, Mehujael, Methushael, Lamech), and his children, Tubal-Cain and Naamah, are in the eighth generation. Yet Noah is in the tenth generation through Adam's son Seth, and we portray Noah as being roughly the same age as Tubal-Cain and Naamah. How can this be if they are two generations apart?

The answer is really quite straightforward, but since we have had people ask about this, it is worth addressing here. The simple answer is that the men in Tubal-Cain's lineage were older on average when each one had his son of record. Let's explore that just a little bit.

We know the age of each patriarch from Adam to Noah when his son of record was born (an average of 117 years), but Genesis 4 does not include the ages of Cain, Enoch, Irad, et al., when their son of record was born. Assuming Cain was born one year after Adam and Eve were created (have you ever considered that Cain may have been just one year younger than his parents?), then the average age upon having their son of record of the men from Cain's son, Enoch, to his descendant, Lamech, would need to be around 175 years. Since Methuselah, Lamech, and Noah were all older than 175 when each had their son of record, this average age is well within biblical precedent. In fact, if one man in Cain's line was approximately 500 years old (like Noah was) when his recorded son was born, then the rest of the men could have averaged about the same age at the birth of their son as the men in Seth's line.

Did Lamech lead a pre-Flood empire?

While studying Genesis for the Ark Encounter, an interesting thought occurred to me (Tim). At the end of Cain's line in chapter 4, we read about a man named Lamech. This man is the first polygamist mentioned in Scripture, and he also boasted about killing someone. Four of his children are named: Jabal, Jubal, Tubal-Cain, and Naamah. The three male children are all cited as being leaders in particular industries: livestock, musical instruments, and metalworking. In the back-of-the-book section of the second book in this series (*Noah: Man of Resolve*), we will explain why we made Naamah a gifted singer.

Why would one family feature leaders in at least three industries? Perhaps they were exceptionally smart and creative. However, many people prior to the Flood were surely very intelligent. Perhaps the reason is that Lamech ruled over a particular area, and he placed his children in charge of these trades.

In our story, we made Lamech a ruler in the land of Havilah. He is an ambitious man who manipulates people to do his bidding. When Noah first encounters him, Lamech is friendly to him because he sees an opportunity to improve his own situation through trade. We will see much more of Lamech and his family in the second book.

Why does Havil have so much gold?

In our story, the city of Havil features a large amount of gold. It can be seen in decorations on buildings, in the expensive gift gallery, and throughout the palace. The basis for this is found in Genesis 2:11–12. There we are told about the first river that flowed out of Eden. Named the Pishon, this river skirted the land of Havilah. The Bible states that there is gold in this land, and that the gold of this land is good.

Since Tubal-Cain was known as an instructor of metalworkers, we made Havilah's capital city, Havil, a place where all sorts of metals, including gold, were readily available.

In our novel, Noah marries the daughter of his grandfather's cousin (his first cousin once removed). In our day, this would be considered incest in many places, so why was it acceptable for so many biblical characters to marry close relations?

Skeptics have long attacked the biblical account of creation because we are told that God made Adam and Eve. Then Adam and Eve had Cain and Abel. After killing Abel, Cain moved away and had children of his own. So who was Cain's wife?

The most natural answer to this famous question is that Cain married his sister. Although it is possible that he married a niece, the objection remains because he married someone very closely related to him. And to make the objection even stronger, the skeptic reminds us that the Bible forbids marriage to a close relation in the book of Leviticus, so how can we claim that many of these people married their kin?

First, we need to understand that the law against close intermarriage in Leviticus 18 was not instituted until two-and-a-half millennia after God created the world. The main reason incest is outlawed in many places is because it can be harmful to the offspring of such a union. Since brother and sister share many of the same genetic mistakes passed down through their parents, these mistakes would be passed down and likely amplified in their children. But early on, marriage to close relations would not have caused these sorts of problems for the offspring because humanity did not have as many genetic problems. As the centuries passed, more and more mutations occurred in our genes, and this genetic load eventually reached the point where it became dangerous for the offspring of closely related parents. This is why the law against such relationships was necessary in Leviticus 18.

Second, the Bible tells us that Eve was to be the mother of all the living (Genesis 3:20), and it also states that after Seth was born, Adam and Eve had sons and daughters (Genesis 5:4). Originally, brother married sister. It sounds gross to us today, but there were no other options, and it would not have the same stigma attached to it as it does today.

Third, some Christians object to this answer because it seems like incest. Some have claimed that God created a different people group so that Adam's children had someone to marry. But such an act would mean that Eve was not the mother of all the living. Also, this objection ignores the fact that Abraham married his half-sister, Sarah. Their son, Isaac, married his first cousin, Rebekah. And their son, Jacob, married two of his cousins, Leah and Rachel. So there are plenty of examples in Genesis of close intermarriage.

Finally, before you get the idea that creationists have a big problem on our hands, you should consider the incest problem we would have if evolution were true. Not only would all of humanity have needed to come from a single pair, or a small community of early humans, but every single plant, animal, and microbe supposedly evolved from the first one-celled organism. Why do skeptics think it is a problem for all of humanity to arise from two people when they believe that all of humanity and every plant and animal came from a single organism?

If it never rained before the Flood why did the story include rain and rainbows?

In our story we mention several instances of rainfall in the pre-Flood world. You may wonder why this deserves mention in this section. Well, many Christians believe the Bible teaches that it never rained prior to the Flood. The primary argument comes from the second chapter of the Bible.

> This is the history of the heavens and the earth when they were created, in the day that the LORD God made the earth and the heavens, before any plant of the field was in the earth and before any herb of the field had grown. For the LORD *God had not caused it to rain* on the earth, and there was no man to till the ground; but a mist went up from the earth and watered the whole face of the ground (Genesis 2:4–6, emphasis added).

Yes, the text states that God had not caused it to rain on the ground. But what period of time are these verses describing? The answer is that these verses state that up until the sixth day of the creation week, God had not caused it to rain on the earth. Is it a safe assumption to extrapolate from this verse through the next 16-plus centuries and claim that it never rained until the Flood? Perhaps, but the text certainly does not demand such a view.

Another argument is based on Hebrews 11:7, which states that Noah built the Ark by faith after being warned by God of "things not yet seen."

Some supporters of the "no rain before the Flood" position claim that the "things not yet seen" refer to rain and other effects associated with storms. But Hebrews does not necessarily have ordinary rainfall in view. In all likelihood, the phrase in question refers to the Flood and its effects.

A third argument used by those who do not believe it rained prior to the Flood is based on the idea that the early earth had some sort of water canopy around it. This is based on a certain understanding of the events on the second day of creation when God separated the waters below the expanse (or firmament) from the waters above it (Genesis 1:6–7). This proposed canopy somehow created an ideal environment around the globe, blocking harmful rays and permitting longer, healthier lives. However, there are numerous scientific problems with the canopy theory, such as the fact that it would have created a massive greenhouse that would have destroyed life on earth. Even more important is that Genesis 1 also states that the sun, moon, and stars are in the expanse, so that would mean that "the waters above" should probably be understood as being beyond the stars instead of some sort of canopy around our planet.

The final argument given to support the "no rain" position has to do with the rainbow. Following the Flood, God made a covenant with Noah and all the inhabitants of the earth, human and animal, that He would never again destroy the earth with a Flood (Genesis 9:9–11). Regarding the sign of this covenant, the Lord stated, "I set My rainbow in the cloud, and it shall be for the sign of the covenant between Me and the earth" (Genesis 9:13). Supporters of the idea that it never rained before the Flood claim that this was the world's first rainbow, so it must not have rained before.

There are at least three big problems with this statement. First, we know it had rained for 40 days and 40 nights beginning at least a year before God announced this covenant. And it undoubtedly rained following those first 40 days, so if sunlight shone through at all during this time, then we should expect a rainbow to appear as well. Second, rain does not even need to fall for a rainbow to form. If waterfalls existed in the pre-Flood world, then a rainbow would appear in the mist that inevitably forms if sunlight reached the water droplets in the air. Third, and most importantly, the Bible does not claim that this was the first rainbow. God used the rainbow here as a sign of the covenant He made. Nothing in the text necessitates this as the world's first rainbow.

If rainbows had appeared before, then what we see here is an example of God attaching special meaning to them at this point. He did the same thing with the Passover lambs roughly a thousand years later. When the Lord told Moses and the Israelites to sacrifice lambs at Passover, He did not invent lambs at that point; He attached special significance to them at that point in history.

In our view, the arguments used for the "no rain" position are not compelling enough to adopt such a position, but at the same time we want to acknowledge the plausibility of such a view. However, since many creationists have heard and repeated these claims as found in the Bible, we wanted to take the opportunity to challenge these assumptions and encourage readers to look closely at the biblical text so that they could learn whether their beliefs are based on Scripture or tradition.

Why does Noah have anger and pride issues when the Bible describes him as a righteous man?

The Bible certainly tells us several times that Noah was a righteous man, but we have several reasons for giving him these character flaws. First, the Bible's description of Noah as being a righteous man had to do with his character at the time God called him to build the Ark. He may have sinned regularly in his first several centuries, and undoubtedly struggled with sin throughout his life.

Second, every story needs to see the protagonist change during the course of his journey. This is especially true in a coming-of-age tale like this one. Readers want to relate to a character, so they need to see a realistic person instead of an idealistic one. They need to see him struggle with difficult situations, make mistakes and learn from them, see the consequences of his decisions, and grow as a person as a result of his experiences.

Third, the fact that Noah needed God's grace (Genesis 6:8) reveals he was not perfect. While it would be nice to think of him as never struggling with any sin, we realize he was just as human as we are, and surely battled the desires of the flesh regularly. This made things tricky for us because the Bible only tells us about one mistake made by Noah, and that episode of drunkenness happened years after the Flood (Genesis 9:21). Many novels about Noah use this event in his life as justification for giving him a disposition toward drinking alcohol. While this may be reasonable, it is a bit overdone in these books, so we decided to give Noah a couple of other sinful issues to struggle with.

The two main areas where our Noah struggles are pride and anger. The pride issues are more subtle in the book, but they can be seen a few times as he admires his own appearance or focuses too much attention on himself. Pride also rears its ugly head in the way Noah is tempted by Naamah, although he does a great job in handling his most difficult encounter with her.

The anger issues are more noticeable. He allows his frustrations to boil over in chapters 14 and 18. But in each case, his temper subsides before too long. Why would we give him such a temper?

We decided to borrow characteristics from the Apostle Paul for aspects of Noah's personality. Like Paul, Noah was a preacher of righteousness (2 Peter 2:5), something we will see him become in the next two books. In the Bible, these men seemed to share a common boldness, willing to stand before anyone at any time and proclaim the truth, regardless of personal harm that may come to them. Paul endured flogging, imprisonment, and many other punishments because of his desire to spread the gospel (2 Corinthians 11:24–27). While the Bible doesn't give us any specific instances about Noah's boldness, there is little doubt he strongly contrasted with the rampant wickedness of his day.

People with this sort of boldness seem to share a righteous anger toward sin, which is a good thing, but there is a fine line that can quickly be crossed when that righteous anger is personalized and becomes a sinful temper. There are signs that Paul had a fierce temper. Prior to his conversion to Christianity, we read that Paul was "still breathing threats and murder" against Christ's disciples (Acts 9:1). Years after his conversion, the high priest ordered Paul to be struck. In the next verse, Paul immediately responds with a strong insult, saying, "God will strike you, you whitewashed wall!" (Acts 23:3). It is hard to overstate how offensive that remark would have been at the time. After being informed that this man was the high priest, Paul recognized his outburst was wrong (v. 5).

Like so many other sins, if not all of them, temper stems from human pride, and Paul was not immune to that. He had a major falling out with Barnabas because of John Mark, whom Paul refused to travel with, thanks to John Mark deserting them on a previous missionary journey (Acts 15:36–41). Paul highlights his prideful failings when he openly admits his daily struggle to do what is right and not do what is wrong (Romans 7:15–19).

If this godly man who wrote 13 books of the New Testament can struggle with pride and anger, then it is certainly believable that a fellow preacher of righteousness, Noah, could struggle with the same issues, particularly at a young age.

Why is the serpent god called Nachash?

By the end of the first book, readers learn about the false god Nachash (pronounced nah-KOSH). Bible readers may be familiar with some of the other pagan gods and goddesses mentioned in Scripture, such as Dagon (1 Samuel 5:7), Ashtoreth (1 Kings 11:5), or Molech (1 Kings 11:7), but Nachash is not mentioned — at least not in English Bibles.

Genesis 3 describes man's rebellion in the Garden of Eden, typically referred to as the Fall. The serpent deceived Eve, and she ate from the tree of the knowledge of good and evil — violating the one prohibition God had put in place. Then she gave some to Adam and he ate. Adam's sin brought sin, disease, suffering, and death into the world. God also cursed the serpent and the ground at this point.

So where does Nachash fit into all this? Nachash is a transliteration of the Hebrew word used for serpent in this passage. This explains why we chose to use a serpent idol to represent Nachash and have Noah refer to him as the Great Deceiver.

Christians generally recognize the serpent as Satan (Revelation 12:9), but Genesis does not make this identification for us, and somewhat surprisingly, neither does any other place in the Old Testament. So readers should not expect Noah or anyone else in the novels to refer to Nachash as the devil or Satan, which leads to the next question.

Why did Noah seem to have a fairly limited understanding of God and the things described in Genesis 1–5?

Early in our story, Noah and Aterre have a conversation about the Creator, and Noah doesn't seem to know how to properly address each of the issues. Some readers may wonder why we portrayed this faithful biblical hero in this way, but we have two major reasons for this decision.

First, at this point in our story, Noah is a young man who has not encountered beliefs contrary to those he was taught from his childhood.

He does not have years of experience to draw from in knowing how to respond to challenges to his beliefs. In our day, this situation would be like an average recent high school graduate being drawn into an important philosophical and theological discussion.

Second, modern readers often assume that biblical characters knew much more about God and His plans than what they may have. We tend to think that they should be aware of everything the Bible mentions about the people and times in which they lived. Some Christians assume that these characters even knew about teachings that would not be revealed until the New Testament.

The main problem with this latter idea is that the Bible describes a concept that has come to be called progressive revelation. Numerous verses could be cited to illustrate this, but the following passage explains it well.

> Now to Him who is able to establish you according to my gospel and the preaching of Jesus Christ, according to the revelation of the mystery kept secret since the world began but now made manifest, and by the prophetic Scriptures made known to all nations, according to the commandment of the everlasting God, for obedience to the faith (Romans 16:25–26).

As he frequently did, the Apostle Paul spoke of a "mystery" that had now been made manifest. When using this term, Paul refers to a concept that God had hidden from the generations before him but had been revealed in his day, such as God's plan to establish His church (Colossians 1:24–27), end times teaching (Romans 11:25; 1 Corinthians 15:51), and the content of the gospel (Ephesians 6:19).

As far as we know, there is an enormous amount of biblical information that Noah was not privy to. It is possible that God had revealed some information to him or others that is not recorded for us in Scripture, but even if this were the case, we cannot know the details of this revelation.

So if Noah was unaware of later revelation, would he have been familiar with all the things written in Genesis 1–5? Many creationists have adopted a view known as the tablet model, which states that the Book of Genesis was written by multiple people, including Adam, Noah, Shem, Abraham, et al., and then later compiled by Moses. Personally, I believe there are some strong arguments against such a view, but even if this model turns out to be correct, it would not guarantee that Noah, as a young man, would have been familiar with all the details at that time. After all, the earlier records may have been passed down to him hundreds of years later.

Another assumption made by many creationists is that Adam knew Methuselah and that Methuselah would have passed this information down to his grandson Noah. It is true that Adam lived 930 years, long enough to be alive during the first two centuries of Methuselah's long life. However, this fact does not guarantee that the two men would have known each other. Methuselah was the seventh generation after Adam. Given their very long lives, it is very possible that these people had dozens of children.

For the sake of argument, let's assume a minimum number of children for each of the men listed between Adam and Methuselah. The Bible names at least one son for each of these men and then states that after they had other "sons and daughters." So each of these men had at least five children — an extremely low number for people living over 900 years. If each generation had five children on average, and each of those children averaged five children, then by the time Methuselah was born, Adam would have had more than 78,000 descendants. But remember, that number is assuming a small number of children for people who may have been capable of producing offspring from at least age 65 (Genesis 5:15, 21) to over 500 (Genesis 5:32). If each family averaged a dozen children, which is probably still a low number in such a long lifespan, Adam would have had over 35 million descendants at the time Methuselah came along. Why should we assume that he happened to know one particular great, great, great, great, great grandson named Methuselah?

The truth is, we cannot know for certain how many people were on earth at that point, and we cannot know if Adam knew Methuselah. In fact, we cannot even be sure that Methuselah and Noah knew each other. In keeping with our goal of challenging stereotypes, we decided to minimize the amount of biblical information from Genesis 1–5 that Noah may have known, at least as a young man. In our story, he is aware of some of the key events in these chapters, such as creation and the Fall, but he does not know all of the details. If these events were not faithfully recorded or passed on to him at this point in his life, legends based on the events would surely develop, making it hard for him to know what really happened. For example, he knows of Enoch's disappearance, but he is not entirely sure what happened to him. Since the time of Babel, many cultures passed their histories to the next generation through storytelling and song. Perhaps some of the people living prior to the Flood did the same.

Traditions would be another way to hand down this information, but as is often the case, a tradition gets passed down while the meaning behind it becomes muddled or lost. An example of this is seen with the Zakari assuming a strange position while praying. This practice comes from a tradition handed down to them derived from a key event in Genesis, but they have lost the truth behind it. Readers will need to wait until the third book in the series to learn why they do this.

Finally, one tricky element in our story has to do with the way in which an individual related to God prior to the Flood. As Christians, living after Jesus Christ's death, burial, and Resurrection, and after the Holy Spirit came on the Day of Pentecost, we have the advantages of hindsight and having the Spirit dwell within us. We also have 66 books in the Bible to guide us as we seek to live in a way that pleases the Lord.

The people of Noah's day did not have these advantages, so how could they know what they should do to please the Lord? They would need to rely on the truth passed down to them, however much that may have been. Some people, like Cain (Genesis 4:6) and Enoch (Genesis 5:21–24; Jude 14–15), had the opportunity to hear directly from God, just as Noah would in the years leading up to the Flood. Perhaps other people had this privilege as well. Even if the people did not have access to these first two options, they still had a God-given conscience to help them discern between right and wrong.

We see examples in the early chapters of Genesis that people made sacrifices to the Lord. Abel offered the "firstborn of his flock" (Genesis 4:4), and after the Flood, Noah offered sacrifices from every clean animal and clean bird (Genesis 8:20). So these individuals must have had some comprehension of their sinfulness and that the cost of sin was death. This practice almost certainly came from the first sacrifice when God killed at least one animal to provide "tunics of skin" to clothe Adam and Eve (Genesis 3:21). These sacrifices may have become mere ritual for some people, but in the cases of Abel and Noah, we know they were righteous men (Matthew 23:35 and Genesis 7:1), so we have every reason to believe that the proper reasons for offering sacrifices were passed down to Noah. Our novel depicts Noah's recognition of the right reasons to offer sacrifices at his coming-of-age ceremony and just prior to his wedding.

ENCOUNTER THIS

Since we worked on the Ark Encounter project, we had the unique opportunity to include details in our story that can be seen in various exhibits. We were also able to influence the design of certain elements so that they connected with our story. If you visit the Ark Encounter in Williamstown, Kentucky, you will be able to see the following items that were included in the story.

Chapter 3: As Noah looks over the family farm, he recalls memories of daydreaming at the top of Sacrifice Hill as he watched boats travel the river. An illustration of young Noah watching a boat on the river while carving a small boat out of wood is shown in the *Who Was Noah?* exhibit on the second deck. This illustration also includes some earth shakers (sauropod dinosaurs) on the other side of the river. In Chapter 9, Noah told Aterre that he had occasionally seen earth shakers when he was younger.

Chapter 4: Meru, Lamech's pack animal, called a lunker in the story, is an extinct animal known as a macrauchenia. Two theosodons, a smaller variety of this kind of animal, can be found in an animal enclosure on the second deck.

Chapter 5: Noah's father, Lamech, and grandfather, Methuselah, appear early on in the story, and Lamech appears later as well. Portraits of these two men can be viewed in *Noah's Study* on the second deck.

Chapter 6: In our first scene from Naamah's point of view, we learn that her father, another man named Lamech, has married a second wife. In the *Pre-Flood World* exhibit on the second deck, there are six large panels depicting the world's descent into darkness. The second panel depicts a man with two wives and includes the Bible verse that mentions Lamech's polygamy. Later in the same exhibit, this king and his wives can be seen in a large diorama depicting a drunken feast.

Chapter 10: The knife Noah and Aterre fashioned from the large tooth can be seen sitting on a shelf in the *Library* on the second deck of the Ark Encounter. Although Noah and Aterre never see the animal it came from, the description of the scene and the details provided by the Varelk make it obvious that the "dagger tooth" creature is a type of Tyrannosaur. Two juvenile tyrannosaurs are on display in an animal enclosure on the second deck.

Chapter 14: After Noah and Aterre leave Zakar, a large animal lumbers across the path in front of them on their way to the river. This awkward creature, unnamed in the story, is called an anisodon. This creature can be found in a large animal enclosure on the second deck.

Chapter 18: Noah travels to Iri Geshem to become an apprentice shipbuilder. After months of frustration, he finally gets his opportunity. The *Who Was Noah?* exhibit on the second deck includes an illustration of Noah learning the trade of shipbuilding from Ara. In *The Interview* film, Noah mentions learning the trade from Emzara's father.

Chapter 20: In the chapter where Noah proposes to Emzara, he hands her a carved animal called a keluk in our story. This carved animal can be found in the *Library* on the second deck of the Ark Encounter. A keluk is what we named the pre-Flood version of the giraffe, and we made it Emzara's favorite type of animal. This fact is mentioned by the animatronic Noah in *Noah's Study* on the second deck, and there is a picture of her guiding two of these animals into the Ark in the *Doors of Bible* exhibit (part of the *Why the Bible Is True* exhibit) on third deck.

Chapter 30: During her wedding, Emzara's father hands her a letter he had written when he offers his blessing on her and Noah. Emzara can be seen reading this letter in *Noah's Study* on the second deck. Three of the items used in the wedding ceremony can also be seen on a shelf in that exhibit: the blindfold around Noah's head at the start of the ceremony, the engagement armband Noah made for Emzara, and the cord used to wrap the couple at the end of the ceremony.

Chapter 36: In the final scene of the first book, the massive idol of the serpent is revealed in Havil. Each of the following exhibits include artwork showing a version of the serpent idol in pagan cities: *The Pre-Flood World* (second deck), *Who Was Noah?* (second deck), *and Flood Geology* (large mural on third deck).

These statements are accurate as of the opening of the Ark Encounter. Exhibits may be modified in the future, so certain details may change.

Borrowed from the Bible

Since the Bible does not give us details about Noah's early years, we needed to use artistic license to tell the story. To keep the story more closely tied to the Bible, we decided to borrow and slightly adapt some of the concepts found in the novel from other portions of Scripture. The Question and Answer section explained that we borrowed aspects of the Apostle Paul's personality in our depiction of Noah's personality. Here are some other examples where we borrowed ideas from other portions of Scripture.

Chapter 12: When the Zakari develop a plan to rescue the children, Erno tells them to spread around the camp and pull out two torches to make the kidnappers think there are more people in the woods than there really were. This plan is loosely based on Gideon's strategy for defeating the Midianites found in Judges 7. With an army of only 300 men, Gideon's men spread out into three companies, surrounding the Midianite camp. Each man held a trumpet and a torch hidden inside a pitcher. When Gideon blew his trumpet, the 300 men blew their trumpets and smashed the pitchers. The cacophony confused and scared the Midianites and the Lord used Gideon to win an important battle.

Chapter 20: Noah agreed to work for Ara for more than five years, at which point he could marry Ara's daughter. While we set up Noah's working relationship with Ara as an apprenticeship, the concept was borrowed from Genesis 29. Here, we read the account of Jacob working seven years for Laban for the right to marry Laban's daughter, Rachel. Of course, Laban deceived Jacob by giving him Leah instead, so Jacob agreed to work another seven years for Rachel. Another similarity to this account is the fact that Jacob traveled far to stay with a relative. In our story, Noah travels a long distance to work with Ara.

Chapter 21: Naamah's visit to the seer is loosely borrowed from 1 Samuel 28 where King Saul consults a medium in order to find out from Samuel what his future will be. At this point in our story, Naamah knows some things about the true God, but she does not have a good understanding of His ways. She desperately hopes that the seer will tell her that she will not always be under her father's rule, which she has grown to despise. His words will play a huge role in her life as she seeks to find the one who will fulfill them. Saul's visit to the medium would end in tragedy as Samuel appeared and told him that he would die later that day. Readers will need to wait to see how this encounter turns out for Naamah. For a detailed explanation of this passage about Saul and the medium, please read my two-part article, "King Saul, a Witch, and an Elohim," at http://midwestapologetics.org/blog/?p=1273 and http://midwestapologetics.org/blog/?p=1382.

Chapter 30: Some of the wording and symbolism found in the marriage ceremony is taken right from the creation of Adam and Eve. As Noah's father explained, the cloth over Noah's face represented the deep sleep Adam was put into by God. Emzara repeats God's words about the woman being a helper for the man. The use of the cord to bind husband and wife together at the ribs is drawn from the fact that Eve was made from Adam's rib.

Chapter 35: Naamah's attempt to seduce Noah is similar to the efforts made by Potiphar's wife to seduce Joseph in Genesis 39. Of course, there are differences between the two situations. Potiphar's wife made numerous attempts over several days to lure Joseph, and he eventually ran away from her. In our story, Noah also behaved admirably during the temptation, but circumstances prevented him from running away.

Dear Reader,

Thank you for choosing this book. We hope you've enjoyed the story so far and are looking forward to the next installment in the series. In the novel, Aterre had plenty of questions about God. While trying to make sense of our world, perhaps you've wondered about many of the things Aterre questioned. Noah did not have all of the answers for his friend, but he trusted in God and believed that answers could be discovered. And he was right. The answers are available if you are willing to search for them.

Today, we have access to details about God and His plan that were unavailable in Noah's time. We have the Bible, God's written Word that tells us all we need to know about God and His plan for our lives and this world. The Bible tells us that we have all sinned against God. In other words, we have rebelled against our Creator. The Bible says that the wages of sin is death. That is, what we have earned through our sin is God's judgment. We need His mercy and forgiveness.

If you really want to know what God is like, then look at Jesus Christ. The Bible explains that Jesus, God's Son, came to earth as a man and lived a perfect life. He died on the Cross and rose again to life to pay the penalty we owe for all our sins. In order to be right with the Most High, you need to acknowledge that you have failed to live up to God's expectations — you've sinned and stand in need of a Savior. Trust that Jesus' sacrificial death and Resurrection are enough to cover you, and ask God to forgive you of your sins.

In light of what God has done for you, commit yourself to living for Him. Read the Bible to learn more about our Creator and how to follow Him faithfully.

> Jesus said to her, "I am the resurrection and the life. He who believes in Me, though he may die, he shall live. And whoever lives and believes in Me shall never die. Do you believe this?" (John 11:25–26).

ABOUT THE AUTHORS

Tim Chaffey is the Content Manager for the Ark Encounter and Creation Museum. A former pastor and teacher, Tim is also a leukemia survivor and competes in half-marathons with his wife and son while his daughter cheers them on. He has earned advanced degrees specializing in apologetics, theology, and church history. Tim maintains a popular blog (www.midwestapologetics.org/blog), contributes regularly to *Answers* magazine and the Answers in Genesis website, and has authored over a dozen books, including *The Truth Chronicles* series and *In Defense of Easter: Answering Critical Challenges to the Resurrection of Jesus*.

K. Marie Adams has an obsession with words that once resulted in her being grounded for reading too much. Later, it served her well as she worked for many years at a bookstore and as a literature and grammar instructor. Now, as a graphic designer, her love of language goes by the fancy name of typography. K. Marie also volunteers for several ministries dedicated to rescuing young girls from modern-day slavery.

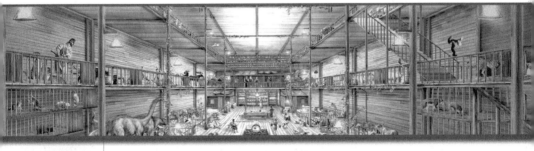

THE REMNANT TRILOGY
BOOK 2

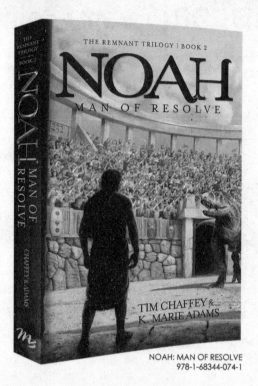

NOAH: MAN OF RESOLVE
978-1-68344-074-1

Packed with action, adventure, and heartbreak, the second installment of the Remnant Trilogy continues the imaginative and respectful look at the life of this hero of the faith as God shapes him into the man who eventually saves humanity's future.

As wickedness increases across the land, Noah and his loved ones endure painful consequences of a world bent on evil. King Lamech expands his rule through deception and force, but does his kindness toward Noah hint that things may change?

Noah and Emzara explore their world and their eyes are opened anew to the creative genius of the Most High, yet mankind's wretchedness threatens to upend their peaceful corner of the world. While tracking down the perpetrator of a malicious crime, they are tested by tragedy and must decide if they will sacrifice everything for truth and justice.

After years of serving God, Noah reaches a crisis of faith due to his mounting frustrations with the proliferation of sin and the apparent silence from the Creator. Thrust into a series of perilous situations, Noah's deepest convictions are challenged. His response will direct his course and change the world forever.

NOAH

MAN OF RESOLVE

TIM CHAFFEY &
K. MARIE ADAMS

Thank You

While our names can be found on the front cover, we recognize that many others played a significant role in helping us complete this book.

The team at Master Books, we can't thank you enough. Tim, thanks for choosing not only to read a work of fiction, but to publish it as well. Brittany, Laura, Katie, and others, you've been a delight to work with, and you make even the mundane fun.

Reagen, thanks for taking the manuscript we sent you and making it shine. Thanks for challenging us in every area of writing fiction and for applying your editorial expertise to produce a consistent, dramatic, and engaging story.

Casey, thanks for the long walks of plot discussion, the living room chats of character dissection, and the countless bowls of popcorn. We rely so much on your understanding of English grammar and your attention to details. We'd say you have a thankless job, but here you are being thanked . . . and you completely deserve it.

Ben, thanks for putting up with a word guy and an artsy girl. You take our spoken ideas and particles of thought and make them come alive on canvas in ways we couldn't have even dreamed. Knowing many will judge the book by its cover, we're so glad that you are the one helping us stand tall.

Janice, thanks for your countless prayers, words of encouragement, and happy reminders of ways we can make many details even better. Tony, thanks for the brainstorms on the plot. Steve, thanks for your editorial assistance in the nonfiction sections.

To all those in our lives, who shape our writing by walking out the experiences of the day to day with us, we love you and thank you.

Most of all, we thank our Lord and Savior, Jesus Christ. Thank You for dying in our place and then conquering the grave. Thank You for revealing so much about who You are through Your word and world. Thank You for godly examples like Noah and for growing our own faith and understanding of You as we wrote this novel.

First printing: June 2017
Second printing: January 2019

Master Books®, P.O. Box 726, Green Forest, AR 72638
Master Books® is a division of the New Leaf Publishing Group, Inc.

ISBN: 9781683440741
ISBN: 978-1-61458-601-2 (digital)
Library of Congress Number: 2017940467

Cover design by K. Marie Adams; cover illustration by Ben Iocco

Please consider requesting that a copy of this volume be purchased by
your local library system.

Printed in the United States of America

Please visit our website for other great titles:
www.masterbooks.com

For information regarding author interviews,
please contact the publicity department at (870) 438-5288.

Master
Books®
A Division of New Leaf Publishing Group
www.masterbooks.com

CONTENTS

DEAR READER,

Thank you for joining us for another look at what Noah may have been like in the years prior to the Flood. In the first book, we followed Noah on a coming-of-age adventure when he left home to work as a shipbuilder's apprentice. He faced many challenges along the way as he learned more about the world beyond his hometown. He stood for justice, met his wife, resisted temptation, and faced a growing evil in the land. Book Two picks up right where book one ended.

As we mentioned in the opening of the first book, we realize that so much of the story we are telling is made up. The Bible provides scant information about the world in which he lived and what Noah was like before God instructed him to build the Ark. Our story is rooted in those small details revealed in the first six chapters of Genesis.

We certainly do not want to be guilty of adding to Scripture, so we have spent considerable space near the end of both novels explaining why we depicted people, places, and events in certain ways. We stated in the first novel that one of our objectives in writing these stories was to use fiction to help readers learn to discern between fiction and biblical fact. That may sound like a strange goal for a novel, but stories can be used as powerful teaching tools. One need look no further than the parables taught by Jesus. While our story is not a parable or an allegory, it is intended to teach biblical truths in the context of fiction.

We have intentionally avoided many of the stereotypical views about Noah that are not spelled out in Scripture in an effort to challenge the reader to pick up the Bible and pay close attention to what it actually states. The nonfiction section in the back of the book is also designed to help the reader distinguish between fact and fiction, as well as highlighting areas where the novel intersects with exhibits that can be seen at the Ark Encounter theme park in Williamstown, Kentucky.

Welcome aboard for another journey as we respectfully imagine what life may have been like for our great, great . . . grandfather Noah.

Sincerely,

Tim Chaffey and K. Marie Adams

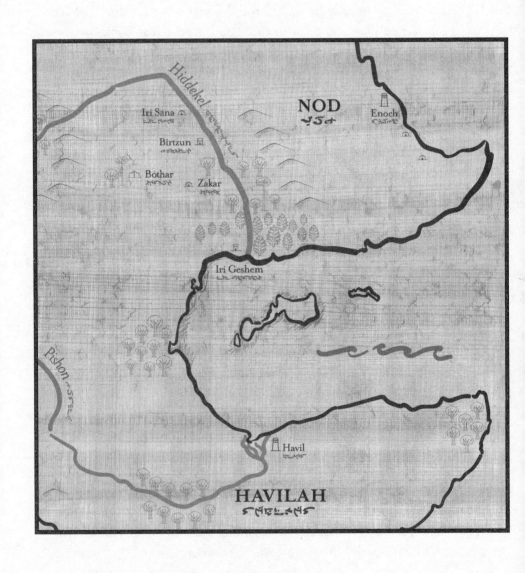

CHAPTER 1

Havil — Noah's 46th year

Emzara sprinted behind Noah, her eyes on the flap, flap of his robe as they fled the courtyard and the golden stare of the serpent idol Nachash. Her weary mind ran circles around the events of the day: the excitement and pleasure of exploring a new place with her new husband, his enjoyment at her delight when she picked out Tubal-Cain's extravagant surprise gift. And later, the knock at the door, the guards grabbing Noah, the dread that he had been killed. And now this: Noah returned safely and the guards saying it was all a misunderstanding. *So why the rush?* As sickened as she was by what she had seen tonight, the sensuality and godlessness of the ceremony didn't pose a serious threat to their lives, right? *Why won't he look me in the eye?*

Without warning, Emzara crashed into Noah's back as he halted in the middle of the street. She grabbed onto him to steady her balance. "Sorry."

Unfazed, Noah reached out his arm and stopped Zain. Pointing to one of the guest homes, he whispered, "I sent Farna straight to the boat, so tell his crew to pack everything immediately and meet us there as soon as possible."

"What happened?" Zain asked. "Why are we in such a hurry?"

"We have to leave before that ceremony ends. Naamah's preoccupied for now, but Garun told me I'm not safe in this city. Be on alert for her guards."

Zain gave a curt nod. "Is it something you've done?"

"No, quite the opposite actually." Noah glanced back down the road. "I'll explain later."

"Let's hope they've already resupplied the ship for the return trip," Zain said.

"Indeed."

Zain paused and looked back toward the city square. "One more problem. We have no idea where Ashur is."

"Ashur." Noah sucked in a breath through clenched teeth. "Now what?"

"You two grab our things," Zain said. "I'll tell the crew to get going, and then go look for Ashur."

"With that crowd?" Emzara's voice shook.

"What choice do we have?" Zain's question hung in the air for a moment before he continued. "You get to the boat. The important thing is to have you leave safely. If I'm not back, go without me."

Noah held up an arm. "But . . ."

"You're the one in trouble, not me or Ashur. We'll find our own way back, if necessary. Let's go."

Noah reached out and gripped the councilmember's arm, delaying his momentum. "May the Creator guide and protect you."

"And you, my friend. Now go."

Grimly, they made their way to their luxurious quarters. Zain hustled to the house on the left, while Noah and Emzara entered their lodging. The room was completely dark and unguarded.

Emzara turned to light a wick, but Noah stopped her with a hand over hers.

"No, let's work in the dark."

She frowned, peering up into his face and wishing for the light just so she could read his expression. "Very well."

Hurriedly, they grabbed their belongings. Emzara laid one of Noah's tunics on the ground in a long rectangle and arranged their folded garments on top. Strands of piks and pikas, clothing, and a few toiletries gave shape to the growing mound.

In her haste, she bumped into Noah, and a bottle of ointment flew from her hand. It shattered in a far corner, filling the air with the sharp scent of herbs and spices. "Sorry."

Already turning away to resume his work, Noah said, "Leave it. Are you hurt?"

"No, but look at me." She put a hand on his arm, her eyes searching out his. "Please tell me what happened."

For the first time since he had been returned to her, Noah held her gaze. "I promise I'll tell you everything, but there's no time right now." He bent down and kissed her forehead, muffling his voice against her skin. "We need to hurry."

* * *

Naamah twirled, her bare feet tracing the same intricate steps to the dance that she performed earlier in the evening. Tap, tap, tap-tap-tap. In the final steps of the choreography, her toe gracefully patted against the sandstone flooring that lined the gardens on top of the palace. She dipped her left shoulder and glanced over it to where the seer lagged slightly behind, his lanky frame dark against the backlighting of the torches. Laughing, she ran back toward him and swirled around several potted kalum trees, enjoying the spicy aroma their flowers gave off.

"How did I do tonight?" she asked, looking up at him and hoping he approved.

"Very well, my child." The old man lightly patted her cheeks, as a father who was proud of his child would do.

"Did I?"

"Yes, your singing mesmerized the people. Hearing your talent in person was greater than I imagined."

"I'm so glad." Unable to keep still, she spun as they walked toward the waist-high parapet marking the edge of the expansive rooftop garden.

"You're a natural leader, and tonight you received some of the recognition you deserve."

Naamah glowed under his high praise and leaned against the low stone wall. "There were so many people. Look at all the lights below, even this late at night."

They both peered out at the city, which still bustled. Pockets of people moved about the streets below, laughing with their companions and calling out good-naturedly to other groups that passed by. The sheer number of lit windows indicated that the celebratory atmosphere moved

11

beyond the streets. Music and drumbeats sounded out from a variety of places.

She flung her hands wide. "Isn't the city magnificent?"

"It's quite a sight. And you are its only princess."

"Yes, I am. Everyone got to watch me."

"And as priestess." He stroked the serpent image atop his staff. "Introducing them to Nachash was your greatest achievement tonight. Against the backdrop of your talents, the people saw the beauty in following him."

Naamah pressed her hands together and trembled with excitement. "I can't wait for next year's celebration. I'll dazzle them even more."

The seer gave a patient chuckle. "I have no doubts, but listen to me." He grabbed her hands. "Tonight was only a first step for you. With my guidance, you can achieve power you've never dreamed of. The success you now feel — and deserve — is only a glimpse of what is to come."

"More?"

He swept his arm out. "All that you see here — the might of your father's soldiers and the skill of your craftsmen." He shook his head slowly. "It's nothing compared to the power available through Nachash."

Intrigued, Naamah looked up and rubbed her chin, pondering the implications.

"The first time we met I saw greatness and giftedness in you. And power — that few can possess and even fewer will be able to resist."

Naamah leaned in closer. "Show me. Teach me everything."

A crooked smile spread across his lips. "Patience. It takes time. I'll guide you in the ways of Nachash, and as you learn, your power and wisdom will grow."

Hearing the rustle of leaves, Naamah stepped back as she glanced around. "Who's there? Speak."

Nivlac stepped forward from the foliage into the well-lit patio area, accompanied by Tsek, a mountain of a man. Nivlac bowed. "Princess, the king's captain has a message for you." Nivlac retreated to his post a short distance away.

Tsek bowed. "Evening peace, Princess. I'm here on behalf of the king. He wishes to inform you that he's pleased with your part in the festivities. Because of your efforts, the people learned how great a leader they have. Now they have a god worthy of the leader who has done much to build this city into what it is. And you, Naamah, played a part in that."

Naamah stiffened as Tsek droned on. *It's just like Father to take what should've been a simple compliment and make it all about himself.* Discouraged, she looked up at Tsek's strong jaw line as she waited for him to finish. *Power? Can I really be as powerful as the seer promised? Could I turn Tsek's loyalty to me instead of my father? Imagine that. His own captain following me.* She grinned.

"I'm glad that you're pleased with your father's report of the evening's successes."

Pulled suddenly from her reverie, Naamah blinked quickly, attempting to speed up her brain's responses. "Of course. I'm happy as long as my father is happy."

Tsek bobbed his head. "Do you have anything you want me to take to the king in reply?"

She looked at the seer, who had taken a seat a short distance away, while she searched for the right phrase. Stepping close to Tsek, she brushed an imaginary speck from his broad, tanned shoulder, being sure to let her hand linger longer than necessary. She cast him an alluring look as she backed away. "Tell the king that my victory rests in his vast accomplishments."

Tsek searched her face before replying. "I shall relay that. And may I say that, personally, I thought you were the highlight of the evening."

She flashed him a broad smile. "You are most kind, Tsek. Thank you for bringing words from my father." She dismissed him with a small wave of her hand.

He bowed and looked back at her twice as he walked through the garden.

The seer rejoined Naamah, wearing a slight frown. "That was not the type of power I was alluding to."

With a flip of her head, she tossed her hair over her shoulder. "Oh, I care nothing for him, but it wouldn't hurt to have his complete loyalty." She turned around to look at the city again. "There is, however, someone that I'd like to bring to his knees before me. Do you think you could help with that?"

"Perhaps. Tell me what's on your mind."

"A man slighted me twice. He dismissed me once a while ago and again just today." She let tears gather at the corner of her eyes, playing the role skillfully and without hesitation.

"Would this be the man your guard mentioned this evening? Noah? The shipbuilder?"

She bit her lip and nodded.

"And just what do you want to do?" He gently touched her shoulder.

She wanted vengeance. *But how?* "I — I . . . never mind."

"Capture this man's wife so that he has to beg you for her life."

Once hidden in the recesses of her mind, her darkest thoughts became clear. And yet, the seer spoke them calmly and with even tones, as if he were simply discussing what would be served for the next meal.

Naamah's eyes widened. "How — how did you know?"

The seer looked steadily at her. "I've been trying to tell you that the power I can teach you is beyond anything you've imagined."

Still awed by his ability, she stared into the wrinkled face before her.

"If you're bent on making this man pay, then call your guards to go get his wife. But I must say, you're setting your ambition too low."

She shook her head, brushing off his disapproval. "Maybe I am. But if I put this behind me, then I can focus more fully on what you have to teach me." She raised her voice so that the sentry stationed on the terrace might hear her. "Nivlac!"

Her most dependable guard hurried across the roof and stood before her. "Yes, Princess."

"I have an urgent mission for you."

CHAPTER 2

"About halfway there," Noah said as they crested a rise in the road. "Are we going too fast for you?"

"No, I'm alright." Emzara ducked behind Noah's broad shoulder, thankful for his presence. The whole moon was bright and cast many shadows over the cobbled streets they raced through. Since Havil was built into hilly terrain, several retaining walls rose up, supporting other roads that followed the curvature of the landscape. The way the roads crisscrossed over each other reminded Emzara of a braided hairstyle in which lengths of hair looped and intersected and were tucked out of sight behind other strands. *I sure hope Noah knows where we are.*

Her lungs burned as she followed Noah down yet another hill, but the distinct sound of the waves slapping the shore told her they were close. Suddenly, Noah stopped and gently moved her against the stone retaining wall that towered over their heads on the left. Little bits of grass poked brazenly between the edges of some of the rocks. The cool grit grated against her skin as she looked up at her husband's face. Making no noise, he jerked his head in the direction of the wall, signaling her to move toward it, before flattening himself against it.

Emzara tucked herself even farther into the protective shadows. "What is it?"

"We're close to the shore. I just want to make sure we can reach the boat without any interference." He leaned forward and scanned both directions. "Looks clear from here. Come on."

They walked quickly toward the beach. Finally reaching the gravel road that ran parallel to the water, she spotted the gentle curvature of the peak which formed the bow of their boat. The light hanging from the edge was lit. *Farna and the crew are on board!* Rejuvenated, Emzara readied herself to burst toward it, but Noah stopped her and pointed.

Four guards sat where the dock met the shore, blocking the path. Emzara shrank back and followed Noah, ducking out of sight behind a large building. She looked at him wide-eyed, wondering if he would come up with a solution.

He blinked. "So what now?"

"I'm scared." She ventured the words as quietly as she could.

Noah pulled her close and she clung to him. "Hang in there," he whispered against her ear, tendrils of her hair brushing against his cheek. "It's not over yet."

"What can we do?"

"I don't know." Noah let out a breath of frustration.

"Are they from Naamah?"

"Hard to say, but I don't think so. They're not paying too much attention." Noah ruffled his hair. "How do we get through?" He lightly pounded his forehead with his fist, as if such an action could speed up his thoughts.

Be brave. Don't give up now. Suddenly, an idea came to mind. She placed a hand on his chest and looked at him with a gleam in her eye. "Let's go swimming."

"What?"

"Well, you're not as fast as Aterre, but we don't need speed, just silence. Forget about using the dock. Let's swim to the boat."

"They'll see us for sure." He stared at the sky. "Unless those clouds block the moonlight." He pulled his head abruptly back down and looked at her. "Wait. I didn't know you could swim."

"I grew up on the water, with a shipbuilder for a father. Of course I can swim."

Noah shook his head and tightened his grip on her, pride and amazement spreading over his features. "I could just kiss you right now."

She tilted her head and studied his eyes as he looked into hers. His love and admiration shone back at her without a trace of deception or guilt. Whatever had happened earlier with Naamah, his conscience was clear. She smiled. "Well, since we have to stay here for a bit, what are you waiting for?"

He eagerly accepted her offer. Suddenly pulling away, he looked at her closely.

"Em, you should know what happened earlier tonight. And I'd rather tell you sooner than later."

"Very well."

"Here." He led her parallel to the water, circling around to approach the boat from the other side. Hiding behind an outcropping of trees, they made their way close to the shoreline, putting them more than two hundred cubits from the guards.

"There, I can see them between the leaves of the brush."

"So tell me about today." She nestled close to him.

"Em. . . ." Noah paused, looking serious. "This whole thing . . . the arrest. . . . All of it was a setup. Naamah, she, uh, offered herself to me."

"What?" Emzara took a step back so she could see his face.

"She staged the execution so she could pretend to rescue me. She wanted. . . ." He stopped.

Emzara gently rested her hand on his cheek, and he drew a deep breath.

"The whole point," he went on, "was to get me to her room where she did her best to seduce me. One moment we were talking about the ceremony, and the next I had to keep my eyes closed."

The gaze he fixed on her showed no deceit, but she couldn't stop the question hovering on her lips. "So nothing happened?"

"Absolutely nothing. She repulses me."

Emzara balled up her fists while she turned and glared at the ground. *How dare she! How dare she try to take my husband!* For a long moment she stood there, warring with the anger at Naamah and, she realized, even at Noah.

Closing her eyes, Emzara pulled in and released a deep breath. No. She could not blame Noah for being pure, for being blind to Naamah's trap. Unsure of what to say, she softly leaned her head against her husband's chest.

"I got out of there as soon as I could. Garun was on duty, and he helped me reach you at the ceremony. He also cautioned me that she may not give up and might seek revenge as soon as the ceremony's over."

17

She shuddered. "I need to know. Were you ever attracted to her?"

Though she wasn't looking at him, she felt Noah shake his head. "I can't deny that she's beautiful and talented, but she could never measure up to you in any way. You completely captivate me."

Straightening her shoulders, she turned back to face him. "I trust you. It's hard to hear, but I'd rather know than not."

Noah nodded. "And I wanted you to know right away, but not in front of the others."

The two sat together in the silence as Noah watched the sky. She closed her eyes and silently thanked the Creator for giving her a faithful husband. After some time, Emzara's thoughts drifted to home. She imagined walking hand-in-hand with Noah near the waterfall where he had proposed to her, but her brief reverie ended as Noah kissed her forehead. "It's as dark as it's going to get. And you have some swimming skills to show me."

Emzara reached up and brushed his face with her hand. "Do you really think this is a good plan?"

Noah nodded. "We'll make it."

She pursed her lips and turned away. *Why are you always so optimistic?* Then she shook her head, realizing that his confidence was one of the many aspects she admired about him. "Well, either way, we're in this together." She hitched up the loose fabric that hung around her ankles and wove it into the sash in the middle of her garment, noting that her husband was fully aware of her preparations. Queasiness struck her as her mind pictured his earlier encounter with Naamah, but it dissipated as she reminded herself of his faithfulness to her. "Ready?"

The two eased slowly into the cool water, packs strapped around their waists. They paddled noiselessly into deeper water, and she could feel the tug of the extra weight from the soaked belongings. Kicking harder and keeping her nose above the water, she concentrated on the safety of the boat. Noah kept close to her as they made slow progress. *Just a few more strokes.* She kept her limbs beneath the water, ensuring silence and minimal splashing.

"Stop!"

She slowly turned toward the dock, still paddling in place to keep her head above water. The guards now stood and blocked two figures from stepping onto the dock.

Noah gestured for her to hurry. "I don't know what's going on, but let's take advantage of the diversion."

When the side of their vessel loomed above them, Noah pulled himself aboard, then turned to haul up the sodden bundles Emzara handed to him. She held up a hand, and he lifted her from the water with a gush of sound that made her wince. Across the deck, a crew member turned.

Emzara held up a finger in front of her mouth, and the man's lips snapped closed as he recognized her. A familiar voice rang out from the shore, causing the crewman to spin in that direction.

Ashur!

"Look, we simply want to get onto our ship. That one." There was a pause, as if the unseen speaker were pointing. "We've no interest in the other. Why would we try to steal the king's vessel, when we're with the company that brought it?"

"He speaks truth." Farna's strong voice joined the conversation. "You may let them pass."

"You know this man?" one of the guards asked.

"Of course," Farna said, sounding almost bored. "He came with our delegation. Ashur, what are you needing this time of night?"

"We couldn't sleep after the festival, so we decided to pay you a visit."

It's Zain! Emzara slid behind a large cargo crate, squatting so Noah could crouch over her as they both peeked around the corner to see the action on the dock.

"Do they have your permission to proceed then?" the guard called.

"Sure." Farna chuckled. His sandals made a hollow slap as he jumped onto the dock and strode toward the cluster of men. "Well, maybe not the shorter fellow. You may want to detain him."

One of the soldiers reached for Ashur but was stopped by his leader's hand on his chest. "He was being sarcastic, Kotic."

"Sorry about that." The guard pointed to the other side of the dock, where Lamech's boat rocked in the gentle swell. "The king wants to make sure his new acquisition is protected."

"Can't be too careful," Farna said. He led Zain and Ashur to the boat and helped them climb aboard. Keeping his voice down, he said, "Now we just need Noah and Emzara."

Noah shifted and stuck his head out from behind the crate, speaking barely above a whisper, "We're here."

"How did . . . ?"

"We saw the guards and didn't want to risk it."

Farna took in their soaked state and then looked at his crew. "Get us moving now." He turned back to Noah and Emzara. "Two of those men are the ones I've been teaching to sail the ship. But I'm glad you played it safe."

Noah turned to Ashur. "I can't believe Zain found you so fast. What happened?"

Ashur shrugged. "I was having a good time when I looked up and noticed that you had all left. I made my way through the crowd, toward the guesthouses, and ran into Zain."

Zain shook his head. "I'm just thankful I didn't have to wade through that mob again." He shot Noah a sober look. "Naamah was already gone, and things were rapidly getting out of hand."

Farna gestured with his hand and stated in a husky growl, "Loose the ropes, men. Let's get out of here."

The crew jumped to obey, freeing the boat, then grabbing pushpoles to shove away from the dock.

"You there!"

Emzara looked up to see about a dozen men with torches approach the dock. The leader called out again. "You! Guards!"

The four soldiers stood at attention as Emzara ducked out of sight.

"Have you seen a man and a woman come this way? We're under orders from the princess to find them."

"No woman, sir. Just the captain and crew and a few of the delegation."

"Be on lookout. No one gets on or off that ship."

On the deck, the puddles left by Emzara and Noah now glowed faintly gray as the first flush of dawn eased over the horizon. "Guess it was worth that swim."

He flashed a grin. "Completely worth it."

"Why is that ship moving?" the leader of the newcomers asked.

"It's — hey! Stop!"

"Move." Farna barked the order, and their sail shot up, flapping then stretching taut as the wind filled it. The ship jerked forward.

Emzara wrapped her arms tightly around her middle as the men on the dock rushed into the king's ship.

Farna glared at the sail. "Come on," he muttered, rapidly tapping his fingertips. "From where they sit, they can still cut us off."

Emzara stood with the others, watching breathlessly as the bow of the Havilite ship pivoted, facing theirs. A few hard shoves from the shouting men would make Farna's warning a reality.

Suddenly a long screech accompanied by a dull groan filled the early morning air. A yell and two distinct splashes followed. Emzara gripped the side of the boat. *What now?*

Farna swabbed his face and let out a laugh. "Looks like they forgot their lessons already."

Puzzled, Emzara squinted toward the other boat. The last upright of the dock was severely bent. In fact, the whole dock looked lopsided, and the stern remained in its original position. *It's still attached!* In their haste and inexperience, the new crew had forgotten to check all of the moorings and the last one held their ship firmly in its grip. Two crewmembers were in the water. One swam for the dock, and the other struggled to stay above water. A guard on the boat quickly shed his armor and jumped in to help him.

Breathing a sigh of relief, Emzara turned her eyes to what she hoped would be her last view of Havil before taking her place at Noah's side.

CHAPTER 3

Iri Geshem — Noah's 49ᵗʰ year

Noah kissed Emzara on the top of the head and loosened his embrace. "I'll be home in a little while."

Emzara glanced at Tubal-Cain and Adira, who were busy saying their farewell for the evening, and then at Aterre, who rested on a low bench on the other side of the room. Shaking her head at Noah, Emzara curled the left side of her mouth. "Behave yourself."

"Me? Of course." He chuckled and hitched a thumb toward Aterre. "I'm not the one you need to worry about."

"Mmhmm." She gave him a quick kiss. "Let's go, Adira."

"I'm coming."

As Emzara turned to leave, she called back over her shoulder, "Don't let my husband get too silly tonight."

Tubal-Cain laughed. "I'm sure he'll do that on his own."

"Evening peace, Zara." Aterre's playful tone demonstrated he had no intention of heeding her request.

"And that's our sign to leave." Emzara shook her head as she held the door open for Adira. She took a final glance at Noah and smiled. "Evening peace, boys."

Noah smirked and watched her for a moment before closing the door. He picked up his leaf brew from the low table and relaxed on a cushion across from Aterre.

Aterre shifted to make room for Tubal-Cain. "I hate to say it, but pretty soon you won't have to let her go each night."

Sitting down, Tubal-Cain sighed. He put his feet up on the table in the center of the room. "Our wedding can't come soon enough."

"You two complement each other well." Aterre turned up his palms one at a time as if weighing one against the other. "She's pretty and sweet, and you're ugly and grumpy."

Tubal-Cain slapped Aterre's arm with the back of his hand. "You sure you aren't thinking about Zara and Noah?"

"Oh, them too."

"Well, if that's how it works," Noah said, "then I must be all sorts of dreadful things, because Em is wonderful in every way."

Tubal-Cain pretended to gag. "Stop him before I lose my evenfeast."

Noah grinned and threw a pillow at him. "As if you're any better. Lately, it's always 'Adira this' and 'Adira that.' And you aren't even married yet."

"He's right," Aterre said. "She's all you talk about."

Clasping his meaty hands together behind his head, Tubal-Cain reclined. "Beats discussing the weather or blacksmithing." He eyed Aterre before continuing. "She's all I want to think about every waking moment of each day."

"Ugh, you two are intolerable." Aterre held his palms up. "Since when did our game nights turn into this?"

"Since Adira agreed to be my wife." Tubal-Cain let his words trail off as if he were daydreaming about her.

"Not again." Aterre let out an exasperated sigh while the two other men laughed.

"So you really don't care what your father will think?" Noah asked, eyeing Tubal-Cain.

"I wouldn't say that I don't care. Of course I want my father to like her, but we're so far from him, I'm not sure it'll be an issue."

"But isn't the son of a king supposed to marry another person of high status?" Aterre asked.

"I've heard of that in other places, but my father's the first king of Havil, and he hasn't been in that position very long. I'm not sure if he's even given much thought about his successor. That will probably be centuries from now."

23

"I can't imagine you being the king of Havil," Aterre said.

"Really? Why?"

"I just don't picture you enduring the strict schedule and all the formalities." Aterre tilted his head. "And there's that whole ugly and mean thing."

A not-so-gentle nudge from Tubal-Cain resulted in a lighthearted wrestling match.

Ignoring the two of them, Noah sipped his brew before setting the vessel on the stony floor. Across the room, salty air wafted through the open window facing the beach, carrying a soft chill along with it. To Noah's right, a short hallway led to Tubal-Cain's room across from a kitchen and dining area.

Beyond the outer wall of the house to Noah's left stood Tubal-Cain's busy forge. In just three years, the blacksmith had taken on two apprentices, and he still needed another one to meet the steady supply of orders for his metal implements. Noah himself often came by on days off to learn the basics.

"Your place looks like it's almost ready," Noah said.

Tubal-Cain tried to catch his breath. "And I have you to thank for that. I've told you before, you're the best woodworker I've ever seen."

Noah winked. "I know."

Aterre cleared his throat. "And you have me to thank for getting you and Adira together."

Tubal-Cain laughed. "Yes, I suppose I should thank you for the hundredth time for locking Adira and me in the forge's office so that I'd be forced to talk to her."

"You're welcome," Aterre said. "Come to think of it, Noah, I'm the one that brought you and Zara together, too."

"Yes, and I believe I've already thanked you a hundred times. Isn't that enough?"

Aterre grinned. "Once more would be nice."

"Thank you for embarrassing me in front of Em."

Tubal-Cain stroked the short beard on his chin. "You know, you should open up a shop where you find matches for people. You could call it, You'll Thank Me Someday."

The three men laughed as Noah and Tubal-Cain tried to outdo one another over names for the proposed store.

Noah sat up straight and looked at Aterre. "Wait, I have a better idea. A much better idea."

"Well, it can't be any worse than the last one." Aterre dramatically dropped his head into his hands.

Noah pointed at his friend. "Since you played such a key role in helping each of us find a wife, I think we should return the favor."

Tubal-Cain bolted upright. "That's a great idea. It's our turn to play matchmaker."

Aterre shook his head. "I was wrong. It could be worse."

"No, this is perfect." Noah squinted as he pretended to size up Aterre. "Let's see. I've got just the right person in mind."

Aterre feigned disinterest. "Who?"

Noah tried to stifle his amusement. "How about Pohal?"

Aterre crinkled his nose. "No thanks."

"Why not? She's a good baker," Tubal-Cain said. "You'd be well fed and. . . ."

"Not interested."

"Why not?" Noah asked, knowing full well the answer. Aterre frequently complained about her squeaky, high-pitched voice. "Just think, she could sing you to sleep every night."

Aterre snorted. "No, thank you. I'd rather listen to Taht sing a lullaby."

Through momentary breaks in his laughter, Tubal-Cain said, "I've got one."

Aterre rolled his eyes. "This ought to be good."

"What about Bakur's niece, Ehiluel?"

Aterre folded his arms. "Nope. Not interested."

"What's wrong with her?" Tubal-Cain asked. "She's nice. She's pretty. She's intelli — oh, that's the problem. She's smart."

"No, that's not it." Aterre folded his arms across his chest. "I'm just not attracted to her."

"Fine, so you're not interested in the pretty type." Tubal-Cain looked at Noah and shrugged. "Picky picky." He stared at the floor before shifting his gaze back to Aterre. "I know!"

Aterre rolled his eyes. "How long do I have to put up with this?"

"As long as it takes," Noah said, enjoying the chance to tease his friend.

"Fletti, the stonemason's daughter."

"Are you crazy?" Aterre asked.

Tubal-Cain feigned offense. "What? I think she likes you."

"Yeah, she asked about you the last time I saw her." Noah leaned in and winked. "She said she wanted to kiss you."

"Ah, I knew it," Tubal-Cain said. "She's the one."

Aterre shook his head. "Right, like she'd say that to either of you madmen."

Noah angled his head to one side and challenged his friend. "But what if she did?"

Aterre yawned. "I'd rather kiss a grendec."

All three erupted in laughter.

After several moments, Noah tried to catch his breath as an idea came to mind, but it only made him laugh harder. Finally, he held up a hand and fought to put on a serious face. "Alright, I found your perfect match. Last one."

"It'd better be." Aterre's expression showed that he had grown weary of this game.

"Who is it?" Tubal-Cain asked before taking a drink of his leaf brew.

Noah strained to keep his composure. "She lives close by."

"Who?" Aterre asked.

"You're comfortable around her. She's got several qualities to make the ideal wife and . . . she's not *too* much older than you."

Noah waited to allow the tension to build. When he could no longer hold it in, he blurted out, "Nmir!"

Aterre stared at Noah in disbelief. "She's probably 600!"

Tubal-Cain sprayed the contents of his mouth all over the table as he keeled over in raucous laughter. Stoically, Aterre crossed his arms until he cracked and joined Tubal-Cain's merriment.

Noah reared back and howled until his stomach hurt.

The cacophony almost drowned out a knock at the door. Being closest to the entrance, Noah barely heard the sound and pulled himself up, desperately trying to gather his wits.

Another knock sounded, followed by a woman's voice. "Hello? Are you still open for business?"

As if he had been bitten, Aterre jerked to his feet and pushed his fingers through his hair. "I'll get it."

Tubal-Cain blocked his path. "She's asking for the blacksmith. That's me." Tubal-Cain walked to the door and opened it. "May I help you?"

"Evening peace." The woman's soft voice stood in sharp contrast to the male jocularity moments earlier. "I'm sorry for disturbing you this late at night, but the latch to our bovar pen broke, and we need it repaired as soon as possible."

Tubal-Cain took the damaged copper part from her. "Certainly. Please, come inside."

Noah started to introduce himself, but then he recognized her as Jitzel, Cada's daughter. No longer the little girl who brought water to her father's farmhands on hot days, Jitzel had transformed into a beautiful young woman. Standing nearly as tall as Aterre, her braided brown hair dropped to the middle of her back beneath her broad shoulders. Her strong, dark arms reminded Noah of his mother's arms — arms that had labored outdoors for countless days.

Her light brown eyes blinked. "Oh, hello, Noah. I haven't seen you in so long, but Aterre talks about you from time to time."

Noah nodded. "It's good to see you again."

Jitzel looked past Noah and quickly glanced away. "Aterre. What are you doing here?"

Aterre hurried to join them near the door. "Evening peace. It's um . . . I, uh . . . what happened to the gate?"

Jitzel peeked up at him and blushed. "I'm not sure. All I know is that Father wants it fixed right away. And I . . ." She looked at Aterre again. "And since I was already planning to head into town, here I am."

"You came to the right place." Tubal-Cain bent down to tie on his sandals. "I can bend this piece back into shape, and that should last you for a little while. But give me a few days, and I'll make one that's much stronger."

"Wonderful." Jitzel turned away from Aterre and faced Tubal-Cain. "Father will be so grateful."

"I like when the boss is happy," Aterre said. "Jitzel, what . . . why were . . ." He took a deep breath.

Noah had never seen his friend flustered like this before. *Is this what I was like around Em? Oh, this is going to be amusing.*

"Why were you planning to come into town tonight?" Aterre finally asked.

Jitzel smiled and looked away again.

A knowing grin crept across Noah's lips, and he wished his friend would look over to catch his expression, but Aterre was too absorbed to notice.

"I wanted to pick up a few supplies." She gestured to the small pack slung over her shoulder. "And I haven't been across the river in a long time. I guess I missed seeing different faces."

Tubal-Cain stepped past her into the doorway. "The tools I need are in the shop. Anyone want to join me?"

Although longing for some playful revenge, Noah decided not to embarrass Aterre. At least for now.

"I'd like to see your workplace," Jitzel said before following him outside. She glanced over her shoulder. "Are you coming too?"

"We'll be right there." Noah put a hand on Aterre's shoulder to prevent him from rushing after her. Keeping his voice down, he asked, "Would you rather continue stammering in here, or do you prefer to make a fool of yourself in the shop?"

Aterre tensed. "Don't you dare say anything."

"No wonder you weren't interested in any of the women we mentioned." Noah grinned.

"I mean it, Noah."

"So now you know how it feels to be on the other side. It's not easy, is it?"

"I hate it. I wish I could say the right words around her."

Noah chuckled. "I could do it for you."

"Don't. I work for her father, and. . . ."

Noah raised his eyebrows. "That didn't stop you from embarrassing me in front of Em."

Aterre's eyes widened. Noah had rarely witnessed this level of desperation in his friend. "Please. I'm begging you."

Sighing, Noah held the door open. "I'll behave."

Aterre eased his shoulders. "And in return for that, I promise never to set you up with anyone ever again."

"Haha. Deal."

They stepped outside, into the fading light, and Noah spotted Tubal-Cain and Jitzel close to the forge. "Come on, Aterre. Don't let her get away." He jogged to catch up to them, Aterre on his heels.

"Jitzel," Noah said, "it's already getting pretty dark, and this will take a little while." He grinned at Aterre. "I think one of us should make sure you get home safely."

"Thank you, Noah," she said. "That's very sweet of you, but . . ."

"I'm sure Aterre wouldn't mind, would you?"

Aterre scratched the back of his neck and looked at her. "No, um, I mean, I'd be happy to walk you home." He inhaled. "That is, if you don't mind."

Jitzel blushed. "I'd like that. Thank you."

Aterre flinched and bit his lip.

"I think that's his way of saying, 'You're welcome,' " Tubal-Cain said.

Jitzel looked away. "I know. He doesn't talk much."

"Who? Him? He talks all the time." Tubal-Cain paused and then slowly lifted his head as he seemed to grasp the situation.

"Does he?" A bemused expression crossed Jitzel's face, and she laid a hand on Aterre's forearm. "You're so quiet at work when I bring you your midmeal."

"That sure is strange." Noah caught Tubal-Cain's attention. "Any idea why he'd be so quiet at work?"

Tubal-Cain looked straight at Jitzel. "I can only think of one reason." He held up the broken latch. "I'd better repair this so you two can enjoy your evening together. Just the two of you. Walking and talking."

Aterre froze and Jitzel stared at the floor. But she didn't let go of his arm.

CHAPTER 4

Ara's shoulder and arm muscles flexed as he strained to pull the recently secured beam out of position. Shifting his stance, he grunted as he pushed against the wood. Finally giving up, he sat down on the deck and looked at his son-in-law. "These new brackets from Tubal-Cain are much better. The joints are as strong as a superglider's bite."

Noah nodded, eyebrows raised. "Didn't I tell you that?"

Ara stretched his fingers before curling his arm up to show off his bicep. "You did, but they needed to be tested by a strong man."

Noah snorted. "Hmm. When Tubal-Cain gets back, I'll ask him to check. You're getting too old for this."

"Too old? I'm not even 300. Just reaching my prime."

"That's good timing then. If these new joints hold up in the water, I think business will really take off."

After guzzling his drink, Ara set the jar down and stared across the beach toward town. "We might be able to double, even triple the size of our boats."

"And what about crossing the sea?"

"I think it might be possible for our next model." Ara turned to Noah. "But I'm not sure anyone here is anxious to do that anymore."

The image of the massive serpent idol on the platform in Havil flashed through his mind, followed by a memory of Naamah in her room. Noah shook his head to banish the recollections. In spite of the inauspicious trip to Havil, he still craved adventure. He wanted to take

30

Emzara on a long voyage to explore the world's unknown wonders. "Perhaps not anywhere near Havil," he said, "but I think the world might be a bigger place than we've imagined. I want to see it."

Noah stood and jumped from the boat onto the sand. He thumped the partially constructed hull with his palm. "So how big do you want to make the next one?"

Ara joined Noah and they walked toward his office. "We'll need to do a lot of planning, but we'll probably start with something about 50 percent larger, and if that works, we'll gradually increase the size. We have to work with the ratios still to make sure it's as sturdy as possible. You aren't the only one who'll want to cross the sea. We're going to have trouble filling all the orders once word gets out that the ships are strong enough." Ara stopped and looked back at the water, saying nothing for a long moment as he stared off across the waves.

"Is something wrong?" Noah asked.

"Maybe. Speaking of stronger boats, Zain told me that Bayt is back in town."

"Bayt? Is he the man who wouldn't listen to you and nearly drowned?"

Ara nodded. "Then he came back here and tried to destroy my business. Hopefully, time has calmed his anger."

"That would be . . ." Noah broke off as he spotted something out in the bay, far beyond Ara's ship anchored in the shallows. "A boat is heading this way." He pointed to the vessel. "Who do you suppose it is? Not Farna — he would come from the river."

"And he's not due for another week at least." Ara held up a hand to block the glare. "Could be from one of the coastal towns I've worked with in the past."

The men continued watching as the ship steadily came nearer. At last Noah could make out a yellow banner above the sail. A sinking feeling hit his stomach. "That's the boat we made for King Lamech." Noah sighed. "And just when I hoped we were finished with that wicked place."

Ara narrowed his gaze at the boat. "Should we be worried?"

Attempting to count the number of people on board, Noah squinted. The light from the morning sun reflected spectacularly off the water, making it impossible to discern individuals yet. "I'm sure there's no threat of attack. But I'd definitely be concerned about the influence they might have here. And if Naamah's there, I'd rather not stick around."

"Emz told me about that." Ara put a hand on Noah's shoulder. "I'm proud of you. Thank you for honoring my daughter and the Creator."

Noah nodded. "I believe the Most High protected me that night." He shuddered and looked Ara in the eye. "Thank you for raising Em to follow the Creator."

Ara tightened his grip. "If our trust in the Most High is to be tested by the Havilites, I'm glad to have you by my side." He looked up and down the empty beach trail. "I think we're going to have to be the welcoming party. Stay with me?"

Nodding, Noah walked toward the point on the shore where the boat would likely land. Using a hand to shade his eyes, he strained to make out the figures on board. "I see the king, and it looks like he has about four guards with him, as well as some women. But I don't recognize them." He let out a deep breath. "That's good."

As the ship neared, about a dozen curious townsfolk arrived on the beach. Noah motioned for them to come over and then spotted Emzara leaving her office. He waved to get her attention.

Emzara hurried to join him. "What's everyone doing?"

"Looks like King Lamech decided to pay us a visit."

"If Naamah is here . . ." Emzara balled her hands into fists.

Noah stepped close to her and rubbed her shoulder tenderly, lowering his voice. "I don't see her. But no matter what happens, we need to stay calm and treat our visitors with respect."

"With the same respect she showed us?" Emzara mumbled under her breath before slowly turning to Ara. "Baba, you're on the council now. Can't you just tell them to leave?"

He shook his head. "Not without consulting the rest of the elders. And I don't think it would be wise to make enemies. We'll greet them and be respectful. Let's take this opportunity to show them how followers of the Most High live." He put an arm around his daughter. "Imagine what could happen if their king started following the Creator."

Relaxing her shoulders, Emzara nodded.

Noah and Ara approached the water as the craft reached the shallows. Noah raised his voice and held up a hand. "Morning peace, King Lamech. I'm surprised to see you."

Dressed in a blue-trimmed golden wrap, the king smiled broadly from his place at the bow. "Ah, young Noah. Morning peace to you. How good to see you again."

Noah stepped into the water and caught the rope a guard threw down as the vessel slid to a halt. He looked up at the king and pointed to his left. "Our pier is over there on the river. But this should be fine here until the tide rises late in the day." He held a hand out to the king. "Let me help you."

Ignoring the proffered hand, Lamech leapt down with a splash that sent water halfway to Noah's chest. He stretched his arms out and yawned, making the scar on his right cheek bunch into a knotty red line. "It feels good to be on land again. Took me three days to get used to all the motion."

"I know what you mean." Noah chuckled.

Lamech glanced back at the Havilites on the boat. "Do you mind if they come ashore as well?"

"Of course not." Spotting Garun among the group, Noah gave him a quick nod. It settled his heart a bit to know at least one person on board followed the Creator. He hoped for an opportunity to talk to him soon.

A half-dozen splashes sounded as several men jumped into the shallows, each holding a bundle above his head. When Garun and another guard had debarked, they turned to help a slight, middle-aged man and the three young women hop from the deck. Even wading through the shallow water, the girls moved with a grace that reminded Noah of the dancers who had performed with Naamah in the king's dining hall during his first visit to Havil.

One of the remaining guards stepped to the bow. "Sir, do you want me stay here with the boat?"

Lamech pointed to the river. "You and Bachamel take it to the pier and tie it up." He turned to Noah. "If that's alright with you."

Noah nodded. "It'll be more secure there. So what brings you to Iri Geshem?"

"Oh, I got tired of sitting in Havil all the time. I needed to get out and see some of the world. What good is a ship if you never sail it? So I thought I'd tackle a few tasks in one trip. Put the new ship through its paces, travel the world a bit, and stop in here to see how my son is doing."

He glanced at his surroundings and patted the ship's hull. "And this must be the place where you built my boat."

Noah gestured to Ara. "Actually, this is the man who designs and makes the boats. I work for him. This is my father-in-law, Ara. Ara, this is King Lamech of Havil."

The king grinned. "You invented these incredible vessels?"

"I did. I trust yours is sturdy."

"Indeed, it is. I'd like to talk to you about ordering several more."

Without warning, a bitter laugh sounded from somewhere in the small crowd. "Why would you want to do that? You're lucky to be alive, riding in one of Ara's boats."

Noah spun to locate the source of the angry voice, and it did not take long to recognize the speaker. A short man with a long, scraggily beard pushed his way to the front of the group of villagers. A ragged wrap wound about his wiry frame, and a long dagger hung from his belt. His wild eyes, full of hatred, shot Noah a glance before locking onto Ara. He looked very much as Noah imagined he would. Apparently, time had not cooled Bayt's anger.

Noah pointed at the man and stepped forward. "If you had followed Ara's directions, then. . . ."

Ara put his hand on Noah's chest to stop him. "Don't worry about him. My work speaks for itself."

Noah took a deep breath, nodded, and then moved back to stand by Em.

Lamech measured Bayt for a moment before shaking his head. He faced Ara. "As I was saying, I'd like to talk to you about ordering several more ships."

Ara raised an eyebrow. "Sounds like a discussion for later." His words came out slowly, and when Noah caught his eye, he could clearly read the reluctance there.

Lamech, too, seemed to sense Ara's hesitation. His gaze shifted from the older man to Noah, and then to Emzara. "And you must be Noah's lovely wife he spoke so highly of. I remember seeing you sitting by my wife, Adah, during the ceremony."

Emzara smiled, but Noah could tell it was forced. "Yes sir. I'm Emzara."

"A beautiful name for an even more beautiful woman."

34

Some of the coolness left Emzara's smile as Lamech took her hand. "Thank you."

"You and your husband are always welcome back in Havil." Releasing Emzara, he turned to Noah and gestured to Tubal-Cain's workplace. "Is my son around? That looks like a forge over there."

"You have a keen eye. That's his shop, but he isn't here today." Noah bit his lip and looked down. He knew Tubal-Cain wanted to share the news, but this unforeseen situation changed things.

"I suppose he's out looking for ores around here," Lamech said.

Noah chuckled. "He'd better not be — at least not right now. He wanted to be the one to tell you this, but he just got married. He and his wife, Adira, planned to be away for a few weeks to celebrate. They should be back within a week."

Lamech's eyes narrowed, and for the briefest instant, Noah thought he glimpsed anger in the flinty eyes. "Married? Tubal-Cain? Without sending word to me?"

"Adira's perfect for him." Emzara took a step forward, and Lamech's mask slipped back into place as he turned to meet her sparkling eyes. "She's smart, funny, beautiful, and is completely devoted to your son. You should see them together. And she follows the Creator. . . ." Emzara flinched and broke eye contact with the king. "And she, uh, she's my best friend. Everyone loves her."

Lamech arched an eyebrow and smiled. "Well, if she's anything like you, then I'm sure my son will be very happy."

"That he is." Noah tilted his head toward the boat he and Ara had been working on earlier. "Would you like me to show you around the shipyard?"

"Maybe later. I wonder if you might show us a place where we could lodge while we're here. Perhaps that friend of yours has space? I'd like to rest in a bed that isn't rocking on the waves."

Noah looked questioningly at Ara.

"Sir, allow me to take you to Ashur's," Ara said. "Noah has an errand to run, and then he can catch up with us in town."

"Thank you." He held out an arm and smiled at the gathered townsfolk. "Please, lead the way."

"Certainly. Come with me." Ara took several steps before stopping. "Ah, just a moment. I've forgotten. . . ." He hurried back to Noah.

"An errand?" Noah kept his voice low.

"Yes. We'll take a longer route. Run and inform the council members about this." He turned to leave and raised his voice so the king could hear him. "Meet us at Ashur's when you're finished."

"I'll see you there."

Ara hustled to catch up to the unexpected guests, and most of the bystanders followed the entourage toward Sarie's Bakery on the road that Noah and Aterre had taken to the shipyard during their first visit to Iri Geshem.

Emzara sidled up to Noah. "I'm coming with you."

Noah squeezed her hand. "I hoped you would." He led her to the road to Ara's house, which would allow them to take a shortcut into town. "As soon as we're out of view, we'll need to move quickly."

"I don't like this," she said. "Lamech — coming here. I don't like it at all. Did you see his face when you told him of Tubal-Cain's marriage?"

"I did, and I don't like him coming here, either. I don't want anything to do with Havil anymore — especially their serpent god." Noah picked up the pace a little. "I hate what he stands for, but I must admit, he's never been anything but kind to me. He can be quite convincing, can't he?"

"He's very cunning. I can see why people follow him." Concern spread across her face. "You don't think Baba will fall for his lies, do you?"

"Never. He's the last person that would. He's not happy about this surprise visit either."

They turned off the road and ran past Ara's house. The trail led through the grove of milknut trees and next to their own home before ending at the beach where Aterre had embarrassed Noah in front of Emzara years earlier. As the sand penetrated his sandals, Noah smiled inwardly, recalling the awkward moments that led to his first sunset with Emzara.

The sun had nearly reached its zenith, and the morning's coolness had given way to warmer air. Sea birds squawked as they flew overhead, while others trotted along the shore, pecking at the moist ground after every wave. Noah and Emzara ran west along the shoreline until they reached the path that led straight to the middle of town. They turned at the second crossroad, and from there a short jaunt took them to Zain's residence.

A well-groomed trail wound through a wide array of colorful flowers that gradually gave way to rows of large niti trees. Tucked away in the shade, Zain's two-story, mud-brick home was one of the oldest in town.

A narrow path to the left led to a well that always reminded Noah of the one on his father's farm.

Noah knocked on the door. "Zain, are you here?"

Moments later, Zain stood in the entryway. "Ah, Noah and Emzara, morning peace. What a pleasant surprise. Please come in." He stepped aside and gestured for them to enter.

Piles of folded garments separated by color rested on shelves along the back wall. Seated in the middle of the room, Zain's wife, Kmani, skillfully slid a shuttle through the strands on a large loom. She stopped and stood, motioning for them to enter. "Welcome." She started to step over a pile of garments, but seemed to have second thoughts about her ability to clear the pile with her short legs. After zigzagging around piles of fabric, Kmani met Noah and Emzara just as they stepped inside, giving Emzara a warm hug.

After shutting the door, Noah put a hand up. "We'd love to stay and visit, but there's no time. I have troubling news. King Lamech and nearly a dozen Havilites just arrived."

Zain's eyes opened wide. "What? Here?"

Kmani looked up at Noah. "What does he want?"

"He said he wanted to try out his ship and visit Tubal-Cain, but he may have other motives. We weren't sure how to handle the situation. It was such a shock."

Emzara pulled her hair back and tied it up as she spoke. "Baba thought it'd be best to be on our guard while extending hospitality to them."

Zain pursed his lips. "That's probably wise. No need to start a feud with Havil. Where are they now?"

"They're taking the long way to Ashur's," Noah said. "Ara wanted me to inform the council members immediately and meet him there. You're the first one on the way."

Zain's eyes shifted to Kmani, and he took a long breath before turning back to Noah. "You two go and warn Ashur. That should give him a little time to get ready for visitors. Let him know that I'll be there soon with the other council members."

Noah nodded.

Zain turned and kissed Kmani's forehead. "I'll be back as soon as possible."

CHAPTER 5

Ashur's eyes grew wide. "The king is in Iri Geshem? Now? And he wants to stay here?"

"Yes, he'll be here very soon," Noah said.

"How many people were with him?"

"About a dozen, including several guards and a few women."

"That's wonderful. Imagine, the king staying at my inn." As if realizing what he'd just said, Ashur frowned. "I mean, that's terrible. I'm not ready for such an important guest."

"What can we do to help?" Emzara asked. "We don't have much time."

Ashur's gaze darted around the dining hall. Several customers were scattered about the room, savoring their meals and enjoying one another's company. "Noah, can you clean the empty tables and straighten the chairs?"

"Of course."

Ashur pointed down the hallway to his left. "Emzara, would you mind preparing a couple of the guest rooms?"

"I can do that," she said. "Which ones?"

"I'll show you in a moment. I'll be right back." He hurried through a door in the back.

"He seems rather excited about it." Emzara bit her lip. "Almost too excited."

Noah kept his voice low. "I think he really enjoyed himself in Havil. I'm not sure he agrees with the rest of the council on this matter."

Emzara crossed her arms and leaned back slightly. "Certainly that can't be true. How could anyone from Iri Geshem want anything to do with Havil after seeing that ceremony?"

Noah shrugged one shoulder. "What if that someone didn't really follow the Creator?"

"You think Ashur doesn't . . ."

"I'm just thinking out loud, but sometimes he seems too interested in wealth and pleasure. Havil has plenty of both. I think your father suspects as much too."

Emzara opened her mouth to speak just as Ashur re-entered the room.

Ashur tossed two cloths to Noah and set a bucket of water on the table beside him. "These are for tidying up out here. Emzara, come with me, and I'll show you which guest rooms you can prepare."

Noah plunged a rag into the water and wrung it out while Emzara followed Ashur up the stairs to the second floor. The establishment boasted four guest rooms on the second floor and four on the ground level. Widely considered the best place to eat in town, the spacious dining hall often filled to capacity in the evening. Noah turned his attention to the nearest unoccupied table and wiped it down, all the while keeping an eye and ear out for the group from Havil.

Before long, Ashur led a couple down the stairs and then to the last room on the right. "I'm sorry about the inconvenience. You can stay for half price tonight."

Noah finished cleaning the tables and set the bucket near the door to the kitchen. He planned to ask Ashur what else needed to be done, but decided to check outside for the Havilites first. Looking out the front door, Noah saw a large crowd of people across the town square with Ara and Lamech at the front. He moved quickly to the landing and called to the second floor. "They're almost here."

A door slammed shut. "Coming." Ashur hurried down the steps, his sandaled feet slapping against the wooden boards. "Thank you, Noah. I owe you one."

"You're welcome. They're still on the other side of the fountain, but I thought you'd want to greet them outside."

Ashur nodded. "Thanks again."

"Do you mind if Em and I use the back exit? I'd rather not be here for this meeting."

Ashur shrugged. "I suppose if you want to. I need to go." He took a deep breath and darted out the front door.

"He sure was in a hurry."

Noah spun around at the sound of Emzara's voice. He crossed the floor and took her hand. "I am too. Let's get out of here."

He picked up the bucket and set it inside the kitchen. Ashur's kitchen hand was busily kneaded a pile of dough while, to his right, a large iron soup pot simmered above coals, giving the room its pleasant aroma. "Smells great, Enika. Ashur said we can use the back door."

"Oh, I didn't even see you. Be sure to stop in again sometime."

As they stepped into the narrow alley behind the inn, Emzara's hand flew to her stomach and then to her mouth. "Whew, I don't feel well all of a sudden. I hope I'm not going to be ill."

Noah gently rubbed her back. "Are you alright?"

"Yeah, I think so." She inhaled slowly and leaned against the building. "What do we do now?"

"After they arrive, we'll join the crowd from behind and observe." Noah wiped sweat from his forehead. He cast about and spotted a large wooden box under a nearby tree. "Do you want to rest over there for a while?"

"That sounds good." She took his hand and followed him to the shade.

Noah sighed as he sat down. "This is much better."

She reclined against him as he wrapped both arms around her. Grinning, she locked her dark brown eyes onto his. "No, *this* is much better." She closed her eyes, a contented smile etched across her tender lips.

As she rested, Noah caressed her cheek with his thumb. Her eyes moved beneath her eyelids and her nostrils flared ever so slightly with each breath. Leaning in, Noah kissed her forehead, taking in the spicy sweet fragrance of the oil she used in her hair. He tilted his head back and closed his eyes. *Creator, thank You for Emzara. What have I ever done to deserve her?* The sound of the approaching crowd turned Noah's thoughts away from his wife. *Most High, please give our council members wisdom regarding this unexpected visit. May we always seek to serve You.*

Emzara sighed. "Did they have to get here so soon?" She sat up. "We'd better go."

Before leaving the alley, they peeked around the corner and saw roughly 40 people gathered between the fountain and Ashur's inn. Ashur stood before Ara and the king, exchanging pleasantries, while the people fanned out in a semi-circle beyond them.

"Are we trying to hide?" Emzara asked.

Noah furrowed his brows. "No, but I got the impression that your father wants us to be cautious, and I agree. Let's just observe from the back. If we get a chance, I'd like to talk to Garun too."

"Oh, I didn't realize he was with them."

"Makes sense. He's been here before, so he could teach them about our city and practices." Noah took her hand and stepped out into the street. "I'm glad Nivlac isn't here."

She wrinkled her nose and frowned. "Me too."

Noah looked down the road toward the sea. *No sign of Zain yet.*

Noah and Emzara slipped into the crowd, maneuvering themselves just close enough that they could hear what was being said at the front.

"It's an honor to host you and your group during your stay," Ashur said. "Would you like to see the rooms now?"

The king put up a hand. "Thank you. My daughter spoke highly of your inn, and I am looking forward to a fresh meal. But first, I would like to address the citizens of Iri Geshem." He paused and his gaze shifted from Ashur to Ara and back again. "May I?"

"Of course." Ashur held out his hands and raised his voice. "Brothers and sisters, King Lamech of Havil would like to speak to you."

The crowd quieted, and Lamech turned to face them, taking a step back as his gaze swept from left to right across the group. With shoulders back and chin up, the king's posture matched his regal position, the dark brown scar stretching from his right cheekbone to ear only adding to the aura of fierce strength he exuded. "Men and women of Iri Geshem, thank you for kindly welcoming me and some of my people to your city. We have traveled a long way to visit you and to thank you for the marvelous ship made by my new friend, Ara."

Without a smile, Ara nodded once in acknowledgment.

"Just as you have learned about metalworking from my son, Tubal-Cain, we would like to learn all we can from you." The king looked directly at Noah, whose height caused him to stand out behind the three rows of people in front of him. "Noah may have told you that we've constructed a place of learning, what I call the House of Knowledge. I've dispatched scribes to cities throughout our region to record any

41

of the wisdom and discoveries they find. Just imagine what we might accomplish for the good of all people if we could learn from each other."

Lamech smiled broadly and opened his arms wide. "With your blessing, of course, I'd like to learn what we can from you." He tipped his head toward one of his subjects, a man dressed in a fine silken wrap, much like the one Noah had worn in Havil. "To show our appreciation for your cooperation in this endeavor, I have prepared a bit of a gift and a brief demonstration of a fraction of what Havil could share with you."

The man opened a small chest and pulled out a handful of golden piks. Excitement grew as he handed out a small gold ball to each person in the crowd.

"I understand that you may not be familiar with gold in Iri Geshem," the king said, "but Havilah has the finest gold in the world. A beautiful metal and so easy to shape, I am sure you will find endless uses for it."

The townsfolk chatted excitedly as each received his or her gold. "It is beautiful," a woman next to Noah said as she stared at her gift. Meanwhile, Ara spoke to the king, but the commotion prevented Noah from being able to hear him.

After a few moments, Lamech held up his hands and the crowd quieted. "I hope you are pleased with that gift. Ara has informed me that I'll need to speak to the town council before any official arrangements are made. But, in the meantime, I'd like you to enjoy a small demonstration of Havil's beauty and talent."

The three Havilite women stepped forward. Joining them were three men dressed in matching blue wraps. One held a stringed instrument, another a wooden flute, and the third carried a drum. In perfect harmony, the women allowed their overwraps to drop to the ground. Two wore light blue silken gowns and the third's was a royal blue. The dresses were much more modest than the ones worn by the dancers in Havil, but still accentuated their attractive bodies.

As the musicians played, the women danced and clapped along to the tune. Thankfully, this show was also more reserved than the performance that exuded sensuality during Noah's first trip to Havil. After a few moments, the dancer in the darker outfit started to sing. Her strong voice perfectly accompanied the music.

She looks like one of the dancers Ashur spoke with at the king's table. Noah glanced at Ashur, who was engrossed. Noah put an arm around Emzara and looked into her eyes. "I'd rather watch you."

A strong hand gripped Noah's arm, distracting him from Emzara's answering smile. "Did you inform the councilmembers?" Ara asked.

Keeping his voice low, Noah said, "We told Zain and Ashur. Zain said he'd get the others immediately."

"They'd better hurry," Ara said. "I think our fellow citizens like what they see from Havil. We need to stop this before it goes on too long, but I don't want to act alone."

"What about Ashur?" Emzara asked. "He's on the council."

Noah snorted. "Look at him. Do you really think he wants any of this to stop?"

"He's right, Emz. Ashur refuses to see Havil as a danger."

The music came to a stop, and the entertainers returned to their former places. Two guards armed with black staffs stepped forward, each clad in Havil's customary light brown leather tunics partially covered by metal armor. They moved about 15 paces in front of the crowd and roughly five cubits apart before turning to face each other. In unison, they looked at the king, who responded with a nod. Both men assumed a fighting pose similar to the one Aterre had shown Noah years earlier. Following a brief pause, they tapped the two staffs together between them.

Without warning, the guard to the right yelled and spun toward his opponent with blinding speed. His strike would likely have broken the other man's leg, except that the second guard deftly blocked the blow with his own staff. A flurry of attacks, blocks, and dodges ensued. The men moved so quickly, effortlessly, and skillfully that the action soon mesmerized Noah. *I wonder how Aterre would fare against these men.* He glanced at Garun, who was positioned near the man who handed out the gold. *Can Garun fight like that?*

As the crowd grew, a few newcomers asked if anyone was going to stop the fight, but they were quickly shushed and informed that it was a demonstration.

The soldier who blocked the first attack intercepted an overhead swing and then ducked and swept the legs out from under the other man. In one continuous motion, he finished the sweeping stroke and spun completely around, swinging his staff high above and then down with reckless velocity at the other guard's head. He hit the ground when the tripped soldier moved at the last possible instant and then kicked the attacker in the chest. Still on his back, he sprang to his feet in one sudden motion and raised his staff above his face just in time to thwart another blow. The two men squared off and slowly spun in a circle, studying each other's movements.

Lamech clapped. "Excellent!"

The guards stood tall, nodded to the king, and then tapped their staffs together. As they moved back to their position near Garun, the assembly applauded.

"There he is," Ara said, pointing to the road to the beach.

Zain ran to them. "What's happening?"

Ara kept his voice down. "They are winning over the people. We need to do something."

Zain nodded. "Right. Let's talk to the king."

Ara and Zain walked around the crowd and joined Ashur near Lamech.

"King Lamech, I'm surprised to see you again," Zain said.

"Ah, Noah's steadfast companion — Zain, I believe it is?"

"That's right. I am one of the council members of Iri Geshem." Zain swung his arm out, palm up. "As are Ashur and Ara."

The king beamed and put his hand on Zain's shoulder. "Perfect. We have much to talk about."

"Indeed we do, but we cannot decide on these matters without the rest of the council," Zain said. "I just spoke with two of the other members, and we will not be able to meet together until tomorrow evening."

"Oh, believe me, I understand what that's like." Lamech looked around the town square. "That's just fine with me. As I mentioned before you got here, I want to learn all I can from your people."

Zain dipped his head and pointed to the town hall at the end of the square. "Our meeting will take place in that large building over there."

"I look forward to it." The king yawned. "Now, if you don't mind, I'd really like to see just how comfortable one of Ashur's rooms is."

Ashur chuckled. "I'm sure it'll seem just like your own room at the palace — when you close your eyes."

The king laughed and cuffed Ashur's shoulder. "I like it already. I hope the food is good too." He turned and called his subjects over. "Come. Let's see where we'll be staying."

44

CHAPTER 6

Noah and Emzara crossed the square toward the front of the council building. The air held a trace of coolness. The sun hung just above the horizon, causing the looming shadow of the building to stretch far across the grounds. He whistled lowly at the sight of the throng of citizens waiting to enter the structure. "I think we're in for a long night."

Emzara slipped her hand into his. "Looks that way."

"I sure hope we can find a peaceful resolution to this situation." Noah cleared his throat. "I really don't want to be part of this."

She pulled his hand up and kissed it. "You'll do great, if they even ask you to speak. Whatever happens, I'll be right there with you."

"Then I have nothing to worry about."

To avoid the cluster of people at the portico, Noah and Emzara turned left before the building and headed for the side door as Ara had instructed.

As they slipped into the hall, Noah glanced at the growing mass of people trying to enter through the main doors. "There's no way everyone will fit in here."

Extra benches and chairs occupied every available spot inside the hall, but they were filling up fast. Seated at the front of the room behind the large wooden desk, Iri Geshem's elders conversed quietly among themselves. As chairman, Akel had settled in the middle seat. To his right were Ashur and Oban, a farmer from across the river who was well into his 500s. To Akel's left sat Zain and Iri Geshem's newest councilmember, Ara.

As Noah and Emzara found their reserved spots in the front left row, Emzara waved to Ara.

"I don't see Aterre." Noah bit a fingernail as he watched the room fill up, although the bench to their right remained empty, having been set aside for the contingent from Havil. The overflowing crowd pressed up against the back and side walls, and their hushed conversations indicated that Noah was not the only nervous citizen. The doors stayed open to allow people in the lobby to witness the meeting.

Akel stood slowly and stretched out his arms for silence. "Please, let us begin our meeting by seeking the Creator's favor." He lifted his hands up near his face. "O Most High, Maker of heaven and earth, we ask for Your guidance during this meeting. Give us the wisdom to follow and honor You."

The old man eased himself back into his chair. "I know many of you are excited about our guests, while others are not too thrilled about their visit. Before we invite them into the hall, I'd like to ask that you treat them with respect, and please let us conduct this meeting in an orderly fashion. If you have questions for the Havilites, there may be an opportunity for you to ask them near the end of our time. Thank you."

Akel signaled to two men standing at the main doors. Moments after exiting, they reappeared with Lamech and some guards. Gesturing for the Havilites to enter the hall, each attendant stepped to one side.

In his typical manner, Lamech strode into the room with head held high and shoulders pulled back. Unlike his public appearances in Havil, the king was not wearing his crown and royal robe, but his blue and red silk wrap still stood out from the linen garments worn by the locals. His eyes scanned his surroundings before focusing on the council members. He stopped at the front of the room. "Council members of Iri Geshem." Holding out an arm, he turned toward the audience. "And citizens of Iri Geshem. Thank you for kindly hosting us in your fine city. I bring you greetings from the great city of Havil, the jewel of the sea."

"Thank you for agreeing to meet with us in this setting." Akel motioned to the empty front row. "Please, be seated."

The king nodded and allowed two of his soldiers to enter the row before him. Two more followed him, including Garun, and they all sat down in unison.

Akel cleared his throat and spoke loudly. "We have called this special session of the council to discuss your arrival." He looked at Lamech. "I know some of our citizens may have questions they'd like to ask. I've informed them that they may have the opportunity later, if you find that agreeable."

The king stood again and smiled broadly while surveying the crowd. "Of course. I'd be happy to answer any question or address any concern you may have."

"Thank you," Akel said. "And I'd personally like to thank you for allowing Tubal-Cain to live with us. He's a fine young man, and his skills have greatly benefited our people."

Lamech nodded. "Nothing pleases a father more than knowing his children are such a help to others."

Emzara squeezed Noah's arm and whispered in his ear. "Too bad the same can't be said about his daughter."

Akel continued, "I know you spoke to several people yesterday in the city square, but would you mind explaining to the council your purpose for coming here?" Akel leaned back slightly. "I want to make sure everyone has the same information before we proceed."

"Council members." Lamech's focus swept from the right side of the table to the left. "Once again I thank you for receiving us. I'm pleased to see that your hospitality has not waned since the last time I visited your lovely town."

Akel scratched his cheek. "You've been here before?"

"Long before I was king of Havil, I passed through with my father. I believe we were here only for an evening. It was much smaller then, but delightful nonetheless.

"But let me speak about this trip. Our purpose is fivefold. First, I had a desire to try out our fine vessel made by your very own councilman, Ara."

Lamech turned to the audience. "Second, I wished to visit my son." He chuckled. "But my timing seems to be off for that.

"Third, I wanted to see more of the world. Meet new people, as well as visit old friends. With such a magnificent boat, I can discover the unknown wonders of the coast from Havil to Nod."

He paused, steepling his fingers before his lips as if considering his next words. "Which leads me to my fourth reason for coming here — I

47

started an initiative nearly four years ago — a House of Knowledge. It's a massive building." He scanned the walls and ceiling of the hall. "You could probably fit 50 of these rooms in it."

Gasps and chuckles filled the air, while from somewhere behind him, Noah heard an accusation of exaggeration.

"You think I'm joking?" Lamech raised his voice over the general murmur. "It's as large as my palace. Ashur, do you think 50 of these rooms could fit in my palace?"

Ashur laughed. "I wouldn't be surprised if you could fit a hundred of these rooms in it."

The king snorted. "You see, I am not jesting. Havil is a magnificent city, grander than anything you've ever seen. But I'm getting ahead of myself." He looked up as if trying to recapture his previous thoughts. "This House of Knowledge — our goal is to fill it with the world's combined wisdom and knowledge. I have sent scribes throughout Havilah and the surrounding lands to record what people have learned regarding medicine, agriculture, animals, religion, metallurgy, music, and technological advancements. Just think what we might be able to accomplish if we worked together and combined all our understanding." He pointed to Ara. "Thanks to your ships, we can already travel farther and faster. Imagine being able to sell your wares to a distant land. What if we could find a cure for the sicknesses in our world? We might even witness men or women live for over a thousand years. The possibilities are endless."

Akel raised an eyebrow when Lamech mentioned an extended lifespan. "Do you really believe that?"

Noah scratched above his ear. *Several people have lived into their 900s. Why does a thousand years seem so strange to Akel?*

Lamech shrugged. "I don't know the limits of what's possible. But I am willing to work hard to make this world a better place." After an awkward silence, Lamech continued. "Our final reason for coming here is that we'd like to establish official trade relations between Havil and Iri Geshem. At this point, with so few ships, I doubt there would be much trade, but I'm looking toward the future when travel between our cities could take place regularly and perhaps be much quicker."

Folding his arms over his chest, Lamech fell silent, though he continued to stand.

"Was there anything else you'd like to say before we deliberate?" Akel asked.

"No, but I'll gladly clarify anything, if needed."

"I'm sorry you missed your son. It is a pity, after you have come so far." Akel put both hands on the desk in front of him, pausing as if to further convey his sympathy. "It seems to me that we really only need to discuss your last two reasons — our potential contributions to your House of Knowledge and the question about a trade agreement. I think it would be fair to let you know that before we sent our first group to Havil, we'd decided against establishing official trade relations with your city. We'd heard rumors about certain practices, and we would like to keep those influences out of Iri Geshem." Akel glanced both ways down the table at his colleagues before fixing his sights on Lamech. "That was a few years ago, and today we have a better understanding of what your city and people are like. At this time, I'd like the other elders to share their concerns, now that you're here to address them."

Lamech's stoic expression changed little during Akel's discourse. When the elder finished speaking, Lamech bobbed his head once and then walked several paces toward the council. "Rumors you say? I find it strange that a wise and upstanding person like yourself would make a decision based on rumors."

Glancing around, Noah saw several townspeople nodding their agreement as Lamech continued in an almost injured tone. "I confess I hadn't dreamed you'd be so accusatory after everything I've done to show my goodwill toward you all."

Ashur leaned forward and addressed Akel. "Well, since I've been to Havil twice now, perhaps I should speak. That way you'll all know I'm speaking about truth and not rumors."

Noah took a deep breath and squeezed Emzara's hand. *Please let this go well.*

"Just a moment." Akel held out a hand toward Ashur and then directed it at the king. "Would you have a seat and make yourself comfortable?" The words were more of a declaration than an invitation, and for the second time, Noah caught a glimpse of anger on Lamech's face. It was slight — nothing more than a glint in the king's eye — and it vanished in a heartbeat.

When Lamech had settled on his bench, Ashur addressed the crowd. "On our first voyage to Havil, we were concerned about the impact certain practices could have on Iri Geshem, particularly activities we had heard were prominent in Havil. It's true that the Havilites, by and large, don't follow the Creator, as most of us do, but I believe that the potential benefits of trading with them outweigh the risk." He glanced at the king. "I've learned much from them during my two trips, and I hope they might learn from us as well, including, perhaps, the value of obedience to the Creator."

Oban, the beardless elder whose name Noah forgot during his first visit to the council meeting four years ago, shifted in his seat to face Ashur. "I remind you that such an agreement would stand at odds with our previous decision, which was not based on pragmatic concerns about business opportunities but on a desire to remain true to the Creator."

Zain set down his pen and pushed a small scroll to the side. "Like Ashur, I have also visited Havil twice." He looked at Lamech. "And while I thank you for your hospitality toward us, I don't believe it would be in our best interest to establish official relations. We certainly don't wish to make enemies of anyone, particularly with those who have shown us kindness. Our desire is to live at peace with all of our brothers and sisters throughout the land. My concerns are primarily based on what we observed at the ceremony, which directly opposed our beliefs. Here, we worship the Most High, the Creator. But you openly encouraged your people to worship the Serpent, the Great Deceiver. I don't believe such an action is something we can simply overlook."

"I'm glad you mentioned that, Zain." King Lamech brushed his robe, looking as comfortable as if he were ordering his next meal from a servant. "I've learned much in my time as king. When I started, I believed that I needed to use religious ideas to win the support of the people. That whole Serpent religion event was a mistake, a means to an end, if you will. I've since learned that the best way to lead my people is through setting a good example."

"Are you saying that your people no longer worship the Serpent?" Zain asked.

The king shrugged. "There are probably some who still hold those beliefs, but it wasn't too long after that ceremony that we stopped promoting them."

Noah studied Garun's face, but the guard sat perfectly still, his pose hiding any emotion.

"That would be a step in the right direction." Zain leaned his elbows on the table.

Ara cleared his throat. "I have a question that pertains less to your ability to run your city and more about the way you run your family. As anyone here can testify, Tubal-Cain is a fine young man. Many of us had the opportunity to meet your daughter as well when she visited, and she seemed to get along well with folks. But I've heard many disturbing things about her since she's returned to Havil."

The king held up a hand. "If you're referring to her role in the ceremony as priestess, I can assure you that this is another area where things have changed. You're correct, Ara, my daughter should never have been involved in something like that."

Ara took a deep breath and slowly let it out. "I was not referring to her role in the ceremony, but to her actions just prior to it."

The king opened his mouth to speak and then tilted his head to one side. "What actions?"

"She used your guards to arrest Noah, and they even detained Zain for a time. When Noah was brought to her chambers, she attempted to seduce him, though she knew he was a married man. Why would your daughter act that way?"

"I have not heard of this until now." The king slowly shook his head and looked at Zain. "You were really arrested by my guards? Did they mistreat you?"

Zain's eyes narrowed slightly as he nodded. "After they stormed into the guest house, threw Emzara on the ground, and said they were going to execute Noah."

"What?" Lamech turned toward Noah. "This is true?"

"It is." Though he wasn't thrilled about being brought into the conversation, Noah twisted halfway around so that both the council and audience could hear him. "I'd rather not discuss all the details in this setting, but it is true that Nivlac barged into our quarters, made false allegations, and threatened to execute me. After the soldiers dragged me to the courtyard, they acted like they were going to sacrifice me to the Great Deceiver. And that's when Naamah stepped in. She stopped Nivlac, but I have reason to believe that was part of the setup to have me brought to her room."

Lamech tilted his head back and closed his eyes as if coming to a realization. "I had no idea, but that explains much. When I found out that our dock had been damaged, I asked around and learned it was because she sent guards to detain you after the ceremony. She never gave me a straight answer about why she had done it, but now I understand."

Lamech faced Noah. "If she really did all that you said, then I'm very sorry for her behavior. I'd have put a stop to it immediately, if you had let me know, but I will certainly deal with this upon my return."

"I'm glad to hear it, sir." Ara sat up straight. "However, the fact remains that her actions reflect negatively on your leadership. Since you're the one who put her in a position of authority, which she abused, it calls into question the decisions you make as a leader. All the more reason for us to be reluctant to establish an arrangement with your city."

"Holding one person responsible for the actions of another is a harsh standard, council members. However," Lamech sighed, "I don't believe in blaming others for what happens under my watch. What my daughter is accused of doing is clearly wrong, and as I said before, I'll certainly deal with it upon my return. I'm afraid there is little else I can offer at the moment. If Noah had brought it to my attention at the time, we might have avoided this whole unpleasant conversation."

Ara strummed his fingers on the desk, his scowl deepening. "Not to belabor the point, but your daughter said it would make sense for Noah to have two wives because you, her father, also have two wives. The Most High created marriage to be between one man and one woman. What makes you think it's acceptable to violate the Creator's standard for marriage?"

Lamech sighed. "I do have two wives, but I only took a second wife after her husband died. She needed someone to care for her. Before I was made king, there was considerable violence around Havil. I helped bring an end to that." He rubbed his eye. "One of the many unfortunate consequences of such violence is that when married men are killed, many widows are left without a means of support. You may not agree with my decision, but I believe this was a way for me to care for a woman and her family."

Ara stroked his beard and then leaned forward. "Intentions, no matter how good they may seem, do not justify disobedience to our Creator." His face reddened slightly and his voice rose in volume.

"Oh, Baba, be careful," Emzara said under her breath.

"Zain told me that you also eat the creatures of the sea." Ara looked unflinchingly at the king. "Another direct violation of the Creator's standards."

Lamech held Ara's gaze. "Who's to say that those old stories about the first man and woman are even true? I've heard other myths about our origins that included no such prohibition. Are you really willing to negate what could become a very profitable trade agreement between us for the sake of your religious traditions? This would just be a business arrangement and has nothing to do with what the Creator may or may not have commanded us to eat."

Ara hit the table with his fist, making more than one person in the hall jump. "These things are never just business!" He rubbed his eyes with the fingers of one hand, and said more quietly, "In any trade agreement, ideas are exchanged, and it's precisely the types of ideas that you've admitted to that we don't want in our city."

Akel stood and held up both hands. "Please, everyone pause for a moment." He glanced at Ara and then the king. "There's no need to let our emotions, no matter how justified, get in the way of reaching a well-reasoned conclusion."

"My sentiments exactly," Lamech said.

Ara let out a deep breath. "Forgive me if I've allowed my feelings to color the council's decision."

Akel slowly shook his head. "There is nothing to forgive because there's nothing wrong with being passionate about these matters." Akel turned to address the crowd. "However, I question whether we're right to require adherence to our rules from those who do not share our view of the Creator." He shrugged. "Why should we expect someone to hold to our standards if they don't believe in our God?"

During a prolonged silence, Noah's insides twisted. *We might not hold them to our rules, but I wonder if we should trade with them so that we can try to help them understand the Creator's ways.*

"Are there any more questions for the king?" Akel asked his colleagues. When no one spoke up, he continued. "The council has no further inquiries. However, I'll now allow others to speak."

Murmurs spread through the audience, but no one spoke up.

Akel rubbed his forehead. "If there are. . . ."

"I have a question."

Noah and Emzara exchanged glances and turned to look toward the back of the room.

Aterre stood near the door, barely visible in the crowd standing behind the rows of benches. "I'm sorry it's not directly on point. I was going to save it until later, but since he mentioned the violence from several years back, I decided I'd ask now." Aterre stood on tiptoe so he could look at Lamech, but the king remained seated. "I'm from the land of Havilah, not very close to your city, but in the region."

"Yes. I figured that out right away." The king grinned but only turned his head enough to see Aterre from the corner of his eye. "It's good to hear familiar speech. Well, almost. You sound like you're from the western lands."

"Indeed, my accent usually gives it away." Aterre chuckled. "Anyway, my question has to do with my family. You see, about ten years ago, my village was raided in the night. My family was taken, and, from what I saw before fleeing, many people were killed. But I've never stopped wondering what happened to my mother and sisters. Do you know if there are slave traders in the region? And if so, would there be anyone you know who could help me find my family, if they are still alive?"

Lamech bowed his head. "I'm sorry to hear about this. What's your name?"

"Aterre, sir."

The king's back rose as he inhaled deeply. "Aterre." He said the name as if savoring the taste of a fine drink. "I know there's been some slave trading, particularly in the west. We've been trying to put a stop to it. I will look into this matter for you." He put a hand on the shoulder of the guard to his left. "Talk to Bachamel here and give him all the details you can. In fact, you'd be welcome to return with us to search for them."

"Thank you, sir. Maybe I will be able to go soon." His head popped up over the crowd again, and he smiled at Noah and Emzara. "But I have some important matters to take care of here first."

Akel waited for a few moments before speaking. "Thank you, Aterre. I pray that your search will not be unfruitful." He cleared his throat. "Regarding the matter of official relations with Havil, I suggest that we refrain from making a decision at this time until we can see for ourselves that the reforms Lamech mentioned are moving forward. Any objections from the council?"

The council members offered their agreement, although Ashur failed to hide his displeasure.

"Then it's decided. King Lamech, I appreciate your willingness to endure our questioning."

The king nodded. "I fully understand your decision. You show much wisdom in not rushing into these matters without all the necessary information. If you'd like to see Havil for yourself, you're welcome anytime."

"Thank you." Akel sat up straight. "Now, regarding the other matter. I think there's an easy solution. You say that you've sent scribes throughout your land to record information."

"Yes."

Akel put his palms together and pointed his hands at Lamech. "Then I assume that you've brought a scribe with you on this journey."

"Yes, we did," Lamech said. "Bedin is our most gifted scribe. I'm sure you could learn much from him, just as he could learn from your citizens."

"For the sake of clarity, are you simply seeking to leave him in Iri Geshem for a certain amount of time to record what he learns from us?"

"That's mostly correct. I'd like to leave one of my guards here as well." Lamech looked at Garun, seated to his left at the end of the bench. "Garun would be perfect for the job. He was here before, and I believe many of your citizens already know and like him. And you won't have to provide for them. They'll cover their own expenses."

"Please give us a few moments." Akel stood and motioned for the other elders to gather around him.

Noah looked at Garun, still practically motionless, as if he were a statue. He leaned close to Emzara's ear. "It'd be great to have Garun here again."

She rested her head on his shoulder. "Do you think they'll agree to it?"

"Not sure. Four of the five elders don't like Havil, but this request doesn't seem to be asking a whole lot. However, I'm not sure Lamech truly has the best intentions."

"I was thinking the same thing."

"May I have your attention." Akel eased himself down in his chair. "The council has unanimously granted the request of the Havilites to leave Garun and a scribe in Iri Geshem until the scribe completes his work."

Lamech stood and bowed slightly. "Thank you. It's my sincere hope that you'll soon see for yourselves the changes being made in Havil and that we might trade openly in the future."

"We shall see." Akel leaned over and spoke briefly to Oban.

Oban stood and raised his voice. "At our normal council meetings, we'd ask if anyone has any new business to bring up, but this was a special meeting to address the requests of the Havilites, so no further business will be discussed tonight. Evening peace to you all."

CHAPTER 7

The sea breeze ruffled Noah's hair as he watched the vessel from Havil drift out of view on the right side of the bay. Hidden for much of the morning by gray clouds releasing a steady drizzle, the sun peeked through a clear patch in the sky, hinting that the afternoon might grow warmer. Sea birds squawked and screeched as they glided over the coast, dipping and rising in their chaotic flight patterns.

Noah folded his arms as his eyes traced the movements of one of the larger birds. "I'm glad that's over."

"I am too." Emzara smiled. "I'm surprised they left so soon. I thought he'd at least stay until Tubal-Cain and Adira returned."

"I thought so too. Perhaps Lamech was more annoyed about the council's decision than he let on."

Emzara pushed a stray lock over her ear, and the wind immediately whipped it free again. "Well, I'm happy they aren't here anymore."

They stood there in silence for a moment while Noah studied her face, a half smile creeping over his lips as his mind wandered back to the day nine years ago when they had stood in this very place and he had finally worked up the courage to tell her how he felt about her. After a time, she looked at him, her delicate brows puzzled. "What?"

"Nothing." He sighed. "I suppose I should go do some work on my day off. Thanks to our unexpected and uninvited guests" — Noah cast an exaggerated glance at Garun — "I'm behind on my work."

Garun chuckled. "And I was beginning to think you were just lazy."

"Not me, but that describes him pretty well." Noah nudged Aterre, who stood beside him, digging one toe into the sand.

Aterre looked up from the ground. "Huh? What did you say?"

"Were you even listening?"

"Sorry, no."

"Is everything alright?" Emzara asked.

Aterre bit his lip and stared at her for a moment. "Yeah, I'm fine. Listen, I need to get over to Cada's."

Emzara tilted her head. "I thought you had the day off too."

"I do, but I need to. . . ." Already walking away, Aterre turned and called over his shoulder, "there's something I need to check on."

"Will we see you later?"

Aterre just raised a hand in reply, and Emzara turned to Noah with a questioning smile. "Is he alright?"

Noah shrugged. "I don't know. He's been distracted like that for a little while."

Bits of metal clinked as Garun shifted his position. "Maybe he's thinking about finding his family. King Lamech did say something about helping him."

Noah's pulse quickened at the thought of a rescue attempt, but his excitement rapidly dampened. "But if I'm going to help him, as I promised I would, that would mean. . . ."

Emzara looked down and fidgeted with her bracelets. "Another trip to Havil."

"Maybe I can go in your place," Garun said. "When I get home, I can do some checking around. Do you know his mother's name?"

Noah stared across the bay at nothing in particular. He slowly shook his head. "I don't think I've ever asked him before. I'll find out."

Emzara pressed her hands together. "Forgive me for changing the subject. Garun, I never had the chance to thank you for warning Noah to get us out of Havil immediately."

Garun turned toward her with a small bow. "It was the least I could do after learning what Naamah planned. I was relieved when I heard that your group escaped." His prominent cheekbones rose as he smiled. "One thing's for sure. You'll never need to question Noah's love for you. The way he withstood Naa —"

"I know." Emzara's features softened as she glanced at Noah. "He told me what happened." She stepped forward and lightly kissed Garun's cheek. "But thank you for the reminder of my husband's faithfulness."

Noah smiled at Garun and gestured to Emzara with his chin. "I knew I was married to the most wonderful woman in the world."

Emzara drew back and pointed at him. "And don't you forget it." She took his hand and gave it a squeeze. "I have to check on Baba. He wasn't feeling well this morning. Enjoy the shipyard. I'll see you at even-feast. Garun, would you like to join us?"

"I'd love to, but I need to get back to Ashur's soon. Maybe tomorrow night?"

"I look forward to seeing you then." Emzara held Noah's hand against her cheek for a moment, then sighed and let it go. "Until this evening."

Noah watched her walk down the hill toward the trail through the milknut trees. As she moved out of sight, he joined Garun close to the edge of the hilltop. "Tell me something."

"What is it?"

"How can your king be so likeable at times?" Noah scratched the back of his neck. "He's been so nice to me, and offering to help Aterre. . . ." He shook his head. "But then there was the serpent ceremony and Naamah . . . and every now and then, I would catch this look. . . ."

After scanning every direction, Garun's eyes met Noah's and his countenance turned serious. "Because he's very good at what he does. He tells people what they want to hear, and when they're not paying attention, he uses his power to do whatever he wants anyway. By the time the thing is done, people rarely challenge him."

Noah held up a palm. "So was he just telling the council what they wanted to hear?"

Garun nodded and frowned. "Much of the time. He told several outright lies last night, but I couldn't say anything then. He would have exiled me and my family, sold us into slavery, or worse."

"Executed?"

"Possibly. It wouldn't be the first time he's gotten rid of someone who disagreed with him." Garun looked down. "He lied about the serpent ceremony. He hasn't put an end to it. If anything, it's grown larger each year. And he hasn't stopped Naamah from participating." He pursed his lips. "She's more involved in Nachash worship now. Ever since . . ." His gaze drifted to Noah and his eyes glinted. "Ever since that night you were there, she's been following the teachings of a strange man, a seer."

"A seer?"

"He's supposedly able to communicate with spirits."

"The spirits of those who have passed on?" Noah stroked his chin.

"More disturbing than that." Garun said. "I've heard some of the ideas he teaches her. He says that the Creator is just one of many spiritual beings, or gods, who run this world. They believe Nachash is the most powerful god, so they follow him. They think he'll reveal secrets about this world that will allow them to become the most powerful people on earth."

"Do you think these spirits exist?" Noah asked.

Garun breathed deeply. "I wish I could say that I thought it was a hoax."

"But you don't."

"No. They've learned things that no one should be able to know." He looked away. "But I think it's come at a cost. Naamah is different. She was always spoiled, but she used to smile and have a good sense of humor. Now. . . ." He shook his head. "She's cold and — I'm not sure how else to put it. But it's sad and, at times, more than a little frightening."

Noah put a hand on Garun's shoulder. "I'm sorry to hear that. Tubal-Cain will be unhappy to hear it as well."

"I'm sure he will. He was always so good to her. But I think when he left, and" — he cast Noah an apologetic look — "when you rejected her, she stopped caring about anyone else. Now she just craves power and control."

"Just like her father." Noah folded his arms again.

"Yes. They make a dangerous team." Garun tugged on the sleeve of his tunic to straighten it under his armor. "I was wrong about her sending the guards after you that night."

"What do you mean?" Noah asked. "The guards did come after us."

"Yes, but they were sent to capture Emzara."

"Em? Why?"

"For revenge. She wanted to make you beg for Emzara's life."

Noah put his thumb on his upper lip as he pondered this new information. "Does she still want that?"

Garun shrugged. "I don't know. I haven't heard her mention either of you for quite some time. As I said, ever since you left, she's been obsessed with this seer and the power he offers. She spends her days in the House of Knowledge for the most part."

"I guess that's a good thing." Noah adjusted his stance. "There isn't much we can do about it anyway, except take great care if we ever return to Havil. Which, judging from what you're telling me of Lamech, I'm not sure we'll ever do. What were some of the other lies he told at the council meeting?"

"His whole story about taking a second wife was false. Taking a second wife allowed him to flaunt his rebellion against the Creator's ways and show the people that he could do it without any consequences." Garun snorted his disgust. "His cant about leading his people by example was spot on, though. His example emboldens them to act wickedly too."

Noah shook his head. "He sounded so convincing."

"That's one of the reasons he's the king. He knows how to manipulate people into doing exactly what he wants."

"Even if it means worshiping the Great Deceiver."

Garun let out a breath as he nodded.

"So what about the scribe?" Noah asked.

"Bedin? What about him?"

"Is he really here to study our culture, like the king said, or is he here to spy on us?"

"I think he is here to record what he learns." Garun shrugged. "That's one thing Lamech didn't lie about. He really is pulling together knowledge from all over the world. He's determined to discover the path to longer life."

Noah looked askance at Garun. "How?"

Garun chuckled. "I don't know. But maybe it isn't as crazy as it sounds. According to the old stories, Greatfather Adam and Greatmother Eve were created to live forever. Maybe there's a way to at least prolong one's life."

Noah considered this, but Garun went on before he could comment.

"When I was a boy, I remember when our town received word that Greatfather died. They said he returned to the dust, just as the Creator said he would." Garun crossed his arms. "At the time, my grandfather told me what had been passed down to him by Ma'anel — one of Great-father's sons. He said that the Most High created Greatfather from the dust of the ground and Greatmother from one of his ribs. They lived in a beautiful garden, but they were only there for a few days until the Serpent deceived Greatmother and she ate from the forbidden tree. After they sinned, the Creator banished them from the garden and cursed the ground."

"Only a few days?"

Garun shrugged one shoulder. "That's what I was told."

"My grandfather told me many of the same details, but I never heard that part," Noah said. "Also, he said that Greatfather was 930 years old when he died."

"That's what I heard too. In fact, I think the king is determined to live longer than that, so he can be seen as greater than the first man."

"He's definitely full of pride."

"Yes he is." Garun snorted. "But what he doesn't know is that he'd have to surpass 985 years to outlive Ma'anel. Then again, maybe he does know that, since he mentioned something at the council meeting about living over a thousand years."

Noah bent down to pluck a long blade of grass from the hillside, wondering about Lamech's statement. *Did the Creator set a limit on how long people could live? If He did, how could Lamech ever hope to break it?* Cupping the grass between his hands, Noah lifted it to his lips and blew a long whistling note.

He grinned at Garun's startled look. Suddenly, his thoughts shifted away from pondering such mysteries and to the man before him. "How did you ever become one of Lamech's guards?"

"Before Lamech came to Havil, I was part of the city guard. I trained men to defend themselves and to fight. But I always taught that fighting was only for self-defense." Garun bent and plucked a blade of grass of his own, but instead of raising it to his lips, he began shredding it, his mind on the past. "When Lamech arrived, he brought Sepha's teachings with him. He joined the guard and quickly rose through the ranks — you've seen him. He used his considerable charisma to entice our men to Sepha, promising not only skill and discipline, but power. Before long, he joined the town council." Shaking his head, Garun tossed the wad of shredded grass onto the ground, where the breeze tickled the strands, teasing them apart and scattering them across the hillside. "They never knew what hit them. Lamech — when he knows what he wants, he's like a force of nature, inexorable and undeniable. With the support of most of the guards, he eventually assumed control of the city and made himself king. He assigned me to guard Tubal-Cain and Naamah."

A quiet bitterness tinged with self-recrimination had crept into Garun's voice as he told his story. Noah watched the fibers of Garun's grass dance and twine among the still-standing blades, trying to figure out how to ask his next question without causing his friend more pain. "Why did no one stand up to him?"

"I ask myself that all the time. I wish I had done something right away, but I was blind. I don't think anyone could have imagined how quickly he'd rise to power and how wicked he really was."

"So what was Havil like before he arrived?"

"I'm sure it wasn't as good as I like to think it was. I can't blame the king for everything." Garun gazed across the water and rubbed his hand over his chin with a sound like sand blowing across stone. "We had problems to deal with, like violence and theft. You don't have that many people together in one place without some trouble. But since Lamech, people seem to be unashamed of their evil acts." A contemplative smile crossed his lips. "You know, I think I might take you up on your offer."

"What offer?"

"To move here."

Noah raised an eyebrow. "You'll want to collect your family, of course." He paused. "I know someone who has a boat."

Grinning, Garun gripped Noah's shoulder. "Let me give that some more thought. For now, I should get back to Ashur's to help Bedin. We're moving into that guest house today."

Chapter 8

Emzara pinched another piece of dough and arranged it with the others on the thin clay dish. Fussing over the placement, she ensured the proper spacing, then she turned to stoke the coals at the base of the stonework oven, readying the temperature so that it would be just right when she placed the tray inside.

She replaced the cover on her starter for the next time she made bread and wound the leather cord tightly on the lip. As she raised it to the shelf, she bumped it against the edge and her other hand rushed to protect and steady the clay pot. With her second attempt, she succeeded in carefully replacing it on top of the dark-stained wooden ledge.

After grabbing the broom, she glanced at the corner where a bowl sat upon a crate. *Not yet.* Shaking her head, she tried to focus on her methodical sweeping, which sent dirt and bits of food swirling around her bare feet.

The small house Noah and Aterre built had started out relatively plain, but Emzara's touches soon made it a home. After the wedding, Aterre moved in with Ara, and Noah expanded the kitchen and dining areas. It was more rustic than her childhood home, but it was theirs. *And it takes less time to sweep.*

She flicked the broom twice more before losing resolve. *I need to know.* Dropping the handle, she rushed over to the bowl. She barely flinched when the broom hit the ground behind her. Picking up the container, she stared at the contents. There was no mistaking it. Cradling the little hollowed-out bowl of sprouting grain pods, she danced around

64

the room. She moved into the bedroom and placed the bowl next to their bed before pirouetting back through the doorway and into the well-lit main room.

Moments later, the smell of fresh bread brought her whirling thoughts back down to earth. *Alright, Em. You've had your reward. Now it's time to get back to work.* She grinned, and placed the fresh bread rounds into a square cloth. She tucked the edges of the fabric in and tied up the four corners, then set the packet on the table as she scooted her feet into her sandals and bound the straps around her ankles. Taking up the warm bundle and balancing it on her head, she left the house and joined the familiar path to her father's place. Looking to her right, she tried to spot Noah and Garun where she had left them earlier on the scenic overlook, but they were gone.

It still felt foreign to knock at her old home, but Emzara forced herself to rap on the front door before she stepped in. "Baba." Her eyes quickly adjusted to the darker space, and she realized he must have heard her approaching because he already hovered near the door.

"Emz! So good to see you." Ara pulled her in for one of his embraces.

She soaked in the comfort of her strong father and her soul warmed, knowing he was always there for her.

"I don't often see you away from the shipyard anymore." He winked. "Now that there's another man in your life."

A sympathetic smile tweaked the corners of her lips as the two of them walked into the house. "Baba, I know you weren't feeling well this morning, so I brought some bread rounds for you. And it gives me an excuse to stop by and give you some care as well."

"Ah, how you spoil me. I'm doing much better. I could've even worked today, but . . ."

"But someone who is very wise and who loves you very much gave you orders to take it easy."

"Well, we've always called you 'Boss' for a reason." His eyes crinkled up at her as he eased his body back into a pile of soft cushions near a low table in the main room.

Emzara set her bundle down in front of him and reached for an empty cup. "Here, you try one of these while I get you more water."

She made her way to the kitchen. *It's still so hard to believe. I just want to burst with this secret.* Beaming, she placed the dipper into the drawn bucket of water and refilled the mug. After forcing herself to pause and allow her facial expression to return to what felt normal, she hurried back to her father.

"Here's your —" Before she knew what was happening, she bumped into a low table and lost her footing. Awkwardly trying to right herself, she flailed for a moment and tumbled into a heap next to her father. The contents of the cup shot forward in an arc, as if at a slowed pace, and deep spots formed on the cushions and on the front of her father's tunic. "Oh, how clumsy of me!" Losing all control of her emotions, Emzara burst into tears.

Ara snorted. "It's completely fine, Emz." He laid a hand on her shoulder, causing her to sob harder. "With the balmy afternoons we've been having, this will dry in no time." He waved the worst part of his damp garment before her, emphasizing his words of comfort.

She wiped her filmy eyes. "I — I'm sorry!"

"What's wrong? You're not usually like this."

"I know." Emzara sniffed, trying to regain control of her emotions. *What is wrong with me?*

Rubbing her back in little circles, he tried to peer into her face. "This isn't about spilled water, is it? Tell me what's going on."

"Well . . ." Unwanted tears pricked at the back of her eyes again and made their way to the corners. She blinked. "I've thought it may be possible for a while, but as of today, I'm pretty sure I'm carrying your grandchild." She looked sheepishly into his face.

Now tears formed in his eyes and he hugged her tightly, muttering barely discernable prayers of blessing and thankfulness under his breath.

It's more real telling someone else. She shook her head in renewed wonder, awe, and disbelief at the joy that flooded her heart.

"Tell me more." Ara pulled back, looking ready for one of the heart talks they had so often shared when she was a girl.

"Well, a while ago Kmani and Nmir told me early signs to be looking for." She flushed a little and bypassed the specifics. "I noticed some and wondered, but felt so unsure. I — I didn't want to be wrong." Emzara shrugged before continuing. "So I tried wetting kernels of certain grains that Nmir showed me with — well, you don't want those details. Anyway, if they sprout, then that's a good indication. I waited as long as I could before checking today, and here we are."

Ara's wide grin matched her own. "So there will be a new little one here in several whole moons. Does Noah know?"

She shook her head. "I haven't had a chance to tell him yet."

"Finding out that you'll be receiving a gift of life from the Creator is a unique joy. I remember when your mother first told me her news about you. I jumped up and shouted. She laughed that bubbling laugh of hers, like bangles making music together. We were so happy. Although," he touched her cheek and smiled, using his thumb to wipe away a tear that lingered there, "it definitely made her cry more quickly as well."

"What happened next?" Emzara pulled her knees to her chest, cherishing every detail about her mother.

He closed his eyes and spoke slowly, as if savoring every word of the precious memories. "In the whole moons to come, we talked and planned as if your coming was the first and only of its kind on this earth. She worked to prepare linens for you, delighting over each. We'd guess what you might be like and talked often about you — even until just before daybreak. I was almost 200 and she was just a little younger, but we felt as giddy as 20-year-olds, yet as endowed with all the responsibility and respectability of people who are 900." Ara paused.

"What else about Amma?"

"We had this game together. I'd made a little wooden bed for you — so tiny. She'd hide it each day, and I had to find it when I came home from work. Some days it'd be in the kitchen. Another day, I found it on a branch in one of the trees outside. She was very creative. Sometimes it was with the animals, or even tied to the coastline as a little boat. Each day I'd bring it back and as I cleaned it, she'd tell me a story about you. With the kitchen, it was about how you'd be a great cook. When it was on the water, the tale was all about the many adventures you'd have. The last place she hid it was on our pallet. She whispered to me that you'd come into both of our hearts and lives to stay."

Emzara felt full, hearing how much her mother had delighted in her while she was still in the womb.

"You know, she left us too soon," Ara said. "Nmir was there to help with the birth, but once you came, your mother struggled to recover. We placed you on her chest and she glowed. I'll never forget the tenderness and love shining from her whole being. But that couldn't defeat whatever was at work inside her body."

He bowed his head in his hands and Emzara wept with him. "I miss her so." Ara cleared his throat and smiled deeply. "You have her hair, her gift for seeing the world for what it can be, and her strength of character. With all she and I discussed about how you'd look and behave, you've surpassed our every dream."

Emzara held his hand. "I wish I'd known her."

"Everything alright? Why all the tears?" Noah's voice filtered into her world, expanding it from the one her father had just shared. She rose to her feet, glided to Noah, and kissed his cheek.

"Yes." She tilted her head up while reaching for one of his hands and placing it on her still-flat middle. "I'm a little emotional right now because, as I just told Baba, someone might soon be calling you Baba."

"What?" His mouth agape and eyes wide, Noah held her at arm's length.

Emzara beamed, nodding.

Ara stood and Noah looked askance at him. "She's — I mean — we're — baby?"

Both father and daughter laughed. Although Noah's words were far from eloquent, his face spoke volumes. He held on to her tightly.

"So you're happy?" She spoke softly into the folds of cloth draped over his shoulder.

"I couldn't be happier." He raised her chin, and she saw a glimmer in his eye that spoke of mischief. "So does this mean I'm going to have to put up with more of this kind of behavior for a while now?" He wiped her eyes and cheeks gently.

Emzara worked to form her lips into a small pout, which wobbled as she struggled to hold back the grin that wanted to burst forth like the morning sun. "And if you are?"

"Worth it." Noah peeked at his father-in-law. "Well I certainly didn't expect to come over tonight and get this news. I was just going to tell you about goings on at the shipyard."

"That can wait." Ara placed his hands on the couple, creating a loose circle. "I've been thinking about this event for some time now. And I want you to have this place. We'll trade. A small house like yours is perfect for an old widower, but with the 40 or so children you'll be having, this will be a much better home for you and all my grandchildren."

"Only 40?" Noah tipped his head to the side and winked at Emzara.

"One at a time. We both come from unusually small families." She reached out to her father. "I can't take your home from you."

"You're not taking it. I'm giving it. Trust me, I've thought about this for a while, long before meeting this fellow."

Noah turned serious. "It's an amazing gift. I — 'thank you' doesn't seem like enough."

"Your care for my daughter is more than enough." Ara paused before adding playfully. "Think about it. If you didn't take her off my hands, this place would belong to her someday anyway."

"Hey!" Emzara placed her hands on her hips.

Noah suddenly reached toward her midsection. "We can't wait to meet you, little one. You're a wonderful gift from our Creator."

Placing one hand over Noah's, Emzara used her other one to grab Ara's hand and situate it near hers and Noah's. "Amen."

"What's this? It's too small to be a community dance." Aterre's sudden entrance broke the close circle, or rather expanded it.

"Aterre!" Emzara extended her arm.

Aterre picked up one of the fresh bread rounds that sat forgotten on the low table. He waved it in the air as he strode over to the group. "Why do you all look as guilty as if you've been caught taking one of these when you're not supposed to?"

The group stared silently until Noah cleared his throat. "Well, maybe it's because I just learned that I'm a father."

Aterre looked quickly back and forth between the couple for confirmation. "You're serious?"

"Yes." Emzara looked down, feeling her cheeks heat up. But then both she and Noah were smashed into a big hug from their friend and everyone was laughing.

"That's wonderful!" He released them. "When?"

"Well," she smoothed the front of her wrapped dress, "it could be anywhere from six to eight whole moons."

Aterre shook his head before clasping his hand firmly on Noah's shoulder. When he didn't speak, Emzara wondered if he was holding back tears. "Well, when he comes," he said at last, the mischief in his voice belying her suspicions, "I'll have plenty of stories to tell him about his father."

"Or she." Ara said as he wrapped an arm around his daughter.

"Oh, I'll be sure she knows too." Aterre took a large bite of the bread.

"We'll have to see that you're far away from here by the time our child is old enough to listen to the yarns you'll spin about me. You'd probably claim to be a faster swimmer."

Emzara grinned as she recalled that special evening.

"But I am," Aterre mumbled with a mouth full of food.

"Or that I ran terrified from a grendec on our journey."

"You tried, but the pace you call running doesn't really qualify. As I recall, you shivered behind Taht for protection."

Emzara laughed, delighted by the banter.

"See? Your stories are so far from reality. My little boy" — Noah glanced at Ara and emphasized his next words — "or girl, needs to know the truth about how strong and handsome and brave I really am. We can't have Uncle Aterre around too much."

Aterre's demeanor suddenly calmed, puzzling Emzara. "Well, you may get your wish. Because it looks like I'll be moving to Cada's farm after the harvest."

All three turned in unison as he scratched his head. "I asked Jitzel to be my wife tonight, and she agreed. I've purchased a plot of land from her father, and we'll be married once the harvest is in."

Emzara squealed, clapping her hands together in excitement. "This is such great news!"

"You finally got up the nerve to ask her?" Noah asked.

"At least I didn't need your help to do it like you did with Zara. That's another story I'll get to tell your child."

"Well there will be plenty of versions to each story with you, me, Baba, and Noah retelling them."

"At least there will be three of us telling the truth about me." Noah sank back into a cushion.

"Hmm, I don't know about that." Emzara flashed him a playful glance as she joined him. "I might have to come up with a version of my own."

Aterre threw his head back, and his infectious laughter compelled the rest of them to join in. Emzara nestled into Noah's side, enjoying the camaraderie and joy that the fellowship of this group brought. She peeked at her father.

Ara, beaming with joy, caught her look. He winked and mouthed the words "I love you."

Chapter 9

Whistling a tune, Noah lifted the large hatchet from its hook on the wall of the shipyard's supply room. He walked out of the building and across the beach. The half moon and stars provided more light than the pinkish glow on the eastern horizon signaling the coming morning. The ever-present lapping of water on the shore blended with squawks of seabirds searching for their first meal of a new day.

Usually asleep at this time, Noah rose early after tossing and turning throughout the night, unable to contain his excitement over the announcement of Emzara's pregnancy. He had spent a long while watching his wife rest peacefully while he imagined what their child would be like. Finally, he gave up on any illusion of slumber and decided to get an early start at work. Despite the lack of rest, Noah still felt fully alert. *Creator, thank You for giving us a child. Help us to raise him,* Noah chuckled softly, *or her, to love and serve You.*

He set the heavy tool down and started to turn back to get more supplies when a faint orange glow farther down the beach arrested his attention. *Is he back?* Moving quietly toward the glimmering light, Noah smiled when he heard the unmistakable sounds of the blacksmith's forge. He hurried to the building and peeked through a thin gap between two boards in the outer wall. Tubal-Cain, back to the door, was bent low feeding chunks of charcoal to the furnace. Noah gently pushed the door open just enough to sneak through it. Stealthily, he entered the shop and tiptoed across the floor until he stood a few cubits behind the blacksmith.

"Hey!"

Tubal-Cain jolted. He scrambled to catch his balance and spun around, wielding a metal bar above his head.

Noah held his hands up. "Whoa! Easy. It's just me."

Tubal-Cain paused for a moment before recognition spread across his face. With a deep breath, he set the tool down. "Noah." The blacksmith stepped forward and embraced him. "It's great to see you. What are you doing here so early?"

"That's what I was going to ask you. I didn't realize you were back."

"We made it home late last night." Tubal-Cain leaned against a worktable. "I needed to check on the shop since I haven't been around for a few weeks."

"Everything look alright to you? From what I've seen, your apprentices have been doing a fine job."

"I think so."

"So, how was it?" Noah asked.

"Our trip?" Tubal-Cain smiled broadly. "Zain was right. That place is the most beautiful spot on earth. You'll have to take Emzara there sometime. There was a massive waterfall that you could walk behind, and the trees." He stretched his arms out wide. "Noah, some of them had trunks bigger than this shop, and they must've been more than 200 cubits tall."

"Sounds amazing." Noah glanced to the side. "But you missed all the excitement around here."

"What excitement?"

"Your father showed up. In fact, you just missed him. He left yesterday."

Tubal-Cain's smile faded. "What did he want?"

Noah sat down and filled Tubal-Cain in on the details, carefully avoiding the disturbing specifics he had heard from Garun the day before.

"I wish he'd stayed for one more day." Tubal-Cain bit his lip and stared at the wall for a moment. "You know, we were never very close, but it still would've been good to see him."

Noah gazed out the window at the back of the shop. Even though this angle hid the water, the early sunlight revealed a blue sky with a few wispy clouds. A playful smile crossed his lips. "That wasn't the most exciting news though."

Tubal-Cain cocked his head. "Really? What was?"

Noah shrugged. "I guess I should tell you before Aterre does. Let's just say that it won't be long before Baby Noah is here."

"Baby Noah?" His eyes shot wide open. "You mean Zara's . . . that's great!" Tubal-Cain enthusiastically clapped Noah's shoulder.

Wincing a bit, Noah tried to conceal the discomfort caused by the hard hit. "I guess we might have Baby Emzara instead."

"That's fantastic. I can't wait to tell Adira." He paused. "No, I'm sure Zara will want to do that."

"I think you're right. Maybe the two of you can join us tonight and Em can tell . . ."

A gut-wrenching wail rang out in the distance.

Tubal-Cain looked around. "What was that?"

Noah jumped to his feet and bolted for the door. With Tubal-Cain right on his heels, Noah raced down the beach road toward the sound of the cry. As he rushed past the shipyard office, he spotted Emzara staggering down the path from Ara's house. "Em!"

She glanced up, dropped to her knees, and screamed. Her hands and robe were dappled with blood and tears streamed down her face.

Noah's heart sank. He sprinted to her and slid to his knees, catching her as she collapsed in his arms. "What's wrong?"

She dug her fingernails into his back and gasped for air. "They . . . he's . . ." She moaned in agony, unable to force another word out.

"This blood. Are you hurt? Is it the baby?" Helplessness filled Noah's body. He held her out in front of him as he checked her for any injury. Finding none, he brushed aside a stray piece of hair from her eyes. She hid her face in his chest, sobbing. He looked up in confusion at Tubal-Cain.

With concern etched across his face, Tubal-Cain said, "I'll check it out." He ran toward Ara's house.

Emzara pulled back a little and her terror-stricken eyes met Noah's momentarily. She opened her mouth to speak but quickly buried her face into his shoulder, her body wracked by sobs.

Holding her tight and unsure of what else to do, he stroked her head softly as she attempted to gather herself.

At the sound of hurried footsteps behind him, Noah turned his head. "Nmir."

"What's wrong?"

"I don't know."

The old woman knelt beside them and rested a hand on Emzara's shoulder.

Emzara slowly turned toward Nmir. She let go of Noah and her lower lip trembled. "Ba . . ." Whimpering and shaking her head, Emzara fell into Nmir's arms.

Tubal-Cain stepped out of the house, his face downcast.

Noah stood and ran to him. "What happened? Where's Ara?"

Wiping his eyes with a blood-streaked hand, Tubal-Cain bit his lip and looked away.

His mind racing to make sense of the anguish of Emzara and Tubal-Cain, a miserable thought sprang into Noah's mind. "No. Please, God, no."

Tubal-Cain turned back to Noah and shook his head. "He's dead." He held up his hand to show the blood. "Someone killed him."

Noah's stomach contorted into a knot and he bent down, putting his hands on his knees. Through hot tears he glanced back at Emzara, who was being cradled by Nmir.

Tubal-Cain put a hand on Noah's back. "That's not all."

Noah groaned from deep within his being.

Tubal-Cain pursed his lips and looked to the sky as he stammered and covered his mouth. His grief-stricken eyes met Noah's and he voiced the name on Noah's mind. "Aterre too."

"No!" Breathing seemed impossible as he dropped to his hands and knees. Overwhelmed by sorrow and pain, he felt as if his heart had been ripped from his chest. Time seemed to slow. The milknut trees blurred in his vision, and everything went silent except for the throbbing pulse inside his ears. He heaved, but only air came up.

His gaze locked onto Ara's front door. He reached for it as his grief turned to anger. Forcing himself to his feet, he balled his fists as his anger turned to rage. Seething through clenched teeth, Noah started for Ara's house. "I need to see."

Tubal-Cain blocked his way. "Don't. Go to your wife."

Noah plowed into him, but the blacksmith stood his ground and wrapped his brawny arms around him.

"Let me go." Noah thrashed against him. "Let go." He twisted, but could not break free. "Let me . . ." Noah moaned and slumped in Tubal-Cain's grasp, his fury draining.

"There's nothing you can do for them, but Emzara needs you, and you need her." Tubal-Cain let him go.

Noah nodded and shuffled over to Emzara. He lowered himself to the ground next to her.

Emzara let go of Nmir. She hugged Noah and they wept together.

Chapter 10

E at this now, both of you."

Noah groggily lifted his head off Emzara's shoulder. He blinked, trying to orient himself. *How long has it been since. . . .* Unable to finish the sentence in his mind, he glanced at the sun, which was well past the peak of its path.

"Eat." Nmir held out a platter filled with bread slabs topped with honey and dried vinefruit. The commanding tone of her voice pulled him from what seemed like relentless waves of thought threatening to pummel him into mental unconsciousness. The scent of her savory flat-seed stew added a welcome greeting, further drawing him from his grief-tossed haze.

Limp, he watched as she set the tray on a flat grassy section at their feet. Awareness finally took root after she took out three bowls.

"Em, here." He guided her gently to the ground. She moved slowly, almost as if she were a child, discovering certain motions for the first time. As they ate, some of his strength returned. *Where is Tubal-Cain? I've never had someone close to me die before. Who could've done this?* The image of Bayt and the long dagger on his belt flashed through his mind. Clenching a fist, Noah felt his temperature rise, and the urge to race off and find the man filled his body.

Breathing shallowly, he glanced at Emzara, and he knew he needed to stay by her side for now. She had managed to consume a half a piece of bread, but her bowl of stewed flatseed lay untouched, slightly askew in the grass. He reached over her lap and held the bowl out. "Please."

Tears welled up in her eyes and, understanding her mute plea, he set the bowl back down. He looked helplessly at Nmir. "Thanks for this. I . . ."

She fidgeted, twisting the overwrap that was tied to her midsection. "I had to do something." Dried trails of darker brown traced down her cheeks like the crooked texture left behind in the wet sand from a retreating breaker.

"Come." His voice cracked and he tried again. "We share this sorrow."

She took his extended hand and sat across from them. Time stretched on before she finally spoke. "There's much to be done before nightfall. Time for grief will be later."

"I don't know what's next. I've never done this before."

Emzara looked up slowly, a distant look in her eyes. "I can only remember going to one burial. It was for the old innkeeper. I was only 15, but I remember them lighting the torch and the family standing huddled by it."

"Torch?" Noah asked.

"It's placed at the head of the burial mound and is kept lit for seven days in honor."

"If you ask me, it's to give the family something to do," Nmir said.

Emzara's wry, half-smile almost appeared. *Trust Nmir to see the practical side of things. She's often right.* Noah tapped his nose with the broad side of his thumbnail, and his wife responded to their secret communication with a soft smile, declaring her love for him as well.

Gone. Ara and Aterre. They're gone. The realization hit him afresh and anguish tore through his midsection. He had needed that lightness of spirit even if just for a moment, but the pain at remembering almost undid any good from the temporary reprieve.

Suddenly, Tubal-Cain's strong hand squeezed Noah's forearm. Standing next to him were Zain, Cada, and Garun, each with a shovel in hand. "We've come to prepare for the burial." Tubal-Cain's voice was deeper than normal, revealing that he had been weeping.

"Let's get this over." Cada's flat voice matched his expression.

He lost his best worker, a friend, and his soon-to-be son. Noah shook his head in frustration, realizing for the first time all the suffering that would stem from this tragedy.

"Here's a shovel, if you're up to it." Zain handed the tool to Noah.

"I'm coming too. I need to focus on something else." Emzara stepped forward, face flushed, but Nmir grabbed her.

"I need you. We'll have to fix up a meal for those who come to mourn, and I can't do it alone."

Tubal-Cain nodded. "Adira's back at your house, Zara, with Kmani. They've got the linens for wrapping Ater —" His word caught in his throat, so he lowered his head and buried it in the palm of his hand.

"And Jitzel will come later with the rest of my family." Cada's stone face barely moved as he spoke. "She . . . needed some time still." He leaned his head back as a tear ran down one of his dark cheeks.

Emzara nodded slowly and Noah dropped his gaze, finding it difficult to imagine what Jitzel was going through. *What would I have done if something had happened to Em?* He shook his head, trying to banish the dreadful thought from his mind. "Thank you all for coming. We . . ." He gulped and gestured to Emzara and Nmir. "We couldn't do this without you."

The group turned and the men made their way around the side of the house. Noah fell into step behind Garun, thankful for the momentary silence. Stopping beside the low grassy mound that marked the grave of Em's mother, Noah pointed to the ground adjacent to it. "Right here."

"And the other one?" Zain asked in a somber tone.

Forcing his thoughts to the task at hand, Noah glanced at Cada. "Here or at your place?"

Cada's puffy red eyes looked away. "Here. I think it would be too tough of a reminder for my daughter at our place."

Noah nodded. "Over here then." He walked several cubits beyond the first mound, plunged the sharp blade of his shovel into the ground, and hoisted a scoop of fresh soil to the side. He simply watched the blade slice into the soft sandy soil and cleanly come up again. Slice. Lift. Drop. Slice. Lift. Drop. The repeated action consumed his mind as he zeroed in on the sounds and the fresh memory of Bayt's crooked grin. The tool dove deeper with each thrust, allowing Noah's anger to fuel his work. With each load his frustration grew and tears dropped freely from his eyes. Soon, the rhythm from his implement was joined by a second scoop as Tubal-Cain joined him. When Noah stopped to catch his breath, he scanned the group. *Where's Aterre?* He dropped his shovel as the pain stabbed him anew and cut through him just like his spade had pierced the earth.

* * *

Wind from the sea just beyond rippled through his hair and whipped across his face. The salty fragrance brought Noah a measure of peace, and he inhaled desperately. The sun hung low on the horizon, but for the first time the radiant oranges, pinks, and purples brought no joy.

Deep within his soul, he silently pleaded with his Maker. *Most High, You have made all things. Surely nothing is too difficult for You. Oh, how I wish the sun would return in its course to last evening and You'd stay the hand of the murderer and spare the lives of Your faithful followers. I don't want to face another day without them.*

Noah paused before placing a shovelful of earth over Aterre's grave. The two fresh mounds joined the older grass-covered one. Each berm stood about knee-high and was several cubits in length, although much narrower in width. The bodies of his friends rested on separate wooden planks and were wrapped with linens. Aterre had been placed first, and then Ara, so that he was right next to Biremza's resting spot. Silently, the men steadily piled soil on top, grading the surrounding landscape and packing it in tightly.

Using his forearm, Noah wiped sweat from his brow and resumed his work, eager to finish the task before losing the sunlight.

Emzara sidled up to him, an unlit lantern in her left hand held aloft. "This one's for Baba. We're almost ready to begin."

Cada carried a similar lantern toward him. "This is for Aterre."

Hand in hand they stepped to Ara's mound. Letting go for a moment, Noah drove the lantern's post deep at the head of the rise, making sure it would stand. He paused, remembering the face that had looked so kindly upon him when he and Aterre first arrived. The face that had been firm but patient with him as he picked up the new trade and learned the skills needed for shipbuilding. The face that shed tears of joy as he gave his daughter away in marriage. The face that only yesterday had been so happy to hear of the new life. Uncontrollable sobs wracked him and he reached out for Emzara's hand. Instead, her body crushed him with a fierceness born of deep pain, love, and even desperation.

A wail pierced the descending twilight. Then another one rang out. Soon several voices rose in their loud expressions of grief. The deafening sound caused Noah to hold Em even tighter as they too, joined in. Oddly, the incredible closeness of friends and family mixed simultaneously with the sorrow of separation. As the cries continued, a bucket of cool mud was passed to them. Emzara smeared streaks of it down Noah's arms before marking her own. "This is to remind us that Greatfather Adam was formed from the ground, and we are made from the same substance. And because of his rebellion, we each die and return to that ground."

In the dim light, people from town followed suit and covered themselves in long stripes of mud from their cheeks, down their chest and arms, to their legs.

Zain stepped forward, his streaked face illuminated by the torch in his hand. He spoke loudly, accentuating his words while lighting the two lanterns. "I light these lamps this evening to honor Aterre and Ara. They were our dearest friends, our family, and we loved them. And we know they loved us deeply in return. Our town wouldn't be what it is today without Ara's vision in his work or his wisdom on the council. And who of us hasn't laughed along with Aterre, whether through his quick wit or his playful spirit. He gave us joy in life. To Noah, Emzara, Nmir, Cada, and Jitzel, you have our support."

Zain hung the torch on the stake Noah had placed. Raising his hands, he continued, "Creator, receive these two men and enable us to be better because of their examples of faithfulness in serving You. We are again reminded of the ultimate price for disobeying You." His voice softened. "We are also thankful for Your mercy that allows us to live each day."

Sounds of assent murmured through the crowd and then died down as each paused in a lengthy silence. An old, bulky man stepped forward from the gathered throng. It took Noah a few moments to recognize Akel with the streaks of mud across his body. He carried a large wooden crate and placed it before the two newly raised places of earth. "Let each person here take a flower cutting from this box and place it on the sites where our dear friends lie. When you have finished saying farewell, the women have prepared evenfeast at Noah's and Emzara's home. You are welcome to gather there."

Noah twined his fingers through Emzara's. "Almost done. Can you make it?"

She looked up at him gratefully, her red eyes shining with tears in the light of the torches. "I have you." She squeezed his hand, and together they moved to lead the procession in placing flower cuttings on the graves.

CHAPTER 11

Carefully guided by the hand of an expert, the carving knife slid gently along the side of the wood, trimming a thin strip from the block. After several more passes, the back of the large-eared tusker began to take shape. Noah set the piece on the table next to the fresh shavings. He brushed the dust from his fingers and used the back of his hand to rub his eyes, which were sore due to the countless tears shed over the past week.

Noah blinked and took a deep breath, fighting the urge to start weeping again. Whittling helped take his thoughts away from the recent tragedy. *And another carved animal may brighten Em's spirit a little.* Normally, the shipyard would be the perfect place to find sanctuary for his weary mind. But with Ara gone, Noah could not bring himself to head to work today. Everything about the place reminded him of his father-in-law.

He stood and lifted the hatch on the wall that faced east, propping it open with a small beam he had fashioned. Breathing in the warm morning air, Noah looked through the window at the grove of milknut trees. He grimaced when he heard hammering in the distance. *Bakur and Fen must be back at work. The mourning period is officially over.* He shook his head. *I need to get over there.*

Noah spun quickly toward a couple of soft knocks on the door. It had been four days since anyone had stopped to check on them. Emzara was still in bed, as she had been for nearly the entire week since the burials. She had only eaten bits of a few meals and was inconsolable at times.

The knocking started again. "Noah, are you home?"

A partial smile tugged at his lips as he recognized the voice. "I'm coming." Noah opened the door. "Zain, it's good to see you."

Zain's expression showed sympathy. He held out a basket bedecked with flowers and filled with bread rounds and a couple of small, covered clay bowls. "Kmani wanted me to deliver these." He tipped his head toward the bowl closest to Noah as he handed him the goods. "She made your favorite berry spread."

Noah gladly took the basket, and his stomach grumbled, reminding him that he had not eaten since midmeal the day before. "Please thank her for us."

Zain nodded. "I will." He looked off into the distance and then down at his feet before back up at Noah. "I'm sorry to disturb you, but you really need to get to the town hall immediately."

Noah tilted his head. "Why? What's going on?"

"It's Garun. Some of the people are blaming him for . . ." He paused as if searching for the right words. "For what happened. And they want the council to meet to decide on his punishment."

"Garun?" Noah tapped a finger against his lips. "I don't think he would ever do that."

"I didn't believe it either," Zain said.

"Wait. Why do you need me for a council meeting?" He ran his fingers against the stubble on his face. *I haven't shaved in a week.*

"I'll tell you on the way."

"Alright, I'll be right back after I let Emzara know where I'm going." Noah walked toward his room, setting the basket on the table along the way.

He opened the bedroom door, and Emzara rolled to her side and looked up at him through despondent eyes. Kneeling next to her, he gently rubbed her shoulder. "Kmani sent us some food. I think you should try to eat something." He slid his hand to her belly and smiled. "Our child is probably hungry."

Her eyes glistened as she forced a smile. "I'll try." Her gravelly words barely surpassed the volume of a whisper.

Noah bent over and kissed her forehead. "I need to go to the town hall. Garun's in a lot of danger, and Zain's waiting for me." He stood to leave.

"Noah, wait." Emzara cleared her throat as she pushed herself into a sitting position and slung her feet over the side of the bed. She reached out and hugged him around the waist. "Be careful."

He softly stroked her head. "I will, and I'll be back as soon as I can. I love you, Em."

She let go of him. "I love you too."

Noah hurried into the front room and quickly strapped on his sandals. He dipped a piece of bread into the berry spread and made for the door. Stepping into the sunlight, he squinted in Zain's direction. "Let's go."

Walking at a brisk pace across the beach, Noah devoured his snack in three large bites. The food combined with the wind in his face and the exercise invigorated Noah. For the first time since the murders, the mental fog lifted from his mind. Savoring the last morsel in his mouth, he said, "Kmani's bread was tremendous."

"It always is." Zain turned onto the path that led away from the beach and to the center of town. "You asked me to ask about Bayt to see if he might've committed the crimes. I was told that he was on his way out of town the morning you saw him on the beach. No one I talked to has seen him since that day."

Noah breathed in through a clenched jaw. "But he might have decided to stay out of town until that night so that we wouldn't suspect him."

"That's possible, but why would he even bother showing his face at all? If he had planned to murder Ara, it would make more sense if no one knew he was around."

"Or that's just what he wants us to think."

Zain shrugged. "Maybe, but I have my doubts. It's no secret he didn't like Ara, but I don't think he wanted him dead. Besides, I'm not sure he's capable of beating Aterre in a fight."

Noah remained silent while trying to weigh this new information.

"You should know that the council wishes for you to fill Ara's position."

Noah pointed to himself. "Me? I'm so much younger than everyone else."

"You make it sound like I'm so old." Zain chuckled. "I thought you knew that our rules say that if a council member dies, his heir has the right to replace him until the next choosing. So, for now, that makes you his successor. The next term comes around in eight whole moons. If you want to continue, and if the council believes you're a good fit, then you could become a permanent member."

"That's quite an honor. I'll need to speak with Emzara about it."

"Of course. But depending on how things are going with Garun, you may need to fill that role as soon as possible." Zain stopped and grabbed Noah's arm. "The people accusing Garun and Bedin are out for blood. They believe that since the crime committed was murder, then the penalty should match. They are talking about executing them."

Briefly, Noah clenched his jaw and fists. "In many ways, that sounds like a fair punishment, though I don't know if I could ever make the decision to put someone to death." He pulled free from Zain's grip. "But Garun's innocent."

Zain let out a breath. "That's how I feel too. But you are in a unique position."

"How so?"

"You were close to both victims. As Ara's son-in-law, only you or Emzara could bring formal charges against the suspected killers. That being said, you were also Aterre's best friend, and since he and Jitzel weren't married yet, you'd be the natural person to bring charges for him as well."

Noah stared straight ahead, processing Zain's words. "So you're saying that people might listen to me, if . . ."

"If you can get them to calm down, and especially if you're on the council."

"And you'll help me?"

"In any way I can."

As they neared the town square, raised voices echoed off the buildings. Noah sprinted to the end of the road to the source of the cacophony. On his left, at the steps of the town hall, approximately 30 people stood, raising their fists and shouting at the two men bound closely together to one of the pillars Noah had carved.

Noah dashed toward the gathering. Ashur and Oban stood helplessly on the top step. Garun and Bedin seemed to be unharmed, but probably not for much longer. The whole scene looked similar to the way Noah pictured a disciplinary sentencing in Iri Sana that his father described to him during his childhood. A man's wagon beast had died, so he stole one that belonged to his neighbor and dumped the dead one in its place. His crime was eventually discovered. As penalty, he was tied to a post in the street and whipped 20 times. Then he had to return the animal and pay a fine.

But they don't want to only whip Garun. Noah swiftly picked his way through the crowd and climbed the five short stairs.

"Murderers!" Ethlin, from the front of the mob called out and pointed in Garun's face.

Stepping between him and Garun, Noah raised his arms to the side and gestured for the crowd to calm. "Please, my brothers."

"They murdered Ara and Aterre." Ethlin's voice maintained its volume.

Noah held up his hand, palm out. "Please, let's talk calmly."

"But your friend and father-in-law," said a man to Noah's left. "These men should be put to death."

Noah closed his eyes and breathed deeply, struggling to keep his emotions in check. "Please." He directed a thumb at Garun and the scribe. "They aren't going anywhere. Let us discuss these accusations in a peaceful manner."

Zain called out, "Let's listen to what he has to say before we make any sudden decisions. After all, he was close to both of the men who were killed." Slowly, the crowd quieted.

"Friends and neighbors," Noah said. "Thank you for honoring the seven-day mourning period and for your desire to see justice done." Scanning the crowd and confident they were willing to listen, Noah continued. "Believe me, no one wants justice for the tragedies more than I do. Aterre was my . . ." He averted his eyes and sucked in a breath through his mouth. *Creator, help me.*

Noah stood up straight, facing the group again. "He was my best friend for nearly ten years, and he was the best friend a guy could ever want. I could tell you so many stories about him." He smiled and shook his head. "But now is not the time. And Ara was my father-in-law, my mentor, and my friend. Apart from my wife, no one will miss him more than me." Noah brushed away a tear from his left eye, but his confidence rose with each completed sentence. Talking about them in this setting helped ease the intense ache inside.

"So what do you think we should do with these men?" Ethlin asked.

Noah turned and faced the accused men for the first time. Bedin's eyes were wide with fear, and Garun smiled grimly as he looked Noah in the eye, before shaking his head and dropping his gaze.

Noah slowly turned back to the group and sighed. "I think we should set them free."

85

"What?" Ethlin asked, and many others echoed his response.

"I agree that the person, or people, who did this deserve death, but I don't believe Garun is guilty."

Ethlin put a hand on his shaking, bald head. "No one's ever been murdered in Iri Geshem until these two showed up."

Noah nodded and out of the corner of his eye caught a glimpse of Tubal-Cain quickly approaching the scene. "I know the timing looks bad, but if they were guilty, then why would they stick around during the mourning period? They could've easily snuck out of town to avoid being accused and captured."

"That's true, but maybe they knew we'd think about that, so they decided to stay," Ethlin said.

"Maybe, but that's quite an unnecessary risk to take." Noah's thoughts drifted back to the day King Lamech arrived. "Let me ask you something, Ethlin. Did Garun put up a fight when you seized him?"

Ethlin smirked. "No, but there were four of us."

"You're lucky then." Noah returned the smirk. "Garun could've easily defeated all four of you. He's trained many of Havil's guards, and you've seen what they're capable of."

Ethlin's grin vanished and he took a step back, looking unsure of himself for the first time. Suddenly, his countenance brightened. "So he would certainly be capable of the murders."

"No doubt, but he has proven his good character to me." Noah considered mentioning the fact that Garun had probably saved his life in Havil, but decided to keep those details hidden from Bedin. "If he says he didn't do it, then I believe him. And if he can vouch for the scribe, then I'll take his word on that too."

Noah looked at the Havilites. "Garun, were you involved in murdering my father-in-law and friend?"

Garun returned Noah's steady gaze. "I promise that I had nothing to do with it, and I don't believe Bedin did either. We were in the guest house your town provided that entire evening."

"Is there anyone who could verify your claim?" Ethlin asked.

Garun paused before speaking. "Bedin met with a farmer that night, and their meeting went very late. But the man wasn't there all evening."

Noah motioned for Zain to join him. "Since you're the ranking council member gathered here right now, I wish to express that I have

86

no intention to accuse these men of murder. I ask that you set them free. However, I want to stress that I plan to do everything I can to find the murderers, and if we find any evidence that leads back to Garun or Bedin, then I'll reconsider my decision."

Zain put a hand on Noah's shoulder and addressed the people. "I believe Noah has spoken wisely. Are there any further objections to this plan?"

"If we set them free and someone else gets killed, then what?" Ethlin asked.

"We're all new at this, so I understand your reluctance to set them free. If something else happens, then we need to investigate and try to find the killer, just like we should be doing now," Zain said.

Ethlin's chest heaved a couple of times as his demeanor softened. "That's all well and good, but we need someone to keep an eye on them for now."

Zain adjusted the wrap slung over his shoulder. "I think that's fair." He looked at Ashur. "Do you still have a room available for them?"

Ashur bit his lip before nodding. "Yes, I have room, but I can't keep a close eye on them at all times."

Zain clapped his hands together. "Very well, they stay at Ashur's, and if they want to leave the inn for any reason, they need to notify him first. Does that work for everyone?"

Ashur frowned and no one else objected.

Oban stepped away from Ashur and whispered something in Tubal-Cain's ear. Tubal-Cain looked confused at first, but then his eyes lit up with understanding.

Zain gestured to Garun and Bedin. "Free them."

Chapter 12

"This whole situation makes me nervous." Ashur scowled at Garun and Bedin, both of whom were stretching their limbs after Noah loosed their bindings. "How much longer do you plan to be in our city?"

Bedin shrugged. "Perhaps two more weeks before I complete my interviews."

Ashur harrumphed. "I'll go prepare their room."

"We'll take them to collect their belongings from the guest house," Zain said. "That ought to give you enough time."

Ashur walked away and acknowledged the plan with a dismissive wave of his hand.

Noah waited until Ashur was out of earshot and then tilted his head toward him. "What's he so mad about?"

"I don't know," Zain said. "If he thinks they really are the murderers, then I could see why he'd be nervous."

"Then why didn't he speak up when he had the opportunity?" Noah asked.

Tubal-Cain reached the top of the stairs and stepped into their small group. Speaking quietly he said, "I think I might know the answer. Oban just told me that Ashur's been secretly housing a guest ever since the day after the murders."

"Who?" Noah's mind raced.

"You think it's the murderer?" Zain asked.

Tubal-Cain shook his head. "I don't know, but Oban says that arrangement will explain why Ashur doesn't want these two to stay with him."

"Noah, you go with Tubal-Cain. I'll stay with them." Zain pointed over his shoulder to Garun and Bedin. "We'll get there as soon as possible."

Garun grabbed Noah's arm as he turned to leave. "Thank you for trusting me. You saved my life."

Noah tipped his head and half-smiled. "I guess that makes us even." Though his words were light, inside, his bruised heart ached anew. When had life become this series of life debts earned and redeemed?

Garun snorted. "Let me know if I can help."

"I will."

His mind churning over what awaited them at Ashur's, Noah hurried across the square with Tubal-Cain at his side. "Any ideas about who this guest is?"

Tubal-Cain shook his head. "No, especially since Oban seemed pretty certain he's not the murderer. I just don't understand why anyone would want to . . ." Tubal-Cain flinched. "Sorry. I don't mean to keep bringing it up."

Noah gave him a grim smile. "It goes around and around in my head like a calic chasing its tail. Sometimes I feel like I'll never escape it, and not because you keep bringing it up." He straightened his spine, turning his mind away from futile regrets. "But the only thing I can give to Ara and Aterre now is justice, so I'm focusing on figuring this out."

"Well, since Ashur's in a foul mood, let's make sure we use some tact."

Noah chuckled. "You don't think I should just march in and demand that he deliver the murderer to us?" Laughing felt good, but at once guilt stabbed him, as if he had disrespected the dead.

Tubal-Cain winked. "That's probably not the best idea."

Noah pulled the door to the inn and held it open for Tubal-Cain. After following his friend inside, he moved to their favorite spot in the nearest corner. The large open room was sparsely populated, indicating that midmeal had not yet been served. Wafting out of the kitchen, the unmistakable scent of Ashur's mouthwatering bread reached Noah's nostrils and reminded him of his hunger. Noah waved over Ashur, who stood behind a counter, wiping down drinking jars.

Ashur avoided eye contact until he reached their table. "Noah, I'm really sorry about Ara and Aterre. They'll truly be missed."

"I appreciate that."

"If there's anything I can do to help, just let me know. Would you like some midmeal? Enika just made Momma Kylel's stuffed specialty."

"Smells great, but not right now," Tubal-Cain said.

Noah raised his eyebrows. "He may not want some, but I sure could use it."

Ashur brightened and leaned toward Tubal-Cain. "You sure you don't want any?"

Tubal-Cain shrugged. "Adira will have something for me when I get home."

"We actually came to talk to you about something important." Noah rubbed his growling stomach. "But we can discuss it while I eat."

An uneasy look passed over the innkeeper's face, and he twisted the cloth in his hands. "Of course. I'll go get your plate."

Tubal-Cain lifted one finger from the table, pointing at Noah. "So do you want to bring it up, or do you want me to?"

"It's probably best if I do it." Noah grinned. "After all, you suggested we use tact."

Tubal-Cain smiled. "Well, then I'll be the muscle if we need to make him talk."

Lowering his voice, Noah ran his finger along the smooth wood of the round-topped wooden table. "Actually . . . he sure likes your father and your city, so he may be willing to talk to you."

"Maybe. When I first moved here, he talked to me quite a bit. But over the past two years or so, he hasn't said much."

Through the kitchen door to Noah's left, Ashur appeared with the meal. He crossed the floor and set down a plate laden with spicy baked pebble beans piled under two large halves of a tangy green vegetable, each filled to the brim with an assortment of grains, beans, and vegetables. Two chunks of bread completed the arrangement. The delicious aroma made his stomach rumble in anticipation. Ashur handed him a clay vessel. "And here's some water."

"Thank you. It looks so good, as always." Noah held out two copper piks.

Ashur reached for the pieces but then withdrew his hand. "This one's on me. Enjoy." He turned to leave.

"Wait, Ashur. I need to talk to you for a moment." Noah motioned to a nearby chair at an empty table. "Please, join us." As Ashur grabbed

90

the chair, Noah shoved a few of the hot, sand-colored pebble beans into his mouth and savored their spicy flavor.

Ashur sat back from the table and crossed his arms. He glanced nervously at Tubal-Cain and then at Noah. "What is it?"

Noah folded his hands together and looked out the square-cut windows that faced the main street of the town. "At the town hall we discussed the need to figure out who killed Ara and Aterre and why they did it."

"And you're certain it wasn't your friend Garun?" It seemed as if Ashur emphasized *friend*, but Noah chose to overlook any insinuation.

"I really doubt it. Garun helped us all escape Havil the last time we were there."

Ashur rubbed his beardless chin. "So what does that have to do with what happened here?"

"It speaks to his character. I trust him. Besides, what would he stand to gain by their deaths? He had no quarrel with them." Noah scanned the room then focused again on Ashur, satisfied that the three other customers were far enough away to not overhear him. "I've heard that you've been keeping a certain guest here since the day after the murders. Is that true?"

The innkeeper fidgeted and glanced at Tubal-Cain.

"So it is true," Noah said. "Who is it?"

Ashur shook his head.

"Ashur, tell me. We need to figure out who the murderer is, and even if you believe your guest to be above reproach, he might have seen something." Noah kept eye contact with Ashur until the chiseled-faced man looked down.

After releasing a deep breath, Ashur pointed at Tubal-Cain. "Not with him here."

Tubal-Cain raised his eyebrows. "Me? Why won't you say it in front of me?"

"Yeah, what's wrong with Tubal-Cain?" Noah asked.

"Nothing, but I just can't say anything with him here." Ashur turned away. "You'll understand why when I tell you, Noah."

Tubal-Cain stood, towering over Ashur. "You'd better tell him when I leave."

"Don't worry. I will. It's nothing against you, but you must trust me on this."

"Fine." Tubal-Cain reached across the table and snatched a portion of bread from Noah's plate. "Now, I'll go." He smiled at Noah as Noah slapped at his hand but missed.

"Hey, thief, get your own bread." The memory of meeting Aterre seared Noah to his core, but he blinked and willed himself to move on.

Tearing off a huge bite with his teeth, Tubal-Cain walked out of the building.

Noah turned his gaze from the door to Ashur. "Now tell me about this guest of yours."

"I think I'd better show you." Ashur slid his chair back across the wooden floor. "I'll be right back." He stood and headed toward the staircase to the upper rooms, and Noah wondered for a brief instant if Ashur would try to flee. *Guess that's where Tubal-Cain comes in as the muscle.*

Noah took a couple of deep breaths as he imagined what he might do or say if Bayt returned with Ashur. *But why would he make Tubal-Cain leave?* Shaking his head to clear his thoughts, he returned to his meal. After a week of barely tasting a morsel, the hearty, flavorful assortment of vegetables, the warm bread, and spicy baked pebble beans reminded him how much he appreciated food. He closed his eyes and breathed in deeply to relish the flavors. *Creator, thank You for the delicious foods You've made for us to enjoy. Please help us find the murderer and may justice be done.*

A creak on the stairs jolted Noah. He tried to hide his surprise when a lovely young woman followed Ashur toward the table. She wore a long wrap with a red border stitched into the edges. Her dark hair was pulled tightly back and then dropped behind her neck. Tilting his head, Noah wondered where he had seen her before.

Ashur directed her to his recently vacated chair, and then he sat in Tubal-Cain's spot. Scooting his seat close to hers, he made introductions. "Noah, this is Navea."

"Noah." She bowed her head slightly.

"Hello." Noah furrowed his brow. "You look very familiar."

She flashed a wide, beautiful smile. "That's not surprising. You've seen me a couple of times."

"I have? Where?"

"The first time was in the royal dining hall in Havil," Navea said.

Noah raised his chin in acknowledgment. "That's right. You were one of the dancers that dined with us."

She bit her bottom lip and nodded quickly.

Noah pointed toward the city square beyond Ashur's front door. "And you were one of the dancers that performed out there when the Havilites arrived in town?"

"Yes."

Pleased with his recall, Noah popped a succulent, red orb into his mouth. Suddenly, he leaned forward. "Wait, what are you doing here? How did you get here? I watched your whole group leave on the boat. Well, everyone except Garun and Bedin."

"That's why I wouldn't bring her out here until Tubal-Cain left," Ashur said.

"Um," Noah rubbed the back of his neck. "I'm not following you."

"Let her explain."

Noah turned to Navea but she sat quietly, her eyes downcast as she played with a strand of her hair. "So how did you get here after I saw you leave on the boat?"

"It's alright." Ashur put a hand on her arm. "You're safe here. And Noah deserves to know."

"I did leave on the boat, as you said." Navea paused and took a deep breath. "We sailed until your city was out of view, and then the king ordered our crew to move the boat close to shore. We sat there at anchor all day, then, early that evening, King Lamech and three of his guards jumped into the water and swam to shore."

"What were they doing?" Noah asked, though the truth sat like a rock in his belly.

"I don't know. They didn't say." As if by habit, she glanced over her shoulder and then relaxed a little. "They were gone for a long time, well into the night. When I realized no one was watching, I slipped into the water and swam for the beach."

"Why?" Noah tilted his head as his eyebrows scrunched together.

Navea rubbed her arm and gave Noah a look that made him feel like a child, naïve and foolish. "You don't know what it's like to work for the king. For years now, I've been free in name only. To Lamech and Naamah, I've been a slave, kept for their pleasure like a caged songbird. It used to be different, at least, with Naamah. We used to enjoy each other's company. I thought . . ." Her eyes glistened, but she clamped her lips into a hard line and swallowed. "I thought we were friends. But then her father made

93

her Nachash's priestess." The bitterness in her voice made Noah wince. "It was like he was pitting us against each other, using me to manipulate her."

She paused, staring out the window as if seeing something other than the street outside. "I didn't care about the honor or the ceremonies, but Naamah wouldn't believe me. She's changed so much — and the changes aren't good. She only cares about power. She's just like her . . ." Navea closed her mouth and shook her head.

Noah nodded. "So what happened after you came ashore?"

"I made my way back here."

"Why here?"

She shrugged and glanced at Ashur. "It seemed like the right thing to do. Ashur always treated me very kindly, so I thought he might be willing to take me in and give me work."

"Did you see the king or the guards again?"

Navea shook her head. "No. I got a bit lost on my way here. I ended up sleeping in the forest and then found my way in the morning."

Mind churning, Noah shuffled through and picked one follow-up thought. "Do you believe they came back here that night?"

She massaged her temple with her thumb. "I'm not sure where else they might've gone, but I don't know this area."

Noah clenched his jaw and studied Navea for signs of deception. "Let's assume they did come back. Do you have any idea why they'd kill my father-in-law and friend?"

She didn't seem shocked at the idea, but met his eyes calmly. "I don't know. If I had to guess, it probably had something to do with the council meeting. Before that, he acted like he always does. He was outgoing and" — she checked over both shoulders — "and arrogant."

"And afterward?"

"After the meeting, he didn't say a word to any of us except his guards." Navea bit her lower lip and stared at the ceiling. "Even on the boat, when we were all in pretty tight quarters, he only spoke privately with his men. It was very strange."

Noah and Ashur exchanged a look, and Ashur shrugged one shoulder. "Ara *was* aggressive in his questioning."

"Yeah, a little," Noah said. "But he wasn't rude. Certainly nothing that would warrant such a violent reaction. And he wasn't the only one to question the king."

"No, but he was the last to speak," Ashur said. "Maybe the king thought Ara was responsible for the rejection of his trade proposal."

Noah's thoughts tossed from one to the next like waves in a stormy sea. The king's kindness toward him in their personal interactions made it hard for Noah to imagine him carrying out such atrocities. But based on Garun's insights, he saw the possibility. He fixed his view on Navea. "Do you believe he'd respond that way to some basic questions?"

"Some disrespectful questions." Ashur held up a hand toward Noah to let him finish. "At least from the king's point of view."

Navea trembled and fear stole into her eyes. "Promise me you won't tell the king about our conversation — or that I'm here at all."

Noah arched an eyebrow. "I don't plan on ever seeing him again. But yes, I promise."

Navea pushed her hands into her lap and lowered her head. "Yes, I think he'd be willing to kill someone he thought was getting in his way."

Fury rose inside of Noah, and he fought to control his emotions. "But why Aterre? What did he ever do?"

"Seems like he was just in the wrong place." Ashur let out a breath and ran his fingers through his dark wavy hair. "Noah, you should know what Zain told me. When they cleaned up Ara's house, it was apparent there was quite a struggle that night. Ara's body only had a couple of wounds, but Aterre's. . . ." Ashur looked away and swallowed hard. "But Aterre was slashed all over. It seems like he gave his life trying to protect Ara."

Noah slammed a fist on the table, causing some food to spring off his plate. Burying his head in his hands, he wept. The agony wrenched his body. "Why?"

Ashur put a hand on Noah's arm. "I'm very sorry."

After a few moments, Noah slowly lifted his head and glared at Ashur through tear-filled eyes. "Why didn't anyone tell me this before?"

"Because of the mourning period." Ashur smiled sympathetically. "And because we knew how hard it'd be for you to hear it."

Noah tipped his head toward Navea. "And her. Why didn't you say something sooner?"

Ashur nodded and repentance showed in his eyes. "I know I should've. But for her safety, I didn't want to say anything the day she showed up." He scratched the back of his neck. "And then I didn't want to interrupt your mourning. And then it became more difficult each day, since I should've said something right away. Trust me, I wasn't trying to keep anything from you, but this morning, when I saw the mob going after Garun and Bedin, I didn't want the same thing to happen to her."

"That would explain your attitude this morning," Noah said.

"Yes, I'm sorry for my rudeness. I knew that having them here would force me to say something before I was ready."

"Noah," Navea said, "I'm very sorry if my presence here is adding to your grief."

Noah closed his eyes and took a few deep breaths. *I need to speak with Garun and Tubal-Cain.* He unclenched his fists and held her gaze. "No, it led to this information. If I think of anything else to ask, should I look for you here?"

"I think so," she said.

"At least for now," Ashur said, patting her hand. "Once things quiet down, I'd like to help her find a more permanent arrangement."

"I understand." Noah stood. "Thank you for the meal and the information."

He strode purposefully across the floor and shoved the door open so hard that he nearly hit Zain with it. The council member jumped back, bumping into Bedin, who followed closely behind, his arms full of belongings. A little ways down the street came Garun, lugging a cart loaded with items.

"Sorry," Noah said.

Zain smiled. "No harm done."

"I have to go right away, but you need to talk to Ashur. He's just inside." Noah pointed to Garun. "And I need him to come with me."

"Is everything in order?" Zain asked, suddenly serious.

"Not yet."

"We'll take Garun's things in. Remember our agreement this morning. You'll be responsible for him."

"Understood." Noah put a hand on Zain's shoulder. "Thank you."

CHAPTER 13

"Can't you just tell us who was at Ashur's?" Tubal-Cain asked as he walked with Noah and Garun past the shipyard.

"Not yet. I don't want to explain it more than once, so we'll wait until I can tell Em too." Noah smiled inwardly at the irony of his situation. His suppressed anger smoldered against Havil and their king, yet now the two people whose help he needed most were the Havilites walking with him.

Typically, while staring across the sea to his left, he contemplated the adventures that lay beyond, but today was different. Today, the surf softly splashing the shore brought no delight and only reminded him of the long days working on the beach with Ara. He turned his eyes away from the water. The long road to Sarie's Bakery steadily rose as it reached into town. Memories of his first jaunt down that hill flooded his mind. The excitement of taking in a new city, the satisfaction of reaching his destination, and the hope of soon becoming an apprentice shipbuilder caused a short-lived smile to appear on his lips. It quickly vanished when he remembered that Aterre had been at his side through it all. It seemed no place in Iri Geshem was safe from memories of Ara or Aterre. *Will this hurt ever go away?*

"Noah?" Tubal-Cain nudged him with his elbow.

Noah lifted his eyes. "What?"

"Garun asked you something."

"Oh, sorry." He looked at Garun. "What is it?"

"I just wondered if you or Emzara would like me to help with anything — get food, do some chores, you name it." Garun held out a palm. "I want to help."

"I can't think of anything like that right now, but I'll need you both to help me with something else soon enough."

They continued straight ahead as the main road turned north. The trail through the milknut grove led immediately in front of Ara's house before reaching the small home he shared with Emzara. *The home I built with Aterre.* He gritted his teeth and stared at the sparse canopy above. *I can't escape them. Do I want to?*

Averting his eyes as they passed Ara's dwelling, he cringed. Ashur's words stung all over again. *It seems like Aterre gave his life trying to protect Ara.* "Why wasn't I there to help?" The words came out louder than he intended.

"You were where you should have been. In your home, with your wife. You can't blame yourself for what happened," Garun said.

Tubal-Cain frowned. "And you probably would've been killed too. And where would that have left Zara? She needs you to be strong."

Noah forced a smile. "It's just . . ." He froze. Laughter emanated from his home, which lay just ahead of them. His heart leapt at the sound of his wife's joy. "That's Em." He spoke softly and put his arms out to halt his friends.

"Adira too." Tubal-Cain put a finger to his lips. "Let's not spoil the moment."

As the group slowly crept forward, the discussion in the house became clearly discernable.

"Remember that time when Aterre told Noah that he had developed a new kind of bean brew and Noah took a huge drink of it?" Adira's voice carried beyond the delicate fabric coverings that hung over the square holes in the walls to allow light into the interior.

"And it was really just bean brew made with seawater." Emzara giggled. "He spit it out all over the table."

Laughter resounded from both women, and Noah gave a lopsided smile. "How was I supposed to know?" He spoke softly then shook his head at the memory of the taste. "It was like drinking brown salt."

Garun put a hand over his mouth to suppress the snicker that crinkled his eyes.

"What about when Baba and Noah challenged Tubal-Cain and Aterre to a race in those two-man boats," Emzara said. "And they gave them one that leaked."

"And they sank right in the middle of the bay." Adira forced the words out in between giggles. "Tubal-Cain was embarrassed because it happened in front of the large crowd that had gathered for the Harvest Day celebration."

"And Aterre wouldn't even talk to Noah until the next day." Emzara chuckled and then sniffled. "And now it makes sense why — Jitzel was watching."

"Serves him right," Adira said. "He always took every opportunity to embarrass us around the men or vice versa."

"Yeah." Emzara dragged the word out. "I miss them so much."

"Oh, I do too. Come here."

Emzara's muffled sobs barely reached Noah's ears. He motioned toward the front door. "Let's go."

As Noah approached, Emzara asked, "Remember when Aterre hid in the kitchen?"

Noah swung open the door. "And he startled Adira."

Both women jolted.

As Noah entered he said, "And she broke the tray over his head."

Smiling at her husband, Emzara hurried to him and wrapped him in a tight embrace.

"He deserved it," Adira said with her hand over heart. "And so do you." She winked.

Noah pulled Emzara's head against his chest and breathed in her familiar scent. He looked at Adira. "And what I wouldn't give to have him here so you could do it again."

Adira smirked. She stood, placing her hands on her hips and tilting her head saucily. "I'd be more than happy to do it too."

Tubal-Cain crossed the floor and kissed his wife. "Sounds like you two are having a good time."

She sighed. "We've been trying to remember all the hilarious moments with them."

Noah released Emzara. "Any time with those two was a good time."

"It sure was." Emzara turned to Adira. "I'm glad you came over. I really needed it. Oh, Garun. You're here. I didn't even see you. Welcome."

99

Noah held up a hand. "Adira, can you stay a while? I have some news to share with everyone."

"About what?" Adira asked, returning to her seat.

Noah pointed to the few low benches that lined the walls. "Why don't all of you have a seat." He grabbed a chair from the table, as well as the basket delivered by Zain earlier that morning. Sitting down across from the group, he placed the food between him and the others. "Help yourselves."

Noah waited until each person had taken a snack. "What we discuss in here is private. I may want to bring Zain into it at some point, but for now, it stays among the five of us. Agreed?"

"Sure," Tubal-Cain said, and the others nodded.

"Oh, and one more thing. We'll need to talk about Havil, so Garun and Tubal-Cain, you two need to decide if everyone can speak freely about these matters without fear of repercussions."

"What do you mean?" Tubal-Cain squinted and shook his head. "This sounds serious."

"It is. Look, I trust both of you. But there are some sensitive things to discuss. Given your positions in Havil, a prince and an important palace guard, I want to be clear. If one of you says something that reflects poorly on your city or some of its residents, the other one won't seek retaliation."

Garun glanced at Tubal-Cain and spread both hands out, palms up. "Say whatever needs to be said. As you mentioned, this is a private meeting."

Tubal-Cain nodded. "Same goes for me. But you need to tell us who was at Ashur's."

"I will, but just not right away." Noah searched for a place to start. "Garun, except for Adira, we've all seen how Tubal-Cain's father acts in public. What's he really like behind closed doors?"

Garun stroked his chin with his thumb and index finger. "What specifically do you want to know?"

"Do you trust him?"

Biting his lip and sneaking a peek at Tubal-Cain, Garun slowly shook his head side to side. "Only to do what he thinks is in his best interest."

"And what if someone gets in his way?" Noah asked.

"Then I wouldn't want to be that person."

"What do you mean?" Noah worked to draw out his answers, noting that the guard understandably spoke much less freely in Tubal-Cain's presence.

"Well, they usually end up imprisoned." Garun looked at the floor. "Or worse."

"Where are you going with this, Noah?" Tubal-Cain asked. "What does my father have to do with anything?"

Noah turned and met Tubal-Cain's stare. "We've been friends for about four years, and our wives are best friends. You know I wouldn't ask these things if I didn't believe I had good reasons for it."

"I know. I'm just confused." He set aside his plate of food and drummed his fingers on his knee.

"Fair enough. Just a couple more questions and then I'll explain." Noah leaned forward. "Do you believe your father would do almost anything to get his way?"

"He's very ambitious." Tubal-Cain reclined and ran his fingers through his hair. "There are some pretty bad rumors about him. Some say that he's killed a bunch of people. I've even heard someone say that he killed his own father, my grandfather, on the way to Havil." He took Adira's hand. "But I've never seen any of that."

"But do you think he is capable of doing it?" Noah asked.

"Capable? Definitely." Tubal-Cain shrugged. "But willing? I'm not sure. Maybe? If he were angry enough. Why are you asking about him? You said he left town early in the morning well before the murders."

"He did." Noah glanced at Garun, "But what if he came back to go after someone that had gotten in his way?"

"Are you insinuating that my father killed Ara and Aterre?"

Noah took a deep breath. "After you left Ashur's, he brought his secret guest to meet with me. I was very surprised to see her."

Tubal-Cain raised his eyebrows.

Emzara's eyes narrowed. "Her?"

"Yes, one of the dancers from Havil. Her name is Navea."

"Yeah, I sort of know her," Tubal-Cain said. "She's a friend of Naamah's. Or was."

"Didn't she leave on the boat?" Garun asked.

"She did." Noah took a deep breath, then recounted Navea's tale about the king and his guards swimming to shore and how she ended up at Ashur's.

When he finished, Tubal-Cain stood and began to pace. "Did she accuse my father of the murders?"

Noah shook his head. "She said she never saw them again after they left the ship, but she did say that his whole demeanor changed after the council meeting."

"But that doesn't prove anything," Tubal-Cain said.

"No, it doesn't. But it raises some questions. Why did his attitude change from that point on? And why did he and three of his guards swim ashore and disappear for a long time?"

"I don't know. What possible motive could he have? What happened at the council meeting?"

"Baba stood up to him." Emzara sat up straight and her dark eyes snapped. "He questioned him about having two wives, eating animals, and the lack of wisdom in putting your sister in a position with so much authority."

Garun leaned forward. "I overheard him that night telling a fellow guard that the shipbuilder wrecked the opportunity for a trade agreement. He wasn't happy."

Tubal-Cain's wide eyes met Noah's and then shifted to Emzara. "If my father did this" — he lowered his head — "I'm so sorry."

Adira put her arms around her husband.

Noah paused to give them a moment. "If he did this . . ."

"Then he alone is responsible for it." With tears in her eyes, Emzara walked over and put a reassuring hand on Tubal-Cain's shoulder. "We'd never hold this against you."

Tubal-Cain nodded his thanks, then his eyes narrowed. "We need to find out for sure."

"How do we do that?" Adira asked.

Tubal-Cain sighed. "We go to Havil and ask around. I have several people I trust who would tell me if they've heard anything."

"I do too," Garun said. "There are a couple of palace guards and many others in the city that do not approve of the king."

Tubal-Cain held out his hand. "You should stay with Bedin. If my father secretly brought guards to Iri Geshem then I say we go to Havil in secret."

"Is it safe for us?" Adira asked.

Tubal-Cain pulled her close. "As much as I'd like you by my side, I'd prefer that you stay here. If my father hears that we're in the city, he may demand to meet you. And if he's the murderer, then I don't want you near him."

"If you think I'm just going to let Noah walk around Havil after what happened last time —"

"He wouldn't have to." Tubal-Cain held up a hand to interrupt Emzara. "We have a small beach home outside of the city. It doesn't get used anymore, so we could stay there while I check around."

"And while you do that, Noah could find my family and help them pack up to move here." Garun smiled at Emzara. "Don't worry. My place is also outside of the city."

"Are you sure you still want to move here?" Noah asked. "After this morning?"

Garun met Noah's eyes. "Even more so. Those people were misguided, but they thirsted for justice and they listened to reason. And justice and reason should always go hand in hand. I want my family to live in a place like this, under leaders like you and Zain."

"It's settled then. I'll help with the packing too." Emzara stepped to Noah and put an arm around his neck. "You aren't going without me."

Noah pulled her down so that she rested on his lap. "Why do I get the feeling that I won't be able to convince you otherwise?" Peering at Tubal-Cain, he asked, "When do we leave?"

"Since we don't want Bedin to know our plan and alert my father, we leave right after he finishes his work here. Garun, you'll need to take him to the next town and return here when you can. We'll be back with your family soon after."

CHAPTER 14

Havil — Noah's 49th year

Looking upward and into the sunlight, Naamah inhaled deeply. She paused, allowing the warmth to cradle her darkened skin. She loved the seemingly slower trek the sun made during the warm season. Completely alone, she reveled in the center's open-air design. *Mmm, my House of Knowledge.* Her fingers traced their way down one of the gilded stone columns. Three intricately carved intertwining serpents gracefully wound their way around the curvy forms of vinefruit. The light stone was smooth and cool to her touch. Brushing her cheek against it, she closed her eyes and enjoyed the contrast of the sun's heat to the staunch pillar's chill.

The sound of a bird calling from outside disturbed her quiet enjoyment of simple things and she hastened on her errand. Her sandals slapped against the stone floor as she made her way from the center toward one of the adjacent rooms. The House of Knowledge stood two stories high, but the ceilings of each floor were tall enough that a man standing on another man's shoulders would not be able to touch the brilliantly hued, frescoed top.

Naamah loved the way this massive square structure made her feel so small. Fourteen rooms on each floor surrounded the atrium, and they acted as entryways to smaller nooks. Two large open entrances stood on either end. This place awed her. The sheer number of scrolls able to be carefully organized and stored in the 84 rooms tingled her sense of anticipation. After just a few years, nearly 4,000 documents filled a tiny fraction of the edifice, and they beckoned to her to not remain small and insignificant in her world.

She gazed at a freshly painted map of the known world; the land shape resembled a semi-circle with an opening on the right side. Her city stood in the middle of the lower half and much of the land in its immediate vicinity was charted. Directly above Havil to the north she spotted Iri Geshem. *Just across the Great Sea.* To the west stood a large region marked as "unknown." *What of Nod at the northeast tip of the map, or the wild lands north and west of Iri Geshem?* She ached to know more of the secrets they held.

Realizing she had daydreamed long enough, Naamah passed through the expanse of that area to the room beyond, where high, thin windows allowed light to peek its way through. Square shelves about two cubits in length formed a geometric pattern on the walls to either side of her and each stored a number of scrolls. After rolling a small, wooden staircase over, she climbed up and reached the place where she had last left off. Clutching the three scrolls from that cube, she made her way back down and then eased onto a plush cushion near the window. Unfurling bits of the rolled papyrus, she skimmed the looping and curving text for information about Sepha.

Aha. Here we go. She reclined in her seat and became absorbed in reading until a light appeared beyond her scroll. She blinked, shaking herself from her reverie, and turned her head slightly toward the sound of soft-padding footsteps. In the now-dim room, a human outline appeared. She sat up straight, and her muscles tensed without warning. As the figure lit a hanging lantern, the visage of the seer came into focus.

"You've been here awhile. Anything to report, my princess?" His soothing tones calmed her the way her mother's soft caress on her cheeks used to when she was a small child.

"I've learned much." She beckoned with her hand, and he lounged on the cushion next to her.

"Tell me."

"This scroll talks of lands that have practiced Sepha since the dawning of days."

"Ah, very good."

"There's a place called Bothar. Apparently, they're very far to the north and west. It seems as if their large city was much like Havil, but there's a strange mystery about it."

The seer nodded, encouraging Naamah to continue.

"A scribe from the west met someone who spent several years living there. Some of what he wrote is . . . well, it makes me uncomfortable." Her tutor's eyes displayed concern, and she plunged ahead. "The people of that town are allowed to . . ." Her eyes scrunched as she held back tears. "The men as an act of worship will go to a temple, where young children are waiting . . . in special rooms . . ." She buried her face in her hands, not wanting to continue.

"Hush, child. I'm surprised that bothered you so."

Her head jerked up, her eyes wide. "Why would you say that? The children. . . ."

"Did you read about the results?" At her silence, he went on, "What did it do for the devotion to Sepha?"

"It increased greatly. The amount of people coming to the temples tripled in a single year."

"Yes." His voice savored the word, drawing it out. A smile played about his thin lips. "I'm shocked that you don't see the great benefit. With all you've done to get our people to follow Nachash, I'd have thought you'd be excited with learning a new method to increase their devotion."

"But the young children."

"They got to play an incredible role in nurturing the people's devotion. Don't you see the honor they held?"

"Yes, but why so young?"

"How would you do things differently?"

"What about someone like me?" She spoke quickly. "Wouldn't it be better if we could get women my age who long to play a greater role in promoting devotion to their god?"

He gazed at her face and frowned. "Someone *like* you, yes. But not you. You're the princess."

"But, why not me? If I could give myself wholly to the cause of Nachash, I would!" Her passionate voice echoed against the dim walls. "It'd be my greatest act as princess."

"No!" He sat upright with a jerk.

She recoiled slightly at his volume. "No?"

The seer cleared his throat. "I want something greater for you."

"What could be greater?"

He settled back and calmed his voice. "Think of how pleased Nachash would be if you were in charge of this idea of yours. You'd accomplish so much more if you were responsible for bringing this to Havil. I'd be so proud."

Her face flushed in pleasure at being back in his good favor. *And something like this — which would add ardent followers — would certainly please our god.*

She longed to hear his praise again. "You like my idea?"

"Certainly. Continue to learn more about how you could implement this here." He tapped the scroll on her lap.

"Oh, that reminds me" — she glanced down at the flowing text — "there was a mystery surrounding Bothar."

"Go on."

"Well, a number of years after beginning this new temple practice — here, let me find the place." Naamah rolled up the right side of the scroll and unraveled the left as she searched for the details. "Ah, here's what the informant told the scribe."

> I have always stayed on the edge of society, watching, recording, but never taking part. However, just today, twelve more have given up the inner spirit and left their bodies to this world. There is wild speculation about what is causing the sickness. It seems that death usually arrives within two weeks of the first symptoms. As a precaution for my own safety, I have settled in a small abode much farther away from the city and have spread word that I have perished. I shall continue to write about the strange death toll in the city from here.

Naamah moved her finger down the page, searching for the part she wanted to show the seer. "And there's a tragic ending here."

> The entire city of Bothar is no more. Within the span of just a few whole moons, the city went from a thriving cultural center to being abandoned. More people were needing to be buried than those who felt well enough to accomplish the task. The stench of burning piles pervades the city. I have watched from

my secret place this week as the last remaining citizens have succumbed to the strange sickness that caused both young and old
to leave their life here on this earth.

Naamah looked up into his deep-set eyes. "What could cause all
that?"

The seer remained silent, but his expression implored her to speak
her mind.

"Do you think it's because of what they did to those children?"
Naamah shuddered. "Because, if so, we should never bring this to Havil."

"Nonsense, you should have more wisdom than that. You yourself
called it a mystery, and if the scribe had known the cause, he'd have recorded it. Instead of trying to link the deaths in Bothar to their practices,
think about how great those customs made their devotion. Don't forfeit
great advancement and power because of the unknown." The irritation
in the seer's typically calm voice alerted Naamah to his displeasure with
her question.

Naamah stared at the scroll as she contemplated his words. "You're
right." She straightened up and tossed her head back, forcing her straight
dark hair behind her shoulder. "I'll start working on this program then.
It's just . . . well it's just too bad that . . ."

"That what?"

"The annual ceremony is in two whole moons. I wish I had discovered it sooner so that we could be ready by then."

"I'm certain there's enough time. You can use your influence with
the palace. Don't forget to practice those incantations I've taught you. If
you promote it properly, women will beg to be priestesses of Nachash."

"You really think so?"

He stood and offered her a hand. "I know it. Now, let's talk about
how."

CHAPTER 15

The crowded city streets bustled. Emzara craned her neck to see the tops of the buildings. The towering stucco edifices were taller than she remembered. *Guess they've been busy in the last four years.* She tripped on a gap in the cobblestone roadway, causing her to look down at the broken surface, pockmarked as it was with holes where stones were missing. *Maybe they should have put some of that construction effort into repairing this road.*

Noah's strong back just in front of her comforted her among the unfamiliar sights all around. She'd expected to recognize more, but the city seemed utterly alien. *A lot has changed here in Havil. Although, maybe it's just my focus that has changed. I was paying attention to Noah last time, and this time we're on a dangerous errand. Or maybe it's because we're on the outskirts of town that I don't recognize all this.*

On some level, she knew the rationalization for what it was: an attempt to make sense of something that bore no logic. The city was more different than her four-year absence could justify. Yet the fact of it remained, and she could do nothing but walk on, following Noah as they headed to Garun's house. Shaking off her unease, she took in the brilliantly colored signs announcing in bright paint a variety of shops: weaponry, woven and wrapped cloths, and jewelry.

She gave a wide berth to another large gap in the street and nearly ran into an elderly woman. Turning, she said, "I'm so sorry," but the woman had vanished. Puzzled, Emzara held her baby close, protecting the tiny form as she scanned the street. There was no sign of the old woman, and Emzara dropped a kiss on the soft fuzz of her baby's head. "Tera." She whispered the name aloud. A perfect combination of *Ara* and *Aterre* for her perfect little one. She smiled as she remembered her father telling her that *Emzara* was a combination of his and her mother's names. Tera barely shifted in the tightly wrapped cloths that served not only to hold her close to Emzara but also to keep her arms free for other tasks.

"Em, are you coming?" Several steps ahead, Noah paused and looked back. She hurried to catch up. The shops thinned out and soon the cobblestone road turned to dirt and became noticeably narrower. Squat dwelling places stood tucked together on either side, with very little room in between. *If this is where Garun's family lives, I'm glad they'll get to move to Iri Geshem soon.* The wind moaned through the branches of a tall tree, sending a chill through her body.

As if on cue, a voice called out from behind them. "You two, stop!"

Noah turned around and grabbed her right hand with his left. "Run!"

She sprinted after him, but based on the sounds coming from behind them, they were not making much headway. Her breath came in short gasps, each one like a knife in her side. Somehow Tera was still sleeping, even with the extra jostling. *Thank you, Most High.*

"Stop or you'll wish you had." The voice from behind them rang with authority.

"Noah, I — the baby . . ."

"We'd better do what he said." Noah's pace slacked and he turned to face their pursuers, pivoting so that she was shielded behind him.

"Noah and Emzara," a man with an evil grin said. His eyes were in shadows, giving his face a ghastly hollowness that struck terror deep within her. "We've been looking all over for you, and here you wander right into our city." Eight guards walked around their leader and encircled the young family, cutting off any hope of escape.

A weight settled within Emzara, like a milknut dropping from a tree and hitting the sandy ground below with a thud. But something about his words struck her as off. They'd been looking for her and Noah? But Lamech had been to Iri Geshem — surely Naamah knew where to find them.

"What do you want with us?" Noah asked.

His boldness both pleased and scared Emzara.

"Step aside." Another voice sounded from behind the guard.

Emzara adjusted her shoulder wrap to further conceal Tera. *Where are all these people coming from?*

Lamech appeared and headed straight toward her.

"King Lamech! But — I — I thought these were Naamah's guards." The words escaped from her mouth before she could stop them.

"Naamah's guards are also my guards, of course." He stepped closer, forcing her to return his gaze. The power and hate in his eyes revealed at once that he had killed her father and Aterre. She swallowed hard. *And now it's our turn.*

"Why have you stopped us, sir?" Noah asked.

"You have something that we want. Something we need."

"What's that?" Noah's voice growled low and instinctively Emzara knew he was readying himself to protect them with his life if need be.

"We've been looking for her." The king pointed directly at Emzara and she quaked inside.

"Me? Why?"

"Get away from her." Noah stepped directly in between his wife and the king.

Before she even saw them move, two soldiers were there, restraining Noah and yanking him out of the way.

Lamech stroked Emzara's cheek with the back of his hand.

She twisted away, being careful to protect her child.

Lamech laughed. "Not you."

Confused, Emzara drew Tera closer to her body.

He sneered. "The child. Take her." Noah broke free and lunged at Lamech, but the king shoved Noah aside as if he weighed nothing at all. The two guards seized him again and one struck him with a club, rendering him unconscious.

Crying out, Emzara struck at Lamech's hands as he reached for Tera. When he brushed aside her blows, she came at him again, this time going for his eyes, her fingers bent like the claws of an animal.

Stars exploded in her vision as he struck her across the cheek, sending her to her hands and knees in the dirt. Pushing aside her outer wrap, Lamech wrenched the cloth wound around Emzara's torso and seized the baby.

"No!"

Awakened by the noise and rough treatment, Tera's loud cries mingled with her mother's sounds of anguish. Still too dizzy to rise, Emzara clung to the king's robe with all her strength. "You can't have her! Not without me!"

Lamech flashed a grin, his large teeth gleaming. "You're welcome to come along." He handed Tera to a guard and with a flick of his wrist beckoned two other soldiers. They hauled Emzara to her feet and shoved her toward the city, back the way they had come.

Somehow, in a blur, they were standing at the base of the middle steps of a large edifice Emzara recognized as the central structure of the ceremony on their first visit. Tears blinding her vision, Emzara stumbled as a guard shoved her up the stairs. The edges dug into her shins and she clamored behind Tera and Lamech, trying to reach her dear baby girl. "Where are you taking her?"

A woman's loud cackle echoed across the expansive courtyard, pulling Emzara's focus to the top of the platform. There stood Naamah, dressed in one of Emzara's own gowns. *Where did she get that?*

"Oh look, it's Emzara." Naamah stepped forward and stared into Emzara's eyes. A wicked grin spread across her face. "The one who has so captured my Noah over there that he won't even look at me, but I'll soon fix that. Once you're gone, he'll have nowhere else to turn."

Emzara followed Naamah's gaze. Held up by two armed men, Noah slumped against a low wall, his head lolled to one side.

"And there's the new symbol of your love. A child. Bring her to me!" Naamah beckoned a nearby guard.

Emzara could barely stand to look as the woman held onto Tera. She clutched at the baby awkwardly as if she had never held one before. "Wake him."

A guard picked up a pail and pitched its contents in Noah's face. The water splashed against him and he shuddered. His eyes slowly registered consciousness, and a look of terror crossed his face as he saw Naamah with his child.

"Look at me, Noah. Now will you have me? I'm dressed for the part in this rustic dress. I'm even carrying your child."

Her laugh drove shivers of fear through Emzara. "Please." Emzara uttered the only word that would come out of her mouth as she fell to her knees in a feeble attempt to reclaim her baby.

Naamah held Tera out with two arms and inspected the child. "Well, it's too late. Now you'll regret ever refusing me." She stood in front of the large serpent statue so its head curved over hers.

"Finally, I have all I need." She held Tera aloft before placing her on a golden altar. "Remember those children Noah rescued before he even met you? Well, Nachash desires the blood of innocents, and your child will take the place of those Noah stole."

Emzara shrieked and struggled to wrench herself away from her captors, but she was no match. They stuffed a cloth in her mouth and held her face in the direction of Naamah.

Naamah closed her eyes and hummed an eerie tune. As her volume rose, the molded head of the serpent grew in size and started swaying. Emzara froze in terror — such a thing could not be. But before her eyes it morphed from a statue into a moving golden being, the head raised and poised over the writhing form of her daughter. Tera's high-pitched cries pierced her mother's heart. As the serpent moved to strike, Emzara screamed with all her might.

"What's going on, Em?"

Someone was shaking her and she sat up, narrowly avoiding collision with Noah's face as he hovered over her. "Where's Tera?" She gripped his upper arm and clung to him as if her sheer force would result in a faster answer. A cold sweat drenched her forehead and her heartbeat raced.

"Who's Tera?" In the semi-darkness, she saw the confused look on her husband's face, and anger at his stupidity stabbed through her heart.

"Our daughter! Is she — is she dead?" The painful word barely crossed her lips.

"Em, you were having a dream. You're still pregnant." He stroked her cheek, and she relaxed her grip on him slightly. "You're safe here in the ship's quarters."

"A dream." She breathed deeply, trying to shake off the sick horror of what she'd seen, but the vivid memory was still etched in her mind. "It was so real." She rested against him, silent for a while. "Do you think it's wrong for us to be traveling to Havil?"

Noah kissed the top of her head. "No. We're going to find answers. If we discover that Lamech is truly to blame, we need to protect others from being hurt or killed by him — his crime must be punished. We're

113

also getting Garun's family to safety. It's just your fears coming out while you're sleeping."

"I guess you're right. But, Noah" — she grabbed his hand and placed it on the growing bulge in her midsection — "I want you to promise you'll be careful. This baby becomes more real to me each day. There are times when I think I can feel her inside of me, moving around. And we need you." Her gaze found his. "Even if it was just a dream, we know Havil is a wicked place. I have a terrible feeling that something evil grows there. And it's *seen* us."

He moved to wrap her in an embrace, but he didn't try to reassure her again. Instead, she felt his stubble scrape her ear as he nodded. "I know."

He shifted so they were both lying on the narrow bed, with her head nestled on his chest and his hand on her belly. For a long time they were silent, allowing the fear to dissipate into the darkness and peace to return.

Noah's chuckle rumbled under her ear. "Her, huh?"

Emzara smiled. "Well, I have no way of really knowing. I just keep thinking of this baby as a girl." She looked up at him. "I kind of like the name Tera."

CHAPTER 16

"T his is probably my favorite part of the journey," Noah said as he watched the waves crash into the shore hundreds of cubits away.

"Sitting and staring at the water?" Tubal-Cain asked. "Looks pretty boring to me."

Noah yawned and pointed at a small gap in the distant forest. "See that opening there?"

"Between the trees?"

"Yeah."

Tubal-Cain slid a crate along the deck and sat on it next to Noah. "What's so exciting about that?"

"There's a small river flowing through there." Noah shifted in his seat to face his friend. "I like to imagine what it'd be like to travel up that waterway with Em and do some exploring. Do any people live there? If so, what are they like? What animals live in the forests? Em would love to discover new creatures. And what about those hills way back there? Is that where the river starts?"

"You know what I think about when I see those hills?"

"The metals you might find there?" Noah asked.

"Exactly."

Noah snorted. "Your musings aren't as exciting as mine."

"Maybe not to you." Tubal-Cain leaned back on his hands. "Since you like sitting and thinking so much, I've got a serious question for you."

Feeling the prick of exhaustion behind his eyes, Noah longed to head below deck and fall asleep next to Emzara, but he already expected very little rest on this secret mission. Emzara and Tubal-Cain assisted in the seafaring responsibilities where they could, but they relied upon Noah's growing expertise to captain the vessel. Yet, despite the somber cause for their voyage and the long days and nights, he had largely enjoyed the first 12 days of the trip.

"Okay, just a moment." Noah pretended to write something on the large scroll spread out on a bin to his left.

"What are you writing?"

He glanced at the map. "I'm adding details about those hills. It says, 'Tubal-Cain's metals' right there." Noah tapped the page.

Tubal-Cain stretched his neck to see and chuckled, his amusement spreading to form laugh lines around his eyes. "No, you didn't."

Noah smirked. "I've just been updating it from our previous trips. There are still some blank areas because we've sailed past them at night." Noah rolled up the map and wrapped a string around it. "What did you want to ask me?"

Tubal-Cain scratched behind his ear. "Do you think we'll ever see them again?"

"Those hills?"

"No." Tubal-Cain shook his head. "Aterre and Ara."

Noah's smile disappeared.

"I mean, do you think there's more than this?" The blacksmith waved his arm from left to right, indicating the whole world.

Noah watched the mildly undulating water distort his long, early morning shadow, enjoying the light, cool breeze as it passed through his unkempt hair. He sighed and stretched a hand out toward Tubal-Cain. "What do you think?"

"I'd like to assume there's something after this life. Some of the older people in our city say we were made from the ground, just like the people of Iri Geshem believe. But they say that we return to the ground and that's it."

"They think the person just ceases to exist?" Noah asked.

"Some of them do."

Noah tilted his head. "That might explain why so many people in your city live the way they do."

Furrowing his brow, Tubal-Cain asked, "What do you mean?"

"Well, think about it. If this life is all we have — if there's nothing after it — then you may as well live however you want. Seek pleasure and power, instead of serving the Creator and helping others."

"I can see what you're saying, but I think you're overstating it a bit." Tubal-Cain looked up and squinted. "Some of those people are very kind to others. They don't just live for pleasure and power."

"Hmm." Noah rested his chin on his fist. "I guess I could argue that they desire to have others think well of them and that's selfish, but I'd rather not judge their motives, particularly since I don't know them."

"Well, that's good. I'd hate to think you pretend to know everyone's motives." Tubal-Cain stared across the water. "After all, couldn't someone turn it around on you and say that you serve the Creator for selfish reasons too — that you're hoping to somehow get His favor?"

"I guess it could look like that from someone else's point of view," Noah said. "But the main reason I serve the Creator is to thank Him for giving me life."

"I can see that, but we're getting away from my initial question. What do you think happens after death, if anything?"

Noah slowly drew in a breath. "I'm not really sure. I've heard several ideas about it."

"Like what?" Tubal-Cain leaned forward.

"Well, remember the Zakari people I told you about?"

"The ones whose children were kidnapped?"

Noah nodded. "Their elder told me that the people who stole their kids, the people from Bothar, practiced the dark arts. They tried contacting spirits, either people who had already died or some other kind of spiritual being."

"So if they contacted the spirits of people who had died, does that mean after death we just roam around the earth and no one can see us?" Tubal-Cain scratched the prickly growth on his face, which seemed to be growing in twice as fast as Noah's attempt at a beard. "Doing what?"

"I'm not sure — waiting to give advice to those who contact them?" Noah shrugged a shoulder. "I guess that's what the people of Bothar believed."

Tubal-Cain drew back. "That's really weird. What did you mean about the other kind of spiritual being?"

"Garun told me . . ." Noah stopped and quickly regretted mentioning his earlier conversation with the king's guard.

"Told you what?"

Noah shook his head. "Never mind."

Tubal-Cain crossed his arms. "No, not never mind. Tell me."

Pulling a tiny sliver of wood from the rail above the hull, Noah said, "I'd rather not."

"It's about my sister, isn't it?"

Noah slowly turned and nodded.

The distinct clinking and scraping of copper and silver reached Noah's ears as Tubal-Cain fidgeted with the leather money pouch that hung from his belt. "Just tell me."

"Garun told me that he's heard her mentor — they call him a seer — telling her about the spirits that he communicates with. The seer told her that the Creator is just one of many spiritual entities. Originally, He made the world that we see and another realm that we cannot see — one that's inhabited by spirits or gods. The Creator was the most powerful spiritual being." A frown grew on Noah's face. "But as time went on, and as more people turned away from Him, other gods, like Nachash, turned against Him and became stronger. Apparently, this seer thinks that Nachash is now the most powerful, or that he can become the most powerful spirit if he has the most followers."

"Do you think she buys into that?" Tubal-Cain asked.

Noah let out a deep breath and spoke softly. "I have a feeling that she'll believe it if it means more power."

Tubal-Cain's forearm bulged as he tightened his grip on the leather bag. "And do you think these spirits actually exist? Besides the Creator, of course."

"Garun thinks they're real because the seer knows things that he shouldn't be able to know. He didn't give me any examples, so I'm not entirely sure what he meant."

"And do you believe that Nachash is becoming more powerful than the Creator?" Tubal-Cain asked, his dark, heavy eyebrows nearing each other.

"I sure hope that isn't happening." Noah lowered his face into his hands and massaged his forehead. "I guess I can see how it might look like that, especially to people in Havil, who think that the city's become so grand because they follow Nachash. But it doesn't really make sense to me that one of these spirits could become more powerful than its Maker. If the Most High created these spirits, then it seems like He could just as easily destroy them."

"That makes sense, but we got off subject again." Tubal-Cain huffed and pointed to Noah. "What do you believe happens when we die?"

Noah thought back to childhood conversations with his father. "I've always believed that the Creator will reward those who faithfully serve Him."

"What sort of reward?"

"My guess is that we'll get to live with Him."

"As spirits?" Tubal-Cain said. "Obviously, our body remains here."

Noah raised his gaze to the sky. "I'm not sure. I think we'll have some sort of body."

"Really? Why?"

Noah chuckled. "You ask a lot of questions." He faced his friend. "My grandfather's father was a man who walked closely with the Most High. He used to warn people that the Creator was going to come to earth someday and judge the wicked people."

Tubal-Cain smirked. "My father said that where he grew up, there was a man like that who visited the city several times, and many of the people mocked him for his rants. As my father told it, this man would walk through town and shout about the coming judgment that never came." A grin spread on his face. "Everyone made up labels for him. They didn't want to use his real name because it was the same as the name of the city, and they didn't want to be associated with him."

Noah looked at Tubal-Cain, then the ship's deck, and then back at his friend. "Wait. Your father is from the land of Nod, the city of Enoch, right?"

"Yes."

One side of Noah's mouth turned up slightly. "That's the name of my grandfather's father."

Tubal-Cain's smile disappeared rapidly. "You mean, the man who warned the city of Enoch about judgment . . ."

"Is my grandfather's father." Noah nodded.

"Forgive me. I didn't mean to disrespect your family."

"You were just repeating what your father told you. I know you wouldn't intentionally say something bad about my family."

"Nah, just you." Tubal-Cain slapped Noah's shoulder and laughed. "So why did you bring up your grandfather's father in the first place?"

"He decided to visit the land of Eden with Berit, my father's —"

"The cursed land?" Tubal-Cain held up both palms. "Sorry, interrupting again."

Noah smiled at his large muscular friend apologizing like a child. "You've heard the rumors, too. Well, I think this might be why they started." Noah adjusted his wrap to cover his shoulder. "As they approached the land, Enoch simply disappeared."

"What do you mean 'disappeared'?" Tubal-Cain asked. "Did he wander off and become lost?"

Noah shook his head. "No, I mean he vanished. One moment he was walking with Berit, and the next moment" — Noah snapped his fingers — "he was gone."

Tubal-Cain stared through wide eyes.

"My father believes God just took him from the earth."

"Why?"

"Our best guess is so that he wouldn't have to face any more of the evils in this world."

"And because of that, you think he's living with the Creator and that we may live with Him after we die?"

"That's right."

"And since his body was taken too, you think that we may have some sort of body when we're with the Creator?"

Noah shrugged. "Like I said before, it's my best guess."

Tubal-Cain sat up straight. "Well, it makes sense to me, and I like it."

"You do?"

"Of course. It would mean that Aterre and Ara are with the Creator right now."

Noah nodded and forced a tight smile. "I like it even more now."

An anguished cry came from below deck, and Noah tensed and spun toward the opening. "Em?"

He hurried to the stairs and made his way down to the low-ceilinged quarters under the deck. Ducking to avoid crossbeams, Noah blinked several times, trying to force his eyes to adjust to the dark quarters lit only by an oil lamp affixed to a nearby shelf. "Em, what's wrong? Where are you?"

There was no figure on the bed, only tousled blankets. A low moan emanated from the foot of the knee-high cot. As he rushed there, Noah's breath caught at the sight of his wife huddled on the floor.

"Em . . ."

Emzara rocked quietly back and forth. Her ebony curls clung to her cheeks. Her long lashes were pinched between her tightly closed eyelids. Even in her discomfort, her beauty gripped Noah's heart. Another subdued moan escaped from her. Her leg violently shot out and she gripped the base of the bed as if in extreme pain. He rushed to her side. Her labored breathing worried him. "Em, what's going on?"

She grabbed his hand with her free hand and for a few moments squeezed with a grip he did not know she possessed. Pain surged through his fingers, reminding him of one of Toman's intense greetings. "Em?"

Suddenly her features relaxed. She released her grasp and reclined against the wall, limp.

Is she dead? The thought vanished as instantly as it came to mind when she took a deep, shaky breath. Noah breathed a sigh of relief.

"I . . ." She held up a bloodied cloth. Combined with Em's pain and heavy breathing, the pieces came together. He had been only a boy when his second sibling was born too early, but he remembered the day vividly. It was not until the birth of Misha a few years later that the light in his mother's eyes finally came back. But the unknown child was never forgotten.

Returning to the needs in front of him, he held Emzara tenderly as she sobbed. Then together they wept over yet another loss.

Chapter 17

Land of Havilah — Noah's 49th year

Holding a bag of supplies in his right hand and with his left gripping one end of a large basket stuffed with clothing, Noah trudged through the shallow water with Tubal-Cain, who held the other end of the oversized container. As they neared the shore, Noah handed Emzara the sack. "I think this is the last of the items that we'll need for now."

Emzara placed the bag on top of a small crate on the beach and arched her back. Silently she took in their surroundings.

Needing a rest after three trips from the boat, Noah walked toward his wife and placed a hand on her shoulder as he took in the clean, glimmering sand and listened to the water gently lapping the shore.

She shrugged off his caress. "Leave me be."

Sighing, he turned and went to sit on the sand beside Tubal-Cain, facing the sea. Noah couldn't resist feasting his gaze on the display of God's creation before him. "It's very beautiful." Enticed, he stretched a foot back into the refreshing liquid.

"Indeed. I spent a lot of time in this water as a child." Tubal-Cain tilted his head toward the nearby woods. "I used to find the slimiest creatures under rocks or logs in that forest, and then I'd put them in my sister's hair."

Despite his revulsion of Naamah as an adult, Noah tried picturing her as a young child like Misha, and struggled to stifle a laugh. "I'm sure she loved that."

"She squealed like a baby, and I'd get in trouble every time." Tubal-Cain leaned back on his hands and chuckled. "It was worth it."

Noah watched Emzara from the corner of his eye to see how she would react to the discussion about Naamah, but she never flinched. She remained the stoic shell of herself that she had become in the past few weeks. A band of longing tightened around Noah's heart, and he ached to see her usual good humor and ready smile return. Losing her first child would have been difficult enough, but going through it just weeks after losing her father and close friend had been nearly unbearable. Surprised by her lack of tears in the first few days after the loss of their baby, Noah did his best to comfort her. But her demeanor eventually shifted from plain apathy to occasional outbursts of exasperation. While he didn't like that she vented her anger at him, at least she came alive during those moments. In between these explosions of anger, she retreated. Not sure what to do, Noah eventually stopped trying to console her, and she rarely spoke to him. Privately, he wondered if she blamed him for everything.

He sighed and watched the boat, anchored about 50 cubits away, as it bobbed softly on the surface. The broad-leafed trees of the forest lined both sides of the narrow lagoon. Noah recognized most of them, but he spotted a couple that seemed foreign to him. *I'll have to check those out with Em.* He let out a sigh, realizing the futility of that now. Colorful flowers topped low-lying plants near the water's edge, their cheery petals a marked contrast from how he felt. A variety of animal chirps and clicks called out through the still morning air. "It's a good thing we arrived at this point during the daylight, or I fear we may have sailed right past that little inlet."

"We would've realized our mistake soon enough," Tubal-Cain said. "The lights of Havil aren't too far away."

"We're that close?" Emzara asked, taking sudden interest.

Tubal-Cain shrugged. "It's a pretty long walk, but close enough for me to get there, check around a little, and return before it's too late this evening."

Emzara paced back and forth. "And you're sure your family won't be visiting this place while we're here?"

"I really doubt it. If they're planning another Serpent Ceremony three days from now, like Garun said, then they'll be too busy making arrangements for that."

Noah climbed to his feet and motioned to their belongings. "Let's get all this inside."

Two quick jaunts up a sandy trail from the shore to the beach home completed the task at hand. Noah set his second load on the wooden floor of the main room.

Emzara dug out some supplies from the largest container. "I'll fix firstfeast right away." She pointed at Tubal-Cain. "That should give you the energy you need for a long day."

"Where should we stay?" Noah asked.

Tubal-Cain tipped his head toward the hallway that began in the middle of the back wall between the front room and the kitchen. "First chamber on the right."

Noah took his time moving their supplies to the guest room. Frustrated by his inability to provide solace for Emzara and by her seeming indifference toward him, Noah tightened his grip on the door handle and pushed harder than necessary. He stepped inside and closed the door. After dropping his physical burden, Noah moved to the large, low-lying pallet adorned with multiple cushions and sat down, determined to release his emotional burdens. Emzara had every reason to sulk, but so did he, and sooner or later, she needed to break free from her mood. He did everything he could think of to be there for her, but she seemed disinterested in all of it. A tear formed in his eye as he pictured her smiling face on the evening she told him he would be a father. *Em, I need you back.*

Noah lay back on the bed and stared at the ceiling. *Creator, forgive me for my reluctance to speak to You these past weeks. I don't understand why You've allowed all of these terrible things to happen recently. I can't bear this pain alone. I know You're here, but I want Em by my side too. If I've done something to hurt her, please help me to make it right.* He closed his eyes and wiped the tears from the sides of his face. A strong sense of conviction washed over him. Gathering his thoughts, Noah continued to pray. *Although I don't understand all that is going on, I trust that You will always do what is right. Even if it hurts.*

After letting out a deep breath, Noah stood and dried his eyes and cheeks. As he stepped into the hallway, he overheard Emzara asking Tubal-Cain something about the house. He entered the main room and Emzara's countenance immediately dimmed; being run through with a grendec's tooth would have hurt less.

"So many memories in this place," Tubal-Cain said as he breathed in deeply. "It still smells the same as I remember."

Noah offered him a weak smile. "How often did you come here?"

"Only about twice year. But I haven't been here since" — he scratched his head — "maybe about 12 years ago. Once I started working with the smiths on a regular basis, I didn't have the free time."

"Firstfeast is ready." Emzara spread three plates on the table between them. "It's not much, but I'll bake some bread today, and we'll have a grand evenfeast tonight."

"And maybe I'll bring some food back from the city," Tubal-Cain said.

Noah glanced at the assortment of nuts, dried fruit, and sliced vegetables on the tray, and his stomach growled. Ever amazed at her gift for making an inviting feast out of even the slimmest of provisions, he selected a few from each of the options and dropped them in the bowl in front of him. After stirring them together, he paused before taking a bite. "This looks wonderful, Em."

She looked down at her bowl and started eating.

Noah suppressed the urge to vent his frustration and glanced at Tubal-Cain, who returned a sympathetic half-smile.

"Well, as soon as I finish, I'll head into Havil with my new disguise." He grinned and rubbed the beard he had grown during the voyage. "I'll check with some people I trust to see if they've heard anything about what happened in Iri Geshem."

"And you'll make sure they don't say anything about the three of us being here?" Noah asked.

"Of course." He shoved another fruit slice into his mouth and talked around it. "Just wait for me here, and I'll be back before you know it."

"What if someone recognizes you and tells your father?" Noah asked.

Tubal-Cain nodded. "I've thought about that. If my father finds out, then I'll act as if I were planning to pay him a surprise visit. If I get caught up in the city, I'll send word to you through someone I trust."

Conversation lagged and the three fell silent as they ate. *Em, I miss your lively banter during a meal.* Suddenly, his once-hungry insides changed on him and tightened. He lowered his spoon and pushed his bowl away.

"Is there anything you want us to do while you're gone?" Emzara broke the quiet as she combined all the leftovers onto one plate.

Tubal-Cain stood and swiftly rewound his wrap over one shoulder. He grabbed Emzara's hand and put it in Noah's. "Yes, talk to each other and rediscover the love you've always had together." He whirled and moved toward the door. "I'll see you tonight."

"Be safe," Noah called out as he squeezed Emzara's hand and watched her.

She slowly raised her head and met his gaze. Looking away, her lip trembled. "Noah, I . . . I . . . don't . . ." Emzara slipped out of her seat and slid over to hug him. "I'm sorry."

Noah stood and held her tight. Afraid to spoil the moment, he silently waited for her to speak.

Emzara brushed his cheek with her lips and backed away, wiping her eyes. "Can we go for a walk?"

Noah lifted her hand and kissed it. "Of course."

Without another word, she led him outside. Turning toward the beach, she whispered "Which way?"

Noah pointed to the west side of the lagoon where some trees that he did not recognize stood. "Over there."

They left the trail to the beach and waded through long grasses until they reached the edge of the woods. Watching Emzara, Noah smiled to himself as he thought about their different perspectives on life. A setting like this inspired him and ignited a need to examine all the various types of wood around him. But she would normally be on the lookout for any animals that might cross their path. Her fascination with God's creatures had grown with each passing year, and now he hoped that these new surroundings would rekindle some passion in her.

"I'm sorry that I've been cold." Emzara pushed her hair back with her free hand. "I just. . . ." She shook her head. "You didn't deserve that."

Noah put an arm around her shoulder and pulled her close. "Em, I don't know what I did wrong, but you know you can always —"

"You didn't do anything wrong. You did everything you could to cheer me up." She stopped and put her hand against his cheek as her eyes welled up. "I've never felt so lost, so helpless, and I never should've pushed you away. Forgive me."

He nodded and placed his hand over hers, keeping it on his cheek.

"I was so focused on my own anguish that I barely even thought about the pain you were feeling." She leaned in and rested her head against his chest. "Every time I saw you, it made me think of our baby and that it was my fault — that I was inadequate to be a mother or to be your wife — and all the heartache rushed back in."

Holding her tight as she wept, Noah kissed the top of her head. He wanted to tell her of his suffering as well, but he decided to remain silent and allow their embrace to begin healing their wounds.

Emzara finally pulled back slightly and looked into his eyes. "I'm still working through my feelings and thoughts, but I'll try to include you when I can. It might take some more time though."

He cleared a tear from her cheek with his thumb. "Em, I love you."

Her eyes flashed their old sparkle. "I love . . ."

Embracing her tightly, Noah dipped his head and planted an impassioned kiss on her lips, which she returned. Weeks of grief seemed to retreat, and the joy they once shared flooded back into his soul. With their lips still pressed together, he slid his arms around her lower back and stood to his full height, lifting her off the ground in the process.

Emzara pulled back first. Noah loosened his grip, allowing her feet to slowly drop to the ground. "Promise me something."

"What?"

"That whatever tragedies arise in our future, we face them together." He tucked a strand of her hair behind her ear. "I need you more than ever in those times."

She bit her lip and looked at her feet. "I'll . . . try."

A loud cracking sound in the distance drew their attention.

"What was that?" Emzara asked.

"Not sure. Let's go see."

Noah quietly led her through the forest toward the disturbance. A snort and then some stomping filled the air. Suddenly, the crashing noise rang out again.

"Over there," he said as he shifted course.

Unrecognizable sounds emanated from an animal as it bellowed and snorted. Emzara wet her lips and slowed her pace slightly as they closed in. Movement in a small clearing ahead made Noah dart behind a wide tree several cubits in front of them.

"What are those things?" Emzara asked.

Noah shook his head, which she probably didn't see, since her attention never left the two brownish-green creatures. He craned his neck to get a better view. Staring each other down, they stalked about on two legs in a large circular pattern. Noah estimated they stood about Emzara's height but were at least twice that long from head to tail. Their most unique feature was the large bony mound on the top of their heads.

The animal closest to them stomped, reared back, and then charged its foe. The other beast lowered its head and dashed in. The spectacular collision echoed through the forest, and the two combatants slowly returned to the edge of the clearing. A snort from one creature triggered an angry blast from the other.

As they marched around their ring, Noah peeked at Emzara. As if she sensed his gaze, she glanced back at him, eyes full of wonder and an ear-to-ear smile etched on her face, before turning back to the observe the confrontation. The stomping of feet signaled another dramatic charge. This time Noah kept his focus on his wife, relishing her reactions as she marveled at the Most High's creativity.

She winced at the thunderous crash that generated a moan from one of the beasts. Noah turned back to the battle, but it was clearly over. The creature on the other side of the clearing raised its head in the air and let out a victory cry. The other staggered away, hanging its head.

Ducking back behind the tree, Emzara gripped Noah's hand and leaned close to his ear. "Incredible."

"Have you ever seen anything like that?"

Emzara shook her head. "Not quite like that. Some male bleaters spar with each other but never so violently." Her eyes lit up. "I can't wait to draw them."

A settled feeling returned to Noah's soul, as her apathy faded. While neither of them would ever be the same, he hoped that this was the beginning of a new normal.

CHAPTER 18

"I'm worried about Tubal-Cain." Emzara paced across the floor and peeked out the front door of the beach home. "It's getting pretty dark, and he should've been back by now."

"He'll be fine. Besides, looking outside repeatedly isn't going to get him here any sooner. There are better ways to pass the time." Noah patted the cushion next to him on the bench. "Come here."

She closed the door and leaned against it, folding her arms in front of her. Scrunching her face, she considered his invitation before slowly making her way to him. She paused, grabbing a piece of cloth from the table.

"So here's what I drew," she said as she sat beside him. Her fingers gracefully smoothed the fabric piece over his lap. The clear lines she had sketched caught the moment of impact. Looking at the colliding animals, he could almost hear the crash of skull meeting skull. "I feel like this often lately." She pointed to the smaller one on the left. "He's the few little pleasures left in life." She shifted to the larger creature and Noah saw the detail in the hardened features about the face. "And he's the pain. Even when they meet, everything hurts."

Noah held her and massaged her head. His insides warmed as she melted in his embrace and a tiny smile appeared on her lips. He tilted his head back, and with his eyes, he followed the wooden trim near the ceiling to the closest wall and then toward the hallway. *Nice craftsmanship.* The house easily outsized their own place, but it was not as grand

129

as Noah had anticipated, based on the king's dwelling in Havil. Other than a couple of small woven tapestries on the front wall, the space was rather bare.

"So tomorrow is when we get Garun's family?" Emzara asked.

Noah's focus returned to his wife. "That's the plan, unless Tubal-Cain has something else in mind." A faint, yet familiar voice from outside arrested his attention, but he furrowed his brow when it was joined by an unrecognized female voice. "Speaking of Tubal-Cain, I think he's back, but it doesn't sound like he's alone."

The woman's words grew louder as she neared the house, and Emzara stiffened. "That's not Naamah, is it?"

Noah placed a reassuring hand on her knee and shook his head. "Doesn't sound like her."

A couple of rapid knocks hit the door before it opened. "I'm back." Tubal-Cain stepped inside and located Noah and Emzara in the meeting room. "I didn't plan on bringing someone with me, but if anyone can help us, she can." Tubal-Cain held his hand out and welcomed his guest into the room.

"Hello, Noah. It's been a long time." The woman pulled the wrap away from her head and let it drop down her back, revealing her long black hair. Her face was oval with pronounced cheekbones, giving her a refined and dignified appearance. A lone freckle graced her left cheek.

Noah stood and leaned forward as he struggled to recognize her. "Hello, it's good —"

Emzara leapt to her feet. "I've seen you before. You sat in front of me at that ceremony."

The woman smiled at Emzara. "Yes, I remember you." She spoke in low tones, even and confident. "You were the pretty girl looking around for your husband." She dipped her head toward Noah. "It looks like you've found him."

Emzara grabbed Noah's arm. "I did." She released Noah and stepped toward their guest. "We were never introduced. I'm Emzara."

The woman tilted her head forward slightly. "And I'm Adah. It's very nice to meet you."

Adah? Noah shot a look at Tubal-Cain. "Adah? Queen of Havil?"

She sighed. "Please, just call me Adah. There's no need for formalities here."

Tubal-Cain closed the door and held a hand toward Adah. "She's my father's second wife."

Noah raised his eyebrows as he stared at Tubal-Cain.

The blacksmith held up a palm. "Don't worry, we can trust her."

"Tubal-Cain has told me briefly why you three are here." She blinked twice and opened her mouth as if to say something else, but then closed it.

Emzara brushed Noah's forearm reassuringly and looked at Adah. "Can I get you some water?"

"No, thank you, dear, I'm fine."

Noah and Emzara returned to their spots on the bench while Tubal-Cain moved two chairs across from them.

Once everyone was seated, Tubal-Cain gestured to Adah. "She'll be staying here for a few days just as if she were on a small retreat, and I've asked Kenter, her personal guard and my friend to keep watch. We haven't had a chance yet to talk many specifics, but I think you'll find what she has to say interesting. Adah?"

"So you want information on Lamech?" She placed her hands elegantly in her lap, all emotions masked.

"Why don't you start with what you noticed when he got back," Tubal-Cain said.

Sitting perfectly upright, Adah said, "He was a little frustrated about your council rejecting his trade proposal, but he didn't seem all that upset — not nearly as angry as I would have expected since things didn't go his way. Usually when he's rebuffed, he completely loses his temper." She glanced at the floor. "I thought he might've calmed down on the long trip, but Kenter told me something else."

"What was that?" Emzara asked.

"It seems that Lamech bragged to Zillah — Tubal-Cain's mother — that he'd carried out a bit of revenge before leaving the city."

Noah moved to the edge of his seat and his heartbeat raced. Aware of the pain rekindling in both him and Emzara, Noah pushed onward. He needed to know. "Did he specify what that revenge was?"

Adah took a deep breath and let her gaze drift toward the ceiling. "He killed two people, a troublemaker and someone else who was just in the way."

Tubal-Cain sat up straighter. Obviously, this was news to him, too.

131

Emzara put a hand to her mouth and tears filled her eyes. "Oh, Baba."

Noah embraced her, and his neck and head grew hot. He had expected a stream of emotions if he discovered the identity of the murderer, but he was not prepared for the anger that flooded his mind. He imagined the king slipping into Ara's house with a team of guards to carry out their attack. Closing his eyes, he breathed deeply and focused his thoughts on Adah. "Those people were my best friend and my father-in-law."

"How could you marry such a monster?" Emzara glared at Adah.

Adah shook her head softly, saying nothing. Finally she offered Emzara a sympathetic expression. "I'm sorry to hear it was your father." She turned to Noah. "And your friend."

"How?" Emzara buried her head in her hands.

"It's not what you think." Adah rubbed her forehead and looked down. "I didn't have a choice. I already had a family. One night, a group of raiders attacked our village. They killed all the men, including my son. And I still don't know what happened to my daughters. They were tied up and led away. I assume they were sold into slavery."

Noah held his head in his hands and shuddered. "Did you get your daughters back? How did you meet Lamech?"

"He led the group that attacked the village."

Emzara's jaw dropped momentarily. "And you married him?"

Noah winced at her tone, and the queen's eyes flared with long-simmering anger. "Not all weddings come from love. I was forced to marry him. It was marry him or die." Adah's gaze slid out of focus, and she stared blankly at the wall behind them. "At that point, my only thought was to stay until I could find out what happened to my girls. But my plans changed when I gave birth to twins." She gave a bitter laugh, and Noah's heart clenched as he recognized a strong sense of resignation and self-loathing that he had recently caught glimpses of in Emzara.

When Adah continued, her smooth voice had changed, carrying a hiss of rage as she spat out the words of her story. "And I've hated nearly every moment of it. If it weren't for my boys, I would've run long ago. But I'm afraid of what they'll become with him as their father." She sighed. "Oh, what I wouldn't give to be free of him." Her voice grew quieter. "He even bragged about murdering the young man."

Noah felt his heartbeat quicken. "Excuse me. Did you say that he bragged about killing a young man?"

She nodded. "Isn't that what I mentioned earlier?"

"No." Noah shook his head. "You said it was a troublemaker and someone who got in the way."

Adah lifted her head in understanding. "Oh, well yes, the troublemaker was the young man. Kenter specifically told me that Lamech boasted about killing a young man who had injured him. I didn't know what he was talking about because he didn't have any injuries when he came back."

Emzara's eyebrows scrunched together as she faced Noah and mouthed, "What?"

"Are you sure?" Noah asked.

"That's what Kenter said."

Emzara's gaze flicked from Noah to Adah and back again to Noah. She spoke softly. "So Baba wasn't the target."

"No, that would mean that Aterre was," Noah said. "But what did he . . ."

Adah leaned in and tilted her head to one side. "What did you just say?"

"I was just confused because we were sure my father-in-law was targeted, but it sounds like they were after my friend instead."

"Yes, but what did you call your friend?"

"His name was Aterre."

Adah sank back in her chair. "I thought that's what you said." She forced a smile. "I haven't heard that name in a long time. That was my son's name too."

Noah's mouth dropped open as memories tore through his mind. *Aterre's village was attacked and so was Adah's. His mother and sisters were taken. Aterre slashed the face of the man who grabbed him, and Lamech has a huge scar on his face. And Aterre's accent was the same as Adah's.*

Noah steadied himself and turned to Adah. "When you first met Lamech, did he have that scar on his face?"

Adah drew back at the strange question. "No, it was a fresh wound." She paused and her lower lip quavered. "What are you saying?"

Noah trembled as he took in a breath through his mouth. "My best friend was also your son."

Sobs rocked the queen's body. All of her austere mannerisms fled. "No!"

Tubal-Cain paused before putting a hand on her shoulder, but Emzara hurried around the low table between the bench and the chairs and knelt beside Adah, reaching for the older woman.

The queen bent down and welcomed Emzara's embrace. She composed herself after several moments and faced Noah. "So Aterre survived the night our village was attacked?" She dried her cheeks with the shoulder portion of her gown. "How did he ever run into you since you live so far away?"

Noah thought back to his first encounter with Aterre and smiled. As Emzara held Adah's hand in support, Noah recounted some of his favorite memories with Aterre, with Tubal-Cain and Emzara adding details along the way, and the queen laughed and wept throughout.

When Noah finished talking about Aterre's relationship with Jitzel, Adah said, "I'm so glad to know that he escaped that night and met all of you. As you said, he always was full of mischief. Did he ever mention us?"

"He always wondered what had happened to you and his sisters," Noah said. "In fact, after his wedding, he was planning to come here to look for you. He even asked the king about help . . ." Noah clenched his jaw and slammed his fist on the table.

"What is it?" Emzara asked.

Noah's breathing increased and his face flushed. "That's how Lamech figured it out." Noah pointed at Adah. "Aterre asked about his mother and sisters at the council meeting. The king even talked about recognizing his accent."

Having recomposed herself, Adah held onto her placid, stately demeanor, but her shaking hand reached to clutch Emzara's.

Noah scrambled to his feet and paced the room. "What a wicked . . ." He grabbed a cushion and threw it against the wall and yelled in anger. "He needs to pay for what he's done."

He turned back to the women to find Emzara staring at him with wide, sympathetic eyes. Tubal-Cain moved toward the door and waved his hand to instruct Noah to join him. "Let's get some air. I have an idea."

Noah followed Tubal-Cain a short distance from the house. The cool, fresh air greeted his lungs, and he took it in greedily. Suspended just above the treetops ahead of him, the nearly whole moon lit up the evening. The dew-drenched grass soaked Noah's feet as he walked. "So what's your plan?"

Tubal-Cain stopped and faced Noah. "The annual Serpent ceremony is in two days. What if we told the crowd that my father murdered two innocent people in Iri Geshem?"

"How would we do that?" Noah pointed to the house. "Emzara won't let me go near the city."

Tubal-Cain stroked his beard. "I can do it. I could interrupt the beginning of the ceremony. I'm sure the people would be surprised to see me and allow me to speak for a few moments."

"You would openly stand against your father?" Noah crossed his arms. "I appreciate your desire to expose his evil deeds, but you might end up dead too."

"I don't think it would happen."

"Why not?" Noah asked.

"Because I think the crowd would turn against him if they knew what he was really like."

"And what if they didn't?"

Tubal-Cain blew out a breath. "That's a risk I'm willing to take."

"You need to think about Adira now, too. What would she do without you? And what do you think she'd do to me if I came home without you?"

"She'd probably kill you." Tubal-Cain slapped Noah's shoulder. "See, it's a good plan."

Noah laughed and sensed some of his anger settle. "Do you really think the people of Havil care what he did? They seemed quite willing to follow him the last time I was here."

"Yeah, but not if they knew what kind of man he really is. They believe that he's just a man who helped expand their city, but I don't think they would put up with him murdering innocent people — especially when they find out he killed the son of his second wife."

"I know I wouldn't follow him." Noah stared at the ground. "It still seems quite risky."

"That's because it is." Tubal-Cain adjusted his wrap. "But do you have any better ideas?"

Noah tried to come up with another strategy to turn the people against the king. "Are there others who would stand with you?"

"You mean besides you?" Tubal-Cain chuckled but let it fade when Noah remained quiet. "I know this is serious. You and Zara don't have to take part. I'm sure we'd have the support of the guards Garun talked about, along with Adah. And I've got several friends in the city who would join us and tell others too."

"I don't think Emzara and I can lose another friend right now."

"Look, maybe this will work, maybe it won't. But I've got to try something. As much as I'd like to deny it, he's family and so I'm partly responsible. I may be the only one who can stop his evil influence."

"What if this crazy plan of yours succeeds, then what? Would you take over as king?"

Tubal-Cain drew back. "Whoa. I never even thought of that. I don't have any interest in ruling." He rubbed a hand over his eyes, thinking it through. "I'd probably appoint a group of trustworthy elders to run the city."

Noah sat on a nearby stump. "Look, we still have a day to think this over. It'll give us something to do on the way to Garun's."

Tubal-Cain took the spot next to Noah. "That's right. I almost forgot about that. If we do this, I'll need to go into the city again tomorrow, and you can go to Garun's."

"Okay. Obviously, I'd like to see what Em thinks."

"Definitely. I'm open to other ideas, too." He looked in the direction of Havil. "We just need to be careful who hears about it. I don't think my father would go easy on anyone conspiring against him."

Noah looked over his shoulder at the house. "Maybe Adah will have some ideas. She certainly doesn't seem to care for your father. I'd imagine she's contemplated turning against him."

Tubal-Cain nodded. "Let's find out."

CHAPTER 19

Noah dodged a large puddle in the trail, but his foot slipped on the soft ground, nearly causing him to fall. Gathering his balance, he scraped some of the mud from the side of his sandal by wiping it in the tall grass that grew alongside the path.

Pausing atop a small rise, Noah studied the route Tubal-Cain had indicated before they parted moments earlier and then surveyed his surroundings. Behind him, the waves of the sea continued their endless ebb and flow. Far to his left, dark rainclouds hovered over Havil as the sun peeked through a tiny gap. On the horizon beyond the city, a single column of smoke rose from one of the high hills. Noah did a double-take. *That's strange. I've never seen a fire emit such a tall plume before. I hope it doesn't come any closer to Havil.* His skin tingled with the memory of the intense heat and smoke during the blaze in the Zakari's barn. He shuddered and took a deep breath, remembering the burning pain in his lungs.

Between him and the strange smoke cloud, the palace climbed above the surrounding buildings, and for the first time, Noah noticed a variety of trees on the building's roof. For a moment he marveled at the architectural prowess that could create such a building. Then his gaze moved on to another edifice. Standing nearly as tall and wide as the king's home, rose a building that Noah guessed to be the House of Knowledge. At the sight, his wonder gave way to a stab of anxiety. *Creator, please protect Tubal-Cain in the city today.*

A warm breeze from the west drew his eye to the lighter-colored clouds rolling in and offered Noah hope that his garment would dry quickly. He faced into the wind toward the wider road he and Tubal-Cain traveled that morning. Thoughts of Emzara prompted a smile to spread across his face. She had risen before anyone else to prepare firstfeast, and by the time Noah and Tubal-Cain left, she was heavily engrossed in a conversation with Adah. *I'm glad Em has someone to keep her company today.*

Noah moved down the narrow path as it meandered past a handful of farms, through a small meadow, and then entered a grove of trees. A couple of bushy-tailed rodents scurried about before him, while a scattering of chirps, peeps, and squawks filled the air. A buzzbird zipped past his head and hovered over some blossoms to his right. The tiny radiant bird mesmerized him as it flitted quickly from one blossom to the next. *I wonder if planting some of those flowers at home would attract buzzbirds.*

Just as Tubal-Cain had mentioned, the trail split near the far edge of the grove. Noah followed the path to the right and marched purposefully toward the house directly ahead. Nestled between two of the rolling hills and shaded by several tall trees, the large, sturdy-looking wooden home featured two levels and an attached shed. Smoke curled out of the stone chimney running up the near side. *This must be the place.*

Noah checked his wrap's inner pocket and then turned onto a thin trail that led to the front door. He ascended two short steps and knocked. Unsure if he had rapped the door hard enough, Noah waited a moment and then reached to hit it again but stopped at the sound of faint footsteps approaching from the inside. A small rectangular portal, just under Noah's eye level, slid open from the inside.

"Can I help you?" a woman's voice asked.

Noah stooped and met her gaze through the slot. "Yes, my name is Noah, and I'm a friend of Garun, a palace guard of Havil. Is this his home?"

The woman eyed him warily. "It is, but he's not able to talk to you right now."

Noah bowed his head respectfully. "I know. He's across the sea in Iri Geshem, my hometown, and he sent me here with a message for you." He pulled a small scroll from his pocket and, mushing it slightly, slid it through the opening. "Here."

Still peering through the tiny slit in the door, he watched as she took the missive and slipped the rope off one end. After unrolling it, she quickly skimmed its message. "How can I be sure it's really from him? This isn't his handwriting."

"He said he doesn't write well and asked me to do it for him. He knew you'd know it was from him if you read the back."

She turned the page over and her eyes brightened. "Just a moment." The small window closed and after a few scraping and clicking sounds, the door opened. The woman waved Noah inside. "Quickly, come in."

Noah entered the house and she shut the door behind him. The fireplace to his left highlighted a rather plain sitting room. The dining area lay beyond it and a wooden ladder to his right led to the second floor.

"Welcome to our home, Noah." The woman nodded slightly before pushing her dark hair behind her shoulders. Her small face supported a tall forehead, with thin eyebrows, small eyes, upturned nose, and firm lips all spaced compactly. "I'm Laleel, Garun's wife. I guess being married to a palace guard makes me a little wary."

"I understand." Noah placed his hand to his chest and smiled. "I'm sure your husband would be glad to know that you're careful."

Gesturing to a low bench near the fireplace, she said, "Please, have a seat. I'll be right back."

Noah thanked her as she shuffled from the room. He sat where she had indicated and stretched out his legs.

Laleel soon returned with a clay vessel and handed it to him. "Have some water."

"Oh, that's very kind." He took a drink and delighted in the coolness it brought to his mouth and throat.

She held up the note and her brown eyes lit up to match her smile. "Thank you for bringing word from my husband. It's a pleasure to meet you in person. Garun told me about the man that rejected the king's daughter." Laleel's shoulders drooped and she frowned. "It breaks my heart to see how that girl's turned out. She had so much potential, but she's too much like her father."

Eager to change the subject, Noah asked, "So what do you think of the message from Garun?"

"He wants me to bring the family to Iri Geshem with you right away?" She gave him a shrewd look. "What's the hurry? Are we in danger?"

Noah glanced around. "I assume it's safe to speak here."

She slid onto a seat across from him and fixed her gaze on his face. "Yes, it's just me and my girls, and they're in the barn feeding the animals."

"There's nothing to worry about right now. But Garun fears that Havil may soon become too dangerous for followers of the Creator, and he isn't sure how safe it'll be for him to be around the palace anymore."

Laleel leaned back and crossed her arms over her chest. "Yes, we thought this day might come, but I didn't think it'd be so soon. What happened?"

Noah closed his eyes, regret and pain washing over him again. "The king murdered my father-in-law and my best friend." He turned away. "If you don't mind, I'd rather not talk about it in further detail."

Suddenly, the floor vibrated, causing Noah and Laleel to exchange glances. The clay vessel nearly fell to the floor, but Noah grabbed it just before it slipped off the bench. The surface and walls creaked and groaned as the gentle shaking continued for a few moments.

"What's that?" Noah asked. "I don't remember that happening when I was in Havil before."

"I'm not sure, but it's happened a few times this past week." Laleel scanned the room, her shoulders hunched. "I'm really sorry to hear about your loved ones. When do we need to be ready to leave?"

"We have some business to attend to tomorrow evening and plan to leave right after that."

"Business? At the ceremony?"

Noah hesitated. He did not plan to discuss the ceremony, but it seemed Garun's wife's mind was as sharp as her eyes. "It looks that way."

"Garun hates going to those awful events."

"I don't blame him. Once was enough for me."

"And yet you plan to go back?" Laleel asked.

The muscles in Noah's jaw tightened. "We have some unfinished business. It's probably best if you don't know."

She pursed her lips. "I see. Well, if Garun trusts you, I trust you." She stood at the sound of a door opening beyond the dining area. "But there's a slight problem with his instructions."

"And what's that?"

She looked toward the other room. "Come in here, all of you."

Three young girls entered. Noah guessed the oldest was close to Misha's age. The two smaller ones were at least ten years younger, although they looked quite different from the taller girl with a lighter brown complexion. "I thought Garun said he had two daughters at home."

"That's the problem. We now have three." She smiled at the older girl and spun to face Noah. "Will you have room for all of us on the boat?"

"Of course." He found it difficult to look away from the eldest girl; she reminded him of someone, but he could not decide who it was. Her face was turned down, but beneath her long, straight black hair, he saw her delicate countenance. The edges of her eyes trailed back, running parallel along her high cheekbones. Her long lashes lay softly against her skin, and her wide nose protruded only slightly from her face.

Laleel held out a hand and the older girl joined her while avoiding eye contact with Noah. Putting a hand on the shy girl's shoulder, Laleel said, "This is Zedakal, and she just joined our family this week."

Noah raised an eyebrow. "I don't understand."

Laleel flicked her wrist toward the younger girls. "Please go out to the barn for a little while." Once they had gone, she said, "The king's daughter recently implemented a program where they take girls of Zedakal's age, and they prepare them to serve as prostitutes for Nachash."

Laleel's scowl was so fierce that Noah almost wished Naamah were there to face it. Here was a woman who could stand up to the princess, if ever there was one. Zedakal, however, stood with her head down. Her shoulders gave a slight shiver as she buried her face in her hands.

Noah scrunched his nose and averted his gaze at the thought of the horrors she'd possibly faced, understanding now why she shrank from him and clung to Garun's wife. "Naamah is doing this? She needs to be stopped."

"And just how would you do that?" Laleel asked.

Some of the bluster went out of him. "I don't know," he admitted. He looked at Zedakal. "How did you escape?"

As the girl remained silent, Laleel hugged her. "She ran away a few nights ago. I found her curled up in a corner of our barn." She raised her small chin. "I don't intend to let anything else happen to her."

Noah imagined Garun's pride in his wife's actions. "But what about the family she was taken from? Shouldn't you return her to them?"

141

Zedakal shook her head rapidly and her hair flew about in cascades, like a melad shaking its mane.

"No," Laleel said. "She was a slave. They all were — all the girls that the king's daughter took for this program. I imagine they have people looking for her even now. And that's the reason I was suspicious of you when you came to the door."

Speechless, Noah slowly shook his head and clenched his fist. Sadness mingled with anger until the line between them blurred.

"Zedakal is free now." Laleel lifted the girl's chin and stroked her cheek. "I'd like her to come with us to Iri Geshem, if she is willing."

Zedakal nodded her head and then buried it in Laleel's shoulder.

Laleel gave a tiny smile. "It looks like you'll need to make room for four of us on the boat."

"Gladly."

"We'll be ready to travel tomorrow." Garun's wife held up a palm. "Where would you like us to meet you?"

"I'll return here to help you," Noah said. "Then you can just come with me."

Laleel glanced around the room and shrugged. "That won't be necessary. The girls and I can manage."

"Are you sure?"

She nodded. "It won't take us long. Just tell us where to go."

"Well, ironically, we're staying at the king's beach home. It's a rather long walk down the western road."

Laleel's eyes grew wary. "The king's? Why would you possibly be there?"

"I came here with Tubal-Cain — he's a friend." Noah held out a hand to reassure her. "He isn't like his father or sister at all. He follows the Creator."

Laleel raised her eyebrows. "That's encouraging. I wish he were ruling in place of his father."

"I agree," Noah said. "Maybe someday Havil will be a different place." He considered Zedakal, who darted her glance away when she saw him looking at her. "For now, though, we'd be better off almost anywhere but here."

CHAPTER 20

"Open up." Naamah's commanding voice resonated from outside the locked door of Adah's room. Clutching the light wooden box to herself and trying not to think about the contents, Emzara spun and looked wildly at Adah. Her new friend motioned to a curtained balcony to the right of her massive bed. After ducking behind the fabric, Emzara crouched down.

Thankful for the height of the railing on the third-level terrace, Emzara stayed low and glanced at her surroundings. Other than a low table, a few benches, and several poles with unlit oil lanterns hanging from them, the balcony held few furnishings. A heavy curtain that hung over the columned entryway back into the room was on her right. That and a large potted plant against the railing were the only means of concealment should Naamah come out here. Her heart pounded. *What are we doing? It all seemed so simple when Adah and I talked in the comfort of the beach home. This isn't simple anymore.*

The holes in the box next to her were necessary, but she hoped they were small enough to keep the contents inside. She shuddered, thinking about how close she had cradled the container against her body. She gently moved it an arm's length away and focused on the conversation inside.

"So this time, you and my mother are to be seated at the top of the main platform, one on either side of Nachash's statue. Da wants everyone to see that his queens are just as involved as his daughter is. Now, here's the order of the ceremony."

Emzara let her thoughts about what had led to this situation drown out Naamah's voice. Was it only this morning that Noah left for Garun's family? And now it must be beyond the time for midmeal. She hoped her insides would remember the few smaller items that she and Adah purchased to munch on as they traveled through the city. A grumbling stomach would be as good as a gong with Naamah standing so close.

Angry footsteps paced inside the large room just beyond her, and she clutched at her knees in an effort to make herself smaller. *Get it together, girl. You'll be in a far scarier place tonight.* Her tense muscles persisted until she reassured herself that Naamah seemed to have no intentions of coming outside.

She rested her head against the curtain, pushing it into the pillar behind it and thought back to the morning. She and Adah had bonded instantly over their shared anguish of losing close family. Adah's ability to understand the loss of a child acted as a balm to Emzara's grieving spirit. However, it was not long until their sorrows were overtaken by another emotion. The words between them repeated in her mind as clearly as when they had first been spoken.

"It's not fair that he can just get away with something that hurt us so badly."

"I know." Adah looked down and twisted a thick bangle on her wrist.

"I just wish there was more we could do."

"Like what?"

"Well he took the life of your son. He took the life of my father, and I hold him responsible for the death of my child as well. He deserves more than humiliation tomorrow."

Adah spoke their thoughts aloud. "He should die so that other lives can be spared from his evil."

Emzara nodded. "Yes. But . . ."

A loud slap broke Emzara's reverie. "I don't care that you're the queen. You will not speak to me like that. And yes, you will wear this special garment that was made especially for tomorrow. The seer demands it." She barely heard the faint sound of cloth hitting the stone floor.

"The seer!" Adah's scornful tone rang out. "I will not take orders from him. Even if you try to hit me again." Suddenly the queen's voice softened. "Naamah, I know you and I have always been at odds, and I understand why. But I can't help but be concerned for you. I don't like how you've changed under his influence. He's leading you into some very dark places. You're no longer the happy, beautiful girl I'd occasionally see around this place. You're angry now and too hungry for power. It's going to come back to bite you someday."

Ironic choice of words, Adah.

"You're just envious because my father replaced you with me as first in his affections. And yes, you'll wear this because I'm in charge of the celebration." A chair scooted on the floor.

"We'll see about that. Don't bother me again."

"Oh, I have no intention to. Besides, I thought you were supposed to be at the beach house until tomorrow."

"That was my plan, but I remembered that I'd invited a few ladies to the palace and will be entertaining them for dinner tonight in the main hall."

"Then I'll just inform Da not to concern himself with you tonight. And I'll make sure mother looks her finest." Emzara pictured the flash in Naamah's green-flecked brown eyes. Shaking her head, Emzara knew that comment did not hurt Adah as intended. The door slammed shut.

Moments later, Adah made her way outside and leaned back against the solid stonework that lined the balcony. "Are you okay?" She kept her voice low and her head level. Concern filled her eyes, but anyone seeing her from the town below would just see the back of her head and assume she was alone, enjoying the fresh air.

"Yes, but I'm concerned for you. Did Naamah slap you?"

Adah placed a hand softly on her own cheek. "Yes, but that's not important now. Let's discuss our plan."

"I still can't believe that all just happened."

"I know, but it actually helps us. Now, Naamah will inform Lamech that I'm here and that I have visitors tonight. I'll stay on one of the couches in the main hall, and it'll look like I fell asleep where I was after a long night of hosting."

"But will that really make you above all suspicions?"

"I'll be surrounded by well-respected ladies and several guards all night. There's no way I could legitimately be blamed for anything that happens up here."

As she pondered Adah's words, Emzara stared past her, noticing the beautiful scenery beyond the southern edge of the city for the first time.

Rolling green hills stretched as far as she could see. The telltale patterns of crops interspersed with small patches of wooded areas blanketed each rise. Straight in front of her, a path, wide enough for at least two large wagons to pass each other unhindered, extended from the city wall and divided the landscape in two. Smaller trails broke off from the road, connecting the small farms dotting the countryside.

"Are they still in there?" Adah stared at the box.

Emzara nodded.

"Good. Stay in here until after you hear that his room is empty. If I know Lamech at all, once he hears from his daughter about the ladies I'm hosting, he'll be sure to look his finest before joining us for evenfeast."

"How will I know when it's clear?"

"Don't worry. Because our rooms are adjoining, it's easy to hear any commotion in there." She rolled her eyes in contempt. "And it can get noisy since he makes a grand deal out of even the simplest things."

"That's when I slip into his room?" Emzara asked.

"I don't think so. That's too risky."

"But he deserves to die."

"And I'd rather you didn't. You can hide in here. In fact, come with me." Adah reentered her room. Emzara "walked" forward on her knees, using one hand to keep her skirt from getting tangled, and carefully holding the package away from her body with the other. She stood up once she was inside and the curtain had fallen back in place.

"What are you thinking?" After setting the box on a side table, she arranged some scrolls that had been lying there to partially cover it.

"Here — where is it?" Adah rifled through several long and expensive cloths hanging on hooks. "Ah." She held up a length of cloth the same tawny color as a young bovar. "This is similar to what our servant girls wear. Let's wrap it around you, so that if someone discovers you, they'll think you're one of my maids tidying up in here."

"So I stay here, but what about . . ."

"You'll hear when the king makes it back to his chambers." She walked over to an ornate wooden door to the right of her main entrance and placed her hand on it. "This leads to his room. When you open it, you'll see a little hallway only about six cubits in length, and on his side there's a thin golden tapestry. It's slightly transparent so don't have any lamps lit in here."

"So I wait until all is still and then carefully open this door. Sounds easy enough. Then I'll just crawl and release the contents before coming back here and making sure this door is shut tight."

Adah nodded. "I certainly don't want any of those things to get in here."

"Adah, what if what Naamah said was true? What if her mother comes back with the king?"

Adah shrugged, "I'd be very surprised if that happened. Naamah was trying to upset me, but the king's affections shifted away from Zillah after I arrived."

Later, as Emzara sat in the darkness listening intently for any movement in the adjacent room, her mind raced through memories of her father and Aterre. She placed a hand on the box and imagined the movement inside, aware of the calamity these creatures could deliver. *Am I no better than Lamech? Willing to kill someone just because they wronged me?* She shook her head emphatically, changing the direction of her thoughts. *Don't back down now. There's no comparison. Aterre was only defending himself, and Lamech killed him and Baba for it. A serpent bite is a fitting end for the king. And besides, I'm not really the one killing him.*

Her breath snagged in her throat as she heard the unmistakable confident tread of the king entering his room. He behaved just as Adah described. *You think you're so powerful; well you're no match for the Creator. Most High* — she immediately and instinctually leapt into prayer, but for some reason, she just couldn't ask Him for help. *I guess I'm in this alone.* She sighed internally but then shifted her focus back to her task. *Sounds like the king is alone too. Good.*

After everything grew silent, she waited for what seemed like eternity. Taking a deep breath, she silently opened the door and took hesitant, soundless steps toward the tapestry. She held onto her precious cargo of death, before laying it on the floor. She lifted the lid and slipped back into the hallway.

CHAPTER 21

They're gone. They're gone. The refrain played repeatedly in her mind as Emzara ducked around a massive needle tree a good distance from the palace. Immense relief rushed through her at not having the box of serpents close by anymore. The thought of having them as her companions for most of the day caused her to shudder.

Although the thick cloud cover kept her hidden from the moonlight as she wound her way through the streets of Havil, it posed other complications. *Let's see, I've passed the big needle tree, so the twisted post is the next landmark.* On their way to the palace in the morning, she took note of things that stood out every so often to aid her on the way back. But the darkness made everything look different. As she veered left, the misshapen tree trunk on the corner of the lot came into view. The shadowy form of an oil lantern still perched atop the odd structure, but as she had suspected, it was not being used.

I wonder how successful Noah was in his errand today. He and Tubal-Cain are probably back already and wondering where I am. She trembled with her whole body, feeling very alone in the darkness. After all her actions of the day, would she still feel alone after she returned to Noah? *Will he be angry? Or will he understand?* Her palpitations continued as she spotted the small grave mound on the edge of someone's property, showing her she was on the right track. A strange sensation coursed through her. Her whole body vibrated again, but this was different than the shivering. *It's like the whole ground is trembling with me.* When the eerie tremors passed Emzara increased her pace.

After what seemed to be the length of a couple night watches, she finally picked her way through the trees and brambles at the edge of the royal beach home. Light from within flickered and danced its way outside the window, giving her a small measure of comfort. Thankful to be back, she also dreaded the explaining that needed to be done. Taking a deep breath, she slowly eased her way through the door and right into a face full of dark textured fabric. She clung to Noah and returned his fervent embrace.

"Are you alright? Where have you been?"

Guilt slithered through her at the fear in her husband's voice. "I'm fine." She gulped, hoping to calm her voice with the next sentence. "I had an errand to run with Adah. I didn't realize it would take so long."

Noah guided her to the sitting area outside of the kitchen then held her on his lap. Clinging to him, she savored the comfort of his nearness and feared that this might be their last moment of closeness after he found out what she had done. He turned her slightly so she nearly faced him and cupped her face in his strong hands.

"I've been so worried about you. Where could you have possibly gone that would have you getting back so long after the deepest dark? And like this too." He brushed at her cheek and a bit of caked dirt landed in her lap.

His touch stung, and she figured that she probably cut herself on the journey back. Fidgeting, she eased her face from his hold and tucked herself under his chin, nestling against him. "I'll tell you," she said just above a whisper, "but please don't interrupt."

Slowly she recounted her day, her chin lowering with each revelation. Hearing their plan aloud and in Noah's presence made her recoil within herself. As penance, she held nothing back, forcing herself to tell him each horrible detail, not even trying to rationalize it as she had before.

"So Lamech is likely dead?" he interrupted for the first time, as she neared the end of her account.

She met his eyes for a moment before dropping her gaze. "I . . ."

She sensed his head turn away. "You murdered the king?"

"What? No, I couldn't go through with it." She gripped the front of his tunic. "I was there, crouched behind the tapestry in his room, the box of serpents in my possession. I pulled the lid off and stole out of the room, but then something came over me. I just couldn't do it, so I snuck

149

back in and covered the box, thankful that the creatures were still in it." She shuddered, waiting for his verdict.

His eyes flashed with an unreadable expression before he pulled her close, squeezing the breath out of her.

She relaxed in his arms, wishing to stay this way forever.

Finally, he sighed. "I'm so glad you're back safely. And I can't tell you how . . . how . . ." He paused and his lower lip quivered. "How glad I am that you didn't let those serpents loose."

"Me too." As she lay there against him, the day's troubles started to fade away, and she savored the rest that they found in each other.

"What made you stop?" he finally asked.

"Two things." She toyed with the embroidered edge she had sewn on the folds of cloth by his neck. "No matter how much he hurt us, and no matter how much I think he deserves to die, I was never entirely comfortable with the idea Adah and I came up with. Eventually, I saw how in my anger and desire for retribution, I was willing to become just like Lamech. Obtaining vengeance would probably feel good, like Adah said, but could I really live with myself knowing I'd murdered a man? Would you ever look at me the same way again? Would you even want to see me?"

He brushed a finger softly over her bottom lip. "And the other thing?"

"I — I tried to pray to the Creator, and it was the first time I ever remember Him feeling so distant. I couldn't seem to reach out to Him. That's when I caught a glimpse of the future if I carried it out." She blinked back tears and verbalized the question at the front of her thoughts. "Do you hate me?"

He kissed the tip of her nose. "Never."

"But what I tried to do was so wrong."

"Yeah," he pulled her head close against his chest. "But it wasn't just you."

"Adah certainly was willing to help. And little wonder with her life as it is now, plus hearing about Aterre. But. . . ." Her large eyes focused on him. "But it was my idea. She simply gave assistance in carrying it out." Her cheeks deepened in shame and her words trailed off.

"I love you."

She looked up, almost shocked.

"Remember, the Creator never treats us how we deserve. Think about Greatfather Adam. Before banishing him from Eden, the Most High offered a sacrifice, allowing our first parents to live instead of instantly carrying out the sentence of death." He kissed her on the top of the head. "I'm proud of your courage. And I'm glad you thought about what the Creator would think, and that you chose to follow Him instead of your own way."

Peace washed over her as the last lingering feeling of isolation faded and she lifted her lips to her husband's.

"Do you really have to do that here?"

Tubal-Cain's voice snapped her back to reality and caused her to blush.

"Can't believe you're still up," he said.

"We're just catching up." Noah grinned as he turned to face their friend.

"Is that what you call it?" He returned a wry smile before scooting up a chair. "Well, as long as we're all still awake, I may as well tell you the little that I've found out about the ceremony."

Emzara stayed silent, allowing Tubal-Cain to talk. But at the moment she cared nothing for the ceremony or Lamech or anything else. For the moment she was content to just be in Noah's arms. Still, she couldn't help but listen as their friend recounted his information.

"It's supposed to be bigger than ever, so my father definitely lied to the town council — what a surprise. There'll be a raised platform for invited dignitaries from all over the land, kind of like where you described being seated last time."

Emzara yawned and reclined against Noah. With her eyes shut, a contented smile crossed her lips as he held her, and before long she lost the fight against the slumber and drifted away.

CHAPTER 22

Noah awoke for what seemed to be the tenth time during a fitful night. Lying flat on his back, he yawned and rubbed his eyes. Sunlight pushed its way through the dark cloth covering the small window in their room of the beach home.

He turned his head slowly to face Emzara. If his night was restless, hers was even more so. She had tossed and turned, and twice awakened shaking and rambling about another bad dream. Noah smiled at her now resting peacefully. He sighed as he imagined what life may have been like for them if she had carried out her plan the night before. *Certainly, Lamech deserves to die, but what would the Creator think of Emzara carrying out the murder? And how would Tubal-Cain take it? Lamech's still his father.* He shuddered and thanked the Most High for staying Emzara's hand.

Determined to let her sleep, Noah quietly slipped out of bed and dressed himself before heading to the sitting room. Pulling back the cloth to let in some early morning light, he scanned the room, deciding what to do first. His mind made up, he entered the kitchen and dipped his cup into the bucket of water he'd drawn from the well the night before and then grabbed a handful of nuts and a malid fruit from the table. He chomped into the luscious produce and relished its blend of sweet and tart flavor and crispy texture.

He moved back to the open window and stared at the scenery before him. Surrounded by taller trees, a handful of malid trees grew along the dirt trail to the house, and several birds stalked under them in the grass looking for a morning meal. Dozens of colorful flowers had just begun to open their petals to drink in the sunlight of the day.

"Looks like a beautiful morning."

Noah spun to see Tubal-Cain entering the room. "Morning peace. I didn't know you were up yet." He took a swig of water and set the cup on the front room's table before sitting on the nearby bench.

Tubal-Cain took a seat across from him. "I've been up for a while. I didn't sleep well." He snorted. "I guess you could say that I'm a bit nervous about tonight."

"I would be too." Noah tossed a few nuts into his mouth. "It'd be hard enough to stand up to a king in front of such an audience, but the fact that he's your father . . ." Noah shook his head. "I'll pray that the Creator gives you the courage."

"I appreciate that." Tubal-Cain crossed his arms. "Just be ready to back me up if I need it."

"My husband will be doing no such thing." Her hair braided and wrapped in a twisting fashion around her head, Emzara stood in the doorway and looked at both men.

Noah held out his hand, inviting her to join him.

"I get it, Zara. I know you don't want him in danger. Neither do I."

Noah took her hand and guided her to sit beside him. "I didn't realize you were awake."

"I've hardly slept. I just decided to stop trying." She leaned against him and looked at Tubal-Cain. "If there's going to be trouble, I need to be by his side."

"What are you saying?" Tubal-Cain tilted his head.

"*We* will be there to support you." Emzara put her hand on Noah's chest. "If you need it."

Noah drew back and his eyes narrowed.

"It seems like you haven't run this past Noah yet," Tubal-Cain said.

She chuckled. "I just did." She kissed Noah's cheek. "And what does my handsome husband think of the plan?"

Noah scratched the back of his neck. "I don't want you in danger. . . ."

"And you think I want you in danger?" Emzara asked. "Being separated from you the last time we were here made me feel so helpless. I won't go through that again."

"You didn't let me finish. I don't want you in danger, but if Tubal-Cain's willing to risk his position or even his life to see justice done for your father and Aterre, then the two of us sure better be willing to do the same."

"My thoughts exactly." Emzara grinned. "My intelligence must be rubbing off on you."

Noah snorted and turned to Tubal-Cain. "I guess we're in."

"You realize what you're signing up for, don't you?"

Emzara leaned forward. "Death has been our life recently. And maybe it means nothing, but on our way here, I faced death in a dream about Havil. I say we have nothing to lose."

Noah clasped Tubal-Cain's shoulder. "We're in this together."

A knock at the door caused a round of nervous glances. Tubal-Cain spoke softly. "Are we expecting anyone?"

Noah raised his head as he remembered what day it was. Keeping his voice down, he said, "Garun's family."

The banging on the door started again. "This is the palace guard. Open up immediately."

Emzara shuddered. "What do we do?"

Tubal-Cain smiled broadly. "It's not locked, Kenter. Come on in."

The guard opened the door and entered the house followed by Adah.

Emzara's hand flew to her chest. "You scared me, Kenter. Don't do that again."

"I'm sorry, lady. I was hoping to scare your husband. Noah, it's good to see you again."

Noah let go of Emzara's hand before climbing to his feet. "It's good to see you as well."

"What brings the two of you out here this morning?" Tubal-Cain asked.

The queen stepped in front of the guard, but Emzara spoke first. "I think I know." She stared at the floor. "I'm sorry, Adah. I was right there. Everything was going as planned, and then something deep inside me wouldn't let me do it." She studied the wood grain around her feet.

Adah held her head high, but her eyes remained unfeeling. "I've lived with things the way they've been for so long, I can last a while longer. My situation is not your fault."

Emzara stepped back and wiped a tear from her cheek. "Thank you. But what are you going to do now?"

"I'm not sure." Adah looked at Tubal-Cain. "What are your plans?"

"It's better if you don't know. That way, if things don't go well and my father questions you or Kenter, you can truthfully tell him that you knew nothing about it."

"But you're planning something for tonight's ceremony?" Adah asked.

Tubal-Cain pursed his lips and shrugged.

The queen looked at Noah. "Well?"

Noah copied his friend's response.

Adah sighed. "Thank you for considering my situation, but I'm really . . ." She stumbled and Kenter helped her regain her balance.

Noah steadied Emzara as the room seemed to sway a little side to side. As the wooden structure creaked and groaned, a basket of bread rounds fell off the table in the kitchen. Suddenly, the shaking stopped.

Adah patted Kenter's shoulder. "Thank you. Another one of those rumblers."

Noah scratched his chin. "I felt that yesterday too. What is it?"

"I don't have any idea," Adah said. "They started before the last whole moon, but they're getting stronger and more frequent."

Kenter pointed in the direction of Havil. "I've heard some people say that it's because of that smoking hill on the other side of the city, but I don't know how a hill could make the earth shake."

A true earthshaker. Noah smiled to himself as he thought of the mighty beasts with the same name.

An awkward silence settled over the group until a large animal bellowed outside the house.

Noah spun and looked out the window. A massive lunker that reminded him of Meru tugged a wagon full of crates and baskets up the trail. Garun's wife and the three girls walked ahead of it toward the house. "Garun's family is here." He pointed to Kenter. "Can you open the door?"

Kenter pulled the door and moments later, Laleel entered with her two younger daughters.

"Hello, Kenter," Laleel ducked her head as she greeted him. "I didn't expect to see you here." She hesitated upon seeing the prince. "Tubal-Cain, sir, I barely recognized you with your beard."

"It's good to see you, Laleel." Tubal-Cain spread his arms out wide. "Welcome."

She continued to scan the room and froze when she spotted Adah.

"Do not fear," Adah said. "I will say nothing to the king." She flashed a grim smile. "In fact, I envy you."

Wondering what had become of the runaway slave girl, Noah peeked out the window again. There she stood, petting the large animal on its shoulder, then she turned and walked toward the house.

Laleel introduced her two daughters to the group, who greeted them in turn.

Adah turned and put a foot on the edge of the low table so she could retie the leather straps around her ankle.

"And the newest addition to our family." Garun's wife gestured toward the door, imploring the girl to come in, which she eventually did, with her eyes downcast and her face flushed. Laleel said, "This beautiful young lady is Zedakal."

Adah spun around, and her sandal, which she had not finished securing, slipped off her foot. "Zedakal?"

The girl peeked out from beneath the hair hanging in her face.

Adah slowly approached her and bent down to see her face. "Kal?"

The recently freed slave looked up slowly, her eyes wide. "Mam?"

"Kal!" The queen swept the girl into her arms and held her tight.

"Oh, Mam, I missed you so much," Zedakal said as she returned the embrace.

Shocked, Noah stared at the two. *Mam? This poor girl is Adah's daughter?* Noah smiled and grabbed Emzara's hand as he watched the reunited mother caress her daughter and whisper into her ear. Suddenly, Noah's jaw dropped. "Wait."

"What's wrong?" Emzara asked.

Noah pointed at the queen. "If she's her mother" — he shifted his finger toward the girl — "then that would make her . . ."

Emzara squealed. "Aterre's sister!"

Adah and Zedakal, still hugging, turned in unison, each with ear-to-ear smiles on their faces and tears of joy streaking down their cheeks.

Emzara released his hand and bolted toward the girl.

Zedakal focused on Emzara. "You knew my brother?" she asked as Adah stepped slightly back, still leaving her hand on the girl's arm.

Emzara bit her lip and nodded before reaching out and hugging Zedakal.

156

The girl blinked rapidly. "I don't remember you" — she glanced at Noah — "or him. But I was a lot younger back in the village."

Noah shook his head. "No, we're not from your home. We've known Aterre for the past ten years."

"What? How?" She shook her head as her voice trailed off.

Adah beheld her daughter. "Your brother wasn't killed the night of the attack. He ran far away, and that's how they met him."

"Really? Where is he now?" She frantically looked around the room.

Adah rubbed her eyes. "He was killed recently."

Noah and Emzara explained some of the details about Aterre's life. Along with the others, Noah's emotions ran the gamut from joy and amusement to sorrow and anger.

With tears in her eyes, Zedakal thanked them for the stories. "I'm glad you got to meet him. He used to pick on me and pull my hair, but he helped take care of us when Da left home."

Noah decided not to belabor the fact that Aterre's father abandoned his wife and children, opting instead to keep the focus on happier elements of Aterre's life. "Well, Zedakal . . ."

"You can call me, Kal. Mam always did, and so did Aterre." The sides of her mouth curled up shyly. "He called me lots of other things too."

"Okay, Kal. Well, I couldn't figure it out yesterday, but now I know who you reminded me of." Noah crossed his arms. "You're very much like him. You have the same look in your cheekbones and noses. Your smile is so much like his — well, yours is much prettier — and you have the same accent."

Adah put a hand on Laleel's shoulder. "How did she end up with you? Is she your slave?"

Laleel looked offended. "We don't own any slaves." She nodded to Kal. "Would you tell the story?"

Kal indicated the bench next to Noah. "Do you mind if I sit? I'm a little tired from the long walk."

Noah moved aside. "Please."

Kal sat down as the others gathered around her. She looked at the queen, and at her reassuring nod, began her story. "I was sold into slavery after we were separated. For about eight years, I worked on a farm in the south. My owners weren't too harsh, but it was hard labor. Then a couple years ago, they gave me to a family in Havil to pay off a debt."

She rested her forehead on her hand. "They were terrible people. If something wasn't exactly the way they wanted it, they'd beat me and I wouldn't eat that day. But then it got worse." Looking down at her fingers in her lap, she twisted them nervously and spoke in measured tones as if detached from her own experiences. "The man of the house started to take notice of me. He . . ." She fell silent and leaned against her mother.

Fiery rage spread through Noah's body. He glanced at Tubal Cain, and seeing the tightness in his jaw, Noah knew they both wanted justice to be served on behalf of this young girl.

Kal took in a deep, determined breath. "Anyway, then when the princess started recruiting young women in the city for her new priestess program, I was noticed and taken away to become one of her . . ." Again she stopped.

"One of her what?" Emzara asked.

Like a mother bird protecting her nest, Laleel stepped forward and put a reassuring hand on Kal's bent head. "At the ceremony tonight, Naamah's going to introduce her latest idea. She rounded up over a dozen young women from the city who are going to help her *serve* Nachash."

"What do you mean 'serve'? How?" Tubal-Cain's voice was firm and his eyes narrowed into slits.

"You won't like the answer."

Tubal-Cain folded his arms. "Tell me."

Laleel glanced at the queen, who encouraged her to proceed with a nod. "Naamah will tell the people that the most effective way for them to worship Nachash is to unite with one of her priestesses."

Tubal-Cain's posture turned stiff and rigid. "She's turning them into ritual prostitutes?"

"I'm afraid so," Laleel said, glancing at her two young daughters.

Listening intently, the two girls displayed compassion but no comprehension of Kal's horrors. Their innocent young eyes showed only a sadness that mimicked their friend's reactions.

"What's wrong with her?" Tubal-Cain asked himself before looking directly at Laleel. "Where did you hear this?"

Garun's wife turned to Kal.

"It's true," Kal said. "I was supposed to be one of them, but I was able to sneak away one night."

Tubal-Cain glared at Adah. "Is Naamah really doing this?"

"I think so," the queen said. "I'm not aware of everything going on around that place, but I know she's rounded up a group of young women."

"You were able to sneak out," Tubal-Cain said. "Why didn't any of the other girls go with you?"

"They didn't want to." She looked up at the blacksmith as a tear slipped down her cheek. "We all went from being slaves to being lavished with baths, silken gowns, jewelry, and more food than we'd ever seen. For the first time, we were treated like we were important." She shrugged. "Naamah and a creepy middle-aged man kept telling us what a valued role we were to play in Havil. Most of the girls longed for the chance to feel like they meant something to someone, and to have the princess of Havil telling us that we mattered — it was all very tempting to stay."

"So why did you run?" Noah asked gently.

"Even with all the clothes and food that we could want, it seemed like just another form of slavery, especially when they did this." She slid the wrap up her left shoulder, revealing a sizeable mark similar to the one burned onto Elam's arm. "Plus, I knew that all the comforts in the world wouldn't make up for what was coming." Noah barely caught the whispered last few words as Kal hugged Laleel and buried her face into the woman's open embrace.

"So she ran." Laleel took up the story. "She fell asleep in our barn. The girls found her in the morning, and we took her in." Laleel turned to Adah. "You're her mother and a queen of Havil. Should she stay with you from now on?"

Adah's chin quivered. "I wish she could, but after what Lamech did to Aterre, I can't risk it."

Kal reached out and gripped Adah's garment. "Come with us, Mam."

Adah knelt and hugged her. "I would if I could. But I have two small sons back at the palace. I can't abandon them."

"Then bring them too," Kal said.

"I can't — at least not now. Lamech would never let us go. He would hunt us to the ends of the earth." Adah looked up at Laleel, her eyes wet. "Can she stay with you in Iri Geshem until I can find a way to escape with my boys?"

"Of course," Laleel said. "I'm sure Garun won't mind."

"And we'll help out in any way we can," Emzara said.

Noah grinned and looked into Kal's face. "We'll have to swap more stories of your brother. I have many tales of how his devious ways have gotten me into trouble."

With tears still running down her cheeks, Kal smiled up at him. "Oh, I'd like that." She paused and her eyes twinkled. "And you should know that he always said I was the mischief master."

The whole room erupted into laughter and Noah relished seeing Aterre's good humor and spunk shine through his sister.

CHAPTER 23

"I look ridiculous." Noah peered at his reflection in one of the four fountains built outside the western gate of the city. He fidgeted with the preposterous cap on his head and wondered how anyone could think it was in good taste to wear one. He snorted as he studied the blue paint Adah had put around his eyes. "I'm sure to blend in with the crowd looking like this — as long as it's a crowd of mimicbirds." Running his fingers through the four weeks' growth on his chin, he added, "And I can't wait to shave this beard."

Emzara slid her hand across his lower back and snickered. "I think you look handsome." She stared into the water. "I'm the one that looks ridiculous."

"You're always lovely." Noah pulled her close and grinned playfully. "Even with all those white streaks on your face."

Leaning close to his ear, she said, "Let's make sure we don't start these trends back home."

"There's no chance of that."

As Noah adjusted his outfit, Emzara wrapped the end of her garment over her head and then down around her chin and tucked it in, revealing only her face. They stepped toward the city gate and fell in line with other travelers. Sentries swiftly checked each person, ensuring no weapons entered the city. After passing the guard station, Noah and Emzara soon found themselves shuffling along the main road through the smiths' section of town.

Noah pointed to a window near the top of the palace ahead and to their right. "That's Tubal-Cain's room, and that large shop over there is where I met him."

Emzara squeezed his hand tightly. "I'm afraid that I'll never see him after tonight."

Trying to mask his own concerns, Noah forced a smile. "He'll be fine."

She rolled her eyes a little and her lips curled up. "You're not very convincing. But thank you for trying."

"You're right. I'm nervous too." He held her gaze. "And not just about him. I don't want tonight to be our last few moments together, but if we're doing the right thing, then it's worth dying for."

She brought his hand up to her cheek and closed her eyes. "I'm sorry for bringing it up. Let's try not to think about those things. We're supposed to look like we're glad to be here."

Noah straightened and put an arm over her shoulder. "Let's go."

The crowd thickened as they drew near the large entrance into the massive courtyard. While walking in silence, Noah thought through their plan and wondered if it was the best approach. Their goal was to arrive early and find a spot close enough to the stage to influence the multitude yet far enough back so as to not be identified by Lamech, Naamah, or anyone else who might recognize them. The fact that the sun still hung well above the horizon in front of them indicated plenty of time before the ceremony's start.

Eventually, they spilled into the courtyard and were able to move faster as the throng spread throughout the grounds. Noah and Emzara walked purposefully toward the palace wall on the right, hoping to find a spot beneath where Tubal-Cain planned to appear.

Four guards approached them from the left. Noah turned his head and reached his arm out to stop Emzara. "It's Nivlac," he said under his breath.

Emzara's eyes grew wide, and after hesitating briefly, she bent down to dust off her sandal, keeping her face turned away from the guards.

Noah flinched when one of the soldiers brushed against him as they passed by. He continued to watch them from the corner of his eye until they were out of range. Breathing a sigh of relief, he glanced up at the palace wall. A silhouetted figure moved past the window in Naamah's room, sending a chill down his spine as his mind flashed back to that fateful night four years earlier. "Let's go."

Keeping their heads down, Noah and Emzara picked their way through an ever-thickening mob. Noah occasionally peeped upward to locate Tubal-Cain's designated spot.

"I don't think we're going to get any closer," Emzara said as they met a wall of people.

Noah scooted behind a taller man who would prevent anyone on the stage from spotting him. "This is probably close enough." Nodding toward the corner of the building, Noah said, "He should be right up there."

Noah and Emzara talked quietly as they waited for the ceremony to begin. A loud group of people to their left passed around a small container and they each took turns sniffing the smoking contents inside. The pungent odor invaded Noah's nostrils and momentarily covered the stench of so many bodies packed together on a warm evening. As the sun neared the horizon, Emzara edged up to him and rested her head against his chest.

Noah put an arm around her. With nothing else to do but wait, Noah's thoughts drifted to his precious wife, so he pleaded with the Most High for her safety and thanked Him repeatedly for the treasure she had been to him. *Creator please protect each of us, frustrate Naamah's plans, and expose Lamech as the murderous villain that he is. I pray that the citizens of Havil would seek to follow You.*

Suddenly, the crowd hushed to an eerie silence. In the distance behind him, a slow but steady drumbeat grew in intensity and frequency. To avoid standing out, Noah and Emzara turned around with those nearby and watched the procession. Beginning at the palace entrance, approximately two dozen girls traipsed toward the lone tree in the middle of the courtyard. Half of them wore white silken gowns, and the other half sported yellow garments. Flanking them on either side, musicians played a variety of stringed and metal instruments and drums. The procession turned right at the tree and moved to the center stairway, where the musicians and women in yellow danced and spun their way up the steps while those in white slowly walked between them. Suddenly, they stopped when the first pair of dancers and corresponding musicians reached the next-to-last stair.

The instrumental tones softened and a woman in a long, flowing black gown approached the top of the procession. Her hair stretched high above her head before fanning out like a fountain. White and yellow streaks hid much of her face, but Noah knew exactly who she was. As the crowd cheered, he turned to Emzara with a disgusted look. "Naamah."

Emzara gripped his hand with strength beyond her size.

Naamah's lovely voice rang out, silencing most of the crowd, and the music grew louder. As she sang, the girls in the procession resumed their routine. Each pair bowed low before the princess when they reached the top step before moving to the stage. The young women in white formed a semi-circle behind Naamah, and the others continued dancing as they made two symmetrical lines extending outward from the tips of the semi-circle.

Quiet at first, shouts of disapproval grew sporadically. Noah spun around to find the detractors then leaned to Emzara's ear. "I guess some people don't care for her or her song."

"I wonder what will happen to them," she said.

"Not sure, but this might bode well for Tubal-Cain and us."

After ending her song, Naamah raised her arms and shouted en-thusiastically, "People of Havil. It's my great pleasure to welcome you to another celebration of our great god Nachash."

Someone lit a basin filled with flammable fluid in front of the giant serpent statue. Flames leapt up to illuminate the golden atrocity, drawing loud cheers from the audience.

Once it quieted down, Naamah snapped her fingers, and the girls in white moved closer to her, tightening the semi-circle. "I have a very special announcement to make about these beautiful young women. They've been selected to be the first priestesses to assist you in your worship of Nachash."

She paused as applause erupted from the crowd. "Yes, they are lovely. And for those who desire to devote yourselves wholly to Nachash, you'll have the opportunity to discover just how lovely they are. We've learned that Nachash is pleased when one of his followers engages in an act of sacred union with one of his priestesses."

Emzara leaned close to Noah. "I think I'm going to be sick."

Noah nodded.

Eyes wide, Naamah jerked her head back at the subdued response she received. "Do you not understand what I'm telling you? You'll now have greater opportunities to worship Nachash."

Applause broke out, but it was mixed with a significant amount of jeering, including from several people near Noah and Emzara. They joined the chorus of dissenters.

Naamah held up her hands and laughed haughtily. "Maybe you don't understand what I'm talking about. Give it a chance, and I'm sure you'll see how *special* this opportunity is."

The disapproval sounded louder than the excitement as the mixed responses continued. From somewhere behind them a disgruntled voice yelled. "You stole my slave for this. How is that a special opportunity?"

Noah smiled and looked at Emzara. "I didn't expect this."

Her lips curled up. "I didn't either. Maybe there's hope for this city after all."

Naamah huffed and paced the stage. "Listen to me!" Instantly the crowd quieted. "Apparently, this idea will take a while for you to get used to. Let us move on to the moment you've really been waiting for. People of Havil, please welcome your king." Naamah and all the other young ladies stepped aside to allow Lamech to take Naamah's place in the front of the platform.

Much of the crowd erupted in praise again while Noah searched the corner of the palace above him for any sign of Tubal-Cain.

"My people," Lamech said. "Please welcome your queens, Zillah and Adah."

Four guards carried a richly ornamented throne on which Zillah sat to a place of honor on Lamech's right. On the opposite side, the same procedure was simultaneously done for Adah. In unison, the guards lowered the chairs to the ground.

"People of Havil, we have much to celebrate this evening." Lamech strode to Zillah's chair as he continued. "Our city is thriving, and our House of Knowledge behind me receives new reports every week. This year we'll be sending out more scribes than ever before, and we'll send them even farther."

He paused while the applause roared. "In fact, I just returned from a trip to visit my son and we left a scribe there. So our initiative has already reached north across the vast sea." The king strutted toward Adah's chair next and put his arm on it. "We had a bit of a problem while we were there, but I left them a powerful reminder that they'd better not get in our way."

Noah's insides twisted and he fought to keep his last meal from re-surfacing as he stretched his neck forward and caught a glimpse of a man standing on the parapet above. *Tubal-Cain!*

The king placed a hand on Adah's shoulder. "Adah and Zillah, listen to me; wives of Lamech, hear my words. I have killed a man for wound-ing me, a young man for injuring me." He stepped forward and raised his voice. "If Cain is avenged 7 times, then Lamech 77 times." He raised his arms to the sky. "Yes, this slash on my face was returned 77 times. Hear me! The same thing will happen to anyone who gets in our way!"

As the crowd roared their approval, Noah stood motionless in his shock. *Lamech admitted what he's done and they're cheering. Cheering! Now what do we do?* As the people slowly quieted, a voice above Noah rang out.

"Murderer! The king is a murderer! He slaughtered innocent people!"

Stunned at the audacity of his friend to continue forward with their plan, Noah remained rooted to the ground. Heads spun toward the roof of the palace, and Lamech squinted as he tried to locate the origin of the taunt.

Noah closed his eyes. *Please Creator, protect Tubal-Cain and let the people recognize the truth about Lamech.*

"Guards, seize that man who would dare insult me."

"Murderer! You're a murderer!" Tubal-Cain remained hidden in the shadows as he accused his father. "People of Havil, do you really want a king who murders innocent people?"

Murmurs spread through the crowd and a smattering of jeers rose up.

The king lifted his sword high above his head. "How dare — bring him to me now! No one speaks to me like that. I am the king! I am the most powerful man —"

Without warning, the terrain beneath them shook violently. People on both the ground and the stage screamed and shrieked as they strug-gled to remain standing. The earth's intense movement reminded Noah of a large wave under a boat. Deafening cracking sounds boomed across the square. A fissure opened up in the middle of the center steps, and Lamech leapt to one side to avoid falling in it.

Huge chunks of the massive wall on the other side of the courtyard fell to the ground. Noah's gut turned. Something snapped above him and instinctively, he pulled Emzara away from the palace's edge. He looked up as the site of Tubal-Cain's defiance collapsed merely cubits away from their previous location, silencing the screams of the people now beneath the rubble.

Emzara dug her fingers into Noah's hand as terror filled her eyes.

Pandemonium ensued and then suddenly, as abruptly as it started, the violent quaking stopped.

"Listen to me!"

Noah glanced up and saw Naamah at the front of the stage yelling loudly, but her voice was muted by the cacophony around them. "Nachash displays his wrath against those who rejected his priestesses. Do not defy him again!"

Noah grabbed Emzara's arm. "We have to find out if Tubal-Cain is alive and then get out of here."

Chapter 24

Noah tried to push through the panicked crowd but quickly found it nearly impossible to make any progress. The collapsed wall of the palace had created a makeshift exit from the square and some of the citizens clambered over the debris trying to escape. Others struggled in vain to lift the wreckage off those crushed under it.

Filled with dread, Noah realized that Tubal-Cain might be among the deceased. Still clutching Emzara's arm, he drove ahead and did his best to avoid being trampled until a massive gray cloud in the distance caught his eye. Noah pointed to it. "What's that?"

Emzara's height hindered her ability to see beyond the crowd. She bounced on her toes, "I can't see it."

Noah's jaw dropped. In the rapidly fading light of the sunset, an immense cloud of smoke shot upward into the sky. *The smoking hill just exploded!*

Minor vibrations shook the ground again. A small chunk of the palace wall dropped on the person next to Emzara, causing her to lurch sideways into Noah, hand pressed to her mouth in horror. Pieces of rock fell as the tremor continued, and many people around them changed course, deciding to head for the northern gate. Just then, a blast of wind swept through the courtyard, nearly knocking Noah to the ground.

Accompanying the wind, a deafening boom, louder than any thunderstorm, rattled through the square, forcing him and others to cover their ears. Undeterred, he forged ahead. Veering right, Noah and

Emzara reached the location where they expected to find Tubal-Cain. His heart sank when he gained a clear view of the devastation. Nothing stirred among the rubble and he climbed over the stones searching for his friend.

The earth continued its trembling, and a group of guards arrived and studied the ruins. "Find the man who spoke against the king," the leader said to the others.

"We don't know what he looks like," another one said.

"Just find someone in this mess who looks like they could've done it. The king ordered us to capture him, and I don't want to come back empty-handed."

Understanding the risk, Noah refrained from calling out the black-smith's name. Afraid of being identified or caught up in the ever-expanding cloud emerging from the distant hill, Noah turned to Emzara. "We need to get out of here."

"But. . . ."

"I don't think we can help him now."

Defeated, they retraced their steps and, after some initial slow-going, made it to a thinner section of crowd for a while, which allowed them to dodge around the people more easily. After nearing the spot they had occupied throughout the ceremony, they moved quickly toward the western gate. As before, they kept their heads down and did their best to avoid the guards stationed at various points in the square.

Destruction surrounded them. Massive sections of the wall on the north and west sides now rested in ruins. People wailed as they picked through the carnage, and Noah passed two bodies bent awkwardly, lying motionless on the ground. He assumed they had been trampled by the terrified crowd.

As they neared the exit, the motion of the earth finally settled. Noah aimed for the middle of the cluster of people to avoid being spotted by guards. Keeping his hands on Emzara's shoulders to ensure they stayed together in the chaos, he shuffled into the horde trying to leave the square. As their advance slowed, the gravity of the situation engulfed his whole being. He glanced up at the massive arch above the exit. *What if that collapses while we're under it?* He fought the urge to turn back and assist some of the wounded people. *What can I really do for them? I'm not trained as a healer.* Besides, getting Emzara back to safety remained his priority.

169

They finally passed under the gate, and their pace immediately increased a little, although they dodged several large pieces of debris. Moving in lockstep with the masses, they passed Tubal-Cain's shop and the other forges, one of which had collapsed while another was ablaze. With each intersection they crossed, the crowd dispersed slightly and their speed increased even more. At the outskirts of town, Noah breathed a sigh of relief when he saw the abandoned guard checkpoint.

Once they reached the western road outside of the city, Emzara touched his arm. "I need to stop for a moment."

Noah led her a few steps off the trail to avoid the trickle of passersby. He gently rubbed her back as she bent over to catch her breath. "You alright?"

She turned her face toward him and the moonlight glistened off her teary eyes. "Tubal-Cain is . . ." She sniffed and shook her head.

"You don't know that."

"That whole area of the palace collapsed. How could anyone survive that?"

Noah bit his lip, looked away, and took a deep breath as he struggled to ward off tears and display confidence.

"Do you think Naamah is right, that Nachash did that?"

Noah scowled. "Why would you even think that?"

"I don't know." She wiped her face. "Maybe because the one person brave enough to take a public stand against the wickedness seems to have been targeted in the destruction."

Gazing back on the city, Noah swallowed hard, trying to push away the sorrow of losing another close friend. The stars above the city, so bright and sparkling earlier in the evening, now disappeared one by one behind the thick blanket of smoke spreading across the sky. As another celestial body vanished, so did his hope that Tubal-Cain had survived. Each moment he spent thinking about it, the more distressed he became. He closed his eyes hard and clenched his jaw. *Just get out of here.* Trying to block the desperate thoughts from his mind, he touched Emzara's cheek. "We need to keep moving."

She nodded and followed him back onto the road. "I'm sorry."

Noah reached an arm around her. "There's nothing to be sorry for. If he didn't make it" — he pulled her against him tight — "at least he did what's right. I'm proud of him."

The bright whole moon hovered over the road ahead, spilling its light on the earth. *Won't be long before that smoke blocks out the moon, too.* An eerie silence hung over their trail, with only the sounds of his breathing and the soft crunching of dirt beneath their footsteps.

Eager to break the stillness and force his thoughts elsewhere, Noah pointed to an upcoming road on their left. "That's the way to Garun's house."

Emzara squeezed his hand but kept her face down.

Noah straightened. "What if all that destruction came from the Creator as a judgment against the Havilites for following Nachash?"

She turned her face to him and shook her head ever so slightly. "Then why would He let Tubal-Cain die?"

A large figure stepped out from behind a tree on their left and strode toward them. "He didn't."

"Tu . . ." Emzara released Noah's hand and hugged the man. "You're alive!"

He chuckled. "It appears that way."

Noah waited impatiently for his wife to step to the side before embracing his friend. "It's so great to see you." Noah released him and they continued down the path together. "How did you survive that fall?"

"I didn't."

"Um?" Noah gestured from his friend's feet up to his head. "Clearly, you're alive."

"I mean I didn't fall." Tubal-Cain stroked his beard. "When everything started shaking, I jumped through the window into Jubal's room. The whole wall and some of the floor instantly collapsed behind me. So I sprinted down the hallway and snuck out the side door. Then I came here to wait for you."

"Praise the Most High, you're safe." She sighed and lifted her eyes up to the sky.

Noah grinned at his wife. "Well said, Em."

Abruptly, her arm shot out and she pointed up. "The moon."

Noah drew back as he beheld the evening light. "It's red."

"That's strange," Tubal-Cain said. "Have you ever seen anything like that?"

"Farna told me that there are times during certain whole moons, when the earth moves between the moon and the sun, that it turns a

171

brownish color. But I think this is different." He searched the heavens. "I think that cloud of smoke is causing it to look red."

"When the earth moves?" Tubal-Cain asked. "Don't you mean, 'when the sun and moon move into the right position'?"

"No, it looks that way, but I said it correctly." Noah thought about describing how Farna taught him to use the stars to track the planet's movement and to chart their progress during a voyage, but they needed more space between them and Havil. "I'll explain on the boat. We should go."

"What's that?" Emzara brushed something off her arm.

Noah held out his hand and watched as tiny gray pebbles struck him.

"Is it rain?" Emzara asked. "It doesn't feel wet."

"Amazing." Noah turned back toward the city. "I think it's from that hill that burst into the sky."

"Is that what happened?" Tubal-Cain asked. "I was wondering where all the smoke came from and why the air is like a blast from one of the furnaces in my shop. I guess I was too busy trying to escape the palace."

More small pellets bounced off Noah's arm. "We really do need to move."

Noah described what he had seen as they started for the beach home. Tubal-Cain reminded them of Kenter's statement about the smoking hill causing the earth to rumble, sparking a lively discussion of how a hill could cause quakes and then burst open. As they reached the halfway point, the substantial amount of dust in the air sparked a coughing attack in Tubal-Cain.

"It reminds me of ashes from a fire." Emzara slid the end of her wrap over her nose and mouth to filter the air. She encouraged Noah and Tubal-Cain to do the same.

With their makeshift masks in place, the gray dust no longer hindered their breathing, but it irritated their eyes. Before long, they left footprints in the accumulating, obnoxious gray flakes. Noah urged them to move quickly, motivated by thoughts of sailing away.

After a long stretch of silence, Tubal-Cain pointed to a dim light ahead. "There it is."

With safety from Havil in sight and longing to breathe clear air again, Noah encouraged the others to run the rest of the way. Reaching the front door, he pulled it open and allowed Emzara to enter first. They shook out their clothes and hurried inside. Garun's wife and the three girls sat in the main room.

"Tubal-Cain, I'm sorry about the house," Laleel said. "The ground shook so hard that part of the roof caved in over the bedrooms." She pointed to the kitchen. "And those shelves collapsed."

Noah quickly recounted a few of the events of their evening. Feeling a sense of gratitude for his friend, Noah especially enjoyed telling about Tubal-Cain's boldness in accusing the king of his crimes.

"Well, I'm glad you're safe. But how terrible about the people who were hurt or killed. I wonder if I knew any of them." Laleel glanced at Noah. "Are we still planning to leave in the morning?"

Noah shook his head. "I think we need to leave immediately. We don't know if the king or others will come here to get out of the city. Plus, we have no idea how long that gray dust will be falling. The sooner we leave the better."

"I agree. We've already loaded our belongings on the boat like you asked." Laleel stood and wrung her hands. "There's just one problem. A huge wave hit after the shaking, and it pushed the boat onto the shore."

Noah's eyes widened. "How far up on the shore?"

"Not far," Zedakal said. "A little bit of it is still in the water."

"Let's go check it out." Noah cuffed Tubal-Cain on the shoulder and turned to Emzara. "Make sure all our things are packed."

As he followed the blacksmith toward the water, Noah said, "So the smoking hill bursts and scatters all this ash" — Noah looked around at the falling debris — "the moon turns red, the ground shakes, and there's a huge wave? I don't understand. What could cause all of that?"

"I don't know, but right now I'm not concerned about that. I only want to know that we can get out of here." Tubal-Cain stepped onto the beach. "I think we can push that back in the water."

Noah squinted in the low light. "I hope the hull isn't broken, or else it'll be a short trip." He put his hands on the hull and Tubal-Cain joined him on the opposite side of the bow. "Ready, push."

Noah shoved with all of his strength, and the boat shifted a little in the sand. He adjusted his grip and dug in his feet. "Push!" The ship slid a couple of cubits before moving it became easier, and before long, Noah found himself standing in the shallows with the vessel floating next to him in the lagoon. "I'll get things ready here if you'll go get the women."

Tubal-Cain turned and called over his shoulder as he ran. "Be right back."

Noah climbed aboard and checked all of the equipment. After pulling up the anchor, he found two pushpoles and shook the ash off of them. "This stuff is everywhere." Satisfied that everything was secure, Noah closed his eyes and offered the Creator a brief prayer for safety.

Emzara reached the boat first. She handed Noah the large basket of goods and then climbed onto the deck.

Tubal-Cain assisted Laleel and her daughters up after tossing some of Noah's supplies onto the ship. He reached out, forming a foothold with his hands for Zedakal to step in. "Here Kal, or should I call you little sister?" He shrugged. "Not that I want to take your brother's place, but we are sort of family."

She gingerly put her foot in his hands. "It's been a long time since I've had a big brother."

Tubal-Cain pushed her up and over the side and then scrambled aboard. "Let's go."

Noah handed him a pushpole, keeping one for himself. He stepped to the bow and shoved one end into the sand, pushing them deeper into the water.

"Hurry," Emzara said quietly as she pointed to the house. "Someone's in the house."

Noah spotted the faint light moving around in the home. "Push harder."

They drifted away from the shore, and soon the pushpoles no longer reached the seafloor. Noah ran to the sail and opened it, tying it into place. As the powerful warm wind drove them toward the open sea, a person carrying a torch walked to the shore and peered toward them. "Is someone there?"

Noah tapped Tubal-Cain on the shoulder. "Who is that?"

"I'm not sure. Probably one of my father's guards," Tubal-Cain said.

"Do you think he saw us?" Emzara asked.

Noah shook his head. "I don't think so." He took hold of the rudder control. "Let's get out of here."

CHAPTER 25

450 years later, Iri Sana — Noah's 499ᵗʰ year

"Farewell, big brother." Jerah grinned as he locked his grip on Noah's forearm and squeezed, his jaw tightening from the exertion.

"Peace to you, little brother." Noah returned the favor, causing Jerah to wince.

Pivi folded her arms. "Still as competitive as ever." She kissed Noah's cheek. "Be sure to greet Emzara for us. We really missed her. What's it been? Fourteen years?"

Noah nodded. "I think so. I know she'd love to see you again. As I mentioned before, you're welcome to visit us any time."

"Maybe we will. Now that Marneka is married we'll have more time available." She looked at Jerah and sighed. "Plus, I'd love to get to the sea again, if I can ever get my husband to leave the farm." She leaned in close. "I think he's just afraid of rumors about bandits on the river."

Noah shrugged. "Well, you do need to be careful, but I've never heard of them attacking the larger boats — they're well-guarded. If you visit, I'll be sure to take you for a small venture on the sea in one of our new ships."

"We'll hold you to that." Jerah helped Pivi into one of the seats on the wagon hitched to their lunker and then climbed into the spot next to her. "Farewell, Noah."

Noah smiled. "May the Creator watch over you until we meet again."

"Always great to see you," Pivi said.

Noah slapped the beast's rump and the animal lurched forward. He watched his brother as they pulled away on their short trip across a few fields to their own farm. Normally, they would walk, but this time a wagon had been needed to haul all the supplies for their daughter's wedding. Shaking his head, Noah's mind drifted back to the marriage ceremony the day before. Marneka, the 31st and youngest child of Jerah and Pivi, made a beautiful bride, but, though the celebration exhibited the traditions acknowledging the Creator, Noah had grieved the lack of sincerity. From his few brief discussions with Marneka's new husband, he had gathered the man had very little interest in walking with the Most High.

The thought made him ache for his wife. His beautiful, godly Emzara, who followed the Creator in spite of all they had endured. He looked at the festive pattern woven into the edge of his fine celebration clothing. Thinking of his wife's efforts in fashioning it made him miss her even more.

Emzara had decided to remain in Iri Geshem to manage the shipyard while he was away, but Noah knew another reason existed. Watching all her nephews and nieces get married broke her heart since she wanted nothing more than to have a family of her own. Four and a half centuries had passed since they lost their unborn child, and Emzara had never conceived again. Yet her faithfulness to her husband and their Creator never waned. *God, would You watch over Emzara too? I know I've asked this countless times before, but please allow us to have a child. Have we not faithfully served You all these years?*

Wisps of despair crept into his mind as he replayed the recent taunts from some of the younger citizens of Iri Geshem. *What's the point in serving the Creator if He never answers? Your God can't even give you a child.* Noah shook his head. "Don't listen to their lies," he said under his breath.

He turned and walked back to his parent's house in the hues of early evening. So much had changed, but some things remained the same. His childhood home had been rebuilt and expanded three times to accommodate his many younger siblings. Yet, as he caught the tangy scent of the familiar springal trees, memories from his early years came rushing back. Even though the row of trees looked different, the thought of chasing Aterre through them remained etched in his mind.

Noah strolled along the stone front wall of the house and entered the large sitting room. On the bench along the far wall, his father sat reading a scroll.

"Son." Nina pulled a slab of braided bread rounds from the oven and placed the hot flat stone on the large table in front of her. "Do you really need to leave so soon? I just baked these for you."

Lamech rose and stood behind her. "You know she doesn't like people leaving here empty handed."

"Or empty bellied." Noah patted his midsection. "Yes, I need to leave now. You know Valur's boat is nearly always on time. Plus, I miss Emzara, and she'll need a break from the shipyard." Eager to hide his frustration with life and people and even with God, Noah stepped forward and embraced her, turning his head so she couldn't read the despondency in his eyes. "I love you, Mother."

After a long hug, she released him. "I love you too, Son."

"It's been great to see you again." Noah smiled tiredly before turning to face his father. "Where's Grandfather? I thought for sure he'd be in here once he smelled fresh bread." Methuselah planned to stay one more evening before returning to his own place the next day.

Lamech rolled up the scroll and set it beside the bench. "Out back, waiting to send you off with his blessing, I suppose." He stood and hugged Noah tightly. "God be with you on your journey."

"Thanks, Father." Noah held him tightly, treasuring the rare moment with his father. He let go and bent to retrieve his bundle of items.

"Here. I also gathered a few things from the feast for you to take with you." Nina held out a bulging satchel, laden with remnants of her good cooking.

"Thank you, Mother. I'm sure this won't go to waste." Noah kissed her cheek before grabbing both bags in one hand and scooping up a couple of fresh bread rounds in the other. He headed for the doorway, nearly as anxious as the first time he had left home and longing to be alone with his thoughts.

Noah walked outside and headed toward the rear yard. He spotted a familiar figure seated near the edge of the house. "Grandfather, I'm headed to the Hiddekel now to catch the boat."

Methuselah stood. "Do you mind if I walk with you?"

"I'd love that, but are you sure? The sun's descent is nearly complete."

"I may be old, but I can still handle a walk like this. It keeps me feeling young. Besides, I want to talk to you."

Noah stretched a welcoming arm out wide and Methuselah attempted to pilfer one of the rolls. It tore apart and less than half remained in Noah's grip. "Hey!"

Methuselah took a quick bite and the bread slurred his words. "I though' you're off'ring one."

Noah chuckled and fell into step with his grandfather. "I suppose you can have it as payment for your company. I always enjoy our talks."

A smile spread on Methuselah's wrinkled face. Although his 870th birthday would come soon, he still displayed the energy and mobility of a man two centuries younger. "As do I."

"What topic should we cover this time?" Noah asked.

Methuselah cocked his head to the side. "Do you remember before you left home all those years ago when I said that my father was the godliest man I'd ever known and that I saw some of that same spirit in you?"

Noah thought back almost half a millennium to his coming-of-age ceremony and how the events of that night led him straight to Emzara. "I remember."

"As you've gotten older, that spirit seems to have grown. You've kept your commitment to honor the Creator." Methuselah put a hand on Noah's arm. "But there's something different this trip. You seem distracted, and I've rarely seen you smile. What's troubling you?"

Noah sighed and tipped his head back to look at the tinged hues of gold and pink beginning to weave their way across the sky. He debated playing it safe by just sharing his everyday frustrations over the growing corruption in the world. In his younger years, those who openly opposed the Creator remained largely confined to certain cities and regions. But as the centuries passed, the immorality of those places had spread like a wildfire and had infiltrated Noah's beloved Iri Geshem long ago. Thankfully, a slight majority of the city's aging council members continued to enforce policies consistent with the ways of the Most High. *But it's only a matter of time.* Noah shook his head. He had shared those concerns with his grandfather before. His recent unease arose from deeper within his soul.

He turned to the wise man beside him. "Is it truly worth it? Following the Creator, I mean."

178

Methuselah drew back and ran a hand through his thin gray hair. "Of course it is. Why would you ask that?"

"This world. Everything. I don't know." Exasperated, Noah let his arms drop. "I'm nearly 500 years old, and I've followed the Most High my entire life. But what good has it done?"

His grandfather tipped his head forward a little but remained quiet.

"Every year the evil grows in our lands. Nachash is worshiped throughout half the world, and I know many people in Iri Geshem follow that abomination now. And it's hardly any better here. The Nodites' vile influence is all over this region. You saw the marriage ceremony. Marneka and her new husband have very little interest in the Most High. And I don't think it bothers Jerah and Pivi at all." Noah clenched his fists and increased his pace. "If the Creator truly is the Most High, then why doesn't He put a stop to all the wickedness?"

"You wish for Him to stop people from acting as they please?" Methuselah asked.

He knew his grandfather despised the vile behaviors all around them but had learned long ago to cut right to the middle of an issue instead of griping about peripheral matters. Noah huffed. "No. I wish He'd warn them so that they'd know He's real and would follow Him."

"My father used to warn them on behalf of the Creator."

"Grandfather, please tell me the truth. Did he really walk with God?"

"Yes. He was a very godly man."

"I believe that, but that's not really what I meant." Noah pulled his eyebrows together and turned his head away from Methuselah. "Did the Creator actually speak to him? I guess what I'm asking is" — he ran his hand through his hair — "can we truly know that the Most High exists or are we just supposed to hope that our beliefs are right?"

"I never heard the Creator speak to him, but I believe He did. That's why he went to the city of Enoch — to warn the people."

"Right. That was so long ago. Where's the judgment that he talked about?"

"I don't know. I've learned that the Most High does things when He chooses to, and not always when we want Him to. Maybe He's waiting for someone else to warn the people." A coy grin spread across Methuselah's lips.

"Who? Me?" Noah stepped over a small depression in the trail.

With a gleam in his eye, Methuselah nodded. "I told you that you have some of my father's spirit. Why don't you do it?"

"I've stood up for the Creator for centuries, but lately, I've been so . . ." Noah shook his head and his jaw tightened. "Why should I? After all I've done for Him, what has He done for me? We still don't have any children, and we never will. For 450 years Emzara and I have pleaded with Him for a child, and what response have we received? Nothing. Silence. Why should I continue doing what He wants?"

His grandfather hesitated before putting a hand on Noah's arm. "He's given you all that you have. Your life. Your breath. Your health. It's all from Him. And He's given you a wonderful wife. Is Emzara not enough of a gift for you?"

"Of course she is." Noah blew out a long breath and the heat in his face slowly dissipated. "But my frustration is for her too. You can't imagine how much she wants a child. She helped our friends, Tubal-Cain and Adira, raise all 17 of their children, but it's not the same as having your own. The best time we ever spent together was when Jerah and Pivi allowed the twins to stay with us for about half a year. She talks about them so much. And that was over 50 years ago. For once, she had a small taste of what it'd be like to be a mother."

"I'm sorry that you two haven't been able to experience the joy of raising your own children. I truly am. I don't pretend to know how difficult that is." Methuselah pulled Noah to a halt so he could face him. "But let me ask you this. Did you know that many of Jerah's children reject the Most High's ways?"

"Yes, I've heard Father talk about that," Noah said. "It saddens him greatly."

"It saddens me, too, but not as much as it hurts Jerah and Pivi. They were devastated each time one of their precious children walked away." The old man stared at Noah. "Maybe that's why you remain childless."

Noah straightened and rubbed his arms to keep warm. "What do you mean? You think my children would turn away from the Creator?"

Methuselah held up his hand and shook his head. "No, that's not what I was trying to say. I meant that maybe the Most High is sparing you the pain that would come if your children did refuse to follow Him."

"Do you really think that?"

Methuselah shrugged a shoulder and began walking again. "I'm just thinking out loud and trying to give you a different perspective on it. I believe the Creator will honor your faithfulness, but I certainly don't know what He has planned for you."

As Noah massaged his temples and sighed, a tiny spark of hope ignited within. "I wouldn't expect you to know that. I appreciate another viewpoint, as well, but it doesn't really change my situation. This wedding reopened the wound of our barrenness. Look at Marneka. She's not even following the Creator, but she'll probably have children within a short time."

Methuselah remained silent, his eyes sympathetic.

"I know everything I have is from the Creator. And He's blessed me greatly. I could probably sell the shipyard and never need to work another day in my life. Yet I have no one to leave any of it to."

"I didn't realize shipbuilding was so profitable."

"We make the best boats. We get orders from all over world, even though people could order from local shipbuilders for less. But what good is that? I just wish I could do something more meaningful than making boats. To pour my life into raising a child of my own would be so satisfying."

"It is. Well, at least it is until they complain to their grandfather about why the Creator isn't doing what they want Him to do." Methuselah placed a hand on Noah's shoulder. "I'm joking, of course. You're a blessing to me and to everyone else I know. Think of what you've accomplished. Your boats carry food and supplies to people everywhere. What about that long voyage you and your wife took to finish mapping out the earth? Was that not meaningful?"

Noah pursed his lips. Many years earlier, he and Emzara along with Tubal-Cain and Adira journeyed around their enormous land mass. It took much longer than he anticipated because he had misjudged how far they would need to sail. But it had been worth it. Even with all the wicked people, the world still held myriad wonders, and during the voyage he had often found himself marveling at the Creator's handiwork. Emzara had discovered scores of spectacular animals and delighted in studying and drawing them. *We wouldn't have been able to do that if we were raising a family.* He sighed. Even the memory of that fulfilling adventure held no comfort for him now.

Reaching the river's edge, Methuselah stopped. "Let me ask you this. Where do you get this idea that the Creator owes you something?"

Noah stepped back, his eyes wide. "I . . ."

"Do you forget that we're created from dust, just like the stuff that's been at our feet this whole walk?" His grandfather's voice was firm yet gentle. "Is not His forgiveness the greatest gift of all?"

Noah bowed his head, not ready to give up his anger, but understanding the wisdom in his grandfather's words.

"Listen. I understand your frustration. But you need to think about whether you're wholly worshiping the Creator, or if you're worshiping the idea of having a family. We serve Him because of who He is, not because of what He gives." Methuselah turned to face his grandson squarely, gripping both of Noah's arms and waiting for him to look up before speaking again. "You don't have to accept this right now, but you have the strength of character to stand for the Most High in these evil times. Don't let your disappointments get in the way of what He may be calling you to do. Continue to serve Him in spite of how you feel and resolve to follow Him no matter what."

Noah stood up tall. "I have a lot to think about."

"Good. You'll have plenty of time for it on your trip home." He slapped Noah on the back and grinned knowingly.

One corner of Noah's mouth turned upward.

"There it is."

"What?" Noah crossed his arms. "I finally smiled?"

"Nope." Methuselah pointed past him. "There's your boat."

"Grandfather, thank you. I needed this walk."

CHAPTER 26

Novanam — Noah's 499ᵗʰ year

"As always, it was good to travel with you, Valur." Noah released the old man's corded forearm. During the week, Noah had wrestled with the thoughts that still plagued his soul, though he had also spent plenty of time helping Valur with the physical demands of running a boat. But even as he worked, he felt his soul preparing for peace, drawing nearer each day to the resolution that would sustain his spirit.

The captain's smile revealed a couple of missing teeth, prominent reminders of the story Valur had told Noah about a violent passenger on his boat many years ago. "You're always welcome on my vessel." The man tilted his head. "Or should I call it your vessel, since you built it?"

"Hardly." Grinning, Noah shook his head and slung his bag over his shoulder before stepping onto the gangplank. "May the Creator watch over you."

"And you as well. Be sure to greet your lovely wife for me, and make sure she comes with you next time so I'll have better company."

"I will." Noah pivoted and eyed the bustling town of Novanam. After marching down the long ramp and reaching land, he turned left in hopes of finding a vacancy at his favorite inn.

"Hey, Noah."

Noah looked up to see Valur calling to him from the ship's deck above.

The sailor patted the rail. "Remember, bigger boats."

"I'll see what I can do." Noah chuckled, enjoying their traditional farewell in memory of Recharu. He and Valur had partnered up to take over a share of the business when Deks retired. Then Valur had become sole owner when Recharu passed away nearly a century ago. It was Recharu who had first requested larger boats after Noah's maiden voyage with them as a young man.

After securing a room and dining at the inn, Noah walked through the city streets. Once a brief stop for the river runners, Novanam now boasted a few thousand residents and had grown into a major stop for the increased boat traffic on the river. Noah estimated that only a small percentage of the people there followed the Creator, and it was not uncommon for fights to break out in the tavern district at night, due to a combination of strong drinks and strong men.

Noah steered wide of that area as he headed for a place that had provided him a peaceful respite on a few occasions. Before reaching the top of the hill on the road to Zakar, he turned down a little-used dusty trail to his left. Part of him longed to continue on the main road and visit his friends in the forest village, but he thought back to his grandfather's words and craved the time alone to reflect and continue praying to the Creator.

Ducking under broad leaves and carefully dodging thorny plants, Noah regretted not purchasing a clearing blade in town, but the trail soon opened up. Mature trees surrounded him on every side, shading out the undergrowth until it dwindled into almost nothing. He climbed up a large log lying to his left and sat down. Staring out over the city of Novanam and the river just beyond it reminded him of his childhood years watching the occasional boats and dreaming of adventure. Now, centuries later, he had experienced more adventure than he had ever imagined and built just about every large boat on the Hiddekel.

Noah slowly closed his eyes and took several deep, relaxing breaths as he listened to the birds chirping and forest animals scurrying about. Without a single man-made sound in the air, he smiled and cherished the tranquil surroundings, occasionally opening his eyes to watch the light glisten on the crystalline water far below. His thoughts drifted back to his frustrations and the recent conversation with his grandfather.

He's right. Who do I think I am, that I can force the Creator to bless me? A battle between selfishness and gratitude raged deep in his soul. Absently breaking a small branch into pieces, he wrestled with himself. Noah took a deep breath. *Creator, do You know what I'm feeling right now? I have no legitimate right to hold on to all this anger, but I find myself unable to let it go. Help me.* He paused. *Help me let it go. Forgive me for doubting Your goodness. You have given me so much to be thankful for, and I often take it for granted. Thank you for Emzara and her tremendous love and support over these many years. Help us to serve You in spite of our disappointments.*

Noah stopped as relief spread through him and the burden eased a little. As he breathed in a new sense of contentment, he became keenly aware of the silence. All the animal noises, as well as the gentle breeze, had ceased. The perfect stillness made him a little nervous, and he slowly opened his eyes to something even more alarming. Gone were Novanam, the river, and the opening in the woods before him. In their place, a forest full of tall, straight trees rested on the edge of a large, relatively flat field with the sun high overhead. Having worked with wood his whole life, Noah was certain he knew every kind of timber in the world, but these were foreign to him.

Instead of resting on the log as before, Noah found himself standing, his mouth agape. He blinked hard. *This must be a dream.* He shook his head, trying to clear it. Only then did he sense a presence behind him. Somehow in the midst of silence, he knew he was being watched. He turned slowly, then stood motionless. On the edge of the forest, a babbling stream flowed beside an old, small stone house and an outbuilding he was sure he hadn't passed earlier.

"Noah."

The voice came from his right, although *voice* might not be the right way to describe it. Instead, it sounded like thunder mixed with raging waters. But his name was clearly discernable.

Fear and peace grappled for control inside Noah. Conflicted, he wanted to run away, but at the same time, he longed to turn and see who had called his name. A chill ran up his spine, causing his arms and legs to tingle and his neck hair to stand upright. As he turned, a bright glow appeared in the corner of his view. He closed his eyes, took a deep breath, and faced the light.

As he cautiously opened his eyes, comprehension eluded him. Hovering just above the ground between the two largest trees in the forest, a flame of fire, not much larger than a man, burned brightly, but it did not consume anything around it. Captivated, Noah gazed at the beautiful yet terrifying sight. The light emanating from the flame seemed to pierce his entire being.

"Noah." The intimidating, thunderous voice resounded from the flame.

Instantly, Noah dropped face first on the ground. Fear surged through his frame, and he felt as if every particle of his body would tear apart. Too scared to think, let alone speak, Noah focused on trying to breathe.

"Do not be afraid, Noah, for you are greatly loved."

Noah's fear waned a bit as the voice took on a hint of a whisper that somehow mingled with the thundering. Keeping his face averted, Noah struggled to speak. "Who . . . who are you?"

"I am the God of your forefather Enoch. I am the Most High, the Creator of heaven and earth."

Noah had never imagined how frightening it would be to meet the Creator, and he instantly regretted the times he had wished that the Most High would speak directly to him. The words finally registered in his mind. *Enoch was telling the truth.*

"Yes, Enoch told the truth and walked faithfully in My ways."

Trembling over the realization that the Creator knew his very thoughts, Noah asked, "What happened to him?"

"I took him so that he would not face death."

"Forgive me for being so bold to speak. Is that why You are here now — to take me?"

"No. I have heard your prayers and have come to speak to you. The whole earth has corrupted itself, and the descendants of Adam have grown exceedingly wicked. I am grieved that I made them, so I am going to destroy this world with a flood."

Keeping his face toward the ground, Noah's mind whirled and he managed to ask, "A flood?" *What about all the people?*

"You are concerned about the people. Do you believe that I will do what is right?"

Still trying to come to grips with the situation, Noah nodded. "Yes, I know You will do what is right. What do you want me to do?"

"You are to build an ark of gopherwood. It will be for you, your wife, your sons, your sons' wives, and the creatures that I bring to you."

Noah played the words back in his mind and tried to make sense of them. "Sons? But I don't have . . ." Hope filled his soul, and he fought to control his emotions. "Thank You, Most High." *Build an ark of gopherwood.* "How large will it need to be?"

"You will receive that information when the time is right."

"What should I do until then?" Noah waited for a response, but he sensed that the flame was gone. He slowly looked up and discovered he was back in the clearing. Shakily, he climbed to his feet and scanned his surroundings. The sun hung low in the sky, casting long shadows from the trees, and the log he previously sat upon was about ten cubits away. The unusual trees and little dwelling place were gone. *Strange.* Noah concentrated on committing the Creator's message to memory. "The whole world?" he asked himself.

As Noah turned to leave, he tripped over a rock and nearly fell, dislodging the relatively smooth stone in the process. He bent over, picked it up, and set it in the spot where he found himself after the vision. Hastily, Noah gathered six more stones and set them all up in a pile as a memorial. Kneeling down near the stones, Noah prayed to the Most High and thanked Him for speaking directly to him. "My grandfather's father warned people about Your judgment. I'll warn them about the flood, if that's what You desire."

Near the end of his prayer, Noah's thoughts meandered back to the Creator's words about the ark's future inhabitants. With an ear-to-ear smile crossing his face, Noah stood. *Sons?* He shook his head and laughed. *Amazing.*

Chapter 27

Iri Geshem — Noah's 499ᵗʰ year

The warm wind whipped through Noah's dark, gray-streaked hair as he surveyed the city that now sprawled on both sides of the river. Iri Geshem's population had multiplied many times over, and Noah guessed it was one of the ten largest cities in the world. Elegant three-story homes lined the western shore to his right, while smaller domiciles cluttered the eastern bank.

They drifted past the old wharf where the river boats used to be loaded and unloaded. A few fishing boats were tied to the ancient docks where he had first set foot in town. All cargo ships now traveled directly to the large port near the city's central district. But before reaching their destination, the small river runners needed to pass under the bridge.

Two centuries earlier, Noah had assisted with the construction of a wooden crossing that spanned the broad width of the river. This allowed produce from the farmlands of the east to quickly reach the city. Wide enough for a pair of animal-drawn carts to pass by each other, the structure rested on a series of piers. The trickiest part of the design was creating the system that pulled two significant sections of the deck back in order to permit the boats to sail through without damaging the bridge or the ships.

Noah studied the mechanisms of the lift as they floated by. *Those hinges will need to be replaced soon. I'll let Tubal-Cain know that he should check them.* As he turned his attention to the city to his right, mixed emotions bombarded him. The fact that so many people in the city refused to walk in the ways of the Creator frustrated and saddened Noah, but he changed his focus to his wife. Knowing he was only moments away from seeing her for the first time in nearly two whole moons, he could hardly resist the urge to dive into the water and run down the beach road to reach her faster.

A hand grabbed his shoulder. "You look like a giddy child again."

"I feel like one, too." Noah faced his longtime friend, Farna. "So, just a couple more runs before you turn the business over to your son?"

"Yeah, I'm getting too old for this. I love being on the water, but I'm looking forward to living out my remaining days relaxing on my small farm up the river." Farna signaled to a member of the crew, and the ship turned right as it entered the bay.

"I'll definitely miss having you around. Em and I will have to stop in from time to time."

"I'd like that. We can kick back and discuss the old days before . . ." Farna looked around and spoke quietly, "before the Nachash followers spread everywhere."

Noah sighed. "I hope they turn from their evil ways before it's too late." He waved to the workers at the shipyard as the craft drifted across the bay, but no one returned the greeting. *Must be too focused on their daily work. That's good.* A smile automatically crossed his lips when he saw the hill where he and Emzara had enjoyed their initial sunset together. The boat crept toward the long pier ahead and Noah bounced on his toes in anticipation. He watched the shoreline closely, hoping that Emzara would be there to greet him.

As one of the crew tossed a rope to a dock worker, Noah asked, "You'll have my crate delivered to the shipyard?"

Farna nodded. "As always."

"Excellent."

When they finally docked, Noah said a brief farewell to Farna and his crew and practically leapt to the pier, only to be stopped immediately by a cargo inspector. Moments later, the man finished his examination of Noah's bag, satisfied that it was free of any taxable items. Slinging his belongings over his shoulder, Noah ran to the beach, weaving in and out of crates and cargo wagons along the way. He turned right and hustled across the sand toward the familiar milknut grove, but running through the soft sand tired him out more than he remembered. He slowed to a walk to catch his breath as he reached the trail that led to the house.

Before reaching home, he passed by the once-small place he and Aterre built. It had been expanded over the centuries, but it currently needed several repairs. Garun and his family had lived in it for several years before finding a place of their own. After that, it had served at various times as a home for a few of Tubal-Cain's children, a storage place for shipyard items, and a guest home, but now it was vacant.

Honoring Ara's wishes, Noah and Emzara had moved into her childhood home. Although it was difficult for the first few years to be reminded regularly of the tragedies, they eventually opted to remodel the interior. As the exterior came into view, he reveled in the peace the sight gave him. It looked almost the same as it did when Ara lived there, thanks to Noah's regular maintenance and Emzara's meticulous care of the grounds.

No longer able to contain his anticipation, Noah ran the remaining distance and entered his house. "Em, I'm home."

"I'm in here," Emzara called from the sitting room.

Part of the renovations included moving their sitting room away from the front door. Puzzled that Emzara had not come running to greet him, Noah dropped his bag on the floor and hurried to the room on the opposite side of the wall on his left. "You won't believe . . ." Noah stopped when he saw several people in the room.

"Welcome back!" Several voices mingled together in greeting.

Tubal-Cain stood before him. "Great to have you back."

"It's good to be back. Although, I didn't want your face to be the first one I saw when I got home." Noah chuckled as he scanned the room. To his right, Adira, Zain, and Kmani sat on one of the large cushioned benches, but he had eyes only for Emzara. As his beloved approached, he held his arms out wide.

Emzara engulfed him in a massive hug, her familiar fragrance washing over him as he closed his eyes and cherished her touch. "I missed you."

"And I missed you too." As he pulled away, he saw three more guests. To the left of where Emzara had been, reposed Elam and Zedakal, with a very young girl sitting on her lap. "What a pleasant surprise. I didn't expect you to be in town." He took Emzara's hand and followed her to

190

her recently vacated spot. She sat and scooted close to Zedakal, giving Noah space to sit beside her.

"So what's everyone doing here?" Noah asked as he settled in to get comfortable.

"We couldn't turn down Emzara's offer of evenfeast to celebrate your return," Zain said. "And we wanted to surprise you. Looks like it worked."

"It sure did, and I look forward to that meal as well." He leaned forward and turned to Elam. "I was just near Zakar a couple weeks ago. What are you doing in Iri Geshem?"

Elam pointed at Zain. "I had some business with Zain this week, and when I heard you were returning soon, we decided to extend our stay. Emzara was kind enough to offer one of your guest rooms to us. My father sends his greetings as well."

"Please give my regards to him and the others in your village when you return," Noah said.

"I will."

Emzara patted Noah's knee. "I needed some company since you were away so long. Besides, they brought their daughter, and I couldn't pass up the opportunity to play with her." She held her arms out to the little girl. "Come see Memma?"

Elam's daughter's green eyes sparkled as she smiled with a drool-covered fist against her mouth. She leaned forward for Emzara to catch her.

Emzara hugged the child. "Noah, say hi to Rayneh. Rayneh, can you say 'Noah'?"

Rayneh played shy and buried her face against Emzara.

Noah gently placed his hand on the child's head and stroked her wispy, light brown hair. "It's great to meet you, Rayneh." He looked at her parents. "Congratulations on another beautiful child. She's adorable. I didn't know you were going to have any more."

Elam and Zedakal had met about ten years after she moved to Iri Geshem with Garun's family, when, as an aspiring seamster, Elam accepted Zain's offer of an apprenticeship at Noah's recommendation. He and Kal bonded deeply during those years when he lived with Noah and Emzara. Noah thought back to the many things they had in common. Both had been kidnapped when they were young. Both had scars on their upper arms resulting from efforts to blot out the awful marks burned into their flesh. And Noah had played a role in rescuing both of them, although much more directly in Elam's case. After Elam finished his apprenticeship, they moved to Zakar, where the people were ecstatic to learn she was Aterre's sister. The Creator blessed them with nearly two dozen children, all adults by now, so this little one surprised Noah.

Kal smiled. "We didn't either, but we're thrilled to have her."

Noah loved Kal's smile. In it, he saw Aterre again. Though he sometimes struggled to remember exactly what his friend looked like, some of Kal's expressions refreshed his memory. Noah touched Emzara's arm. "Well, I'm very pleased you're all here, and I look forward to catching up with everyone. But if you don't mind giving us a moment, I need to speak with my wife privately."

"Right now?" Emzara's eyes widened. "Is everyone well? Your parents?"

Noah nodded and stood. "Everyone is fine. This shouldn't take long. I have something very important to tell you and I really can't wait."

"Oh, well I have some news for you too." Emzara kissed Rayneh's cheek and then handed her back to her mother.

Kal grinned and nudged Emzara with an elbow.

"Alright." She reached for Noah's hand and he pulled her up.

"Whatever it is, you can just say it in front of us." Zain chuckled and slapped Noah's leg with the back of his hand. "We're like family here."

Noah smirked. "And I plan to tell all of you later, but Em needs to hear it first."

The women whispered to each other and Kal put a hand over her mouth to contain her giggles.

Noah shook his head slightly, feeling as if he had missed an inside joke. *I'll ask later.* "Come on."

Noah led Emzara back through the front room and down the hall to their room. After closing the door behind them, Noah placed his hands on her cheeks and kissed her. He pulled back and looked into her eyes. "I love you. It's so good to be back."

Reddening a little, Emzara said, "It's good to have you back, and I love you too, but what did you need to tell me that couldn't wait?" She took a couple steps back. "Or was your plan just to get a longer kiss?" She grinned.

192

Noah snorted "No, but I'm not going to pass up the opportunity." He gestured to their bed. "You may want to sit down."

She arched an eyebrow and slowly sat on the edge of their sleeping pallet. "I'm ready."

Noah let out a deep breath. "This is going to sound very strange, but I can assure you it's true."

Emzara cocked her head and squinted, clearly confused.

Noah swallowed and glanced at the floor. "He spoke to me, Em."

"Who?"

"The Creator."

Her eyes snapped wide open. "What? Are you teasing me?"

Noah held her gaze. "No, He truly did."

"What do you mean?"

Noah shook his head. "I'm not really sure how to describe what I saw." Without warning, his eyes welled up. "It was surreal — the most amazing thing I've ever experienced. He was terrifying and beautiful at the same time."

Emzara reached forward and placed her hand on his arm. "What did He say?"

"He said He was going to destroy the world with a flood because of all the wickedness."

She covered her mouth. "What? When?"

"He didn't tell me." Noah sat down next to her and lightly rubbed her back.

Emzara lowered her head, stared at the floor, and spoke slowly. "What will happen to everyone?"

Noah grimaced. "I wondered that too, and I've been thinking about it the past two weeks." He turned to face her. "He told me something else too. He said I need to build an ark."

Emzara faced him. "A boat?"

"Yes, it'll be a big one, but I'm not sure how big."

"Larger than the ones you already make?"

"I think so." Noah bit his lip. "He said that He would send animals for us to take on board."

She straightened. "How many animals?"

Noah suppressed a smile. "I don't know."

"Wait." Emzara gestured to Noah and then herself. "Us? We'll be spared? Why? What about our friends and everyone else?"

"Believe me, I've been trying to understand His message, and we can talk about that later. But Em, there's more." No longer able to hold it in, Noah grabbed her shoulders as his volume increased. "He said that it'd be for those animals, along with you, me" — he gave her a quick peck on the cheek — "and our sons and their wives."

Emzara's jaw dropped and she put a hand to her chest. "Our . . . sons?"

"That's what He said." Noah chuckled. "So I guess that means the flood won't happen for a while since . . ."

Placing a gentle finger over his lips, she smiled and her glistening eyes danced. "Maybe not as long as you think." She grabbed his hand and placed it on her stomach. "We already have one on the way."

Her midsection bulged slightly and he stared at her, dumbfounded. "How long have you known?"

"Since right after you left." A tear streaked down her face. "You don't know how hard it was not to be able to tell you until now."

Noah hugged her tightly. "Praise the Most High. He has answered our prayers." The strange behavior of the women in the other room suddenly made sense. "So all our guests already know, don't they?"

She pulled back and wiped the corners of her eyes with her fingertips. "Yes. They're here to celebrate with us."

Noah kissed her again. "Then let's go celebrate."

CHAPTER 28

"It was so good to see everybody again. And Elam and Kal — what a surprise." Noah leaned close to his wife. The flickering light from the oil lamp picked up the sparkle of her eyes as the two sat on their favorite overlook by the sea. Though it was too dark to enjoy the view of the water other than the occasional crest of a small wave, his ears stayed attuned to the rhythmic splashing below them. Near the docks to their right, workers loaded and unloaded crates from large seagoing ships his company built. The lights from the city and the harbor dimmed Noah's view of the evening sky. "It's even better to see you."

Emzara snuggled in close and breathed out a happy sigh. "I've missed you. So much has happened while you were away." She put her hand to her midsection and smiled as she slowly shook her head.

Noah wished he knew a way to prolong the evening and simply take in her nearness.

"And your experience is beyond anything we've imagined." She paused and her voice turned somber. "But your news about the flood made it more difficult to enjoy the time with our friends. Did the Creator say anything else about it?"

"He spoke of how wicked this world had become and that He was grieved that He made people. Can you imagine the Most High being grieved?"

"Why shouldn't He be?" Emzara shrugged. "We're saddened by it too."

"I don't know. I suppose I imagined that He wouldn't have emotions like we do." Noah stared at one of the smaller boats in the harbor, where two men busily pulled their fishing net out of the water. Now commonplace, fishing was once unimaginable. Noah dropped his gaze as he recalled the first time he saw someone eating fish. King Lamech's impudence had deeply troubled him at the time, but over the centuries, Noah had grown accustomed to the idea and it rarely bothered him anymore. Suddenly that old revulsion rose to the surface. "But you're right. Man has rejected the Creator in every conceivable way. Why shouldn't He grieve? And why shouldn't He send a flood?"

Emzara started. "How can you say that?" She looked up into his eyes. "Our friends follow the Creator. Why should they be killed?"

Noah stroked her hair above her ear. "I asked Him what would happen to all the people." He thought back to his meeting with his Maker. "Actually, I didn't even ask the question. I simply thought it, and He knew my mind."

Emzara's eyes widened. "What happened?"

"He asked me . . ." Noah gulped, "He asked, 'Do you believe that I will do what is right?' "

"What did you say?"

"What could I say? How could I begin to disagree with the One who knows my thoughts? The One who made me? Of course, I believe that He will do what's right."

In the dim light, she turned her large brown eyes toward him and the softened, higher pitch of her voice foreshadowed her tears.

"So Adira, Tubal-Cain, Kal, Elam . . . Rayneh. . . . Can they come with us or will they just . . . be gone?" She clung to him.

"I don't know what's going to happen." He groaned. "The promise was for us, our sons, and their wives." Ever since receiving the Most High's message, the weight of it had settled on his shoulders like a massive wooden ship beam. His mind fumbled with the knowledge of what the future held and all the details yet unknown, although sharing it with Emzara lightened the burden a little.

"Our lives have been marked by seeing loved ones die. And now you say there's much more to come? How can I bear this?"

He hugged her to himself. "I don't know." Tears rolled down his face and his chest tightened. "It's not easy." She sobbed in his arms, and all the emotion that he had kept locked inside for weeks finally broke free.

After some time, she took in a shaky breath, and he peered into her face, wiping her tanned cheeks with his thumbs.

"Em, God told me not to be afraid and that He loves me." Noah looked up and briefly closed his eyes. "He also confirmed that what we heard about my grandfather's father is true."

Emzara returned a thankful half-smile and rubbed the wet trails on his face with her fingertips. "That's amazing, but. . . ."

"Here's what I have to believe. We know from what happened with Greatfather Adam that even though the Creator warns of death, He's merciful in the outcome. We don't know what that will look like for this situation. Maybe He'll allow our friends to join us, but even if He doesn't, I know we can trust Him. We have to."

She nodded slowly.

"We should take comfort that the flood must be many years away."

"So what do we do until then?" She put her hand in his and his pulse quickened.

"We start by enjoying the time we have with the people we love, and we think about how we'll complete the task that lies ahead."

"We're not alone in this you know."

Noah touched her midsection and smiled. "I know." He stood swiftly and brushed off his garment. "Do we still have that young bleater?"

She rose, tilting her head as her eyebrows came together in the middle. "Yes."

"I know it's late, but let's consecrate our actions before the Most High through a sacrifice and seek His direction."

Emzara clasped her hands together and nodded.

197

CHAPTER 29

As Noah walked backward with his hands on Emzara's slightly rounded abdomen, she rolled her eyes. "Are you ever going to hold my hand again?"

"You've had 450 years of that. Right now, I need to be ready in case he kicks."

"I haven't even felt that yet, so I think you'll have to wait a little." She picked up her pace, causing him to stumble slightly. "It's good to have you home, but we'll never make it to the shipyard at this rate."

With an exaggerated sigh, Noah fell into stride with her and placed an arm around her back. "It's good to be back." He looked up at the familiar milknut trees, and she followed his gaze. The massive shoots at the top of each trunk boasted dozens of long, slender leaves that waved like graceful fingers and provided a comforting canopy overhead. She loved how the early morning light pierced through the foliage to dapple the soft forest floor below.

"It's nice to have company again on the way to work."

"You've had him with you." Noah tipped his head toward her midsection.

She smiled. "True. Although not quite the same."

"Well, I grant you I may be a better conversationalist than he is."

"You keep saying 'he.' So you're pretty sure this is a boy?"

Tears formed in the corners of Noah's deep brown eyes. "I'm positive."

"I still can't believe the Creator actually spoke to you."

"Nor can I."

"I don't want to consider all that stuff right now, but tell me what you're thinking about this ark." Emzara kept her voice soft, still in awe of having a mission from the Most High and still trying to wrap her mind around all it portended.

"Well, I think God's placed us in a perfect location. We already have the shipyard and all the tools and materials we'll need. We're right on a harbor, which should be perfect, and we have many skilled people who could help. It's almost like He planned this."

She grinned at him before turning somber. "And I like that we won't be traveling — it's less risky for the baby." Noah reached up and squeezed her shoulder, drawing her closer to him. Fresh emotions from the loss of their first child welled up from deep within her. "But now we have a second chance."

"More than that. The Creator said 'sons.'"

Her smile returned. "Sounds like we'll have our hands full."

"And not just with them, but with animals. Lots of them. You should love that part."

She clapped her hands together. "It looks like studying them all these years will be useful after all." She marveled at the Creator's foresight. During their travels, she had always wanted to stop whenever they sighted unfamiliar creatures, in order to draw pictures of them and document their habits. And before it was shut down to make space for the expanding city, Emzara had helped out at a farm dedicated to treating injured animals. "It's as if the Creator's been preparing us all our lives for this."

"I was just thinking the same thing."

"Extraordinary." She drew the word out in awe of the Creator's wisdom and her responsibility. "Do you realize that this will have to be bigger than any ship you've made so far?"

"Much bigger. I've always wanted to build bigger boats, even back when I was your father's apprentice, and I've had success. Think about the breakthrough we had a century ago when I learned that wood pegs can make the hull stronger than anything we'd tried before that. It seems like the Most High has every detail worked out."

She squeezed his hand. "Remind me of this if I forget to trust Him."

"Of course."

"You've already started thinking out the plan for building it, haven't you?"

Noah's grin gave away his answer.

"I thought so."

"I'll need to construct some scale models to learn which proportions will be best. There's still a lot to figure out." Noah flexed his hand, revealing his eagerness to begin.

He stared at the ground silently for a few moments. "The last thing my grandfather told me was that he saw in me the same spirit that his father had. He encouraged me to warn people of the Creator's judgment." Noah looked up at her. "This impending flood gives me an urgency to tell others about Him and His ways."

She stopped and faced him. "Will you say anything about the flood to them? To our friends?"

"I — I don't know. Probably not yet. It's still too new. But I'll do my best to persuade people to follow Him."

"Count me in."

"There you are!" Tubal-Cain's loud, frantic voice cut into the peace of their walk as he ran toward them from the shipyard.

Noah tensed. "What's wrong?"

"Word's just getting out. Three of our council members were found dead this morning in the town hall."

"What?" Noah's and Emzara's startled responses mingled into one cry.

"Zain?" Noah asked.

Tubal-Cain nodded grimly. "He's one of them."

"No!" Emzara's scream muffled as Noah pulled her against him.

Noah's chest heaved shakily.

Emzara sniffed. "And the other two?"

"Kanael and Te'arek."

Noah shook his head as Emzara tried to absorb the information. *How could three people die at the same time, unless —*

"Adira was talking to Maiava when I left to see if she could learn any other details. But, I think it's obvious that this was no accident."

Emzara gasped. "Those are the last three members committed to the Most High."

Noah took in a long breath. "Does Kmani know yet?"

"I don't know, although . . ." Tubal-Cain stopped as Adira rounded the side of the old office building and rushed toward them.

"Maiava couldn't say much," Adira tried to catch her breath, "but she was able to tell me in private that it looks like they were poisoned during or after the council meeting last night."

"Poisoned?" Noah asked.

A loud clanging of deep tones from the town's emergency gong grabbed the group's attention.

"Guess we're being summoned to the crier's post." Tubal-Cain turned as he spoke.

"Stick together," Noah said.

Emzara walked alongside Adira as they followed Tubal-Cain's long, hurried stride while Noah brought up the rear. They marched up the hill toward Sarie's and found a large crowd had already gathered at the broad intersection. As the city's population increased, they had implemented a series of outposts by which news could be disseminated quickly. The council dispatched runners to inform the citizens gathered at each station.

Tubal-Cain led them up against the wall of the former bakery. He and Noah strained to see over heads, but the tightly packed crowd made any visibility impossible for Emzara. Glancing back over her shoulder, she pulled Adira close.

"Make way," a loud voice shouted ahead of them.

She turned her eyes up to the small platform that had been built about eight cubits off the ground between two large poles. Before long, the speaker climbed the rungs of the left post and stood above the crowd.

The gathering hushed as they waited.

"The words of Ashur, councilman of Iri Geshem. 'Tragedy has struck our great city.'" The crier's perfectly enunciated words carried over the assembly without being yelled. "Three of our cherished council members died mysteriously last night: Zain, Kanael, and Te'arek. As difficult as it will be to mourn for them, you need to know that we may all be affected by more than just grief." He paused to allow the crowd time to process.

Carefully, the messenger produced a small scroll from his wrap and held it above his head. "I have a message from the master healer." He unrolled the document and cleared his throat. "I have examined the bodies to see how all three could have died at the same time. There was no sign of violence, and I have concluded that they all had the same strange illness."

Emzara pressed herself against Noah, feeling reassured by his nearness. She imagined the high-pitched, nasal tone of the healer as the crier relayed his words.

The citizens murmured and many tried to back away from each other only to bump into the people behind them. A woman's voice called out, "Will it spread to others?"

"He wasn't sure, but he added a precaution. Ah, yes, here it is. 'If anyone has had contact with any of the deceased in the last week, they should go home immediately and remain there until the master healer declares it is safe to come out. Make sure you bathe in a blend of warm water, salt, shavings of milknut fruit, and three leaves from a red orb plant. If you experience any sudden pains or convulsions, hang a white cloth from your front door and a healer will be sent to you.' "

The crier rolled the scroll up and slipped it back into a pocket. "Following the private burial today, there will be an official week-long mourning period concluded by a gathering seven days from now in the square. That is all."

Questions immediately filled the air, and the messenger instructed the crowd to ask them in an orderly manner. At the same time, the gathering began to disperse. Emzara followed Noah as they weaved through the onlookers, and before long, they were on their way to the shipyard with Tubal-Cain and Adira.

"I don't believe it," Tubal-Cain said.

"Neither do I." Emzara shook her head. "I don't like this at all."

"Sickness?" Adira rolled her eyes. "Why would they gather everyone together only to tell them they need to avoid contact with each other?"

"With Zain gone, who will lead the council?" Emzara asked.

"Probably Ashur." The blacksmith squinted and clenched his jaw. "I suspect he's behind all of this somehow."

Emzara held up a palm. "So do you think the master healer is part of some conspiracy?"

Tubal-Cain shrugged. "Could be. He'd do what Ashur says if he thinks it's in his best interests. But maybe they were poisoned so that their deaths look like an illness."

Adira ran her fingers through her hair, pushing it behind her shoulders. "It's all a lie. Who's ever heard of such a silly cure? There's something they aren't telling us."

"Obviously, they intend to replace the three council members with people who agree with their wicked ways." Tubal-Cain slammed a fist into his open palm. "Zain didn't deserve this. He was a good man."

Emzara knew her husband's silence meant he was deep in thought. "Noah? What do you think?"

He shifted his focus from the road before them and held her gaze. "This changes everything." Noah grasped her hands.

"What do you mean?"

With a grim look, he glanced at Adira and Tubal-Cain. "We can't stay here. It's not safe for us."

"Where will you go?" Tubal-Cain asked.

Noah sighed. "I'm not sure. Probably Iri Sana at first, but I don't know if I want to stay there either."

"Just until things settle down, right?" Emzara said.

Noah shook his head slowly. "I can't see that happening. I'm afraid we won't be coming back."

"But this is our home." Emzara pulled her hands away from him. "We can't just give up and move away when something bad happens."

"Em, once the mourning period is over, Ashur and his followers will have complete control of the council." Noah stroked his temples. "Do you really think they'll allow followers of the Creator to just go about their business? They'll make it illegal to serve the Most High, and you know what that means?"

Emzara imagined some of the horrors she had heard about from cities where Nachash worship flourished. Shivering as she pictured herself going through unspeakable torture, she beheld Adira for a moment before turning back to her husband. "What's your plan?"

"We have a week. It'll take a few days to load a boat with the necessary supplies, and I think we'll need two of them." He pointed to her midsection. "You'll leave town with our son when the first one is loaded and head to my parents' house. I'm sure Garun and Laleel would be willing to go with you."

"What about them?" Emzara faced her long-time friend. "We can't leave them here."

Adira glanced at Tubal-Cain. "Most of our children are around here, so we'll stay put for now?"

Tubal-Cain nodded curtly.

"But if what Noah says is true, then you'll be in danger." Emzara swallowed hard.

"Maybe not right away," Tubal-Cain said. "Ashur's afraid of my father. I doubt he'd do something to us. If things turn out as poorly as you anticipate, then perhaps we'll join you in a short while."

Adira grabbed Emzara's arm. "Promise me that you'll stop in Iri Dekkel and tell our son what's happened. Tell him not to visit here until he gets news from us."

"That's a better plan," Noah said. "Em, instead of going all the way to Iri Sana, go to Purlek's and wait for me. We can travel together from there."

Emzara sniffed and her lower lip quivered as she watched her husband. "And when will you leave?"

"As soon as the second boat's loaded." Noah kissed her head. "I should be well on my way before the mourning period is over."

"Do you think they'll guard the bridge to make sure no one leaves?" Tubal-Cain asked.

"I don't think so, but if they do, there are ways around that." Noah turned his head to make sure no one else could hear their conversation. "The hinges on the lift need to be replaced and require the care of a certain blacksmith. Of course, it makes sense to work on it at night so you aren't interrupting normal business traffic."

"And if a certain boat happens to come along while I'm working on it?" Tubal-Cain asked.

Adira put a hand on his chest. "Then you pretend like you didn't see it."

CHAPTER 30

Iri Geshem — Noah's 499ᵗʰ year

I'd prefer that you come with me." Noah looked the elderly man in the eyes. "But I understand that you want to stay close to your family."

Bakur leaned his 810-year-old frame against the outer hull of one of the ships under construction. "I'm sorry to see you go, but I understand why you must. So what becomes of the shipyard?"

Noah slowly surveyed the flurry of activity around him. Over a dozen employees scurried about as they neared completion of another pair of ships for Malrak, a major port to the southwest. As the business had expanded in the past century, Noah had replaced a few run-down buildings and built a large warehouse for lumber, tools, and other supplies. Even more impressive, a giant four-story construction barn butted up close to the sea. Reserved for constructing the 100-cubit-long cargo vessels, this outbuilding allowed the shipwrights to work in any weather, and it contained moveable platforms for easier access to even the tallest portions of the ship.

Noah smiled to mask his pain at leaving it all behind. "If you won't come with me, then it's all yours."

"What is?" Bakur asked.

Noah spread his arms out wide. "All of this. The shipyard. The whole business. The house. It's yours." He pointed to the small river runner that he had been loading all morning. "Except that one, of course."

The old man shook his head. "I never asked for . . ."

"I know, but if anyone deserves it, you do," Noah said. "There's no one else I'd rather see it go to. After all, you helped train me."

Bakur stared off into the distance and a smile slowly crept across his lips. "Those were the days, weren't they?"

"They sure were." Noah placed a hand on his shoulder. "I've already written up the papers in your name. They're in my office."

"I can't believe this is happening — that you're really going through with this. It's all so . . ." Bakur turned his head up as if searching for a word. He shrugged and said, "so sudden." He sighed. "Make sure you add a line to the effect that the business reverts to you if you ever decide to come back."

"I can do that, but it won't be necessary. I have a new calling." He glanced toward the city. "Besides, I doubt I'll be safe here for much longer."

Bakur nodded grimly. "You've made a lot of enemies around here by doing what's right."

Noah had stood against the younger generations' practices for a long time, and a growing number of them resented him for it. Being a success-ful businessman and occasional member of the council earned him some respect, but based on the snide comments and angry looks, most of the town's burgeoning population was not going to miss him.

"Well, for what it's worth, I'm grateful for your example over all these years," Bakur said. "I'll truly miss you and Emzara."

Noah nodded. "And we'll miss you and many others. We'll get everything finalized later. Right now, I need to finish loading the ship."

After enlisting the assistance of two younger employees, Noah headed for the warehouse to finish the tedious process of moving items to the boat. Two days earlier, Noah had finished loading Emzara's boat with many of their belongings, along with various tools and devices necessary for shipbuilding, though he was careful to leave plenty for the shipyard to run efficiently. She had left with Laleel and Garun the night before last, and he could almost feel the distance between them grow with every moment he delayed.

When most of his items were packed away on the ship, Noah went to his office and stretched out on the nearly vacant floor. Closing his eyes, he smiled as memories rushed through his thoughts. This room had been his second home for centuries. He could have ruminated for weeks on the memories he'd made here, but a knock at the door stirred him from his daydream.

Noah rolled over and pushed himself up. "Come in."

The door opened and Pav, one of the young men who had helped him load the boat, stepped in. "Sir, Bakur said there are guards from the city waiting outside. Everyone is required to head to the city square immediately."

Noah raised an eyebrow. "Did they say why?"

"The memorial celebration for the fallen council members."

"That's not until tomorrow."

Pav shrugged. "It must have been moved up a day for some reason."

"I see. Thank you. I'll be out shortly."

"I'll let them know." Pav turned to leave.

"Pav, wait." Noah gestured for the young man to enter his office. "Did the guards see you?"

"No, sir. I was inside and Bakur told me to fetch you."

"Great. How'd you like to earn three weeks' pay for a short errand?"

The young man nodded excitedly. "What do you want me to do?"

Noah slipped a gold pikka from the leather band around his neck. "Wait in here until everyone's gone, and then take my riverboat to the old docks."

Pav's eyes followed the golden disc in Noah's hand. "On the river? And what if they stop me at the bridge?"

Noah nodded. "You shouldn't have any trouble, but if they ask where you're going, just tell them your boss wanted you to take it for a short ride on the river. If they tell you to get to the ceremony, ask them to let you use the old docks so you can get to the square faster." Noah flipped the pikka to Pav. "I'll make sure you receive two more if you complete the task."

"I will. Thanks. I'll stay out of sight until the guards are gone." Pav headed to the next room.

Noah adjusted his wrap and took a deep breath, contemplating why the council would have changed the timing of the ceremony. Bowing his head, he focused on his recent encounter with the Creator, and a sense of awe and responsibility washed over him. *Creator, I promised I would serve You. Help me to remain true to my word and faithful to You.*

Moments later, Noah marched down the long hallway and stepped outside. Over at the main building, a guard directed his employees toward the road while two more approached from Noah's right. Each sentry sported a leather jerkin under a bronze chest plate and shoulder covers along with a long dagger in a sheath hanging from the left side of his belt.

"Noah," the man on the left said.

Spinning to face them head on, Noah said, "Morning peace."

"Sir," the guard said without changing his stoic expression. "We have orders to take you to the council right away."

Noah tilted his head and smiled when he recognized the speaking guard as Elnach, a grandson of Ashur and Navea. "For what reason?"

Elnach shook his head. "The council chairman didn't say. He just told us to find you and bring you to them."

"The chairman?" Noah asked. "They've already selected a new leader?"

The guard nodded. "Ashur. He wanted you to join them for the memorial."

Noah pursed his lips and turned toward town. "Then I shouldn't keep your grandfather waiting."

They led Noah on the shortest route to the city's central district, which took them through Iri Geshem's old city square. These days he typically avoided the area altogether. He hated the increasing violence and blatant immorality, and he struggled to block the vile images that it burned into his mind. Sadness and disappointment washed over Noah as they passed through the area. Ashur's old inn served as a brothel, and rumors persisted that he still owned the place despite his public denials. The ancient town hall stood in disrepair while functioning as a shop selling idols and potions designed to enchant their users. Rickety shelters leaned against many of the buildings, and a foul stench filled the air from the garbage and human waste dumped in the open square. Shaking his head, Noah tried to comprehend how so many denizens lived in this squalor and how his beloved city had come to this.

People still milled about — taking their time to get to the memorial. A woman, obviously from the brothel, almost bumped into him as she laughed with her male companion. Noah quickly sidestepped her, but in the brief moment they exchanged glances, her eyes told a story of misery. In a darkened alleyway, two ragged young boys sat, their heads bent low. Noah had often offered jobs and mentoring to those in need, though few had accepted over the years, most choosing to continue searching for worldly ways to numb their pain. *Oh, Most High, surely You didn't create us for this. Use me however You will to show them the life that comes in following Your ways. And God, if that means . . .*

"Going to the memorial?" A confident voice interrupted Noah's prayer. "You'll need one of these." Holding up a small animal idol, the salesman started his pitch. "With so much death around, Zsanom is the only one to protect you now."

Noah turned away and held his arm out, refusing the offer. He picked up his pace, eager to break away from this environment.

The guards grabbed Noah's elbow and turned him onto the broad street that led straight to the central district. Now beyond the malodorous area, Noah took in a deep breath of fresh air, trying to clear the disturbing effects from his spirit. Hundreds of citizens marched toward the square in the distance; most stepped aside for Noah and his armored escorts.

The sounds of construction grabbed Noah's attention as they neared the massive theater, where crowds frequently gathered to be entertained by plays and other activities. Initially, the dramas showcased talented performers from around the world acting out epic adventures or gripping tragedies. In his days on the council, Noah often took Emzara to the shows, where they enjoyed the best seats in a section reserved for council members and dignitaries. But Noah stopped attending many years ago. In the past few decades, most of the performances had degenerated to the point of focusing on coarse jesting and sexually immoral behavior. Recent renovations expanded the theater even more to allow for sport and often featured warriors who fought to the death to entertain bloodthirsty audiences.

Noah beheld the newest construction project attached to the theater's southwest side. Roughly the size of the shipyard's largest barn and featuring extremely thick stone walls, the addition spread up half the outer wall and around the outside of the theater. A stone ramp dropped below ground through a large tunnel. *That must be the new entrance to the lower levels Zain told me about.*

They ambled past the arena and under the imposing gate that led into the central district. Tens of thousands of people moved about the expansive square as they waited for the ceremony to begin.

"Over there." Elnach nudged Noah and pointed toward the new town hall, a towering edifice that dwarfed all the other extravagant buildings around it both in size and elegance. The sunlight reflected off the hall's white stone façade causing Noah to shade his eyes with his hand. A sprawling balcony jutted out from the third floor, allowing those on the terrace to look over the entire square.

Elnach led Noah to a reserved section on the ground that featured about 25 rows of benches. It was roped off and guarded to prevent any unauthorized admittance. Beyond that area, an immense crowd had gathered. Noah was ushered to a seat near the middle of the reserved section, giving him a perfect view of whoever would address the crowd.

"Why so close?" Noah asked.

Elnach shrugged. "I believe many of the business owners will be in this area." He and the other guard turned and marched back the way they had come.

From high above, a metallic clang sounded twice, alerting attendees to get ready for the ceremony to begin. Fashioned by Tubal-Cain, the huge bronze disc hung at the top of the town hall and could be heard throughout Iri Geshem. *Where is Tubal-Cain?* Noah scanned the crowd but did not see any of his friends. He recognized some of the people around him, but at best they were merely acquaintances. The wife of a man who owned a tavern in the old city scowled at Noah. Apparently, she still held a grudge against him from when he, along with the majority of the council, rejected the initial proposal to allow the establishment of such drinking halls in town. Noah shook his head. *That must have been 200 years ago, and it was changed soon after that.*

The metal plate was struck again. On the platform above, five council members dressed in traditional white garb strode to the edge of the terrace and dropped into their ornate seats. Four spots remained empty; one belonged to Ashur, and the replacement council members would fill the other three. Ashur walked to the middle of the group and gestured with his arms for the crowd to be silent.

"Citizens of Iri Geshem, thank you for arriving on short notice to honor the lives of three faithful servants of our city. This past week has been very difficult for all of us." Criers stationed strategically throughout the square echoed each line of his speech so that everyone heard the proceedings. "This tragedy has affected each one of us. We've lost dear

210

friends and tremendous servants of our great city, but we know that they would want us to move forward and take every opportunity to ensure that Iri Geshem has a bright future."

He motioned to his fellow councilors. "We've been in constant meetings throughout the week, deliberating on what to do next. We decided to replace our fallen members so that your council would have every advantage as we make important decisions. So please welcome your new council members."

Although he had anticipated that the new elders would not be followers of the Creator, Noah's heart sank as he watched his concerns become reality. He did not know the first woman mentioned, but the serpent markings on her arms told him enough. The man was a wealthy merchant and the other woman was an apothecary who peddled the intoxicating substances often used in Nachash worship. Both had repeatedly stood against the previous council's efforts to maintain the Creator's ways in the city, and they made no secret of their contempt for Noah.

Another clash from the bronze plate rang out. Music filled the air from all directions as shouts resounded from the north side of the courtyard, causing Noah to turn. A large wagon pulled an enormous object toward the middle of the square by a team of six lunkers. Having seen a similar event in Havil in his youth, Noah shook his head, knowing full well what rested beneath the cloth. He spun back to glare at Ashur, only to see the chairman looking straight at him with a wicked grin. Noah scanned the crowd for an escape route, but he realized that dozens of guards now surrounded his position.

Once the lunkers stopped, Ashur spoke again. "Today is a monumental day for Iri Geshem. We will finally cast off the restrictive rules of those who follow the so-called Creator. Today, our marvelous city becomes even greater as we officially dedicate it to the mighty Serpent, Nachash."

As the covering dropped from the stone serpent, cheers erupted from the masses. Gold glimmered in a long line along the back of the figure, and red stones filled its eye sockets. Similar to the idol in Havil, the stone abomination stood roughly twenty cubits tall, with its body coiled at the base and its head erect, as if poised to strike.

When the people finally quieted, Ashur continued. "The new council's first act is designed to foster unity among our citizens and loyalty to our true god. When you hear the music play, you will bow down to Nachash.

All who refuse will be arrested and will face banishment or worse." He stared directly at Noah. "We cannot permit such treasonous acts to go unpunished." Ashur held his arms up high. "Are you ready?"

A deafening shout instantly sounded from the populace, and a chill swept through Noah. At the same time, a confidence he had never known before surged through his body. The hairs on his arms and neck seemed to stand and yet he struggled to repress a smile.

Ashur lowered his arms. Instantly, drummers throughout the courtyard beat on their instruments in rhythm. People all around Noah spun to face the idol and hastily dropped to the ground in obeisance.

Defiantly, Noah folded his arms across his chest and refused to budge, keeping his back turned to the serpent god. Ashur's lust for wealth and control stirred feelings of pity inside Noah. Nevertheless, he knew Ashur's disobedience would soon be punished. *Creator, be with me and guide my actions. May these people realize that You are the Most High and that the Serpent is the Great Deceiver.*

The music paused as Ashur held up a hand and looked around the square. "Did you not hear the music?"

Noah followed Ashur's gaze around the square and noticed a few dozen people standing.

"You will have one more chance to honor Nachash," Ashur said. "If you refuse to bow, you will be arrested promptly."

The music started again, but Noah stood tall, sticking out like a taroc next to a group of buzzbirds. Ashur grinned at him, as did several other council members as four guards approached.

The captain spoke. "You were ordered to bow!"

Noah raised his voice. "I bow only to the Cre —" A sharp pain exploded in the back of his knees, dropping him to the ground. Noah looked up and realized it was Elnach who had struck him.

"Bow!" Elnach held a staff above his head, ready to deliver another blow.

Noah stood quickly despite the searing pain in his legs. "The Creator is the Most High!"

Another blow to his legs caused his knees to buckle, but he caught himself before hitting the ground. As he tried to right himself, he glimpsed a fist just before it crashed into his face. Suddenly, he fell backward and everything faded to black.

CHAPTER 31

Noah raised his bound hands and pushed them against his head to quell the throbbing that gripped his attention the moment he regained consciousness. He carefully opened his eyes, trying to take in his unfamiliar surroundings. Daylight streamed in through a thin opening at the top of the stone wall to his right. He cringed after taking in a breath of the stale, pungent air.

"You're finally awake."

The familiar voice slowly registered in his head. *Tubal-Cain.* Noah rolled onto his left side to face his friend. "They went after you too?"

The blacksmith rested against the wall, each arm stretched to the side by ropes tied to his wrist on one end and a ring in the wall on the other. His head sank. "And Adira, but I don't know where she is. They arrested dozens of people."

"I'm sorry. We all should've left with Em."

"It's not your fault, Noah. We knew the risks, but we wanted to stay near our children and their children." Tubal-Cain sighed. "I just never imagined things could change so rapidly."

"We should've seen it coming, though. Ashur's been trying to get control of the council for decades."

"And in his first move, he arrests everyone who would dare oppose him. Ruthless."

"Ara warned me about him so long ago, but I don't think even he ever imagined it would come to this." A sharp pain stung Noah's leg as he attempted to stretch it out, a painful reminder of the blows from Elnach.

Wincing, he forced himself into a seated position and leaned against the wall opposite Tubal-Cain. "Speaking of arrest, do you have any idea where we are? This isn't one of the holding cells near the town hall."

"No, it's not." Tubal-Cain lifted his head and looked toward the wooden door on the far side of the room. "That's the only way in or out. I think we're in the lower level of the old theater. It sounded like there was some cheering a while ago, but it was pretty muffled in here."

Noah's eyes widened as a cruel thought formulated. "And we're going to be part of the entertainment, aren't we?"

"That seems like a strong possibility."

Twisting his wrists, Noah tried to slide his restraints off. "Any chance of us breaking out of here?"

Tubal-Cain shook his head. "Not likely. I've tried."

Noah fell still as hopelessness washed over him. Then he smirked. "Well, you'd better hope they don't make us fight to the death. I think we both know who'd win that one."

Tubal-Cain snorted. "Only because I'd let you."

"And I'd never fight you." Suddenly serious, Noah shifted his weight, trying to find a comfortable position. "No matter what happens today, I want you to know how grateful I am for your friendship over the years. I couldn't ask for a better friend, and I know Em feels the same way about Adira."

"And we think the same about you and Zara, but don't get too mushy. Besides, I don't think Ashur would have the guts to kill me if he thought it would upset my father." Tubal-Cain glanced up and his eyes glittered with unshed tears. "To be honest, I'm worried that he'll want to make an example of you."

Approaching footsteps captured Noah's attention.

"He's in this one." A man peeked into the locked room through a small opening near the top of the door. "One moment." Metal pieces clinked together before the latch slid out of its place. The door opened and two guards carrying torches entered the cell.

The man on the right pointed to Tubal-Cain. "There he is."

As the guards stepped to either side and placed their torches in the sockets on the wall, a woman dressed in a long black gown walked between them, holding her chin high and shoulders back. The left side of her head was shaved, but her dark black hair hung down behind her right arm, which bore the unmistakable emblems of Nachash. A high-ranking soldier followed close behind her. She cocked her head to the side. "Tu?"

Noah's heart sank and he quietly dipped his head, hiding his face from Naamah. He watched Tubal-Cain from the corner of an eye.

Tubal-Cain's head flinched backward. "Amah?"

She let out a mocking laugh. "Ah, brother, it's been a long time."

"Yes, it has. What are you doing here?"

Naamah raised her chin. "Haven't you heard? This city belongs to Havil now, and it's time for them to meet their princess and high priestess."

"What? How. . . ."

"You'll know soon enough."

"Where's my wife? Is she safe?" Tubal-Cain fought his restraints.

"How should I know?" She bent down in front of him. "I'm sure we'll find her, and if you cooperate, I can guarantee her safety."

"Cooperate?" Tubal-Cain leaned back. "What do you want?"

"That's for Da to decide." She snapped her fingers and turned to leave. "Guards, take him to my father."

Noah dipped his head even lower, but a man's armored legs soon filled the edge of his view. A strong hand grabbed his chin and forcibly twisted his face upward. Recognition filled both captor and captive at the same moment. *Nivlac!*

A wicked smile opened on the guard's lips. "One moment, Princess. Look what I found."

She turned and fixed her gaze on Noah. Her mouth widened in a slow, sinister smile as she recognized him. "I'll be there soon," she said over her shoulder, without taking her gaze from Noah's face. "I'd like to have a few moments to talk with my old friend Noah before he makes his debut in the arena."

"Naamah, don't do this," Tubal-Cain said as the guards untied the ropes from the wall and bound his hands together.

"It's not up to me. Perhaps you can persuade the king to spare his life."

Noah looked past her to Tubal-Cain. "Don't worry about me. Honor the Creator no matter the consequences."

Tubal-Cain climbed to his feet with the guards' assistance. "I will. Farewell, Noah."

"May the Creator keep you."

215

"Enough!" Naamah stiffened and faced the guards holding Tubal-Cain. "Get him out of here."

The two sentries pulled the rope binding the blacksmith, leading him out of the room while Nivlac took up a post near the door.

Naamah laughed derisively. "Ah, Noah. This certainly looks familiar. Just you and me. And your life in my hands again." She paced in front of him. "And to think, you could've prevented all of this. You and I could've ruled Havil and the rest of the world together, but you were too self-righteous and too naïve. Tell me, where is your wife now?"

Silently thanking the Creator that Emzara was safe far up the river, Noah said nothing and kept his head down, only able to see Naamah's feet as she stopped in front of him. He recoiled when her hand touched his cheek.

"Still intimidated by me, I see. Very well. Perhaps she'll be in the crowd, cheering you on as you face your death." She pivoted. "Help him to his feet."

The dry ground crunched beneath Nivlac's footsteps. He grabbed Noah under the arm and pulled him to his feet.

"That's better," Naamah said. "Look at me."

Noah stared at the ground until Naamah snapped her fingers. Nivlac grabbed Noah's hair and yanked his head back.

Naamah stretched her arms to the side and slowly spun around. Her attractive form had diminished little over the centuries, but somehow she seemed to have aged much more than her contemporaries. Her eyes lacked the beauty and spark that had inhabited them so long ago. Her face was wrinkled like that of someone a century older, though she tried to mask it with various paints and dyes. "Do you regret your decision now, Noah?" She brushed his cheek with the back of her hand and then gently slapped him. "What a shame. We could've accomplished so much together, but today will be your last, and I'll continue to be the most powerful person in the world."

A surge of confidence rushed through Noah. He straightened, drew back his shoulders, and stared defiantly at her. "I will not die today."

One side of her lips curled up and she unsuccessfully tried to stifle a laugh. "You amuse me. But I promise you, you will die today."

"I don't think so." Noah shook his head. "But even if that happens, the Creator will bring me back to life."

216

Naamah's jaw dropped and she stared at him. "The Creator? After all this time, you're still trying to serve a defeated God? Most of the world follows Nachash now. He has overthrown your insignificant God." She snickered and strode away before turning and marching back. "Tell me, Noah. What makes you think you'll live beyond this day?"

Something in her expression and tone showed a tinge of doubt. Noah's confidence rose even more. "Because I haven't finished the task He has given me."

"The task? The Creator gave you a job to do?"

Noah wondered if he should remain silent, but his desire to see everyone follow the Creator won out. Still, he did not want to give away too many details. "Yes. He's going to destroy this world with a flood. Only a small number of people will be spared."

"Let me guess, you're supposed to be one of those people."

Noah nodded.

A vicious grin curved Naamah's lips. "Well, this day just got better. Not only will your life come to a spectacular end in the arena, but so will belief in your weak God when the people see your demise."

"And when you're proven wrong, then what?" Noah asked. "The Serpent is a fraud, Naamah. Turn to the Creator while —"

She slapped him. "Don't you dare address me without my proper title! I am the high priestess of Nachash, and you'll soon learn the meaning of true power." She spun and walked to the door.

He watched her go, saddened by her eagerness to follow the Great Deceiver. Nivlac held the door open for her, and a massive human frame appeared on the other side of the opening. The top of Naamah's head barely reached his waist, and his torso and head remained a mystery because they were higher than the door frame. Each of the giant's legs measured about as large as Noah's whole body.

"Your father is waiting for you." The man's deep voice rumbled through the cell just before the door shut.

Is that what I'll face in the arena? Noah took in a deep breath before slumping to his knees and stretching forward. *Creator, my life is in Your hands. I believe You'll rescue me today because I trust You to fulfill Your plan. I don't know how You'll do it, but I ask that others will have the opportunity to hear the truth about You.*

CHAPTER 32

Naamah walked swiftly beside her gigantic guard, rage fueling her steps and allowing her to keep pace with him. What was it about Noah that always made her feel powerless? She no longer felt any attraction toward him, but his words still sliced through her and made her feel helpless. The lack of control she felt around him was the same as when her then-beloved father brought home a second wife all those hundreds of years ago. *Really? You're not going to die today?* She smirked. *We'll see about that.*

A gaping door stood at the end of the wide passage, but the hulking figure at her side opened up a smaller door to their right, which led to a snaking path up to the main platform. Approaching Tu, who waited by the entrance with his armed escort, she tossed her hair behind her back with a flick of her head and straightened her shoulders.

"What's going on, Amah? Why are you and Da here?" His old pet name for her sparked something from deep within, but she squelched it.

Four guards accompanied them through the smaller exit; two led the way while the other two followed. Her giant companion left her side in order to enter the arena from a route more suitable for his size.

"We took over the town. Well, it was handed over to us. No battle necessary." She allowed Tubal-Cain to walk beside her and he leaned his head occasionally to avoid the low ceilings. "The king plans to make Iri Geshem our northern capital."

"Come on, Noah's not here, and you don't have to brag in front of me."

She leveled a cold look at him. "I'm not kidding. Once you see him, you'll know the truth."

He shrugged. "So what does he want with me?"

"You're his son, why shouldn't you share in his greatest achievements?"

"He's always left me alone before now."

"Well, you're not young anymore. Maybe he thinks it's time you started showing loyalty to your family."

"Oh, I'm not young anymore, huh?" His face lit up with his unique grin.

Naamah kept her visage expressionless, hoping to hide her thoughts from him. *Oh, Tu, when's the last time I've seen a genuine smile from anyone? I didn't realize how much I've missed you.*

"You know," he said, "you're not so young yourself." He winked at her. "And what's this new look you've got going on?" He pointed to the intricate design on her shoulder, where embedded ink interwove with lines of delicate scar tissue to form twisted vines and snakes in the branches of a Sepha tree. She had endured countless needle pricks and fine knife work to shape the image and raised skin, which covered her shoulder and a good portion of her arm, and extended down her back. Yet she had received it so long ago that she had almost forgotten it was not naturally part of her. "Nachash has been very good to me all these years."

"Pardon me for saying so, but I don't believe that. You still look beautiful, sister, but the look in your eyes and the wear around them tell me a different story. You seem wrecked by Nachash."

Anger flared again, and she sneered. "How could you say that? Don't you realize I could have any man in this arena if I so chose? But I doubt that anyone in this place is worthy of me."

He groaned and shook his head, but the pity in his eyes drove her onward. "I have more power than ever before. In moments, and with barely a nod of my head, people run to do my every whim: whether that's to sentence someone, to start a new project, or to simply call someone to bring me a piece of exotic fruit from the south country. I have it all."

"You seem to. But you've forgotten the most important thing, that which makes life truly meaningful."

"And what's that?" She spat the words at him.

"You've chosen to ignore the Creator and His ways. Instead, you're a slave to your own passions and pride."

"Enough! The Creator is a weak God worshiped by weak-minded people desperate to justify their own failure to rise in this world. You will speak no more to me about this, and if you know what's good for you, you won't breathe a word of it to Da." She turned away slightly and bit her lip, frustrated that she used an informal name for their father in this setting. It was a sign of weakness that he flustered her, but if he noticed, his unchanged expression did not show it.

Naamah stepped in front of him and held her head proudly. Seeing the sunlit entrance ahead of them, she was glad his opportunities to harass her had come to an end.

One of the guards hurried out through the exit to announce their arrival to those seated in the place of honor. After he returned, he motioned to the guards in the rear. "You two, escort the Prince and Princess of Havil to their waiting areas atop the platform." The soldiers instantly obeyed, grabbing Tubal-Cain's restraints and forcing him forward as Naamah followed.

The back wall temporarily blocked their view of the sizable audience, but Ashur's annoying voice welcomed the people to the dawn of a new era of prosperity and peace. He pontificated on how the King of Havil had arrived just in time to save them from whatever evil killed three of their leading citizens. "And now, give your king the honor due to his greatness."

A deafening roar split through the arena, making her ears ache, while reverberating through her chest. Soon the voices quieted, and Naamah imagined the king's fist raised high, commanding their attention.

Lamech's voice thundered through the crowd. "My people, as your first king, I'm indebted to your loyalty. Let us celebrate the peaceful transition and the prosperity to come." A slight pause followed before he yelled, "Let the games begin."

The crowd erupted again. Having witnessed it in Havil and a few of the other cities they controlled, Naamah could picture the scene clearly: a small company of captives shuffle their way into the center. Once the guards return to safety, a door opens, allowing whatever wild beast lies behind it to come and prey upon the hapless victims. As elsewhere, the roar of this crowd revealed their enjoyment of the sport. She sneaked a sideways glance at Tubal-Cain, who was still heavily guarded. With his eyes closed, his broad shoulders quivered as his lips moved silently. Even the sentry fumbling to untie her brother's bonds failed to interrupt his focus.

You haven't seen anything yet. She laughed low in her throat, thinking about how powerful she was compared to him, that even this death sport had little effect on her emotions.

"And now, my people," King Lamech called out, "I give to you Nachash and unity."

From their place behind the platform, Naamah and Tubal-Cain followed their cues and entered through the heavy brocade fabric that draped on either side of the open doorway. The deafening applause thundered again as she confidently took her place on the king's right. The newly unveiled statue of Nachash towered above them to her right.

"Let me introduce you to two people whom you may have already met. The first is Naamah. She, my only daughter, is high priestess of Nachash, and quite a sight to behold. Am I right?" He paused, letting the crowd show their approval.

The volume of praise filled her heart, and she breathed in the moment, holding her fist high in the air. As they chanted her name, she twirled and sashayed a bit, accentuating her best features in a spontaneous dance, spurring the crowd into more of a frenzy.

"The next . . ." the king waited for silence, "the next is my oldest son and heir, who has lived among you as one of your own for centuries. Your favorite blacksmith, Prince Tubal-Cain!"

Amid cries of delight, a guard directed Tubal-Cain to sit in the large throne made for him on Lamech's left. He leaned toward the king and shook his head slightly, "You know I want none of this."

"Quiet, you fool!" The king scowled at his son. The vehemence of his words caused the tight curls of his coiffed hair to dance about his shoulders. "You will do as I say."

"My good people." He straightened the crown on his head. "Tubal-Cain and Naamah are brother and sister, they are my children and they will demonstrate before you their loyalty to Nachash and their unity to this new, wonderful nation. Bring forth the sacrifices!"

Two scantily clad, stone-faced women came forward, each with a baby in her arms. They stood in front of the towering serpent statue, its golden head held aloft, forked tongue ready to receive innocent blood.

Lamech gestured to a guard who quickly handed him a knife. He held it out to his son. "And now, here is my son to offer the first official sacrifice of Iri Geshem, the northern chief city of Havilah."

The color drained from Tubal-Cain's face, and he folded his arms across his broad chest, refusing to take the dagger.

Shock rippled through the crowd, slowly silencing their cheers.

Come on, Tu. It's just one baby. Naamah tapped her foot on the stone flooring.

Anger churned in their father's eyes as he stood and approached Tubal-Cain. "You will do as I command."

Tubal-Cain held his head high. "People of Iri Geshem," his voice rang out as clearly, if not clearer and louder, than the king's, "I am not a prince of Havil. I am but a servant of the Most High, and He never asks for the blood of a child. Only the Great Deceiver demands the sacrifice of a baby."

The people jeered and shouted their disapproval.

Lamech, in his anger, whirled and stood before his throne once more. When the crowd quieted, he spoke loudly. "If your squeamish, sensitive nature cannot handle the demands of sacrifice, then at least bow before Nachash."

Unfazed, Tubal-Cain shook his head. "Never." He turned to the crowd. "Friends, I beg you, turn from your ways. Remove the shackles of fear and bondage brought by Nachash and embrace the one true God, the Creator."

Naamah watched the unfolding power play between her father and brother as both tried to sway the masses to their way of thinking. *Just bow, you fool.*

"My son, you talk of fear." Lamech rubbed his hands together. "You say your worship of the Creator frees you from fear?"

"Yes."

The king held out his arms. "Good citizens, he lies. Bring out his wife!"

Tubal-Cain gasped as the guards brought Adira to the center of the stadium and one of them shoved her. With disheveled clothes and hair, she staggered and fell to her knees.

"She will die if you do not bow." The king flashed a grin at Naamah before fixing his gaze on his son. "Surely you fear that!"

"Stay true to the Creator, Love!"

The plaintive cry of the bound woman annoyed Naamah, and she hissed. "Just bow! Don't you see that you could lose everything?"

He pierced her with his eyes. "Rejecting my Creator would be the worst loss of all."

The crowd yelled out a variety of taunts. "This is unity?" "You can't even control your own offspring!" "We want blood!"

"Tu, she will die if you don't bow." Naamah's voice squeaked in desperation. *Ugh, why do I feel so powerless?*

"You have one more chance to show your loyalty." Lamech narrowed his eyes on his son.

Tubal-Cain stood silently.

"Very well." He held up one finger toward a small entryway into the arena. "Bring it out."

A pithoct entered the area, snarling and tugging against its restraints, which were held by a pair of strong warriors. The beast bared its two long upper teeth, locked its eyes on its prey, and roared.

Why wouldn't Adira tell him to bow? Now she's made Da look bad in front of all these people. I hope it's a slow and agonizing death for her. Naamah watched the proceedings in front of her intently, hoping to catch the full measure of pain and justice.

"Listen to me! As your king, I know what you want and what you need. Nachash will have his unity and his blood. Not even my son will get in the way of that."

Alarmed at the undertone of pure hatred in his voice, Naamah turned just as her father lifted the sacrificial dagger he still grasped. His hands quivered only slightly before driving it into the lower right side of her brother.

"No!" The scream escaped Naamah's lips before she could stop it. *Tu! How did it escalate to this?*

Adira shrieked and ran toward them.

Tubal-Cain slumped against the railing, keeping his eyes on his wife.

"A kingdom cannot allow such treason to exist." Lamech stepped forward, bent down, and lifted Tubal-Cain's legs up and over the railing. "Die with your wife, Traitor!"

Naamah fought to control her emotions as she watched her brother fall into the arena and hit the ground with a thud just as the guard released the furry beast. It took every bit of her self-control to resist charging her father to push him over the rail as well. She glared at the back of the king's head with all the hatred she could muster. *Someday, you'll die for this.*

The beast slowed as it seemed to contemplate which of the two victims it preferred first. Keeping its distance, it circled around the couple, stalking them, as Adira tried to shield her wounded husband. Finally, it charged.

Tubal-Cain ripped the dagger from his side, scrambled to his knees, and pulled his wife down behind him. As the beast leapt, Tubal-Cain yelled and jabbed the blade upward as the pithoct struck him. The animal moaned as it collapsed on its target. Screeching, it hopped awkwardly to the side before stumbling, a dark red spot growing on its white-furred chest. Lying on its side, the creature kicked its legs for a few moments and then stopped moving.

Tubal-Cain remained motionless as well, except for the barely noticeable rise and fall of his chest and a slight turn of his marred face to look at his wife. She knelt at his side and pulled his wrap away from the dagger's previous location. Blood oozed from the gaping wound, causing her to slump over him and wail. He struggled to lift his left arm and drape it over her.

Unable to watch his demise, Naamah turned away. Seething rage increased with each breath.

Tubal-Cain's wife screamed in agony, and it echoed through the arena, causing some to laugh while others looked on in shock.

Having heard similar cries many times before, Naamah knew her brother's life had just ended. *Tu! How could you be so stubborn and ignorant? How foolish to give your life for nothing.*

"Take her," Lamech said to the giant guard, who had just entered the arena, while pointing at Adira. "Put her with the next batch of prisoners."

Naamah glared at her father. His smile showed his delight in the turn of events. *You wanted this to happen all along.* She paused in her thoughts and looked up at the giant serpent next to her. *O Nachash, grant me strength and wisdom to exact revenge on him.*

CHAPTER 33

Noah lurched forward and stumbled to keep up as the enormous guard yanked the rope tied about his wrists. The immense man easily covered four stairs at a time, practically dragging Noah up the steps. Above the pounding in his ears from his heartbeat and his panting for air, Noah still easily discerned the roar of the crowd in the arena.

They reached level ground and stopped in what had been one of the four large foyers in the theater's early days. Remodeled over the years, the cavernous room now seemed to serve as a staging area for whatever bawdy entertainment happened to be on the schedule. Huge timbers stretched upward to support the sloped ceiling, which also served to hold hundreds of spectators above it. Racks of weapons and armor lined the wall ahead. To their right, countless shelves of colorful garments and headwear rested behind three reflective metallic panels.

As they approached the large iron gate that led to the arena floor, the room grew lighter, allowing Noah to finally take a long look at his giant escort. Rumors of giants in Havil and other places abounded, but he had assumed the tales were merely exaggerations of tall individuals. The reality proved to be more impressive than the stories. The man easily surpassed six cubits. Musclebound like Tubal-Cain, only much larger, the man pulled Noah as if he exerted no effort at all. His left fist, roughly the size of Noah's head, clenched the rope, while his right hand swung freely. Iron armor covered his chest and midsection. A long, thick spear hung across his back and strapped to his belt, and a massive sheathed sword rattled and swayed along with its owner's loping gait.

To avoid the discomfort, Noah fought to keep up. "Will they even give me a weapon to fight you?"

The giant stopped before the gate and angled his shaved head down toward Noah before snarling. "I wish they would. You'd make a good meal."

Noah turned away in disgust. Was the man simply trying to scare him or did he really eat people?

A deep, rumbling laugh escaped from the titan's mouth. "I'm told they have something special planned for you."

Noah grinned. "So does the Creator."

The giant's free hand moved with blinding speed to grip Noah around the neck. With just one arm, the oversized man picked Noah off the ground and raised him until they were face-to-face. Huge, hate-filled, bloodshot orbs glared at him, and for an instant, fear surged through Noah's body.

Noah felt as if his eyes would pop out of his head — that is, if his head did not separate from his body first. With breathing or screaming an impossibility, he kicked and swung his arms wildly to break free, but striking at a stone wall may have been more effective.

"Don't you ever speak of the Creator around me." He spat in Noah's face and tossed him to the ground.

Gasping for air, Noah wiped saliva from his face with his shoulder. He groaned and struggled to stand, hoping to avoid being dragged again.

As a roar resounded from the crowd beyond the gate, the giant glared at Noah. "Time for you to die."

Noah cleared his throat, trying to collect himself. "Not today." He had imagined those words coming out stronger than the hoarse whisper that escaped his airway.

The huge man snorted before he bent over and grabbed the gate with his free hand. With metal creaking and groaning in protest, the giant heaved the iron bars above his head in one swift motion until it latched in place.

A crowd buzzing with excitement roared as Noah's attendant stepped out of the shadows. He yanked the rope, causing his captive to stagger before falling to the ground. The giant laughed as he dragged Noah across the arena floor.

The afternoon sunlight assaulted Noah's eyes while the hardened soil scraped his arms and legs as he flailed about, unsuccessfully trying to scramble to his feet. Finally, the man stopped. Noah peeked through the dust cloud around him only to see the giant looming over him.

"Get up, morsel." The deep voice bellowed above the cacophony. The colossus drew his large blade and stuck the point of it in Noah's face. He scowled and then quickly severed Noah's bonds. He sheathed his weapon and walked back toward the gate.

Noah unsteadily stood and glanced around. Several thousand people packed the benches throughout the stands; most jeered him with curses and other vile taunts. He spun around to face the reserved seating, knowing it was where Naamah, Lamech, and others who sought his death would be located, but a blood-soaked wrap on the ground beneath them grabbed his attention. A moment later, he realized a body lay beneath the garment.

Moving a few steps closer, Noah stopped and his stomach tightened when he recognized the lifeless eyes of Tubal-Cain staring back in his direction. He clenched his fists and fought the simultaneous urges to scream and weep. Laughter from the audience barely registered in his ears as his pulse quickened and his neck burned with anger. Gathering himself, he let his eyes drift up to the platform above. *God, please repay the king for this evil.*

Seated on a throne, dressed in a glimmering, gold-flecked robe, and wearing a large, ornately designed golden crown, King Lamech raised a hand and the crowd noise subsided to a murmur. Ashur, Navea, and the other council members sat behind him on the elevated platform in smaller and less decorative chairs. Naamah stood beside the king, but her earlier amusement had vanished. Glaring at her father as he stood to speak, she seemed pale and ill. On a large pedestal at Naamah's right stood a golden serpent idol nearly twice the height of a man.

Lamech directed a finger to the arena floor. "Noah, my old friend, it pains me that we meet again under such conditions. You have been charged with a capital crime against your own city. They say that you refuse to honor our chief deity, Nachash. Tell me Noah, are you guilty of such treason?"

Noah thought of the Creator's promise to give him sons and to flood the earth. He dusted off his arms and cleared his throat as conviction filled his mind. "I'd rather commit treason against the Great Deceiver than deny the Most High, the Creator of heaven and earth."

227

Angry shouts and obscenities streamed from the audience as Lamech raised an eyebrow. He waited for the crowd to fall silent before he spoke. "Noah, you have just condemned yourself to death, but because I am a merciful king, I am willing to give you another chance." Lamech turned to the iron gate and with his hand beckoned someone to enter the arena.

The giant returned, but this time he pulled seven captives in tow. The gate slammed shut behind them, and a pain struck Noah's heart as he recognized Adira, Elam, Kal, and even little Rayneh among the prisoners. Adira stared blankly at the body of her husband as she walked behind the towering man. Kal fought against her bindings to hold on to Rayneh, who cried out to her mother and father for help. Attempting to rush to her side, Elam tripped when the guard tugged the rope, eliciting uproarious laughter from the crowd. Finally, the procession stopped some 15 cubits to Noah's right, and the audience awaited the king's words.

Lamech ordered the giant to remove the binding ropes from the prisoners and then held a hand out toward Noah. "As I said before, I am a merciful king, but even the most compassionate leader cannot allow sedition to undermine his rule. I will give you one more opportunity to do what is right." He pointed to the large idol near Naamah. "Kneel before Nachash now and proclaim your allegiance to him. If you refuse, not only will you face a terrifying death, but you will condemn these seven people, including one little child, to the same fate. What will it be, Noah?"

Noah shook his head slowly at Lamech, astonished by the depths of his wickedness. A fleeting thought encouraged him to obey the king to spare his friends. He could always plead for the Creator's forgiveness later. But he quickly dismissed the pragmatic idea. The king could not be trusted to keep his word about sparing them, but more importantly, Noah would never deny the Most High. The God he had recently encountered was far more terrifying than anything Lamech threatened, and more deserving of devotion than any other.

Elam shouted encouragement to Noah, urging him to stand for the Creator. The colossal guard immediately silenced him with a swift backhand that sent Elam tumbling.

Creator, what I do now, I do for You. Please show these people Your power. Noah let out a breath and stood tall, holding Lamech's gaze. "You speak of mercy but know nothing of it. It will not be my hand that kills these people today. King Lamech, you and you alone will be guilty of

228

their blood." Noah turned to the crowd and shouted as loud as possible. "I serve the Most High, the Creator of all things. Before Him alone will I bow, for only He is worthy."

"And I, as newly appointed king of this city" — Lamech walked closer to the platform's edge — "cannot allow Nachash, the Splendor of the World, to be disrespected in such a way. If your God does not let you kneel to another to spare the lives of your friends, then the Creator is a cruel monster." An evil grin streaked across his face. "And speaking of cruel monsters." He turned to Naamah and chuckled.

Dread settled in Noah's stomach. What vile scheme could trigger such an amused response?

Naamah stepped forward and leaned against the rail. "Just think, you could've been sitting up here by my side, but now . . ." She scoffed and then held her arms out wide, raising her voice for all to hear. "Moments ago, Noah told me that he wasn't going to die today." Laughter broke out in the audience, and when it quieted, she continued. "Then he said that even if he did die, the Creator would bring him back to life."

An eruption of insults and jeers rained down on Noah. People he recognized and had treated kindly over the years now mocked him for his faith and clamored for his blood.

Naamah waited several moments before gesturing for the crowd to listen. She smirked at Noah. "You still think you won't die today?" She laughed and then nodded to her father.

Lamech signaled to the guards standing above the large wooden double-door gate on the opposite end of the coliseum from where Noah had entered. The loud clacking of the gate's massive latch popping open drove the spectators into a fevered pitch of excitement.

Noah stared at the gate, his mind racing to figure out who or what would soon emerge from the other side. *Most High, my life is in Your powerful hands.*

A thunderous roar shook the wooden doors and echoed through the stadium. Having heard such a roar only a few times in his life, Noah cringed. His thoughts returned to the night he and Aterre had fled from the carcass of a dead earthshaker as a grendec approached. *Oh no.* Terror gripped Noah and his body went rigid. Suddenly, the same peace as when he encountered the Creator washed over him. Noah's dread instantly vanished. He took a half step forward as if readying for battle.

As the crowd anticipated the monster's entrance, the giant laughed behind him.

Noah glanced at Naamah. "I will not die today." He kept his words quiet enough so that only she and those in her immediate vicinity heard.

Naamah raised her eyebrows and waved to the guards above the gate.

In the stillness of the moment, Noah spoke loudly as he turned to face each part of the crowd. "People of Iri Geshem. Nachash is the Great Deceiver and the old stories are true. Just as he tricked our Greatmother Eve, he has misled the world, and now you, into following him. The Creator is the true God, and He is going to wipe this world out with a flood. Denounce your false god, turn from your wicked practices, and serve the Most High."

Laughter and jeers mixed in abundance for a brief moment until an earsplitting crash flung the massive wooden doors wide open. Only the beast's head emerged from the shadows at first. Perched more than eight cubits in the air, the gaping maw displayed dozens of long bony daggers. The grendec's greenish-yellow eyes locked onto Noah, and the creature stepped into the arena, revealing gold and jewel-encrusted covers on the two large horns above its eyes. Two absurdly small arms dangled from its torso, while brown and gray scales rippled over unbelievably powerful leg muscles as the horned grendec took three large steps in Noah's direction. Its lengthy tail swayed wildly behind it, striking the wooden door on the left and splintering one of its panels.

Noah stared in wonder at the mighty creature, but remained calm. *Almost too calm.* With no fear at all, he wondered anew how the Creator might rescue him from his deadly foe.

Only about 40 cubits away, the beast stopped, lowered its head, and looked directly at Noah. Opening its mouth wide, it let loose the loudest roar imaginable, mingling with the cries of the audience.

Noah flinched at the sound before taking a step toward the dagger-tooth. The creature twisted its massive head one way and then the other. Without warning, it rose and faced the crowd opposite the king, eliciting screams from some of the people sitting in its view. Its nostrils flared and fury grew in its left eye. The grendec charged the audience, the ground seeming to shake at each step.

Noah drew back as he recognized the danger. The arena had not been built to exhibit such a large creature, so the wall only extended about six cubits up from the ground, putting the front two rows of on-lookers within reach of the beast.

As people directly in front of the monster scattered, the grendec rushed in without slowing. Turning its head at the last moment, the animal blasted into the wall, using its massive neck and shoulder as a battering ram. Stone and brick shattered and a section of the barrier — some three cubits to either side of the impact — crumpled to the arena floor, dumping screaming citizens to the ground in the process. The monster snapped its powerful jaws around the body of a man as he fell, instantly silencing his horrific cry. The weakened wall continued to crumble and spill spectators into the arena.

A child shrieked behind Noah. He spun and saw the giant standing over Zedakal, holding the back of her head with one hand while his other hand gripped the handle of the massive spear he had run through Kal's midsection with such force that it stuck into the ground beneath her.

Elam yelled and scooped Rayneh up as he ran with the other prison-ers away from the titan toward Noah. Setting his daughter down, Elam directed her to Noah before he hurried to the fallen body of Tubal-Cain and picked up the sacrificial blade that lay beside him.

"Elam, No!" Noah picked up Rayneh and sprinted toward his friend. "There's nothing you can do for her now."

Adira arrived near her deceased husband and dropped to her knees beside him.

"Come on." Noah motioned frantically for her to get moving.

She shook her head and waved for him to leave. "Farewell, Noah. Tell Emzara that I love her." She grabbed Tubal-Cain's hand and held it against her tear-stained face.

The giant withdrew his spear, and Kal's lifeless body slumped to the ground. With blinding speed, the huge man spun and bounded toward them.

Elam finally turned and followed Noah toward the growing crowd of people attempting to flee through the double gate the grendec had en-tered through. Noah glanced over his shoulder and saw the giant pulling his weapon out of Adira's back as she fell across her husband's body.

Quickening his pace, Noah tried to force the horrific images from his mind. A moment later, a long, bloodied spear zipped between Noah and Elam and lodged itself in the ground. A spine-tingling shout rang out behind them.

Elam looked back and dropped to the ground just as the giant's massive blade flashed over him, hitting nothing but air. In a seamless maneuver, Elam rolled to one knee and swung his own blade behind him, striking his attacker. The blow opened a gaping wound in the middle of the man's large lower leg muscle.

The giant stopped and reached for his leg, allowing Noah, Rayneh, and Elam to decrease the gap between them and the exit. Turning to look back, Noah watched as the warrior looked up from the wound, grinned, and gave chase.

Noah tightened his grip on Rayneh and hurried into the midst of the crowd with Elam right beside them. The horned grendec continued its pursuit of the moving targets, pausing occasionally for a deep, thunderous call.

Without warning, Elam grunted as he fell to the ground, and his weapon bounced out of his hand, landing near Noah's feet. A massive hand clamped around Elam's ankle.

The giant stood upright, dangling Elam upside down by one leg and raising him so that their faces were even.

Rayneh screamed for her father.

Noah set the girl down, shielding her with his body, and picked up the long dagger by his feet, yelling to distract the murderous guard.

Ignoring Noah, the giant opened his mouth wide and leaned in as if planning to take a bite out of Elam's neck. Just before his teeth met flesh, the grendec's massive tail struck the colossus in the back, sending him sprawling forward toward Noah while Elam crashed to the ground.

Instinctively, Noah raised the dagger to protect himself just as the giant slammed into him, knocking him backward and forcing the air out of his lungs as he hit the ground.

Groaning loudly, the guard reached for Noah before yanking his hand back to his side as a howl bellowed from his lungs. The sacrificial blade stuck firmly to its hilt in the giant's side.

Noah scrambled to his feet and then helped Elam stand. "Let's go."

The brute tried to get up, but upon reaching his knees, the large guard yelled and clutched at his side again as he dropped to the ground.

He grasped the handle of the weapon as his own blood dribbled through his fingers. Wincing, he pulled the sword from his flesh and hurled it at Noah, missing his mark by less than a cubit. The weapon clanked harmlessly against the wall. Noah rejoined Elam and Rayneh as they blended with the crowd and hurried out of the arena.

CHAPTER 34

Emzara sat on the deck of the river runner, her back against the cabin. She turned to look for the late afternoon sun, but the thick fog still obscured it. Whenever it peeked through the mist, it looked more like the moon than the sun. As the craft made its way upriver, she barely glimpsed the ghostly tops of the tall trees along the shore as they moved slowly past.

Clutching the soft, handmade blanket from Adira in her lap, Emzara thought over the events since Noah had made it home up until the moving secret farewell two days ago. Her gaze shifted to the blanket, and tears pricked her eyes as she replayed her last moments with Adira. Following an emotional hug, her friend had handed her the intricately patterned weave. "It's for your new little one. Take it with all the hope and love I'm giving you."

"Zara?"

Emzara peered across the deck and barely discerned the outline of Laleel as the woman approached. Beyond her, Garun kept his back to them as he piloted the boat. Hastily wiping her eyes with her fingertips, she placed the blanket back down on the small wooden chest near her. "Yes?"

"What are you doing?"

"Just thinking, I guess. And enjoying the stillness."

"This is a good place for that." Laleel reached down and touched the spread. "What's this?"

Emzara smiled. "Oh, it's a gift from Adira for my baby." She tucked it into the chest before standing. "I guess I'm being overly sentimental, but I've been going through some of my old keepsakes."

"Will you tell me about some of them?"

Emzara read the care in Laleel's questions and it warmed her. She nodded before kneeling and pulling out a few items from the chest. "Well, this is the eye wrap that Noah wore for our wedding. These are beads from our anniversaries. And this" — she held up an old scroll — "is a letter my father gave to me on my wedding day. It's probably my favorite possession." She sniffed and closed her eyes. "I'm sorry, I'm not usually like this." Emzara tucked her head in embarrassment.

"There's nothing to be sorry about. I'm glad you thought to bring those along." Laleel walked to the railing. "I'm sure it helps. You've had huge changes in the last few days. And bringing something to remember those you love is a good idea."

Emzara joined her. "I'm not the only one going through big changes. I'm grateful you and Garun came with me."

"We wouldn't have it any other way." Laleel rubbed her hands together to warm up. "So how are you feeling?"

"With the baby?" Emzara let out a short joyful laugh. "I'm sorry. It still sounds strange to speak about my own child."

The wrinkles on Laleel's forehead became more pronounced as she smiled warmly. "Yes, with *your* baby."

"Better than I expected. Although, the motion of this ship is getting to me, and I feel sick in the morning."

"I'm sure you know that's to be expected. Your desire to look through those precious things is probably due in part to the baby too."

Emzara smiled as a cherished memory popped into her mind. "That's right. I remember during some of Adira's pregnancies, she would cry while looking through the baby clothing their older kids had worn."

"I was the same way."

Emzara slowly lifted a finger to point at her. "You were the same way?"

Laleel winked. "I guess I just hid it better."

Emzara stifled a laugh and then grew somber.

"What's the matter?" Laleel asked.

"I miss Noah, and I'm worried about him. He should've left when we did."

"He said he'd be on his way before the mourning period ended. They never stopped us at the bridge, so it doesn't seem like there's much to worry about." Laleel gently rubbed Emzara's shoulder.

"I know, but it's more than just Noah. I'm worried about our baby. The circumstances are so similar to the last time I was pregnant."

Laleel raised an eyebrow. "When were you pregnant? I've known you for over four hundred years."

Emzara patted her wrap near her knee to straighten a wrinkle. "It was right before we met. We were sailing to Havil when I lost our child. I was grieving the sudden deaths of two of the people dearest to me."

"Your father and Aterre?"

Emzara wiped a tear as she nodded. "And now things are so similar. Zain was just killed, and here I am on a boat worrying about losing Noah and our baby."

Laleel took a deep breath and grabbed Emzara's hand. "But this time is also very different. You told me yesterday that you have a promise from the Most High that you, Noah, and *your children* have yet to fulfill." She softened her tone and pointed to Emzara's midsection. "I know it's not easy, but cling to that promise. The Creator is faithful."

Emzara remained silent for a while, wrestling inside. *Can I trust You to do what You've promised with all that's going on? What am I saying? Of course, I can depend on You.* She nodded slowly, but then a smile spread on her lips and her confidence rose. "You're right. I may not know everything that's going to happen, but I must believe that Noah will be well. The Creator will protect him."

"Protect him and give you children," Laleel said.

Emzara folded her arms tightly against her body as if hugging herself would keep the warm feelings from escaping. She let out a breath. "I've always referred to Him as the Most High. Well, since that title accurately describes Him, then I know He will make good on His promise."

"And when He does, then you'll tell me more about this promise?"

"When Noah decides the time is right." Emzara yearned to tell her about the flood, but she had yet to grasp all the ramifications of the worrisome news. She forced her thoughts back to the promise of sons. "Oh, speaking of children. We should be pretty close to where Adira's son lives."

"That's right." Laleel turned toward the bow of the ship and called out to her husband. "Any sign of . . ." Her voice trailed off as her eyes followed something in the water.

"What is that?" Emzara leaned in and squinted as they floated past a large wet cloth that appeared to be wrapped around a box or barrel. Near one edge of the fabric, a dark round mass jutted out. As she turned to question Laleel, she glimpsed a human foot at the edge of the cloth on the water's surface. Gasping, Emzara covered her mouth.

Laleel's hand flew to her chest. "I see it. Garun!"

"You'd better come up here," he said. "Something's wrong."

As Emzara and Laleel neared the steering control, Emzara rubbed her forehead. "Did you see that body?"

Garun nodded. "And there was one on the other side too." He angled the boat toward the eastern shore and pointed ahead. "Look there."

Through the patches of fog, blackened silhouettes jutted out from the land. The once proud buildings now depicted harsh angles and missing pieces. The overall landscape reminded Emzara of an animal's lower jaw with jagged teeth, and she instinctively shuddered. Faint wisps of smoke trailed above the destruction.

"Am I seeing this right?" Laleel's voice was a mere whisper. "Is that Iri Dekkel?"

Emzara's heart sank. "Oh no, Purlek."

Garun motioned for his wife to grab the steering arm. "Here, take this." He cleared his throat, but his voice still came out raspy. "Keep it pointed toward the wharf. I've got to slow us down." He hurried back to the mast and quickly dropped the large sail.

"Who could have done this?" Laleel asked as she held the control steady.

"I don't know." Emzara scanned the beach for any survivors.

"Do you know where Purlek lived?"

Emzara closed her eyes, trying to recall from her trip 14 years earlier. "I think I know where his forge is."

"That's right. He's a blacksmith like his father." Laleel peeked over her shoulder and called out. "Hurry up." She smiled at Emzara and spoke quietly. "Or else you'd better find something to hang on to because I have no idea what I'm doing."

Emzara chuckled before bending down and grabbing two pushpoles. She tossed one to Garun as he approached and then moved to the right side of the deck to help him guide the boat safely to the dock. Painted words on a post confirmed they had reached Iri Dekkel.

"Strange." Garun tossed a rope around a mooring. "No other boats. Is that normal here?"

Emzara shook her head. "I don't think so. Maybe they fled."

"Or maybe whoever destroyed the town also stole the boats," Laleel said. "Did you come across any other boats in the night?"

"Just a handful of fishermen," Garun said. "Maybe they went upriver."

"Do you think it's safe for us to be here?" Emzara asked.

Garun nodded. "My guess is that this all happened last night. Some of the wood is still smoldering, but I don't see any flames. Plus, you're with me." He winked at Emzara as he took his wife's hand.

The three stood looking at the burned and gutted remnants of the town. A shiver passed through Emzara's frame. There was something eerie about seeing the remains of what had once been the home to hundreds of people. *Will the whole world look like this after the flood that the Creator's going to send?*

"Where's Purlek's forge?" Laleel asked.

"This way." Emzara led them down the road into town and turned left at the first cross street. A crashing sound to their right jolted them. "What was that?"

Garun nodded in the direction of the noise. "Part of that building just collapsed."

"Do you see any people?" Laleel spun all the way around, scanning the village. "What's happened to them?"

"I don't know, but it can't be good," Garun said.

They continued walking toward the north end of town. Charred remains of homes and shops seemed to be all that was left of Iri Dekkel.

"Is it much farther?" Garun asked. "We shouldn't leave the boat for long."

"We're almost there." Emzara increased her pace and the others matched her. "If I remember correctly, it's just at the end of this road."

The street turned slightly before leading under a grove of large trees lining both sides. The houses stood farther apart in this section of town and appeared to have suffered less damage.

As they crested a small rise in the road before a steady downhill, Emzara pointed. "It's right down — oh no."

The small blacksmith shop she remembered lay in ruins. Three of the walls still stood, but parts of the roof had collapsed. Emzara tried to sprint, but her legs refused to move as quickly as she wanted, no matter how much she urged them.

Garun sped past her and arrived at the forge first. "Purlek!" He pulled two stones away from where the door once stood and called out the blacksmith's name again. He continued shifting the wreckage and calling out.

"Anything?" Emzara asked as she reached Garun.

"No." He pressed on, clearing the entryway.

Laleel picked her way around some debris to the right. "I'm going to check around back."

Emzara peered inside as Garun moved another block. With no sign of Purlek, she stepped back just as Laleel disappeared around the corner. "Wait, I'll come with you." Emzara trekked to the side of the shop and followed a small trail that wove through a copse of large-leafed trees. Keeping her eyes on the rubble, Emzara strained to find any sign of her friend's son.

A cry from Laleel gave her a start. "Garun! Back here!"

Emzara dashed past the trees and found Laleel tugging on a large beam.

"Help me with this. I can't move it."

Tracing the timber from its nearest end to the opposite side, Emzara discovered the source of Laleel's urgency. Under the plank, stones, and other debris, a man's legs extended back toward the building. *Purlek!* An instantaneous sense of grief fled as a surge of energy flowed through her body. She joined her friend and the beam rocked slightly.

Garun soon rounded the back corner of the house. "What is it?"

"He's under here." Laleel leaned back, using all her weight to pull.

"Hold on." Garun quickly examined the scene. "Zara, step back."

Emzara tilted her head and narrowed her eyes, but she obeyed.

He quickly removed two large stones and slid a third one to the side. "Alright, now try."

Together, the three lifted the beam and moved it toward the shop. Then they feverishly worked to clear debris off the man, Garun lifting the heaviest pieces while Emzara, because of her condition, only worked with lighter objects. Finally, the rest of the man came into view. Dried blood fastened some of his dark curly hair to his neck. Scrapes and cuts marred his muscular arms and back. His right leg contorted at an odd angle.

Tears filled Emzara's eyes as she stared at the battered frame of a young man to whom she had been like a second mother. The memory of teaching Purlek to bake bread rushed through her head. Just then a small movement caught her eye. Her imagination must be playing tricks on her. *How can I tell Adira?*

"Is he dead?" Laleel asked.

Garun bent low and gently placed his fingers on the front of Purlek's neck. He bit his lip and looked at his wife. Suddenly, his eyes went wide. He leaned in close to Purlek's face while repositioning his fingers on the man's neck. Garun's jaw dropped. "He's alive."

CHAPTER 35

A swarm of humanity converged in the staging area under the arena. With no cover of darkness to hide them, Noah pulled his wrap over the top of his head in an effort to prevent anyone from recognizing him. He followed Elam and Rayneh as they fled the arena floor. They passed a woman screaming a man's name as she watched the people stream past her.

Making their way through designated routes, they marched slowly up the large ramp along the outside of the building. Keeping his head down, he listened to the hurried conversations around him. Several people spoke about the grendec, marveling at the creature's strength and ferocity; a few even laughed about the man it devoured. A pair of women wondered if the giant would survive his injuries. Another man made a crude comment about Naamah's appearance.

Finally, the crowd emptied onto the main street. The late afternoon shadows provided slight relief from the heat. Noah pointed ahead and to their left. "This way."

Far behind them, the massive metal plate rang out in a pattern, alerting the guards to prevent anyone from leaving the city.

Elam switched Rayneh to his other arm, and they jogged for several blocks toward the old city square. The tiny girl clung to him, her face buried. Her curly locks displayed a hint of almost gold in some places, if the light caught them just right. "They'll close the gates. What's your plan to get out of here?"

"We need to reach the old docks," Noah said. "If everything went as planned, I'll have a boat waiting there."

Just before the old square, they turned left on a road that led straight to the Hiddekel. Now separated from the arena's crowd, they slowed to a brisk walk. The shock of everything that had just occurred wore off as they walked. Rayneh squirmed and cried for her mother while Elam tried unsuccessfully to calm her. With tears in his eyes, he looked at Noah. "What do I tell her? I don't even know how I'm going to get through this."

Noah shook his head. "I don't have the words to say to bring you any comfort. I'm so sorry about Kal." He stared at the ground and his own eyes welled up. "And Tubal-Cain and Adira." His heart ached and his midsection tightened, threatening to bring him to his knees. Kicking at a stone on the ground, he longed to scream, but the last thing he wanted to do was draw attention to his little group. That final thought helped him refocus on the danger at hand. "I'll do whatever I can to help, but right now we need to get out of the city or we'll be right back in that arena."

Elam nodded. "I know."

They passed the old rundown bakery. Children played a game in the street, paying little attention to Noah, Elam, and Rayneh. Noah cast a look at the shipyard down the road to his right. *I'll likely never see it again.* "Come on. We're almost there."

Jogging again, they moved quickly toward the river. Noah's concern increased with each step because the boat was nowhere in sight. As they neared the docks, his mind raced to consider other possibilities, but the familiar hull of his ship soon became visible beneath a tree branch on the left side of the road. "There it is. We should hurry."

Elam rushed ahead and jumped onto the deck. He set his daughter down and grabbed a pushpole.

Noah loosed the mooring and threw the rope into the boat before hurrying aboard. "Push. I'll get the sail up."

Elam shoved his pole against the shore and grunted as he forced the boat away from the bank.

Noah untied the knot around the sail and hoisted it into place. He tied it off, and a steady breeze soon drove them farther into the river. After pointing the boat in the right direction, he grabbed a pushpole and assisted Elam, but before long the river grew too deep and the poles were of no use.

"Stop!" A commanding voice rang out from the shore.

Noah put his pole down and spotted a group of guards, roughly a hundred cubits away. "Take her below." He glanced at the sail as Elam grabbed his daughter and rushed to the hatch. "Come on, we need more wind."

"Wait!" The guard's voice lost its edge. The blue shoulder cover on his uniform identified him as a low-level officer. "Is that you, Noah?" He leaned forward. "It is! Noah, the shipbuilder, there's no reason to flee. King Lamech enjoyed your actions in the arena so much that he wishes to formally pardon you. Come back with us and you can return to your life at the shipyard."

Noah shook his head in disbelief as they steadily drifted away. "Do you think I'd ever trust that lying murderer to keep his word?"

"Very well. Have it your way." The officer signaled to his men. Each guard pulled a curved bow from his back.

"Stay below," Noah shouted to Elam. "They're preparing to fire at us." As the distance between them and their would-be captors increased, so did Noah's sense of security. He kept the boat aimed across the river as he watched the officer and his men. Typically, the vessel should be driven at a sharper angle, particularly in this wide area with its slow-moving current, but the pressing concern at the moment was to move out of the archers' range before heading north.

Each guard fastened a string to his bow and nocked an arrow. They raised their weapons and directed them at Noah. "This is your last warning. Turn back, or we'll fire."

As the officer dropped his hand, Noah dove behind a shipping crate. One arrow whistled overhead while two struck the hull. A third collided into the opposite side of the crate while a light splash indicated that another had fallen short of its target.

Now nearly halfway across the river, Noah peeked around the box just in time to see two guards move along the row of archers, lighting the tip of each new arrow already nocked. Ducking down, Noah prepared for another volley. He hoped they were beyond reach after two fizzled in the water, but the splintering of wood to his left dispelled that notion as a flaming arrow lodged itself in the hull. Noah peeked around the corner just as two more buzzed past the boat. With a thump, a third one hit its target.

As the guards reloaded their bows, Noah assessed the damage. He peered over the side and noticed a burning substance covered the area around the arrow. He dipped his hand into the water and splashed some onto the flames, causing them to spread. Confused, Noah watched as the liquid seemed to feed the fire. Before dropping behind the crate again, Noah checked their trajectory. They were drifting too far down the river and straight toward the eastern part of the city. It would soon be too late to sail beyond the gate and past the city wall.

Another round of arrows launched, but only one found its mark, igniting a small crate. Noah emptied it and tossed the box overboard. The blaze danced on the river's surface without extinguishing. Shaking his head, Noah hurried to the steering mechanism and angled the craft to the northeast. Looking back, he watched a few fiery missiles drop harmlessly in the water, but one flew directly over his head and ripped through the sail. The tiny hole would have been of little consequence, but the gooey material from the arrow stuck to the canvas and burned wildly.

Making some quick calculations, Noah spun the boat to allow the current to carry them to the eastern bank. The wind momentarily pushed the sail and they picked up speed until the fire damage tore the material apart. They would have to take their chances in the city. He looked back toward the distant shore as the final few arrows fell short.

The guards hurried down the river road toward the bridge.

"Elam! Come up here."

"Are we out of range?" Elam asked as he poked his head above deck. He glanced at the sail. "Oh no. What do we do?"

"There's no time for me to raise the spare. We need to reach the shore as soon as possible and then run." He pointed to the guards. "But we'll have to hurry. Grab a pushpole and get ready. How's Rayneh?"

"She's scared, with good reason. She doesn't really understand what's going on." Elam grabbed the pole and stood near the edge of the deck.

Smoke poured from the back and side of the craft as the flames continued to chew away at the hull. The boat coasted ever closer to the bank. While no guards waited on the eastern shore yet, the archers had arrived at the bridge and started across.

"We should be shallow enough by now," Noah said.

Elam shoved his pole deep into the water. He grunted and the vessel veered slightly to the left. "Just barely." He repeated the process multiple times as the guards closed in.

244

Noah grabbed the other pole and together they drove the boat toward the beach. "Get your daughter."

Elam dashed down the short flight of stairs and reemerged with Rayneh in his arms.

"Brace yourself." Noah grabbed a large box to avoid losing his balance as the boat slid to a grinding halt. They all pitched forward with the landing. "Come on."

Noah grabbed a sack of food and two small bags of gold piks and pikkas before splashing down into the knee-deep water. He turned around and took the little girl from his friend, allowing Elam to jump off the boat.

"Where are we going?" Elam asked as they hurried to the shore.

The soldiers were about halfway across the bridge now and Noah picked up his pace. "You'll see."

A middle-aged fisherman stood on the beach and looked quizzically at them. He set one end of his pole on the ground and placed his hand above his eyes, squinting as the fading sunlight reflected off the water.

Noah looked away and sprinted up the road. After reaching an intersection, they turned right and headed into an older section of the city down a street lined with fruit trees. Thankful for the deepening shadows, Noah led them toward one of the few farms that still stood within the city wall. An old, tattered shed occupied a small piece of land near the side of a large white stone house. A few cattle grazed in the small pasture. Sneaking around to the right, Noah and Elam ducked under a fence. Noah led them behind the outbuilding, where they pulled back one of the wood panels and slipped inside. Fumbling in the dim interior, Noah found a ladder and climbed up to the second floor. He reached down and lifted Rayneh up and waited for Elam to join them.

Noah directed them to the large piles of hay stashed around the room. "We can hide in those until late tonight."

"Where are we?" Elam asked.

"It's Cada's farm. Aterre used to work here." Although it was now too dark for her to see it, Noah smiled at Rayneh, wishing for all the world that she could have met her uncle.

CHAPTER 36

A pair of guards searched the entire lower level of Cada's old shed. One of them tipped over a shovel just before declaring it all clear, and Noah held his breath, fearing the noise would wake the sleeping Rayneh. But the little girl continued her slumber. For some reason, the guards never checked the hay loft. Perhaps they were unaware of it. Noah let his breath out in a silent sigh of relief as he remembered Elam's decision to pull the ladder up to the second floor.

Noah waited a long while after the guards departed. "They're gone." He peeked over the edge and carefully lowered the ladder. "We'd better get moving to where we can get out of the city while we still have the cover of night."

Elam nodded and cradled his daughter close as Noah made his way down the rungs. Noah hoped that her dreams provided some peaceful respite from the pain and confusion of the day's events.

The two men took turns carrying the sleeping child as they darted through alleys, hid behind trees, and snuck around buildings. Rayneh stirred occasionally but never fully awoke.

After arriving at the familiar home just before the deepest dark, Elam quietly slid the key into its slot and gently opened the door. Noah handed Rayneh to him before stealing one last glance down both directions of the street. He slipped inside the house behind Elam, closed the door, and breathed a sigh of relief.

"Kmani." Elam spoke just above a whisper as he moved through the sitting room. "Kmani, it's Elam. Are you still awake?" He paused and tilted his head as he listened for a response. He moved to the hallway and stopped. The door at the end cracked open and faint light seeped through the gap. "Kmani, it's Elam."

The elderly woman froze and stared down the hall, her eyes searching the darkness. She pulled a lantern around her rotund frame and held it up, illuminating her smile as she spotted her unexpected guests. "Elam. Noah. What are you doing here?" She increased the lamp's brightness. "Putting that key we gave you to good use, I see."

"Sorry for waking you, but we need to get out of the city." Elam pulled the key from his pocket and handed it to her. He hugged her with his free arm. "I don't think I'll need this again."

"Guards stopped by earlier looking for you and they searched the house. Here, let me take her." Kmani held out her short arms and took Rayneh, who jostled a little before nestling up against her. With a tip of her head, she gestured back down the hall. "Downstairs."

Noah stepped to the side, allowing Elam to move past him and open the entry between the sitting room and dining area. After Kmani walked by, Noah followed them to the stairway and closed the door behind him.

"How are you doing, Kmani?" Noah and Emzara had stopped over to comfort the grieving widow the day before Emzara left town, and he had been stunned at how calmly she seemed to be handling Zain's murder. She told him that although it was painful, she was not surprised by it, given the city's descent into all sorts of evil activities and the fact that her husband had long been at the forefront of the resistance against them.

"Each day is difficult," she said as she reached the bottom of the stairs and handed him the lamp. Noah used the flame to light a second lantern near him on the wall. The cellar instantly seemed larger as the glow illuminated the space. The room served as a storehouse for their textile supplies as well as a cool environment in which to keep food preserved longer. He turned his attention back to Kmani.

"We'd been together for more than 700 years," she said. "I'm grateful for the time the Creator gave us, but at the same time — and I don't know how else to describe it — it seems like half of me is missing." She tilted her head and frowned toward Elam, who sat on the floor against the wall, his head buried between his knees as he wept quietly. She covered Rayneh's ear and looked up at Noah. Grimacing, her voice came out just above a whisper. "Kal?"

Noah pursed his lips. "Kal, Adira, and Tubal-Cain were all killed in the arena." He closed his eyes before the tears escaped. "Tubal-Cain was gone before they brought me out, so I don't know how it happened."

"The king stabbed him for refusing to worship Nachash, but he didn't die right away." Elam wiped his eyes and took a deep breath. "He killed a wild beast that was meant for Adira before succumbing to his wound. We were forced to watch it all through one of the gates."

A knot formed in Noah's midsection as the terrors of the arena flooded his mind again. His bottom lip quivered as he thought about Tubal-Cain being killed by his own father. "That's the second time he's taken the life of my best friend." Self-pity nearly engulfed him, but, glancing at Rayneh, he suppressed it. Yes, another dear friend was lost to him, but the little girl would grow up without her mother, and Elam would never see his wife again — at least not in this world. *How would I feel if that happened to Em?* He cast a sympathetic look at Elam.

"Come now." Kmani tapped Elam. "There'll be plenty of time for that later, and you're right to do it. But not now. Those guards may return at any moment, and you need to get your little girl out of here." She caught Noah's attention and gestured to a large shelf unit holding all sorts and colors of fabric. "Behind that."

Noah nodded. "Do we need to move the whole unit?"

Kmani shook her head. "No, the bottom half of the middle section pulls out, but it's heavy. Just pull some of the material out first. I can repack it later."

"You aren't coming with us?" Noah hung the lantern on a hook near the shelves. "Aren't you in danger here?"

She smiled. "I think Ashur prefers to let me suffer in my grief for Zain. Besides, if he wanted to kill me, I'd already be dead." She adjusted her hold on Rayneh. "Don't you worry about me. Zain made arrangements in case something like this ever happened. I'll head to my son's place in a month or so."

"I'm sorry it's all come to this."

Her eyes glistened in the low light. "So am I."

Noah grabbed a pile of folded linens from the large bin before him and set them on a table to his side. He repeated the action two more times before Elam joined in the work. With half the container emptied, the two men pulled it away from the wall.

Elam snatched the lantern and held it in the recently vacated space, revealing a dark drape hanging from the back of the shelving unit. "It's behind this?"

"Yes," Kmani said. "Just push it to the side."

Elam slid the curtain to the side and then ran his hand along the wall, searching for the small hollow that served as a handle. Once he found it, he slipped a finger behind the little opening and pulled back. A door, lower than Noah's waist, swung open, exposing a couple of steps down to a hidden tunnel that Zain had dug out shortly after building the house nearly a century earlier.

"And this will take us under the wall?" Noah asked.

Kmani nodded. "Yes, take the lantern with you. There's an abandoned shack up against the woods about 200 cubits past the wall. When you reach the end of the tunnel, just look for the door above your head. It's built into the floor of the shed and hidden behind some debris in the corner. Before you open it, listen to make sure all is still."

Elam kissed the old woman on the forehead. "Thank you for everything."

She teared up afresh. "I know you're overwhelmed by all that's happened, but be strong for your daughter." She rubbed his shoulder. "I'll miss you all very much."

Blinking back tears, Elam said, "I love you. You and your husband were wonderful mentors to me. I hope we'll see you again." He turned and crawled backward into the opening. "Don't worry, Noah, the tunnel is taller once you get inside."

Noah hugged Kmani. "May the Creator keep you safe."

"And you as well." Kmani gently handed Rayneh to Elam. "Be careful, and get as far away from here as possible."

Noah waited for her to move out of the way before following Elam into the tunnel, carefully holding the lantern off the ground as he ducked under the low opening. After a few steps, the ceiling allowed him to stand, although not to his full height. "Noah, take this." Kmani reached down and handed an empty waterskin to him.

"Thank you." Noah mustered a smile that tried to convey half a millennia of gratitude. "Oh, I almost forgot." He pulled two gold pikkas from a small pouch. "Please make sure that a young man named Pav at the shipyard gets these."

Kmani nodded and a tear dripped off her cheek. "I will. Farewell." She sniffed and closed the door.

Noah held the light aloft and studied the tunnel before him. A handful of scraggly roots poked through the dirt ceiling above. Wooden beams stretched from the floor to the top every five to six cubits, and a crossbeam connected them along the ceiling. A few streaks of water appeared on the clay that formed much of both sides up to Noah's shoulders. He walked past Elam. "Let's go."

Keeping his head down, Noah led the way through the tunnel. After approximately 60 cubits, the passageway veered left. Just beyond the turn, a tree root had forced its way through a section of the wall, spilling enough dirt to block nearly half of their route.

"We must be under the forest," Elam said. "That means we're past the wall."

"I believe so. It shouldn't be too much farther. Stay quiet until we're sure no one is in the shed."

A few uneventful moments later, they neared the end of the tunnel. Noah dimmed the light and stopped before the ladder set into the left wall. Glancing up, he spotted the hatch. He put a finger to his lips, reminding Elam to be silent.

Rayneh wriggled in Elam's arms, trying to get comfortable. He stroked her head and held her close. After a long silence, he spoke in a whisper. "Noah, if something happens to me. I want you and Emzara to raise Rayneh as your own."

Noah smiled and touched the little girl's cheek. "We'd be honored. But don't talk like that. We're going to make it."

"You think it's clear up there?"

Noah shrugged. "Well, let's find out. I'll go up first." Noah carefully slid a latch that unlocked the door above him and then slowly cracked it open. He climbed the ladder and peeked through the gap. With no sign of intruders, Noah finished his ascent, which led him to a small area behind a wall of crates. A gap between the crates and the far wall opened up to the rest of the shack. He squeezed through the breach. Confident that they were alone, he retraced his steps back to the tunnel exit. "It's all clear." Noah stooped low, set the lamp on the floor, and took Rayneh from her father.

Elam climbed up the ladder and closed the door. "It's safe?"

"I think so. I'll take her for a while." Noah nodded to the far wall. "You can get past the crates over there."

After retrieving the lantern, Elam followed Noah's directions, and they soon reached the front door. "Where do we go from here?"

"North, through the woods. We need to avoid the main roads at least until we're a long ways from the city. And keep the light dim."

"Good idea." Elam took a deep breath. "Are you ready?"

Noah nodded and then closed his eyes. "Creator, please protect us. We thank You for helping us get this far and pray that You'll lead us safely through the rest of the night."

Elam patted Noah on the shoulder and then opened the door. The men stepped out into a glade, hurried across the clearing, and entered the forest. They walked through patches of woods intersected by swaths of fields. When the lights of Iri Geshem could no longer be seen, they slowed their pace a little.

They reached a road marked by deep wagon wheel grooves. "If I'm not mistaken," Noah said as he pointed left, "this road leads west to Kadzen."

"That's the first town on the river, right?" Elam rubbed his tired eyes.

"Yeah." As the threat of death seemed less imminent, the stress of the day's events started to take its toll. Noah stretched his neck and shoulders. "We could go that way and take the river road until we find a boat heading north. But for now, I think we should stay off the roads. After the sun rises, maybe we can find the old trail along the eastern edge of the forest. It'll be a little out of the way, but we should be able to move faster. And I really doubt that troops will be sent that far to find us."

"They probably think we're still in the city. I'm sure glad Zain built that tunnel." Elam yawned. "Let's go with your plan, but I'd like to rest a little first."

Noah motioned to the forest across the road. "Let's find a place in there to hide."

They scampered across the path and down a short hill into the woods. A small stream babbled before them. Noah leapt over it and then filled the waterskin. Both men drank from it before Noah topped it off again and slung it over his shoulder.

The forest offered little resistance due to its sparse undergrowth. While this allowed them to move steadily, it also afforded them very few places to hide. As the eastern sky developed a faint glow, signaling the coming dawn, Noah pointed to a grove of large trees where the brush grew thicker. "That looks like a good place."

Elam found a level piece of ground near one of the trees and reclined. After taking Rayneh, he adjusted his wrap to cover her tiny frame. "I'm glad you're still resting, sweet one. We'll get through this together."

Noah set the lamp, bag of food, and water on the ground. Reclining against a tree a few cubits from Elam, he wrestled with all that transpired in the past day. He remained silent as Elam sniffled, giving his friend some privacy as he grieved an unimaginable loss. Iri Geshem's addiction to violence had now claimed the lives of so many people that Noah loved. Yet, even though the vivid images of brutality remained fresh, his focus stayed elsewhere: the peace and boldness he possessed in the midst of the most terrifying moment of his life. *The Creator protected me and gave me the courage to warn the people.*

Settling his head on his crossed forearms that rested on his knees, Noah closed his eyes to pray. He thanked the Most High for watching over him in the arena and asked Him to protect Emzara, Laleel, and Garun as they traveled the river. *God, please comfort Elam as well.* Noah's prayer continued until he nodded off. His head jerked up before he let it down on his arms again. His thoughts drifted to Emzara and their unborn child, and then sleep overtook him.

"On your feet!" A sharp voice rang out. It seemed distant at first, but Noah quickly realized it did not originate in a dream. "Up. Now."

Noah opened his eyes and his heart sank. A spear was pointed directly at his face only a fingertip away. *Why did I fall asleep?* He blinked hard and his eyes adjusted to the bright morning light. *Elam?* Noah looked over to see two guards standing over his friend with spears aimed at him. Noah slowly raised a hand. "I'm getting up." As he carefully climbed to his feet, he held out both hands. "We're unarmed."

"What about him?" The guard pushed his spear closer to Elam.

"He's only carrying his daughter," Noah said. "Please don't harm them."

The guard gestured to the man on his right. "Get them up."

As a soldier bound Noah's hands behind his back, two others prodded Elam to his feet.

"Sir, what about the girl?"

"Let her father carry her, but bind him around the waist," the man in front of Noah said. "We'll let the captain decide their fate."

Only then did Noah realize why their accents sounded strange. The half dozen soldiers wore red and black uniforms bearing the unmistakable emblems of the famed Nodite army.

Enjoy a glimpse of Book 3 in the compelling Remnant Trilogy

CHAPTER 1

Iri Geshem — Noah's 499ᵗʰ year

Turning her head to dodge the brilliant reflection of sunlight off the glimmering façade of Iri Geshem's town hall to her right, Naamah marched toward the guest mansion reserved for foreign dignitaries. Jaw set in an angry line, she twisted the oversized iron bracer covering her left arm from elbow to wrist and stared at its intricate patterns.

Led by Nivlac, a quartet of guards flanking her increased their pace to keep up. Even after her many protests, they still accompanied her. Iri Geshem's seedy characters always posed a slight threat, but the soldiers had remained on high alert since the day before. A mixture of outrage and grief had overtaken the town after the debacle in the arena and the chance remained high that someone might seek revenge for loved ones lost. Still, being surrounded by overprotective men at all times did nothing to improve her mood, and she maintained a stony silence throughout their trek.

Two soldiers manned the doors into the residence. Normally, the gold trim along the frame, a sign of Havil's influence in this city, would bring her happiness, but she was in no mood to be amused. The guards pushed the doors open and stepped inside as she approached.

The bearded man on her left nodded. "Welcome back, Princess."

Ignoring him, Naamah stormed ahead into the spacious foyer. She glanced around, hoping there would be no delay. To her right, a small group of people spoke quietly around the low table in the sitting room. They fell silent at the sight of her, but she turned away without acknowledging them. The lavish dining hall to her left sat vacant except for a servant girl preparing the place settings. Besides Nivlac, the guards remained near the door.

Naamah moved to the stairs and ascended to the second floor. She turned left and hurried to her guest room at the end of the hall.

"Princess." Nivlac gently touched her arm. "Is there anything I can do to help?"

She opened the door, jerked away from his touch, and glared at her loyal guard. "Just wait out here."

He drew himself upright and faced the hallway. "As you command."

Naamah shut the door behind her and tossed her green-hemmed cloak on a bench. She slid her shoes off and dropped onto the bed. As she loosened the strings on the bracer, regret and sadness filled her entire body. *How long has it been since I've felt this way?* She adjusted the metal and retied the cords, fitting it more comfortably, even though it was clearly made for a man's large forearm. Studying the remarkable craftsmanship, her thoughts raced back to her brother's final moments in the arena. She shook her head in an attempt to rid herself of that memory. Thankful for the opportunity to spend some time in Tubal-Cain's shop earlier in the day, she stroked the one memento she had found to remember him by.

As she repositioned herself, an object pressed against her stomach. Withdrawing the small dagger from the pocket of her wrap, Naamah held it in front of her eyes and slowly twisted it about. For a brief moment, the thought of plunging it directly into her own chest raced into her mind. She raised the knife and gripped the handle with both hands. Taking a deep breath, she recalled her father's smile as Tubal-Cain died. She lowered the blade and inserted it into its slot in the bracer. *Not while Da is still alive.*

As she stared at the armband her brother had crafted, Naamah said, "And I'll wear this until he's dead." She fell back onto the bed and closed her eyes. *Why wouldn't you bow, Tu?* Her lip quavered and she squeezed her eyes tight, successfully preventing a tear from escaping. *All because you came to this city with Noah.*

Gathering her wits, she sat back up and gazed out the large window to her right. In her mind she watched the giant drag Noah into the arena, leaving him standing helplessly beneath her as the grendec entered and

256

the crowd roared. No matter how many times she replayed the next moment, the outcome never changed. Brimming with a quiet confidence, Noah looked at her and said, "I will not die today."

Her heart pounding, she clenched a fist and slammed it into the bed. "How did he know?" *What if he's right? What if the Creator is more pow* — "No!" Impossible. Noah was just lucky. *No matter. He'll soon be back in our custody, and there will be no escape. How dare he try to make a fool of me in front of everyone!*

Naamah stood and moved to the reflective plate on the wall. She ran a hand through her hair, pushing all of it over to the right. After straightening her gown, she held up her left arm to examine how the bracer looked on her. A hint of a smile grew on her lips as she focused on the hilt of the dagger. *I like it.*

A knock at the door ripped her attention away from her reflection. "Not now, Nivlac."

The door creaked open. "Princess, the king told me to update you on the search." The voice was not Nivlac's.

Naamah gasped, but briskly straightened her shoulders and lifted her chin. "Enter."

A guard stepped into the room and knelt before her. Keeping his head down, he said, "Every exit to the city has been blocked since yesterday. As you know, we stopped him from fleeing the city by boat. Our —"

"Where is he?" Naamah tapped her foot.

The guard hesitated and dropped his head even lower. "Still no sign of him, but he must be in the eastern part of the city. Our men have been searching every home."

Naamah grabbed a small vase off the shelf beside her and smashed it onto the floor, shattering it into dozens of pieces. "Find him!"

The man flinched. "Yes, Princess."

Glaring at the back of the man's neck, she slid the dagger partway out of the armband. Letting out a breath, she replaced the blade with a clinking of metal. "You weren't sent out to come back empty-handed. Return without him again, and you'll be fed to the grendec."

He nodded. "Yes, Princess."

"Get out!"

The soldier stood and bowed before spinning around and hustling out of the room.

Naamah kicked a clay shard across the floor. *Tubal-Cain is dead and Noah's free.* "Ah!" Her breathing quickened as her anger kindled. Trying to shake the image of Tubal-Cain's bloodied corpse from her mind, she paused and let it fuel her temper instead. She scratched an itch near the top edge of the bracer, the irritation increasing her rage even more. Her eyes locked onto the handle. "This comes off today."

Stepping carefully over shattered pottery, she reached for her shoes and pulled them on. "Nivlac!"

He stepped into the room, and his eyes darted from the mess on the floor to her. "Yes, Highness."

Controlling the tone of her voice, Naamah asked, "Do you know where my father is?"

"I believe he's in a meeting with leaders from the city."

Biting her lip, she contemplated how to take revenge. *Yes, that should work.* "Very good. That's all."

Nivlac nodded. "Would you like me to inform the king that you'd like to see him?"

She strode past him. "That won't be necessary. Follow me."

Rushing down the hall, Naamah allowed the memory of Tubal-Cain's murder to drive her forward while ignoring all the warnings that rang inside her. *I don't care if this is a deadly mistake. It's worth the risk.* As she reached the middle of the passage, she turned left and pushed the double doors open, then stepped confidently into the spacious meeting hall. The city's council members reclined on lush cushions around a low table loaded with colorful fruits and vegetables along with a variety of meats. Skimpily clad male and female dancers twirled and twisted near the musicians on the far side of the room.

Seated at the opposite end of the table, her father handed a tray of food to a young woman dressed in a tawdry outfit standing at his side. His eyes lingered after her as she stepped away. Only when the girl had disappeared through the servants' entrance in the corner did he turn to face his daughter. "Naamah, please join us."

Nivlac remained at the door as she glided around the council members and stopped about ten cubits before the king. As she bowed her head slightly, she glimpsed the hilt of the dagger at her wrist. She raised her voice for the benefit of everyone in the room. "Father, why did you murder Tubal-Cain?"

The music stopped and Lamech raised his eyebrows. "Murder?" He snorted. "That's called justice, my dear. He disobeyed direct orders from both of us. He needed to be punished for his treason."

"But he was your son, and my brother!" Her tone grew sharp and accusatory. "You never should have put him in that situation."

"He sought to undermine my rule." The king raised a finger and pointed at her. "And you'd better watch yourself."

"Pah! Are you threatening me?" Naamah stepped closer, defiantly challenging his authority and anticipating a blow to the face as he had dealt her several times before. But at over 700 years old, he was weaker and slower than he had once been. He would never see the dagger until she had planted it deep into his chest in an act of self-defense. "Without Nachash's followers, your rule would crumble."

Anger burned in his eyes as he glanced at the council members, many of whom wore shocked expressions. He stood and took a step toward her. "If you ever speak to me that way again —"

"What? You'll kill me just like you've killed your son?"

"Enough!" Lamech raised his hand to hit her, but he froze when the twin doors burst open.

Jolted by the interruption, Naamah turned to see two guards dash into the room just as she placed her hand over the bracer.

"Sir!" The guard who entered first dropped to a knee, and his companion followed suit. "Please forgive the interruption. I bring a critical message from Commander Tsek!"

Behind the Fiction

Just like in the first book in the Remnant Trilogy, *Noah: Man of Destiny*, the initial part of this non-fiction section, *Questions and Answers*, is designed to address certain questions that readers may think of during the story. Many of these issues will be apologetic in nature. That is, in this portion of the book, we will respond to numerous challenges raised by skeptics and critics. The goal is that these novels will also help you defend the truth of Scripture.

You may have noticed as you read the novel that several things didn't line up with what you may have expected. This was done on purpose to help break certain stereotypes about Noah and the pre-Flood world that many Christians assume are from the Bible, but aren't actually found there. We want you to see clearly what comes directly from the Bible and what comes from traditions people have developed over the years.

The second feature in this non-fiction portion is what we call *Borrowed from the Bible*. Since the Bible only includes scant details about Noah's life and times, we must use artistic license to flesh out his story. We certainly do not wish to be seen as adding to Scripture and want the reader to understand that these are works of fiction, with the exception of the few details that come straight from the Bible. In some places we curbed the amount of artistic license taken by drawing from other biblical accounts instead. In *Borrowed from the Bible*, we highlight certain events and customs in our story that will be somewhat familiar to those who know their Bibles.

The third special feature is entirely unique to this series. We had the incredible opportunity to work behind the scenes at the Ark Encounter for the past few years. Tim was involved in the planning of nearly every exhibit and was responsible for writing or overseeing all of the content while K. Marie took part in designing various aspects of several spaces on the Ark. We wanted to use our experience to bring this series to life in a creative manner. As such, many of the objects and animals described in the book are on display in the Ark Encounter, so visitors to the theme park can see part of what Noah witnesses in our story. The *Encounter This* section lets the reader know what these items are and where they can be found.

We hope you've enjoyed reading about what may have been, while learning to better discern between fact and fiction.

ANSWERING QUESTIONS
RAISED BY THE NOVEL

SPOILER ALERT! Many of the answers to questions in this section reveal key points in the storyline of the novel. If you have not read the story first, some of these details will spoil important events in the book.

How long were Adam and Eve in the Garden of Eden?

In chapter 7, Garun told Noah that the first man and woman were in the garden for only a few days before being banished. This was new information for Noah, and likely for many of our readers as well. Many Christians assume that Adam and Eve spent quite a while in the Garden of Eden with the Lord before they sinned and were subsequently banished, but does the Bible support this notion?

In keeping with our approach from the first book to steer clear of popular ideas not specifically found in the Bible, we decided to introduce this topic to encourage readers to closely consider the biblical text. The truth is Genesis does not tell us precisely how long Adam and Eve lived before they rebelled, but it does give us some parameters to make an educated guess.

The Bible provides an upper limit to the amount of time that passed before man's first sin. Adam and Eve had their son Seth when Adam was 130 years old (Genesis 5:3), which took place after Cain murdered his brother. This figure cannot be the upper limit since we must first allow enough time for Cain to grow old enough to offer sacrifices and kill Abel. Let's assume a minimum of twenty years for those details, which would bring our upper limit down to about 110 years.

With the maximum time limit set, let us take a look at the lowest amount of time they could have been in the garden. Adam and Eve were created on the sixth day of the creation week (Genesis 1:26–27), and at the end of that day, we are told that everything was "very good" (Genesis 1:31). God rested on the next day, a day that He blessed and sanctified (Genesis 2:1–3). We can be quite confident He did not curse the ground on that day. So the earliest Adam could have sinned would have been on the eighth day.

There is a strong reason to believe they were in the garden for a very short amount of time. Our first parents were perfect when they were created. That is, they had no defects or flaws that would prevent them from having children. On the sixth day, God told them to be fruitful and multiply. Since they were married from the start and capable of producing children in obedience to God's command, how long might it have taken before Eve conceived a child? It seems likely that this would have taken place within the first few months.

We know that she did not conceive a child until after they were expelled from the garden. This is the order in which the biblical narrative is explained — expulsion from the garden in Genesis 3:23–24, and Eve conceives a son (Cain) in the next verse, Genesis 4:1. But we can also be pretty confident about this because if she had conceived Cain prior to eating the forbidden fruit, then Cain would probably not have been born with a sin nature, which he obviously had.

So with all of these details considered, it seems like Adam and Eve would have been in the garden for a very short time, perhaps less than a month, before they rebelled. The view passed down to Garun in our story is based on this line of reasoning.

Some Christians object to the brief timeline before sin because they say that Adam and Eve had to have time to walk with God in the garden. While this idea of our first parents walking with God is commonly taught, the fact is that the Bible never explicitly teaches it. Nowhere does the Bible claim that Adam and Eve walked with God in the garden, and yet many Christians have taught this idea as if it came right from Scripture.

In all likelihood, this notion is based in some way on Genesis 3:8, which states, "And they heard the sound of the LORD God walking in the garden in the cool of the day . . ." (NKJV). It seems like many people have just remembered some of the wording in this verse and assumed that it says Adam and Eve walked with God. But that's not at all what is going on here. This verse appears immediately after our first parents rebelled against the Creator. They are not taking a leisurely stroll with God; they are hiding from Him as He comes to announce His judgment.

Much more could be discussed on this subject, but those details are far beyond the purpose of the original question. However, if you would like to learn more about the arguments for and against this idea, please read Tim's article, "Did Adam and Eve Walk with God in the Garden?" and the many comments that follow it, at http://midwestapologetics. org/blog/?p=1349.

Did anyone live longer than Methuselah?

In our story, Garun told Noah in chapter 7 that one of his ancestors, Ma'anel, a son of Adam, lived for 985 years. It is not uncommon to hear Christians claim that Methuselah lived longer than anyone in history, but that is not necessarily the case.

The Bible tells us in Genesis 5:27 that Methuselah lived a total of 969 years, and it does not mention anyone living any longer than that, so it is possible that he had the longest lifespan of any human. However, the Bible only gives us the age at death for a tiny fraction of the people who lived prior to the Flood. From Adam through Noah, there are only ten people whose lifespans are recorded, and yet there may have been many millions of people who lived prior to the Flood. So it is certainly possible, if not rather likely, that someone outlived Methuselah.

Of course, Ma'anel is just a fictional character. The Bible mentions that Adam and Eve had other sons and daughters (Genesis 5:4), but it only names Cain, Abel, and Seth. For more details about whether people really lived so long, please see the back pages of the first book in this series, *Noah: Man of Destiny.*

As part of this conversation in the book, there was a reference to King Lamech seeking to live a thousand years. The king also voiced his idea to the council of Iri Geshem in chapter 6. This goal fits well with his boastful character, but there was another reason to bring this idea into the story. God warned Adam that he would surely die on the day he ate the fruit from the tree of the knowledge of good and evil (Genesis 2:17). Just what did God mean by saying Adam would die that *day* when we know Adam lived for 930 years? Biblical commentators have proposed several ideas about how Adam may have died in some sense that day. Certainly, his relationship with God was instantly marred by sin. Many Christians refer to this as spiritual death. There may have been physical implications as well in the sense that Adam's body would now endure sicknesses and other ailments, so to some degree, he began to die on that day.

Not as popular as these first two views, some have proposed that God meant Adam would not live a thousand years, since elsewhere the Bible explains that to God a day is like a thousand years (2 Peter 3:8). We definitely would reject any attempt to insert a thousand years whenever the word *day* is used because the context frequently rules out such a possibility, as it does for the days of creation in Genesis 1 and the days that Joshua and the Israelites marched around Jericho (Joshua 6). Nevertheless, it is interesting to consider how it might fit in some of the places where the term is used in the context of judgment, as it is in Genesis 2:17. While this view may be unlikely, we thought it would be interesting to see the wicked King Lamech hold such an idea and strive to defy his Creator in a unique manner. The reader can probably guess whether the king will be successful in this endeavor.

Why would Noah's culture use a judicial concept not mentioned until after the Flood?

In chapter 11, one of the men in the crowd, Ethlin, accuses Garun and Bedin of murdering two people in Iri Geshem. Consequently, he believes that they deserve to die for their crime. The idea that the punishment should fit the crime is popular throughout the world, but it is not mentioned in the Bible until shortly after the Flood. In Genesis 9:6, the Lord told Noah, "Whoever sheds man's blood, by man his blood shall be shed; for in the image of God He made man." So why did we put this concept into the pre-Flood world?

The answer to this question is probably rather obvious. The concept seems to make pretty good sense in many cases. If someone steals an item from you, then according to this perspective, the thief would need to make restitution in some way. They could return the item, reimburse you for the cost, or replace it at their expense. In the case of murder, then the murderer has essentially forfeited his life.

Did Noah endorse the notion that an idea is true because of how he felt about it?

Postmodernists hold to an idea that views truth as subjective — truth is whatever one wants it to be. We each have our own truth, they say, and there is no overarching truth that is true for every person (besides that statement, of course). This view can often be seen in the way many

Americans talk about religious beliefs. It is not too uncommon to hear someone say, "It doesn't matter what you believe, as long as you're sincere."

This type of argument is also used by some Christians who reject the biblical concept of the lake of fire as a place of eternal torment for the wicked. Since they do not understand how God could sentence someone to this fate or they just do not like the idea, they seek to reinterpret the many passages that teach it. For the record, I am not thrilled about the idea of people I know who will suffer eternally for their sins, but instead of reinterpreting Scripture, I trust that God really means what He inspired to be written in the Bible about those matters. This truth motivates me to share the gospel of Jesus Christ with an unbelieving world. Sincerity or feelings cannot be used as an accurate test for truth.

In chapter 16, while sailing to Havil, Noah and Tubal-Cain discuss the afterlife. You might remember from the first book when we explained why we did not give Noah knowledge of all the details found in Genesis 1–5. As far as we know, Noah and others of his time had not been given clear revelation from God about what happens after death. He certainly could have known that our bodies return to the ground, as God told Adam in Genesis 3:19. This is observable at every burial, so one might assume more of a naturalistic view of death — that there is no afterlife and our bodies decay in the ground. But is that all Noah could have known, apart from direct revelation from God?

Ecclesiastes 3:11 states that God has put eternity in the hearts of men. This is generally understood to mean that man has been given some sense of his own existence beyond his physical life. If this is accurate, then Noah and others in his day may have believed in an afterlife. Also, if Noah knew that God had taken Enoch from the earth to heaven, then he might come to believe that one would enjoy a physical existence with the Creator after this life is through.

This was the rationale behind the discussion between Noah and Tubal-Cain. Near the end of it, Tubal-Cain said that it made sense to him, and he liked it because it would mean their dear friends were with the Creator at that moment. Noah added that he now liked the view even more. Notice, he did not say that he believed it to be true more than he had before, just that he had a stronger appreciation for his view. So in our book, Noah did not subscribe to the idea that something must be true because of how he felt about it.

Were there diseases in the pre-Flood world?

In chapter 14, Naamah spends time in Havil's grand library, the House of Knowledge. While she's there, she reads about Bothar, an important city far away to the north that has been decimated by a strange disease. Readers may remember this city from the first book as the place where the kidnappers were planning to take Elam and the other Zakari children.

Biblical creationists believe that diseases would have been non-existent in the beginning. But over time, due to the effects of sin, which would include genetic mutations, diseases would increase to what we observe today. That being said, some people have asked me if I believe there would have been diseases in the pre-Flood world. Well, we wrote this detail into the book to raise this very issue.

We know from the fossils found in sediments laid down during the global Flood that certain diseases existed at that time. Evidence of cancerous tumors has been found in dinosaur remains buried in the Flood. So if animals suffered from diseases, then humans probably did as well. When we consider how diseases are frequently transmitted in our day, it is easy to see how the same things may have occurred in the exceedingly violent and decadent world prior to the Flood.

Did women suffer miscarriages in the pre-Flood world?

In chapter 16, Noah and Emzara suffered further heartbreak as she lost their first child not long after learning she was pregnant. We know that people of that time would have had fewer genetic mistakes than we do today since they were closer to Adam and Eve, so would women have had to undergo the sorrow of losing a child in the womb?

The Bible does not give any specific examples of women miscarrying prior to the Flood, although by the time God gave the Law to Moses, people were familiar with this concept. The Lord told the Israelites that if they obeyed Him, He would bless them and that no one would be barren or suffer miscarriage in their land (Exodus 23:26). Centuries earlier, after suffering unimaginable personal tragedy, Job expressed that it would have been better for him if he had been stillborn (Job 3:16).

After Adam and Eve sinned, the Lord made a statement that might be relevant to this discussion. He explained that the pains a woman suffered during childbearing would be greatly increased. While miscarriage is not specifically mentioned, there was at least the indication that bringing forth children would be quite difficult.

Many of the people living prior to the Flood were extremely wicked, so many of them surely engaged in harmful practices that might contribute to poor prenatal care, such as violent behavior and an unhealthy diet. Given these factors, it seems quite reasonable to assume that women suffered miscarriages prior to the Flood, although at this point it probably would have been rarer.

Finally, we would like to clarify that the novel does not blame anyone in particular for Emzara's miscarriage. Some people might get the impression that since she was under extreme duress in the weeks leading up to the event that she brought it on herself. While it might be natural to think that way, we did not seek to attribute blame to her. Sometimes terrible things happen in this world without a direct connection to one's own behavior. The fact that she was a sinner living in a sin-cursed world where good things and bad things happen to the righteous and the wicked was reason enough for this to occur.

Would the pre-Flood world endure earthquakes, volcanic eruptions, and other natural disasters?

In chapters 23 and 24, the city of Havil was devastated by a violent earthquake triggered by a volcanic eruption. Is such a scenario consistent with the popular creationist model of a single pre-Flood continent? In other words, if there were no continental plates sliding against each other, could an earthquake have occurred?

The major fault lines, or fault zones, in our world today exist along the boundaries of continental plates. However, there are plenty of fault lines that occur far from continental boundaries. So even if the pre-Flood supercontinent did not have fault zones along continental boundaries, it could have had fault lines in the midst of the land mass.

On the third day of the creation week, the Lord caused dry land to appear. Creationists generally believe God raised the ground up from the water. This enormous amount of geologic activity could have included faults. Residual movement of these faults from the third day could have triggered earthquakes following that time.

Volcanic eruptions occur when molten rock, called magma, forces its way to the surface of the planet. A violent eruption, like the one described in the book, occurs when the pressure in a magma chamber becomes so great that it forces its way through the volcano's conduit and escapes through the vent. While the vent allows for a certain amount of pressure to be released, there are times when the pressure becomes too great for a slow and steady release through the vent. Movement of magma beneath the surface can also cause tremors prior to the eruption. This is why the people in and around Havil were able to see smoke from the volcano and feel tremors in the days leading up to the blast.

Finally, Romans 8:22 explains that "the whole creation groans and labors with birth pangs." The reason the whole world suffers is due to man's sin. So earthquakes, volcanoes, and other natural disasters are almost certainly included in the groaning of the whole creation, and this has been going on since the Lord cursed the ground because our first parents sinned in the Garden. Verse 19 states that all of creation eagerly waits for the time when God will make all things new. In the new heavens and new earth, there will not be any earthquakes or other natural disasters.

Did Noah really believe the earth traveled around the sun?

In chapter 24, we see Noah express a basic understanding of a heliocentric solar system as opposed to a geocentric solar system. He told Tubal-Cain that the earth occasionally moved between the sun and the moon, which caused the moon to have a brownish appearance. Would Noah have known this information given that so many people up until the 16th century A.D. held to the belief that the sun and other heavenly bodies orbited the earth?

It is true that geocentrism was popularly held from the time of the Greek astronomer Claudius Ptolemaus (Ptolemy) in the second century A.D., and it was not widely rejected until the time of Nicolaus Copernicus. However, roughly four hundred years before Ptolemy, Aristarchus of Samos proposed a heliocentric model of the solar system.

We regularly discover that ancient people had a better understanding of the heavens than is generally supposed. Archaeological discoveries throughout the world have shown that ancient people used the stars for navigation and timekeeping, which was one of the reasons God created them on the fourth day (Genesis 1:14). Very early records of eclipses have also been discovered. Incidentally, lunar eclipses demonstrate the roundness of the earth since the moon passes through our planet's shadow, revealing earth's curvature. At the Ark Encounter, visitors can view a globe of the pre-Flood world in Noah's Study.

We cannot be sure what Noah did and did not know on this subject, but based on the discoveries from the ancient world, it is not unreasonable to think that people in the pre-Flood world had a fairly good understanding of the heavens.

Did people really have huge families prior to the Flood?

In our story we mentioned a few families as being rather large. For example, Noah's brother and sister-in-law, Jerah and Pivi, are described as having 31 children and we mention that Tubal-Cain and Adira had 17 children. Is it realistic for a couple to have so many children?

The Bible does not tell us how many children certain individuals had prior to the Flood. Cain's descendant, the evil king in our series, had four children that are mentioned. The men in the line from Adam to Lamech, Noah's father, in Genesis 5 each had at least five children (one is named, and then we are told that they had other sons and daughters).

The novel is actually probably too conservative on the number of children in a given family. A Russian woman from the 18th century is believed to have given birth to 69 children, and she only lived about 75 years. There are more than a dozen women reported to have given birth to more than 30 children in the past few centuries. In the pre-Flood world, men lived much longer lives than they do today, so women presumably did as well. If a woman who lives fewer than a hundred years can give birth to over 30 children, then it is quite believable that a woman who lives for many centuries could have dozens of children.

At this point in our story, Jerah and Pivi are nearly 500 years old. You may recall from the explanation in the first book that we proposed that people during that time would have aged slower. So a 500-year-old person would look similar to a 50-year-old today. Consider that Pivi could have become pregnant from the time she married until she was around 450 years old. That would mean that she had over 400 years to bear children. Even if she had just 1 child every 10 years, she would have had 40 children. The fact that we only gave her 31 kids is probably an underestimation of the size of many pre-Flood families.

Why was God portrayed as a large flame?

Perhaps the trickiest decision we had to make in writing these books is how we were going to depict God when He spoke with Noah. The Bible simply tells us that the Lord spoke to Noah, but it does not say how He did that. Throughout Scripture, God communicated with people through various ways. The following list gives some of these means.

- Appearing as a man to Abraham in Genesis 18
- A burning bush to Moses in Exodus 3
- Still small voice to Elijah in 1 Kings 19:12–13
- In a vision to Isaiah in Isaiah 6
- In a dream to Nebuchadnezzar in Daniel 2

When God appears in some type of physical form in the Old Testament, theologians identify the occurrence as a theophany, from the Greek words for "God" and "appearance." In this case, the Bible does not even say that God appeared at all. He may have simply spoken to Noah without appearing. So there were plenty of options available to us that would have been consistent with how God speaks to people in the Bible.

We chose to use a vision combined with an appearance similar to the burning bush for several reasons. The use of the vision and some of its details will be significant in the third book, *Noah: Man of God*.

Having the Lord appear as a flame tied together several biblical concepts. As mentioned above, Moses saw God as a burning bush, but the bush was not consumed. In our story Noah saw a single flame, but there was no bush or anything else for the flame to burn.

When describing the way God revealed Himself to the Israelites at Mt. Sinai, the Bible states that "the sight of the glory of the LORD was like a consuming fire on the top of the mountain" (Exodus 24:17). This idea is repeated in Deuteronomy 4:24 and 9:3. Also, Exodus 13:21 states that "the LORD went before them by day in a pillar of cloud to lead the way, and by night in a pillar of fire to give them light."

272

One of the earliest appearances of God in physical form recorded in Scripture occurred when the Lord established His covenant with Abraham, called Abram at the time, in Genesis 15. Abraham gathered the sacrificial animals God instructed him to bring, and then the Lord put him into a deep sleep. God, in the form of a fire pot and flaming torch, passed between the animals that had been sacrificed. Much could be said about the significance of this event, but the point here is that we have another example of God appearing to someone as a fire.

The single flame was essentially an attempt to combine aspects of these ideas while remaining unique. After all, there are differences between each of these appearances, so we did not want to copy any of them in every detail.

Why did God only give Noah part of the details about the Flood and the Ark in this book?

When God appeared to Noah in our story, He described just a fraction of what we read in Genesis 6. Would it not have been better to simply quote exactly what God said to Noah so that someone does not think we were attempting to take away from God's Word?

The short answer is that we will include the entirety of God's message to Noah at the appropriate time. As mentioned in Chapter 26, Noah will hear from the Most High again.

We do not know if the Lord's message to Noah about building the Ark was delivered all at one time even though this seems to be the most natural way to understand the text. However, we need to remember that the Bible does not always include every detail. It is quite possible that God revealed certain aspects of His plan to Noah at various intervals, but when the text was eventually recorded, the writer (Moses) simply put all of the communication into one segment.

This is also the reason Noah did not receive all of the information about the Ark at this point. He does not know at this point how large it will need to be, how many decks to build, or any of the other details that God revealed in Scripture. He just knows that he will need to build an Ark large enough for eight people and plenty of animals.

Our decision to divide the Creator's instructions into at least two portions had more to do with storytelling than any clues from the text.

We wanted God's statement about Noah having sons after centuries of childlessness to be an opportunity for Noah to trust God at the heart of his greatest frustration. He had grown discouraged over the years, so he could have responded in various ways upon hearing about having sons. He could have laughed as Sarai did in Genesis 18:12 when God promised that she would have a child in a year's time. He could have doubted the message as Zacharias did in Luke 1:18 when the angel told him that he and his wife would soon have a son (John the Baptist). Instead, we chose to have Noah respond with complete trust in what God told him, which underscores why the Bible identifies him as a righteous man. His confidence in the Lord will continue to grow as he sees the Creator's faithfulness.

Didn't Noah have 120 years to build the Ark? If so, shouldn't God have spoken to him 20 years earlier than He did in the novel?

In our novel, Noah was nearly 500 years old when God first spoke to him. The notion that he had 120 years to build the Ark would mean that God would have spoken to him when he was about 480 since the Flood struck in Noah's 600th year. This idea is a rather common misconception among Christians. I cannot count the number of times I have heard people say, "Noah had 120 years to build the Ark." This is based on Genesis 6:3, but there are at least two problems with this view.

When the Lord gave Noah the details about the Ark, He told him that He would establish a covenant with Noah, his wife, his sons, and his sons' wives (Genesis 6:18). So it sure seems as if the sons were grown up and married when God told him to build the Ark. Since the oldest of Noah's sons was born when Noah was 500 years old (Genesis 5:32), and the Flood came in his 600th year, then Noah would have had much less than 120 years to build the Ark. In fact, he would have had fewer than 100 years to build it, since we need to consider how long it would take for the three boys to be born and to grow up and get married (perhaps 25–50 years), and then subtract that number from 100 to figure out the maximum amount of time for building the Ark (approximately 50–75 years).

The second problem with the idea that Noah had 120 years to build the Ark is that the verse it is based on, Genesis 6:3, is not even about the timing of the Ark's construction. In the first book, we briefly discussed two popular views about the meaning of this verse in which God stated,

"My Spirit shall not strive with man forever, for he is indeed flesh; yet his days shall be one hundred and twenty years." Many people believe it refers to God's judgment on man's lifespan. Prior to the Flood, many of the men mentioned in Genesis 5 lived beyond 900 years. The only two exceptions in the line between Adam and Noah were Enoch (365) and Lamech (777). For God to drastically reduce man's lifespan would indeed be a severe judgment.

Others believe this verse refers to a countdown to the Flood. That is, from the point God made the announcement there would be 120 years before the earth would be destroyed by the Flood. Even if this happens to be the correct view, notice that it would still not mean that Noah started building the Ark at this time. In fact, God commanded Noah to build the Ark 11 verses later.

Finally, in an *Answers* magazine article about the construction of the Ark, I wrote about the following problem in thinking it took 120 years to build the Ark.

> Consider the implications of building such an enormous boat out of wood over the course of many decades. Exposed to the elements, wood tends to warp and decay as it endures heat, cold, and changes in humidity. Imagine trying to complete one part of the Ark decades after another section had been built. The earliest parts of the construction might need repair by the time the Ark was finished.

To read the rest of the *Answers* magazine article, please see "Fantastic Voyage: How Could Noah Build the Ark?" at www.answersingenesis.org/noahs-ark/fantastic-voyage-how-could-noah-build-ark.

Were there really giants prior to the Flood?

In the dramatic arena chapters in our story, Noah encounters a giant guard that would have easily outsized anyone alive today. We depicted Noah as a fairly tall man. While our story never uses modern units of measure, like feet and inches, we decided that Noah should be about 6'2" tall to match how he is depicted at the Ark Encounter. The reason he is that height is based on the 20.4-inch cubit that was chosen for the construction of the Ark Encounter. But even at that height, Noah only reaches the man's midsection. Were there really giants in ancient times or is this idea just a tall tale?

Genesis 6:4 states, "There were giants on the earth in those days, and also afterward, when the sons of God came in to the daughters of men and they bore children to them. Those were the mighty men who were of old, men of renown."

This verse appears at the end of one of the most controversial and misunderstood passages in the Bible, which is one of the reasons Tim decided to write his ThM thesis on this subject. People have long disagreed over many of the details included in Genesis 6:1–4, particularly the identity of the "sons of God" who married the "daughters of men" (Genesis 6:2). Scholars generally adopt one of three views regarding the sons of God. Some believe they were godly men in the line of Seth, others believe they were tyrant kings who viewed themselves as divine, and others believe they were angelic beings who left heaven to marry women. The ministry that built the Ark Encounter, Answers in Genesis, does not hold an official position on the identity of the sons of God. For a balanced overview on this topic, read my article from *Answers* magazine, "Battle Over the Nephilim" at www.answersingenesis.org/bible-characters/battle-over-the-nephilim.

So where do giants fit into this picture? Well, they are often viewed as the offspring produced by the sons of God and the daughters of men. This idea is sometimes disputed as well. Some people will say that the giants were already on the earth when the sons of God and daughters of men had children. However, a close look at the Hebrew language favors the former view. Regardless of one's position on that debate, Genesis 6:4 states that there were giants on the earth in the days before the Flood, and it describes them as "mighty men" and "men of renown."

But does the word translated as *giants* in Genesis 6:4 actually refer to physical giants? After all, many English Bibles use the word *Nephilim*, which is a transliteration of the Hebrew word. Some popular level writings contend that this word means "fallen ones" and comes from the Hebrew verb *naphal* ("to fall"). However, this is unlikely since the Hebrew language follows patterns when a term is used as a basis for another word. Please bear with me for a brief discussion of technical details in this paragraph. In this case, to transform the verb *naphal* into a word that means "fallen ones," the word would be *nephulim*. To convert it into a noun meaning "those who fall" would yield the word *nophelim*. Notice that neither of these terms is spelled the same as the word in Genesis 6:4 ("Nephilim"), and there is a pretty good reason for that. The term *Nephilim* is likely the Hebrew plural form of the Aramaic noun *naphil*, which means "giant."

The translators of the Septuagint, the name given to the Greek translation of the Old Testament begun in the third century B.C., translated Nephilim as *gigantes*. You can probably tell just by looking at it that *gigantes* means "giants." It is interesting that every single Hebrew and Aramaic lexicon that I have examined lists "giants" as the primary meaning of *Nephilim*, and not one states that it means "fallen ones."

When we compare Scripture with Scripture, we find another reason to view the term in question as meaning "giants." *Nephilim* appears two more times in the Bible, and both occurrences are in the same verse. Numbers 13:33 records the words of the spies who returned to Moses and the Israelites after searching the land of Canaan. They said, "There we saw the giants (the descendants of Anak came from the giants); and we were like grasshoppers in our own sight, and so we were in their sight." Both occurrences of the word "giants" in this verse translate to the term *Nephilim*. Notice that they are described as being very large people. Some commentators have argued that the spies were lying about seeing giants in the land because the previous verse states that the spies gave a "bad report." However, the term translated as "bad report" does not refer to a false message but to a true report of bad tidings. Furthermore, the narrator of this passage, Moses, already explained in verse 22 that the spies had seen three giants known as Anakim. In fact, the Bible describes several other people groups in the land of Canaan and surrounding regions as giants: the Amorites (Amos 2:9–10), the Emim (Deuteronomy 2:10–11), the Zamzummim (Deuteronomy 2:20–21), and the Rephaim (Deuteronomy 3:11–13). Since Moses wrote both verses in which the word *Nephilim* appears, and the context of each passage describes some of the physical attributes of these individuals, it makes sense to interpret them consistently as being giants. At the Ark Encounter, we depict a couple of giants in the Pre-Flood World exhibit. We made them to be about the same size as Goliath — six cubits and a span, which is nearly ten feet tall. The giant in the novel is described as being about the same height.

Why did you depict the giant as a cannibal?

Legends and other stories of giants often describe them as having a taste for human flesh. The cyclops Polyphemus from Homer's *Odyssey* is probably the most infamous of cannibalistic giants, but he is not alone. In fact, Odysseus had previously lost his entire fleet of ships except for one when they stopped at the island of the Laestrygonians. The residents of this island were giants who sunk Odysseus' ships by hurling huge rocks at them, and then they speared Odysseus' men as one would spear fish and carried them off to feast on them. The popular story of Jack and the Beanstalk also features a giant with a hankering for human flesh.

In our story, the giant guard is not a very nice character. He made a comment about wanting to devour Noah and then attempted to take a bite out of Elam. What was the rationale in making this guy a cannibal? Was it simply to make him scary and unlikeable or was there a biblical and historical basis for it?

It turns out that ancient Jewish writings also connect giants to cannibalism. The book of 1 Enoch, which is not part of the Bible, was penned sometime between the writing of the Old and New Testaments. Obviously, it was not written by Noah's great grandfather Enoch, although the work pretends to be from his hand. The book describes events prior to the Flood and mentions giants who consumed all the things grown by men, but "when men could no longer sustain them, the giants turned against them and devoured mankind" (1 Enoch 7:1–5). Another popular non-biblical Jewish writing from the intertestamental period, the Book of Jubilees, describes the pre-Flood giants as cannibals. This book has been called "Little Genesis" because it describes portions of Genesis and then adds details. While expanding upon Genesis 6:1–4, the controversial passage about the sons of God and the giants, Jubilees says that lawlessness increased on the earth after the giants were born and that all flesh became so corrupted that "they began to devour each other" (Jubilees 5:1–2). Neither of these books belongs in the Bible because they were not inspired by God, although Jude 14–15 does quote from 1 Enoch.

Where do these ideas come from? Were they just invented to make giants seem more terrifying or might they have a basis in reality? As strange as it may seem, there may be biblical support for this notion. When the Israelite spies returned from searching out the land of Canaan, they said, "We went to the land where you sent us. It truly flows with milk and honey, and this is its fruit. Nevertheless the people who dwell in the land are strong; the cities are fortified and very large; moreover we saw the descendants of Anak there" (Numbers 13:27–28). As pointed out in the response to the previous question, the "descendants of Anak" (the Anakim) were described as giants. Notice that the spies had nothing negative to say about the land itself — they praised it as a land flowing with milk and honey. But then a few verses later, as they are trying to persuade the people against trying to conquer the land, the spies stated, "The land through which we have gone as spies is a land that devours its inhabitants, and all the people whom we saw in it are men of great stature. There we saw the giants . . ." (Numbers 13:32–33). What happened in those few verses? Did the spies change their mind about the land itself? Did they say it was a great land and then immediately go back on their word and say that the land was undesirable? I doubt it. Look closely at what they said about the land in verse 32. They claimed that it was "a land that devours its inhabitants," and then they immediately went on to talk about the giants in the land. By using *land* to refer to the land's inhabitants, a figure of speech known as synecdoche, the spies may very well have meant that certain people of the land literally devoured its inhabitants. No wonder the Israelites were so afraid of trying to enter the Promised Land at that time, although they should have trusted that the God who freed them from Egypt through many signs and wonders could have safely brought them into the land (which He did 40 years later).

Commentators offer a variety of possible meanings to the statement about the land devouring its inhabitants, so I would refrain from claiming that the interpretation mentioned in the previous paragraph must be the correct one. Nevertheless, I do believe it makes the best sense of the context, it helps explain why the Israelites were terrified of trying to enter the land, and it offers some intriguing connections to other ancient literature about the location and behavior of these giants. For more details on this subject, please read Tim's blog post "Giant Speculations" available at www.midwestapologetics.org/blog/?p=1139.

Where did you come up with the various people and place names in the books?

Coming up with unique names for the people and places was often a challenge. Obviously, there were some characters taken right from the

Bible, such as Enoch, Methuselah, Lamech, Noah, Tubal-Cain, Naamah, Jubal, Jabal, Adah, and Zillah. However, many of our characters were simply made up, so how did we come up with their names?

Some people have suggested that we should have used names that are common in the Bible, as many other historical fiction novels about biblical people have done. But there were a couple of reasons we did not want to do this.

The first reason we avoided using names from the rest of the Bible is that most of the biblical names are post-Babel. Since God confused the languages of the people at that time, we can be rather confident that the pre-Flood tongue (and pre-Babel for that matter) would have been different in most cases. Most of the names in the Old Testament are Hebrew names, but it is quite unlikely that the Hebrew language existed prior to the Flood. Although some Christians believe it was the original language, I do not find the arguments for this view to be compelling.

When we borrowed a name from the Bible, we typically limited ourselves to names that are found prior to the Babel account in Genesis 11. For example, the names Elam and Ashur (Asshur) are found in Genesis 10:22, and some of the names we chose were slight variants to names in these chapters. Oban is similar to Obal (Genesis 10:28) and Ara is similar to Aram (Genesis 10:23). Some of the place names are right out of the Bible: Havilah (Genesis 2:11), Nod (Genesis 4:16), the Hiddekel River (Genesis 2:14), and Eden (Genesis 2:8).

At times, we simply made up the name based on what sounded like a good name for that character and others were based on names of real people. For example, two of the characters in this book have names that I discovered while watching rugby, so I adapted their names for our characters.

The second reason we often avoided borrowing names from later portions of Scripture has to do with the way many biblical characters are named. You may have noticed that many biblical characters have "el" somewhere in their name. Here are just a few: Israel, Elijah, Elisha, Daniel, Samuel, Michael, Gabriel, and Ezekiel. These two letters are one of the titles for God, so it was common for a person to have a name with "el" as a prefix or suffix. This existed in the pre-Flood world as well: Mehujael and Methushael (Genesis 4:18) and Mahalalel (Genesis 5:12). So we used "el" in some of our names: Parel, Akel, Jitzel, and Elnach (a combination of El and Nachash, an obvious sign that his par-

280

ents did not fear the Creator). But there is another popular prefix and suffix found in much of the Old Testament that we were very careful to avoid using for our characters. Many biblical characters have part of God's personal name in their own name. As a prefix, it frequently appears in names beginning with a "J" (Jehoshaphat and Jehoram), and as a suffix it typically takes on the "iah" ending (Isiaiah, Jeremiah, and Jedidiah). The reason we avoided this title will be explained in the response to the next question.

Why does Noah only use three titles for God?

You may have noticed throughout the first two books that Noah and others have only referred to God as the Most High, the Creator, and God. The Bible uses multiple titles for God, such as the Almighty (Genesis 49:25), Ancient of Days (Daniel 7:22), and Holy One of Israel (Isaiah 41:14). Another title that occurs frequently is Lord, but we intentionally avoided using it because most English Bibles use it to translate two very different terms. When it appears as "Lord," it is typically a translation of the Hebrew word *adonai*, and it often means "master." Many English Bibles use the word "LORD" to translate God's name, YHWH (Yahweh).

When God spoke to Moses after the Israelites were commanded to make bricks without being given any straw by the Egyptians, He made a very interesting statement. He said, "I am the LORD [YHWH]. I appeared to Abraham, to Isaac, and to Jacob, as God Almighty, but by My name LORD [YHWH] I was not known to them" (Exodus 6:2–3).

What did God mean when He said that He appeared to Abraham, Isaac, and Jacob, but He was not known to them by His name, Yahweh. The most straightforward way of understanding this sentence seems to be that God said the patriarchs did not know Him by His personal name. However, this would be a strange thing to say since the divine name is used 162 times in Genesis, and 34 of those occasions come from someone speaking God's name. It is possible that when Moses wrote Genesis, he inserted God's personal name in several places to replace *adonai, elohim*, or another title for God, but this cannot be proven. Consequently, some commentators conclude that God meant that the patriarchs did not really know God's covenant-keeping nature, while others propose that God's statement should be understood as a question. That is, perhaps

God asked, ". . . but by My name, Yahweh, did I not make Myself known to them?"

We may not be able to know for certain how this verse is to be understood. However, there is one very interesting piece of information that I have not shared yet, which explains why we avoided using God's name in the novel. We have seen that many people prior to Moses had "el" as part of their name, but there is not a single example of anyone being identified with part of God's personal name prior to Exodus 6:3. In fact, the first time we see someone with part of God's personal name in the Bible is found just 17 verses later, and it happens to be the mother of Moses, Jochebed. Prior to this passage, she was called "a daughter of Levi" (Exodus 2:1) and "the child's mother" (Exodus 2:8). Could it be that Moses called her by a new name after learning God's personal name? We know that he changed his successor's name to include the divine name when he changed "Hoshea" to "Joshua" (Numbers 13:16). And after the time of Moses, the Bible includes scores of people whose names reflect knowledge of the divine name.

Perhaps they really did not know God's personal name prior to Moses. Since this is at least a possibility, we decided to refrain from naming anyone with part of the divine name, and we also kept people from calling Him by that name. We also did not have anyone call Him "Lord" because of how easily it can be confused with "Lord." At the same time, we realize they may well have known God by His name, but we thought it would be interesting to explore this angle a bit in the story.

Why was Noah so confident that he would not die in the arena, or that if he did die, that God would bring him back to life?

During their brief conversation in the dungeon, Naamah told Noah that he would die that very day. Noah confidently replied that he was not going to die that day, but then he added that even if he were to be killed, the Creator would need to raise him from the dead. Two chapters later, Noah reiterated that he would not die that day.

The source of his confidence that he would survive the arena was his strong faith in what God had told him. He knew that God would preserve his life until he built the Ark and survived the Flood. But he also added one small caveat. If he did die, then God would raise him from the dead. Why did he mention this detail?

This idea actually comes from the life of Abraham, so this idea was borrowed from the Bible, but I wanted to address it here because of its length. Hebrews 11:17–19 states, "By faith Abraham, when he was tested, offered up Isaac, and he who had received the promises offered up his only begotten son, of whom it was said, 'In Isaac your seed shall be called,' concluding that God was able to raise him up, even from the dead, from which he also received him in a figurative sense."

Have you ever wondered why Abraham was willing to sacrifice Isaac? This passage tells us that he concluded, or some translations say he reasoned that God was able to raise Isaac from the dead. What a marvelous picture of faith! Not a blind leap in the dark, biblical faith is a well-reasoned trust in the perfectly good character of the all-powerful Creator.

God called Abraham to do something that most of us would never carry out, yet this great man of faith knew that God had already promised him that the whole world would be blessed through Isaac. Obviously, since Isaac had no offspring at this point, there would be no way for God to keep His Word if Abraham sacrificed Isaac, unless something else happened. Abraham figured it out. He knew that God always keeps His promises, so he believed that even if he sacrificed Isaac, God would need to bring him back to life so that He could fulfill His promises.

We wanted Noah to have a faith similar to Abraham's. Even though he faced a situation that seemed as if it would lead to certain death, he stood firm in his faith and demonstrated why he is called a "preacher of righteousness" (2 Peter 2:5).

Why did you make some of the characters, like Naamah and Tubal-Cain, so different than how many Christians have imagined them?

We have mentioned that one of our goals in writing this series is to encourage readers to take a closer look at Scripture because so many wrong or unsupportable ideas about Noah and the early chapters of Genesis have become popular in the Church. For example, in the first novel, we mentioned rain in a few chapters even though many have been led to believe that it had never rained before the Flood. This allowed us to discuss the issue in the back of the book. In the same way, by countering many of the stereotypes about the biblical characters, we are able to discuss them here and urge our readers to examine the Bible.

Tubal-Cain is often described as a wicked and violent man. The blasphemous 2015 film *Noah* depicted Tubal-Cain as a murderous villain. The late biblical scholar Meredith Kline also described Tubal-Cain's father, Lamech, as a king, but then went far beyond the text in stating that Lamech's "policy was one of tyranny, a tyranny that reckoned itself through the power of the sword of Tubal-Cain more competent for vengeance than God himself" (Meredith Kline, "Divine Kingship and Genesis 6:1–4," *Westminster Theological Journal*, 1962).

We wanted to counter these ideas about Tubal-Cain by seeing him as a man who eventually comes to believe in the Creator through Noah's influence. Although he was raised by a boastful murderer, there is no guarantee that he would have followed in his father's footsteps. Some of Israel's godly kings had wicked fathers. This truth shows us that there is always hope for people who were raised by ungodly parents.

With Naamah, we went the opposite direction. Many Christians believe that she was Noah's wife. A fifth century A.D. writing called the Genesis Rabba identifies her as such. The rationale behind this is that there does not seem to be a reason to mention Naamah in the genealogy, particularly since the text says nothing else about her. While identifying her as Noah's wife is within the realm of possibilities, it certainly is not the only way to understand the biblical text. An ancient Jewish tradition viewed Naamah as a pagan woman who sang songs to idols. Unlike her brother and half-brothers (Jubal and Jabal), no role is ascribed to Naamah. However, her name may come from the Hebrew root *n'm*, which means "to be lovely," or it may be derived from a different Hebrew root that is spelled identically and means "to sing." This is why we made her a beautiful singer who is also an idolatress.

The book of Jubilees identifies Noah's wife as Emzara. Of course, this name is likely just invented by an ancient writer, and it probably means something like "ancestor of Sarah." Jubilees 4:33 states that she was the daughter of Rake'el. While we liked the name Emzara, we did not want to give the impression that we viewed Jubilees as being divinely inspired, so we named her father Ara instead. Finally, if we discover someday in heaven that Noah's wife was Naamah, you can be sure that we will apologize to her for how we portrayed her in this series.

Did the pre-Flood world have large cities with massive buildings and temples?

By the time our story fast-forwards 450 years, Iri Geshem and many other cities are depicted as being heavily populated with huge buildings. But were the pre-Flood cities really like this? After all, these types of cities and megastructures do not seem to appear in historical records until well after the Flood. So why did we describe the cities this way?

There are a couple of points to consider when discussing this issue. First, we have no archaeological record of what the pre-Flood cities were like. These places were entirely devastated by the Flood, so it is highly unlikely that any trace of them will be found.

The second factor to consider is that the Flood would have caused what may be called a technological reset. Apart from what was on board the Ark, all of the world's technology would have been wiped out. Noah's family would essentially restart civilization, but within the next several generations, society would undergo another technological reset at Babel. As people scattered from that place in their various groups, they would have taken what they knew with them. Consider what would happen to a group that had little to no knowledge of agriculture, or if another group knew very little about construction. This is the reason we see multiple civilizations spring up around Europe, Asia, and Africa all around the same time, yet some of these groups were hunter-gatherers and some planted crops. Some people lived in cities while others lived in caves.

With these two factors in mind, we see that we cannot look back to our earliest archaeological records to get a clear view on the pre-Flood society. Since the Bible does not really describe what the cities were like at that time, other than highlighting man's excessive wickedness, we were left to imagine what they could have been like. At the Ark Encounter, we made the decision to portray the pre-Flood world as being somewhat like the classical Greek or Roman cultures, at least in terms of technological achievements. They had civil societies based on laws and were capable of amazing feats, but they were also extremely decadent. So our story will remain consistent with that decision. Since ancient Greece and Rome had massive buildings and temples, we will include similar structures in the pre-Flood world.

ENCOUNTER THIS

Since we worked on the Ark Encounter project, we had the unique opportunity to include details in our story that can be seen in various exhibits. We were also able to influence the design of certain elements so that they connected with our story. If you visit the Ark Encounter in Williamstown, Kentucky, you will be able to see the following items that were included in the story.

Chapter 11: The chapter opens with Noah trying to figure out a way to pass the time while grieving over his tragic losses. He begins carving an animal out of a block of wood, and it is mentioned that the back of a large-eared tusker started to take shape before he put the project down. This carving based on an elephant-like creature modeled after *paleomastodon* can be seen on a shelf in Noah's Library on the second deck.

Chapter 15: In this chapter, Emzara has a nightmare of having her child taken from her, and then she is forced to watch as the child is sacrificed to the serpent idol. While this was just a dream for her, the Ark Encounter depicts a similar scene in the Pre-Flood World exhibit on the second deck. There is a large diorama featuring a pagan temple with people offering their small children as sacrifices to the serpent god.

Chapter 16: While traveling to Havil to find out whether their suspicions about Lamech were correct, Noah is shown working on a map of the coastline they are sailing past. This map and a wider map of the world can be seen hanging on a wall in Noah's study on the Ark's second deck.

Chapter 17: In this chapter, Noah and Emzara witness two strange creatures involved in a clash. Dinosaur lovers may have recognized the creatures being described as *pachycephalosaurs*. These dinosaurs are usually recognized by the large bony crest on top of their skulls. It is generally believed that these were used for sparring with other males, perhaps to earn the right to mate with the females in the group. Two *pachycephalosaurs* can be seen in one of the cages on the Ark's second deck, although they are juveniles at this point, so they have not yet grown the large bony crest.

Chapter 23: In one of the more disturbing moments of the book, Naamah announced the institution of ritual prostitution during their annual serpent ceremony. The people were told that they could engage in a high form of worship by uniting with one of the temple prostitutes. These sorts of religious practices were quite common in the ancient world. The pagan temple diorama from the Pre-Flood World exhibit, mentioned above in the chapter 15 description, shows people meeting outside of some rooms on the side of the temple, and it is apparent that they are there to take part in ritual prostitution.

Chapter 25: While Noah is walking with his grandfather Methuselah, he thinks about the widespread wickedness in the world contrasted with the many wonderful things to see in creation. In Noah's Study on the second deck of the Ark, people can ask questions of the animatronic Noah figure. In two separate responses, he references the world having been such a beautiful place but now had been overrun with corruption. To hear these responses, ask Noah what the world was like before the Flood and why his globe only has one land mass.

Chapter 30: As Noah is being led through the old city square and is distraught over how decadent Iri Geshem has become, a man tries to persuade Noah to purchase an idol from him. Noah puts out an arm and turns away. An illustration conveying this scene can be found in the *Who Was Noah?* exhibit on the Ark's second deck.

Chapter 32: In the dramatic sequence when Tubal-Cain is forced to choose between serving the Creator or saving his wife, we describe a unique creature that is brought into the arena. We called it a pithoct, but the creature being described is known to us today as a *thylacosmilus*. This cat-like animal featured two large saber-like teeth and grew to about the size of a jaguar. They are thought to have been marsupials, so the females may have had pouches. The Ark Encounter features two of these very cool-looking creatures on the second deck.

Chapter 33: After his arrest, Noah is brought into the arena where he encounters two foes that no one would ever want to encounter in such a situation. The guard who drags him into the arena is a giant warrior, but the more terrifying creature is what comes through the door moments later. The "horned grendec" seen on the book's cover is based on a *carnotaurus*, a *T. rex*-like dinosaur with horns on its head. The Pre-Flood

World exhibit on the second deck features a large arena diorama featuring this dinosaur and a giant guard. The arena in Iri Geshem is described as being quite a bit larger than the one shown in the Ark. Also, if you visit the Ark Encounter, take a very close look at the giant in that diorama. One of the authors of this book, Tim, posed for the images used to 3D print the giant, so the character looks just like him.

Borrowed from the Bible

Since the Bible does not give us many details about Noah's life, we needed to use artistic license to tell the story. To keep the story more closely tied to the Bible, we decided to borrow and slightly adapt some concepts found in elsewhere in Scripture and work them into Noah's story.

Major spoiler alert! Do not read this section unless you have first read the novel.

Chapter 23: In the serpent ceremony in Havil, Lamech boasted about killing a young man who wounded him. Of course, this plotline goes all the way back to the first chapter of the first book and forms the basis of Aterre's tragic story. He was the young man who wounded Lamech in self-defense. This boast of Lamech is taken directly from Genesis 4:23–24.

Chapter 23: During the same speech mentioned above, in response to being called a murderer, Lamech boasted about being the most powerful man in the world, although he was unable to finish his sentence because a violent earthquake interrupted him. This concept of judgment immediately falling on a boastful king is found in the Bible. In Daniel 4:28–33, Nebuchadnezzar boasted about all that he accomplished even though he had been warned to humble himself, and immediately God caused Nebuchadnezzar to live like a beast for seven years. In the New Testament, Herod Agrippa gave a speech causing the people to hail him as a god. We are told in Acts 12:20–24 that he failed to give glory to God, so an angel of the Lord immediately struck him so that he was eaten by worms and died.

Chapter 25: After our story jumps forward 450 years, we learn that Noah and Emzara are still childless and that they have been praying for a child throughout those centuries. Of course, if you are familiar with the account of Noah in the Bible, you know that he will eventually have three sons. The idea of a barren couple praying for a child is not uncommon in Scripture. Hannah prayed for a son and eventually gave birth to Samuel (1 Samuel 1:10–11). We do not specifically read about Abraham and Sarah praying for a child, but we know they longed for a son, and even though they tried to fulfill God's plan in a different way, Abraham trusted the Lord (Genesis 15:1–6). Our story probably parallels the experience of Zacharias and Elizabeth in the New Testament. She was barren and both were advanced in years. When Zacharias entered the temple to fulfill his priestly duties, an angel appeared to him and announced that his prayer had been heard and that he and Elizabeth would have a son. Unlike Noah in our story, Zacharias did not believe at first and was struck with muteness until his son, John the Baptist, was born (Luke 1:5–25).

Chapter 26: In our story, when God appeared to Noah in a vision, we borrowed several ideas from other portions in Scripture. The Lord opened by saying, "Do not be afraid, Noah, for you are greatly loved." Many times in Scripture when God or an angel appears to a person, the first words often spoken are, "Do not be afraid" (see Genesis 15:1 and Matthew 28:5 for some examples). The line about being "greatly loved" comes directly from Daniel, who was told multiple times by an angel that he was greatly loved (Daniel 9:23, 10:11, 19). Since Noah is described as being righteous, like Job and Daniel (Ezekiel 14:14, 20), we thought it was fitting for Noah to hear from God that he was greatly loved too. Finally, when Noah replies to God, he begs forgiveness for daring to ask a question. We borrowed this concept from Genesis 18 where Abraham pleaded with God to not be angry with him for asking about possibly sparing the city of Sodom on behalf of a certain amount of righteous people that might be found in it (Genesis 18:22–33).

Chapter 26: After the Lord appeared to Noah in our story, Noah tripped over a stone and knocked it loose from the ground. He decided to stack several rocks together as a way of remembering the place where God spoke to Him. Jacob did something similar to this in Genesis 28:18. He stood one stone on end and poured oil on top of it after the Lord appeared to him during the night in a dream. When the Israelites crossed the Jordan River into the land promised to them, God instructed them to take 12 stones from the river and set them up as a memorial to what He had done for them (Joshua 4).

Chapter 31: When the city of Iri Geshem is taken over by the Havilites, one of the first rules they make is that everyone must bow down to an image of Nachash. Of course, the city council made sure that Noah was in attendance, knowing full well that he would refuse to bow and they would have an excuse to arrest him. This scenario is quite similar to the situation faced by Daniel's three friends, Shadrach, Meshach, and Abednego, in Daniel 3. They refused to bow and were subsequently thrown into the fiery furnace. In our story, Noah refuses to bow to the statue, so he is arrested and eventually brought into the arena, presumably to meet his doom.

Chapter 33: In another scene reminiscent of the Book of Daniel, Noah finds himself in the coliseum being ordered to bow before a false god or face what would seem to be certain death. In Daniel 6, King Darius signs a law forbidding anyone to petition any man or god over the next 30 days, or they would be thrown into the lion's den. The entire plot was a setup by the Medo-Persian governors and satraps who were envious of Daniel. They knew Daniel would refuse to follow such a law, and after he continued praying to the true God, they brought him before the king who reluctantly ordered for him to be thrown into the den of lions. The Lord miraculously delivered Daniel, and those who accused him were then thrown into the lion's den. Similarly, in our story, Noah is delivered from a terrifying beast while some of those calling for his death met their own end.

Dear Reader,

Thank you for continuing our tale of Noah's life, as we have imagined it. As you probably know by now, one of our goals in this series is to encourage readers to carefully study the Bible so that they can rightly discern fiction and biblical fact. And the main reason we want readers to examine Scripture is so that they might learn the most important message we could ever tell — the gospel, the good news that Jesus Christ died on the Cross for our sins, was buried, and then conquered death by rising on the third day.

As we explained in the first book, Noah could not have known all of these details since he lived long before they occurred. However, the Bible describes Noah as a righteous man who found grace in the eyes of the Lord. Even though he lived in an extremely wicked world, he faithfully completed the tasks that God gave him, and he trusted that God would remain true to His promises.

We also live in a time when many people are opposed to God's truth. In an effort to make the gospel message more appealing, some Christians teach that trusting in Jesus will make everything better in this life. While God does grant joy and peace to believers, Jesus taught His followers to deny themselves (Luke 9:23) and to consider the cost of following Him (Luke 14:25–29). We are also told that godly people will suffer persecution (2 Timothy 3:12).

In the climactic chapters of our book, Noah and Tubal-Cain refused to compromise their faith in the Creator even in the face of death. Serving God was more important than life itself. The same can be said of those who follow Jesus today. We understand that He gave His life on the Cross for us and grants eternal life to those who trust in Him, so His followers should be willing to give up everything for Him. This commitment to follow Him at all costs is not derived from efforts to obtain salvation. It is rooted in a desire to love and serve Him because He has first loved us and obtained salvation for us (1 John 4:15–19).

What about you? Have you placed your faith in the risen Savior, Jesus Christ, and are you willing to stand for Him no matter the cost? The reward of serving Him makes it all worthwhile.

Jesus said, "Blessed are those who are persecuted for righteousness' sake, for theirs is the kingdom of heaven" (Matthew 5:10).

ABOUT THE AUTHORS

Tim Chaffey is the Content Manager for the Ark Encounter and Creation Museum. A former pastor and teacher, Tim is also a leukemia survivor and competes in half-marathons with his wife and son while his daughter cheers them on. He has earned advanced degrees specializing in apologetics, theology, and church history. Tim maintains a popular blog (www.midwestapologetics.org/blog), contributes regularly to *Answers* magazine and the Answers in Genesis website, and has authored over a dozen books, including *The Truth Chronicles* series and *In Defense of Easter: Answering Critical Challenges to the Resurrection of Jesus.*

K. Marie Adams has an obsession with words that once resulted in her being grounded for reading too much. Later, it served her well as she worked for many years at a bookstore and as a literature and grammar instructor. Now, as a graphic designer, her love of language goes by the fancy name of typography. K. Marie also volunteers for several ministries dedicated to rescuing young girls from modern-day slavery.

THE REMNANT TRILOGY
BOOK 1

NOAH: MAN OF DESTINY | 978-0-89051-972-1

Most people think of Noah as the man who built a large ship and spent months caring for thousands of animals. But who was he and what events shaped who he would become? *Noah: Man of Destiny* takes readers on a captivating, coming-of-age journey through the pre-Flood world. Noah learns more about the Most High while standing against a sinister belief system emerging throughout the land. Whether escaping legendary beasts, tracking kidnappers, or pursuing his future wife, Noah acquires the skills he will need when God calls him to his greatest adventure: surviving the global Flood. Explore what it may have been like for a righteous man to relate to God before the Bible was written.

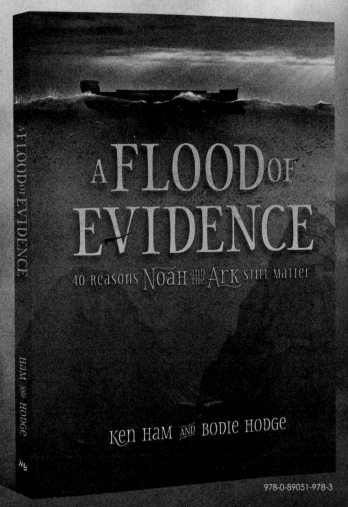

NOAH

MAN OF GOD

TIM CHAFFEY &
K. MARIE ADAMS

First printing: May 2018
Second printing: September 2019

Master Books®, P.O. Box 726, Green Forest, AR 72638

Master Books® is a division of the New Leaf Publishing Group, Inc.

ISBN: 978-1-68344-105-2
ISBN: 978-1-61458-662-3 (digital)
Library of Congress Number: 2018939633

Cover design by K. Marie Adams; cover illustration by Ben Iocco

Please consider requesting that a copy of this volume be purchased by your local library system.

Printed in the United States of America

Please visit our website for other great titles:
www.masterbooks.com

For information regarding author interviews,
please contact the publicity department at (870) 438-5288.

Master Books®
A Division of New Leaf Publishing Group
www.masterbooks.com

Thank You

The Remnant Trilogy has been quite an adventure for Noah and the authors. Crafting a novel takes a considerable amount of time and energy, and often involves many more people than those whose names appear on the cover. We wish to say a heartfelt "thank you" to all those involved, especially to the following people.

Tim Dudley and the great team at Master Books. Thank you for your patience with us, for taking a chance on some novels, for being so easy to work with, and for turning out a great product.

Reagen Reed, thank you for lending your editorial expertise. Our stories are so much stronger and cleaner as a result of your efforts.

Casey, with the amount of work you put into this series, your name could easily appear on the book covers. Thank you for all of the brainstorming, editing, rewriting, and everything else you did to bring these stories to publication.

Ben, thank you for another outstanding cover. We know that people should not judge a book by its cover, but if they decide to make such judgments, we are certain they will like these novels.

Janice, thank you for your prayers and proofreading.

To our great, great . . . grandfather Noah, thank you for your faithful example in walking with the Lord. Without it, we would not be here. We hope our stories have done justice to your godly life.

Finally, thank You to our Lord and Savior, Jesus Christ. Thank You for the gifts You have given us and the opportunity to write these stories. We pray they will bring honor and glory to Your matchless name. Thank You for the gift of salvation You have offered through Your sacrificial death, burial, and Resurrection.

CONTENTS

DEAR READER,

Thank you for reaching the third and final volume in *The Remnant Trilogy*. We hope you have enjoyed reading them as much as we have enjoyed writing them.

As we have mentioned in the first two books, our intent has not been to add to Scripture while sharing this imaginative retelling of Noah's life. In fact, our goal has been practically the opposite in that we want to help readers discern between the fiction we have created and the facts recorded in the Bible.

So far, our story has traced Noah's life from his youth up until the months before his oldest son is born. Can you imagine waiting hundreds of years before the birth of your first child? Can you envision working on the same construction project for decades, knowing that once you finish, the world will be destroyed? Now imagine what it would be like to do those things as one of the few godly people remaining, while the world around you becomes more and more wicked to the point that God was grieved that He had made man (Genesis 6:6). These are just a handful of many unique aspects of Noah's life that we pondered as we developed this work.

If you read the preview of this novel at the end of the second book, please be aware that the first chapter in this book is extended. So if you skip the first chapter here, you will be missing some important details in the story.

Settle in and get ready for the exciting conclusion of *The Remnant Trilogy*. Thank you again for joining us on these adventures.

Sincerely,

Tim Chaffey and K. Marie Adams

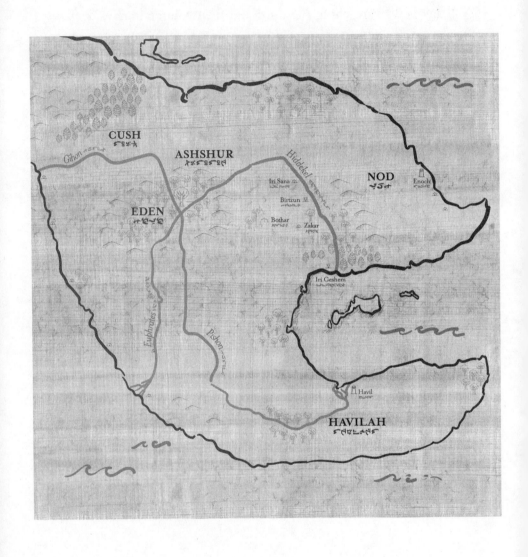

CHAPTER 1

Iri Geshem — Noah's 499th year

Turning her head to dodge the brilliant reflection of sunlight off the glimmering façade of Iri Geshem's town hall to her right, Naamah marched toward the guest mansion reserved for foreign dignitaries. Jaw set in an angry line, she twisted the oversized iron bracer covering her left arm from elbow to wrist and stared at its intricate patterns.

Led by Nivlac, the quartet of guards flanking her increased their pace to keep up. Even after her many protests, they still accompanied her. Iri Geshem's seedy characters always posed a slight threat, but the soldiers had remained on high alert since the day before. A mixture of outrage and grief had overtaken the town after the debacle in the arena, and the chance remained high that someone might seek revenge for loved ones lost. Still, being surrounded by overprotective men at all times did nothing to improve her mood, and she maintained a stony silence throughout their trek.

Two soldiers manned the doors into the residence. Normally, the gold trim along the frame, a sign of Havil's influence in this city, would bring her happiness, but she was in no mood to be amused. The guards pushed the doors open and stepped inside as she approached.

The bearded man on her left nodded. "Welcome back, Princess."

Ignoring him, Naamah stormed ahead into the spacious foyer. She glanced around, hoping there would be no delay. To her right, a small group of people spoke quietly around the low table in the sitting room. They fell silent at the sight of her, but she turned away without acknowledging them. The lavish dining hall to her left sat vacant except for a servant girl preparing the place settings. Other than Nivlac, the guards remained near the door.

Naamah moved to the stairs and ascended to the second floor. She turned left and hurried to her guest room at the end of the hall.

"Princess." Nivlac gently touched her arm. "Is there anything I can do to help?"

She opened the door, jerked away from his touch, and glared at her loyal guard. "Just wait out here."

He drew himself upright and faced the hallway. "As you command."

Naamah shut the door behind her and tossed her green-hemmed cloak on a bench. She slid her shoes off and dropped onto the bed. As she loosened the strings on the bracer, regret and sadness filled her entire body. *How long has it been since I've felt this way?* She adjusted the metal and retied the cords, fitting it more comfortably, even though it was clearly made for a man's large forearm. Studying the remarkable craftsmanship, her thoughts raced back to her brother's final moments in the arena. She shook her head in an attempt to rid herself of that memory. Thankful for the opportunity to spend some time in Tubal-Cain's shop earlier in the day, she stroked the one memento she had found to remember him by.

As she repositioned herself, an object pressed against her stomach. Withdrawing the small dagger from the pocket of her wrap, Naamah held it in front of her eyes and slowly twisted it about. For a brief moment, the thought of plunging it directly into her own chest raced into her mind. She raised the knife and gripped the handle with both hands. Taking a deep breath, she recalled her father's smile as Tubal-Cain died. She lowered the blade and inserted it into its slot in the bracer. *Not while he is still alive.*

As she stared at the armband her brother had crafted, Naamah said, "And I'll wear this until he's dead." She fell back onto the bed and closed her eyes. *Why wouldn't you bow, Tu?* Her lip quavered and she squeezed her eyes tight, successfully preventing a tear from escaping. *All because you came to this city with Noah.*

Gathering her wits, she sat back up and gazed out the large window to her right. In her mind she watched the giant drag Noah into the arena, leaving him standing helplessly beneath her as the grendec entered and the crowd roared. No matter how many times she replayed the next moment, the outcome never changed. Brimming with a quiet confidence, Noah looked at her and said, "I will not die today."

Her heart pounding, she clenched a fist and slammed it into the bed. "How did he know?" *What if he's right? What if the Creator is more pow—* "No!" Impossible. Noah was just lucky. *No matter. He'll soon be back in our custody, and there will be no escape. How dare he try to make a fool of me in front of everyone!*

Naamah stood and moved to the reflective plate on the wall. She ran a hand through her hair, pushing all of it over to the right. After straightening her gown, she held up her left arm to examine how the bracer looked on her. A hint of a smile grew on her lips as she focused on the hilt of the dagger. *I like it.*

A knock at the door ripped her attention away from her reflection. "Not now, Nivlac."

The door creaked open. "Princess, the king told me to update you on the search." The voice was not Nivlac's.

Naamah briskly straightened her shoulders and lifted her chin. "Enter."

A guard stepped into the room and knelt before her. Keeping his head down, he said, "Every exit to the city has been blocked since yesterday. As you know, we stopped him from fleeing the city by boat. Our—"

"Where is he?" Naamah tapped her foot.

The guard hesitated and dropped his head even lower. "Still no sign of him, but he must be in the eastern part of the city. Our men have been searching every home."

Naamah grabbed a small vase off the shelf beside her and smashed it onto the floor, shattering it into dozens of pieces. "Find him!"

The man flinched. "Yes, Princess."

Glaring at the back of the man's neck, she slid the dagger part way out of the armband. Letting out a breath, she replaced the blade with a clinking of metal. "You weren't sent out to come back empty-handed. Return without him again, and you'll be fed to the grendec."

He nodded. "Yes, Princess."

"Get out!"

The soldier stood and bowed before spinning around and hustling out of the room.

Naamah kicked a clay shard across the floor. *Tubal-Cain is dead and Noah's free.* "Ah!" Her breathing quickened as her anger kindled. Trying to shake the image of Tubal-Cain's bloodied corpse from her mind, she paused and let it fuel her temper instead. She scratched an itch near the top edge of the bracer, the irritation increasing her rage even more. Her eyes locked onto the handle. "This comes off today."

Stepping carefully over shattered pottery, she reached for her shoes and pulled them on. "Nivlac!"

He stepped into the room, and his eyes darted from the mess on the floor to her. "Yes, Highness."

Controlling the tone of her voice, Naamah asked, "Do you know where my father is?"

"I believe he's in a meeting with leaders from the city."

Biting her lip, she contemplated how to take revenge. *Yes, that should work.* "Very good. That's all."

Nivlac nodded. "Would you like me to inform the king that you'd like to see him?"

She strode past him. "That won't be necessary. Follow me."

Rushing down the hall, Naamah allowed the memory of Tubal-Cain's murder to drive her forward while ignoring all the warnings that rang inside her. *I don't care if this is a deadly mistake. It's worth the risk.* As she reached the middle of the passage, she turned left and pushed the double doors open, then stepped confidently into the spacious meeting hall. The city's councilmembers reclined on lush cushions around a low table loaded with colorful fruits and vegetables along with a variety of meats. Skimpily clad male and female dancers twirled and twisted near the musicians on the far side of the room.

Seated at the opposite end of the table, her father handed a tray of food to a young woman dressed in a tawdry outfit standing at his side. His eyes lingered after her as she stepped away. Only when the girl had disappeared through the servants' entrance in the corner did he turn to face his daughter. "Naamah, please join us."

Nivlac remained at the door as she glided around the councilmembers and stopped about ten cubits before the king. As she bowed her head slightly, she glimpsed the hilt of the dagger at her forearm. She raised her voice for the benefit of everyone in the room. "Father, why did you murder Tubal-Cain?"

The music stopped and Lamech raised his eyebrows. "Murder?" He snorted. "That's called justice, my dear. He disobeyed direct orders from both of us. He needed to be punished for his treason."

"But he was your son, and my brother!" Her tone grew sharp and accusatory. "You never should have put him in that situation."

"He sought to undermine my rule." The king raised a finger and pointed at her. "And you'd better watch yourself."

"Pah! Are you threatening me?" Naamah stepped closer, defiantly challenging his authority and anticipating a blow to the face as he had dealt her several times before. But at over 700 years old, he was weaker and slower than he had once been. He would never see the dagger until she had planted it deep into his chest in an act of self-defense. "Without Nachash's followers, your rule would crumble."

Anger burned in his eyes as he glanced at the councilmembers, many of whom wore shocked expressions. He stood and took a step toward her. "If you ever speak to me that way again—"

"What? You'll kill me just like you've killed your son?"

"Enough!" Lamech raised his hand to hit her, but he froze when the twin doors burst open.

Jolted by the interruption, Naamah turned to see two guards dash into the room just as she placed her hand over the bracer.

"Sir!" The guard who entered first dropped to a knee, and his companion followed suit. "Please forgive the interruption. I have urgent news!"

Glaring at Naamah, the king said, "This had better be important. What is it?"

"The Nodite army," the first guard said.

Lamech broke eye contact with Naamah. "What about the Nodites?"

The second sentry lowered his gaze. "They were spotted one day's march from here and are headed this way."

A few gasps and nervous chatter broke out from the others in the room. Lamech raised his hand to silence his guests and turned to Iri Geshem's new chief councilmember. "Get your security commanders here immediately."

Ashur nodded once and whispered something to the man next to him, who abruptly stood and dashed out of the room.

Glancing again at the dagger hidden against her forearm, Naamah dismissed the urge to stab her father while he was distracted. *Patience. It must be in self-defense or in private.* She cautiously stepped away, hoping the news would make him forget her insubordination. Upset that her plan had been foiled, she clenched her jaw tightly until she remembered the small vial tucked inside a hidden pocket of her gown. She spotted the drinks on the table and the faintest of grins tugged at the corner of her mouth.

Lamech barked a command, causing Naamah's heart to skip a beat.

The first guard shot to his feet. "Sir?"

"Find Commander Tsek and tell him to gather my war council right away. The city gates and the river shall remain closed and guarded. No one enters the city without inspection and no one leaves. Noah is the least of our problems now. If the Nodites have any spies here, we cannot allow them to get out."

The man nodded and raced toward the door with his companion on his heels.

"King Lamech," Ashur said as he climbed to his feet. "Might I suggest that we reconvene in the city planning hall downstairs? It's larger than this room and has a model of Iri Geshem that may be useful in planning our defense."

Lamech's gaze shifted to Naamah. His lip curled, as if promising retaliation to come, but then he turned away. "Very well. Prepare the room."

Chapter 2

"Ashur." Naamah grabbed the councilman's shoulder as she watched her father stride out of the meeting hall. Gesturing toward the table with a tip of her head, she said, "The defense meeting will take a while, so it would be wise to have the drinks brought to the room."

Ashur nodded. "Understood, Princess." He signaled two servants with a snap of his fingers. "Help me take the food and drinks downstairs."

Naamah released his shoulder. "Have you ever defended the city from attack?"

The determined look of a man who had spent his life advancing his career through any means necessary gave way to wide, fear-stricken eyes. "We've never had the need. What will we do? Can we win?"

A smirk crossed her lips. "Have no fear, Councilman." She emphasized his title to remind him that he was beneath her. "Our king, my father, has never lost a battle."

Gathering himself, he let out a breath. "Thank you. I must hurry." Ashur scurried across the floor and picked up two large trays of food with the practiced ease of a former innkeeper.

While everyone busied themselves with the change of location, Naamah discretely withdrew the small vial from her hidden pocket, removed the cover, and slipped it under the wrist end of her bracer. Holding her hand up so that the powder would not spill out, she pretended to study the metal armband as she marched to her father's place setting. She leaned forward over his cup only to freeze upon hearing Ashur's voice.

"Don't do that," he said.

Momentarily seized by fear that her scheme had been uncovered, she recovered herself, then straightened her shoulders and glared at the councilman. He shrank back and nearly dropped a tray. "I'm sorry, Princess. I didn't intend to issue an order to you." He took a breath and gave her a half smile. "I only meant that you don't need to carry any of this. My servants and I will handle it."

She nodded. *I should've known the fool was too blind to know what I'm doing.* "Thank you, Ashur. I was only reaching for this fruit to take to my room while I wait for everyone to assemble."

"My apologies. Help yourself." He steadied the platters and headed for the door.

Naamah leaned forward again and grabbed a ripe green malid. Glancing around the room, she pulled back and carefully passed her wrist over her father's cup, the most ornate one on the table, and allowed the vial's powder to fall into the intoxicating beverage. After replacing the cap on the poison, she bit into the crispy fruit and grinned. *Father, today your pride will serve me well.* She cupped the malid with both hands. *You'll soon be avenged, Tu.*

Holding her head high, she exited the room and returned to her private chambers, where she closed the door behind her and placed the tiny container back into her hidden pocket. Allowing a slight chuckle to escape her mouth, she whispered, "Goodbye, Father."

* * *

A short, stout soldier pointed away from the part of the model representing the city's main gate. "Do you think the Nodites will attack from the sea too?"

The king set down his cup and wiped his mouth. "They might. But we'll be ready for them. If Tsek ever gets here, that is. Where is he?"

"He's here, sir," called a guard who stood near the door. He stepped aside as the mountainous commander hustled past him.

Tsek stopped a few paces before Lamech and bowed his head. "My king, the messenger told me about the Nodites. What's your plan?"

"Send our fastest ship to the islands." Placing a hand over his mouth, Lamech stifled a cough. "Get the reinforcements here immediately. No time to spare."

16

"Yes, sir." Tsek spun and lumbered out of the room.

"What defenses do you have in the eastern city?" Lamech asked a middle-aged officer from Iri Geshem.

"We have sentries at each watchtower along the wall and two battalions at the ready. But even if the Nodites breached the eastern barrier, there's only one bridge to the main city. Our concern has always been to protect this side."

"A wise decision," the king said.

As Lamech and the war council worked out the details, Naamah listened closely while gazing about the space. The city planning hall gleamed with white stone walls stretching high above to a ceiling that continued to climb upward to a central peak. Six metallic concentric rings dropped from the middle, each successive circular piece hung about two cubits lower than the one above it, and all flickered brightly with dozens of burning wicks. Naamah guessed that oil flowed through the middle tube and the armatures that held up the rings to provide a steady fuel supply. She envisioned reworking the piece as one large coiled serpent.

Beneath the grand chandelier, an extravagant scale model of Iri Geshem sat on a dais encircled by over a dozen men who excitedly pointed at various sections of the city as they deliberated. Her half-brother Jubal sat among them but never spoke. His musical abilities were unmatched in the world, but he had little aptitude for leading men into battle. Nivlac occasionally participated in the discussion, although he was better suited to serve as chief of security than war strategist. Still, despite his shortcomings in this setting, she valued having a loyal servant in the king's inner circle.

A hint of a knowing smile crossed Naamah's face as her father coughed again and took another swig. Beads of sweat appeared on his reddened forehead. As she turned away to hide her delight, a twinge of regret threatened to overshadow the satisfaction. Memories of a few enjoyable times with her father flashed into her mind, but she quickly dismissed them with thoughts of her imminent ascension to the throne. Focusing again on the conversation around the miniature replica of the city, she forced herself to consider how she would take charge when the poison finished its mischief.

"So our main objective is to delay the Nodites' attack until our reinforcements arrive." Lamech reached for his stomach and grabbed the edge of the model with the other hand.

Nivlac lunged to assist him. "Are you alright, sir?"

The war council fell silent as the king dropped to his knees and retched repeatedly. He reached for his throat and gasped for air. "Help me." His weakened voice barely exceeded a whisper.

"Father!" Naamah knelt next to him and placed her hand on his back. "Call a healer!"

Jubal stood and echoed her command before joining Naamah at their father's side, carefully stepping around the vomit. Other councilmembers stood at a distance, watching the king with great concern. Ashur sprinted out of the door, yelling for a healer to hurry.

Groaning, Lamech attempted to stand, but he lost his balance and tumbled forward. Despite Naamah's best effort to catch him, he spun as he slipped from her grasp and fell into the foul mess on the floor. Eyes wide open, he stared at Naamah. "Help." The breathless word barely escaped his throat as the muscles in his neck constricted.

"Help me sit him up so he can breathe," Naamah said to Jubal.

Jubal bent down to help her, but the stench caused him to turn away and cover his nose. He gestured to Nivlac to take his place.

Nivlac knelt and slid his arms under the king's shoulders as Lamech struggled for air. The guard's eyes met Naamah's for an instant, but in that briefest of moments, they told her he was aware of the situation. "I've got him, Princess." He lifted the king to a sitting position and dragged him to a clean area of the floor.

Having witnessed the effects of this particular poison on victims many times before, Naamah knew what to expect. Typically, the poor soul would suffocate in moments. She glanced at her father's cup. Her heart sank when she saw that it was still over half full. Had he consumed enough poison to kill him? Staring at the drink, she knew what she needed to do next. She pointed to the cup. "Nobody touches that. I think he's been poisoned." She stood tall, but before she could say anything more, Ashur rushed into the room followed by a short, gray-bearded man carrying a large bag. Ashur directed him to the king as Nivlac and others made the pathway clear. Ashur caught Naamah's attention. "This is the master healer."

Naamah stepped in front of the short man. "This is your king. Save his life or you will lose your own. Understand?"

"Please." The man peered around her to see his patient. "I'll do what I can, and you should probably call on Nachash for his intervention."

"Of course." She moved aside, caring little to ask for the deity's help in this matter. "Hurry."

The little man stooped beside the king, who writhed on the ground still red-faced and fighting for each breath. "Sir, if you can understand me, please open your mouth."

Lamech moaned in agony before his whole body went limp and his eyes shut.

Naamah strove to suppress her anticipation of her father's final breath.

The healer glanced at Nivlac. "He must open his mouth or I can't help him."

Nivlac looked for Naamah's approval, and she nodded in return. He placed two fingers from each hand into the king's mouth and pried it open.

After a brief examination, the little man dug into his bag and pulled out two small, covered clay jars. "Don't let him close his mouth." He opened the first vessel and withdrew a pinch of fine black powder and placed it on the back of Lamech's swollen tongue. "Give him a sip of water and make sure he swallows that."

"Here." A Havilite commander lowered a cup to the king's lips and poured a bit of its contents into his mouth.

Nivlac closed the limp ruler's mouth and tipped his head back.

Lamech gagged, and a few spurts of water escaped his lips despite Nivlac's efforts to prevent it.

The healer opened the second jar and hastily smashed the tiny green leaves in it with a pestle. Satisfied with his progress, he gestured for Nivlac to repeat the process.

Shortly after the administration of the second dose, Lamech's body contorted and then suddenly stiffened. The king remained motionless.

Naamah's silent hopes were dashed yet again when her father's chest slowly rose and fell.

"He'll need to rest," the healer said. "I think he's going to live." He turned to Naamah. "Princess, I believe someone has poisoned your father. If you don't mind, I'd like to stay with him until he wakes. He may yet need some more treatment."

"Of course. Thank you for saving his life. You'll surely be rewarded." She took a deep breath and imagined dumping the poison right into the healer's mouth as his reward. "Ashur, have two of your men take the king to his room with the healer. I want them to stay there until further notice."

"Yes, Princess." Ashur called the guards near the door and relayed Naamah's instructions.

The two men lifted the king up and carried him out of the room. The healer followed closely behind them.

"What are we going to do now?" Ashur asked.

Jubal cleared his throat and stepped forward with his chin held high. "I will lead us in my father's absence."

Naamah fixed an icy stare on him. "You will do no such thing, little brother. Go back to your music and parties and leave the war to those of us who are qualified to discuss such matters."

Jubal looked around the room for support, but no one dared to challenge Naamah. He shrank back and sat down.

"No one else leaves this room without my permission." Naamah picked up the king's cup. "We need to find out if this was poisoned, but first—" She snapped her fingers. "Nivlac!"

Just as overeager to please her as he had always been, Nivlac hustled to her side and stood at attention.

"Go fetch Commander Tsek. Make sure that ship is sent to the islands, just like my father wanted, but in light of the circumstances, we need Tsek here to help us plan the battle."

"Yes, Princess." Nivlac turned and headed toward the door.

"We have no time to delay." Naamah directed the remaining members of the war council to return to their positions around the city model. She scanned the faces of each man to ensure their full attention. "We have a lot going against us at the moment. The Nodites are at our door, and from what we've just seen, someone in our midst does not wish my father to be the king. This is no time for fear or division." Her voice rang out in confidence, and the expressions in the room revealed a general willingness to follow her. "We must go forward in honor of the king. We will see to it that in this darkest time, with foes all around, we shall not be overcome."

Ashur beat a fist against his chest. "So be it. Princess Naamah, the one who will lead us to victory!"

She feigned humility, smiling softly and shaking her head while exulting on the inside.

20

"Hail, Naamah." The man to her right, a respected guard from Iri Geshem, bowed his head toward her.

The rest of the council followed his lead, and she longed to savor their praise, but an attack was imminent and required everyone's full attention. She held up her hand, and they quieted. "As the king said before, our main objective is to delay the advancing troops until our reinforcements arrive. The Nodites will undoubtedly approach the main gate, so we'll need most of our forces there to give the illusion of a vast army. That will give them pause and buy us time." She held her arms out to the side. "Ashur!"

He straightened and then bowed low. "Yes, Princess."

"You're a leader of Iri Geshem. You'll lead the investigation into who tried to topple our great city from within by poisoning the king. The rest of us will defeat the Nodites. Victory will be ours!"

CHAPTER 3

Iri Dekkel — Noah's 499th year

Emzara stared blankly at the wall opposite where she sat on a large woven mat. The golden hue of the evening sun cast shadows from the surrounding foliage onto the sand-colored canvas of the tent. Sighing, she played with the band tied around her upper left arm. The carved medallion carried the same rainbow design as the wooden one Noah had tied on her when he had asked her to marry him. *How long before you get here, my husband?*

At Garun's insistence, they had moved across the wide river from Iri Dekkel for protection in case some of the people who decimated the city returned. Lamech's former guard had silently taken in the surroundings and selected a small clearing in the undergrowth. Using ropes and wooden pegs from the ship's supplies, he created a framework to support the large piece of fabric. Now Emzara and her still-unconscious charge rested under the tent while Garun busied himself with the finishing touches.

Small breaks in the trees allowed them to watch the river without being seen from the opposite shore. The surrounding forest also served to block much of the cool wind that had picked up earlier in the evening. Thankfully, Garun's shelter intercepted any stray drafts that occasionally made their way into the clearing. Biting a nail, she glanced at the severely injured man lying on elevated bedding about three cubits from her. A large purple-and-black bruise on the side of his chest stood out like a gold pikka among a pile of silver piks. Dried blood coated parts of the

22

fabric under a pair of wooden braces holding his lower leg in place. Although hidden by a cloth at the moment, thoughts of the large gash and bump on his head made her wince.

Grateful that he remained asleep after he stirred slightly, Emzara sighed. *Everything in my life is about waiting right now. I don't know if I can take much more of just sitting here until the next thing happens.* A beautiful pattern from the shadows of the leaves danced all about her. Fluttering, they crossed and then moved apart from one another in the breeze. *I wonder if this is how the Most High views our lives: events slowly unfolding as we run about interacting with each other.* The wind ceased and the leaves stood still. She stared at the silhouette of a lone leaf. *And then we're alone while we wait for more movement. But I'm never really alone, because the Most High sees me.*

O Creator, waiting is hard when you think you have the answer but you have yet to see proof. You chose Noah to build Your ark, so I know he will be safe, but I would be happier if I could see him, hold him. My view of life is obscured, just like I only see the shadows from within this tent, but You see all the detail and colors of the leaves as if from the outside. And You know just how it will all unfold.

Feeling movement inside of her, she looked down and the corner of her mouth rose. Emzara placed both hands on her belly. *I guess not all waiting is bad.*

"One more thing." Garun stood at the opening of the tent. He held up a thick, dark cloth. "I just need to attach this to the top so that you have a little privacy curtain. I'll hang a second one on the other side for me and Laleel. That way we can still hear if he makes a noise."

"Do you need me to get up?" She put weight on her hand and moved her feet out, readying herself.

With shoulders hunched and knees bent, Garun began attaching the fabric to the apex of her dwelling. "Thanks. I've got it." He carefully stepped by the back of the tent, making sure not to disturb the bedding near Purlek's head, and continued his work. "There, that should do it. You're sure you don't mind looking after him tonight?"

"Of course not. He's like my son; I wouldn't have it any other way."

Garun looked as if he were going to respond, but with his stooped posture and the tilted angle of his head as he avoided the top of the tent, his focus quickly returned to his task.

Em suppressed a laugh. "Thanks for doing all of this." She gestured to their temporary lodging.

He dropped his head even lower. "Well, I have much more to do." He stepped out from under the flap, straightened up, and stood tall. Arms crossed, he sternly glanced around. Emzara guessed that he was imagining their camp from the vantage point of any potential enemies. But as each chore merged into the next, she wondered if something else was behind his busyness.

After a short jaunt into the woods, Garun returned with his arms laden with branches. He placed the wood beside the campfire, sat next to Laleel, and the two talked in hushed voices while she stirred a clay pot resting above the coals. Laleel frowned and looked over at the tent quickly before turning her attention back to the meal.

Emzara shook her head to clear her thoughts and knelt beside Purlek. Slowly she removed part of the stiffened bandage on his head, taking care not to reopen the wounds. She poured some water into the shallow dish and gently cleaned away some of the dried blood. Sensing a flicker out of the corner of her eye, she looked at his closed eyelids. *Had they moved?* She focused on his face but saw no change.

"I brought you some dinner." Laleel's voice was soft as she made her way inside the tent. "It's a light broth in case he's able to have some. Any signs of waking?"

Emzara sat back on her bed and accepted the bowl. "Well, I don't know. I thought maybe he opened his eyes, but I must've imagined it. What if he's like this for a while? What will happen if we have intruders intent on harming us?"

"Garun said we're to run to our boat and he'll move Purlek as quickly and carefully as he can."

"Good. I wouldn't be able to face Adira knowing we hadn't done all we could to rescue him. But what if he—"

From where she still stood at the tent's entrance, Laleel held up a hand. "Let's not think about that. So far, we're hidden and safe." She swept her arm toward the campfire behind her and laughed, although it came out slightly forced. "I mean, look at this. Garun is so restless he may have a whole village constructed by the time Purlek wakes up."

Emzara returned a small smile, appreciating her friend's efforts to be cheerful. "I don't blame him at all. I'm just as restless on the inside. I'm thankful for all that both of you have done, but it's not easy just sitting here. I know I could do more."

Laleel leaned forward and patted her hand. "Yes, of course you could. But that's not the point. You're helping by letting Garun do all the work, believe me." Both laughed, Laleel's deeper tones melding with Emzara's higher ones.

"Now, you need to eat something." Laleel pointed to the utensil on the bed between them.

Emzara obediently raised a bite to her mouth. When the tiniest sputter of a cough caused both women to look down, Purlek shifted a bit to the side but didn't wake.

* * *

Emzara bolted upright at the sound. She struggled to make sense of her surroundings in the semi-darkness. Heart racing, she blinked several times, willing the fog of sleep to subside. Another quiet moan was all she needed to put together the pieces and rush from her bed, flinging aside the curtain that separated her from her patient.

She bent low and tried to keep her excitement at a whisper to keep from waking up Garun and Laleel. "Purlek. It's Emzara."

His wide-open eyes and a large grimace revealed his pain. He thrashed violently, but winced and lay back. Only the tiny spasms from his limbs told her that this mostly motionless state was purely due to his will.

She used the moonlight to find a tiny bottle in her care bag. Holding it up, she unhinged the cap and dumped a portion into her hand. "Here, this will help. Chew it." She placed a small bark bit in his parted lips and his jaw moved slightly.

"Don't talk, dear, and try to stay still. I know it hurts." She wanted to reach out with a reassuring touch, but she pulled her hand back, afraid to cause him more pain. "You're going to be alright, but it will take some time. Your leg is broken, and I think you broke some ribs, too." She paused and studied his face for understanding. "I'm here on a journey up the river with friends, Laleel and Garun. Do you remember them?"

Gritting his teeth, Purlek nodded slowly.

"It's gotten pretty bad in Iri Geshem, and Noah's taking care of a few things before joining us. We came to see you and pass along greetings

25

from your parents, but found Iri Dekkel in shambles — you as well."
Holding up a waterskin, she gave him drink. "We're safely hidden in the
trees across the river now."

The tension slowly eased out of his face as he raised his head barely
a handbreadth to manage a few swallows before lying back. "Ma-Zara."
His nickname for her came out low and weak.

"Yes, dear."

"They attacked. Suddenly." Each word was measured.

As much as she wanted to know the details, she shushed him. "Never mind that. What's important right now is your recovery. You need
your strength."

"It helps. To talk. Helps me not think. About pain."

"Very well then, go ahead." She blinked back a tear as she recalled
the morning Purlek had been born. The youngest child of Tubal-Cain
and Adira had grown into the spitting image of his father, except for his
eyes. *Those are definitely Adira's.* His broad shoulders, muscular arms, and
sturdy frame made it seem as if he were born to follow his father's profession. Yet despite his strength, here he was before her, helpless, just like
the first time she met him.

"So fast."

"Who were they?"

"Nod—" He blinked hard. "Nodites."

A pit suddenly formed in her stomach. "Nodites?" *So far west?* "Do
you know why they attacked you?"

"No. Barely any warning at all."

Her mind flashed to Noah and Iri Geshem. "We didn't hear anything
about an attack." She rubbed her forehead. *Noah could be in danger.* "Why
would their raiders travel so far? Why now, after centuries of peace?"

He slowly shook his head. "Money? Slaves? Sport?" His eyes dulled.

She sighed. "What do you remember?"

"Hit him."

"Him who? A Nodite?"

"He. Attacked. Home."

Piecing this story together was slow going, but now that he had
begun, she was determined to get as much of it as possible before he fell
back asleep. "He attacked you. And you were at home?"

"Uh — no."

26

"We found you at your smithy, is that where you were?"

"Yes. Just started . . . the day."

"How many showed up?"

"Don't know. A lot." He shifted gingerly and closed his eyes.

A pang of guilt assailed her. "Purlek, you don't have to talk. You should rest."

"It's alright." He took a slow breath between each sentence. "Not. Much more. They burned . . . place."

She gently placed a hand on his arm, the need for contact outweighing her fear of hurting him. "Oh, I don't know how you survived everything. We saw the charred remains."

"Forge." He chuckled, coughed, and then winced.

"Huh?"

"Fireproof."

"Yes it is! So you crawled in there and waited for the flames to pass?" The image of the wrecked building and his body lying under the rubble filled her mind. "But we didn't find you there."

"Came out early. Roof fell."

"Of course. That's the beam we found you under. It must have knocked you out. Thankfully, they'd left by then, but of course you wouldn't have come out until you were sure they were gone."

His labored breathing smoothed into a more peaceful rhythm. He placed his hand on top of hers and forced a smile. "Thank you." He closed his eyes and fell asleep.

Emzara mused over this new information. She considered heading back to her own pallet for some much-needed rest, but dwelled on Purlek's abbreviated retelling of the attack. She shuddered in the dark. With concern for Noah and the possibility of marauding Nodites in the region, sleep would be impossible.

CHAPTER 4

Region of Iri Geshem — Noah's 499th year

Noah readjusted his wrists in an attempt to relieve the chafed area beneath the ropes. The bonds had made the miserable march from Iri Geshem to the Nodite camp even more uncomfortable, especially as he and Elam had to take turns carrying Rayneh. From their capture in the early morning to their arrival in the main camp just after dark, they had rested only twice, during the two brief meal breaks along the way.

Bound by a long rope attached to the center post of the tent, Noah stood in the entrance and gazed across the sprawling field before him. A light but steady rain beat down on the tens of thousands of soldiers preparing for war under the gray morning sky. Warriors worked tirelessly to turn felled trees into what Noah supposed to be war machines. One of the larger trunks rested on a massive wagon while men chopped one end to a blunt point. Upon overhearing soldiers talk about it, he had learned that this weapon would be used for smashing city gates. The other contraptions seemed to be designed for launching large rocks toward the enemy. *Toward Iri Geshem.* A wide range of emotions coursed through Noah as he thought about the city that had been his home for over four centuries. What would happen to Kmani, Bakur, and his other friends if the Nodites broke through? Torn by the desire to see the wicked defeated and the longing to see the city return to its former ways of following the Creator, Noah closed his eyes. *Most High, please show me what to do.*

"Noah." Elam's voice cracked as he approached.

"How's Rayneh?"

"She's finally sleeping again." Elam joined Noah at the tent's door. Their bindings prevented them from moving any farther. Red eyes and pale, puffy cheeks unveiled the effects of mourning his wife's death for the past two days. Whenever his daughter was awake, Elam composed himself, trying to be strong for his little girl, but Noah had heard his friend's grief in the night, while the little girl slept.

Keeping his voice just above a whisper, Elam said, "We have to get out of here." He sniffed and motioned toward Rayneh. "Noah, the Nodites, you know what they'll do to her if we don't escape soon."

Noah nodded. Every time he heard them recounted, the nefarious Nodite tales sent shivers through his body. This ruthless army showed no mercy to their captives, killing older men and women and sending young men to be worked to death in the mines or fields. Young women, even little girls, lived out their short and miserable existences as sex slaves in brothels. Noah clenched his teeth as little Rayneh's possible future flashed before him. "I know."

Elam held up his bound hands. "I'm sure we could break free from these, but I'm not sure how we would escape unnoticed."

Noah recalled his awe-inspiring encounter with the Creator only three weeks earlier. Drawing confidence from the Most High's message, he took a deep breath. "I know our situation looks bleak, but don't give up hope."

Noah almost reminded Elam of how the Most High had protected them in the arena, but he quickly realized Elam would struggle to see it that way. After all, Kal, Tubal-Cain, and Adira had not been spared. A lump formed in his throat. "I trust the Creator will make a way for us to—"

"You!"

A familiar voice broke his concentration, and Noah searched for its source. Strolling toward them, the leader of the small group that had captured them held his head high and his shoulders back. The other soldiers called him Enil, but Noah was not sure if that was his name or a title. The rounded black patterns tattooed or branded on his cheeks made him easy to recognize.

"Me?"

"Yes, you," Enil said as he reached the top of the small rise on which the tent rested. His armor clanked against itself as he moved, and raindrops slid off the smooth metal surfaces. "The captain wants to see you now." He stepped inside the tent and worked to free Noah's rope from the center post.

Elam pressed his lips together and tilted his head toward Rayneh. "Don't forget about us."

"Never."

Enil stepped past them and tugged the rope, pulling Noah's arms forward. "Come on. Time for your fate to be decided."

"We'll be alright," Noah said to Elam as he lurched forward to follow Enil. As he passed into the drizzling rain, he turned his head for one more glimpse of Rayneh and Elam, hoping that his words were true.

Noah hurried to keep up with the soldier. The wet grass soaked his feet, and the cold rain made for a mushy and uncomfortable walk through the camp. Most of the troops ignored him, but more than a few ridiculed and taunted him as they passed by. The continual pounding and chopping by the men building their war machines nearly drowned out the sound of the mockers.

Ahead and on a hill to the left stood the largest tent in the compound. Four red and black flags, symbols of the Nodite civilization, flapped atop tall posts. Outside the door, six guards, three to a side, stood at attention. The first man to their left wore a colorful patch over one shoulder. He nodded to Enil and tilted his spear toward the tent's entrance.

Keeping his head down, Noah entered the large, dry, well-lit shelter. As their prisoner, he would show deference to their authority — humility would serve him best. The soldier advanced several steps before stopping, and Noah followed suit.

Enil stood tall and rigid. "Captain, here's one of the prisoners from Iri Geshem."

"What's your name?" The man's firm tone matched his position of authority. "Look at me."

Noah slowly lifted his chin and looked at the captain for the first time. Sitting on a low chair behind a table, the man appeared to be smaller than Noah had anticipated. Dark eyes complemented his dark complexion, and his muscular neck and thick forearms would cause any potential challengers to think twice. "I'm Noah."

"Sir, we thought he might be a spy. He and his companion were found in the forest traveling with a very young girl," Enil said. "A clever cover for a spy, if you ask me."

The captain studied Noah for a moment and then set his writing stick on the large scroll sprawled out on the table in front of him. Noah instantly located Iri Geshem, the sea, and the Hiddekel. Undoubtedly, the Nodites were planning an invasion. Two high-ranking soldiers stood to the captain's left and another was on his right. "I didn't ask you, Enil. This man is no spy."

"Forgive me, sir. How do you know?"

The captain gestured with his finger to spin Noah around. "Let me see his back."

Enil turned Noah and then pulled his wrap down to his waist.

"As I suspected. He's no spy."

"Sir?"

Raising his voice, the captain said, "He doesn't bear their mark — the tree with the serpent. Unbind him."

Enil loosened the cords from Noah's wrists and leaned a little closer. "Don't even think about fleeing."

Noah turned back around and returned his wrap to its proper place over his shoulder. Stretching out his fingers, he twisted his wrists in small circular motions, careful not to touch the red skin rubbed raw by the ropes.

"Well, Noah, I am Captain Iradel, high commander of the Nodite army. My men overheard you and your companion talking about escaping from Iri Geshem." The Nodite leader stared into Noah's eyes. "Tell me, why were you running from the city? Did you live there?"

Noah bobbed his head. "I used to live there. My wife and I were in the process of moving."

"But your wife wasn't with you."

"No sir. She left several days before me."

"And why were you moving? Something happen in Iri Geshem?"

How much do I tell him? This foe of Iri Geshem was not entitled to know everything, but lying was wrong. However, Noah's once beloved city now suffered under the influence of another enemy, one already within its walls. Perhaps the Nodites could destroy Lamech's army and Naamah's religious system. *Should I help them?*

"Something did happen." The man rose from his chair and crossed his arms. "We didn't feel safe anymore when a few of the city council-members died last week."

"I already knew about that. Very strange. Three councilmembers die of a mysterious illness on the same day. Does that not seem strange to you?"

"It sounds deliberate to me. I believe they were poisoned." The loss of Zain struck Noah again. His neck warmed and he looked away.

"Of course they were. That's the only reasonable explanation. And you didn't feel safe with the new leadership. Why? Why would the new leadership concern itself with you?"

His bold faith in the Most High had drawn scorn from most people, but some had seen it as a threat. Noah briefly considered sidestepping the real issue. He looked at the ground, deliberating, then back at Iradel. *The Creator will protect me. Somehow.* "Because I follow the Creator, and it seems like the rest of the world follows Nachash."

The captain rolled his eyes. "I care not for religious disputes." He tilted his head as if an important thought had just come to mind. "Nachash, that's the god of Havil. Why would the people of Iri Geshem follow Nachash?"

Noah bit his lower lip as he contemplated how much to tell the Nodite leader. His delay frustrated his interrogator.

The man leaned forward and stared directly into Noah's eyes. "Unless you have some useful information for me, I will not hesitate to order your execution and that of your friend. Understood?"

"The people of Iri Geshem follow Nachash because King Lamech, along with his daughter, have managed to take control of the city."

"What do you mean? How have they taken control? An invasion? A coup?"

"Not an invasion. I'm not aware of all the details because I was in a dungeon when it happened. But I believe they helped carry out the murders of our councilmen. With the only leaders who opposed Havil out of the way, the town's new leadership handed control of the city to Lamech without a fight."

Iradel drew back and glanced at the soldier to his left. "And the king is currently in Iri Geshem?"

"He was yesterday. He presided over a ceremony in the arena where the people pledged their loyalty to him and Nachash."

Iradel snapped his fingers toward the man on his left.

"Yes, sir." The soldier saluted and hurried out the door.

Taking a deep breath, the leader returned his focus to Noah. "And if you were imprisoned, how would you know these things?"

Unsure of the significance of the captain's hand signals, Noah stared at his muddy feet as his confidence wavered. *What did I say that he didn't already know?* Regaining his composure, Noah slowly lifted his head. "Because I was brought into the arena and given the choice to bow to Nachash or to be eaten by a grendec."

The captor raised an eyebrow. "And you forsook the Creator to save your own neck?"

"No. I would never worship Nachash."

"A man of conviction." The captain stared off in the distance for a moment and tapped his chin with his index finger. "How did you survive the arena then?"

"The Most High had other plans."

A smirk crossed Iradel's lips. "And do you think you'll escape death today?"

Noah held up his arms and cracked a wry smile. "I'm no longer bound, and I believe I've already given you some useful information."

The captain snorted. "Indeed. Perhaps you've given me enough to spare your life, but what about your friend and the little girl? Do you have any information to barter for theirs?"

Noah recoiled inside at the not-so-subtle threat. "What would you like to know?"

Iradel stepped around the table and motioned for Noah to follow him toward the tent's entrance. Sweeping his arm across their field of view, he said, "I'm sure you realize we are preparing to conquer Iri Geshem. I already know the layout of the entire city and where they position their soldiers. Provide me with important details about the Havilite forces, how many and where they're stationed, and I'll release you, your friend, and the little girl."

Noah thought of Kmani, Bakur, and a few more friends still within the city. "What will you do to the people once you defeat the army?"

"I have no quarrel with the citizens. If they willingly obey Nodite rule, then they can live peacefully."

The man's straightforward manner impressed Noah. He was not like councilmembers who sought to please everyone and were willing to say whatever they thought a person might want to hear. He was direct, and Noah hoped his response was trustworthy. He took a deep breath. "I have something, but it must be worth four lives: me, my friend, his daughter, and an elderly woman in the city."

"You're in no position to negotiate." The captain crossed his arms again and glared at Noah.

Noah leaned in a little closer. "Wouldn't you like to know how I escaped the city when all the gates were blocked and I was being chased by their soldiers?"

The man gave a half smile and lifted his chin. "You know a secret way in."

"I do. You could sneak many of your soldiers into the city without being detected."

"Very well. Show my men this secret entrance, and I will spare the lives of your friends." The captain turned back toward the center of the tent and called to the two high-ranking soldiers near the planning table. "Prepare your men to march to Iri Geshem by nightfall."

CHAPTER 5

Iri Dekkel — Noah's 499th year

Emzara shifted her weight on the log at the lookout point. The uneven surface and bumpy texture helped keep her awake. Placing her hands on her lower back and arching slightly, she tried to loosen the knot just above her tailbone. The moon hung low in the sky, smothered by a blanket of clouds, so keeping watch was difficult. It was long past deepest dark, and while she scanned the area, she kept her ears on high alert, knowing that they may be the first to deliver an indication of company.

One full day had passed since Purlek had first awakened. His pain level remained high, and he had slept fitfully much of the day, but each time he awakened, he talked a little more. He feared that most of his friends from the village had been slaughtered, but Garun informed him that he had found only a few bodies while searching the town. They concluded that most of the townspeople had fled or been captured as slaves.

Emzara forced the awful thoughts from her mind and focused on the young man. *Thank You, Creator, for the improvements he's beginning to show.* Pleased with how well the herbs were healing the gash on his forehead, she looked up at the night sky and smiled.

Her eyes traced the dark outline of foliage all the way down to the riverbank. From her perch, the trees dipped toward the river. Fallen branches, saplings, and other small bushes kept her mostly out of sight. To her left, the river that led to Iri Sana flowed steadily. To her immediate right stood the main cluster of trees that shielded their campsite from anyone who might be prowling on the other side of the river. She stared past the town, longing to catch a glimpse of Noah.

She tried to shake her anxious thoughts, but they reappeared again after keeping her up most of the night. *What if it only took Noah two days to pack?* She counted silently on her fingers. *He might even arrive here tonight.* She peered excitedly down river but saw nothing. *Bakur and Pav would've helped him. Tubal-Cain would've, too, although he might be more of a distraction.* She shook her head and softly chuckled. Sometimes, those two still behaved like little boys when they were together.

What if something happens to Noah on the way to meet us? A chill marched down her spine and she straightened up. She paced two steps in one direction and then two back. *What would I do without him? This little life inside of me needs his father.*

She bit her lip to keep from sobbing. *Most High, I can't do this alone.* Her thoughts sped faster as she became more frantic. *How would we be able to even build the ark that You—.* She stopped midstride.

"The ark. Of course." *You've promised that Noah and I and our sons and their wives would be on board. O Creator, forgive my restlessness. How could I continuously forget Your promises?*

The evening dragged on, and Emzara's eyes grew heavy. Occasionally, she stood and stretched or paced, trying to stay awake, but eventually she fell into imagining her sweet reunion with Noah and began to drift in and out of consciousness.

The snapping of a twig jolted her and her eyes shot open. As fast as a bounder, her pulse throbbed. She listened closely and peered toward the shore. In the darkness, a figure hunched near the beached rowboat Garun had used to travel back and forth to the abandoned village, while the ship lay hidden nearby among trees that stretched out over the river. Though she kept her eyes fixed on the person, he stood still, stooped as though protecting something in his arms. *Why hasn't the intruder moved? How long was I sleeping?*

Emzara placed her hand on the hilt of the small dagger strapped to her left hip. The darkness almost succeeded in hiding the scene from her view. Carefully watching the placement of her feet to avoid crackling any underbrush, she tiptoed closer for a better look. A sudden movement followed by a light splash mixed with a groan told her that he had moved the craft closer to the river. Throwing off all caution, she sprinted toward the boat thief.

The figure crawled ashore on his hands and knees and looked up at her.

"What are you doing?" She placed her hands near the middle of the boat with a firm grasp and held it steady. The water cooled her feet and ankles.

He glared up at her, and the tension mounted until slowly he lowered his shoulders. "I have to warn my parents. I have to rescue them."

"You will do no such thing." She kept her volume low so as not to alarm Garun and Laleel, but her words carried force behind them. Without warning, he came into full view. She looked back over her shoulder and noticed the clouds no longer blocked the moonlight.

"But if I don't, they could die. Ma-Zara, how can you not care for their safety?" Gripping the edge of the boat, Purlek tried to stand but gave up after failing to plant his right leg. He groaned in pain and dropped back to all fours.

"What are you talking about? You're going to set your healing back." Emzara shook her head. "How could you even get to them in your condition?" With a heave, she pulled the boat mostly onto the shore.

"I'll let the river take me to Iri Geshem."

"Aren't you forgetting something?"

"What?"

"You can barely stand upright."

"Don't need to. I'll be staying in here." He gripped the side of the boat again as if he still planned to go through with his foolhardy scheme. "And I'm only one person, so I'll be able to sneak past the army."

Her hand flew to her chest. "Army! What army?"

He frowned and clenched his jaw. "I told you. The Nodites. We have to warn Iri Geshem and my family."

"I thought it was just a small raiding party."

He looked down and shook his head.

"How do you know they're going to Iri Geshem? We didn't see them on the way here. And if by some miracle you did make it there, then what? Even though you can't walk, you'll rush about and somehow find your parents in time to warn them and protect them — all without getting killed yourself?"

37

He slumped to the ground. "I guess not, but I'm tired of lying around here."

"I understand." She moved around the front of the boat and placed a hand on his shoulder. "Look, I confess that before I saw you, my thoughts were jumbled about Noah."

"Really?" He looked at her and a shock of dark wavy hair fell in front of his left eye. In an instant, she pictured the young rascal of a boy she had loved and helped raise.

"Yes, but we must trust they are in the hands of the Most High. Otherwise we'll go mad."

Suddenly, he flashed his impish smirk. "You know what?"

She narrowed her eyes playfully. "What?"

"You're going to make a really good mother."

"Am I?" Her whole body tingled and she felt as if she were floating.

"Yes. You've already got the mother instincts."

"Well then. In that case, I can tell that you're just changing the subject, Purkly." She emphasized the nickname she had used for him when he was a young child.

He laughed. "Oh, I am?"

"Yes. And there's only one thing to do about that."

"Which is?"

"To send you off to bed with no snack. What do you make of that?"

"Guess I'll have to march off in a huff."

She chuckled. "You can't even do that, but I can assist you back to your bed."

As she leaned down to help him stand, Emzara's foot slipped and she landed with a splash in the cool water.

Purlek grabbed his side and struggled to catch his breath. "It hurts to laugh, but I can't stop."

She scowled up at him, but his magnetic grin drew her in. She swung her arm across the surface of the river and splashed him.

Water dripped down Purlek's face and his wet wrap hung loosely over his shoulder. "Hey, I'm injured."

They both laughed until cracking twigs and rustling leaves grabbed their focus.

Garun burst onto the nearby shore with his sword drawn. "Is everything alright?"

Laleel appeared behind him armed with a blade of her own.

Purlek looked shamefaced. "I was going to sneak away to warn my parents about the Nodites, but she stopped me."

Emzara smiled. "I think your injuries stopped you before I did. I—" Em tried to calm herself, but the oddity of the situation mixed with the lack of sleep hit her at just the right point, and she gave in to another burst of laughter.

Garun and Laleel approached and his stern look caused a pinch of guilt to rise within her, but she failed to control her giggles.

"We need to get the boat back into hiding." Laleel's voice was deeper than usual, with the fuzzy edges of being roused suddenly from sleep.

"I'll do it." Purlek reached for the craft but winced and stopped. "I'm sorry."

"All is well," Garun said. "I'll take care of it. He pointed at Emzara. "You can help him back to the tent."

A small smile broke on the left side of Laleel's face. She turned and looked at the sky, which now held the promise of lightening. "There doesn't seem to be much point in trying to get more sleep at this time. I'll prepare some of Nuca's brew for everyone."

Garun rolled his eyes and shook his head. He pointed at Purlek. "If you're up for it, you can tell us what you two troublemakers were doing out here and what you've been up to since you moved away from home."

Chapter 6

Region of Iri Geshem — Noah's 499th year

Several thousand troops paraded swiftly around the bends and rolling hills along the Hiddekel. Lunkers and other large creatures pulled the war machines under the guidance of their handlers. At times, the only sounds to be heard were the steady pounding of footsteps interrupted occasionally by grunting beasts.

As he reached the top of a small rise, Noah looked ahead to see hundreds of rows of 20 soldiers, each stretching on as far as he could see. The line snaked across a narrow bridge over the river and then veered south on the road to Iri Geshem. Noah had never seen so many people move with such efficiency.

"We're almost there." Noah recognized many of the landmarks from his countless trips on the river, but seldom had he passed them on foot. To his right, a tiny village that usually bustled with activity appeared to be vacant. Perhaps the people had fled to Iri Geshem to hide behind the walls. Whatever the reason for the emptiness, Noah breathed a sigh of relief that the Nodites lacked the opportunity to slaughter anyone here.

A smile crossed his face as he watched the muscles ripple on the shoulders of the pair of unfamiliar furry animals pulling the two-wheeled cart next to him. *Emzara would've already sketched them.* He glanced up at the captain, who rode in the cart, and pointed to the large hill across the river. "You should be able to see the city once you're up there."

"Then this is where you leave us, correct?"

"Yes, sir."

"Enil." The captain gestured to the soldier marching beside Noah. "Take your company and follow Noah to the secret entrance. If you're able to get everyone inside the city undetected, then set Noah and the other two prisoners free. Send word back to me. We will set up camp on the other side of the river, but out of sight from the city wall."

"And the old woman is to be spared?" Noah asked.

"I gave you my word. Enil, see to it."

"Sir." Enil held up a hand and made a couple of signals. Immediately a couple hundred troops moved to the left side of the road. Unlike the rest of the soldiers, these men wore their light armor discreetly under their unmarked, sand-colored robes.

"Thank you, Captain. If possible, please go easy on the citizens and spare the shipyard." Noah rejoined Enil, spotting Elam and Rayneh between two warriors a few rows back. "This way."

Daylight had slipped away early due to the overcast skies, which served as both a blessing and a curse. While making it more difficult to find the small shed, the darkness also kept them hidden from the sentries on the city walls. They waited along the edge of the forest to allow the darkness to grow even deeper.

The wall around the eastern part of the city loomed in the distance. Torches flickered at various lookout posts along the top of it, providing enough light to see a few soldiers standing guard. Suddenly, the distinct ring of metal being struck pierced the darkness. "What is that?" Enil asked.

Noah held up a hand to request silence. Listening closely, he heard four more clangs at regular intervals. "They do that every night to signal a shift change for the guards."

"Let's go," Enil said.

"Wait." Noah stood and pointed ahead and to the left. "It should be up there a little way, but it'll be hard to find at night. You and I should go look and then come back for the others."

Enil motioned for two nearby soldiers to join him. "The four of us will go — just in case you're planning on escaping."

Noah shrugged. "You have my friend and his daughter, so I'm not going anywhere. We'll need to stay quiet. The city is surely worried about reports of your army, so they may have extra sentries posted."

41

"Right," Enil said. "What are we looking for?"

Noah faced the three Nodites. "The tunnel entrance is in a shed on the south edge of a small clearing about 200 cubits from the wall. Let's go."

Staying low, he quickly moved out of the woods and led the trio of soldiers across a glade. As he slowed behind a copse of trees, a low-hanging twig scratched his face. He carefully grabbed the small branch and allowed it to move back into place. "It should be just over there."

"I see something," one of the soldiers said. "Right there."

Noah stared into the darkness in the direction the man pointed. Eventually, the faint outline of a building came into focus. "That's it. Let's make sure it's empty."

"But don't make a sound," Enil said as he moved ahead of Noah.

The four men soon covered the distance to the shed and quietly opened the door. Slipping inside, they found themselves in complete blackness.

"I can't see a thing," Enil said. "Is it safe to light a lamp here?"

"There aren't any windows so it should be," Noah said. "Just keep it low."

A spark flashed to Noah's left along with the muffled clack of two stones striking each other. This was followed by a second and then a third strike before a soft glow emanated from a tiny oil lamp. Noah had started fires using two types of stone before, but the Nodites must have invented a device that made the process more efficient. The man put the fist-sized flame starter into his pocket. Holding the lantern up, he moved toward the back of the room. "I don't see any entrance." He spun and glared at Noah. "You lied to us."

Noah held up a hand. "No, it's there." He pointed to the left corner. "It's behind that wall."

The man with the lamp inspected the corner and soon disappeared through the small opening and the soft glow faded until almost vanishing entirely. He soon reentered the room. "Looks like our prisoner was telling the truth after all. There's a tunnel beneath the floor in there."

Enil turned to the other soldier. "Get the rest of the men, and make sure they are quiet."

The man nodded and stole outside.

"So am I free to go?" Noah asked.

Enil snorted. "Not yet. We need to get everyone safely through the tunnel first. Let's have a look at it."

Noah followed his captors into the hidden room and looked at the hatch on the floor. *Could it have only been two days since I was here? Feels like a whole moon.* "This leads into the lower level of a home built against the inside of the city wall. The woman who owns it is the one you need to spare."

"Then you can go through with me to tell her."

Noah nodded. "It'll be difficult to open the door at the end. It may take a few men to push it open since she keeps a large, heavy bin on the other side to hide the entrance."

"I'm sure we'll manage. And once we're inside?"

"That's up to you. You'll need to cross the bridge if you have any hope of opening the main gate for your army."

"Of course." Enil measured Noah with his eyes. "So how does it feel to betray your own people?"

Visions of the Nodite army overrunning the city generated another wave of guilt. After wrestling with his decision throughout the day, he had thought he was at peace with it, but this new twinge of shame made him second-guess himself. For the first time, he voiced his conclusion out loud, hoping it still sounded appropriate. "The people of this city have already turned against me, but I'm not doing this to get back at them. I'm helping you battle the Havilites while hoping you'll treat the citizens well."

Soft footsteps pulled their attention to the front of the shed. Enil used the first lamp to light his own, and the flickering illumination made the designs burned into his high cheekbones dance. "Have the men kindle some lanterns once they're in the tunnel. I'll direct the rest from here." Enil moved into the other room and spoke quietly to his men.

A long steady stream of soldiers passed Noah before descending into the hole. Their organization continued to impress him. Two hundred troopers dropped into the tunnel faster than he could have imagined.

Elam carried Rayneh into the room and Enil followed closely behind them. "Your friend and the little girl will go into the passageway, too. Once we're safely inside the house, the three of you are free to go."

"I'm ready." Noah gave Elam a half smile and then climbed down the ladder.

The tunnel seemed much different than Noah remembered. Two nights earlier, he and Elam had been in such a hurry that they never really studied the results of Zain's labors. Now that Nodites lined one side of the passage with several lit lamps, Noah saw the extent of the burrow. It was not very wide, but being so long, it still must have been a massive undertaking. *How did Zain do all of this without telling anyone?*

Enil and Noah advanced to the front. Enlisting the help of two soldiers, they forced the small door open. Noah entered the room and pushed the bin farther to the side. Nodite combatants poured into the room behind him.

"Let's go find the old woman," Enil said.

Noah grabbed a lamp and led Enil up the stairs and quietly entered the top level of the home. "Kmani?" He called her name softly as they moved through each room. He knocked on her bedroom door. "Kmani. Are you in there?" Upon hearing no response, Noah cracked the door and peeked inside. He pushed it open and scanned the room. No excess belongings were out. *I hope she's left and is safe.* "She's not here."

Enil grabbed his arm. "How do we get to the palace?"

Noah shook his head. "There is no palace."

The commander crossed his arms. "You know what I mean. Where will the king be staying? And what about the town council?"

Noah headed back to the front room and pointed. "This road outside goes straight to the river, and there's another road there. Go left, and it'll take you all the way to the bridge. That's the easiest way and at this time of night will have the fewest people." Noah took a deep breath. "If you make it that far, the king will likely be staying in the guest mansion on the northeast side of the main square. It's next to the town hall, which is the tallest building in the city. You can't miss it."

Enil shook his head. "I didn't think your plan would work, but you've lived up to your end of the bargain. You're free to go."

"Thank you. If the old woman returns, please be kind to her."

"We're under orders from the captain." He reached into a pocket and produced a small strap with a patch sewn into it. "Here, take this. If you run into any other Nodites and they seek to detain you, just show them this and tell them that Commander Enil, son of Mehetael, has granted your freedom."

Noah nodded and slipped the item into his pocket. He hurried back down the stairs, past dozens of soldiers in the lower level, and waited impatiently for a break in the traffic to slip into the tunnel. Hugging the right wall, Noah squeezed past the line of warriors that stretched halfway down the passage. He found Elam and Rayneh behind the last soldier. The little girl's large round eyes looked up at him, and he wondered how much of this she understood.

"Can we go now?" Elam asked.

Noah clapped his friend's shoulder and produced a smile. "We're free. For now."

Chapter 7

Iri Geshem — Noah's 499th year

After closing the thick wooden door, Naamah leaned against the adjoining stone wall and slid her eyes shut, her long lashes resting against her cheeks and her body abuzz with all that lay before her. The sheer size of this tower and the texture of the cold stone under her palms infused her with a feeling of security and strength.

Nivlac guarded the other side of the door. Beneath him, down a small flight of steps, rows of soldiers stood at attention, waiting for the Nodite army. From this height, she could safely observe the impending battle. *But is that what I want?* To be in the thick of the action where every decision, every movement impacted the future of this world would be far more exhilarating. She walked to the north window and looked down at the lines of her warriors illuminated by torchlight and shuddered in excitement.

The daylight now gone, Naamah reveled in all she had accomplished since she had assumed command. As if she had done it all her life, she ruled over all matters, giving orders regarding troop operations, allocation of city resources, and potential citizen involvement in the battle — all without the king's input. Somehow, that miserable wretch looked like he would survive the poison. *If only he had finished his cup.*

As they awaited the first strike, her army stood in readiness, the majority deployed on the wall as a show of force. There they would remain in readiness until the Nodites attacked or the reinforcements arrived. Tsek, majestically arrayed in his battle armor of gold-plated pieces, strategized with his officers on a wide area atop the wall not far from the tower.

She breathed deeply, slowly. The reinforcements should arrive within a day or two with enough strength to even the odds, if not the numbers — the wall itself would serve as a powerful equalizer. That is, if her scouts had reported an accurate count of the opposition's troops and resources.

She clenched her hand into a fist. "This is it!"

The door opened. "Princess?" The lines on Nivlac's forehead bunched up as he scoped out the tiny enclosure.

"What is it?"

"I heard you speaking and wanted to make sure no one else was in here." He stood close to her and brushed his hand down her bare arm.

"It's just me." She shrugged his hand away. "I was going over the plans and must have spoken aloud."

"Yes, Princess." Undeterred by her coolness, he touched her cheek where her jaw met her throat, his large fingers like sand against the silk of her skin. "I also heard you mumbling last night in your sleep."

Searching his face, she asked, "What did I say?"

He shook his head. "I couldn't make it out."

Naamah breathed a sigh of relief and kept her voice low but stern. "What's tormenting my sleep is the thought of the king lying in his plush bed, regaining his strength."

"Ashur is by his side constantly and vows he will be until the king awakens. He says that is of the utmost importance, so he handed over the investigation to some imbecile."

She rolled her eyes. "The fool. His devotion to my father will play nicely into my plan. This can still work." Naamah grinned, but stopped when her stomach tightened. The healer's skill thwarted her first plan. The next attempt would have to be flawless.

Nivlac raised his eyebrows.

"Don't pretend you don't know. You're the only one who does." Her eyes narrowed. "Of course, I'm upset it didn't work. And now I stand here, poised to lead our army into battle, but we have to wait for reinforcements. And with every passing moment our *precious* king regains his strength, enough to possibly take back his control."

"He's in no shape to lead a battle."

"Not yet, but he was resting better when I stopped by this morning."

"You went and saw him?" he asked.

"Of course. I've got to keep up appearances."

He pursed his lips and nodded, clearly satisfied.

"I will get my chance." She raised her fist, but not her voice. "If only he had died."

"If only." Nivlac bowed slightly and exited the room.

Looking up to the point where the four triangles of the tiled roof met, she whispered, "It's not over yet, worthless king. Now that I've tasted full authority, I will not rest until it's mine alone." She licked her lips, pondering ways to kill Lamech in the battle should he take over. Each idea seemed far-fetched and too easy to be traced back to her. *Now's not the time.*

She glanced out the southern window, over the city and toward the harbor. If only this were her beloved Havil instead of this dung-heap of a town. Then she would have all sorts of secret ways to kill him. She kicked at the stone flooring in frustration. *Focus. Control yourself! Wait until the time is right to take him out. Just like your troops wait for the ensuing battle. To act now is to ensure defeat. Wait. Regain the king's trust and gain the respect and loyalty of these people. Today you will sow seeds that will grow and yield all that you desire.*

Delaying was best. After waiting centuries to assume control, she could be patient a little longer. Long ago her father had called her his tempest, but she had learned to control that inner storm in order to strike out at the best possible moment.

"Soon enough, the Nodites will be here. In the meantime, I need to pray." The slit of a window opposite her let in just enough light from the torches in the street outside. "My army will be victorious because of the might of our god."

Uncoiling the bracelet around her arm, she repositioned the golden object on the narrow window ledge, rewinding the thick links that made up the snake's body. She removed the fanged pendant from her neck and attached the head to complete the venomous figure. She knelt and bowed before it.

"O Great Nachash, I praise you for giving me the insight, the cunning, and this opportunity to rule — even if it's just temporary. No longer will I consider the king my father — that title belongs only to you, Mighty One. Give me the victory I seek. Grant me favor in the eyes of my people." She paused and chose her next words carefully. "Give me a chance to rid this world of that king who doesn't care for your fame, because he seeks only his own glory. Show us your power." Satisfied, she lifted her face from the ground and peered at the figurine still posed above her.

"Ah, if only the seer could witness this moment with me, Nachash. His old eyes would be so pleased to see the culmination of all he's taught me about you." She pictured him sitting in his den back in Havil, his shriveled hands folded over his thin lap. Unfortunately, his age and health prevented him from traveling this distance. If he had succeeded in his quest to find eternal life, then he could have gone anywhere with her. Her shoulders sagged and she sniffed, blinking quickly. Instead of going down that trail, she willed her mind to rove the warm walls of his home, stuffed with scrolls and tablets full of incantations. She threw back her head with a slight laugh. *Maybe somehow he's watching me right now.*

She climbed to her feet, grabbed the snake charm from the ledge, fashioned it once again around her wrist, and hung the pendant back on its chain. Her movements slowed. Somehow, this ritual and prayer seemed incomplete and insufficient.

Nachash, I've sacrificed children to you, my children. The image of Nivlac heading for the door moments earlier flashed in her mind. *Our children. But at a time like this — I brought no child and no blood, just words of prayer. You deserve much more.*

Her eyes narrowed and a dark smile crossed her lips. "Nivlac!"

His face soon wedged into the crevice formed by the slightly opened door. "Yes, Priestess."

"I need your assistance."

He hurried to her. "What would you like me to do?"

"I need Nachash's power surging through me."

Nivlac's eyes wandered up and to the side for a moment before focusing on her. "Very well, Princess." He grimaced, knelt beside her, and placed his hands on her shoulders to steady her. "I'm ready."

Clutching the chain about her neck, she pulled it out from under her clothing. Twice the size of a pikka and all gold, but hollowed out to carry venom, the pendant bore two green precious stones in place of eyes that rested above its opened mouth, which boasted two capped fangs. With a quick motion, she pulled off the small covers, revealing two tiny daggers.

As Nivlac dutifully braced her, she traced the fangs along her arm, and chanted under her breath. The slight pressure left two tracks on her skin. Mesmerized, her eyes gleamed, her hand steady and sure. As she reached the ink on her left shoulder that etched a permanent snake's head, she plunged the two points into the corresponding fangs.

"Ah!" Her left hand seized in a clenched fist and Nivlac fought to hold her steady. "Nachash! Accept my blood and my actions. Above all, accept me, your mistress."

Chapter 8

Her head throbbing due to the venom, Naamah pushed her thumbs hard into her temples as she climbed the stone stairway. During the night, her body had threatened to seize up as the poison spread through her system. For most of the night she struggled even to breathe as her throat constricted and her joints stiffened. The pain had been nearly unbearable.

This was not Naamah's first experience with the venom. She had endured the self-inflicted routine countless times before, so she was confident the dose would not be fatal; although the first time she tried it, she had hoped it would be. Reeling from the people's rejection of her plan to institute ritual prostitution in Havil and the subsequent destruction of the city centuries earlier, Naamah attempted to end her life by allowing a serpent to bite her. She recovered days later, but decades passed before the city returned to its former glory. The people eventually warmed up to her ideas, and within a couple of generations, Havil required all citizens to serve in such a capacity for a minimum of one year. Much to her mentor's dismay, she took part in the custom on important days of the year. With Naamah leading by the example of sacrificing her first child and all eight others since, any child conceived during these rituals was offered to Nachash.

A jolt shot through her arm and stabbed her chest, ripping her mind back to the present. She welcomed the pain with a clench-jawed smile. The lingering effects of the venom typically wracked her body for days.

Still, the brush with death provided a high like no other, capped by the ultimate thrill of doing it in honor of Nachash. Knowing that she always endured the venom gave her the assurance that she could survive the coming battle.

Steadying herself with a hand on the enormous city wall on her left, Naamah pushed forward. The massive blocks forming the 30-cubit high barrier would surely resist a direct assault from the Nodites. As she neared the highest step, the early morning sun peeked over the eastern half of Iri Geshem, forcing her to squint as her eyes adjusted. Atop the wall, hundreds of soldiers armed for battle stood at attention. She hoped their presence would make the Nodites think twice before attacking.

Breaking rank, Commander Tsek approached her and bowed. "Hail Naamah! How is the king?"

"He's recovering well." As much as she hated to say the words, she needed to inspire the soldiers. Willing away the pain, she spoke evenly with just a tinge of enthusiasm. "Thank you for asking about my father. Commander Tsek, are the men ready for battle?"

He swept his arm to the side, indicating the rows of warriors standing side by side. Just behind Tsek, a low parapet, matching its larger counterparts along the wall, served as a barrier between the platform on which they stood and the street far below. The immense double gate rose from the ground level to just beneath the feet of the soldiers ahead and to her left. Three layers of heavy timbers comprised each door, and a massive iron bar lowered into brackets prevented anyone from forcing the entrance open.

Naamah stepped to the side and suppressed a gasp when she saw the expanse of the enemy army positioned outside. Stretching all the way to the river and several hundred cubits back, the black and red armored troops from Nod stood ready for war. Huge wagons with strange contraptions rested near the back of the throng. Pulled by lunkers and pushed by soldiers, another large cart bearing a massive pointed log moved through the middle of the army toward the gate.

"Have you spoken to them yet?"

"Not yet, Princess." Tsek walked toward the wall as a few of his soldiers made way for him and Naamah. "They have spent all morning moving into position."

"And the river? Do we have troops stationed there?"

52

"Two companies. We have saturated the banks with fire liquid so we can ignite it if the Nodites attempt to use the river."

Hurried footsteps on the stairs behind her drew closer. "Princess." Breathing heavily, Ashur stopped a few paces short of her. "We have four thousand citizens who want to join the fight."

Naamah turned to Tsek. "Where do you want them?"

"They aren't trained, so they'll only get in our way up here." The large man scratched his neck. "If the reinforcements don't arrive in time, we'll use them as decoys. For now, gather them in the city square, and I'll send some of my men to train them in some basic maneuvers."

"Thank you, Commander." Ashur turned to leave but he stopped. His eyes grew wide and he pointed toward the Nodite army. His voice trembled as he spoke. "Can we . . . do you think . . . will we defeat that?"

"Have no fear, Councilman," Tsek said. "It's always easier to defend a city than to attack one."

Three loud horn blasts sounded from beyond the wall. "People of Iri Geshem." A booming voice echoed off the stone around her. "Who is qualified to speak with the fearsome captain of the unconquerable Nodite army?"

Naamah and Tsek walked to the edge of the wall, and Ashur followed, peeking over her shoulder. A dozen soldiers in metal armor stood with red and black flags around three men. The man in the middle held a bronze horn and the one next to him held a spear with the blunt end resting on the ground. Behind them, a decorated man stood in a chariot pulled by two large, angry-looking brown creatures. He stared up toward the Iri Geshem troops.

Tsek put his hand in front of Naamah. "Remember, our whole plan depends on delaying them until reinforcements arrive tomorrow."

"I know, Commander," Naamah said. "You have experience in these matters, so I will let you speak to them."

"Very well, Princess." Tsek put his meaty hands on the edge of the wall and leaned forward. "Greetings, Captain of the Nodite army. I am Tsek, high commander of the Horde of Havilah, the greatest force ever assembled, and I serve the majestic King Lamech and the mighty Nachash, the Splendor of the World. What is your business here?"

"Commander Tsek, proud words coming from a man hiding behind a wall. I am Captain Iradel, and I look forward to meeting you in battle.

Indeed, I was pleasantly surprised to hear that the king of Havilah had taken control of Iri Geshem and is currently in the city. It will bring my master great joy to know that his army defeated Iri Geshem and conquered the runaway king of Havilah."

Tsek furrowed his brows at Naamah, who responded with a shrug of her shoulders.

"You mean you do not know your king's history?" the Nodite captain asked. "Then I shall tell you about the cowardly son of the failed usurper?" He paused and peered up at Naamah. "And you must be his witch daughter. Yes, Princess Naamah, I know all about you, too. Indeed, you are attractive, but your beauty and enchantments will not spare your life today. Poor soul, you don't even know your family's history. Did you know that your grandfather was a Nodite?"

Naamah's neck grew hot and she clenched her jaw, her mind racing through a list of incantations for a special curse to call down on the arrogant worm who dared to insult her and her family.

"Yes, he was a prince of Nod. At least he was until he attempted to kill his older brother so that he could become king upon their father's death." He pulled tight on the reins to steady the mighty beasts in front of him. "He was banished, but fate caught up with him when his own son, your father, murdered him in his sleep."

"He lies." Naamah looked at Tsek. "My grandfather died of an illness after being unjustly accused by his older brother and exiled." Words spoken by her father many years ago rushed to her mind. *Just like me.* Somehow, in that moment, she knew the Nodite spoke the truth. She was just like her father, even in her efforts to assassinate him, just as he had done to her grandfather. Her mouth dropped open slightly, but she chased the thoughts away with an arrogant shake of her head.

"That's right, Princess. Your father, the mighty king of Havil, is nothing but an illegitimate child of a failed usurper."

"Your boasts and mockeries are empty speech," Naamah said. "Why are you here?"

"To take this city for the Nodite Empire, of course." He laughed and encouraged the men around him to join in. "But, Princess, perhaps I should be the one to ask why you are here." He pointed his spear directly at her. "Where's your cowardly father? Or what of your older brother,

Tubal-Cain? Why isn't he here in his father's stead?" He scratched his chin. "Of course I know why he cannot be here. It's because your brother was recently murdered by your father. I know all about what's been happening in the city and why your father isn't here. I wonder, do you think he'll recover from his recent poisoning? Do you even want him to, Princess? Serves him right. What kind of man murders his father and son?" He stretched out his arms toward the soldiers on the wall. "How can anyone follow such a monster?"

Naamah clenched her fists and glared at the captain.

"You have two options, Princess. Remain in the city and be killed along with the rest of Havil's army. Or your army can lay down its arms and go home to Havilah and never return. Turn over Iri Geshem to me peacefully, and I'll allow you to leave unharmed."

Naamah crossed her arms and smirked. She spoke softly to Tsek. "Delay them."

Tsek nodded. "Captain Iradel, I look forward to fighting you. While I am impressed with your knowledge of history, I see no reason to fear your army, if it's even fair to call this an army." He gestured to the assembled Nodites. "Surely, you know a direct assault on the city is certain death for you and your troops. Your best option is to starve us out, but we have enough food in the city to last a year. Can you wait so long? Besides you do not control the harbor, so we can import endless supplies. We have no reason to fear you or your little gang."

"Ah, Commander Tsek, if you only knew what I know. If only you knew how many spies I have in the city and how many people from Iri Geshem are prepared to turn on you when the battle starts. . . ." The captain turned and briefly conversed with one of his nearby soldiers, then he withdrew his sword and directed it at Tsek. "You have until this same time tomorrow to leave the city or we will destroy it along with you, your incompetent king, and the witch princess. Commander Tsek, I have no doubts about your abilities, but I do not wish for your ego to bring about the slaughter of tens of thousands. Go speak with your poisoned king. I'm sure the coward will want to be the one to give the order to retreat."

Iradel uttered a command to the beasts, and they pulled his chariot away from the wall. The dozen flagbearers spun and marched back to join the innumerable mob.

Tsek snorted. "That went well. The fool just bargained his own life away."

Naamah let out a deep breath and whispered to herself, "Only if the reinforcements arrive on time."

CHAPTER 9

The soft wind cooled the shaved side of her head as Naamah reached the top of the wall just after dawn. The throbbing in her head and pain in her muscles and joints had subsided early the previous evening. With a full night's rest behind her, Naamah felt invigorated, excited to establish herself as the most powerful person in the world. A victory over the Nodites and her father's eventual demise would see her realize that goal. She quickly located Tsek, and her black gown lightly brushed the ground as she strode determinedly toward him. "How are preparations, Commander?"

Tsek twisted his large frame to face her. "Princess, the men are ready, but the wall and gate will not hold all day. We need those reinforcements."

Naamah stared toward the harbor, but the low light and several tall buildings limited her view. "Still no sign of them."

"No, but at least this wall will prevent the Nodites from seeing them when they do come. The element of surprise will only add to our advantage."

She turned around and scanned the Nodite army. A few dozen guards stood watch in the front of the camp. Behind them, tents filled the road and nearby fields as far as she could see. Milling about in the multitude, a handful of men seemed to be waking their fellow soldiers. Torches blazed outside the large tent in the middle, casting enough light to catch glimpses of activity inside.

"Has the king improved at all?"

Naamah took a deep breath. "I didn't see him, but the healer said he rested well during the night." The healer's face flashed in her mind as she lightly tapped her fingers against the small vial always hidden on her right hip. *After the battle, he'll get his reward for saving the king's life. Then he'll need his own medicine.*

"That's good news. If he's not able to be here, you'll need to inspire the men before the battle starts. Your father has always been great at that." Tsek tipped his head toward her. "I'm sure you will be, too."

"They must fight for Nachash — not for me or the king. He is the one who will grant us victory today."

"Of course, Princess. You need only remind them of that truth."

Closing her eyes, Naamah thought of what to say to the troops. For the first time in her nearly 500-year life, she considered the possibility that she might be killed by an enemy. Occasionally she had feared the king's wrath, and her recent insubordination had certainly put her life in danger, but she had never needed to worry about an outside force. The Havilite army knew no equal in the southern part of the world. She considered the timing that had brought them control of Iri Geshem now, just as the powerful Nodites from the northeast apparently had decided they wanted the city themselves. *We need those reinforcements.*

Naamah walked to the edge of the wall and watched as the enemy camp quickly turned into a hive of activity. Soldiers hustled about, packing up tents and moving their giant war machines into place. The morning dew glistened far beneath her, and the sunlight reflected off the metal armor of thousands of soldiers. As if united by a singular purpose, the Nodites transformed their encampment into a standing army not long after the sun had risen above the eastern wall of the city.

An eeriness hung over the men stationed on the wall. The guard next to her repeatedly shifted his weight and glanced around. His fear would infect the rest of the troops. *Time to remind them who they serve.*

Naamah turned and strode toward Tsek's post on a low platform. The immense commander seemed to be arguing with Ashur about something. As she neared, both men stopped.

"Princess." Tsek stood upright. "The councilman says that two Nodite spies were captured last night in the eastern part of the city."

"Do they represent a threat? I thought we weren't concerned about that area," Naamah said.

"It's true we aren't focusing our efforts there, but" — he glared at Ashur — "I'd like to know how they entered the city and if there are any more of them."

"Are they still alive?" Naamah asked.

"Yes, Princess." Ashur hitched a thumb over his shoulder toward the steps. "Down there."

Naamah smirked. "I'm sure we can persuade them to talk. Bring them to me."

Ashur nodded and headed for the stairs.

Naamah scanned the lines of Havilite soldiers to her sides before glancing at the Nodite army. The captain and his entourage passed through the middle of the legions. The large wagon carrying the giant pointed log rested a short distance before the gate. She cleared her throat and faced the soldiers on the wall. "Men of—"

"Princess!" A messenger ran to her from the top of the stairs.

She glared at him.

"Forgive the interruption." He lowered his voice. "The reinforcements. They're here."

Naamah's eyes grew wide and she looked toward the harbor. "When?"

The man bowed low. "Four ships were spotted entering the port. We expect more, but I was immediately dispatched to bring you the good news before any others could be seen."

Her hopeful façade instantly converted to genuine confidence. "Wonderful. Return to the harbor at once and tell them to meet us at the northern gate immediately. War is upon us."

The messenger saluted and dashed away.

Naamah turned to Tsek. "We still need to delay until our men are in position. Where are those two spies?"

"What do you want to do with them?" Tsek asked.

"We will—" Three loud blasts from a horn cut her off.

The Nodite captain stood in the same position as the day before, with the same formation around him. "Witch princess of Havil." His voice rang out loud and clear, echoing off the stone walls. "I don't see your cowardly father this morning, so he must be living up to his title. Or perhaps he has not recovered from the attempt on his life yet. I assume you're acting in his place. Shall I bid you morning peace or have you chosen war and destruction?"

Naamah largely ignored the insults, but his haughtiness irritated her. Leaning close to Tsek, she asked, "The men know that we are not retreating, correct?"

"I informed them before you arrived."

"Very good." She took a deep breath to squelch her anger. "Captain, indeed my father is ill, but I have consulted with him about your offer." She paused, knowing that every passing moment brought them one step closer to battle readiness. "I told him that we were capable of defending the city."

The captain chuckled, causing those around him to laugh as well. "Very foolish, Witch. If you choose to fight, you will die today."

"I'm not finished." Naamah folded her arms. "The king said that if he were well enough, he would rout your army, but since he cannot be here this morning, he has ordered us to withdraw from Iri Geshem and turn it over to you." Her shoulders curled toward her chest as she lowered her head.

"So the runaway king is going to run again?" The captain held his arms out wide. "A wise decision. Although I must admit that I'm rather disappointed. I looked forward to battling Commander Tsek and hanging your body from the wall of the city before dragging it through the streets."

Naamah glared back at the man, visualizing what punishments she might dole out to this insolent soldier. She imagined him on an altar of Nachash, screaming as she cut out his boastful tongue.

"Princess." Tsek leaned close to her ear. "The councilman has returned with the captured Nodites."

Naamah spun and faced the captives, who were being held near the top of the stairs so as to remain out of sight of the Nodite army. Both men were bound, gagged, and led by Ashur and a pair of Havilite soldiers. The prisoner on the left sported a large swollen gash next to his left eye. The other man's nose veered to the side above a split lip. A grin creased her lips, knowing that these men would soon endure far worse. "Councilman, thank you for bringing them to me. Now I need you for another important task."

"Of course, Princess," Ashur said.

Pivoting to face the Nodite captain once again, Naamah kept one arm pointed at Ashur. "Captain, I will be leading the Havilites out of this city. Since you will be assuming control of Iri Geshem, allow me to introduce you to the head of their council, Ashur." She gestured for him to step to the edge of the wall so the Nodites could see him. "I am sending him to you to work out the terms of our surrender."

Ashur glanced up at her and kept his voice low. "What are you doing, Princess? I don't want to go out there."

Matching his volume, Naamah said, "I need you to stall him as long as possible. Then when you return safely, we'll launch our assault."

"Very well, Witch." The Nodite captain gestured for Ashur to come to him. "Send him out. Enjoy living out your days as a coward. Just like your father."

"At least I'll have *days*," Naamah said to herself.

Ashur stepped in front of her, his hands trembling. "What do I say?"

She slapped him. "Stop it. If you want to be a leader here, then you need to act like one. You had the spine to poison your fellow councilmembers. I think you can handle simple negotiations."

"But what if they kill me?"

Sighing, Naamah shook her head. "If you don't go, you'll die here. The Nodite thinks we're turning the city over to him peacefully, so he won't do anything to you. In his mind, if he wants to kill you, he'll do it once we leave. You have nothing to fear." She walked toward the stairs. "Come. I'll walk you to the gate, and then I'm going to meet our reinforcements."

"Princess," Tsek said. "Don't you want to interrogate these two first?"

"As long as the Nodite army doesn't see or hear them. Find out what you can and inform me when I return. Once the battle starts, hang them from the wall." Naamah turned and descended the steps.

Ashur trailed her. Upon reaching the street, they turned toward the gate and stopped when a familiar female voice called out.

"Ashur."

Naamah wheeled about and childhood memories flashed through her mind as Ashur hurried to Navea.

Navea's colorful wrap and the expensive jewelry around her neck and wrists suited her as a councilman's wife. She smiled wide. "Princess Naamah. It's good to see you again. I'd hoped to spend some time together while you were here. It's been so long."

"Indeed." Naamah forced a hint of a smile at her friend from her youth, but the woman now before her had committed a crime against Havil by running away from her duties as a dancer so many years earlier.

Not that Naamah blamed her. She longed to escape her father's reach as well. Nevertheless, Naamah knew little but contempt for the woman who had nearly stolen her glory long ago. "But we have urgent business at the moment."

"Yes, I know," Navea said. "I have news from the healer. He says the king is awake and wants to see you right away."

"Unfortunately, he'll have to wait. I'm too busy here." Naamah grabbed Ashur's arm. "You must hurry."

"Where are you going?" Navea asked.

"To negotiate with the Nodites." Ashur pursed his lips. "I need to delay them a little longer. The reinforcements have arrived, but it'll take some time for them to get to the gate. We need the Nodites to think we're surrendering the city."

Navea's eyes darted from her husband to Naamah several times. "Is Naamah going too?"

"I have other duties." Naamah wanted to scold her for speaking so informally, but another idea came to mind. "Go with him. It'll calm his nerves to have you along. Don't worry — it'll be safe."

"Of course, if you think it's a good idea." Navea took Ashur's free hand.

Ashur hesitated and opened his mouth, but closed it when he glanced at Naamah. "Let's go." He started for the gate.

Naamah reached into her hidden pocket and withdrew the small vial. "Wait." She threw her arms around Navea and kissed her on both cheeks. "It is good to see you again, old friend. Be safe." She deftly dropped the vial into one of Navea's pockets.

Navea smiled and her muscles relaxed slightly. "I will."

Naamah pulled back and turned to Ashur. "Just treat this like one of the thousands of business deals you've made before. You're merely arranging the terms of conquest before they take control of the city."

He stood tall. "Thank you, Princess. I'll do my best for you and for Havil."

"Guards." With a wave of her hand, Naamah caught the attention of the two men standing next to the small door within the left side of the gate. "Take Ashur and his wife outside to meet with the Nodite captain." She pointed to the next two closest guards. "And take these two with you as well. Ashur is to do all of the talking."

The soldier on the right nodded. "Yes, Princess."

Chapter 10

As Ashur and Navea headed for the gate, Naamah found Nivlac standing by her chariot. He had spent the previous day training volunteers from Iri Geshem in basic combat skills and only this morning returned to serve as her bodyguard. "Take me to the harbor. I want to see for myself how soon we'll be ready to fight."

Nivlac jumped into the two-wheeled cart and grabbed the reins attached to two brown beasts whose shoulders stood at his full height. Their massive furry frames rested atop short and relatively thin legs that ended in sharp hooves. Each animal sported a long, toothy jaw and bore significant tusks on either side of the head, providing a perfect attachment point for a bridle.

Naamah stepped behind her guard and gripped the cart's handholds tightly. "Let's go."

Nivlac barked a command, and the creatures squealed as they charged away from the wall. He guided them down the city's main thoroughfare. Hailing Naamah as she sped by, the newly trained volunteers lined both sides of the streets, ready to support the veteran soldiers when the time came.

Before reaching the expansive city square, they turned left and headed east toward the river. Citizens scurried about. Aware of the danger at their gates, some had barricaded the doors of their homes, but most of them continued with their daily business. *They know that I'll lead them to victory.* In her excitement, her right hand slipped, and she bent her knees slightly to keep from falling. She regained her balance and took a deep breath. Twice, Nivlac shouted for people to clear a path or get run over.

Finally, they pulled to a halt on a ridge overlooking the harbor to the south. Over a dozen ships had run aground in the sand and at least two dozen more were moving toward the shore. Her heart leapt. Victory might be achieved after all. Hundreds of soldiers assembled on the beach, but her gaze locked onto something far more interesting in the midst of the group.

"I wasn't expecting those," Nivlac said.

"Neither—"

"It's the princess!" A gruff male voice barked. "Kill her!"

Naamah flinched and spun to her right while her mind tried to keep up with her eyes. A man wearing a sand-colored robe stood beside the door of a rundown building pointing his sword at her. Though it was mostly concealed by the robe, she glimpsed the insignia of the Nodite army on his armor. At least four combatants ran toward her as several more streamed out of the house.

"Go!" Naamah shrieked and prepared herself for the impending jolt.

Nivlac whistled and then roared at the beasts. The cart launched forward just as the first Nodite grabbed hold of its side. He ran along with it, and just before the beasts outpaced him, he pulled himself forward and leapt into the crowded chariot.

Naamah squeezed forward to avoid the attacker.

The soldier drew a blade but immediately dropped it as Nivlac swung an elbow, striking the man in the head. Undeterred, the warrior reached for Naamah, dodging Nivlac's next attempt.

Sliding down with her back against the front of the chariot, Naamah kicked the man in the stomach. He nearly fell off the back of the cart but steadied himself by grabbing Nivlac's shoulder. Behind him, a number of Nodites were in pursuit. As the soldier reached for her again, Naamah yanked the dagger from her bracer and stabbed him in the leg.

Howling in pain, her attacker reached for his injury. At the same moment, Nivlac struck him in the face and the man tumbled out of the chariot, landing awkwardly and rolling a few times before coming to a stop.

"Whoa!" Nivlac pulled the reins back.

"What are you doing?" Naamah asked as she climbed to her feet. "Get us out of here."

He pointed ahead, where dozens of her troops from the beach raced past her and gave chase to the Nodites.

"Kill them all!" Naamah fought to catch her breath.

"That was too close." Nivlac turned toward her. "How did all these Nodites get into the city? And how many more are there?"

"I don't know." Naamah shook her head. *If only I would've interrogated those spies.* She swept an arm toward the reinforcements a few hundred cubits down the road. "We need all these men at the city gate immediately. Take us down there."

"Yes, Princess." Nivlac drove the chariot toward the beach and pulled it to a stop when one of the captains stepped in front of them and hailed Naamah.

"Captain, I know there are still more men arriving on the ships, but we need every single one of you, and especially the beasts and their handlers, at the front gate now. The battle may start at any moment."

The soldier bowed slightly. "We haven't been here before." He glanced from Nivlac to Naamah. "Can you lead these men where you need them? I'll send the rest as soon as they come ashore."

"Very well." Naamah straightened and pulled her shoulders back. "Tell them to follow us."

As the captain belted out commands to his men, Nivlac turned their animals around. There was no sign of the Nodites who had ambushed her, other than the man she had stabbed. His body lay in a heap in the middle of the road ahead, and a grin spread on her face.

After the first wave of soldiers reached the chariot, Nivlac led them through the streets of Iri Geshem at a brisk pace. Bodies of several more Nodites and a few of their own soldiers lay unmoving near the city square.

A messenger rapidly approached, and Nivlac pulled the beasts to a halt.

"Princess." The runner kept his eyes focused on the ground. "We've killed more than two hundred Nodites in the city and suffered some casualties in the process."

"How did they get in here?" Naamah asked.

"We tortured one of the men to find the answer to that question. He said that they were shown a tunnel under the wall by a man named Noah."

Nivlac frowned and kicked the wall of the chariot. "Did you say Noah?"

The man nodded.

Hatred flowed through Naamah. She glared at the man and clenched her jaw before willing herself to relax. "Did they say what happened to this traitor?"

"They let him go free."

She moved directly in front of the man. "Where's the tunnel?"

"He wouldn't reveal that information." Dropping his gaze even lower, the messenger said, "Our men are searching for it now. They think it's on the other side of the river."

"Find it and figure out where it leads. Then send out trackers to hunt down Noah."

"Yes, Princess." The man turned and sprinted away.

She looked at Nivlac. "I cannot wait to kill him." Naamah turned to the officer closest to her. "The gate is straight ahead. Keep the men quiet. We don't want the enemy to know we have reinforcements." He turned when Naamah tapped him on the shoulder. "Go quickly. We need to tell the soldiers at the gate to be silent or else the Nodites may suspect something."

Nivlac nodded, gave a command, and the chariot sped ahead.

While passing the volunteer recruits, Naamah shushed them. When the chariot stopped near the staircase, she stepped to the ground and leaned close to Nivlac. "Keep these men quiet and make sure the beasts are placed at the front. We have a special surprise for Captain Iradel."

"I will." Nivlac jumped off the cart and hurried for a nearby captain.

Naamah took a deep breath and marched up the stairs. She found Commander Tsek standing at the wall, watching the negotiations. "How is our councilman doing?"

"Princess." Tsek bowed his head. "He looked nervous at first, but he likes talking, so he seems to have relaxed a little." Tsek cracked his knuckles and kept his voice low. "The reinforcements?"

Grinning, she put a hand on his lower back. "Come with me, Commander."

They walked toward the opposite edge of the platform to peer at the street below. The front of a long procession of Havilite warriors cleared the nearest building and entered the intersection. The line, eight men across, stretched back as far as she could see. Near the front, soldiers stepped far to the side to make way for Iradel's surprise. Four large, muzzled, horned grendecs, each led by a pair of giants, stomped to the gate and stopped.

Tsek rested his beefy arms across his barrel chest and smiled. "This should even things up."

"Are your men ready?" Naamah asked.

Tsek lifted his chin and pulled back his shoulders. "The troops on the wall are, but I'll need to briefly speak to the new arrivals. Should we wait for the councilman to finish?"

Naamah shook her head. "I have no more use for him or his traitor wife."

"What about my soldiers with them?"

She shrugged. "If they survive, we'll honor them for their service."

"I'll be right back." Tsek disappeared down the stairs while Naamah walked back to the wall, hid behind a parapet, and peeked at the negotiating parties in the field. A smile formed on her lips as she savored thoughts of leading the people to victory. She stretched out her arms and raised her head, allowing her eyes to roll back. *O Great Nachash. Hear me. Grant me victory today; then nothing can stop you from being worshiped around the whole world — not even the blasphemous king who only seeks to use you for his own power. Through this victory today, the people will see me as their rightful ruler and you as their only god.*

Naamah took a deep breath and refocused her attention on the Nodite army. Thousands of soldiers held their positions as their captain listened to whatever Ashur babbled about. There was no turning back now. Once the battle commenced, she would emerge as the leader of Havil's greatest victory, or she would perish in humiliating defeat. Either way, she would not report back to the king unless the people of Iri Geshem and the army of Havil viewed her as their savior.

"Princess, we are ready." Tsek stopped beside her and waited quietly.

"First, a little misdirection." She cleared her throat and raised her voice. "Captain Iradel of the fearsome Nodite army. Please pardon my intrusion into negotiations. We are ready to leave. As a token of our agreement, we have prepared a grand gift for you and your men."

The captain stood and glared at her. "Why are you still here, Witch? Shouldn't you be sailing away by now?"

"Indeed, Captain. But first, please accept this gift on behalf of Havilah." Naamah spoke quietly to Tsek. "Send out the grendecs and fire upon the enemy as soon as they are distracted."

Tsek nodded and strode to the opposite side of the platform and looked down to the street below. "Send out the surprise."

The clanging and clunking of the huge iron latch being lifted out of place echoed off the stone walls. Hinges groaned and wood creaked as the massive door slowly opened outwardly.

"Now!" Commander Tsek's bellowed command launched a flurry of activity.

Two horned grendecs burst through the gate, their muzzles removed. The first let out an ear-shattering roar as the second sped past it toward the Nodite army. The other two beasts charged right on their heels.

Tsek raised an arm and then dropped it. "Fire!" Archers along the wall launched arrows into the midst of the enemy.

Captain Iradel whipped out his sword, yelling instructions to his men as he and his entourage, which had circled tightly around him, ran back to the Nodite line.

Navea screamed and jumped back, away from the negotiating area. With the wall behind her and the Nodites before her, she turned left and bolted. Her Havilite escorts rushed after her, swords drawn in anticipation of attack.

Ashur hesitated when he saw the grendecs. He looked up at Naamah with wide eyes. "Wait! Not yet!" Glancing back toward the gate, he stumbled as he tried to get his footing. He screamed and dove to the side, dodging the first creature as it rushed into the front line of the Nodites. Unfortunately for Ashur, his lunge put him directly in the path of the next one. His cry ended abruptly as the grendec stomped his midsection into the ground.

Naamah's stomach fluttered in excitement, and she bounced on her toes. Taking a deep breath, she quickly composed herself.

Arrows continued flying while the grendecs wreaked havoc on the Nodites' front lines. The eight giants who had previously handled the beasts rushed forward leading a swarm of normal-sized Havilite warriors into the fray. Half of the titans veered toward the left flank and the other half attacked the right side. The monsters and their handlers cut swaths through the enemy lines before meeting significant resistance. Tsek pressed the advantage and assembled his troops outside the wall. He also ordered two of his men to hang the pair of captive spies from the top of the wall.

After the shock of the surprise attack wore off, the Nodites regained a semblance of organization. Two of the grendecs were cut down, a third lumbered away toward the forest to the west, while the fourth continued to assail the soldiers with its tail and powerful jaws. Meanwhile, the five remaining giants occupied about a dozen men each. Captain Iradel shouted orders, but the chaos prevented Naamah from hearing his words.

The Nodites attempted to reassemble, even though the initial assault had devastated the front third of their army. As the archers on the wall fired volley after volley of deadly missiles, Tsek ordered his infantry to charge. A small team set fire to the large wagon with the pointed tree trunk parked near the gate, while hundreds of soldiers streamed out of the city and joined the fight.

Swords clanged and clashed, javelins and arrows swooshed through the air, and spears frequently found their marks. Soldiers from both sides soon littered the battlefield, and in many places piled one on top of another. While Tsek boldly stood his ground, Naamah took cover behind a parapet when an arrow whistled past her. Peeking out, she was unsure which army held the advantage.

Eventually, the arrows ceased and Nivlac approached Tsek. "Commander, I have an idea." The battle sounds prevented Naamah from hearing the rest of Nivlac's words.

The large commander nodded and then walked to the edge of the platform overlooking the broad way inside the gate. "Send the trainees straight to the front lines! Men of Iri Geshem, the fate of your city depends on you! Fight and save your lives and the city!" A great yell rose from the streets as the four thousand novices raced through the gate. Most were armed with small swords and very few bore armor.

"What are you doing, Commander?" Naamah asked. "They'll be useless out there."

"Almost." Tsek led her to the other side of the platform to watch the battle. "Their sacrifice will give our men a rest while the Nodites must continue to fight. Then we'll make our final strike."

Naamah watched intently as the new recruits crashed upon the front line like a large wave breaking on the beach of the Great Sea. The men battled fiercely, and although they were outmatched by the Nodites' skill, they managed to create significant gaps in the enemy's ranks.

As the Nodites reeled from the influx, Tsek ordered the Havilite soldiers to regroup with the two remaining giants and make straight for Captain Iradel. A narrow strip opened in the Nodite lines as the Havilite warriors rushed toward the enemy's leader.

Dozens of guards formed a barrier to protect their captain, but Iradel recognized the danger a little too slowly. He whirled his chariot around and violently whipped the reins. Just as his animals lurched forward, one of the giants threw himself across them, causing the cart to flip. Trying to climb to his feet, Iradel stumbled sideways. Blood flowed from his head, and he struggled to remain upright. He cried out as Havilite soldiers surrounded him, but his men could not reach him.

The giant stood and unleashed a furious cry as he lifted Iradel above his head. The gesture seemed to take the heart out of the Nodites. Several hundred of their soldiers fled from the battle.

Tsek turned to one of his captains. "Take three companies to pursue those deserters."

Before the man could respond, Naamah stepped forward. "I want one hundred of them kept alive for a grand sacrifice to Nachash."

The captain saluted Tsek and bowed to Naamah. "It will be done."

A great cheer erupted from the remaining soldiers, and the city streets soon filled with citizens celebrating the monumental victory.

Naamah closed her eyes and took several deep breaths, trying to comprehend the weight of what they had accomplished. *Nachash, you have led us to victory, and I will lead the people to worship you alone.*

She followed Tsek down the stairs to meet with their victorious warriors. Soldiers and citizens inside the walls celebrated, stopping only momentarily to bow as Naamah passed them.

Naamah and Tsek walked beneath the massive city gate. Thousands of figures, twisted and bloodied, covered the field before her. Slight movements accompanied by groans indicated that more than a few were still alive, but only a small percentage would survive their wounds. A slash of color caught her eye. Amid the carnage, Navea's crumpled body lay next to the soldiers who had followed her. Naamah gestured to Nivlac and two other guards. "Come with me."

She led them to Navea's corpse. "Take her back to the city for a proper burial."

As the guards picked her up, the tiny vial fell out of her pocket.

"What's that?" Naamah asked, knowing full well the answer.

After setting the body down, one of the men handed Naamah the small container. She opened the lid and lightly breathed in the flowery scent of the powder. She scowled. "It's poison." She looked at Nivlac, eyes going wide, feigning surprise. "The same kind used to poison the king!"

"Princess." Tsek gestured for her to join him near the smoldering wagon with the pointed log. As she drew close, he pointed to the ground in front of him.

Ashur's frame appeared almost comical in its unnatural shape. Although his midsection was all but gone, the lower part of his legs and his upper body appeared almost normal, other than the expression of horror frozen on his face. Naamah exhaled with a disdainful huff and shook her head. "Serves him right for teaming up with his wife to poison the king."

Metal instruments blasted behind her, and a mighty shout went up from within the gate. "Make way for King Lamech."

Naamah spun and faced the city. Dozens of guards led a procession toward her. Carried above the crowd on a bed draped in purple and gold, King Lamech sat propped up by multiple cushions. He nodded slowly as the people cheered him.

Tsek bowed as the king's entourage stopped before them. Naamah quickly lowered her head in a half-hearted bow. *Of course he would show up now to steal my glory.* She approached her father, composing her features. *Be patient. You will find the right moment.* "My king, it's wonderful to see you feeling better on this glorious day. Your enemies have been defeated."

"And the people tell me that much of the credit for the victory goes to you, Naamah." His volume barely surpassed a whisper. He coughed and cleared his throat.

Despite her contempt for the man, Naamah smiled. "Thank you, my king." She swept her arm toward the army. "Commander Tsek deserves some of the praise for his strategy and training of the soldiers. And of course, above all else" — she raised her voice and turned toward the people — "we must thank our great god Nachash for granting us victory. Tonight we worship him with a great sacrifice — a hundred Nodite soldiers!"

The crowd shouted in approval.

Lamech slowly took in a deep breath, "Very good." His pale face showed that he had many days of recovery ahead. "But there is another matter I wish to discuss with you."

"Anything, but first, I need to tell you that we figured out who poisoned you."

He narrowed his gaze at her, a hint of skepticism shone through. "Who was it?"

"Ashur and his wife." She pulled the vial from her pocket and held it up. "We found this on Navea's body over there. I believe it's the same type of poison we sent to them to dispose of their troublesome councilmembers. They must've saved some and thought that they would rule the city if something happened to you."

"And where is Ashur?"

"Right back there." She pointed toward the man's remains and grinned as she spotted one of the giants carrying the defeated captain toward them.

"Are you sure it's the same poison?" Lamech asked.

Naamah folded her arms. "It smells and looks like it, but I suggest we try it out on our enemy to be certain."

"King Lamech," Tsek said. "Forgive the interruption. We've captured Captain Iradel of the Nodites, but I don't think he'll overcome his injuries. You should know that he insulted you repeatedly and accused you of murdering your own father. He also slandered the princess on numerous occasions. I'd love to kill him for you."

Lamech raised a hand. "Wait. Let me see the man who would dare insult me."

The giant set Iradel on the ground at Tsek's feet. "Here is your prisoner, Commander." He tipped his mostly shaved head toward Lamech. One long braided cord of brown hair grew from the back of his head, and it dropped in front of his massive shoulder as he leaned over. "My king."

Blood oozed from Iradel's mouth. One of his legs was badly broken, and his left arm hung limply on his lap. Iradel refused to look up.

Lamech pointed to the vial in Naamah's hand. "Captain Iradel. I'm told you fought bravely. I would enjoy learning more about such a worthy rival before we put you on trial. I'll send a healer to your cell. But first . . . you must be thirsty. Have some water."

Naamah took a cup of water from one of the king's attendants and quickly dumped the poison into it. She lowered it to Iradel, but he tried to swat it away.

"I insist," Lamech said. "Ereg, he looks thirsty to me."

The giant grinned and picked Iradel up again. The captain squirmed and grunted in pain, but the massive man easily restrained him. He held his victim before Naamah and forced him to comply.

Naamah poured the water into Iradel's mouth and the giant squeezed the man's lips shut and plugged his nose.

Iradel kicked his good leg and tried to free himself, but there was no use. After several moments, he swallowed and the giant allowed him to breathe.

"You see, that wasn't so bad, was it? Maybe the next time we offer you hospitality, you'll accept it." Lamech chuckled.

"There won't be a next time." Iradel sputtered blood and saliva as he coughed out the words. "You can kill me, but you will not defeat the Nodite Empire." He took in several short breaths as he reached for his midsection. Finally, he looked straight at Naamah and then Lamech, his eyes bloodshot and full of rage. "We will never yield to" — he bent forward and groaned as he fought to compose himself — "to the coward king and his witch daughter." Iradel dropped to the ground, squirmed in agony, and retched.

Lamech laughed and spit on the Nodite captain. He turned to Naamah and smiled. "Well done, my daughter, great princess of Havil and Iri Geshem. When I heard the good news about the battle, I insisted I be brought here at once to see you. I couldn't bear the thought of what could've happened to you." His demeanor softened, and he attempted to lift an arm toward her, but he only managed to hold it up for a moment before resting it on his lap. "Please, come closer, so I can embrace my marvelous daughter."

Naamah hesitated and glanced around to see if any of his men were ready to attack her when she let her guard down. Would he dare try something in front of the army she had just led in their greatest victory? She forced a smile and climbed onto his palanquin, knowing she needed to respond appropriately to keep up appearances. "It is enough for me to know that you are recovering." She leaned in and wrapped an arm around his neck.

He weakly held her with one arm behind her back and whispered in her ear. "Attempting to kill your own father — you really are just like me."

Naamah stopped breathing as he spoke. Somehow, he knew. She wanted to pull away, but he mustered enough strength to hold her fast a moment longer.

"You will return to Havil and remain there for the rest of your days, however few or many they may be."

Naamah drew back as he let go. She nodded as she glared at him. "Thank you, my king." She stood tall and pointed at Iradel, gurgling as he writhed on the ground. "Ereg, let the poison take him and then drag his body through the streets so the people can see what happens when they stand against Nachash."

CHAPTER 11

Iri Dekkel — Noah's 499th year

Noah stretched out his arms and yawned. The midmorning sun brought warmer air than any day in the past week, and the nap reinvigorated him. After a restless night, Rayneh had finally fallen asleep on a blanket next to him in the wagon, the edges of her lips curled up. *Must be having a good dream.*

"Look who's awake."

Pulling himself up using the edge of the wagon, Noah faced the front of the cart and spotted Elam smiling back at him.

Elam sat on a bench beside Lakh. The old farmer had met them on the road three days earlier and offered them a ride in his large wagon. The two beasts that pulled the cart looked like lunkers but were a bit smaller and faster.

Like Noah, Lakh had decided to move away from Iri Geshem after the deaths of the three councilmembers. He lived a half day's walk outside the city and had grown weary of the escalating wickedness and its influence on those around him. He knew of Noah the shipbuilder, although they had never met before, and his son had told him about what happened in the arena. Lakh listened to Noah's recounting of the events, but despite Noah's assurances that the Creator protected him, the old man concluded that Noah was simply lucky.

During their time together, Lakh frequently reminisced about better days — he even mentioned meeting Emzara once, decades ago, when she had cared for one of Lakh's animals — but he often grew silent when Noah spoke of the Most High. As far as Lakh was concerned, the Creator had abandoned mankind long ago, so the farmer had no interest in serving Him.

"How long before we reach Iri Dekkel?" Noah asked.

"Not long," Lakh said. "It's a short walk beyond those crossroads. I'll leave you there since I'll be heading east."

"We're very grateful for your help." Elam rubbed the back of his neck. "You saved us a few days of walking."

"Enjoyed your company," Lakh said. "It's refreshing to speak with honest men. Not too many around anymore."

"Has there been any sign that the Nodites were this far north?" Noah rubbed his eyes.

"Unfortunately." Lakh nodded. "Their tracks are all over."

Elam furrowed his brow. "The last town we passed had also been pillaged."

"They'll be fine," Noah said to Elam, but he needed to convince himself, too.

"I sure hope so." Elam lowered his head and turned away.

Lakh pulled back gently on the reins and commanded the beasts to halt. "This is where we part ways."

Elam thanked Lakh again and climbed down from the bench. He moved to the side of the wagon and pointed to Rayneh. "Hand her to me."

Noah gently scooped the sleeping girl into his arms and transferred her to her father. He jumped out of the wagon and, stopping before Lakh, reached up and gripped the man's forearm. "Thank you again."

Lakh nodded. "I hope you find your wife. She helped me so many years ago. I'm glad I had an opportunity to return the favor."

"Me, too. Please remember what I said about the Creator. Don't believe the lies spread by Nachash's followers."

"I know you mean well, Noah. But I haven't seen anything that would make me believe the Creator still cares about us. Look around you. Does it look like He's in charge? And if He is, He sure doesn't seem to care much. Now, maybe if I actually heard from Him — then I might think twice."

Noah thought back to the strange mix of fear and peace he had felt in the presence of the Most High. He smiled. "Be careful what you wish for."

Lakh snorted. "Farewell, Noah. And take care of that little girl, Elam."

Noah and Elam smiled and spoke in unison. "Farewell."

The old man snapped the reins and the wheels rolled forward. He turned right and his creatures picked up their pace. Before long, he rode over a small hill and disappeared from sight.

"People just won't listen," Elam said as they started walking north. A sign at the edge of the road informed them that they would soon reach their destination. The path led into a wooded area before it angled to the left.

Noah shook his head. "I pray he'll decide to follow the Creator."

Elam nodded. They walked on for a short while before he spoke again. "Do you think we did the right thing?"

"What do you mean?"

"Showing the Nodites the way into the city."

"It was the only thing I could think of that might persuade Iradel to spare us."

"I know. I didn't mean that to sound like an accusation." Elam lowered his head. "I just can't imagine how many people will die, or already have died in the battle. Why did it have to get so bad?"

Noah thought for a while. "I've asked that same question many, many times. It breaks my heart when I think of my early days in Iri Geshem compared to now. With each generation, it seemed like they came up with new reasons and ways to rebel against the Most High. It was as if they were blind to the fact that they were destroying themselves. They have no hope."

"And no joy." Elam wiped his cheek. "And now Kal is gone." His chest heaved and he blinked back tears.

Noah searched for the right words, but nothing felt appropriate. He placed a hand on his friend's shoulder, and his heart ached for Elam and Rayneh. Guilt pricked at him. While they searched for Emzara, Elam suffered from his unimaginable loss.

Elam stroked Rayneh's light brown hair out of her face and kissed her forehead. "But I still have you."

They rounded the turn in the woods and Iri Dekkel, or what remained of it, came into view. Charred structures lined the dusty road before them. Blackened stone walls still stood in place, but their roofs lay in collapsed fragments of burned timbers. Other than a light wind passing through the leaves and the peeps of a few songbirds, no sound emanated from the town.

"Oh no." The words barely escaped. Noah's stomach tightened and he ran a short distance ahead. "Em!" The birds in a nearby springal tree scattered. "Em!" He spun to face Elam. "I need to check Purlek's place. It's at the end of this street."

Noah ran through the length of the town, yelling his wife's name. Finally, he stopped when he spotted the wrecked forge at the end of the road. His legs felt weak and he dropped to his knees. "Em!" The shaky, desperate cry sucked every bit of air from his lungs and stung his throat. He hit the ground and closed his eyes. "Creator, please help—"

"Noah!" Elam's voice sounded hopeful.

Spinning around, Noah found his friend near the top of the hill, pointing toward the river. "What is it?"

"Hurry up!" Elam frantically gestured for Noah to come to him.

He jumped to his feet and raced toward Elam and Rayneh. The little girl stood on her own and took a few shaky steps before falling. Noah ignored his sore knees and ankles, choosing to focus on getting enough air as he sprinted.

A smile crossed Elam's lips as Noah drew close. He pointed again toward the river. "Look!"

Before he turned, a faint sound reached his ears. Was that his name? Yes, a woman's voice was calling his name. Not just any woman; it was Em. Em called his name! He scanned the beach. There was no sign of her, but still he heard her voice.

"Across the river," Elam said.

Noah looked up, and his heart leapt when he saw Emzara on the far shore, waving to him. "Em!" He waved back and then sprinted for the beach. Glancing around for a boat as he ran, he saw only one, and it had been broken in pieces. He stopped at the edge of the water and called her name again.

His pounding heart and the wide rippling river made it difficult to hear her. She pointed upriver and Noah thought he heard the words, "A boat."

He turned to Elam, who was making his way down to the river. "I think she said the boat is over there."

"So we'll just wait here?" Elam asked.

"You can. I can't wait that long." Noah shed his outer garment and charged into the cool water. When it was deep enough, he dove forward and started swimming. Memories of racing Aterre and goofing around with his brother flooded his mind as the water swelled around him. But a single image quickly consumed his thoughts. *Em!* His adrenaline pushed him forward, but he knew the distance was too far to keep up his fastest pace. Slowing a little, he focused on breathing every few strokes, and he soon fell into a rhythm.

Swimming was easier in his younger years. His joints and muscles never ached then as they did now, but he would gladly endure sore shoulders for the next week if it meant holding Em a little sooner. Every stroke brought him closer to her. Regularly correcting his course, thanks to the river's current, he attempted to keep his strokes even. He checked his path again and saw her wading toward him. She was only a couple hundred cubits away. He plunged ahead, pouring all his strength into every stroke, which quickly made it difficult to breathe.

Em stood up to her waist in the water, beaming with joy and calling his name.

When he could no longer catch his breath, Noah stopped and allowed his feet to search for the river bottom. They found purchase in the soft sand and he stood with his head barely above the surface. He fought for air as he pushed himself toward his wife. "Em!"

"Noah!" She surged toward him.

He reached out and collected her into his arms, pulling her tight against himself. After all he had endured in the previous week, holding her was the greatest feeling imaginable, with just one exception — being in the Creator's presence. He squeezed her and then pulled back and kissed her. "I missed you so much."

"I was so worried about you." Em kissed him again and then wrapped her arms tight around his neck.

Noah did not even mind the pain caused by her shoulder in the front of his throat. He caught movement out of the corner of his eye and turned to see Garun rowing a small boat past him toward the distant shore. Finally, he drew back and looked into her eyes.

Emzara tilted her head to the side a little and furrowed her brows. "Where's the boat?"

"The what?"

"The other boat. I don't see it."

Noah had been through so much in the past week that he had almost forgotten that his other boat had been destroyed after his flight from the arena. Gazing into her eyes made it difficult to focus, but he blinked and allowed his mind to rest on the boat and the flaming arrows. He breathed in and bit his lip. *Where do I start?*

"And is that Elam and Rayneh you were with?" Em tucked a few strands of hair behind her ear. "Where's Kal?"

Noah gulped as he unsuccessfully fought back tears. Images of Kal, Tubal-Cain, and Adira in the arena raced through his head. *I have to tell her about Adira, too.* His lips trembled as he shook his head before burying it against her shoulder and pulling her tight again. "I . . . I'm so sorry." His body quivered as tears flowed freely.

"What's wrong?" Em asked as she kissed the top of his head.

Noah sniffled and tried to steady his voice. "I have terrible news."

Chapter 12

Iri Sana — Noah's 499th year

Noah finished tying the rope to a post he had put in the ground decades earlier. In frustration, he yanked the frayed ends harder than necessary. His left hand slipped and smashed into the pole. "Ouch!" With a lump in his throat he glanced at Garun. "Would you stay with the boat until we send someone here?"

"Of course. Take as long as you need."

Emzara wove her fingers through Noah's. "Your father will be happy to see you. Be strong for him."

Noah squeezed her hand and then kissed it. "I'll try." He put his other hand in his pocket, where a small scroll silently toyed with his emotions.

Laleel carried Rayneh and Elam assisted Purlek as the group walked slowly and somberly behind Noah and Emzara. Every step through the familiar malid orchard felt as if anchors pulled his feet back to the ground. They would reach the house soon enough, but then what? What would he say? What could he say? The late afternoon sun stood in stark contrast to the darkness fighting inside him.

The three weeks on the river since Iri Dekkel had been mostly uneventful. Telling Emzara and the others about Kal, Adira, and Tubal-Cain had wounded Noah's spirit. Reliving each horrific moment sucked the life out of him. Adding to his torment, Emzara's expressions reminded him of the day she discovered that her father and Aterre had been murdered. However, she handled this grief better than he anticipated, occupied as she was with filling a motherly role for Purlek and Rayneh. Noah also suspected that she refused to think too much about it because she often blamed herself for losing their first child after her father's death.

Garun and Laleel handled the pain by keeping busy taking care of the needs of others. Purlek's reaction surprised Noah the most. He mourned for a few days, but after that his focus shifted to the fact that his parents had been killed by his grandfather. He knew he was related to the king and high priestess of Havil but struggled to understand how a man could kill his own son. On several occasions he asked Noah to tell him more about Lamech and Naamah and wondered why they had become so evil. Noah disliked talking about them, but he was glad to see Purlek's pride in his parents' refusal to compromise their beliefs even when their lives were at stake.

Noah enjoyed spending time with the young blacksmith. He had his father's sense of humor, and his laughter brought momentary reprieves from the sadness they all endured on the river. Noah wondered more than once if Purlek would continue with them after his leg healed. A blacksmith would be quite helpful in completing the Creator's task.

Just when Noah sensed the group had moved beyond the initial stages of grief and were looking forward to reaching his father's place, he received the news that ripped his heart again. A ship from Iri Sana traveled south on the river, and it carried a message bound for Noah in Iri Geshem. However, one of the crewmembers recognized him and directed the boat to move alongside Noah's craft. The man handed him a small scroll and offered his sympathies.

Seeing his father's emblem on the scroll, Noah guessed that it contained news of his grandfather's death. As he cracked the seal and unrolled the parchment, he braced himself, but nothing prepared him for what he read. The first several lines were from his mother. She told him how much she loved him and Emzara and how proud she was of both of them. Then she encouraged him to remain steadfast in his trust in the Creator. She ended by telling him that she wished she could see him again. Then his father's handwriting continued the letter and explained that shortly after Noah left the last time, his mother had become extremely ill. A healer moved in to care for her, but her health continued to deteriorate.

Noah's hands trembled as he read the final line. His father's handwriting became especially shaky as it stated that the sickness took his mother's life about a week earlier. Noah's lips quavered and tears blurred his eyes as he reread the line. He covered his mouth and looked at Emzara before his legs gave out and he collapsed on the ship's deck.

"Noah!"

His grandfather's raspy call snapped his attention back to the present. He looked up and spotted the old man sitting in his favorite spot behind the house. A shaft of happiness pierced his dejected countenance. "Grandfather!" He released Emzara's hand and sprinted forward.

Methuselah climbed to his feet and welcomed Noah with a hearty embrace. "Did you get your father's message?"

Noah nodded. "Yes." Tears flowed once again, but this time they were due to a strange combination of sorrow and joy. Seeing a close family member brought unexpected consolation.

Methuselah kissed his cheek and patted his back a few times before letting go of him. He gave Noah a sympathetic smile. "I see that you did us a favor and brought Emzara this time."

Noah laughed a little through his sniffles. "I didn't think I'd be welcomed here again without her."

"You're probably right." Methuselah grinned and then moved to the back door. He cracked it open. "Son, you should come out here."

The door opened all the way and Lamech appeared in the entry. "I was on my way when I heard you shout." He stepped toward Noah and took a shuddering breath before wrapping his arms around him tightly. "I'm so glad to see you, Son."

"I'm so sorry, Father."

Both men wept openly as they embraced. Their shared tears seemed to wash away some of the pain and sorrow. He heard his grandfather speaking to Emzara, but he would let his father determine when their hug would end.

Eventually, Lamech released him and gave Emzara a hug. "It's great to see you, too." He looked at Noah. "But how did you get my message so quickly?"

"It reached us on the river yesterday. I'll explain soon." Noah motioned to his friends. "We have much to talk about."

Lamech nodded. "Come inside, all of you. The house is still set up for guests because of. . . ." Lamech took a few steadying breaths and looked at Noah. "Because of your mother's burial two days ago."

Emzara wrapped the crook of her elbow around Noah's arm.

To his surprise, Noah kept his composure at the mention of the burial. "Father, are any of the farmhands here?"

"Yes." He pointed to the shed where Noah had built his own workshop as a young man. Like every other building on the property, it had been rebuilt several times over the centuries. "They stay in your old place."

"Are they trustworthy? I need someone to watch our ship — it has all of our belongings. My friend, Garun" — he pointed to Laleel — "her husband, is watching it now, but I would like for him to join us."

Lamech scratched his chin. "Bivel is an honest man."

Noah raised an eyebrow. "Jerah's boy?"

"Don't look so surprised." Lamech snorted. "He's a hard worker and I trust him."

"I'll go tell him," Methuselah said. "You go inside and spend time with your son." The aged man strolled toward the shed.

"Thanks, Father." Lamech stepped to the side and held the door open wide. "Please, come in. Noah, lead them to the sitting room. We'll get acquainted once we're inside."

Once everyone entered the homey area, Noah introduced Laleel, Elam, Rayneh, and Purlek to his father.

Lamech welcomed each of them into his home and directed them to sit. "Let me get you something to drink."

Noah followed his father into the kitchen. As they prepared leaf brew, he told his father about the trouble in Iri Geshem, hurrying through details about the arena and being captured by the Nodites so as not to upset the grieving man too much. "We had to flee because it was no longer safe for followers of the Creator. There's much more to tell, but now is not the time."

"So the young man with the injured leg is the son of your blacksmith friend? Why didn't he come with you?"

Noah sighed and shook his head. "Some of our close friends didn't survive. We've all lost loved ones since the last time I was here. Our trip has been a grim one."

"I'm very sorry to hear that." Lamech handed Noah a bowl with mushed malids in it. "For the little girl. Would you take the drinks in? There's someone I'd like you to meet."

Noah nodded. "Who?"

"Just a moment." Lamech walked down the hall and knocked softly on a door. "Evet, would you please join us in the sitting room?"

Emzara joined Noah and helped him carry the refreshments. She set the bowl of mushed malids in front of her seat before turning to Laleel and holding out her arms. "I'll help her eat."

Laleel smiled and handed Rayneh to Emzara. "You'll need the practice."

Lamech reentered the room and looked at Emzara with his mouth agape. "Practice?"

Emzara blushed and patted her stomach with her free hand. "Yes. Are you ready to be a grandfather again?"

He clapped his hands together. "How wonderful!" He glanced at Noah and grinned. "Apparently, the Creator was tired of hearing your complaints."

Noah chuckled and shook his head. "Whatever the reason, He has indeed chosen to bless us."

A young woman entered the room, and Lamech stepped to the side. Her black hair and dark brown eyes complemented her dark complexion. Her muscular arms and broad shoulders accentuated her sturdy build.

"I'd like you to meet Evet. She was Nina's nursemaid and will be moving back home soon."

She nodded. "It's nice to meet you."

Noah stood. "I'm Nina's son, Noah."

"I would have guessed that. You look like your brother, Jerah."

Noah winced playfully. "That wasn't very nice. This is my wife, Emzara." He pointed and then quickly introduced the others.

"Noah," Lamech said. "Evet is Toman's granddaughter."

"Really?" It made sense. Her dark complexion and stocky build certainly came from him. "Remind me never to shake your forearm."

She giggled. "So he's crushed your arm, too?"

"Too many times."

Lamech pointed to Purlek. "Evet, with the young man's permission, would you mind looking at his leg?"

"Of course not." Evet looked expectantly at Purlek.

"Oh." Purlek scooted up on the bench. "I'll try anything to speed up the healing. I'm tired of hobbling along and being a burden on everyone else."

Evet sat a short distance away and asked Purlek to lift his leg onto the bench. The back door opened and more introductions were made after Methuselah and Garun entered.

Noah closed his eyes. *Creator, help me say the right words.* He opened his eyes and slowly scanned the room, being careful to look each person in the eyes before he spoke. "We all know these past weeks have been extremely difficult, but I fear it's only going to get worse. I need to tell you about something I've only told Emzara so far."

He paused and looked at Methuselah. "Grandfather, last time we spoke, you encouraged me to speak boldly about the Creator, as your father did. During my trip home, I resolved to do exactly that, to follow the Most High no matter what. And that's when. . . ." He put his hand on Emzara's knee and squeezed it. His eyes moistened, not from tears of sorrow, but because they always did when he thought about what had happened outside of Novanam. He put his head down. "This is going to sound strange, and some of you may not believe me, but it's true." He gulped and scanned their faces again. "He spoke — the Creator spoke to me."

Methuselah's eyes grew wide and Lamech bolted upright, staring intently at Noah. Purlek hissed when Evet accidentally dropped his leg onto the bench as she spun to face Noah.

"So what did He say?" Garun folded his arms across his chest.

Laleel leaned forward in front of her husband. "What was He like?"

"He was — no, He *is* beautiful . . . and terrifying. He is . . ." Noah dabbed his cheek with the wrap on his shoulder, "indescribable."

Methuselah sat so far forward in his chair that Noah believed he would soon fall on the floor. The old man gestured. "Go on."

"He said that He was the God of my forefather, Enoch, and that Enoch spoke the truth."

Methuselah's eyes welled up, and he glanced at Lamech. "I told you."

Lamech smiled at his father before turning to his son. "What else did He say?"

"This is the hard part." Noah cleared his throat. "He said He is grieved about how wicked people have become, so He is going to destroy this world with a flood."

86

There was silence.

"The whole world?" Lamech asked at last.

Noah nodded slowly. "Everything."

"What? Everything?" Evet asked.

"Does that mean everyone?" Purlek asked. "When?"

"He didn't say when, but I know it's still many years away."

"How do you know that?" Lamech asked.

"You're serious?" Garun's arms dropped to his sides.

Noah shook his head in amazement. "Yes. He commanded me to build a ship. One that's big enough for the animals He's going to send me." Noah smiled at Emzara. "And He said that we would have sons."

Laleel touched Emzara's shoulder. "Sons?"

Emzara bit her lip and nodded excitedly.

"Are you sure you didn't just dream this because you wanted children so badly and now Emzara is with child?" Lamech asked.

Noah opened his mouth, but Emzara cut him off. "No. He told me we were going to have sons before I told him I was pregnant."

Elam stroked his chin. "So that's what you had to talk to Zara about as soon as you returned from your trip. No wonder it couldn't wait."

"Exactly. I had to tell her."

Methuselah twisted to stretch his back. "I told you before that I see my father's spirit in you. He responded the same way as you are now whenever he spoke about the Creator."

"So what's your plan?" Garun asked. "I don't think you can go back to your shipyard in Iri Geshem. How will you build this ship?"

"I was hoping all of you would help me with that."

"Us?" Purlek pointed to himself. "I'm not a shipbuilder."

"No, but I sure could use a blacksmith to remake the tools I lost when my other ship was sunk. And I'll need hundreds of braces and countless bolts."

"Do you plan on building it here?" Lamech asked.

Noah shook his head. "It's not safe. The Nodites just wiped out several cities to the south as they marched on Iri Geshem, and I don't know the outcome of that battle. But no matter who won, it's not safe for us here. If Naamah finds out where I am — and this will be one of the first places she checks — then she'll come after us."

"Where will we go?" Elam asked.

"Far away to — wait, we? You're going to join us?"

Elam looked at his daughter, who was elbow deep in mashed malids. "If the Creator spoke to you, then there's nowhere else we'd rather be. I may not be the best construction worker, but I'll do what I can. I need to send word to my father and children in Zakar. They don't know about Kal yet." His chest heaved and he blinked hard before focusing on Noah. "So where are we going?"

Noah tipped his head toward Methuselah. "A place where no one will follow us."

The old man scrunched his face. "A place where no one. . . ." He leaned back and repeated the words twice before jolting. "Eden? You're planning to go to Eden?"

"But it's forbidden," Evet said. "No one goes there."

"Forbidden? No, but there are many rumors surrounding it, so few people go there. But that's why it's the perfect place for us. It's the last place Naamah will ever consider."

"Aren't you worried about the stories?" Evet asked.

"Not anymore." Noah stood and paced about the room. "I think all of those tales started because of what happened to Enoch, my grandfather's father. But he wasn't punished for going there. The Creator told me that He took him so that he wouldn't die. I think the various legends arose from his disappearance. Besides, I only plan to pass through it to the northwest region of the world. According to the adventurers I've spoken to, it's currently far beyond Havil's reach and sparsely populated. We should be able to find a place to start over."

"Count me in," Methuselah said.

"And us, too," Garun said as he slipped his arm around Laleel's waist. "What about it, Purlek?"

The blacksmith glanced at Evet and then back at Noah. "I don't know. I need to think about it."

"I understand." Noah faced Lamech. "Father?"

Lamech shrugged. "I'm not sure. I need to talk to Jerah first."

"Of course. I'd like to leave in a couple of days. The sooner we leave here the better."

CHAPTER 13

Brushing her hands together, Emzara watched the tiny dust of the flour fall onto the table. The beauty of the light flakes in sharp contrast to the dark-stained wood mesmerized her. Cleaning the last vestige of kneaded dough from between her fingers, she pondered what to do while the bread rose.

An idea struck her, and she padded out the door and then toward the barn. Picking up her pace, she almost skipped to the massive weathered structure comprised of sections of wooden planks and blocks of cut stone. Purlek's well-furnished quarters lay in the heart of the building, which not only housed the farmhands but also provided space for them to stay up with birthing or injured animals.

Arriving at the darker interior, she slowed to a walk so as not to alarm any of the animals. Low whispers reached her ears, and she craned her neck toward the sound. She reached the sheeted entrance to Purlek's room as mingled laughter emanated from within. Emzara listened briefly before slowly backing away with a smile on her face.

"Oof!" She spun quickly and kept her voice at a whisper. "Noah. What are you doing here?"

"Getting crushed apparently." He rubbed the top of his foot dramatically, resting his other hand on a beam for support.

Emzara took his hand and tiptoed out of earshot of Purlek's room. "I don't weigh that much." She lightly slapped his shoulder.

"I was teasing." He held her close and breathed in the spicy scent of her hair like he so often did. "What are you doing here?" He raised his eyebrows.

"Well, I was going to check on Purlek, but Evet beat me to it."

"Is that so?" Noah nodded, but his focus seemed to be elsewhere.

"Noah, Evet and Purlek . . . I think. . . ."

"You think what?"

"I think he's glad she beat me to it."

"Hmm."

"I was only there for a moment, but they were talking about their lives. And there was enough giggling to know they were getting along well. I don't think they'd want me to intrude right now."

"Interesting." A smile raised one half of his mouth. "Well, good for them to be spending time together. You know" — he paused for effect — "I had a similar intent in mind."

"Oh?" She laced her fingers in his and smiled up at him, feeling as if she was the young girl who had fallen for his dark eyes shortly after they met.

"I'd like to have some time with just you. There's something you need to see. Do you have time for a walk?"

"Yes, the bread doesn't need me for a while."

"Come on, then." He guided her out the back entrance of the barn and parallel to the river. Emzara put a hand above her eyes to block the sunlight. Behind them, in the malid grove, Elam and Rayneh played in the soft, tall grasses. Based on her movements, it seemed like she was trying to catch a small insect. Each time she pounced, her curly hair tried to keep up with her movements.

"There's something about seeing a father take care of his little girl," Emzara said.

"So are you disappointed we're having a son?"

Even though she knew he was teasing, she shook her head. "I can't wait to watch you be a father to him."

For several moments the world stood still as Noah embraced her.

"I may have to say that more often," she said. "Four hundred and sixty years and you can still leave me breathless with your kisses."

"I can't believe you remember the number."

90

"Well, I can't believe you still tease me for forgetting number 392." She flashed a saucy smile at him, enjoying the opportunity to tease him. "You'll probably think it's funny for the next 500 years." She turned and walked ahead through the orchard.

"Oh, and now you think you know where we're going?"

His steps quickened behind her and a giggle escaped her lips. "Well, we've been walking parallel to the river. Are we changing direction?"

"Definitely."

She stopped. "Really?"

"Yeah. Our little one will be born soon. That'll change everything."

She softened her voice. "I can barely think about anything else."

"I can't wait to take him on his first overnight trip." He locked her arm in his. "We'll look up at the stars, and I'll explain how grand their Creator is. Then I'll tell him stories about all the adventures his mother and I had."

"Hmm. I can't wait to tell him about how his father looked a daggertooth in the face and shouted, 'I'm not going to die today.'"

"I said that to Naamah."

Emzara held up her hands. "I said daggertooth. I just didn't specify which one."

Noah smiled and shook his head. "So many great things we'll get to share with him."

"And he's going to be curious. If he's anything like his father, he's sure to try some crazy stunts on his own."

"Are you scared?" Noah asked.

"You'd better believe it. Now if we were having a daughter," she shrugged, "then probably not."

"We're not in this alone, and you've had centuries to perfect your skills." He winked at her.

"Careful. Are you calling me an old woman?"

He gave one of his carefree laughs and she joined with him. Suddenly, he quieted and held his hand up to her mouth. He leaned close to her ear. "We're here. Look."

Her eyes widened and she stared. Nearby, a keluk stuck out its long tongue, and she watched in fascination as it helped itself to a mouthful of leaves, chewing slowly and methodically. Its lower jaw moved in opposition to the upper one. She walked closer, grabbing Noah's hand and pulling him with her.

"Hey, sweet one." The animal turned and blinked his long lashes at her.

"I think you've made a friend."

"He's coming this way. Look at the graceful way he moves." She giggled. "Only his knobby knees counteract his poise."

"And you don't think those four furry stubs coming out of his head are strange?"

"Not at all. Those and his gorgeous eyes make him simply adorable." She refused to take her eyes off the creature.

"And to think you used to say such things about me."

She briefly pulled her gaze away from the animal as Noah pretended to be hurt to his imaginary audience. "Maybe now you can see why I like them so much. Guess there's some resemblance."

Noah gave her a goofy grin in response. She could tell his excitement for showing her the animals nearly matched her own joy at seeing them.

"I can't believe it's taken you almost 500 years to make good on your promise to show me one of these."

"Five hundred! You're trying your hand at numbers again. Four hundred and sixty is hardly almost 500." He winked. "But who's counting?"

She straightened and cleared her throat, but realized the keluk had resumed eating and was no longer alone. Three others had joined him. "And there's a baby one!"

"What are you waiting for? Go closer."

Emzara's heart had longed for this moment, and she needed no further encouragement. She joined the little group and headed straight for the center. One of the shorter ones nuzzled her on the shoulder. She reached up and gently felt the knobs on top of the female's head. The baby ambled up to her, and she plucked some leaves and held them out to him. As he accepted the food, she looked up and grinned at Noah, wanting to make sure he saw. He beamed while she laughed at the tickling of the little one's scratchy gray tongue tasting her arm to see if it held any further treats for him.

"Hang on, baby." She scratched behind his ear with one hand while reaching with her other one to get a second helping of leaves. His huge eyes were even cuter up close. She took in the keluks' movements, felt the muscles in their necks, and memorized the contours of their bodies so she could draw them in better detail. The animals lumbered slowly around her, sometimes lowering their heads to take her in as well. It seemed as if they were in a dance, with each movement choreographed. Giving in to the sheer joy she felt inside, she raised her hands — palms up — and circled around in their midst.

All too soon they started to move on. She patted the youngest member one last time and tore herself away from the tiny herd. "Noah, that was—" She let her misting eyes do the talking for her.

"Enchanting — watching you with them."

She intertwined her fingers in his as they headed back. "And well worth the wait. I just wish we weren't leaving tomorrow morning, or I'd come back here."

"Maybe we'll find more where we're going."

"I hope so. That was a wonderful surprise. Thank you. I can't wait to draw them in great detail when we get back. The only problem will be settling on the best pose."

"You'll have several days on the boat. You can sketch all of them if you like."

"Maybe I will."

He rubbed her midsection. "Shall we call our little one Keluk?"

She giggled. "I don't think our son should have such a graceful name."

He shook his head and smiled. "I won't tell Purlek you think his name is borderline graceful."

"Oh, that's awful. Purlek and Keluk is a stretch even for you!" She punched him playfully on the arm before sobering. "So do you think he's going to go with us?"

"I don't know. He hasn't said, and we leave tomorrow."

"And if he and Evet are bonding, maybe he'll make the choice to stay here with her." Her voice carried the sadness she felt at the prospect.

"I think he might stay behind and help Jerah with the farm now that father and grandfather are coming with us."

"Jerah sure wasn't happy with you for taking them with us."

"It was their decision. He could've come, too."

"I know." She leaned her head on his upper arm and they walked in silence for a time.

As they neared the barn, he slowed. "You go on ahead. I'm going to stop and chat with Purlek."

"Noah, thank you." She kissed him on the cheek. "It was wonderful."

CHAPTER 14

Kadel — Noah's 500th year

Approximately two dozen torchlights of Kadel flickered in the evening as light snow flurries whipped across Noah's view. He rewound a blanket around his shoulders and head as a chill shook his body.

Garun rubbed his hands together rapidly. "Iri Geshem may be more dangerous for us, but it sure has better weather."

Noah chuckled and his fingers fumbled as he adjusted one of the ropes holding the ship's main mast. "Indeed. I certainly miss the year-round warm air and sunset strolls on the beach with Em."

"I hope our destination won't be this cold."

"It shouldn't be. We'll be heading southwest for a little while once we get off this boat. And the farther south we travel, the nicer it'll be. Besides, I think snow is pretty rare here. It looks like we just arrived at the wrong time."

"What do you think it'll be like?" Garun put his hands together in a ball and blew into them.

Noah shrugged. "Uninhabited, I hope."

"How about full of godly shipbuilders?"

"Even better." Noah smiled and shivered again. "Would you tell the others that we're here?"

"Of course." Garun strode across the deck toward the large cabin behind them and entered it.

95

An entire whole moon had passed since they had left Iri Sana. Jerah had ridiculed the idea even up to their departure but stuck with his agreement to help Bivel take over the farm in Lamech's absence. To Noah's pleasure, Purlek and Evet had decided at the last moment to join the crew. Under the young woman's care, Purlek's leg had regained most of its strength, but that was not the only thing that grew stronger. Every passing day, the relationship between nurse and patient blossomed, and Noah rarely saw either of them without the other present. *Tubal-Cain would've liked her. She's tough and spirited.*

The journey had been slower and more difficult than expected. The narrowing of the river generated a quicker current to battle, and the cold spell over the past week made each day seem longer, since most of the group remained in the warm cabin. Still, the thrill of a new adventure and the enjoyable company of his father and grandfather kept his morale up.

Garun returned from below deck and readied two ropes as the boat neared the tiny pier already holding three much smaller vessels.

Noah carefully guided the ship to the first mooring on the wharf so that the current would push his boat away from the others. "I don't think they're used to such a large boat."

"This will probably be the biggest one they've ever seen." Garun jumped onto the pier and quickly looped the ropes around two of the moorings.

"Hopefully that fact will entice someone to buy it or trade for it."

Garun shrugged. "If we're going where the Creator wants us to go, then I'm sure it'll work out." After returning to the deck, he moved toward the back of the boat. "I'll drop the anchor just to be safe."

"That sounds good." Noah stretched out his arms and legs as he yawned. "So you'll remain with the others here while I go into the village with Elam and Purlek?" He knew Garun could protect the women and older men better than anyone else on board, and taking two men with him, especially the burly blacksmith, would discourage confrontations with any ruffians.

Garun sighed. "Yes, I'm stuck on the boat again."

He rarely complained, and Noah picked up on his sarcasm. Somehow, Garun managed to find something positive in nearly every situation. "Hey, at least you get to be around some lovely ladies." Elam and

Purlek exited the cabin and walked toward Noah. "And I'm stuck walking around with two smelly men."

Garun nodded toward them. "Well, when you put it that way."

"Want to trade places?"

Garun smiled and shook his head. "No sir."

Noah gestured to Elam and Purlek. "Let's go." He looked over his shoulder at Garun. "Be safe."

"Same to you." Garun waved.

The three men entered the village on the road from the pier. Known as the final outpost on the river, Kadel reminded Noah, at first glance, of many other river towns he had visited, particularly in his younger years. A collection of old wooden buildings lined each of the roadways, and a couple of loud drinking establishments stood close to the river.

"We'll want to avoid these places if possible," Noah said as they neared one of the drinking halls. "They can get pretty rough."

"Do you think anyone here will really have what we need?" Purlek asked.

Noah shrugged. "Adventurers stop here to outfit their trips, so this town may be exactly what we're looking for. We'll know soon enough."

Two women walked hurriedly toward them from the opposite direction. Appearing a century or two younger than Noah, they each wore only a basic wrap and seemed immune to the cold.

"Excuse me," Noah said. "Can you tell me where a merchant or outfitter might be at this time of night?"

The women stopped, and the shorter one with long straight hair smiled at him and then measured Elam and Purlek with her eyes. "Wurnu's place is on the edge of town." She pointed back the way she had come. "Continue on this road and then left on the last street. You'll know it when you see it. You can't miss it."

"Thank you," Noah said as he turned to leave.

"Young man."

Noah stopped and faced the women again.

"No, not you." The taller woman strutted toward Purlek. "I was talking to the young man."

"Can I help you?" Purlek asked.

"You certainly can. Why don't you join us for a drink?" She flashed him a seductive smile. "And then you can keep me warm tonight."

97

Purlek shook his head. "No thank you. Your drink can keep you warm." He turned and walked away with Noah and Elam while the woman called for him a couple more times. Eventually, the women laughed, called Purlek a few inappropriate names, and entered the drinking hall.

"I hope Wurnu has more integrity than that," Elam said.

"Yeah, that's not really the best way for a town to make a good first impression," Purlek said.

Noah put a hand on the blacksmith's shoulder. "I'm proud of you for handling that appropriately."

"Thanks, *old* man." Purlek chuckled. "I'm not interested in a woman like that. And even if I were, can you imagine what would happen to me when I got back to the boat? Evet would kill me, if Ma-Zara didn't do it first."

Noah laughed. "I think Evet could probably do it, too."

"Yeah, she's pretty tough." Purlek wrapped his arms around his chest and pretended to shake in fear.

"You should've met her grandfather — strong as a grendec."

As they marched toward their destination, they kept their heads down and pulled their wraps tight to minimize the effect of the biting wind. Noah told Purlek a couple stories about Toman and speculated about how different his life would have been if Toman's brother had taken him on as an apprentice.

At the top of the hill, they turned left at the intersection. Thankful that the buildings to his right blocked the freezing gusts, Noah scanned the road before them.

"There it is." Elam pointed toward a building on the right that displayed a storefront similar to the other shops on the road but attached to the rear of the structure stood a large barn. A wooden sign hung above the door, identifying the place as Wurnu's Outfitter and Livery.

"Let's hope they have what we need," Purlek said.

"I'm glad they're open." Noah turned toward them and stopped. "I think it would be better if you didn't call me by my name in here. If he documents his transactions, we don't need to leave any records that I was here."

Elam glanced at Purlek and shrugged. "If you think that's best."

Noah hurried toward the door. "Now let's go. I'm freezing out here."

Purlek smiled. "It's not that cold, *Farna*. Must be an old man thing." He opened the door for Noah and Elam.

Noah playfully elbowed him in the stomach as he stepped into the shop. "Is that why you stayed in the cabin all day while Garun and I braved the elements?"

Purlek pulled the door shut behind him, making sure it latched so that the wind did not blow it open. "No, I stayed inside because I was taking care of the ladies."

"I think you mean one particular lady."

"Evening peace, travelers!" A throaty voice interrupted them from behind the counter to their left. "How can I help you?"

A fireplace crackled in the back and emitted enough heat to warm the fairly large room. The proprietor stood about a handbreadth shorter than Noah. A large bald spot on top of his head gave way to long, frizzy, gray-and-black hair that dropped to his shoulders. He wore some sort of spotted animal skin over his midsection and another skin around his lower body. "Are you Wurnu?"

"Depends on who's asking," he said with half a smile.

Noah tipped his head toward the man. "A customer who needs to make a large purchase or trade."

"Then yes, I'm Wurnu." The man stepped around the counter and greeted each of them with a firm shake of the forearm. "What're you looking to purchase?"

A chill ran through Noah's body, and he glanced back at the fireplace. "Can we talk over there?"

Wurnu chuckled. "Of course." He led them toward the hearth. "You must've come from the south. Can't handle this cold. Truth is, it rarely gets this cold, but the past week has been rough." He gestured to some benches. "Please."

"Thank you." Noah chose the seat closest to the fire. "Much better."

Wurnu nodded and held out a palm toward Noah as if to ask him to continue.

"Well, we sailed a large boat up the river, much larger than anything we saw docked here, and we'd like to trade it for several items." Noah loosened the wrap from his shoulder a little. "We need three wagons, beasts to pull them, and food for a few whole moons."

99

"And a map of the western lands, if you have it," Elam said.

"Is that all?" Wurnu chuckled.

"I know it sounds like a lot." Noah glanced around the room. "I'd probably buy several of your tools, too."

Wurnu grinned and rubbed the back of his neck. "It's not that I don't have or can't get what you need, but I don't think you realize how much everything will cost."

Noah folded his hands together and leaned forward. "My boat's worth at least twice as much as what we're seeking in trade. It's only a few years old, and it's made by Ara's Shipyard in Iri Geshem, the best shipbuilders in the world."

The man's eyes lit up. "Of course, I'd need to inspect this boat to see if it's truly worth so much."

"Of course," Noah said.

"Hey, boss," Purlek said as he looked at Noah. "Would you really trade it for so little?"

Wurnu jumped in before Noah could respond. "I'm sure you'd like to see what I have to offer." He pointed to an opening beside the fireplace, which led to an attached barn. "I have several options for wagon beasts, hundreds of tools, and plenty of foodstuffs, but it might take me a few days to get a third wagon here."

"I'd prefer to let my wife make the decision about the animals. She's the expert in that area." Noah looked around at the shop. "While we wait on the third wagon, would you recommend a warm place for us to eat?"

"Yes, of course." He stood and waved an arm toward the rest of the shop. "Let me know if there's anything else you need, and we can wait until daylight for me to examine this boat."

Noah stood and gripped the man's forearm. "That sounds perfect."

* * *

Western Frontier — Noah's 500th year

Noah glanced at the ever-expanding bulge in Emzara's midsection as he slipped his arm around her and scooted close. The cushion beneath her lifted her to his height as they sat on the bench of the second wagon in their tiny caravan. Lamech, Methuselah, Elam, and Rayneh spent much of their time in Noah's wagon. Being the largest of the three vehicles, it served as the group's meeting place and meal room during inclement weather. Garun and Laleel currently took the lead in their smaller wagon, while Purlek and Evet brought up the rear.

The springtime sun slowly sank toward the horizon in the western sky far ahead. The two gray large-eared tuskers hauling the cart plodded along the scarcely used path. Thankful for Emzara's expertise with animals, Noah had quickly learned to appreciate this kind more than lunkers. They provided a slightly faster and steadier pace, and they were far less irritable. In fact, they were often friendly and playful and, despite their bulk, they seemed to enjoy being around little Rayneh. Of course, they were not alone in that area. She was the center of the group's attention whenever they were together.

Noah kissed Emzara's head. "Two whole moons."

She lifted her head from his shoulder and furrowed her eyebrows. "Two? We've been traveling for three."

Noah grinned and touched her stomach. "No. I meant two more until we get to meet our son."

She snuggled against him and softly pushed her head under his chin. "I can't wait to carry him on the outside."

"I can't wait to see that. If the reaction to Rayneh is any indication, our son will be well loved by his people."

"Well, Rayneh probably won't like it when he starts stealing some of her attention." She placed one hand behind his back and rubbed it as she spoke.

Noah sighed. "I love watching her with my father and grandfather. Did you see her at midmeal? Grandfather kept trying to teach her new words, but all she wanted to do was show him her new dance, which is really the same as the old one. She just spins around with a cute grin on her face."

"Mmhmm. You up for a strange question?" Emzara asked.

Noah shrugged his free shoulder. "Sure."

"Well, speaking of Rayneh, did you ever wonder if she might be . . . if she might marry one of our sons someday?"

Noah pushed a loose strand of hair behind her ear. "I've wondered that ever since we escaped the arena. And in many ways, I hope for it.

Obviously, I want her to be on the ark. But wouldn't it be wonderful if Aterre's niece became our daughter-in-law?"

Emzara sat up and stared into Noah's eyes. "You really have given this some thought." She pressed harder against his lower back in the spot that gave him the most trouble. "And thank you for mentioning Aterre. I haven't thought about him for so long. It would be terrific to have his niece on board." She grinned. "I guess we'd better hope our son has good taste."

"Well, there's a very good chance of that since his father has incredible taste."

Emzara rolled her eyes and then yawned and stretched.

Noah responded automatically with a yawn of his own and allowed his mind to drift while the same scenery passed by in the open grassland. For three weeks, they had seen nothing but wide open plain, the monotony of rolling hills broken only by the occasional small copse of trees or wandering stream. Rarely had they met anyone on the path, and they passed only a handful of tiny settlements and farms. Noah appreciated the peaceful travel and, based on the map Wurnu had provided, guessed that another two weeks might bring them to the outer edge of Eden. How far they would need to move beyond it, he could not yet say, just as he could not know when the Creator would tell him the remaining details about the ark.

Shortly before the sun touched the horizon, the caravan started up one of the largest hills they had observed in the region. As they reached the crest, Garun stopped his wagon and then frantically gestured for the others to stop. He ordered his animals to back up a little and then hurried to Noah and Emzara. "We might have a problem."

"What is it?" Noah asked.

"Come and look."

Lamech peeked out of the canopy that covered the large wagon. "Why did we stop?"

"Bring Elam out here," Garun said.

By the time Noah climbed down from his bench and walked around the pair of tuskers, Purlek had joined the group. "Why did we stop?"

"Follow me," Garun said.

The men followed Garun up the hill, but as he approached the top, he crouched lower and encouraged the others to do the same. He dropped to his hands and knees for the final 50 cubits or so.

Shadowing Garun's movements, Noah finally peered over the top of the hill as a stunned silence fell over the group. Sprawled out in the valley before them stood a settlement consisting of hundreds of tents and thousands of beasts, including herd after herd of bleaters. "Was this place on the map?" Noah asked.

Elam unrolled the map and studied it for a moment before shaking his head. "Nothing is marked here."

"Do we go around?" Purlek asked.

Noah looked at his father. "What do you think?"

Lamech shrugged. "I think you're the leader of our expedition. I know we're running low on rations, so we may want to approach them to see if we can buy supplies."

Noah stroked his beard, which had grown much longer than he liked it during this trip. "What if we emptied one of the wagons? Then Garun and I could drive it to their settlement to see if they are friendly or hostile and ask about purchasing goods."

"Me?" Garun asked.

Noah smiled. "Yes, you. You're the one who complained about always being left behind while we check out new places. Are you afraid?"

Garun chuckled. "I wasn't objecting to your plan. I was merely surprised that you recommended me."

"What do the rest of you think?" Noah asked.

"I think Emzara's going to hate it." Elam faced Noah. "Maybe if someone else went in your place."

"I can go," Lamech said.

"You there!" A voice from the other side of the caravan jolted Noah. A younger man, perhaps in his mid-100s, stepped around the front of the first wagon and approached. He did not appear to be dangerous; a small knife strapped to his belt was his only visible weapon. "What are you doing? Spying on our camp?"

Noah stood and approached the newcomer. "No sir. We're traveling west and were surprised to come across such a large encampment. It's not on our map. We were concerned that we might need to take a different route to avoid any problems. But we also need to purchase provisions, so we were just discussing who would go down there to speak for us."

"Have no fear, travelers. We are a group of peaceful herders. My grandfather grew tired of the violence in the cities to the south, so we've roamed this area for centuries, living off the land and keeping herds. We have an abundance of supplies you could purchase." He gestured to the three wagons. "Come, I'll take you to meet my grandfather. He's always happy to welcome friendly visitors."

Chapter 15

Emzara repositioned her cushion as far to the right as she could to allow the man a spot in the seat next to Noah. Noah reached out a steady hand to guide him and he laid his staff in the wagon bed behind them before settling in.

"I'm Vadid. And you are?"

"Noah, and this is my wife, Emzara."

As Vadid directed the caravan toward the camp, Emzara studied him from the corner of her eye. His hair and beard were shorn close. His garment, a cream linen tunic, fell to his knees, and a belt cinched it at his waist. He wore a dark blue woven outer cloak, bound together in the front by a beautiful metal clasp. Hides encircled his calves and leather cords crisscrossed and held them tight to his legs. His brown shoes reached mid-calf and completed his unique outfit.

"That's one of our herds over there." Vadid pointed left when a sudden animal call drew their attention. A lone man stood in the distance with a staff in his hand. At least ten bovar surrounded him. Soon more herds and farmhands dotted the landscape, and not long after that, clusters of large rectangular tents appeared. Their peaked tops were not much higher than the sides. Pelts or fabrics covered them, and Emzara imagined what each home told about its owners. One had hides haphazardly strewn around the structure, and she pictured a chronicler living there, more interested in the information he wrote than the place where he lived. Another was brightly colored with images painted on the sides, and she imagined a happy young family lived inside. They passed by a plain one, and Emzara stifled a laugh as she pictured someone like Nmir living there.

As she watched, a woman stepped outside, but she bore little resemblance to Emzara's old nursemaid. Instead, this woman looked like someone else from her past. She raced through memory after memory, trying to locate the person's face. Suddenly her mind brought up an image of Kal as a young girl, hugging the woman. She smiled and spoke quietly to herself. "That's who she reminds me of."

"What did you say?" Noah glanced at her.

"Oh, nothing really." Emzara gestured toward the woman. "I was thinking that she reminds me a little bit of Adah. I guess it must've slipped out."

Vadid raised an eyebrow at her. "That's funny. Her name is Adah, too."

Emzara spun to see the woman again. "Could it be?"

Vadid swept his arm in a sideways arc to indicate the whole encampment. "Her son leads our group. Actually, he started it after they fled Havil."

Emzara grabbed Noah's knee. "Stop the wagon." Before they fully slowed, she leapt to the ground and hurried toward the woman. "Adah!"

Though now gray-haired and wrinkled, the still-beautiful woman stood on her front platform and stared.

Before Adah could stop her, Emzara grabbed her old friend by the shoulders and studied the face she had not seen for centuries before wrapping her in a hug.

Adah pulled away. Looking confused, she measured Emzara. "You seem familiar. Where do I know you from?"

Emzara bit her lip and nodded rapidly. "From a long time ago. We were . . ." Emzara looked up as she searched for the words, "we were co-conspirators — well, almost anyway."

Adah's face lit up. "Emzara?"

"Mmhmm."

"How? I mean, what are you doing here?"

"I was going to ask you the same thing."

"It's a long story."

Noah rushed toward them as Vadid and the others secured the wagons.

"Adah" — Noah tipped his head slightly — "it's good to see someone we know so far away from home."

"This is my home now. It has been for a long time." She held out an arm to Vadid, who came alongside her. "Long before Vadid here was even born."

"Good to see you, Grandmother." He warmly took her hands in his own.

"Vadid, where are you taking them?"

"To see the chief. They want to trade with us."

"Perfect. Come with me, all of you." Adah turned her back to the group and started walking.

Emzara looked at Noah and shrugged, then they all followed the elderly woman. None of the dwellings seemed befitting for a leader, but they continued toward their unknown destination.

"Here we are." Adah stopped outside a large but modestly constructed tent.

"This is where the chief lives?" Noah asked. His tone made it clear that he was surprised, too.

"Yes." She opened the leather flap and led them inside.

As her eyes adjusted to the low lighting, Emzara saw the wooden posts that formed the inner frame of the walls. She was amazed at how large and cozy it was. Fur rugs covered most of the floor except for the space opposite the door. There, a man sat next to a bleater in a small pen and the animal bellowed loudly.

"Son, we have visitors," Adah said.

"Be right there." The man wiped his brow with his forearm and then cleaned his hands on a large cloth before looking up at his guests. He opened his arms out wide. "Welcome. What can I do for you?"

Noah stepped ahead of his friends. "Sir, we came upon your settlement, and Vadid mentioned that we could purchase food and supplies from your people."

"That shouldn't be a problem." He glanced at Adah. "Mother, why didn't you just take them to one of the merchants?"

Adah smiled. "I thought you might want to see an old acquaintance of ours."

The chief furrowed his brow and turned to Adah. "Acquaintance? Who?"

"This is Noah, someone you met when you were very young." She laughed. "And, Noah, this is my son Jabal."

Turning back to Jabal, Noah asked, "The musician?"

Jabal snorted. "No, that's my brother, Jubal."

"But you were both talented musicians. I saw you play when I first visited Havil."

"That was a long time ago. I played when I was a child, but I could never compete with my brother."

"You were—" The bleater moaned, and Noah momentarily lost his focus. "You were young, perhaps not even ten years old."

"Jabal?" Laleel asked, her high forehead pinched in thought.

"Yes. And forgive me, you are—"

"I'm Laleel, and this is my husband, Garun. He used to guard your family."

Squinting, Jabal stepped closer to Garun. "I think I do remember you. Well, it's nice to meet you again after all this time." He fanned his arm around the room. "Please, everyone, have a seat and rest from your journey."

Adah sat beside her son, and the others followed her lead, forming a small circle. Only Lamech and Methuselah were missing, since they had remained with the wagons.

"Forgive me for greeting you in such a fashion, but this bleater is about to give birth, and I don't want anything to go wrong. She lost her last baby. But please, tell me about your travels. It's likely to be a while before her little one makes an appearance. Vadid can bring you something to eat and drink."

"Jabal, how did you and Adah end up here, so far away from Havil?" Noah finally asked what Emzara had been longing to know.

"Mother?"

Adah looked into her hands before nodding.

"Well, there's really not much of a story here if you know what my father is like." Jabal shifted in his seat. "After my brother and I grew up, he tried to take over our futures. I started getting really involved in architecture. He fueled that passion, and I became rather proficient in it. However, I noticed several odd things. One day, Mother had a long scarf covering her arms though the day was very warm. Then, a week later, I found her limping. She said she'd stumbled into something."

Jabal sighed. "Honestly, I probably wouldn't have figured it out had I not been walking around the palace late one night when I heard terrible sounds coming from Mother's room." His words picked up speed until they tumbled over each other. "My father. He went into these rages. I think he might have killed her if I hadn't shown up. He stopped as soon as he saw me." Jabal slowly let out a deep breath. "That's when I realized how selfish I'd been. I'd seen only the grandeur of Havil and imagined my own greatness. I didn't even notice the pain my mother was enduring."

"Jabal—"

"It's true, Mother. Anyway, I knew I had to get her out of there. I figured the only way I could keep her safe was to travel as far away from that city as possible. And that's what we did."

A little squeal turned everyone's attention to Rayneh. She had wandered to the pen and stood before the bleater with one little hand clutched to her chest.

Jabal chuckled and lightly patted Rayneh's head. "Would you like to try petting her again?"

She stared at him through wide eyes.

"Here. She might have thought your hand had food in it. If I hold her head like this, you can feel how fluffy she is." He cupped the creature's face in his hands.

Rayneh held out her hand cautiously and plucked up the courage to try again. After making contact, she giggled and pulled her hand away again.

"There. See?" Jabal scruffed the ears of the animal. "I think she likes that."

Noah knelt beside the young girl. "Rayneh, you just met him, but he's your uncle, which means that you're his niece."

"And that makes us family," Elam said.

Noah glanced at Adah. "She's Kal's daughter."

Adah leaned forward. "Kal? Where is she?"

Elam took a deep breath and shook his head. "My wife—" He swallowed hard and fell silent.

"Kal died before we left Iri Geshem." Noah put a hand on Elam's shoulder and sighed. "I'm sorry, Adah."

Adah's mouth curved downward and she slumped. After momentary silence, she considered Rayneh and smiled through misty eyes. "I'm glad I can meet her daughter, my granddaughter."

Emzara pursed her lips, pleased to see the hurting people she cared about finding comfort together. She noted Noah's wisdom in not sharing the details of Kal's death. Adah did not need to learn that Lamech had killed another one of her children.

"And I guess that makes me your nephew." Purlek stepped toward Jabal. "Tubal-Cain was my father, but he, too, is no longer with us."

Jabal lowered his gaze. "I'm sorry to hear about Tubal-Cain. I only knew him while I was a boy, but he was always very kind to us. You look very much like what I remember of him." He grasped Purlek's forearm. "It's wonderful to meet you, Nephew."

Garun cleared his throat and gestured to Jabal. "So you and Adah escaped here?"

"We did. We've picked up many people along the way, others who wish to be free of the growing violence in the cities. We focus on our herds and staying out of everyone's way. We're able to pick up and move whenever the need arises."

Emzara gestured at the large room. "And your knowledge of building created something so cozy and warm, yet strong, protective, and mobile. It's impressive."

"Yes." Evet added. "But I'm surprised that you, as the leader, have a tent that looks no bigger than any of the others."

"No, my son doesn't look like a chief or a king. And that's how he wants it. We've had quite enough of palaces and powerful people. I think my son's humble lodging suits him quite well."

Jabal lowered his head briefly, acknowledging the comments, before looking over at Noah. "So tell me about you and your group."

"Well, your father and sister haven't changed their ways. They recently took over Iri Geshem, which is why we fled. She wants to kill me — has for quite some time now. This time I barely escaped." Noah stood and paced across the floor. "We plan to travel through Eden to the northwestern lands. That should be far enough away from her reach."

"Eden?"

Jabal's face held an odd expression, and Emzara was unable to categorize what it meant.

"One moment." He turned his full attention to the pregnant animal. Still lying on her side, the beast grunted and bleated loudly.

Emzara watched in fascination as this former prince gently encouraged the creature with soothing words.

Jabal kept his eyes on the bleater. "Noah, you may want to rethink Eden."

"Why?" Noah asked, but the loud grunts from the struggling creature nearly drowned his question.

Jabal clenched his jaw as he deftly worked with the bleater. "Garun. Hand me that towel and water basin over there." His focus locked in on the struggle for life in front of him.

"Is the baby in the wrong position?" Evet looked at Adah.

"I believe so. My son's had to deal with this plenty of times before. One of the shoulders is likely caught. He'll have to reposition it before the baby can come."

"There." Jabal scooted back as the spindly, wet newborn suddenly slid out and onto the ground.

Jabal looked pleased as he turned back to the group. "What were we saying? Oh, Eden." He dipped the towel in the basin and washed his hands and arms. "Strange things happen there. I'm sure you've heard the rumors."

"Yes, but they are rumors," Emzara said.

"That's what we thought, too." He scratched his head. "It's a couple weeks' journey to the west. We settled close to that land at one point many years ago, but we suffered for it. We lost nearly an entire herd and a couple of our herdsmen."

"How?" Noah asked.

"The men spoke of a beast so large and terrifying that it could swallow an entire bleater in one bite. It wasn't worth risking any more lives. We decided to stay away from that area forever."

"Sounds like a grendec."

Jabal nodded. "That's what one of the men called it."

Noah sighed. "Well, I certainly don't want to be foolhardy, but we think that the rumors about Eden will keep unwanted people from coming too close to us."

"Suit yourself." Jabal shrugged and stood up. The mother bleater sniffed her baby as it nosed around her looking for nourishment. "Please be careful."

"We will."

Jabal adjusted his wrap and tightened his belt. "So tell me about the food and supplies you need."

"Well, since we're not sure how much longer we'll be traveling, we'd like to restock our wagons with food and purchase some bleaters from you." Noah looked around the expansive tent. "And I wonder if you might have some of these tents to sell."

Jabal smiled. "I'll see what I can do. How many tents would you like?"

"Let's see." Noah stared at the ceiling as he counted on his fingers and mouthed the names of people in their group. "Six, I think."

"Make it five," Purlek said as he stood.

"Who else is sharing one?" Noah asked.

Purlek grinned and pulled Evet to his side.

Embarrassed, Evet stepped back. "But we're not—"

Purlek smiled at her. "I was hoping we could take care of that while we're here."

Emzara beamed, and Noah caught her eye, chuckling.

Evet gasped. "Are you asking me to marry you?"

Taking a deep breath, Purlek looked around the room and then focused on Evet. He took her hand and kissed it. "I'm not good with words, but I know that everything is good when you're near me. Evet, I love you and would do anything to be your husband. Will you marry me?"

She buried her head against his chest and squeezed him tight. "Of course I will. I love you, too."

Purlek kissed her cheek.

Jabal laughed. "It's not every day you get to watch your nephew stumble through a proposal. Let's prepare for a wedding celebration. But first" — Jabal patted Rayneh's head — "I have something I think you might like to help me with. He walked over to a large clay oven and withdrew a fluffy baby bleater from one of the side doors. It blinked its eyes and gave a timid call. "This little one has been left alone by her mother. But we've been able to care for her. We keep her warm in there, but now she needs to be fed. Would you like to help?"

Rayneh hid behind her father. "Uh-huh."

"Wonderful." Cradling the animal with one arm, Jabal grabbed a leather pouch and slipped off the cap. He placed the young one in Elam's lap before sitting down next to him. Then he set Rayneh on his knee and helped her hold the pouch in her chubby toddler hands.

Rayneh giggled as the tiny creature squirmed against her.

"When she's finished, we'll see if the new mother will adopt this one." Jabal pointed to the newborn and mother bleaters in the small pen. "I'll rub some of that afterbirth on this one and hope that the mother will treat her as one of her own."

"Can I help with that?" Emzara asked.

"Of course." Jabal smiled at Rayneh and then looked at her father. "Sometimes, the bleaters who've lost their mothers and are given extra care by those who love them are the ones who turn out the strongest."

Elam put a hand over his heart and nodded at Jabal. "I'm very thankful for our close group here."

Jabal stood and brushed his hands on his wrap. "I suppose we'll need to make some plans for this wedding. The whole community will want to be involved in the celebration."

CHAPTER 16

"I already miss the vast prairie," Emzara looked at Noah as she vigorously scratched the neck of the tusker hitched on the right, causing it to blast a playful honk through its short trunk. She giggled and patted the creature's thick, rough skin. "It doesn't seem like we're getting anywhere. And to make it worse, there are hardly any animals to study, and the sunlight rarely makes its way through."

Noah stared back behind the caravan, searching for a glimpse of the enormous grassland they had traveled for more than two whole moons. But it was long gone now, having given way to the thick forest they had been laboring through for over a week, with no end in sight. Large twisted tree trunks reached nearly 50 cubits high before shooting into a canopy of branches and broad leaves. Smaller plants filled up nearly every open space on the forest floor and thick, thorny vines wrapped themselves around just about everything that stood still. To make things even more difficult, the land had risen on a gentle slope for most of the past three days. Despite all the vegetation, stones marking the edges of an ancient trail occasionally peeked through to guide them.

"Come on, I'll help you up." Noah took her hand as she climbed onto the front of the wagon.

She slowly lowered herself into her seat with one hand on her lower back. "This cushion isn't really helping anymore."

"You should ask Elam if he can make you a larger and softer one."

"That's a great idea." She adjusted her wrap as she tried to get comfortable on the bench. "Do you think we'll get there before the baby is born?"

Noah circled around the tuskers and pulled himself into his spot next to Emzara. He patted her midsection and flashed a half-smile. "I hope so." His curt command set the tuskers in motion. Leaning over, Noah massaged his right foot, digging his thumb deep into his arch. "Just a little rest, then it's back to cutting through more of that stuff."

She tilted her head and stared at him, her eyebrows slightly raised.

Noah knew that look. She sensed his frustration and patiently waited for him to speak it. He sat up and kept his voice quiet. "It's Purlek. I think this slow pace is making him regret his decision to join us. He was excited when we were on the move, but now he's grumbling again about wishing he and Evet had stayed with Adah's people. It was hard enough to persuade them to leave after those two weeks. Now I fear they may turn around and go back."

Emzara sighed. "I saw you talking to him when he gave you a break. I wondered if it was about that again. Do you want me to speak to them?"

"I think he's more likely to listen to Ma-Zara."

A brief smile crossed her face before she shifted into a more comfortable position by reclining and putting her hands on the bench behind her for support. "Do you think it's coming more from him or Evet?"

"It's hard to say, but if I had to guess, I think most of it's from him. She seems pretty content to be part of this group." Noah shrugged. "He grew up in a large city and spent the last two decades in a busy river town." Noah stretched an arm toward their little caravan. "Pushing slowly through this forest can't be the most exciting thing for a young man and his new bride."

"That's what I was thinking. I'll look for the right moment to talk to him." She pushed herself upright and adjusted her cushion again. "Don't get too worried about it. You know that the Most High will make sure we have the right people to do all that He has commanded you."

"I know." Noah looked at the canopy above them and let out a breath. "But that's part of my concern. We have a huge task ahead of us, and I hope I won't have to do all the woodworking *and* metalworking. It would be great to have a blacksmith — and not just to take some of my workload — I love having Tubal-Cain's son around."

She slipped her hand into his. "I do, too."

They rode slowly until it was time for evenfeast; having to hack their way through the undergrowth made for little progress. As he had done for much of the journey, Lamech helped Laleel prepare the cold meal in the large wagon. Since they had left Adah and Jabal, Evet had taken charge of a small herd of bleaters and a couple of bovar, and she worked tirelessly to keep them moving along with the caravan.

Emzara turned around and called to Laleel. "How long until it's ready?"

"We're almost finished."

Without warning, Garun stopped the first wagon and jumped to the ground. Noah halted his animals and called for Methuselah to do the same. Wielding thick blades to help them carry out their path-clearing duties, Purlek and Elam spoke excitedly with Garun.

"What's that all about?" Emzara asked.

"I don't know," Noah said as he stepped down from the wagon. "Be right back."

"Why did we stop?" Lamech asked as Noah walked away.

Noah heard Emzara say something to his father, but his attention remained on Garun, Purlek, and Elam. He joined their small cluster. "Is something wrong?"

Elam shook his head. "You need to see this."

Purlek handed his blade to Garun and then hurried back toward the second wagon. Noah and Garun followed Elam and as they passed the lead animals, Noah noticed the vegetation on both sides, especially the vines, thinned out a little. The trees grew straighter, and there seemed to be an increase of birds chirping and singing.

Elam pointed ahead and to their right. "Look closely."

Noah peered through the foliage, tilting his head and squinting. Finally, in the distance he detected the corner of two stone walls. "Is that a building?"

"Or what's left of it," Elam said. "But look over there." He shifted his finger to the left a little. "Notice anything different?"

Noah scanned the area and his eyes grew wide. "It's a clearing."

"Maybe we're finally getting past the thick part of the forest," Garun said.

"Well, at the very least, we can check out that building." Noah took the blade from Elam and hacked at a low-lying branch hanging across the path. "Come on. Let's get to that clearing so that we can look around after evenfeast."

Garun joined him, and the two enthusiastically chopped, slashed, and cut through branches, vines, weeds, and any other obstructions. Oddly enough, Noah's fatigue waned and he felt invigorated. As they proceeded, the ancient trail came into view again, leading toward the stone structure before veering left.

"Should we stay on the path or head to the building?" Garun asked.

"Looks like the trail leads to the clearing," Noah said. "Let's go there first. It'll be easier on the wagons."

Sweat dripped down his face and his surge of adrenaline quickly faded. Slowing to catch his breath, Noah handed the blade back to Elam and put his hands on his knees while Garun and Elam continued on. The forest over the last hundred cubits before the clearing thinned out even more, allowing the men to move quickly.

Finally, Noah ducked under a branch covered with a fuzzy green plant and stepped into the spacious opening. Drawing a deep breath, he took in the scenery. The surprisingly flat, grassy glade stretched about 500 cubits wide and at least twice that in length, although it was difficult to be certain since the sunlight had nearly faded from the sky. The little herd of bleaters and bovar scampered into the open, snatching greedily at the fresh green grass. All around the meadow, the trees shot high and straight into the air. They looked vaguely familiar, but he could not quite remember where he had seen their kind before. To be fair, most tall trees looked similar in low light. Surprisingly, an orchard grew to their left, and many of the trees boasted ripe fruit.

Elam moved alongside Noah. "Looks like we'll have some fresh fruit for evenfeast."

"Unless somebody lives around here." Noah stepped farther into the clearing and looked in all directions. "Hello!" He waited, but no answer came. Noah stared at the colorful fruit. "Let's enjoy some tonight, but keep track of what we take, and I can pay the owner if there is one."

Garun hacked through the final branch and walked toward Noah, breathing heavily and wiping sweat from his brows with his forearm. "What is this place?"

Noah massaged his right shoulder with his left hand. "Not sure, but I think it seems like a perfect spot to camp for the evening."

"Right here?" Elam asked. "Or would you like to get away from the trees a bit?"

Noah shook his head. "Right here is fine. I'd rather not be out in the open without first checking the place out."

"I agree," Garun said. "I'll organize the camp."

Noah rejoined Emzara at their wagon, and Garun directed them into place. As they had done every evening the trail allowed for it, they formed a triangle with the wagons and prepared to eat in the center of it.

Emzara climbed down from her perch with Noah's assistance and gladly stretched out her legs and back. She turned around and reached for her cushion.

Noah put his hand on her arm. "I'll get it. You just find a way to get comfortable." He pulled the padded seat off the bench. "Is there anything else you would like?"

She nodded. "I'd like to deliver this child so I can be of more use to the group. Everyone wants to help me, and I can barely offer any help in return. I feel useless."

"The Creator is giving you time to rest before our child is born. You won't get much rest after that." Noah gazed into her deep brown eyes and smiled. "I know you don't believe me when I tell you this, but you are more beautiful now than the day we met."

She snorted. "I feel like a lunker, and I probably look like one, too."

"Not at all." Noah measured her with his eyes and winked. "More like an earth shaker."

She laughed and slapped his chest before falling into his embrace as they watched the others set up camp.

Purlek and Elam gathered twigs and branches to start a fire. Rayneh followed her father and carried two small twigs. As they set their loads into a pile between the wagons, Rayneh threw her sticks on top of her father's and beamed with pride before chasing him to grab some more. Meanwhile, Laleel and Evet returned from the fruit trees with a basket full of ripe produce. By placing a board across two small crates, Lamech created a makeshift table. Then he pulled trays of prepared food from the large wagon and set them out. Garun worked on starting a fire using two sparking stones, dry leaves, and a handful of the small twigs. Methuselah sat on the ground and blew into Elam's musical rod, but the shrill sounds

118

it produced assaulted Noah's ears. Despite Elam's attempts to teach him, the old man had very little ability in that area.

"Grandfather. Why don't you let Elam play after the meal and you can think of a story to tell?"

Methuselah held up the instrument and laughed. "You don't like my music?"

"What?" Noah grinned. "I can't hear you. You broke my ears."

Emzara laughed and pulled Noah to the other side of their wagon and stared into the clearing. "This place is beautiful. We should stay here for a while."

Noah yawned. "It would be nice to stop moving, but we have a long way to go before we reach our destination."

She sighed.

"We'll have to look around in the morning." He peered over her head, trying to locate the stone structure, but it was blocked by foliage and ever-deepening shadows. "There's a building somewhere over there that I'd like to check out in the daylight."

"I'm not sure how many more bumpy rides our baby can take."

Noah smiled and nodded. "I understand. I'd rather not make a decision until we know more about this place and everyone gives their input."

She nestled against him. "That seems fair, but unless there is something very dangerous here, you know where I stand."

"Hey, Son," Lamech said. "Evenfeast is ready. Come and join us."

Noah pulled Emzara tight against his side and rubbed his own stomach. "And you know where I stand on that."

Chapter 17

Noah rolled over and carefully adjusted his blanket to avoid waking Emzara. A faint light pushed through the thin covering of their wagon, informing him that the sun would soon clear the horizon. He shifted to get comfortable and closed his eyes. He concentrated on slowing his breathing, hoping to get a little more sleep before the others stirred.

As he drifted toward unconsciousness, a memory flashed into his mind. *Grandfather!* Had he dreamed it, or did he actually see the elderly man steal out of the wagon a short while ago? Noah sighed and looked at his grandfather's empty bed.

Sitting up, he rubbed his eyes and then stretched out his arms and legs, causing several light snaps and cracks of his joints. As he slipped on his shoes, Emzara put her hand on his lower back.

"Where are you going?" she asked through a yawn without opening her eyes.

"To check on Grandfather." He leaned over and kissed her forehead. "He stepped out a while ago and hasn't returned yet."

She peered up at him. "Be careful."

He patted her hand and then crept toward the back of the wagon, trying not to wake his father, Elam, or Rayneh. As he lowered himself from the platform, Noah silenced a groan. His achy feet and knees protested the contact with the ground. In the early dawn, he saw the shadowy humps of sleeping animals, but no sign of his grandfather, so he

120

circled their tiny encampment. Cool, damp grass met each step as Noah looked from side to side. *Where could he be?*

The snapping of a twig from the direction of the stone structure seized his attention. Keeping his voice down to avoid waking the others, Noah asked, "Grandfather, is that you?"

An indistinct figure appeared next to the building and moved forward, holding a hand against the stone wall. "Noah?"

"What are you doing out here?" Noah asked as he cautiously walked toward Methuselah. He climbed over a log and ducked under a couple of low branches.

Methuselah chuckled as he drew close. "I knew it."

Noah raised an eyebrow. "Knew what?"

"This place." He lightly slapped the wall twice. "Last night after we went to bed, I couldn't help but think that I've been here before — back when I was only a child."

"Come on, Grandfather. You've never been here. It's just your imagination." Noah held his palm up. "When did you ever travel so far from home?"

"I told you, when I was a mere child." Methuselah tipped his head back and closed his eyes. "I would've been only about six or seven years old. My father and grandfather took me on a long journey to meet—" Methuselah covered his mouth and clutched Noah's shoulder.

Unsure of whether this was a true story, a dream, or the product of an active childhood imagination, Noah nodded for him to continue. "To meet who?"

Methuselah laughed and then spun to study the small stone building, which Noah could now see consisted of just four low walls and a collapsed roof. "This wasn't their home. It was a place for storing food. I remember going in here" — he pointed to the end of the wall, only about 10 cubits away and started walking along it — "in the door over here."

Now fully convinced his grandfather's tale was imaginary, Noah followed along in hopes of persuading the old man to return to bed.

Methuselah turned left and pointed. "Ha. I told you there was a door."

Noah smirked when he saw an opening with a few scraps of a rotted wooden door collapsed on the floor. "You've already looked at the other sides, so the door had to be over here."

Methuselah ignored Noah's remark. "This was only a shed." He closed his eyes and held up a finger to request a moment to think. Then his eyes shot open and he laughed. He pointed across the glade, almost in the direction of their wagons. "Because their home was on that side of the clearing."

"Whose home, Grandfather?" Noah grabbed his arm to stop him. "Who did you come to meet?"

"You don't believe me? Come." Methuselah gestured for Noah to follow him. "I remember there was a small river behind the house."

Noah huffed and trailed him back to the clearing. *Why won't he answer me?*

As they marched across the glade, Emzara shuffled toward them as quickly as a woman more than eight whole moons into a pregnancy could move. She walked alongside Noah. "What are you two doing?"

Noah shook his head. "Grandfather says he's been here before, but he won't answer my question."

"What question?" Emzara asked.

"He said his father and grandfather brought him here to meet someone, but he didn't say who."

"Did you ask him?"

Noah rolled his eyes. "Two or three times. He keeps talking about *them*, but won't say who *they* were."

Emzara touched his arm. "Maybe you just didn't ask the right way." She took a few quick steps and caught up to Methuselah. Gently slipping her arm under his, she said, "Morning peace, Grandfather."

"Yes, morning peace, child." Methuselah continued his determined walk across the glade, largely ignoring her presence.

Emzara pulled his arm gently and stopped him. "Grandfather. You said you've been here before?"

He nodded. "Yes, so many years ago. I was only a child."

"And who did you come to see?" she asked.

He quirked an eyebrow and snorted. "Who?" He shook his head, apparently amused that anyone would ask such a question. "Why Great-father and Greatmother, of course. This is where they lived." He pulled his arm away and continued his march toward the trees.

Noah's grin from watching his wife and grandfather vanished, and he stopped cold.

Emzara's mouth hung open as she turned and stared at Noah.

For a moment, neither of them could speak. Noah blinked and breathed in. "Did he just say what I think he said?"

Emzara laughed and bounced on her toes.

"It can't be." Noah grabbed her hand and gently pulled her toward Methuselah. "Come on. He said that their home was over this way."

The sun began to bathe part of the field in a soft glow, but the tall trees still cast long dark shadows over the eastern side where they had camped. Methuselah reached the tree line on the southeast corner. He stopped and looked from left to right, giving Noah and Emzara an opportunity to close the gap.

"Do you see it?" Noah asked.

Methuselah stared into the abundance of flora in front of him, a disappointed look growing on his face.

Noah stepped past his grandfather and pushed some of the brush out of the way, searching for any hint of a house. After several moments he turned and faced the old man. "Maybe you don't remember it correctly."

"I was so sure of it." Methuselah kicked at the ground.

"Grandfather." Emzara stood a few dozen cubits to their left pointing into the woods. "You may want to see this."

Methuselah and Noah exchanged an excited glance and then hustled to Emzara.

"Did it look something like that?" she asked.

The old man put an arm around her and smiled. "Just like that."

Noah stared at the house in disbelief. Tucked away behind a couple of fallen and mostly decomposed trees, a stone building rose from the forest floor. The place might have been a little more than half the size of Lamech's house, and like the structure on the other side of the clearing, the remains of a thatched roof had fallen inside of it.

"Listen," Emzara said. "Do you hear that?"

"It sounds like a river." Noah flashed a sheepish grin at Methuselah, who crossed his arms and nodded. A twig snapped and Noah spun to face the camp.

"What are you three doing?" Lamech asked as he approached.

Methuselah pointed at Noah. "Your son was just telling me how good my memory is."

Lamech stared past them. "Is that a house?" He scratched his cheek. "Your memory? What does that have to do with you being out here so early?"

"He says he's been here before," Noah said.

"When were you ever so far from home? And why would you come here?"

"Because his father wanted him to meet Greatfather and Greatmother," Emzara said.

Lamech stared wide-eyed. "You never told me any of this."

"That's because I was so young, and I couldn't remember if it was real or if I had just imagined it."

"So you're telling me that Greatfather lived in that house?" Lamech asked.

"That's right." Methuselah shook his head and chuckled. "I can't believe I remembered this place after more than 850 years."

"What else do you remember?" Lamech asked.

Methuselah closed his eyes and then slowly shook his head. "Maybe I'll think of more if we go inside."

"Let's find out," Noah said. He moved ahead and led them toward the house, picking his way around overgrowth, trying to find the easiest route. "Was there a specific reason your father wanted you to meet them — besides the novelty of meeting the first two people?"

"We came with my grandfather, too." He cocked his head and looked at Emzara while he counted on his fingers. He chuckled. "Jared was your father's grandfather."

Emzara's eyes brightened, and she slipped her hand into Noah's. "I've never heard about any of this."

"I remember my grandfather wanted us to learn the truth about our world from those who were here at the beginning." Methuselah sighed. "Unfortunately, I was so young and it was so long ago that I recall almost nothing of what they said. I remember thinking about how old they were. At that point, they were the only people I'd seen with gray hair. Now we all have it." He touched the top of his head and looked at each of them. "Oh, the serpent. I remember they warned us about the serpent."

"That was good advice," Noah said as he finally reached the front of the house. Like the other structure, this one's door had mostly decayed.

Noah pushed the little bit that was left of it and it simply crumbled to pieces and fell to the ground. The collapsed roof timbers had clearly seen better days. Three of them had decayed all the way through, each leaving two shorter beams on either side of the respective breaks. The significant deterioration in other beams caused Noah to think they were ready to surrender at any time. To his right, a short hall opened to two smaller rooms, a section of the roof still held above them. Instead of thatching, this covering consisted of mud-brick. One large room sat to his left, a fallen stone table occupying the center of the space.

"Don't touch any of the wood," Noah said. "It's too far gone and isn't safe."

"Bring back any memories?" Lamech asked.

Methuselah stared at the two smaller rooms to his right. "Definitely." He stopped at the end of the hall. "My father spent a lot of time with Greatfather Adam all the way back there." After passing the first room, he entered the second and turned to his left. "I don't remember that."

"What?" Emzara asked as she strode toward him.

The old man shrugged. "Painted images, I think. They look familiar, but I can't place exactly where I saw them.

Emzara stared at the walls, her mouth slightly agape.

Hundreds of faded fist-sized images sprawled across the back wall and continued onto the adjoining one to the right. The artwork, directly painted on the stone, had a sense of order, yet some of the depictions converged so closely that they almost wove together. The remaining part of the ceiling blocked much of the light, but it had likely protected the paint from rain over the years.

Emzara tiptoed around debris for a closer look. "They don't seem to be just for decoration."

"I wonder if they tell a story. In fact" — Lamech looked at his father — "Grandfather Enoch had scrolls with pictures much like this."

Methuselah slowly lifted his head. "You're right." He stared intently at the images. "It's too dark to see all of them."

"I'll get a lamp," Lamech said as he turned to leave.

"Grab two, Son," Methuselah said.

"I will."

The left side of the back wall received the most light, but the images there also appeared to have faded more from the exposure. Noah leaned closer to the stone and studied a few of the clearest illustrations. In one, the top half of a man came up from the ground while a wind blew across his face. Or was the wind pushing him into the ground? The next featured several trees. Most of them bore fruit, but two stood apart in the middle, and the one to the left looked too much like the old Sepha skarep tree. Frowning, Noah shook his head. The third image showed four squiggly blue lines emanating from a short central line.

"What do you think they mean?" Emzara asked.

Noah scratched his head, trying to match the sequence with anything he had learned in the past. He glanced to the right to gather a little more context, but decided to wait until his father returned with the light. "I don't know, but I think my father is right. I think they tell a story."

"Grandfather, do you—" Emzara faced Methuselah but stopped her question when she noticed he was praying. Sheepishly, she smiled at Noah. "I guess I'll wait."

Words from Noah's past entered his mind and he snapped back to the first image. "The Creator fashioned our Greatfather Adam out of the dust of the ground and breathed into his nostrils the breath of life."

Methuselah ceased praying and stared at Noah.

"The words from our marriage covenant?" Emzara asked.

Noah smiled wide and touched the picture. "Right here." He stepped back and scanned the two walls. "I think Greatfather might have recorded what happened in the earliest times."

Methuselah nodded. "I think you're right. In fact, they seem to tell the story my father taught me when I was young." His shoulders slumped. "But I failed to pass it on to your father." His eyes watered. "I guess I can do it now."

Lamech reentered the room, breathing heavily and carrying two lit oil lamps. "Here."

Noah took both lamps, handed one to Emzara, and then held his up to illuminate the upper right corner of the side wall.

Methuselah carefully made his way to the lit corner. He closed his eyes, took a deep breath, and let it out. Then he looked at the first several symbols and his lips curled up on one side. "I know what this is describing."

"First, the Creator made the heavens, and then He made the earth out of water. Next, He made the light and separated it from the darkness.

That was the first day." He ran his finger under each symbol as he spoke. On the second day, the Most High separated the waters and created the skies between them." He touched a round symbol with one black half and one white half. "This represents evening and morning. Notice that it appears each time we are shown what the Creator made. On the third day, He created the dry ground and various plants."

"And on the fourth day, he made the sun, moon, and stars, right?" Emzara asked as she pointed to the next series of images.

Methuselah smiled as he looked over the pictures she pointed to. "That's right." He slid a little to his left. "Then He made all the sea creatures and flying creatures on the fifth day."

"I wish I could've seen that," Emzara said.

Noah nudged her with an elbow. "You and your animals."

"Yes, I think you'll like this one," Methuselah said. "On the sixth day, the Creator made all the beasts of the land."

Emzara grinned widely and nodded. "That would've been amazing to see, too."

He reached the point that Noah had figured out earlier. "You were correct, Noah. The Most High made Greatfather Adam from the dust of the ground, and He breathed the breath of life into him. He made a garden with all sorts of fruit trees, and He put two special trees in it: the tree of life and this one" — he pointed to the one that reminded Noah of the Sepha tree — "is the forbidden tree." Then he moved on to the next image and gently waved his hand over the four squiggly lines. "The garden had one large river that split into four." He glanced at Lamech. "I don't remember the names of all of them, but I know one — it flows past your house."

"The Hiddekel?" Lamech asked.

"Mmhmm." Methuselah turned back to the wall. "Then Greatfather named the beasts of the field and birds of the air."

Emzara leaned against Noah as Methuselah paused before explaining the next part.

"After that, the Creator put the man to sleep, and He made Great-mother Eve from his rib."

Sounds of sandals scraping against stone caused Noah to turn around just as Garun entered the room.

"Firstfeast is—" Garun stared at the wall. "What is that?"

"We'll explain over firstfeast," Lamech said. "Is it ready?"

Garun blinked and then quickly nodded. "Yes."

Noah put a hand on Methuselah's shoulder. "We'll come back here after we eat."

CHAPTER 18

Land of Eden — Noah's 500th year

Noah gulped down the water along with his last bite of firstfeast. "Grandfather, let's get back to the house."

Methuselah chewed his food slowly before swallowing and held up his tray to show he still had a little more to eat. "Patience. The markings have survived this long. I think they'll still be there when I finish."

Emzara put her hand on Noah's arm. "Don't get up yet. Let him eat."

Noah blew out a breath in frustration. "Father, you said that you saw some of those paintings before — on scrolls at Enoch's home."

Lamech nodded. "When I was very young."

"Do you think he copied them from here?"

"I'm sure he did," Methuselah said. "He came here a few times to make sure that what he told people was true."

Noah held out a palm toward his grandfather. "So what happened to the scrolls?"

Methuselah pursed his lips and paused for a moment. "Setela probably has them. When the Creator took my father, my older brother inherited the house and land. But he sold those centuries ago and moved toward Nod. We haven't spoken since." Methuselah shrugged. "I don't even know if he's still alive."

Noah crossed his arms. "It would've been nice to know what they said, especially if it's more than what we have here."

Without warning, Emzara winced and pitched forward.

Noah stroked her back gently. "Are you alright?"

She inhaled deeply and slowly let it out through gritted teeth and then repeated the process. Finally, she sat up, looked at Noah, and nodded as she caught her breath.

Evet dropped to the ground in front of her. "Can you describe what you felt?"

"All of a sudden, it seemed like someone squeezed my whole midsection. But then it went away almost as fast as it came on."

"Was that your first one?" Evet asked.

"First what?" Noah asked.

Evet grinned at Noah. "I think you may get to hold your son today."

Noah bolted upright. "What? Today?" He gently grabbed Emzara's arm. "Do you need anything?" Before anyone else could speak, he turned to Evet. "What can I do?"

Evet chuckled. "Well, you can calm down. Labor pains move at their own pace. They're difficult to predict and sometimes women feel them days or weeks before they deliver their baby. Although that one seemed pretty strong. I'd be surprised if it'll be that long." She rested a hand on Emzara's knee. "Tell me when you feel another one."

"I will." Emzara looked into Noah's eyes. "We'll be fine." She smiled and added, "All three of us."

"Come on, Grandson. I'm not going to wait all day."

In his excitement, Noah had failed to realize that Methuselah now stood behind him, ready to leave. Desiring to stay with Emzara, but longing to hear about the rest of the symbols, Noah hesitated. "I—"

Emzara struggled to her feet. "I'm going, too."

Glancing at Evet, Noah asked, "Is that a good idea?"

"Yes, Noah. She'll be fine for now." Evet stood and brushed the dust from the back of her wrap. "Purlek and I will go with you."

Noah jumped up, adrenaline still racing through him. He looked back and forth between his wife and his grandfather and then settled on Methuselah. "Well, what are you waiting for, old man? Let's go."

"We'll clean up around here." Laleel gestured to herself and Garun. "From what you described, it doesn't sound like there's enough space for all of us in that room. We'll come take a look at it later."

"We'll stay, too," Elam said as he bounced Rayneh on his knee.

"Maybe Emzara can put her artistic skills to use and copy the paintings," Lamech said. "After having the baby, of course."

Emzara smiled and clasped her hands together. "I'd love to."

Purlek and Evet walked next to Emzara and Noah as they followed Methuselah and Lamech back to the house. They soon found themselves in front of the scenes on the walls again, and Methuselah summarized what he had said earlier for the benefit of Purlek and Evet. During his review, Emzara endured another contraction, but she insisted it was not too painful.

"This is incredible," Evet said, peering closely at the picture of the trees in the garden. "My grandparents followed the Creator, so I've heard some of these things from them. I've always assumed they were just legends, though, because that's what my parents said."

"Unfortunately, that's what most people are told now." Noah looked at Purlek. "Your parents believed in the Creator. Your father saw just how awful the teachings of Nachash are and how they pervert the truth. And his sister—" Noah stopped, unwilling to utter words that might sound like an accusation against Purlek. Also, despite Noah's disdain of Naamah and all she stood for, he often wondered if he could have done more during her first visit to Iri Geshem to help her understand the truth. *Maybe this world wouldn't be in such a mess.* Noah dropped his gaze to the floor.

"I know that my aunt is the high priestess." Purlek scratched at his nose. "My father warned me about her, my grandfather, and Nachash."

Methuselah moved back to the right side of the room, carrying an oil lamp. He cleared his throat. "Speaking of Nachash." He pointed to the first few illustrations on the next line of images. "The serpent, Nachash, came to Greatmother near the forbidden tree. The Most High had warned man that he would die if he ate from it. But Nachash told Greatmother that the Creator restricted people from eating the fruit of that tree because He didn't want them to become like gods. He tempted her, and tragically, she believed his lie and ate it."

"And then she gave some to Greatfather?" Lamech asked as he touched the wall just under the next picture.

"Yes." Methuselah looked away, with pain etched on his face. "And he ate, too. They both disobeyed God." Moments later, he controlled his emotions and focused on the wall again. "For the first time, they recognized their nakedness and shame, and they made coverings for themselves by sewing leaves together. That's when they heard the Creator in the garden, so they hid among the trees."

Noah took Emzara's hand in his and looked at the others. Everyone appeared to be captivated by Methuselah's words.

"What happened next?" Evet asked.

"The Most High announced His judgment on each of them. The serpent was cursed to crawl on its belly all its days. And I think this picture is showing that Nachash would be at war with the woman, and his offspring would war with her offspring. One of her descendants would bruise Nachash's head, but Nachash would bruise his heel."

"What does all of that mean?" Purlek asked.

"I'm not really sure," Methuselah said and then looked at Noah. "I think the Creator is showing that He offers hope and victory in the midst of judgment. Someday, Nachash will be defeated."

"I can't wait until that happens," Noah said.

"What's that one?" Evet asked, moving toward the next image. "It looks like Greatmother is pregnant."

"That's part of the judgment for their sin, and one that Emzara is going to know all too well in the near future. He promised that women would have great pain in childbirth."

Emzara squeezed Noah's shoulder hard and bent over slightly. "Another one."

Evet took Emzara's other hand and stroked her arm gently until the pain subsided.

Finally, Emzara looked up with a grin. "I guess that was good timing. Maybe you shouldn't read any others about childbearing."

Methuselah chuckled and faced the wall again. "It also looks like there would be some contest or struggle between the man and his wife. And this one is for you, Son." He tapped the image to the left, which showed a man working hard to remove weeds from his crop. "The ground was cursed to produce thorns that would make his work more difficult."

Lamech put a hand on Noah. "And that's where you got your name. Even back then I longed for rest from those toilsome days."

Noah nodded and gestured to their surroundings. "It makes me even sadder, knowing how Greatfather and Greatmother lost so much through their disobedience. All the hard work, all the sicknesses, all the wars, and all the death . . . all because they rebelled."

"That's the next image," Methuselah said. "Man was going to return to the dust. God said man would die if he ate the fruit, and we've sure seen the truth of that statement. But the Most High showed them mercy. Instead of immediately killing them for their sin, which is what they deserved, He sacrificed animals in their place and gave the skins to cover them."

"And our sacrifices today are based on that first one?" Noah asked.

"Indeed. Each sacrifice is a reminder that we deserve to die for our sins, but God has allowed us to use animals as temporary substitutes."

"And then it looks like He sent them out of the garden," Evet said.

"Exactly. The Most High banished them from the garden so that they could never eat from the tree of life and live forever."

"Why is there a fiery sword over the path?" Noah indicated the part of the illustration where two people walked away from a beautiful cluster of plants.

"He stationed guardians and a flaming sword there to prevent anyone from entering again."

Noah scratched his chin as he tried to process everything.

"Come out here!" Garun's shout interrupted their lesson. It sounded like he yelled from the clearing.

Noah crossed his arms and raised his voice. "Can it wait?"

"I'm pretty sure you'll want to see it!"

"We can finish up later," Methuselah said, patting him on the shoulder. "Let's go see what Garun wants."

The group picked their way through the brush again. The trail became a little easier to traverse each time they walked it.

"What was so important?" Noah asked as they approached Garun and Laleel.

"We decided to take a walk around the clearing," Garun said. "You won't believe what we found. Come on." He waved his arm for the group to follow him.

Emzara grabbed Evet's shoulder and reached for her midsection. "Another one. Stay with me." She glanced up at Noah. "You go ahead without me, but don't be gone too long."

"It's not very far," Garun said.

"I'll return soon." Noah kissed Emzara's forehead. "Be safe."

"I will."

"I'll stay with her, too," Laleel said.

The men walked quickly along the tree line to the south. The morning sun lit up the glade and surrounding vegetation. Noah's focus shifted to the massive trees, struggling to figure out why they looked so familiar.

Garun pointed in the distance. "It's up at the little mound."

Noah guessed they still had a hundred cubits or so to cover.

Methuselah let out a little laugh. "I just remembered something else."

"What?" Lamech asked.

"These trees." Methuselah swept his arm to his left. "Look how big they are."

"I think we can see that they're large, Father."

"I know, but when I was here as a boy, my father helped Greatfather plant a lot of these gopherwood trees."

The words echoed loudly in Noah's head. He looked wildly around the glen, shocked that the entire area was surrounded by the tall, straight timbers.

"What's the matter?" Methuselah asked. "Was it something I said?"

Noah nodded toward the forest. "Did you say these were gopherwood?"

Methuselah raised an eyebrow and smiled. "Yes, my father helped plant them. I think Greatfather said they were his favorite. They grow tall and straight and don't have any fruit on them."

"Are you sure?" Noah asked.

"Of course I'm sure. What's the matter with gopherwood?"

Noah's eyes welled up. "Nothing's wrong with them." He looked quickly at each of the men. "I told you before that when the Most High appeared to me, He told me that I needed to build an ark. What I didn't tell you was that He said I was to make it out of gopherwood, but I didn't know what kind of wood that was."

Methuselah laughed. "Well, you do now."

"And now I know why I've seen these before. They were in my vision. And so were the house and the little river. This is what the Creator showed me. He knew I would come here." Noah put his hands on his head and spun around.

Garun stopped and pointed to the mound. "Did you see this in your vision?"

Noah stared at the small rise and then something out of the corner of his eye caught his attention. Directly behind the tiny hill, two massive gopherwood trees, much larger than all the others rose from the ground. He looked back at the raised ground again and then to the trees. "This is the spot." He dropped to his knees, tears of joy streaming down his cheeks. He pointed to the mound. "Right here. The Most High stood right here when He spoke to me."

Lamech knelt beside Noah and put an arm around him. "He has truly guided us here. This field. These trees. He has prepared all of it for you to build His ark."

Noah hugged his father and then shakily climbed to his feet. He sniffled, wiped his eyes, and turned to Garun. "So why did you lead us out here?"

Garun gestured for the group to follow him to the other side of the mound. "This is where Greatfather and Greatmother are buried. Look."

Silence hung over the group as Noah stared at the grave markers bearing the names *Adam* and *Eve*. Overwhelmed by the revelations of the morning, Noah could not even think about speaking. All his life, he had begged the Most High to speak to him, and then in one brief encounter outside Novanam, the Creator had done so, revealing so much more than he had realized at the time. Noah saw now that the Most High had worked everything out long ago, even before Greatfather planted these trees. Awed, he bowed his head and quietly thanked the Creator for His guidance and provision.

"I think we should offer a sacrifice tonight," Lamech said.

They all agreed.

Purlek stepped forward and motioned to the ground in front of him. "I can see the graves of Greatfather and Greatmother, but who is in this third one?"

Noah's attention snapped to where Purlek stood. He had failed to notice it before, but sure enough, a third grave lay before them.

"Noah!"

Elam came running toward them, waving excitedly to get their attention. His smile stretched ear to ear. "It's time. Emzara needs you."

* * *

"Thank you, Evet." Noah refused to take his eyes off the little bundle resting in his arms. For several moments after his birth, the infant had screamed, but he calmed down after cuddling with his mother. Noah grappled with a vast array of emotions as he watched Emzara bond with their child. With the assistance of some wispy tree bark, she had endured all the pains of childbirth, just like Grandfather said she would. Then she held the fruit of her labor and wept with joy. Even after the long struggle, her sweaty, tear-stained, and tired face struck Noah as the epitome of beauty in the world. Finally, after Evet had cleaned up a little, she softly transferred the baby boy to his father. Then she left to give Noah and Emzara time alone with their newborn.

Noah slowly marched around the interior of the tent, which the men had set up for them. The spacious shelters they had purchased from Adah's people would suit the families well until more permanent structures could be built. He had seen tents before, but Jabal had perfected the craft in essentially creating a home that could easily be transported from one place to the next.

Noah carefully stroked the black hair on the tiny head in his arms and beamed. Without closing his eyes, he offered a silent prayer. *O Most High, You are so faithful and so good. Our many years of frustration and disappointment have been overshadowed in one day of unspeakable blessing. Knowing that You guided us to this very spot that You set apart and prepared for the building of the ark — and that You chose me to be a part of it — O Creator, I don't know what to say. And now this.* Tears clouded his vision as he stared at his son. *This. The first of the sons You foretold. My words could never express my gratitude, and I know they surely could never express Your majestic glory and goodness. Thank You.* He pulled the child in a little tighter. *Thank You!* He slowly lifted his eyes toward Emzara.

Breathing deeply with a satisfied smile across her lips, she stared back at him and blinked. "So what do you think?"

"He's perfect. Just like his mother."

"You mean just like his father." She slid herself back a little in order to sit up a bit more. "Do I ever get to hold him again?"

Noah shook his head playfully before placing him carefully on her chest. "I think we should name him before the sacrifice tonight."

Emzara kissed the baby's head. "I agree. Now that you've seen him, what would you like to call him?"

"He should bear the name of an honorable man." Noah knelt beside her and caressed her head. "How about Ara?"

She smiled up at him, but then shook her head. "It's a wonderful name, but I think it'd be too hard for me to say it all the time."

"I understand."

"What if we named him after my mother's father? We only saw him a couple of times over the years, but he was an honorable man. And it'd bring back only pleasant memories to hear his name."

"So you want to name him Japheth?"

Emzara bit her lip and nodded. "If you agree."

Noah beheld his son and mouthed the name Japheth a couple of times. He turned back to Emzara and kissed her forehead. "He looks like a Japheth to me."

She smiled and a tear dripped from her eye. "Come here." As he bent forward, she stretched up and kissed him. "Thank you. He does look like a Japheth." She offered their son back to Noah. "Would you like to introduce him to our friends?"

Noah gave her a confused look. "You want me to invite them in here?"

She shook her head. "Take him outside and introduce them to Japheth."

Noah cradled the baby in his arm and stood tall. "I'd love to." His chest puffed up and he smiled wide as he strode toward the tent's opening.

CHAPTER 19

Emzara leaned her back against the side of the wagon bed, with Japheth cradled in her arms and Methuselah sitting on the bench in front. Initially, she had offered to walk to the mound, but Noah insisted that they take the cart so she had a clean, more comfortable place to sit during the sacrifice. His overprotective care for her well-being reminded her of their time in Havil shortly after their wedding.

As the flames slowly consumed the pair of animals on the altar, she looked at the perfect face of her sleeping son and shook her head, knowing that he would sin just like Greatfather Adam and everyone else. Noah would need to teach him the significance of their sacrifices.

As the evening air cooled, Emzara pulled the blanket snug under Japheth's chin. Noah looked her way. His face was always grim after killing an animal. He raised his eyebrows slightly and Emzara wondered how the birth of their son affected his thoughts. Lamech and Elam stood somberly near the altar, their bloodied arms and tunics a testament to their participation in the ceremony.

"Creator God, we thank You," Lamech prayed, and Emzara looked up toward the heavens. "Thank You for bringing us to this place. We offer up praise to You for Your mighty works. You have continuously shown us Your faithfulness. Like a guard, You have preserved us from the evil intentions of our enemies.

"We praise You for new life. Like a farmer, You will tend to young Japheth and Rayneh as they flourish and grow. Help us to train them in Your ways.

138

"Like a master craftsman, You have a plan for everything and everyone here. You guide and direct us and prepared this place long before we arrived. We marvel at the perfection of Your ways, even though we do not fully understand them.

Please continue to watch over and bless us. May Your holiness and mercy be ever before our eyes, and may the paths we tread be pleasing in Your sight."

As his words faded, everyone remained silent until Rayneh tripped over Purlek's foot. Her bottom lip quivered as he picked her up. "Careful, little one," Purlek said as he brushed off her knee. "There, all better." He tickled her midsection and she giggled.

Rayneh lifted her arms in the air. "Up."

Purlek kissed her chubby cheek and placed her on his shoulders. "Methuselah, what can you tell us about the third grave there that is separated from the other two?"

Methuselah slowly climbed down from the front of the wagon. "This sacrifice is the perfect backdrop to what happened." He paused, and as with other natural storytellers, his demeanor drew everyone in.

Noah moved closer to Emzara and put an arm on hers while the others moved closer to Methuselah.

"Just like you, my dear Emzara" — Methuselah nodded in her direction — "Greatmother Eve experienced the joy of motherhood. Her eldest was named Cain, and their second born they called Abel. Cain tilled the ground and tended the crops, much as you have done, my son." He smiled at Lamech. "And Abel became a keeper of flocks.

"Greatfather had many other sons and daughters, and Cain married one of his sisters, and Abel did the same. But after they were grown and had started families, something terrible happened between them. Cain couldn't stand the way that Abel seemed to thrive. Abel had fathered two sons and a daughter but Cain had no children at the time."

Emzara stroked Japheth's cheek and bent down to kiss his soft skin. She wondered if Cain and his wife struggled to produce children and she understood the pain they might have faced.

A strong, steady gust of wind blew through the camp, and a cloud passed in front of the moon. The telltale scent of a storm filled the air.

"I think we'd better move inside before the rain hits," Lamech said. "We have room in our tent, if you want to meet in there."

"Grandfather," Noah said. "Take Em and the wagon back to the tents. I'll help clean up around here." He turned and raised his voice. "If anyone wants a ride in the wagon, it's leaving now."

* * *

Seated inside Lamech and Methuselah's tent, Emzara resituated the swaddled, sleeping baby in her lap. She thought about laying him down on the pillow beside her, but the urge to watch and feel her newborn breathe overrode her desire for sleep.

"Was he worth waiting for?" Lamech asked, tipping his head toward the infant.

Emzara gave him a tired smile. "Worth every year of it."

"I can't express how proud I am of you and Noah." Lamech's eye twinkled in the soft glow of the various oil lamps in the tent. "Whenever you get tired of holding him. . . ."

"You'll get another chance." Emzara grinned. "Maybe in a few weeks."

With Lamech's assistance, Methuselah slowly sat down between her and Lamech. He turned to Emzara. "But I get to hold him before my son does."

"Of course." Emzara winked at him before glancing around the room. Garun and Laleel played with Rayneh while Elam picked at his fingernails, trying to remove bits of encrusted blood from the sacrifice.

A flash of lightning briefly illuminated the darkness outside the tent, giving her a glimpse of the rain pounding on the roof and sides of the shelter. Emzara gently covered Japheth's ears so that the impending peal of thunder would not wake him.

"Hurry up." Purlek's voice mixed with a laugh as loud footsteps raced closer to the tent's opening.

A moment later, Evet ducked under the flap, trailed by Purlek and then Noah. Her hair and clothing drenched from the sudden downpour, Evet chuckled as she wiped her face with the back of her hand. "I guess we were a little too slow."

"Here." Lamech tossed dry cloths to her and Purlek.

Noah used the inside of his wrap to wipe off his face before making his way toward Emzara. "What did we miss?" he asked as he found a spot beside her.

"Nothing yet," Emzara said.

He held out his damp hands toward Japheth. "My turn?"

Emzara playfully turned her shoulder away from him. "Not while you're soaking wet. But you can have this." She quickly kissed him on the cheek.

"That'll do." He smiled warmly at their child. "At least for now."

She winked at him and then nudged Methuselah. "Grandfather, do you mind telling us more about what happened with Cain and Abel?"

He straightened. "I'd love to."

"You just started telling us about something terrible happening between the brothers." Using an oil lamp, Garun lit the firepot in the middle of the tent.

"Yes." Methuselah squinted and stroked his beard. "Ah, that's right. The young men brought their sacrifices to the Most High."

"Like the one we just offered?" Purlek asked.

"Well, yes, but not quite the same. Abel's sacrifice was like ours. It was the best of the animals in his herd. But Cain offered the fruit of his labor with the land. You can clearly see the images at the house that depict the distinct sacrifices. It reminded me of the lessons my father instilled in me. The Creator was displeased with Cain. He told him that he would be accepted if he did what was right. Sadly, Cain didn't heed the warning."

Noah shook his head slowly. "I can't imagine hearing God and refusing to obey Him. Must have ripped Cain up inside."

"It did more than that. Cain became furious, and rather than dealing with his anger and pride, he gave into it. One day, while the two were alone, he murdered his brother Abel."

A gasp escaped Emzara's lips, and she instinctively clutched at her son. Tears filled her eyes at the thought of what Greatmother Eve must have endured. *Did Cain or another of her children tell her what became of Abel? Or did she sit and wait for days for her son to return?* She shivered and held Japheth tighter.

"Our world is very wicked, but I can see that really wickedness has pervaded our hearts since that first choice to sin." Garun furrowed his eyebrows. "How poisonous it is to rebel against the commands of the Most High."

Methuselah nodded gravely. "God punished Cain and sent him away to wander the earth for the rest of his days. He separated from his parents, taking his wife with him. God was merciful, though, and gave them a family. Cain then built a city in the land of Nod and named it after his son."

"It's such a sad portion of our history," Emzara said.

"Enoch," Noah said as if thinking out loud.

"That's correct," Methuselah said. "Now I think I understand one of the reasons my father kept going back to that place to warn them."

"Because he had the same name as the city?" Noah asked.

"Yes. I think he felt an extra burden for that place."

"So Noah, Rayneh, and I encountered the descendants of Cain when we crossed paths with the Nodite army?" Elam broke a twig and tossed it into the small fire.

"Mmhmm. They became a mighty people." He pointed to Purlek. "If I'm not mistaken, you're one of his descendants."

"I am." Purlek grabbed Evet's hand. "But I'm not like Cain. I want to follow the Creator's ways."

She nestled against him. "I know."

"Many of Cain's descendants believed in the Creator. My father told me about some of the ones he met in his travels." Methuselah shifted in his seat. "Cain wasn't the only one to whom God gave a son after all of this. Greatmother Eve also gave birth to another son. She named him Seth." He gestured to Noah, Emzara, Lamech, and himself. "We're his descendants. I'm not sure about the rest of you."

Garun slid an arm around Laleel. "We're from Ma'anel, one of Greatfather's youngest sons."

"What about you, Elam?" Lamech asked. "Do you know your lineage?"

Elam focused thoughtfully on the crackling flames in front of him. "My father told me we were descendants of Zakar, the second-born son of Abel."

Laleel leaned forward and pointed at both Purlek and Elam. "How interesting that we have descendants of both Cain and Abel here."

"I'm glad you two get along better than your ancestors did," Emzara said.

"Me, too." Elam laughed. "I don't think a seamster is a match for a blacksmith in a fight."

Purlek smiled at him. "You have nothing to fear from me." He shrugged and snorted. "Besides, I need someone to make clothes for me."

Laughter filled the tent, and Emzara treasured the tight bond of friendship within the group. When they all quieted, she asked, "So was there anything else on the wall about Cain and Abel?"

Methuselah closed his eyes and twisted his lips as he thought. "There was. Cain hoped that no one would find out what he did, but the Creator confronted him. He said that the blood of Abel cried out to Him from the ground. Part of his punishment included a promise that the land would not yield its fruit to him."

"Abel's blood cried out from the ground. I wonder. . . ." Elam spoke slowly. "It's been a tradition of my people as we're praying to the Creator to place one ear on the ground."

"I remember the first time I saw the Zakari do that. I meant to ask about it."

"I never gave it much thought, but now that I know our history, I wonder if Zakar started the practice as a way to honor his father." Elam ran a finger across his lips. "Or maybe we do it to receive an answer, as if Abel's blood really does cry out."

"Maybe both," Lamech said. "Perhaps Zakar started it as a way to honor his father, but maybe as time went on, it became more of a tradition detached from its true meaning."

"That makes sense to me." Elam picked Rayneh up into his lap as she ran into him. He kissed her forehead and spoke softly. "We just found out a little more about our people."

She giggled and leaned in until her face almost touched his.

"There is one more thing about Cain," Methuselah said.

"What is it?" Purlek asked.

"God placed a mark on him to protect his life. Anyone who killed Cain would face retribution sevenfold."

"What sort of mark?" Purlek asked. "And who would he need to be protected from?"

Methuselah raised an eyebrow. "Remember, his brothers and sisters were also Abel's brothers and sisters. And Abel already had a couple of sons. Any of those people may have sought vengeance on Cain for his actions."

"And that's what King Lamech boasted about," Noah said. "The last time we went to Havil, he bragged about killing Aterre, and said that if Cain was to be avenged sevenfold, then he would be avenged 77 times."

"Sounds like he knows his history," Lamech said.

"And he also sounds very prideful," Methuselah said.

"More than you can imagine." Noah rubbed the back of his neck.

Purlek stood and helped Evet to her feet. "It's good to learn what happened in the lives of our forefathers, even if it's not always what we want to hear. It helps us make sense of some of the things we encounter today. Thank you, Methuselah, for telling us what you've learned."

As the group exchanged farewells for the evening, Emzara looked down at her tiny son as he rested. His lashes lay in perfect form on his cheeks, like carefully fanned out stalks of grain after the harvest. *I'm going to tell you and your brothers the story of where we all came from so that you can tell future generations. We must never forget.*

CHAPTER 20

Havil — Noah's 530th year

"Careful, you fool." Naamah glared at the servant as he fumbled near the wooden stand, rattling the many glass bottles filled with various potions that rested on it. The man quickly added the new vials to the inventory and rushed out of the room.

Standing at the foot of the bed, Naamah turned and looked at her handiwork. Under her orders, tapestries enhanced with symbols of the dark arts had replaced the gaudy decorations that once adorned her father's bedroom walls. Statues of Nachash had taken the place of the myriad weapons. Additional pillows graced the bed. A new wardrobe to the left held a variety of cloths and towels. The windows bore extra thick fabrics to eliminate all light if needed. The king's chamber was ready for its new occupant.

"Bring him in." She motioned to the man at the door who in turn beckoned to those in the hallway before stepping out of the way. Slowly, six priests carried a stretcher through the entry. A small form lay prostrate on the canvas. Naamah rushed to the seer's side and grabbed his hand.

"Priestess."

"Shhh. Save your strength." Turning to the men transporting him, she pointed at her mentor. "Move him carefully to the bed. His life for yours."

"Naamah, this will not bode well for you if your father finds out."

His breathing increased as four servants carefully transferred him to Lamech's bed.

"You will be by my side while you're sick. I'm doing what I can to make you well, and there's no need to worry about the king. Nachash is on our side."

"But this—"

"Is my father's room?" she finished for him, grinning. "I know."

"Consider everything we've worked for." He tried to sit up on one arm, but after finding the exertion to be too much, he lowered himself back onto the pillows.

"That's exactly what I'm doing. I've had the adjoining room since his precious Adah left years ago. And now I've fixed his room up so you can get better."

"But the king—"

"Is in Iri Geshem ruling and won't be back for several weeks. By our combined wisdom and Nachash's power, you'll be better by then and back in your little hovel, which for whatever reason you love. Until then, consider this your home. I've done my best to bring everything here. See, even your beloved scrolls are close by."

The seer relaxed a little. "Thank you, Priestess."

Naamah busied herself organizing the room, lighting a variety of candles scattered on different stands. Suddenly, a cry emanated from the sick man. She rushed to his side. "What is it?"

"The pain!"

"Melok, bring the priests. Now!" She then gestured at a female servant. "Get the healer. Hurry." Both left the room in haste.

Naamah knelt by the seer's side, fear filling her for the first time. Her knees quivered, and she lowered herself to the floor. She needed to remain strong for his sake. She whispered an incantation over him and gradually increased in volume as her fervor grew.

His face seemed like ash and beads of sweat broke out on his forehead. Could his wide eyes see her fear? Maybe this was the wrong decision to bring him to the palace. Had his condition worsened during the move? Chills swept through her but she pushed back the fear and rocked as she prayed.

"We're here," said a raspy voice at her side.

A group of about 20 concerned priests stood just inside the doorway. Prominent scars from slashing themselves during ritual worship mingled with tattoos of Nachash over most of their bare torsos.

"Begin immediately!" She stepped closer to the seer's head to allow them space. Soon the smell of incense filled the room. Two priests sat down and beat rhythmically on drums. Breathing deeply and closing her eyes, Naamah told herself everything would be well. Surely Nachash would spare the man who meant the most to her.

After what seemed like eternity, she peeked at her mentor, but there was no change. Angry at her helplessness, she looked around for the healer and found him by the door. She pushed aside the priest closest to her and hurried across the room. To his credit, the priest never wavered in his intercession.

She grabbed the healer's shoulder. "You saw him before. Tell me, has moving him here made him worse?" She cringed, hating to vocalize the question that troubled her.

"No, princess, but I fear that these are among his last moments." Concern etched across his face, but she could not tell if it was for the seer's well-being or his own, being the bearer of such unwanted news. For once, her anxiety surpassed her anger, and she did not lash out at him. "Can you do nothing?" *What have I been reduced to, pleading with this insignificant fool?*

"Let me have access to him, and I'll do what I can."

"Fine, but you're not to disturb the priests." She had never put much trust in healers and she certainly was not going to start now. They usually annoyed her, especially since the one in Iri Geshem saved her father's life.

The man tucked his small frame between two of the priests and knelt by the bed. He listened to the seer's ragged, shallow breaths. His fingers poked various places. He held up the patient's left hand and let it drop then repeated the process. Finally, he looked up at her. "It's as I thought. I can do nothing more for him but give him something that may dull the pain. His body is hanging on but I fear his time is very short."

"Fool! You know nothing!"

"He's not responding to the noise in here, to touch, or—"

"Silence!" Naamah straightened to her full height and leveled a withering glare at him. "Thank you for proving to me just how worthless you and your kind are."

He cowered and lifted a small vial to her. "Do you still want the medicine for the pain?"

"Ha! As if that would help." She slapped it out of his hands and it skittered across the floor. "You there." She beckoned to a guard along the wall. When he came quickly to her side, she said, "Restrain this useless man — this pile of refuse. Let him see the might and power of Nachash."

The healer struggled, but he was no match for the raw strength of the soldier. It was like watching a fish squirm in the grasp of a mighty taroc.

Naamah released a loud long wail, which held a single note for several moments and then climbed to a much higher pitch before she took a quick breath. Instantly, the commotion of the priests stopped and they bowed low. Rolling her eyes back into her skull, she bared her arms and moved them in circular patterns over the unconscious seer. Her powerful voice sang incantations he had taught her centuries ago. As she twisted her body and accompanied the eerie sounds with sudden bending at the waist, her fingernails almost grazed the skin of the man she considered to be her father. Low melodic hums came from behind her as the priests added their vocal petitions.

She pulled out a knife and etched a scar on her arm, piercing the skin. Blood oozed and she let it drip onto the seer's bare chest. As the red drops hit his flesh, she breathed deeply, muttering barely above a whisper.

Suddenly, he opened his eyes wide and coughed. His skin reclaimed a tinge of color, and his breathing returned to normal. He held her hand as her tears flowed freely. "Thank you, my daughter."

She bowed her head, silently sobbing as her shoulders shook. After managing to control her emotions, she stood, not caring about the smears of kohl from her black-rimmed eyes. "Praise to Nachash, the all-powerful who has healed his most faithful servant."

The priests in the room repeated her chant.

The healer stared at her from the clutches of the sturdy guard.

"And that's how a true healing is performed." She dismissed them with a wave of her hand and smiled as the guard led his prisoner away. She would grant his release in the morning, after he endured a long night in the dungeon.

Kneeling again, Naamah gently brushed the seer's forehead and temples with a wet cloth while offering prayers of thanksgiving to her god. She adjusted the blankets and tucked the pillows, but left the blood in place. He smiled weakly as he watched her. She finally looked up and noticed they were alone. The warm light from the candles and lamps flickered dimly.

"You saved my life, my dear child." The seer cupped her face with his hands.

"No, it wasn't me. Nachash saved your life. And you helped, through your patient training all these years."

"Ah, but tonight you were his mistress, providing for my healing through your use of his power."

She smiled and let the warmth of his words comfort her.

"Now, my daughter." He brushed her cheeks with his thumb. "You need rest."

"Let me stay with you."

"As you have said, you'll be right in the next room and can hear me should I need you during the night. Be at peace. You've done your greatest service to me already."

* * *

Thrashing from the adjoining room woke Naamah suddenly. Her bare feet hit the floor as she dashed through the curtained entryway. In the moonlight, she glanced at the bed but could not see him. Her heart pounded. She rounded the platform and spotted the seer on the floor, writhing in a tangled blend of man and sheet. The large statue of Nachash cast a shadow on his moving form. He screamed and clawed at the air, causing a shiver of fear to rock her frame from head to toe. Casting about the room wildly, she sensed another presence but saw no one.

Again the seer screamed in pain and jerked his body. She grasped at his hands but missed. Blindly waving in a panic, he scratched her face, and she quickly stepped back. Never had she witnessed anything like this before. She ran behind the towering gold idol and clung tightly to the cold metal. *We saved him today. Why is he behaving this way? Spare his life, I beg — No! I demand it!*

149

Helplessly, she watched from her protected place. The open-eyed but detached man placed his hands on the floor and with strength beyond anything he had exhibited in decades, pushed himself to a seated position. A loud baleful yell emerged from his depths, and she trembled uncontrollably. His eyes locked on hers, but it was as if he stared right through her.

Nachash, what are you doing to your servant? You have the power, save him!

Without blinking, the seer screamed in terror. "The flames! They burn!" Then he collapsed to the ground, his head hitting the floor with a thud.

After many moments of silence, she slowly edged her way around the golden serpent-god, keeping one hand on it for safety. The seer's eyes remained open, staring blankly at the ceiling. *Was he really gone? Or was he under the healing power of Nachash?* She leaned forward, longing to know, but afraid to move much closer.

Without warning, his body convulsed and she jumped back. He wailed again. "The pain, it burns like a thousand fires! O God, what have I d—" His voice caught in his throat. As if someone had extinguished the flame of a candle, a final breath escaped his lungs and his body went limp.

Naamah fell at the molded base of Nachash and let the pain rip her insides to shreds. Feeling smaller and more alone than ever before, she screamed as loud as her lungs allowed. Finally she slumped down and closed her eyes, but only for a moment. The seer's final moments replayed in her mind, haunting her.

CHAPTER 21

Naamah stared at the massive serpent idol behind her father. Not once tonight, in the annual ceremony dedicated to Nachash, had the king credited the mighty god for their victories and prosperity. *How arrogant!* She balled up her fists.

Her temperature rose with the heat of the glare she directed at her father, and his words were drowned out by her hatred and the sound of her own pulse pounding in her ears. She clenched her jaw as she considered how to respond to his irreverence.

Lamech held his arms out and laughed. The roar of the enormous crowd yanked her away from her introspection.

What did he say? Naamah blinked and took a deep breath.

The king strutted back to the gold statue above his throne. He patted it twice and smiled. "Nachash has become more powerful than the Creator by leading the world to follow him."

Naamah relaxed her shoulders a little and lifted her chin, hoping that the king would now give Nachash his due praise and eliminate the need for a potentially deadly confrontation during the ceremony. She wasn't ready to clash with the king openly. Not yet.

Lamech moved proudly toward the front of the stage and beheld the tens of thousands gathered in the vast courtyard. "But just as the serpent sheds its skin as it grows" — the king allowed his gold-bedecked outer robe to slide off his shoulders and drop to the ground — "we have outgrown our need for ideas from the past." He smirked at Naamah before facing the audience and taking a deep breath. "With our defeat of the Nodites, we became more powerful than anyone or anything else — even more powerful than Nachash himself."

"No!" Naamah's scream drew hundreds of gasps from the multitude below. "Don't listen to such profane speech!" She narrowed her gaze at the king. "You—"

Her father scoffed and pointed to a pair of nearby guards. "Bind her."

Naamah reached for the dagger hidden in the bracer, but before she could touch it, a soldier grabbed her wrists in a painful grip, while the other pulled out some rope. She headbutted him, causing lights to explode in her own vision. Her knees buckled slightly as they bound her arms. Her head throbbed as she attempted to focus on her father. "How dare you blaspheme Nachash, the Splendor of the World, the supreme god!"

Chuckling, Lamech swaggered toward her but kept his voice low enough for only those on the platform to hear. "No. How dare you blaspheme and curse me. I am the god of this world now."

Naamah's eyes grew wide, and she struggled to break free from her captors, but their strength far exceeded her own. "Treachery! Blasphemy!"

Lamech slapped her and she tasted blood. "Silence her!"

The guard on her left stuffed a large cloth into her mouth as she writhed and shouted invectives at the king. The pungent odor on the rag nearly made her pass out, but as the blackness closed in on her, she found renewed vigor in her anger. Standing upright and concentrating on taking measured breaths, she ignored the cloth. A second strike from her father did nothing to wipe away the scowl she fixed on him. A tear slid down her cheek from the pain, but it only fed her rage. *Why doesn't Nachash do anything? Why aren't they being struck with another earth shaking like before?*

Turning his back on her, the king returned to the front of the stage and held out his arms. "My people, it saddens me that my own daughter, the princess of Havil and your high priestess for many centuries, has rebelled against me." He waited for the horde to focus on him as he played the victim.

"For several years now, Naamah has sought to usurp my throne." He faced her and shook his head. "Foolish child, did you really think you could keep secrets from me in my own city? I'm well aware of your seditious schemes."

Naamah fought to control the fear rising inside her. *What does he know? What will he do? Prison?* An image of Tubal-Cain's bloodied body on the floor of the arena flashed in her mind. *No, he wouldn't hesitate to kill his own flesh and blood.*

"I know this turn of events may be shocking for most of you." Lamech paced and spoke confidently. "Before announcing her sentence, I will reveal her crimes. When you have heard all, you will agree that my decision is just. First, she has repeatedly challenged my authority as king, both in private and in public, as she has just done again." He stopped several cubits before her and looked into her eyes while speaking quietly. "For the last time."

Walking back across the platform, he feigned sadness. "Imagine. My own daughter inciting treason against the very man who raised her and gave her everything she's ever had." He stood tall and crossed his arms. "But no kingdom can tolerate such dissension and division. And I have tolerated it for far too long."

Lifting a hand above his head, he raised two fingers. "Her second crime is that she attempted to replace me with her mentor during my latest voyage. She moved his belongings into my chambers and even allowed him to sleep in my bed." Once again, he waited for the crowd to express their displeasure and rally behind him. "Men, how would you feel if your own daughter sought to replace you?" He shot Naamah a pained look and placed his hand over his heart.

She screamed at him, but the cloth muffled her cry. His words and actions muddled her thoughts, destroying any hope of escape. *Nachash, help me. We're going to lose everything. Show me what to do.*

"And do you know what happened to this pretender, this would-be father?" After a pregnant pause for effect, he climbed down two steps and sat at the top of the stairs. "The old man died in his sleep on the first night in my room." He shook his head and smirked. "It seems to me that Nachash also disapproved of my daughter's betrayal." His laugh led many in the crowd to mimic him.

A trace of guilt struck her, but she rapidly dismissed it. She seethed at the masterful way her father manipulated the crowd and twisted her actions to be seen in the worst possible light. Always the coward, he afforded her no opportunity to defend herself. *Please, Nachash!*

"But the worst crime of all occurred 30 years ago when we peacefully took over the city of Iri Geshem." He stood again and slowly moved toward her. "For a long time, I tried to deny my suspicions, but her actions have been confirmed. I was poisoned and would've died if it weren't for the fast and skillful work of a master healer." He grinned at her as he spoke of the healer, knowing full well her hatred for their craft.

Holding one arm toward her, he faced the masses. "She put the poison in my cup! She is the murdering wretch who would kill her own father — her king! Now, I ask you, what should I do with such a rebel?"

Thousands of shouts reverberated through the square. "The dungeon! Exile! Death!"

Naamah glared at Lamech and attempted to shout, "I hate you!" but the cloth muffled and distorted the words.

He beheld her and gave her a pained look before dropping his shoulders and lowering his gaze. Slowly, he nodded and faced the crowd again, waiting for the noise to subside. "This is the most difficult decision I've ever made as your king. But in a way, I'm not even making it. My daughter has forced my hand. She has condemned herself through her rebellious actions."

Lamech sighed and turned toward Naamah before his gaze drifted above her head and a wicked smile crossed his lips.

He wouldn't dare! She struggled to break free, but the rope around her wrists held fast.

The king pointed past her. "Put her on the altar she loves so much."

The guards easily dragged her back a few steps and then lifted her onto the blood-stained altar where dozens of infants had just been slaughtered.

"My people, surely it would be just for me to simply carry out this execution in an unceremonious manner. But as a final act of kindness toward her, I believe my daughter would agree that if she must die, she would like nothing better than to give her life as an offering to *her* god."

One guard lashed her feet to separate sides of the slab while the other held her shoulders down.

"Commander Tsek!" The king beckoned the large man across the stage. As Tsek made his way to them, Lamech grabbed the bloodied sacrificial dagger and spun it slowly between him and Naamah, making sure she could see every curve of the glinting blade and his sinister smile behind it.

Tsek stopped beside him. "Yes, my king."

Without taking his eyes off Naamah, Lamech held the jagged knife toward him. "You will have the honor of carrying out the greatest sacrifice ever given to Nachash."

The commander hesitated before shakily taking the blade.

Lamech held up a hand. "Wait." He took a deep breath and raised his voice. "Before Naamah is sacrificed, I will show her one last kindness — an opportunity to speak for herself."

At Lamech's gesture, one of the guards removed the gag from her mouth. She snapped her teeth at the man as he quickly pulled his hand away. Her bindings holding fast, she took in a full breath. Knowing that her fate was sealed, she refused to beg for her life. With a loud and clear voice, she spoke. "The king lies. He seeks to blind you with his crafty words. You know that I have devoted my life to his service. I have sought the wisdom of Nachash for our people and sacrificed much for his intercession. I am innocent of these charges, but my only desire is that Nachash accepts my life as a pleasing offering on behalf of the people." She shook with a level of hatred she had not felt before. "Nachash will judge the king for his actions here today."

Lamech shook his head and mocked her with a sympathetic smile. "Pity. You played your role perfectly for a long time, and there were days that I enjoyed having you around. But now, you're too much of a liability." He stared into her eyes and lowered his hand. "Tsek. Do it."

Naamah's eyes darted to the commander, who remained frozen in place.

"Commander Tsek, did you hear me?"

"Yes, my king." As he slowly raised the dagger, her large brown eyes focused on the man behind the deadly weapon. After what seemed like an eternity, he lowered the blade. "I'm sorry, Majesty. I can't do it."

Naamah released a tense breath.

"Then you will join her." Lamech spun and grabbed the blade's handle. He called several guards over. "Detain Commander Tsek." He stared up at the large man. "After all these years, you defy me."

Tsek did not resist the guards, but he stood tall as they restrained him. "I have no desire to disobey you, but I cannot bring myself to kill the king's daughter."

Lamech snorted and shook his head. "I see now where your loyalty truly lies. I will consider your fate later."

The king clenched a fist and spoke to the audience. "My daughter's treachery has even twisted the loyalty of my most trusted commander. But now her rebellion must end."

Naamah shot a glance at Tsek, but the four guards held him still. "Nachash, save me now. Do not let this wretch get away with defiling your name."

Lamech laughed. "Your serpent god is powerless to stop me because I am now more powerful than he is." He raised the dagger above his head with both hands.

Feeling her head clear, Naamah quickly repeated a spell the seer had taught her years earlier.

Bemused, the king shook his head. "See? Your god can do nothing."

She stared steely-eyed at the sacrificial dagger that she had used so many times before. She stiffened, preparing to feel the cold blade thrust into her midsection. As her whole body shook, she rapidly recited the dark incantation again.

"I'm sorry, Daughter, but there is no god who can save you now." He adjusted his grip on the cruel knife and looked out at the crowd. "I am the most high god!"

Naamah continued chanting as she watched a drop of blood fall from the tip of the blade. It landed on the king's crown, directly on the head of the molded serpent woven around the headpiece. Suddenly, the golden creature turned reddish-green and appeared to move. *Am I dreaming? Did I die?* She blinked hard and watched her father rear back as he prepared to drive the knife into her. The serpent on the crown sprang into action. With the back half of its body intertwined in the crown, its front half slithered down the side of the king's face and plunged its fangs into his neck just as he started to drive the knife downward.

The king shrieked and dropped the dagger as he reached for his neck.

Screams rang out from the crowd as Lamech stumbled. The nearby soldiers jumped back and held their swords toward the small serpent clinging to the king.

Lamech reeled to the side and grabbed his attacker. He tore it away from his neck, ripping flesh away while simultaneously yanking the crown from his head. Staring in horror at the little beast in his hand, he grabbed the arm of the soldier holding Naamah down. "Call the healer!"

Lamech whipped the crown and the attached serpent against the base of the altar and staggered toward his throne.

The guard released Naamah's shoulders and sprinted to the top of the stairway, screaming for a healer.

Naamah lay still and silent, unable to fully believe what she had just witnessed. Slowly, she sat up and scanned her surroundings. Soldiers eyed her warily, and the crowd stood in collective shock. She pointed at her feet. "Nachash has made his decision. Untie me at once."

The soldiers remained still except for Commander Tsek, who pulled away from his stupefied captors. He strode confidently toward Naamah while closely watching the crown near the foot of the altar. He untied her restraints and helped her down from the altar.

Lamech stumbled and fell on his face a few cubits short of his throne. Thrashing wildly about, with blood oozing from his wound, he screamed for the healer and cursed Naamah and Nachash.

"Stop." One of the soldiers pointed his spear at Naamah. His hands shook as he nervously glanced at his fellow guards for support. "The king gave orders."

Her legs weak from the brush with death, Naamah smirked and carefully bent down to pick up the crown. She stroked the serpent before holding the golden prize out toward the guard. "Do you really want to try to stop me?"

The guard withdrew his spear. "No, Princess." He bowed his head and dropped to a knee.

"It's Queen of Havil."

He lowered his head even more. "Forgive me, my queen."

She narrowed her eyes and studied the serpent as it slid in and out of spaces in the jewel-covered crown.

A spine-chilling cry echoed from the base of the throne. The king gasped for air as he struggled on all fours to reach the chair.

"Tsek, come with me." Holding her head high, she marched toward the throne.

Lamech stretched his hand up for the armrest but lost his grip and tumbled to the floor as Naamah arrived. He rolled to his back and stared up at her through fear-filled eyes. "Seventy—" A series of short, labored breaths cut off his words. He groaned. "Seven times."

Naamah loosened the bracer, slid it off her arm, and flung it unceremoniously next to the king. Ignoring his curse of retribution, she stepped over him and ascended the throne. Keeping her gaze on Lamech, she turned dramatically and sat down. "No healer will save you this time."

Lamech reached for his sword, still in its sheath at his waist, but he quickly pulled his hand back toward the gash in the side of his neck as he gasped for air. A final breath rattled out of his lungs, and his movements stopped. His dead eyes remained fixed on the new ruler of Havil.

Naamah lifted her arms and looked to the sky as relief and exhilaration flooded her body. *At last!* She longed to gloat over her father's demise, but first she needed to secure the people's loyalty. "Nachash has punished the king for profaning his great name. Let this be a lesson to all who doubt the power and wisdom of the Great Serpent and his high priestess, the Queen of Havil."

She held the crown out for all to see, and the serpent returned to its position before transforming back into gold. Hands trembling from the euphoria coursing through her, Naamah proudly lifted the crown above her head and slowly lowered it onto her scalp. Closing her eyes, she breathed a prayer of thanks to Nachash for his protection.

The guards from the altar hurried to her and bowed with their faces to the ground. "Hail, Queen Naamah," shouted one of the men, and the others followed suit.

Naamah stood quickly. "Silence." She snapped her fingers and then pointed at the body of her father. "Get that out of my sight."

Stepping down from the throne, Naamah strutted toward the front of the stage. "My people, King Lamech cared only for himself and his power. Now he is gone because he refused to acknowledge Nachash as the rightful ruler of Havil. In my first act as queen, I will correct his mistake. We will exalt Nachash as he leads us into a glorious future."

She spun around and faced the giant serpent statue behind the throne. Slowly, she knelt to the ground, her gaze cocked to watch the crowd below. Pleased that they dropped to their knees as well, she took a deep breath, and with her beautiful voice, she led them in her favorite song of worship.

CHAPTER 22

Land of Eden — Noah's 530th year

Almost to the top. Breathing heavily, Noah lowered himself to the ground. He turned and looked through a small gap in the lush forest around him. Descending tree tops corresponded to the slope he had just climbed. The hill appeared smaller than it felt. In the distance, the large clearing that had been transformed into a tiny settlement was barely visible in the broad woodland.

With the sun high in the sky, he pulled out his waterskin and enjoyed a refreshing swig. He leaned back on his hands and let his mind drift back home as his breathing gradually slowed. Much work had been completed in the last 30 years. At just 20 years of age, his youngest son, Ham, had helped Noah design and construct a sawmill powered by a waterwheel. A satisfied smile crossed his lips as an image of the young boy poring over designs came to mind. *He's going to be a great help in building the ark, especially if he'd stop fighting with his brothers.*

Japheth already stood a finger-width taller than Noah — a fact he often reminded his father of. Under the guidance of his grandfather, Noah's oldest son spent most of his time cultivating and harvesting in the fields with Rayneh. Noah tipped his head back and breathed deeply, pleased that his father had the opportunity to work on the crops with his grandson. Of course, Japheth's aptitude and enjoyment of the work with Lamech meant Noah could focus on something other than farming, which had never been his first love. Growing up together in such a small community essentially forced Japheth and Rayneh to play together throughout their younger years, and now they were virtually inseparable. Shem, on the other hand, did not seem to mind being alone. Born two years after Japheth, he never quite fit in with whatever Japheth and Rayneh were involved in, so he learned to enjoy keeping the bleaters and other livestock. Elam often joined him in the fields. At first, it was to show him how to cut the bleaters' long coats to make clothes and other materials, but the two quickly established a tight bond.

Purlek also used the waterwheel to drive the bellows of his forge. Within two decades, the restless young man had discovered and mined ore deposits in the region, and he used the metals to build the many tools Noah requested. But a few years earlier, his adventurous spirit had diminished when Evet gave birth to a little girl named Kezia.

Thrilled to have another girl in the group after three consecutive boys, Emzara volunteered to help Purlek and Evet whenever possible. She told Noah that Kezia would be their daughter-in-law someday, but she could not decide if Shem or Ham would marry her. Although secretly hoping with her that Kezia would one day be a part of their family, Noah liked to tease Emzara by reminding her that it was not her decision to make. Emzara and Rayneh studied the abundance of animals in the area, drawing or painting them and learning about their diets and habits.

Garun helped Noah build a ship construction barn similar to the one in the Iri Geshem shipyard. Not knowing how large the ark would be, Noah and Garun made the structure in such a way that it could be expanded to accommodate a ship greater than any he had made before. Laleel prepared most of the meals with Emzara's help. On the cusp of 900 years, Methuselah assisted wherever and whenever he could, but he no longer participated in the hard labor.

Everyone in their enclave seemed happy. Everyone, that is, except Noah. Undoubtedly, the Most High led them here to build the ark, but now what? Thirty years had flown past like a taroc chasing its prey, and Noah still did not have any more information about the ark. He often rejoiced that the Creator blessed him with three sons, and that they enjoyed a quiet life far away from the decadence elsewhere in the world. But his heart longed for much more — to have specific direction for this undertaking, but above all to hear from the Creator again.

That lone experience stood above all others, and although terrified by the prospect, Noah desired more than anything to be in His presence again.

He closed his eyes. *Most High, please forgive me for being frustrated, and let my heart rejoice in the blessings You have given me.*

Noah stood, dusted himself off, and turned toward his destination. Dozens of birds flitted about the trees and others sang from their perches as he marched toward the top of the hill. Two small furry creatures frolicked on the trail before him and then scampered up a tree at his approach, making him wish that Emzara would have joined him on this journey.

As he crested the hill, the sound of a waterfall reached his ears from the right. Little by little, Noah spun around and scanned his surroundings. The forest stretched as far as he could see below, and a wide river wound its way eastward. *I wonder if that's the Hiddekel.* Turning farther, he saw that the types of trees in the forest changed abruptly. The towering needle trees gave way to a wide variety of shorter fruit trees, although, strangely enough, none seemed to be in season. As he examined the different scenery, he moved toward the fruit trees. A glint of light in the distance caught his attention. Noah searched for its source, but his eyes locked on to a single tree several hundred cubits away. *Why is that the only one with fruit?*

Suddenly, a flash of light exploded in his face and Noah fell on his back. Shielding his eyes, he scooted backward quickly and looked up, trying to understand the sight. A large flaming sword hovered before him, menacingly spinning in a slow arc in his direction, as if preparing to slice him as easily as a malid.

Transfixed, Noah gradually became aware of two other presences, one on either side of the sword. Standing approximately ten cubits tall, two enormous men — if they could be called men — dressed in glowing white clothing peered down at him. Their massive arms crossed in front, each of them boasted two gigantic wings that stretched upward from their backs and increased their imposing stature, and two more wings stretching far to either side. An immense sword hung from each man's belt. The one to Noah's left appeared a bit taller and thinner, and his hair, if that is what the glowing strands truly were, was a lighter brown than his companion's hair.

Trembling, Noah averted his eyes.

"Fear not, Noah, son of Lamech, for you are greatly loved." The thunderous voice belied the words he spoke.

How can I not fear? Still shaking, Noah willed himself to focus on the source of the sound — the giant being to his left. An image from Great-father's home invaded his mind. *The guardians and the flaming sword at the garden!* "Forgive me. I didn't realize this was the garden."

The protector to the right flicked his wrist, and the flaming sword sped away.

Noah climbed to his knees and lowered his head.

"Do not bow to us. Like you, we are servants of the Most High."

"I'm sorry. I—"

The blinding glow from both beings lessened and they relaxed their stances. "Perhaps you will be more comfortable if we appear like this," the shorter one said.

Noah nodded, still overcome. Shakily, he stood and beheld the guardians.

"Why are you here, Noah, son of Lamech?" asked the taller guard.

"I'm not sure. I'm looking forward to beginning work on the ark, but . . ." he let his voice trail off, aware that he was talking to beings that had been in the presence of the Creator.

"But the Most High has not revealed the rest of the plans," said the shorter one.

Noah nodded.

"You have already begun the work." The left guardian pointed back toward Noah's home. "Have you not been preparing all this time?"

"We have."

"And has the Most High supplied you with all your needs?"

"Yes." Noah lowered his eyes, thinking of the gopherwood trees, ashamed to look back up at them.

"Then why are you frustrated?"

"Because I want to see Him again — to hear from Him." Passion filled his tone.

"That is as it should be."

Noah quickly glanced up and caught a look pass over the taller one's face. *Was that approval?* Emboldened, he dared to ask the question that

162

had been heavy on his soul for years. "Can you tell me when He will speak to me again?"

"When the time is right, He will tell you what you need to know."

"Yes, of course." Noah breathed in his first normal breath since they appeared. "May I ask another question?"

The giants nodded in unison.

Noah pointed beyond them. "That tree with the fruit. Is it the—"

"You must never try to reach it." The shorter guardian put a hand on the hilt of his sword.

"I understand. So the old stories about Greatfather and Greatmother being driven out are true?"

The expressions on their faces transformed into frowns. The left guardian nodded. "After Nachash deceived the woman, and after the man rebelled, the Most High banished them so that they could never reach out their hands and eat from that tree."

It's good to know I learned the truth from my early years. Noah tilted his head. "Are there others like you?"

They looked at each other before the taller being spoke. "There are many like us, and many more not quite like us — the host of the Most High."

"And Nachash? Is he—" Noah shook his head. "Forgive me. *Was* he like you?"

The taller one nodded and lowered his voice. "Yes, Nachash was once like us, but he rebelled against the King of Glory, and now he fills the world with his lies."

"But he will fail." The shorter guardian's countenance brightened. "The Most High has declared it."

"The descendant of the woman will bruise his head, right?" Noah held up a palm toward the one on the right. "How? And how will his heel be bruised in the process?"

"We cannot say. The Most High does not reveal everything, but you can be sure it will come to pass."

"My friend Garun believes there are others like you who work with Nachash. Is he right?"

The taller guardian's face flinched. "Yes. Sadly, others have rebelled against the Creator."

"What will happen to them?" Noah asked.

"The Most High has not revealed that to us," the taller one said. "Like you, Son of Lamech, we only know what the King of Glory permits us to know, and we must trust that He will do what is right."

The other guardian glanced at the sky. "And now you must be on your way. You have much to do before the judgment, and your wife will be concerned if you do not return by dark."

Noah pursed his lips. He had so many more questions, but wearing out his welcome seemed like a poor decision. He nodded. "Thank you."

"Farewell, Noah," the guardians said in unison.

"Farewell." Noah turned slowly, but kept his eyes on the guardians. After several steps, he checked his path ahead to make sure he would not trip over anything. He glanced back and jolted. In a heartbeat, the guardians had disappeared. Staring at their previous location, Noah shook his head. *There is so much I don't understand.*

CHAPTER 23

"Love you, too. I'll see you at midmeal." Noah pulled away from Emzara, and with a bounce in his step, he exited their tent. Scattered rays of sunlight filtered through the tall gopherwood trees surrounding the encampment. A hint of coolness filled the air, though it would likely dissipate soon.

"Morning peace, Noah."

Turning at the sound of the gravelly voice, Noah spotted Methuselah still sitting at the entrance of his tent. "Morning peace, Grandfather."

"Still working on the lifts for the moving platforms?"

"Yes, we're nearly finished with the second one."

Methuselah held out a bag toward him. "Would you take this to Shem on your way?"

"Of course." Noah took the pouch. "What's in it?"

"Some of his favorite dried fruit and a new scroll I've been working on."

Noah grinned. "Well, the scroll will certainly be delivered, but I can't promise the fruit will make it."

"They'd better."

"I'll try to restrain myself." Noah winked before turning to head for the fields. The high-pitched tinging of metal to his left testified to Purlek's industriousness. Down the tree line past the forge, Garun and Ham walked west toward the ship barn, but Noah veered to the right when he approached the crops. As usual, Japheth and Rayneh worked side by side. Today looked like a weed-pulling day, causing a hint of a smile to form on Noah's lips. *Glad I'm not doing that anymore.* Continuing on, he spotted the herd of bleaters grazing on long green grass under Shem's watchful eye as he sat against the trunk of a nearby tree, braiding three cords together to make rope from the material Elam had given him.

Noah was reminded of days long ago as he strode toward his middle son. Shem bore many similarities to Noah in his youth. They both shared a deep interest in following the Creator, his son's trait that gave him the most joy. As a young man, Noah could work with others, but he preferred to be alone in his woodshop. The primary difference was that Shem's independent attitude blended well with his love for animals, an interest he definitely inherited from his mother.

Shem rose to his feet and yawned as Noah arrived. "Morning peace, Father."

"Morning peace." Noah hugged his son and then handed him the bag. "This is for you."

His eyes brightened. "From Great Grandfather?"

Noah nodded.

"Wonderful." He opened the sack and withdrew a few pieces of dried fruit and popped them into his mouth. "These are so good."

"How's the herd?"

Shem nodded as he chewed and swallowed. "They're fine. No sign of any predators."

"No grendecs?"

"How would I know, since I've never seen one before?"

"If you saw one, you'd know." Noah grinned. "But if that ever happens, don't confront it. Just stay out of sight and let it take what it wants. You're more important than every animal combined."

"I know. All people are." Shem tossed a piece of fruit into the air and caught it in his open mouth. He chuckled. "Well, maybe not my little brother."

Noah raised an eyebrow.

"I'm only joking." He spit a seed onto the ground. "Father, did you really do what mother said?"

"Your mother says a lot of things about me. Which one are you talking about?"

166

"Face down a grendec and shout that you weren't going to die?"

Noah laughed and shook his head slightly. "It wasn't quite like that. Yes, I was in the center of the arena, and they released the horned beast to kill me. Your mother wasn't there, so the story has become a little exaggerated. I didn't shout about not dying. I told the princess and those around her that I wasn't going to die."

"Yeah, that's what Elam said when I asked him about it, but then he got quiet. That's where his wife was killed?"

Noah nodded. "And Purlek's mother and father." The old ache of those losses resurfaced as Noah thought of his friends, but it was duller now, like the worn edge of an often-used blade. "Tubal-Cain was my most trusted friend for much of my life. And Elam's wife, Kal, was the sister of my best friend when I was just a little older than you are." Noah clenched his fist and let it out. "And the wicked king of Havil killed all of them."

"Purlek's grandfather?"

"Yes."

He looked toward the fields where Japheth and Rayneh worked alongside his own grandfather. "And she was there, too?"

"Mmhmm. Just a tiny little girl at the time."

Shem shook his head. "It's so hard for me to imagine what it would've been like." He swept his arm from left to right. "All I've ever known is this place and the people that live here. You've been all over the world, seen so many things, and met so many people."

"And so much I wish that I'd never seen." Noah put his hand on his son's shoulder. "I know it's hard for you to understand because everyone here is so kind, but—"

"Except for Japheth."

Noah tousled Shem's hair. "*Everyone* here is so kind. But out there" — Noah gestured beyond the trees — "it's the opposite. The world is full of wicked people. At least it was before we came here. I'm grateful you don't have to see the things I've seen. Trust me."

"I believe you. But it would be nice to see other places."

"You will. Someday." Noah squeezed Shem's shoulder. "I need to get to work. I love you, Son."

"I love you, too."

"Oh, by the way. The reason I said I wouldn't die is because of you and your brothers."

Shem furrowed his brow. "What do you mean? We weren't even born yet."

"I know, but the Most High told me a few weeks before that day that I would have sons. So I trusted that He would protect me because that hadn't happened yet. Either that, or He would bring me back to life."

"You don't have any doubts about the Creator, do you?"

Noah shook his head. "Not anymore. You'll see. The Most High always keeps His promises." He turned and walked toward the end of the field opposite the tents, cherishing the conversation with his son. Of the three boys, Shem asked the most questions about the Creator. Noah loved that he was so interested in the Most High's ways.

Soaking in the morning sunlight, he chose the roundabout path to the shipbuilding barn. It would take him a bit longer than the other route, but the walk would give him time to reflect on matters before the busyness of the day started.

Staring past the trees to his right, Noah spotted the distant hill he had visited many weeks earlier. He thought about his encounter with the guardians as he walked along the edge of the orb plant field. He had told only Emzara about the meeting so far. They had decided to keep it secret until the appropriate time in case the boys allowed their curiosity to get the best of them and tried to visit the site.

His path veered a little to the left and directed him straight toward the burial mounds of Greatfather and Greatmother. The setting always brought peace to his mind and helped him focus his thoughts. Today, his concentration centered on his sons. Being a father thrilled him more than he had ever imagined it would. Watching the boys grow up warmed his spirit, even on the worst of days, when they fought with each other or were less than respectful toward him or Emzara.

O Most High, thank You for providing us with a safe place to raise our sons and for allowing them to grow up around my father and grandfather. Help me to teach them how to live so that if the time comes when they are confronted by this world's wickedness, they will choose to follow Your ways.

Reaching the end of the last crop, Noah turned left toward the ship-building barn, which now stood between him and his tent on the far end of the clearing. Seeing no sign of Garun and Ham, Noah assumed they were already working inside on one of the lifts.

"Noah."

He froze. The hair on his neck stood on end and tiny bumps appeared on his arms. The sound reverberated inside his head as if spoken by a thousand tongues. The voice he longed to hear terrified him while paradoxically calming him. It made little sense. How could he feel such fear while simultaneously enjoying the greatest comfort imaginable?

With his head bowed and eyes averted, Noah cautiously turned back toward the gravesite, fully expecting to see the living flame hovering above the ground. As the corner of his eye caught a glimpse of the fire, he dropped to his knees and pushed his face to the ground. This time heat emanated from the blaze, but just as before, nothing else burned. The light seemed to pierce his entire body, and Noah briefly wondered if a shadow could even form behind him.

"Fear not, Noah. I am the God of your Greatfather Adam and forefather Enoch."

Due to the glorious and awesome presence of the Creator, the instruction to not fear did not put Noah entirely at ease. "Most High. T-t-to be in Your presence — n-nothing can compare."

"You longed for this day, did you not?"

"I have, but I'm not worthy to look upon You." Noah understood well why the guardian called the Creator the King of Glory.

"Noah." The voice, now only a singular sound, soothed his spirit and the fear departed.

"I have seen that you are righteous before Me in this generation. Stand up, for I wish to speak to you as a friend."

A lump formed in Noah's throat and tears filled his eyes. *A friend?*

"Yes, a friend."

A slight smile tugged at the corner of Noah's mouth as he recalled that the Most High knew his very thoughts. He climbed to his feet before slowly lifting his eyes to see his Creator. The flame's intensity softened, but a precise understanding of the scene still eluded his comprehension.

"I have set apart this place for you to fulfill your calling. You have done well by preparing to build. And you have met two of my guardians, but you must not return to the garden." The flame danced as the voice sounded forth.

Noah nodded. "I understand. I'm grateful for all You have given us."

"Noah, the end of all flesh has come before Me, for the earth is filled with violence through them. I am going to destroy them and the earth."

169

Biting his lip, Noah nodded.

"You are to build an ark of gopherwood. Make rooms in it and cover it with pitch, both inside and outside. And this is how you must build it."

An image of a huge ship flashed into Noah's mind. It looked like nothing he had seen before — so much longer than it was wide. Before he could consider the thought further, the Creator spoke again.

"The length of the ark shall be 300 cubits, its width shall be 50 cubits, and its height 30 cubits."

Noah's eyes grew wide as he realized that would be nearly twice the size of anything he had built before. He quickly repeated the numbers to himself, allowing the figures to etch themselves into his memory.

"Make a roof for the ark and finish it, except for the final cubit from the top. Put a door in its side, and make three decks within."

As Noah contemplated the details, the flame grew brighter and heat once again radiated from it. He shielded his eyes with his hand and looked to the side.

"I am going to flood the earth with water to destroy from under heaven all the living creatures in which there is the breath of life. Everything on the earth will die."

The flame calmed again, and a litany of thoughts and questions bombarded Noah's mind. He forced himself to think through what he had just heard.

"Noah, I will confirm My covenant with you. You will enter the ark — you, your sons, your wife, and your sons' wives with you. Of every living thing of all flesh, you must bring two of every kind, a male and a female, into the ark, to keep them alive with you. Of flying creatures after their kinds, of the beasts after their kinds, and of the creeping things of the ground after their kinds, two of every kind will come to you to be kept alive. And you must take for yourself every kind of food that is eaten. Gather it together, and it will be food for you and for them."

"All flesh . . . every living thing . . . every kind of food . . . 300 by 50 by 30." Noah gazed upon the flame, mesmerized by its beauty. He struggled to string together a complete thought until he finally said, "Thank You for entrusting me with this task."

A peace exploded in Noah's frame. He watched as the flame before him quickly faded until it disappeared entirely. Lifting his hands toward the heavens, with tears streaming down his cheeks and his body alive with energy, Noah prayed aloud. "O Creator, You are truly the King of Glory. Thank You for the grace You have shown me — for preparing all of this." Noah stretched his arms out wide, indicating the entire land around him. "You alone will I serve throughout my remaining days." He glanced at the three graves before him. "Until I return to the ground as Greatfather did."

"Father?"

The word barely registered in Noah's ears, but it was enough to distract him. He closed his eyes to focus — to continue his prayer.

"Father!"

Noah jolted and faced the campsite to see Ham standing a few steps away.

"What's wrong?" Ham stood rigid and blinked rapidly.

Noah held out a hand and Ham helped him stand. A smile grew wide on Noah's face as he hugged his youngest son. Noah shook his head from side to side. "Nothing. Nothing at all. Go, gather everyone to meet at the circle."

Chapter 24

His heart pounding from the short run, Noah ducked into his tent and blinked hard as his eyes adjusted to the darker room.

"What is it?" Emzara asked.

He spun to his left and found his wife sitting at her table with several scrolls sprawled out before her, animals sketched on many of them. He took a quick breath and wiped sweat from his brow. "He spoke to me again."

She tilted her head and raised an eyebrow. Slowly, recognition spread on her face and her jaw dropped. "The Creator?"

Noah nodded.

Emzara sprang to her feet and moved around the table. She grabbed his hands. "What did He say?"

Taking a deep breath, Noah tried to make sense of what he had learned. "He called me His friend."

"His friend?" She looked at the ground. "That's kind of strange."

"I thought so, too." Noah shook his head in wonder. "But I'm not complaining."

"And He told you about the ark?"

"Yes. I need to write down the directions before I forget." He pointed to the table. "Do you have a scroll I can use?"

"Of course." She turned toward her supplies, but then stopped and spun back to face him. "What did He say about our friends?"

Noah's excitement faded as he realized the recent conversation included nothing about them. He shook his head. "Nothing."

She narrowed her gaze. "And you didn't ask?"

"Em, I—" He scratched his head. "I can't explain it, but when He was right there before me, I couldn't think like I normally do. He is so wondrous to look at. It's as if all of my concerns disappear in His presence." He kissed her hand. "I'm sorry."

"So what do we do now?"

"Ham is gathering everyone outside so that I can let them know what I heard." A smile formed on his face. "We can finally start."

Emzara furrowed her brows. "And what will you say if someone asks about who the ark is for?"

Noah bit his lip and stared at nothing in particular on the tent wall. "I don't know."

"Maybe we should ask Garun and Laleel what they think first."

Noah thought through her proposal before slowly nodding. "That's a great idea. Would you mind getting them? I need to write down some notes."

"Here." Emzara handed him a small scroll and kissed his cheek. "Be right back."

After unrolling the first portion of the parchment, Noah dipped Emzara's pen into the inkwell and started jotting down notes as he spoke to himself. "Gopherwood. Make rooms. Pitch, inside and out. Cubits — 300 by 50 by 30. Leave one cubit from the roof unfinished. Three decks." He quickly sketched the image of the ship that he had seen as the Creator spoke to him.

"Noah," Emzara's soft voice broke his concentration.

He turned to face her. She stood in the middle of the tent next to Garun and Laleel. "Sorry. I didn't realize you'd returned."

Laleel nudged her husband and smiled. "I know what that's like. Sometimes I have to call his name three or four times."

Garun shrugged. "Guilty." His smile faded and he folded his arms. "Zara said you had something very important to ask us about before talking to the group."

Noah took a deep breath. "The Creator spoke to me again."

Laleel grabbed Garun's arm and looked expectantly at Noah. "So you have the rest of the details?"

Glancing at his notes, Noah rubbed the back of his neck. "It's big. Really big. But I'll share all that with everyone when we go out there. There's one detail I want your advice on."

"Our advice?" Garun wrinkled his forehead. "About the Creator's message?"

Noah swallowed the lump in his throat. "The first time He spoke to me, He said that the ark would be for the animals and for me, my wife, our sons, and our sons' wives."

"And you didn't have any children at that time." Laleel clapped her hands as she bounced on her toes slightly.

"Right." Noah held out a hand. "That's why I was so confident about surviving things in Iri Geshem. I know the Most High will keep His word." Noah shifted his weight to one side. "And this time, He said essentially the same thing, that He would confirm His covenant with me, my wife, our sons, and our son's wives."

Garun lifted his head as if he understood. "And He didn't say anything about the rest of us?"

Noah lifted a finger toward him and nodded. "Exactly."

Emzara placed a hand on Laleel's shoulder. "We're concerned about the rest of you. The Creator didn't say anything about you — whether you'll be on board or not."

Laleel patted Emzara's hand. "Don't worry about us. Noah, didn't you tell us that God will always do what's right?"

"That's what He asked me the first time He appeared, when I became troubled over the idea that the whole world would be destroyed." Noah stared out the opening of the tent. "I know He'll always do the right thing."

"Then you have nothing to worry about," Garun said. "If He wants us on the ark, then that's where we'll be."

"And if not?" Emzara asked.

Garun and Laleel exchanged a look, and it seemed to Noah that their eyes held peace. "We know God will do what's right. For now" — Garun unfolded his arms — "we're committed to helping you build this ark. We'll leave those concerns for the Most High."

"But what do I tell the others?" Noah asked. "I can tell them the instructions for the size and how it's to be built, but what do I say about this?"

"Do you need to say anything about it?" Garun scratched his head. "Just tell them about the ark itself and what we need to do. We can worry about the other issue when the time comes."

"And what if someone asks about it?" Emzara wiped her eye with the back of her hand.

Garun shrugged. "You said that you aren't really sure about the answer. So just be honest and tell them that you aren't sure. It sounds like this thing will take a while to build." He turned quickly to Noah and snorted. "Some of us may not even live long enough to see it completed."

Laleel playfully slapped him on the chest. "Don't talk like that."

Garun grabbed her hand and kissed it. "We'll be alright. Besides, I wasn't talking about you. You don't look a day past 400. Let's stop worrying about things we don't know." He glanced up at Noah. "We have an ark to build."

Noah chuckled, knowing Laleel was well beyond 500 years old. Then he shifted his gaze to Emzara. "Sound good to you?"

"I think so — for now."

Noah briefly studied his notes before moving toward the exit. "Let's go tell them."

Stepping into the late morning sunlight, Noah shielded his eyes until they adjusted to the brightness. Emzara leaned softly against his shoulder as he scanned the gathering and thought about what he would say. Circled about the fire pit, which was barely smoldering from the previous evening, their group quieted down when they saw him. Garun and Laleel took up the bench to Noah's right. Purlek stood near Evet behind the next log while Kezia played with a cloth toy Elam had made for her. To their left, Methuselah relaxed next to Lamech. Japheth and Rayneh sat on the other side of Noah's father, their hands covered in soil. Elam rested on the next bench by himself, with plenty of space next to him for the two young men racing toward them from the field where the herds were kept.

Moments later, Shem and Ham sped into the assembly, with Ham slightly in the lead. As he hurried around the bench to sit first, Shem leapt over the log and quickly sat next to Elam before Ham found a spot.

"I win," Shem said as he pushed dark locks away from his eyes.

Ham shoved his shoulder. "You cheated. I got here first."

"You started first."

"No, I'm just faster than you."

"I wasn't even trying."

Ham shook his head. "Let's do it again. Right now. I'll beat you anytime."

Noah smirked as the squabble reminded him of growing up with Jerah. "Shem. Ham." His words came out loud and firm, but not angry. "Not now. You can race later." He pointed at Methuselah. "Besides, you have no reason to boast. A 900-year-old man made it here before both of you."

The group laughed as the boys folded their arms across their chests. Noah winked at his sons and said, "You'll need to save that energy for something else." He quickly looked around the group again. "Thank you for taking a break from your work. I'd like to make today a day of celebration."

"What are we celebrating?" Methuselah asked.

Noah licked his lips. "The Most High appeared to me again this morning."

Methuselah's smile faded and he scooted forward. Evet picked Kezia up and implored her to listen. Even Shem and Ham stopped whispering back and forth and turned their full attention to their father.

"He said that we have done well by preparing for the building of the ark. Then He gave me some basic instructions."

"How big is it going to be?" Japheth asked.

Lamech held out a hand in front of Japheth. "You can tell us that later. I want to know what *He* was like."

"I'll tell you all about that during the celebration." Noah put an arm around Emzara and squeezed her shoulder. "The ark is going to be huge — bigger than I imagined."

"Will it be larger than the ships you made back in Iri Geshem?" Elam asked.

Noah nodded. "Nearly twice as large as the biggest I've ever made."

Elam's eyes grew wide. "Twice as big?"

"Almost. I have a lot of planning to do." He pointed at his youngest son. "You'll get to use that engineering mind as we determine the best way to do this." Noah looked at his father, Japheth, and Rayneh. "The three of you can keep growing crops for now. At some point, we'll need to start storing up food for the animals. And Purlek, I'm sure we'll need plenty of strong braces for the ship's joints. I'll need your help in planning the best way to build them."

"I'm happy to help," Purlek said.

Noah held his arms out and raised his voice. "We have much to celebrate today. Beginning tomorrow, we start planning. I believe this project is going to take a long time to complete."

Chapter 25

Land of Eden — Noah's 590th year

Emzara set the knife down and carried the plate of sliced vegetables across the room to a small table. "Is the bread almost finished?"

Ducking low, Rayneh stared into the stone oven. "Almost."

Kezia placed a bowl of dipping sauce onto the table. "Do you want me go tell everyone that midmeal is ready?"

Emzara shook her head. "I'll do it. I want to see how the water collection system is coming along. I suppose you could tell your father and anyone else who might be outside."

Kezia smiled. "I can do that." She leaned close to Emzara's ear. "Let's just hope Rayneh doesn't burn the bread again."

"I heard that." Rayneh giggled and tossed a rag at Kezia. It missed and fell harmlessly to the floor. "It was Japheth's fault last time."

Kezia picked up the cloth and threw it back with a laugh. "You won't be able to blame your husband this time."

"We'll be back soon," Emzara said as she walked out of the unfinished space that would eventually be part of the living quarters in the ark. Light spilled in from the long opening along the roof, illuminating much of the ship, an extremely helpful feature, now that the first layer of the hull had been completed.

"I still can't get over how big this is." Kezia swept an arm toward the bow end. "It's amazing."

Emzara stepped around an array of little cages designed for the smallest creatures. Stacked five high and five across with small ramps under every cage to catch and direct each animal's waste, Ham's clever idea would allow the family to efficiently feed and clean up after the animals when the time came. "It truly is. Can you believe Ham designed all these things?"

"He's so smart, and always inventing something. I don't know how he thinks of some of those things."

"Well, he gets that from his father, but his good looks come from me." Emzara waited to see if Kezia would react to her comment about Ham's appearance and was disappointed when the girl said nothing else. *Don't meddle, Em.* After walking silently for a moment, she asked, "So are you enjoying your work?"

"Most days are fine." She shrugged. "But sometimes it seems like we're doing the same thing over and over without making much progress."

"I know what you mean. But then when I think back to when you were born, I remember that this was just an open field with some crops. And now the end is finally in sight."

"That's how I think about it, too. It helps me stay optimistic that our efforts aren't in vain." Kezia turned toward the large open doorway on the opposite side of the ark. "I'll see you soon."

Emzara ascended the ramp to the third deck and found Noah and Garun holding a ladder in place while Ham fastened a long tube plant to a large clay vessel on the storage shelf.

"Is midmeal ready?" Noah asked.

"Almost." She looked up at Ham. "What's he doing?"

"I think it's ready." Ham climbed down a few rungs. "Mother, you're just in time."

"For what?"

Ham jumped to the floor. "Watch this." He knelt down and twisted a valve attached to the bottom of the tube plant. Water gushed into a trough until Ham turned the spigot off.

Garun squeezed Ham's shoulder. "Looks great."

"That's part of the water system?" Emzara asked.

Ham stood and faced her. "It's from the rain we had last night." He pointed toward the ceiling. "It runs down to the edge of the roof, and we allowed some of it to drain into that cistern. We can put a bunch of these in to get fresh water during the flood."

Emzara's lips curled up on one side. "Amazing. You're doing a great job."

Ham pointed toward the middle of the second deck. "I can even run some to the living quarters, so you won't need to come up here to get water."

She touched the tube plant. "Do you have enough of these?

"Not yet, but Japheth found some on the other side of the river. We'll need him to plant a lot more."

"I'm sure he'd be happy to do it," Noah said.

"Well, we can talk to him about it at midmeal." Emzara gestured for them to follow her as she turned to leave. "Let's go."

Noah walked beside her while Ham and Garun discussed specifics about the size and number of cisterns that could be installed.

"Just remember," Noah said as he looked over his shoulder, "I still want to bring a lot of drinking water in the clay vessels."

"We're working that into our calculations," Garun said.

"It's too bad you don't know how long the flood will last," Ham said as they descended the ramp to the second deck. "It sure would make it easier to figure out how much food and water to take."

Noah raised an eyebrow. "Perhaps the Most High has already told us how much we need to bring."

"Did He say something that you didn't tell us about?" Emzara asked.

Ham shook his head. "Father thinks that since the Creator said how big the ark needed to be, there will be enough room for everything as long as we use the space wisely."

Emzara looked up for a moment. "That makes sense. He knows how long the flood will last and how much space we'll need for food and water."

"Mmhmm. I hope your animal records are accurate." Noah pointed to one of the larger animal enclosures near the center of the ark. "We won't have room for too many more cages that size."

"And they take me a while to build," Garun said.

Emzara smiled. "Maybe you men will just have to trust that the Most High has already provided that information, too."

Ham chuckled. "Well, we could always kick Shem out of his bed if we need space for another pair of animals."

Without warning, the ark shuddered, sending Emzara lurching to her left, bumping into Noah as he staggered to maintain his footing.

Timbers creaked and groaned. A basket plunged from a shelf and crashed onto the floor while an array of small cages tipped over and slammed against the deck. *What's happening?* Suddenly, the quaking ship pitched her to her right and Noah held onto Emzara to keep her upright. Then, the shaking ceased as quickly as it had started.

Rayneh used the open doorframe at the entrance to the living quarters to hold herself up. "What was that?"

Emzara opened her mouth to ask Rayneh if she was all right, but stopped when a dreadful thought invaded her mind. *Most High, please don't let the ark be damaged.*

"I wonder if one of the piers broke." Noah seemed to speak the words to himself as he rapidly looked about the space. Then his eyes grew wide. He grabbed Emzara's hand and bolted for the large door. "Everyone outside!"

"What's wrong?" Emzara asked as she tried to keep up.

"I'm not sure, but we don't want to be in here if it collapses," Noah said as Ham and Garun sped past them.

"Wait." Emzara pulled her hand free and spun around. "Rayneh!"

"I'm coming." Rayneh turned the corner from the hall and sprinted toward them.

Emzara held out her arm. "Come on." After Rayneh took her hand, they hurried out of the opening. Emzara squinted in the bright sunlight as Noah directed them down the ramp. Rayneh raced ahead as Emzara focused on the sturdy wooden planks under her feet, sensing Noah's steps pounding behind her.

"Where are we going?" Emzara asked.

"Away from the ark — in case it falls over."

Emzara reached the bottom of the ramp and turned toward the fields where Lamech and Japheth stood watching them.

Lamech held a hoe against the ground with one hand and gestured with the other for them to come to him. "Over here."

Garun and Ham arrived first, and they were followed by Rayneh who ran to Japheth and hugged him.

"Are you alright?" Japheth asked.

She nodded. "Just a little scared. What happened?"

Japheth tipped his head toward Lamech. "That's what we're trying to figure out."

Emzara bent down to catch her breath.

"So you felt it, too?" Noah asked.

"Of course." Lamech tapped the ground with the hoe. "The whole earth shook for a moment."

"Father!"

Shem's call caused Emzara to glance up toward the herd of nervous bleaters. Her middle son ran to them and stopped next to Ham. "What was that?"

An ancient memory surfaced. Emzara looked at Garun and Noah. "Remember what happened in Havil after the ground trembled like that?"

Garun nodded. "That mountain exploded and the city was devastated."

"What?" Ham held his arms out. "You've never told us anything about that."

"Your father can tell you all about it." Emzara smiled at Noah but he seemed distracted by something in the distance. She followed his gaze to see what held his focus. "What are you looking at?"

"I just wanted to make sure there was no smoke coming from that hill." Noah pointed toward the site where he had met the guardians. "Before the explosion in Havil, the hill there had a steady stream of smoke for weeks."

"Do you think this is something different then?" Emzara asked.

He shrugged. "I don't know." He spun to face the ark and swept his gaze slowly from left to right. "It looks fine from here, but we need to make sure it didn't sustain any damage. If one of the piers gives way, it could ruin everything."

"Then let's split up." Shem pointed to the ark's stern. "Ham and I will check this end."

"Good idea." Noah looked at Emzara. "Your mother and I will inspect the bow. Father, would you and Garun examine the middle?"

"What about us?" Rayneh asked.

Noah stared toward the tents. "Go make sure everyone else is alright."

Japheth put his arm around her waist. "Let's go."

"So what exactly are we looking for, Son?" Lamech asked.

"Look closely at the sides of the ark to make sure there is no damage — cracks, popped seams, buckling — that sort of thing. And then examine the piers. Make sure none of them have shifted, bowed, or cracked."

Emzara nervously watched the others draw nearer to the towering structure. "And be careful."

"We will," Ham said.

"Beat you there." Shem pushed Ham's shoulder and took off running.

Emzara leaned against Noah as they walked. "Will those two ever grow out of it?"

Noah gave a small smile. "What? Being competitive? I doubt it. Jerah and I never did."

She shook her head and her mouth turned upward, too. "Boys." Even after all this time, she still did not understand them.

While Noah studied more than a dozen large wooden piers on which the ark's bow rested, Emzara walked around the front of the ship scanning the hull for any signs of damage. Satisfied that everything appeared to be in order, she joined Noah near one of the giant supports.

"Everything looks good from down here," she said.

Noah breathed a sigh of relief. "Glad to hear it. I don't see any damage here either."

Seeing her husband relax, she realized she had hardly drawn a full breath since the ground shook. As she released the tension, Emzara scanned the horizon. *God is faithful.* Approaching footsteps drew her attention toward the tents.

Breathing heavily from his sprint, Japheth stopped and looked at Noah. "What is it?" Noah asked.

"A couple of the tents collapsed. I think Purlek and Evet's suffered the most damage."

Emzara leaned forward. "Was anyone hurt?"

Japheth put his hand on her shoulder. "They're fine, but I think they could use some help." He turned and headed back toward the tents.

"Let's go," Noah said.

Emzara hurried to keep up.

They passed the dwelling shared by Noah's father and grandfather. *It looks fine.* She tilted her head, trying to determine if her own home had sustained any damage. A messy pile of fabric lay on the ground where Purlek's tent once stood. Kezia and Evet held an animated discussion off to one side, but they were too quiet to hear. Purlek sat on the ground with his head down.

Noah walked over to him. "Looks like a bit of a mess, but we're here to help."

Purlek shook his head. "Don't worry about it."

"Are you sure? We can have this back up in no time." Noah's forehead wrinkled as he scrunched his eyebrows.

"There's no need." Climbing to his feet, Purlek glanced at Noah, but his gaze settled on Emzara. "I'm sorry, Ma-Zara."

"What's this all about?" Noah asked. "Sorry for what?"

Evet stepped close to Purlek, who took a deep breath and stood tall. "We've decided to leave."

"No." The word leapt from Emzara's mouth before she thought to stop it. "Have we done something wrong?"

Noah placed a hand on her arm.

Purlek shook his head. "No, it's not because of anyone here. We love all of you. You're our family. Look, Evet and I have been talking about this for several years now, and after Jabal's people made that last delivery of clay pots a few weeks ago, we finally decided it was time."

Emzara blinked, trying to understand. After all these years, she still viewed Purlek as if he were her own son. "But why?"

He swept his arm toward the ark and the fields. "This. This place is all we've ever known together. We've been married for 90 years, and we've spent all of them right here, working on that ark for more than half that time." He shook his head slowly. "I've stayed about as long as I could. I've already made all the braces and fasteners that you'll require, so you don't really need a blacksmith anymore. And if something comes up, we've installed that little forge in the ark — Ham knows how to use it." He looked at Noah. "And so do you."

"Where will you go?" Noah asked.

"To Jabal's people." Evet pushed her hair behind her shoulder. "They've been really kind to us. We'll get to enjoy some new surroundings and have a chance to meet new people." She motioned to Purlek with her eyes. "And they could use a blacksmith."

"For how long?" Emzara wiped a tear from her cheek with the tips of her fingers. "I mean, the flood is coming."

Purlek swallowed and then shrugged. "I don't know. This whole flood thing is just so hard to accept. It's not that I don't believe in the Creator — I do, and I want to follow His ways. But it's so hard for me to think that He'll really destroy this whole world. There have to be other good people out there. Is He just going to let them die?"

Noah stroked his beard. "Purlek, I'm not going to argue with you. You know I believe the Creator will do exactly what He said He would do — even if I don't understand it all. I don't have to understand — I just need to trust Him and obey."

Nodding, Purlek said, "I know." He wiped the back of his wrist over his forehead. "I really admire that about you, but right now, I just feel—" He stared toward the ark and shrugged. "I don't know how to describe it. I've become disinterested in this project over the past several whole moons. I need to try something different."

"And you've really thought this all through? You aren't just scared because of the ground shaking?" Noah asked.

Purlek shook his head. "No, like I said, we've thought about this for a while. But since our tent collapsed, we figured we may as well be on our way instead of taking the time to put everything back together only to tear it down again."

"Kezia?" Emzara looked over at the girl, not sure how to fully form her question.

"We've talked it over with her," Evet said.

"I don't want you to leave." Kezia fought back tears as she pushed her face into Evet's shoulder.

Emzara struggled to control her emotions as it occurred to her that the young woman she had long thought would become her daughter-in-law might soon be departing. Her sadness intensified as she watched Kezia and Evet crying together.

"I'm going to miss you so much," Evet said to her daughter.

Emzara straightened and repeated Evet's words in her mind to make sure she understood them correctly before speaking. "Is . . . is Kezia staying here?"

"We wanted to let her decide. She's old enough." Purlek smiled at his daughter. "Why don't you tell them what you told us?"

Kezia sniffled and looked at Emzara and then Noah. She twisted her fingers together as she spoke. "I believe what you've said about the flood and about the Creator and what He's said about the wickedness in this world. I haven't seen much of it myself, obviously, but most of you have. I want to stay and help with the ark. That is, if you'll have me."

185

Emzara held out her arms and Kezia embraced her. "Of course we'll have you." She glanced at Purlek and Evet. "We'll take great care of her."

Evet smiled as she came close. "We know you will."

Noah put a hand on Purlek's shoulder. "If you truly are going to leave, I want you to do it with the blessing of our whole group. Tonight, we'll enjoy a feast and ask the Most High to guide you."

Purlek gripped Noah's forearm. "That sounds wonderful. Thank you for listening."

Emzara squeezed Kezia tight and prayed silently. *O Most High, if this is part of Your plan, help me to trust You as Noah does. Thank You for Kezia's belief in You and please watch over her parents.*

CHAPTER 26

Land of Eden — Noah's 595th year

Noah set his mallet down and checked the small pile of wood behind him. "I'm going to fetch another load of planks from the mill. Keep working on this row."

Shem drove a trunnel into the two boards, fastening them to the side of the ark. Just as Noah had instructed, he left two finger widths of the wooden nail sticking out to eventually secure the hull's third layer. "Sounds good. Would you refill this while you're there?" Shem handed him his empty waterskin.

"Of course." Noah stood and smiled at his son. The young man worked hard, but Noah knew his passions lay elsewhere. Shem rarely found time to watch the flock and read the scrolls Lamech and Methuselah had written or brought with them, except when Noah encouraged the group to take a break from the ark. Instead of hanging around with Rayneh, Kezia, and his brothers, Shem often spent those days beneath his favorite tree.

"Would you check on Ham, too?" Shem hitched a thumb over his shoulder in the direction of the other hanging platform about 50 cubits closer to the stern. "He left his spot a long time ago and hasn't been back since."

"I will. I'm sure he has a good reason for being away. He's probably helping Garun figure out the waste-removal system."

Shem sighed. "He's always working on something other than the actual ark."

Noah shrugged. "Trust me. You'll be grateful if he gets these systems up and running. Be back in a little while." He watched his son for a moment before grabbing the rope ladder and climbing down about 30 rungs to the ground.

He scanned the length and height of the ship that towered above him. Resting on top of enormous piers, the ark looked taller than it truly was, but even without the supports, the ship was massive. A huge wooden structure above him protruded from the base of the stern end like the shoulder of a large stringed instrument. Noah had begun installing these types of projections on the bow end of his larger ships a couple centuries earlier to help the crafts cut through larger waves. As they designed the ark, Ham had pointed out that without any means of self-propulsion to push the ship into and through the waves, it would be carried along in front of the wind and waves, propelled with them by their combined power. Consequently, the projection designed for the waves to break against, which had always designated the front of other ships, would actually be on the tail end of the ark. It took several whole moons for Noah to reverse his thinking and grow accustomed to calling the stern the bow and vice versa.

"Ah, there you are."

Noah turned and spotted his father walking toward him. "Morning peace, Father."

Lamech glanced at the partially cloudy sky. "Morning peace, although morning is almost past."

"You've been looking for me?"

Lamech bit his lip and kicked at a scrap of wood lodged in the ground. "I've thought about our conversation for a long time now, and I've prayed many nights about it." He raised his head. "I've decided to return home, and don't try to talk me out of it again."

Noah folded his arms and shook his head. "But we're getting so close to finishing the ark. A few more years, and this thing will finally be done."

"And that's why I need to go." Lamech put an arm around Noah's shoulders and led him toward the circle of tents. "If you're right about the flood, then I have to see the rest of my children again."

Noah sighed. Sixty-five years had passed since the Creator last spoke to him, and he still did not know if anyone else would be allowed on the ark.

"I love you, Son, but I love your brothers and sisters just the same — even if the Creator hasn't called them to such a grand purpose. I've lived more than 750 years, and I'd rather die knowing that I reminded all of my children about the Most High than live on without telling them."

Noah turned and watched Japheth pulling weeds from a field. "I understand. I think I'd make the same decision. I knew you were going to insist on this, so I've already talked it over with Emzara and the others. I'm coming with you."

"But the ark. You need to finish the Creator's work."

Noah raised an eyebrow. "I know, and I hope it isn't too presumptuous for me to say this, but I don't believe the flood will start until we're finished here. After all, the Most High told me that I'll be on it."

"Noah, you have your work from the Creator, and I have mine."

"Yes, and part of my work is taking care of family, so I'm coming with you, and so are Shem and Ham, Garun and Laleel, and Elam."

"But that only leaves my father, Japheth and Rayneh, Emzara, and Kezia. Who will protect them?"

Noah's lips curled up on one side. "The same one who watches over all of us."

Lamech shrugged. "Why are the others coming?"

"I think Garun feels like it's his duty to protect me. So naturally, Laleel is going to join us. Elam wants to see how much the world has changed, and I think he wants to find out how the Zakari are doing. I want Ham to look at what others have built to see if it gives him any ideas for things that can help here. And Shem wants to see where I grew up." Noah chuckled. "Em's convinced herself that Kezia will marry either Shem or Ham, so she wants me to find a wife for the other one."

Lamech grinned. "Yes, I've heard her speak of Kezia that way. I think Shem would be content to remain alone. Ham, on the other hand — if he could get his mind to stop thinking about designing things for the ark for a moment, I think he'd see how special that young woman is."

"I think you're right." Noah massaged a tight area in his forearm. "I want them to go because I think it'd be good for both of them to see for themselves how evil the world truly is. They need to know the dangers of forsaking the Creator's ways. I wanted to take Japheth, too, and he really wanted to go, but Rayneh wouldn't hear of it."

"He's wise to keep his wife happy. I'm going to miss those two." He sighed. "And the others."

"I will, too, especially Em." Noah gestured up to the ark with his eyes. "I'm not sure if I'll miss this thing, though. I think a half-year break will be good for me."

Lamech bit off the end of a fingernail and spit it on the ground. "It's too bad you don't have your construction crew who could finish it while you're gone."

"That'd be nice, but I'm sure Japheth and Em will keep things moving here. As much as they can, with the crops and the herds to tend."

"So, six whole moons?"

"I hope to be back that soon." Noah took a deep breath and let it out while staring at the ground. "My goal is to get you home safely and then return here. Whether you are with me on the way back is up to you. But we should wait a few weeks before leaving. That way we'll avoid the coldest weather that might delay us."

Lamech nodded. "That makes sense to me. In that case, I'll work harder around here until then to make up for the time you'll miss."

Noah shook his head. "No, I want you to work less. Spend more time with your family. You may not see them again."

* * *

Hiddekel River — Noah's 595th year

"What are you working on?" Noah asked as he ducked his head and stepped into the cramped quarters.

Sitting at a makeshift desk consisting of two crates, Ham held up his index finger. "Just a moment." His curly black hair hung over his ears and forehead as he moved the pen rapidly across the parchment, drawing whatever his mind devised.

Noah quietly sat down on a cargo box and let a slight smile form. Seeing Ham in this position reminded him of his father-in-law. Ham looked more like Emzara's side of the family, while Shem and Japheth drew comparisons to Noah and Lamech, respectively. Ham displayed the same broad shoulders as Ara, and just like Emzara's father, he often blocked out all distractions as he carefully noted every last detail in his designs. They even wore similar expressions as they worked, brow furrowed, tongue peeking out of the right corner of the mouth.

Ham finally set the pen down, rubbed his eyes, and turned to face his father. "I think I've figured out a good way to build the enclosures for the larger creatures. We can install gates—"

Noah held up his palm. "You can tell me later. Your grandfather wanted to show you something outside."

"Can it wait? I'm right in the middle of this."

"Not when you're sailing down a river. Come on." Noah led Ham out of the room, down a narrow hallway lined with a few more rooms, and then up a short flight of stairs to the ship's deck.

Warm evening air greeted Noah as he emerged from the ship's lower level, and the stench of dead fish assaulted his nostrils. The crew's reliance on the swimming creatures for sustenance upset Noah, but he had broached the subject with the captain only once. As a guest on the boat, he knew it was best to avoid becoming a nuisance.

The vessel looked much like the boat they had sailed to Kadel nearly a century ago, although it may have been a little longer, with a shorter draft to accommodate the shallower stretches of this part of the river. Still, the craftsmanship lacked Noah's skill. Multiple places on the ship flaunted pieces that were hastily put together and sealed with globs of pitch. When he had run the shipyard, he insisted on making sure every piece fit properly. Pitch was only to be used as a final coating — never to patch a mistake.

"There you are," Lamech said as Noah and Ham approached the bow. Shem and Elam stood beside him.

"Where's Garun?" Noah asked.

"He and Laleel went to their room to eat." Lamech gestured beyond the front of the boat. "See those lights ahead? We're getting close to Iri Sana."

"And this is where you lived?" Ham asked.

"Almost. My farm is south of the city. But this land here. . . ." He smiled at Ham and stretched his right arm to the western bank of the river. "This all belonged to Toman, Evet's grandfather."

Shem nudged Ham's shoulder and smirked. "So that would be Kezia's grandfather's father."

Ham frowned at his brother. "Yes, I figured that out." He huffed. "Is that what you wanted to show me, Grandfather?"

"No, not just that. There are several other farms before the city. I've got embarrassing stories about your father from each of them."

Noah cleared his throat. "They don't need to hear those."

"Yes they do," Elam said.

Lamech raised his eyebrows. "Of course they do. Every man needs to know how his father grew up. You think I like it when your grandfather tells embarrassing stories about me?"

Shem chuckled. "We like it."

"Well, then I guess they are worthwhile." Lamech nudged Shem with his elbow. "Did you know your father was scared to greet Toman? The man had such a strong grip Noah complained every time they shook forearms."

Ham snorted. "Sort of like Purlek's grip? That guy is strong."

"No, not like Purlek. Toman would make him seem like a young boy." Noah put his hands a handbreadth above his own shoulders. "He was huge. Strongest friend I ever had. My arm was sore for a week every time he shook it."

"And that next farm." Lamech directed his thumb over his shoulder. "There was a tree there that the boys liked to climb. One day, when he was about 30, Noah tried to impress a young girl who lived there, but he fell out of the tree and broke his arm. Needless to say, she wasn't very impressed."

Shem and Ham laughed.

Noah shook his head. "That wasn't me. Jerah did that."

"I'm pretty sure it was you," Lamech said.

"No, Jerah was the one always chasing the girls. Besides, I've never even broken my arm." Noah smiled at his father. "I think your memory is broken."

"We can settle this when we reach the house. We'll ask Jer—" Lamech yelped before pitching forward. He clutched Noah's arm to keep from falling.

Noah pulled back to keep the man upright, and Elam held him from the other side. Only then did Noah notice an arrow sticking through his father's shoulder. A second arrow whistled past his face. Noah ducked and faced his sons. "Get below deck. Now! Stay down!"

Ham hesitated. "But Grand—"

"We've got him. Go!" A quick glance at the opposite shore revealed a group of bandits rowing a small boat toward them. "Captain, we're under attack!"

The captain and three crewmen stood near the back of the craft. "I see them. Quick! Defensive positions. I'll steer."

The crewmen pulled on a rope, which drew up a wooden wall above the deck to protect them from projectiles. They picked up their own bows and fired shots at the approaching craft. In the distance, a man's yell preceded a loud splash.

"I hit one," the crewman closest to Noah said.

"Keep shooting," the captain said.

Staying low, Noah and Elam guided Lamech toward the stairs as another arrow flew over them and lodged itself in the opposite rail. The boat shifted toward the western shore as the three crewmembers continued firing arrows.

Garun emerged from his room just as they reached the bottom of the steps. Shem stood in the hallway behind him. "What's happening?" Garun asked.

"We're being attacked by bandits. Shem, you and Elam need to take your grandfather and find a place for him to sit."

"Let's see if the captain needs help," Garun said.

"You read my mind." Noah climbed a few stairs and stopped. He raised his voice. "Captain, can we help?"

"Just stay down there! My men have it under control. We're almost in the clear."

Noah grabbed Garun's arm. "Then we need to help my father."

"I'll get Laleel."

Garun hurried back into his room as Noah navigated the tiny hallway to the back of the boat. He entered the dark chamber and located his father grimacing as he sat on a box.

"Stay still. You can't lie back." Ham held the old man steady.

Noah rushed to his side and knelt down. The arrow entered through the back of his shoulder and the tip stuck out through the front. A thin trail of blood trickled down Lamech's chest while another line formed on his back. "Father, look at me. How do you feel?"

Lamech gritted his teeth. "I've been better."

Garun and Laleel entered the room and moved quickly to Lamech's side.

Noah looked up at Laleel. "Tell me what you think. I suggest breaking the arrow back here." He pointed to the shaft near Lamech's back. "Then we can pull the rest of it through the front."

Laleel nodded. "I agree. And I'm sure the captain will have some strong drink on board to help clean out the wound until we get to Lamech's place and find something better."

"Father, what do you think?"

Lamech cringed and sucked in a breath through his teeth as he craned his head, trying to look at the arrow. "Do it."

"If it's safe up there, I'll ask the captain about the strong drink," Garun said as he headed for the door.

Noah glanced around. "Elam, get me a couple of cloths. Laleel, something for him to bite down on. Boys, you need to hold him steady."

Noah stepped around his father and sized up the wound from the back. After Laleel handed Lamech a folded cloth and he bit down on it, Noah gripped the arrow with his left hand where it entered Lamech's shoulder. Holding it as still as possible, he snapped the shaft and dropped it onto the floor.

Lamech grunted as the piece in his shoulder jiggled slightly.

"That was the easy part." Noah inspected the broken shaft sticking out of his father. Lightly gripping the point of the fracture, he twisted his hand around it several times to make sure no loose fragments remained that could break off as it was pulled through the other side.

Elam returned with several cloths. "Ready when you are."

"Alright, let me have one of those." Noah took a rag and returned to his spot in front of his father. After wrapping the cloth around his hand to protect it from the arrowhead, Noah managed to grasp the shaft behind the tip with his thumb and two fingers. "Boys, hold him steady."

"We are," Ham said as a tear slid down his cheek.

Noah stared into his father's eyes. "This will probably hurt a lot. Are you ready?"

Lamech clamped down on the cloth in his mouth and nodded.

"On the count of three. Everyone ready?" Noah steadied his feet and tightened his grip on the arrow. "One—" He jerked so hard that he stumbled backward. Lamech screamed through clenched teeth as Noah regained his balance. He examined the shaft, which looked intact.

Elam pushed cloths against the wound on the front and back to soak up the blood.

Breathing heavily, Lamech spit the cloth out of his mouth. "You said you were going to pull on three."

Noah grinned. "I didn't want you to tense up."

Garun reentered the room with a small container. He handed it to Laleel. "The strong drink." He glanced at Lamech and then at Noah. "Did you get it?"

"Yes." Noah lifted his hand to show his friend the front half of the arrow. "Is it safe up there?"

Garun nodded. "We outran them. The captain said that his men shot three of the raiders. He said it's the first time he's ever heard of someone being attacked on the water this close to the city. Usually they are far upriver. How's your father?"

"I'm glad it wasn't closer to his heart. It just went through the shoulder."

Lamech moaned as Laleel poured some of the liquid into the front wound.

Glancing at the arrow, Garun frowned and then looked at Lamech. He leaned close to Noah's ear and whispered. "Captain also said that the arrowheads are often dipped in poison."

CHAPTER 27

Iri Sana — Noah's 595th year

"Noah?"

Noah opened his tired eyes and looked toward the door. "Meesh?" He stood and embraced her for the first time in over a century. "It's been so long."

As his sister pulled away, she offered a half smile and then stared at the man lying on the bed in the center of the room. "Pivi told me what happened."

"I'm so sorry." Noah sniffled.

"Oh, it's not your fault. That river's been dangerous for years. How's he doing?"

"He's resting right now. He's been waking every so often and talking when he can, but the healer said it won't be much longer."

"Misha," Elina said as she entered from the kitchen. "A bunch of us are in here, waiting for father to wake up."

"I'll be right there." She paused and caught Noah's eye. "Is it contagious?"

Noah shook his head. "No, you can touch him."

Misha walked to her father's side, bent down, and kissed his forehead. She gave Noah another sympathetic smile and touched his shoulder as she walked past him toward the kitchen. "Come and get me the moment he wakes."

Noah returned to his seat. Despite their best efforts to clean the wound with strong drink, herbs, and even fire, the damaged flesh refused to improve. The healer confirmed the captain's suspicions about the arrow being poisoned. Just as she anticipated, red and purple sores had soon spread outward from the injury and now covered much of his upper body and neck. Four days ago, Lamech had lost the use of his left arm, and by the day after that, he no longer possessed the strength to stand.

Garun and Laleel had come that morning to say goodbye to Lamech and then retired to a guest room in the barn to make room for Noah's brothers and sisters in the house. Shem and Ham had also said their farewells at that time. Noah knew Lamech's death would be especially difficult for them because they had never lost a loved one before. Currently, they led games with their younger cousins behind the house. Noah privately hoped one of the young women might catch Shem's eye — by now he suspected Ham harbored feelings for Kezia, a fact his brother never missed an opportunity to exploit for his own entertainment. But even if Shem found someone here, Noah doubted her parents would permit her to travel to Eden with crazy Uncle Noah.

His tiny smile faded as he focused again on his father. Squeezing his eyes shut, he replayed the incident in his mind. *If only the arrow flew a handbreadth higher or to the left, then it would've missed him.* Clenching his fists, Noah prayed. *O King of Glory, please hear my prayer. Was it wrong for us to come here? Perhaps I should have persisted in trying to talk him out of it.* Noah took several deep breaths and slammed his fist on his knee. *I know You created all things and made Greatfather from the dust of the ground. I know You are capable of healing my father. Please do it, and show my brothers and sisters that You are more powerful than Nachash and any other god.*

"Noah," a weak voice said.

Noah lifted his head to see his father looking at him. He grabbed Lamech's hand. "Father."

"Is Misha here yet?" His voice barely surpassed a whisper, but his eyes conveyed love and admiration.

"Yes, I'll go get her."

Lamech gently squeezed Noah's hand and grimaced. "Bring all of your brothers and sisters in here."

Noah licked his lips as his eyes welled up. He nodded and slowly stood. "I'll be right back."

Lamech refused to let go of his hand. "Thank you, Son." After another labored breath, he released his grip. "For bringing me back home."

Noah lowered his head and walked into the kitchen, where 8 of his 11 brothers and sisters quietly talked and laughed, enjoying the rare opportunity to be together. The other three lived too far away to reach in time. A nervous silence settled over them as Noah entered. With a trembling lip, he said, "Father's awake and wants to see everyone right away."

He turned and led them back into the sitting room. Being one of the tallest in the family, he stepped back against the wall and let the others take up the closer spots. Misha hurried to Lamech, knelt down, and hugged him around the neck. She drew back but remained on the floor next to him, gently stroking his head with her hand. Hetel, Noah's second-youngest sister, sat beside Misha, holding Lamech's hand.

Lamech methodically moved his gaze around the room, beholding each of his children. "Thank you all for coming." His words slowly crept through dry lips, but his countenance brightened a notch. "I planned to visit each of you in the coming days, but it looks like I found a way to bring everyone here."

Noah suppressed a laugh, thankful his father's sense of humor remained intact. Two of his brothers chuckled, but Jerah folded his arms on his chest and frowned.

"I want you all to know that since Noah is my firstborn, it's my wish to leave all of my property to him to do with as he sees fit."

Jerah scowled. "How could you? I've stayed here my whole life, and he—"

"But he wanted me to pass it on to you, Jerah."

Jerah raised an eyebrow. "Really?"

"Of course." Noah nodded. "There are only a few things I need to get back home."

Jerah shrugged. "That works." He leaned back against the wall and stared at their father.

"I've spent much of the past century on an amazing project with your grandfather and Noah. He can tell you all about our work later, and when he does, I want all of you to listen carefully to what he says." Lamech winced and sucked in a few deep breaths.

"Your mother and I raised each of you to follow the Creator and His ways." His pace increased a tiny bit. "I know that can be very difficult in our world, where there is so much evil and so many false ideas to distract you. But I have seen the truth of my beliefs with my own eyes. We found Greatfather's house, and it was filled with the truths I passed on to you. The Most High has twice appeared to Noah to prepare him for a judgment that is coming on the whole world."

"He appeared to Noah?" Hetel asked. "What did He say?"

Narrowing her eyes, Elina looked up at Noah and shook her head. "What judgment? What's he talking about?"

"I'll explain all of it later. Let Father finish."

A tear formed in Lamech's right eye as he struggled to look around the room. "My children, with my final breaths, the most important thing I can do is to remind you and encourage you to follow the Most High — no matter the cost. I love you." He grunted and winced again, clenching his jaw and pulling his knees up closer to his stomach. After taking in several short, raspy breaths through his mouth, he finally relaxed and opened his eyes. Immediately, they locked on to something across the room, as if looking past Noah and his youngest brother, Moteh. A broad smile crossed his lips and peace washed over his face. "Now I can finally rest." His facial features stilled and his head dropped onto the cushion beneath it. One last breath escaped his lungs, and Lamech's life ended.

Sobs filled the room, as Noah's siblings hugged and consoled one another. Noah swallowed a lump in his throat and a bittersweet smile tugged at his lips as he thought about his father's final words. The rest he had longed for since before Noah's birth had finally arrived.

* * *

"Tell Emzara that we love her, and that we're sorry we won't see her again," Laleel said.

"I will. Please be safe." Noah faced Garun as Laleel hugged Elam and then walked up a short ramp and boarded the boat on the edge of what had been his father's property.

"Old friend." Garun embraced him. "Please believe me when I tell you that we truly intended to return to Eden with you. But your father inspired me to track down my children and tell them about the Creator before it's too late."

"Do you think you can even find them?"

Garun shrugged. "I have to try." He gestured toward Shem and Ham. "If our situations were reversed, would you do the same for them?"

"I would. It's just . . ." Noah swallowed. "It just hurts, knowing that we'll never see each other again."

"Well, if your ideas are correct about what happens after this life, then you'll see us again. By the way, your words at the burial were exactly what your brothers and sisters needed to hear, and it's what I plan to tell my children. Your father would be proud of you."

"I hope so." Noah rested a hand on Garun's shoulder. "May the Most High guide you. I pray that your children will listen, and that I'll get to see them again when this life is over."

Garun cupped Noah's shoulder. "Thank you." He pointed toward Shem and Ham. "Hey, watch over your father for me."

"We will," Ham said.

"I hope you find your sons and daughters and that they listen to you," Shem said.

Elam hugged Garun. "I pray the Creator blesses you on your way."

"And you as well, dear friend."

Garun turned and joined his wife as she wiped away tears with one hand and waved with the other and the boat slowly drifted away from shore. "Farewell, Noah. You are the truest of friends."

Noah stood with his sons and Elam, watching the vessel sail down-river until it eventually moved out of sight.

"I hate this trip," Ham said. "First Grandfather and now Garun and Laleel."

"I know it's hard, Son." Noah put his arm around Ham's shoulder as they walked back toward the house, where their loaded wagon awaited their imminent departure. Behind them, Elam explained to Shem what he had learned about the Zakari during his trip into Iri Sana earlier in the week.

"I just wish none of this had ever happened." Ham kicked at a rock on the ground but missed.

"So do I. But I'm grateful for the opportunity to see my family one last time."

Jerah stepped out of the back door of the house as Noah's group drew near. "Noah, do you still plan to leave right away?"

"Yes, I need to get home as soon as possible. Besides, if anyone around here remembers that Havil put a price on my head, then I'm in danger, and I'm putting all of you in danger."

"Can I speak with you for a few moments alone?"

"Of course." Noah directed Ham to the wagon. "Make sure everything is ready to go."

After watching the others walk away, Noah faced his brother. "What did you want to talk about?"

"The first thing is that I wanted to thank you for passing your inheritance on to me."

"You're welcome. I have no use for it, but even if I did, you deserve it more. You've spent your whole life here, helping father with the farm."

Noah looked at the grassy field around them and chuckled. "I remember watching you chase Pivi around here when we were young. Sometimes I long for those innocent days."

"So do I." Jerah folded his arms. "The second thing is not as easy to say. I'm frustrated and angry with you for talking father into your foolhardy plan to build your ark. If he never went with you, then he'd still be with us. And he gave his life for what? Preparing for a flood that will never happen."

Noah had anticipated Jerah's complaints about the ark. He raised his eyebrows and nodded. "But it will happen. The Creator told me that it will."

Jerah shook his head. "And if that's true, then things are even worse."

"What do you mean?"

"Father raised us to follow the Creator. We were told that He is good and made everything beautiful. But now you show up and tell me and our brothers and sisters that He is going to destroy this world and kill everyone except for you, Zara, your sons, and their wives." He glanced in the direction of Shem and Ham. "And they aren't even married." Jerah held his arms out wide. "How am I supposed to believe the Creator is good if He plans to kill everyone? The people in the city say that Nachash is the most high. His followers are certainly in charge of this world, so why shouldn't I follow him?"

Noah felt as if someone had punched him in the midsection. "You can't really believe that. Nachash's followers murder infants on their altars and kill anyone who stands in their way. The Creator doesn't force us to follow Him. He made everything perfect, but Greatfather and Greatmother ruined it when they rebelled."

Jerah snorted. "And you believe those legends."

Noah cracked a wry smile. "Those legends are reality where we've been living. We found Greatfather's house and grave, and Grandfather remembered visiting the place when he was a young child. Jerah, the old stories are true."

Jerah scratched his head. "Even if that's the case, why would the Creator plan to kill *everyone*?"

"I just mentioned that the old stories *are* true. The Most High warned Greatfather that the penalty for disobedience is death. We've all disobeyed. You know that. That's why we offer sacrifices every year."

"But don't you think this is too drastic?"

Noah sighed. "I struggle with it, too. It's not as if I want it to happen. But I know that the Creator will do what's right." He tilted his head. "You have to admit that our world is full of violence and unspeakable wickedness. You told me yesterday that it isn't even safe to go into Iri Sana anymore. That would've been unthinkable when we were growing up."

"But it can't be that bad everywhere."

"It's far worse in most places." Noah closed his eyes. "Brother, there are evils in this world beyond your imagination, and I'm sure it's become even worse since I moved away. The Most High showed mercy to Greatfather and Greatmother by allowing them to live. But look around. This is what happens when our sin seems to have little consequence — murder, thefts, ritual prostitution, child sacrifice, and more. By judging the world, He will be eliminating so much vile behavior and giving man an opportunity to start over."

Jerah frowned and pointed toward the house. "Yes, some people are vile. But what about us? What about Pivi and our sons and daughters and our grandchildren? I know we aren't perfect, but what makes you so special that the Creator is going to save you and kill us? Is it just because you're a shipbuilder and that's what it takes to survive a flood?"

Noah swallowed the lump in his throat and shook his head, fighting the urge to justify himself. He knew Jerah and his siblings did not walk as closely with the Lord as he did, but he also knew that he had the same propensity to sin. "When did I ever say that I was better than any of you? What I know — and must believe because of His response when I wondered about all the people — is that the Most High will do what's right."

Jerah stared off in the distance. Twice he opened his mouth to speak before stopping. Finally, he looked straight at Noah. "But why a flood? Don't you think He could have chosen a less painful and terrifying way to do it? Why not just kill everyone in their sleep so they didn't know any different?"

Noah shifted his stance and adjusted his wrap. "I've thought about this for a long time, and I think there are a couple of possible reasons. But before I explain those, you need to know that the Creator has the right to flood the world if He wants to because He made it and all things in it. But He is also good, so He would only do it if it became necessary."

Jerah hesitated as he seemed to consider Noah's words. "So what are the reasons? Why a flood?"

"Right. Well, if He just killed everyone in their sleep, then they would have no warning — no time to cry out for the Most High's forgiveness. With a flood, many people will see the water before it takes them. They will have a few moments to plead with the Creator. Perhaps He will show mercy and forgive them."

Jerah shrugged. "That makes some sense." He crossed his arms. "I still don't like it, though. What's the second reason?"

"This one may be more speculative." Noah pointed toward the road to Iri Sana. "What happens to the old road whenever there's a rainstorm?"

"The water washes out portions of it and we need to fill them back in."

Noah nodded. "That's right. Water is extremely powerful, and it leaves evidence that it's been there. Maybe a reason for choosing a flood is that it will leave vivid reminders of the Creator's judgment — a warning for all future generations."

"You've really thought this through, and I understand those reasons, but it still seems cruel to me."

"I know." Noah's eyes moistened. "And I know you aren't coming with us, and it pains me to think that I won't see you again." Noah embraced his brother. "Promise me that you'll never follow Nachash. Stay true to the Creator, just as Father urged us to do."

Jerah pulled back. "You've given me much to think about."

"I need to go." Noah held out his arm for their traditional forearm shake. "I love you, Brother."

Chapter 28

Western Frontier — Noah's 595th year

Ham scanned the rolling hills. "None of this looks familiar yet. Maybe we passed it already."

Seated behind him in the wagon, Shem pointed ahead and to the right. "I told you: we still need to travel north for a couple more days before we find our trail."

"And you figured that out from looking at the stars last night?" Ham spun to face him. "How is it that I can work out how to build just about anything, but I can't make sense of the stars?"

"Let's take a short break," Shem said to Elam as he put down his game pieces on the seat between them.

"Sure." Elam set his pieces down, too.

Shem leaned forward, sticking his head between his father and brother. "Not the stars — just one star. Remember the one I showed you that's always in the north?"

Ham nodded.

"You check its angle above the horizon, and that will tell you how far north or south you are, right, Father?"

"That's right. We can show you how to do that tonight. Looks like it'll be clear."

The heat of the day finally relented as the sun slowly dropped in the cloudless sky ahead. Nearly three whole moons had passed since they departed from Iri Sana. Instead of journeying north by water for several weeks and then west, they had sought a more direct route due to the dangers of the river. Farms, villages, and a few sizeable cities speckled the landscape during the first three weeks, before yielding weeks ago to the vast open grasslands they now traversed.

"What's that smell?" Elam asked.

Ham sniffed the air. "I don't—"

"It smells like death." Noah frowned.

"That's what I thought, too," Elam said. "Where's it coming from?"

They rode in silence for a short distance while climbing a hill. As they neared the top, Ham abruptly raised his left arm. "Right there."

Noah followed the direction his son pointed and spotted the source of the stench. The dead body of a large, horn-faced beast on the far edge of the ridge grabbed his focus. As he drew back on the reins, the pair of dependable tuskers slowed to a halt. "Let's go take a look. I need to stretch my legs anyway."

"That's the biggest creature I've ever seen. Is that an earth shaker?" Ham asked.

Elam snorted. "No, these are horn faces. Earth shakers have long necks and can be much bigger."

Ham's eyes grew wide. "Bigger than that?"

Noah stepped to the ground. "They can be almost as large as our construction barn."

Ham rolled his eyes. "There's no way."

"It's true," Elam said. "Their legs are like tree trunks and so are their tails."

"Are you just teasing us?" Shem raced past them toward the carcass.

Noah grinned. "No. Why do you think they're called earth shakers? The ground actually trembles when they walk. Besides, there are even larger creatures in the sea."

Shem stopped and covered his mouth as he reached the body. His shoulders slumped and he shook his head repeatedly.

Noah picked up his pace to reach his son.

Shem gestured to the valley as Noah drew near. "It's horrible."

Covering his nose with part of his wrap, Noah's heart sank as he surveyed the scene before him. Strewn about the slope below lay dozens of slaughtered horn-faced beasts. A couple of tarocs picked chunks of flesh off the nearest remains and swallowed them whole. In the distance, some spotted furry scavengers also made a meal of the corpses. Strangely enough, the dead animals lacked their most notable feature, the long pointy horns protruding from their heads. The large stout bodies and fan-shaped frill on the top of their heads clearly identified them as horn faces, but only bloody cavities remained where the beautiful horns once grew. Noah's temperature rose and he balled his fists.

"What could do this?" Shem nodded toward a young animal lying next to a larger one. "Even a little one."

"Not what," Elam said. "Who."

Shem pointed at the nearest beast. "People did this?"

Noah let out a deep breath. "Yes. Notice only the horns are missing. If grendecs or some other beasts had done this, they wouldn't have taken those — they would've eaten the body. Looks like someone killed all these animals just for their horns."

"That means there are people in this area," Ham said. "And by the looks of it, they probably aren't the type we want to meet."

"I agree. We should move on." Noah pointed to a wooded area across the valley. "We'll head for the trees and then travel north, like Shem indicated. Does that work for you, Son?" Noah put a hand on Shem's shoulder.

Tears ran down the young man's cheeks. "I can't believe someone would do this."

Noah guided his son toward the wagon, searching for words that would help. "It's another reminder of how wicked people have become."

Shem punched a fist into his opposite palm. "This makes me so angry."

"And it should. The Creator made man to care for His creation — not destroy it." Noah sighed. "But we have corrupted everything through our sin."

Shem climbed into the wagon and sat down. "I wish I could see what it was like before Greatfather rebelled."

"So do I." Noah cupped his son's shoulder and settled into his seat. He drove the wagon down the hill, dodging several rotting carcasses along the way. Upon reaching the tree line, they turned north and stuck to the edge of the woods. Moments later, the snapping of branches far ahead made the two tuskers jittery. Birds scattered away from the source of the sound, and several furry creatures bolted out of the forest nearly 200 cubits ahead. The unmistakable sounds of massive footsteps filled the air.

"What's happening?" Ham asked.

"What is that?" Shem stood up, bracing himself on Noah's shoulder, trying to see.

Elam shushed the boys and pointed directly to their left. "In there."

"Good idea." Noah quickly turned the tuskers into the woods. Ducking down and pushing a low-lying branch of a needle tree over them, Noah kept his voice low as he said, "We need to stay out of sight."

The heavy footsteps pounded to their right, but the branch-snapping stopped abruptly. Noah halted the wagon about 50 cubits into the forest. "Don't make a sound, but be ready to run if necessary."

All four men watched the edge of the forest. A deafening roar reverberated through the trees, causing them to cover their ears. Fear filled Shem's and Ham's eyes as they looked at Noah.

Noah put a finger to his lips and then pointed for them to keep focused. A few more footsteps shook the ground before the source appeared. An enormous head boasting a huge mouth filled with long, sharp teeth came into view as the beast moved past a small opening in the trees, and then massive legs and a long, swaying tail followed. The beast seemed unaware of their presence as it stomped through the grass toward the fallen horn faces.

Noah leaned forward and spoke calmly to the tuskers as they threatened to bolt. "Easy. It's alright."

White-knuckling the wagon's bench, Ham stared wide-eyed at Noah and spoke quietly. "Is . . . is that a grendec?"

"Yes," Elam said. "It doesn't have horns on its head, like the one your father and I faced." He raised his eyebrows. "But I think this one's much bigger."

Shem turned to face them, his mouth open in shock. He sat silently for a moment as if willing himself to speak and then blinked. "Can we go now?"

"Soon. Let's wait until it starts eating so it's distracted." Noah raised his eyebrows. "Awesome, isn't it?"

Shem swallowed and nodded.

Bone-crunching sounds of the grendec feeding sent shivers through Noah's body. Shem winced, and Ham looked slightly green. Noah prodded the tuskers to advance between the widely spaced needle trees. Once the sounds from the grendec could no longer be heard, Noah encouraged the tuskers to increase their speed a little. Eventually, Shem and Ham relaxed and began chattering about the size of the beast and peppering Noah and Elam with questions about them.

After a while, they came across a small break in the woods that at one point may have been a man-made trail running north and south. "Let's head north for a bit, and then we'll try to cut back to the edge of the forest."

The path made for easier travel. Only occasionally did they need to duck under branches or slow down to clear a path around obstructions. Elam handed out bread rounds that he had baked the evening before in a small, portable clay oven they purchased in one of the villages.

The snack satisfied Noah's grumbling stomach, but he longed for one of Emzara's bread rounds hot out of the oven and dipped in savory root stew. And he longed to hold her again. He knew they were drawing closer, but privately he worried that it might still take several weeks to find Eden.

As they entered a small clearing, Noah stared at an odd sight ahead. "Whoa!" He pulled hard on the reins and stopped the wagon.

"What is that?" Ham asked.

"I'm not sure." Noah stepped out of the wagon and walked toward the edge of a large pit in the ground. The massive hole stretched about 40 cubits across and the walls were at least twice as deep as Noah was tall. Bones completely covered the floor and rose to nearly ground level in the middle. "With all the dark shadows, I almost drove straight into it."

"Do you think it's where the grendec lives?" Shem asked.

"No, this is man-made," Ham said. "Look at the sides of the pit. No beast dug this."

"I think you're right," Elam said. "We should go."

"Don't move!" The voice from above held a firm tone, but it was not angry.

Noah held his palms up and looked into the trees. He gasped as his mind slowly comprehended what he saw. Large wooden platforms and bridges traversed the treetops high above. At roughly halfway up to the platforms, perhaps 15 cubits in the air, five men stood on small tree stands ready to fire arrows at them. "Don't shoot."

"What are you doing here?"

Noah's eyes darted to the man to the right of the one he had been watching. A blood-stained wrap hung loosely over his shoulder, and a long white dagger hung from his belt. The blade might have been made of bone. The man's headgear boasted a design that also seemed to be made of bone and gave Noah the impression that he held a position of authority. "We were traveling through the area when a grendec caused us to go off course. Then we stopped when I saw this pit."

"What's a grendec?"

Noah described the nightmarish creature.

"Ah yes. The giant mouth-killer." The man gestured to the platforms above. "They are the reason we live up in the trees, and" — he pointed to the hole — "why we have the bone pit." He snapped his fingers and three of the men swiftly slid to the ground on ropes.

"Please, we mean you no harm." Noah stepped slightly to the side to shield his sons.

The man smiled. "I believe you. We mean you no harm either, but if you remain down there, harm will likely come to you. What did you call them . . . grendecs? This forest is full of them at night."

The three men approached and looked in their wagon. One of them looked up and shook his head. "No weapons."

Noah shrugged. "Like I said. We were just passing through and didn't even notice your village until you said something."

"What's your name, stranger?" the man with the headgear asked.

"I'm Noah." He quickly introduced the others.

"Noah, I'm called Ek'tura. For your own protection, I invite you to stay here tonight. Then in the morning, you can continue your journey."

Noah glanced at the others. "What do you think?"

"They seem nice enough," Ham said.

Shem kept his voice low. "What if they were the people who killed the horn faces?"

"What if he's telling the truth about grendecs in this forest?" Elam asked.

"It doesn't look like we have much of a choice." An uneasy feeling rose in Noah's chest, but he thought of the monster they had seen earlier and frowned. "Let's stay with them, but remain alert just the same." After the others agreed, Noah looked up. "Thank you. We'd be honored to stay here tonight. I'm very interested to see what it's like living up in the trees."

"I'll be happy to show you." The man whistled two short high-pitched sounds. Immediately, a small platform high above them, suspended by four ropes, slowly lowered toward the ground.

Noah pointed to the descending object. "Is this how we get up there?"

"Yes. My men will escort you, and I'll greet you when you reach the top."

"What about our wagon and animals?" Noah asked.

The man pointed to the opposite side of the bones. "Put the wagon behind those trees over there. The pit will offer some protection, and we have guards out here all night."

"As you say." Noah drove the wagon around the hole and instructed Elam, Shem, and Ham to take any valuable items with them if they could be carried — in case their hosts became too interested in their belongings. Noah hid his string of gold piks and pikkas in a concealed pocket of his wrap, though he doubted he would have use for them again. Shem made a point of grabbing the map.

Soon they joined one of the guards on the lift and were steadily raised into the tree top village. Noah tried to hide his surprise when he stepped off the plank. A platform stood before him with one walkway straight ahead that seemed to connect to an even larger platform. Four small bridges ran to other areas of the village, and from this vantage point, he could see dozens of other bridges, platforms, and even several small buildings.

"Noah, welcome to our home," Ek'tura said as he approached. The top of his head reached only to Noah's mouth, but his musclebound frame accentuated his imposing presence. "Come, let me introduce you to our leader."

Noah raised his eyebrows. *So this man isn't even the leader.* Ek'tura led them straight ahead onto the large bridge, which bounced a little as they walked across it. Much of the architecture and most of the decorations around the platforms and bridges consisted of bones. Some were carved and shaped to resemble birds and beasts while others remained uncut and placed in a pattern. Noah looked askance at a grotesque sculpture of a strange beast devouring a man. *They're infatuated with death.* The uneasy feeling in his chest tightened into a knot.

They stepped onto the other platform and turned right. Huge bone sculptures of birds and beasts lined either side of the area. On the opposite end, a man rested on a large chair made of bones. To his right stood a muscular man with a bald head and serrated spear that seemed to be carved out of a single bone. On his left, a young woman dressed in furry hides and holding a similar spear stared at them as they approached. Her expression exuded confidence, more than making up for her lack of size. Suspended high above the chair, a massive grendec skull angled down at them with its jaw agape.

"My chief," Ek'tura said. "I'd like to introduce Noah and his companions. They were on a journey, and I invited them to stay with us this evening to protect them from the night creatures."

The chief stood and nodded to Ek'tura. "A wise decision. The forest floor is too dangerous in the dark." He stepped toward Noah's group and looked them over from head to toe. "Welcome to our village, Noah. I'm Chief Ov'anit. Where have you come from?"

"Thank you, Chief. We've traveled far from the east, from a city called Iri Sana. These are my companions, Elam, Shem, and Ham."

"I haven't heard of such a place, but that's no surprise. My people do not travel far." He glanced at Shem. "Is something troubling you, young man?"

Shem cleared his throat. "I'm sorry, sir. I'm a little nervous being up this high in the air. And I've never seen anything like this." He gestured to the large sculptures. "I'm trying to get used to it."

The chief smiled. "Have no fear. Our village is very safe." He returned to his seat. "Noah, we'd be honored if the four of you would join us for our evening meal."

Noah nodded. "We're grateful for your kindness to strangers like us."

"Wonderful. It will be ready shortly. Ek'tura, please prepare four extra seats for our guests."

Ek'tura nodded and hurried away.

The meal commenced a few moments later, and although a variety of meats were available, Noah's group found plenty of warm root vegetables, several kinds of bread, and a nut stew to eat. Several townspeople introduced themselves, but most looked at them as a curiosity. Based on the number of people Noah could see elsewhere in the village, he estimated that about a third of the villagers had gathered on the large platform.

More than once, out of the corner of his eye, he caught the young woman from the chief's side watching them closely, the steely expression never leaving her face.

As the feast came to an end, the chief stood. "Noah, we thank you for sharing a meal with us, and we'd like you to join us as we offer a sacrifice to Bak'hana, the god of the forest who has made us successful." He motioned to the grendec skull above his throne.

Noah glanced at his companions before standing. He kept his gaze at the chief's feet and took a deep breath to collect his thoughts. *Creator, please give me the right words to say, and watch over us.* "While I again thank you for your hospitality, please permit us to not participate in this sacrifice. We don't wish to disrespect you and your people, but we worship the Most High God, the Creator of heaven and earth and everything in them." Noah looked at the sculptures that served to constantly remind people of death. "The Creator gives life to all things, including the creatures of the forest. And He doesn't permit us to worship other gods."

The chief folded his arms and stared at Noah as an awkward silence settled over the gathering. The strong man and young woman beside him spoke quietly though rather animatedly with the chief. When they finished, the chief tapped the floor twice with his staff of carved bone. "Very well, Noah. We don't wish you to incur the wrath of your God. Ek'tura will show you where you can rest. May you sleep well. Also, I'd like to speak with you in the morning before you depart."

Noah put his fist to his chest. "Thank you, Chief. I look forward to it."

Ek'tura spoke briefly with the chief before he led them across several bridges to an area that seemed more like a bird cage than a room. Not much larger than the bed of their wagon, the circular wooden floor rested on a large branch jutting out from a tall thick tree. Multiple ropes tied to distant branches and trunks held it securely in place. Its walls were made from hundreds of thin pieces of wood and bone placed vertically from floor to ceiling, if it could be called a ceiling. A few beams crisscrossed above, and leaf-filled branches covered them. Several cushions, furs, and hides rested against the wall.

"I trust you'll find the room comfortable," Ek'tura said. "If you need anything, I'll be just outside the door. I have orders to lock you in."

"Why?" Noah's relief disappeared, overcome by a sense of foreboding. "I thought we were guests here."

"You are, but Chief Ov'anit is concerned for your safety. Some of our more zealous citizens might be offended that you refused to take part in our ceremony. So I'm here to protect you."

"I see. Well, I didn't intend to be offensive." He lowered his head in what he hoped was a sign of peace.

"Do not worry, Noah. I'm one of the best warriors. You'll be safe." Ek'tura thumped his own chest twice before smiling at the group. "I'll be right outside. Please let me know if you need anything."

"Thank you." Noah watched him close the door, but he could still see the man through the dozens of slim gaps between the wall slats.

"Father, is everything alright?" Ham asked.

Noah shrugged one shoulder and kept his voice low. "I'm not sure. Something doesn't feel quite right. Let us pray to the Most High and then get whatever sleep we can. It's been a long day, and I hope to leave early in the morning."

CHAPTER 29

Slowly opening his eyes, Noah hoped for the darkness of night. The primary light shining into their room emanated from the sole torch near the door. *Good, it's not morning yet.* He rolled over for what seemed like the hundredth time, trying to get comfortable and settle his mind. The next day would be difficult if he could not sleep more than a few brief spells. As he drifted off again, he longed for his spot on the bed next to Emzara.

His eyes shot open at the faint sound of approaching footfalls. Had he slept again? There was no way to know. *Who's coming? Maybe another guard to relieve Ek'tura.* Through the gaps in the wall, he spotted the tireless guard seated just beyond the door. Suddenly, Ek'tura bolted upright. "Ar'yel." Keeping his voice low, he asked, "Why are you here?"

"I came to see you."

The soft, feminine response surprised Noah, as did the glimpse of the woman clad in form-fitting skins who now stood near Ek'tura. Noah shifted his head one way and then the next, trying to get a clear view but to no avail. Her face remained hidden in shadow.

"You shouldn't be here," Ek'tura said.

"Why not?" Ar'yel asked, her words lilted with the same accent as the rest of her people. "I know you've been watching me."

The guard breathed deeply and looked away.

"Don't deny your feelings, Ek'tura." She raised a hand to the back of her head, and with a dramatic movement pulled a bony pin from her coiled locks and shook her head, allowing her hair to fall past her shoulders and nearly to her waist. Gracefully, she stepped toward him and dropped the hairpin.

"But the law." Ek'tura took a step back. "No one is permitted to touch you until the grieving period is over."

"I can't wait another whole moon." She stopped just before touching him. "Kiss me."

Again the guard turned his head, but only momentarily. He leaned forward and reached toward her before backing up another step to the railing. "No, it's forbidden."

She placed her hand on his chest. "But you want to."

"Y-yes, but we need to wait."

"No one will ever know." She stretched up to kiss him.

He turned his face away again. "They will," he said as he pointed toward the guest room.

She snorted. "And who will they tell after the morning dawns?"

Something in her tone bothered Noah. *What did she mean? Is it just that we are leaving or are we in danger?*

A half-smile formed on the guard's mouth and he shrugged. "Only the others who have entered the darkness."

"Exactly. Have no fear, brave Ek'tura." She put her left hand around his neck and pulled herself up to kiss him.

The guard hesitated, but then leaned in and closed his eyes.

In a flash, just before their lips touched, Ar'yel slipped her right hand, palm-first into Ek'tura's face. He drew back, but with her left arm pulling him forward and her right pressed into his face, he could not break free. He gave a choking cough, struggled briefly, then collapsed forward into her. She caught him with a grunt, using her slight frame to break his fall before lowering the unconscious man to the floor.

For the first time since she arrived, Noah saw her face. *The woman by the chief's side.* He sat up and shook Ham and then Shem. His voice just above a whisper, he said, "Get up."

One of the boys moaned.

Ar'yel dusted some substance off her hands and then wiped them on Ek'tura's wrap. She withdrew an object from his belt pouch and hurried to the door.

"Elam, wake up." Noah turned but realized his friend was already awake.

A quiet click sounded from the door before it opened. Ar'yel stood before them with a finger pressed against her lips. "Be silent. We have to leave now."

Shem stirred and sat up.

"What did you do to him?" Noah asked.

"Sleeping dust. It won't last long." She glanced over her shoulder. "If we don't leave now, we'll all end up in the bone pit."

"The bone pit? What do you mean?"

Looking frustrated, she pointed straight down. "This isn't a guest room. It sits directly above the pit — surely you saw it yesterday. At sunrise, you'll be dropped into it as a sacrifice to Bak'hana. Let's go."

Noah urged the others to get moving and ordered them to stay silent. Moments later, they followed Ar'yel out the door and across two bridges. After reaching a small platform, she stepped near the edge and felt around in the darkness before her, searching for something. She grabbed it and pulled it close. Only then did Noah see the thick rope in the faint glow of a distant torch.

"This is our way down. I've cut all the other lines, but my people can still get to the ground in a hurry. Go now. I'll follow you."

Elam stepped forward and took the rope. He climbed down and disappeared beneath the platform.

Ar'yel urged Ham to go as soon as Elam was several cubits beneath them. Shem followed his brother.

"I'll go last," Noah said as Shem started his descent.

She tilted her head. "No."

"How do I know you won't cut it while we're climbing?" Noah asked.

She shook her head. "Fine. But I wouldn't go through the trouble of freeing you just to kill you." Once Shem climbed a little lower, she gripped the rope and effortlessly dropped below.

Noah glanced back the way they had come. Ek'tura still lay motionless outside their room. With a deep breath, Noah followed the others. Accustomed to climbing ropes, he descended briskly toward the ground, but he knew his aging muscles and joints would remind him of the action for several days. While focusing on the climb, he listened for sounds other than his own breathing and the slight creaking of the branch above from which the rope hung.

After Ar'yel touched the ground, Noah slid a bit and then let go of the rope before it stung his hands. As he gathered himself, she ushered them forward.

"Wait. What about our wagon?" Noah asked.

"No time." Ar'yel gestured for Noah to hurry. "Besides, your beasts are already dead. Come on." She broke into a sprint and they followed her lead.

A loud yell shattered the peaceful air. "Find them!"

His heart leapt into his throat. Struggling to stay on Elam's heels, Noah ran alongside Shem while torchlights lit up the canopy behind them. Suddenly, a shout turned Noah's attention forward.

"Watch out!" Elam lunged toward them and slammed into Shem just as a blurry figure entered Noah's vision. A man swinging on a rope crashed into Elam and they toppled to the ground. Both men groaned while struggling to get to their feet. As he climbed to one knee, the invader reached for his bone spear, which lay a short distance away.

Ar'yel raced to them, her long hair flowing behind her. She whipped out a knife, and with a scream, drove it into the man's thigh.

He cried out and fell to the ground, clutching at his leg.

With Shem's help, Elam stood up but staggered as he took his first step. He reached a hand to his side and pulled it back to look at it.

Noah's stomach turned as he spotted the dark sheen of blood all over Elam's hand.

Shem ducked under Elam's arm and supported his weight on his injured side. "I'll help you."

"Hurry!" Ar'yel gestured for them to move again.

Shem and Elam soon figured out their steps and then half walked, half ran behind Ar'yel and Ham. Noah followed them, repeatedly looking over his shoulder as the attacker's screams gave away their previous location.

They hustled through the woods, and the yelling soon faded to distant cries.

"Can we slow down?" Shem asked. "He's hurt really bad."

"Not yet." Ar'yel pointed toward a faint light ahead. "Not until we cross that bridge."

Something whistled past Noah and skittered along the ground. *An arrow!* "They're shooting at us. Go!"

Multiple shouts rang out behind them and Ham turned to look at Noah. "They're gaining on us."

Elam stumbled and nearly fell, but Shem caught him and adjusted his position. "I've got you. Come on. You can make it."

The forest came to an abrupt end as they approached the light. The lone torch flickered atop a post at the end of a long bridge.

Ar'yel put a hand up and then gestured to the bridge. "Go quickly. Watch your step!"

Noah peered over the edge of a deep crevasse. Although a hint of orange appeared in the eastern sky, providing the slightest bit of illumination to the land, he could not spot the bottom of the gorge.

Ar'yel grabbed his wrap. "Go!"

Noah stepped onto the bridge. Like those in the tree village, it bounced a little as he hurried across. Grabbing the rope railings at his sides, he made sure each step landed on one of the boards suspended above the seemingly bottomless canyon. Glancing ahead when he reached the halfway point, he noticed only Ham in front of him. Distracted by the moment, he had forgotten to make sure Shem and Elam crossed first. He turned around to see Ar'yel right behind him, holding the torch she had taken from the bridge's entrance. Back at the start of the bridge, Shem struggled to help Elam keep his balance on the unsteady planks.

Despite Ar'yel imploring him to move, Noah stopped. "I have to make sure my son is safe."

As their pursuers' shouts drew closer, Ar'yel pointed ahead. "Go! I'll make sure he gets across." She turned around and swiftly moved to Shem and Elam. A quick, animated conversation ensued, and Elam dropped to his knees while holding onto the rail.

Noah gripped the ropes tightly. "Hurry up!"

Shem glared at Ar'yel. "No!"

"It's the only way," Elam said as he took the torch from Ar'yel.

She pushed Shem forward.

"No, I won't leave him!"

"Run, Shem!" Elam shakily climbed to his feet. "I'll be right behind you."

Noah glanced from Elam to the edge of the forest and then back again. As Shem and Ar'yel drew near, he turned and hurried to the opposite end of the bridge.

Ham stood on the land, waving frantically and urging them to hurry.

As Noah stepped off the bridge onto solid ground, he turned and grabbed Shem's blood-covered arm and helped pull him to safety. Ar'yel crossed immediately behind him.

Elam stumbled again and fell to his knees in the middle of the bridge.

Noah and his sons screamed for Elam to hurry as a dozen men appeared at the forest's edge across the bridge.

Elam faced Noah's group and held the torch against one of the two ropes on which the wooden slats rested.

"No, Elam!" Shem stepped around Ar'yel and moved toward the bridge.

Noah grabbed him and pulled him back before an arrow rocketed into the post near his head.

"Go!" Elam quickly lit the two rail ropes and then fell forward with an arrow sticking in his back. He gasped and placed the torch against the other support rope. "Run!"

Ar'yel pushed Noah away from the bridge. She pointed ahead. "Into the woods. It's too late to save him."

Another arrow zipped past them, and three villagers moved onto the bridge, each wielding a bone spear. The first support rope snapped and the bridge twisted and swayed, causing the men to stumble. They turned around and hurried back to the land. Elam wrapped an arm around the most recently ignited rope, holding the torch in place.

Noah pulled Shem along, and they soon ducked into the woods. Hiding behind a pair of large trees, they turned and watched as the rails burned through. The bridge flipped, and Elam dangled from the lone remaining rope, which burned near his arm. Suddenly, it snapped, and Elam plunged into the darkness.

Shem dropped to his knees and wailed. Noah felt as though a piece of his heart had been ripped from his body. Seeing his son's agony only intensified the pain.

"I'm sorry about your friend." Ar'yel touched Shem's blood-smeared wrap and spoke matter-of-factly. "He wouldn't have survived the wound. You should be proud of him. He gave his life to save all of us." She took a deep breath and spoke with more compassion in her voice. "I'm truly sorry, but we need to keep going. It'll take them only about a day to go around without the bridge, so we must get far away from here."

220

Chapter 30

"I don't think I can travel much farther." Noah sucked in a deep breath through his mouth. His lungs burned and his legs ached. The sorrow and anger of watching Elam die had fueled his flight, but now, as the sun marked midmorning, Noah's strength was rapidly dwindling.

"We're almost there." Ar'yel slowed her pace. "Listen. Do you hear the river?"

Noah bent down and put his hands on his knees. At first, he could hear only his own breathing and the pounding in his ears, but as his pulse slowed and he caught his breath, the sound of rushing water registered in his mind. "I hear it. Then we can stop?"

Ham smiled at him. "You want me to carry you the rest of the way?"

Shem scowled at his brother and kept walking. He had not spoken since the bridge.

Noah offered Shem a sympathetic smile before playfully punching Ham's arm. "I'm not that old. And you're not that strong."

"Once we reach the waterfall," Ar'yel said, rolling and elongating her *R*s.

"What's so special about this waterfall?" Ham asked. "Why do we have to get there?"

"You'll see. Come."

She led them through the forest, and they soon found themselves at the bank of a calm and shallow river. She waded in up to her knees. "Step into the river and take a moment to drink. Then it's essential that we stay in the water."

"Why?" Ham said.

She pointed to their feet. "If my people discover our tracks, they will be able to follow us. The river will hide our trail."

Noah and his sons entered the river. While Ham and Noah enjoyed several handfuls of the cool water, Shem scrubbed the blood from his hands and arms before drinking. Noah closed his eyes, and the image of Elam dangling from the bridge and then falling crept into his thoughts. He clenched his jaw and shook his head. *Be strong for your sons, especially Shem.*

Ar'yel crossed to the other side and walked around, intentionally stomping on the ground occasionally to leave marks and then backtracking over her footsteps.

"Do you want us to do that too?" Ham asked.

"No, it probably isn't necessary. We were careful, so I'm not sure they'll know which way we went. It's just a precaution." She waded back into the water and slipped her shoes off. "Follow me. You may want to hold your sandals, too. They can get stuck in the mud."

She led them upstream through the shallow river. Noah's toughened feet barely noticed the rough rocks scattered along the way. As they progressed, the roar of crashing water grew louder. Before long they rounded a bend and a spectacular landscape sprawled out before them.

Noah stared at the wide wall of water tumbling straight down from some 30 or 40 cubits above and ending in the crystal clear pool ahead. On the left, the needle forest dominated the view, climbing the steep hillside to the top of the falls and beyond. However, a handful of fruit trees grew a short distance from the shore. Immediately to either side of the falls, the water splattered all over enormous rocks that almost formed natural staircases to the middle of the cascading water. To the right, the trees appeared to yield to a large meadow, but Noah could not see too far in that direction.

He cupped his hands, filled them with water, and raised it to his mouth. The cool drink and striking scenery soothed his soul. "This is a beautiful place."

"Yes, it is." Ar'yel flashed a quick smile. "But it gets better."

She led them to the left side of the pool and to the fruit trees. "Help yourself." She grabbed a bulbous red seed fruit from one tree and a malid from another.

The men followed suit and then Noah and Ham chomped into crispy malids. Shem stuffed one seed fruit into his pocket and held on to two more. Ham lowered himself to the ground.

"Not here," Ar'yel said. "We're very close."

Ham sighed and slowly stood. "Where are you leading us?"

"You'll see." She stepped onto the large wet rocks and climbed along the left side of the waterfall. Looking back, she gestured for them to join her.

"Where's she going?" Ham asked, his eyebrows pinched low on his forehead.

Noah looked at his sons. "Let's find out."

They traced her path up the damp stones. As they approached the top, she moved closer to the falls and then disappeared behind the wall of water.

Ham shouted something to Noah, but the deafening roar drowned out the sound. Ham put his hand on Noah's shoulder and pointed where Ar'yel had just stood.

Noah craned his neck to see what Ham attempted to show him, and that's when he spotted a hidden trail leading behind the falls. He followed his sons onto the trail and then behind the thick sparkling veil.

Marveling at the wall of tumbling water, Noah stuck his right hand into it and felt its power as it pummeled his fingers. To his left stood a spacious cavern approximately 10 cubits high and perhaps 20 cubits deep.

Ar'yel sat about two-thirds of the way toward the back on a dry area of the floor. She waved them over. "Now we can rest."

Noah and Ham found spots near her, but Shem kept his distance, sitting farther toward the right side of the room. Noah bit into his malid and then looked at her. "Is it safe here?" For the first time since the meal the night before, he looked closely at her and was surprised by how much she resembled Emzara in her younger years. Her long, dark hair and eyes complemented her brown skin, and her slender build belied the strength she had exhibited all morning.

She nodded. "No one in my village knows about this place."

"How did you find it?" Ham asked.

"I didn't. My husband did. He brought me here a couple of times. He planted those fruit trees many years ago."

Noah drew back. "You're married?"

She looked aside and slowly shook her head. "I was . . . for almost a year. He died a couple of weeks ago. They told me he was trampled while hunting great horned faces." She sniffed and rubbed her eyes.

Shem's jaw clenched, and he slowly shook his head at her.

"I'm sorry about your husband," Ham said while looking down at the partially eaten fruit in his hands.

"Thank you." After a few moments, she gathered her composure and looked up.

Noah waited until she looked his way before speaking. "We should be the ones thanking you for the rescue. Before we speak about that, let me introduce my sons." Noah put a hand on Ham's shoulder. "This is my youngest son, Ham." He gestured toward Shem by tilting his head. "And that is my middle son, Shem. He was very close to Elam — the other man who was with us." Grief filled Noah's heart and he blinked hard. "He was a great friend."

She glanced at Shem. "I understand the pain of losing someone close to you."

Shem pulled his knees up and put his face against them.

After an awkward silence, Noah cleared his throat. "Ek'tura called you Ar'yel. Is that your name?"

"Yes."

"And you're the chief's daughter? I ask because you were standing beside him last night."

"Not exactly. My husband was the chief's son." Ar'yel sat up straight. "In my village, if a man dies, his wife takes his position."

"Interesting." Noah stroked his beard, glad to think about something other than Elam's death. "So why did you risk everything to rescue us?"

"Something you said last night — I couldn't get it out of my mind." She stared past him. "When you refused to take part in the sacrifice, you said that your God created everything and that He gives life to all things, including the creatures of the forest." She shook her head. "For my people, everything is about death, and I was so weary of it — especially after my husband died. You spoke of life, and I. . . ." She sighed.

"What is it?" Noah asked.

"I think I was supposed to rescue you."

Shem perked up and looked at her.

"Why do you say that?" Ham asked as he yawned. He stretched out on the floor and closed his eyes. "I'm listening."

"Ever since my husband's death, I've had the same dream many times." She shrugged. "This will probably sound silly to you. In my dream, I saw a colorful bird fly into our village and land before Ov'anit, the chief. It was so vibrant and beautiful. It was also very old and wise. And it spoke. Its words were unlike anything I'd heard before. It said that the Creator had a message for us, but Ov'anit ordered my people to put it in a cage so that it could be sacrificed to Bak'hana the next day. Each time in my dream, I waited until night and then opened the door to the cage." She looked at all three of them.

"And then what happened?" Noah asked.

She held her palms up. "I don't know. That's when I'd wake up."

"And you think this dream represented our arrival last night?" Noah pointed a thumb to his chest and smiled. "Am I the 'very old' bird?"

She chuckled. "Well, you are much older than almost everyone in my village. Most people are killed before they reach 200 years." She lifted a finger toward him. "And how old are you?"

"I'm nearly 600. It's sad that your people are killed so young. But the bird, you think it represented our arrival?"

"I thought the Creator might have given me this dream so that I'd know what to do when you arrived."

Noah massaged his temples as he considered her words. "But you do not follow the Creator?"

"I don't know much about Him, but I think I'd like to. Why would I worship Bak'hana, the forest god and a god of death, when I could serve the God who gives life and made all things?"

"That's a great question."

She folded her hands together. "Would you teach me about Him?"

"We'd love to." Noah smiled broadly. "But let me ask you a couple of questions first." Noah glanced at his sons. Ham's breathing indicated that he was likely asleep, and though Shem stared toward them, he appeared to be in a daze. "What are you planning to do next? Surely, you can't go back to your people."

"No, they'd kill me." She shook her head. "I was hoping I could travel with you until . . . well, wherever you're going."

"We're heading for the land of Eden. My wife is waiting for us there, along with my grandfather and my oldest son and his wife." A pain stabbed Noah's heart. "She is Elam's daughter. Now, I have to tell her that—" He took a deep breath to gather his thoughts. "You are certainly welcome to—".

"And Kezia," Ham said as he yawned and rolled over.

Noah gave Ar'yel a half-grin as he used his eyes to silently gesture to Ham.

She smiled and nodded as she seemed to understand his meaning.

"Yes, and Kezia. She's the daughter of some of our dear friends. She's probably about your age. As I was saying, you're welcome to join us. We could tell you all about the Creator on the way." An image of Shem teaching Ar'yel about the Most High flashed through Noah's mind. *Could she be the one?* He suppressed a smile.

"I don't know the land of Eden, but I'd be grateful to join you."

"Can you tell me a little more about our escape? You said that our beasts were already dead."

"Yes, after you were taken to the cell, we used them for our sacrifice."

Noah folded his arms and shook his head. "Poor things. And what about the bone pit. What's its purpose?"

"It has a couple of purposes. The grendecs, as you called them, often stalk the forest at night. And they can smell the dead animals in the pit from far away. So they come there and many of them fall in, and they cannot get back out."

"So you use it to kill the grendecs?" Noah asked.

"That's one reason. The other is for sacrifices. If I did not help you escape, when the sun rose they would have opened the floor of your room, and you would have fallen into the bone pit. If the fall didn't kill you, you would've been left there to die."

Noah scrunched his forehead. "That's terrible."

"I know. I told you before. My people think only of death."

"Well." Noah yawned. "I'm very thankful you thought of life."

"I am, too. I already feel free, as if the darkness from deep within me has been removed."

"And are we free? You don't think they'll find us here?"

"No one knows about it. But like I said before, it'll take them at least a day to go around because of the bridge. And by then, we'll be far away.

226

Look." She pointed past Shem. "There's a path through there that will take us north. They'll never be able to find our trail."

"So it is safe to get some rest here?" Noah asked.

"Yes. We should all sleep a little and leave later today."

Chapter 31

Land of Eden — Noah's 595th year

"This is beginning to look familiar," Noah said as he surveyed the various trees surrounding them.

"Not to me," Ham said. "I don't remember being here."

"I don't either, but notice the types of plants that grow here." Noah swept his arm in an arc. "They're the same as the ones near our home. Also, based on my calculations last night, we must be getting close — just a little farther north." Normally, Shem helped Noah make the calculations, but he still had not spoken since the bridge.

"I don't recognize it either." Ar'yel rubbed her arms as if she were cold. "My people never enter the forbidden land."

Noah quirked an eyebrow. She had spoken only a little more than Shem since midmorning, which he found quite odd since she had been extremely talkative after they had left the waterfall cave the previous day. "The forbidden land?"

"Yes. Once we left the needle tree forest, we were no longer in Bak'hana's realm. My people say this land is forbidden. I did not realize this was the place you meant when you spoke of Eden."

"So even if they could track us, we should no longer worry that they'll follow us?"

She shook her head.

He breathed deeply, unaware until this moment the weight of tension he had borne while constantly looking over his shoulder for a surprise attack.

Noah wondered if their refusal to enter the land had something to do with the old rumors about Eden. "Is there another reason they do not come here?"

"What do you mean?" Ar'yel asked.

"Besides the land being outside of Bak'hana's realm? I mean, who decided where his realm ends and another one begins?"

"I don't know. I only know that my people believe they'll die if they come here."

Noah nodded slowly. "And that's why you've been so quiet. Well, we've been living near here — at least I think it's near here — for 95 years."

She smiled and seemed to relax a little.

They walked in silence for a long while. Eventually, they stopped in a small clearing and sat down to eat some of the fruit they had picked from the orchard near the waterfall, along with some wild berries they had found along the way.

Instead of sitting away from the group as he had done since Elam's death, Shem joined them. He broke open a seed fruit and pulled some of the juicy red kernels out, then offered it without a word to Ar'yel, who sat to his left.

She took the fruit and smiled. "Thank you, Shem."

He nodded. "You're welcome."

Noah swallowed a bite. "It's good to hear your voice again, Son."

Shem sighed. "Why did he say that, Father?"

Perplexed, Noah looked askance at Shem. "Why did who say what?"

"Elam. On the bridge when he took the torch, he told me that he could finally repay his debt to you."

Noah shrugged. "He didn't owe me any—"

"Could he have been talking about the time you rescued him from kidnappers? He told me that story many years ago when I asked what happened to his arm."

"Hmm. I suppose he might have thought that." Noah's eyes welled up as he remembered Elam's final moments. "I never looked at it that way. He was a good friend, and I only did what I hope any of us would do in that situation. Besides, I wasn't alone. Rayneh's uncle, Aterre, helped me, and so did Elam's father and several other men from their village."

"That must be what he meant." Shem stared at the ground. "I'm going to miss him so much."

"Shem, the greatest act of love a person can show is to give his life for another." Noah rubbed the back of his neck. "Elam did that for us. As much as it hurts to lose him, we should honor his sacrifice."

"I know." Shem glanced at each of them. "I'm sorry . . . for the way I've been acting." He faced Ar'yel. "I've been blaming you for my friend's death, even though I know you were willing to give your life to save ours — four people you'd never met before. I'm truly sorry. Will you forgive me?"

She tilted her head. "Thank you for such kind words, but I don't know how to answer your question. Forgive — what does it mean?"

"Forgive?" Shem drew back, his eyes wide. "If someone has done something wrong to you or if they owe you something, you can choose to forgive them. It means that you don't count that wrong or that debt against them anymore." Shem looked at Noah. "How would you define it?"

"You did just fine, but perhaps an example would make it clearer." Noah looked at Ar'yel but pointed to Ham. "When my sons were younger, Ham took something that belonged to Shem, a small toy that my wife had made for him."

"What?" Ham asked. "How do you know about that?"

"You'd be surprised how much your mother and I know." Noah grinned. "Shem knew he took it, but Ham denied it. One day, Ham accidentally broke the toy, so he buried it in the ground, hoping no one would find out. Shem knew what he had done, but he never held it against Ham — he forgave him — and he continued to love him as his brother."

"I understand." A small dimple formed in her cheek as she smiled at Shem. "Yes, I will forgive you."

"Thank you." Shem stood and removed his wrap from his shoulder. He ran his fingers along its edge until he located a slight rip in the cloth. He gripped the fabric on both sides of the damaged section and pulled hard, tearing the wrap in half.

Shem held it out to Ar'yel. "I tried to clean it in the water, but it's still stained. It's not much but it should keep you warm."

"That's so kind." She took it and draped it over her shoulders. "Won't you be cold now?"

He shrugged. "I'll be fine."

Upon finishing their brief meal, they headed north. Ham and Noah discussed details about the ark's ventilation system. Shem and Ar'yel followed them as she peppered him with sincere questions about the Creator and their beliefs. By midafternoon they reached a field filled with long grasses.

Noah scanned the large meadow and froze when he spotted something far in the distance above the trees. A huge smile spread on his face. "There it is!"

The others stopped and looked where he pointed. "There what is?" Shem asked.

Ham spun and faced his brother, his eyes full of excitement. "The ark!"

Shem squinted for a moment and then laughed. "We're almost home."

"What's an ark?" Ar'yel asked.

"You'll see soon enough." Shem gestured for her to start walking. "Let's go. We should be able to make it before it gets dark."

A pair of birds shot out of the tall grass to their right, causing Noah to jump a little, much to the delight of his sons.

"Father is scared of two birds." Ham snickered.

Shem elbowed him. "And they were little birds."

Slightly embarrassed, Noah shook his head, trying to think of something witty to say.

Suddenly, the tall grass to their right parted as a furry creature leapt through the air toward them. Ham instinctively raised his right arm to protect his face as the animal slammed into him. He cried out and tumbled to the ground, the beast rolling over him to land just beyond.

Noah caught a glimpse of the powerful creature no bigger than a large bleater and recognized it as a pithoct, the two large fangs extending from its upper jaw making it easy to identify. In a heartbeat, the creature spun around and lunged for Ham again.

Just before the pithoct landed on Ham, Shem swung the solid branch he had been using as a staff and cracked the beast on the side of the head, causing it to land short of Ham. It snarled at Shem, but Shem wasted no time in striking at it again. This time it dodged his blow.

Ar'yel shouted and whipped a rock at the animal, smacking it in the side. Keeping an eye on the beast, she searched the ground for another object to throw.

Noah raced to stand over Ham, holding out his own makeshift staff toward the pithoct.

Glaring at Shem with its cold golden eyes, the creature slowly stepped toward him.

Noah found his opportunity. A quick thrust of his staff found its mark in the monster's midsection.

Angered, the pithoct shifted its focus to him. Shem instantly landed a crushing blow on top of the beast's head. It whimpered and crumpled to the ground for a moment before snarling and running off.

Noah knelt at Ham's side. Blood streamed from a long gash under his right eye. "Where else are you hurt?"

Ham moaned as his left hand reached over to grab the back of his right arm. "My arm burns." He pulled his hand back and looked at it. For a moment, he looked as though he might faint when he saw the blood.

Ar'yel dropped to her knees on Ham's right side. "We need to stop this bleeding right away." She pulled her newly acquired garment from her shoulders and tossed it to Shem. "Tear two long strips from that and then find me a strong stick — no longer than your arm."

Shem quickly tore the cloth and handed the strips to Ar'yel before scanning the ground for a stick.

Ham winced as she lifted his injured arm and briefly examined it. "What are you doing?"

"Can you turn to your side?"

With Noah's assistance, Ham rolled on his left side.

Ar'yel slid one end of the cloth under his arm and then pulled it until the two ends lined up. As she tied an overhand knot and pulled it tight, she said, "You have a very deep cut. If we don't stop the bleeding now, you may lose your arm or worse."

"Why are you tying a knot above the wound?" Ham asked.

"Trust me," she said.

"Got one." Shem hurried to Ar'yel and handed her the stick.

"That should work." She placed it on top of the knot. "Shem, hold this steady."

He reached across her and held the wooden piece in place.

Calm and confident, Ar'yel formed another overhand knot above the stick and tightened it. She brushed Ham's hair from his eyes and stroked his forehead once. "This might hurt for a few moments. Tell me if it gets too tight."

He nodded.

Using both hands, she slowly twisted the wood. "Shem, tear that other strip in half. Give one half to your father to hold against the cut on Ham's face."

Shem followed her instructions as she continued turning the stick.

"Ow!" Ham grunted. "Too tight."

She stopped as she studied his injury. "I'm sorry. Just a little tighter."

He clenched his teeth and nodded as Noah folded the cloth from Shem and gently pushed it against Ham's cheek.

Ar'yel gave the stick another quarter turn and then pointed to the cut. "Wrap the other one around it. Not too tight."

Once Shem finished tying the cloth, she directed him to keep the wood from unwinding. Standing up, she wiped her hands on her outfit. "The knot is keeping the blood from rushing to his arm. We can gradually loosen it as long as it doesn't start bleeding too much."

"Ham, can you stand?" Noah asked.

"I think so." He sat up slowly and then reached for the side of his chest and grimaced. "That thing hit me hard. It really hurts." Planting his left hand on the ground, he carefully climbed to his feet.

"This will only stop the bleeding." Ar'yel pointed to the bandage. "The wounds still need to be treated by a skilled healer or they'll become infected."

"I understand," Ham said.

Noah placed a hand on Ham's shoulder. "Kezia will know what to do. We'll go as fast as you can manage. Do you need any help?"

He shook his head. "Not right now. Let's move."

CHAPTER 32

"Your father will be quite surprised when he gets back. This looks great." Emzara sat on the recessed bench that would serve as her bed in one of the walled-off sections of their living quarters. Across a narrow hallway from her rested a tall storage cabinet for food and dishes. "Are you two sure you don't need my help right now?"

"No, we're almost done with this one," Japheth said.

Rayneh held up one end of a shelf as Japheth secured it to the upright beam. "I hope I'll have time to paint some of these things to make it feel like a home. Once we get the rest of these ledges secure, I think we'll be done with the major elements. We'll let your brothers finalize their own places." She pointed behind her to the open spaces adjoining Emzara's room.

"What about that extra empty space inside Shem's chamber?" Emzara asked.

Japheth moved down a rung on the short stepladder and skillfully used the plumb line to measure the level of another shelf. "Can you hold this steady, Mother?"

Emzara grabbed the bottom of the line and held it against the wall. "Right here?"

"Perfect." He glanced at Shem's room. "I thought we'd make a little drop-down desk for him to use, but I want to wait for Ham to get back. He'll figure out the best way to build it."

234

Rayneh grinned at her husband. "Are you sure you want to encourage Shem to read even more? How's he ever supposed to get a wife with his head buried in a scroll?"

Japheth shrugged. "That's his problem not mine. Besides, Kezia's here, maybe he'll wake up and start to pursue her."

Rayneh chuckled. "Well, I think she'd prefer to have your other brother pursue her."

Emzara smiled to herself but kept silent. *Most High, help me to trust You in this matter. You told Noah that our sons' wives would be on the ark. I believe You.*

Japheth marked the spot on the wall and tapped a fastener into it with a mallet. "There. I've got it."

Emzara stepped back and surveyed the whole area. "You've both worked tirelessly, being in the fields for most of the day and then here until late into the night. I'm proud of you."

Japheth lowered the mallet with a sigh. "Truth is, all the work has helped me not to think about the adventures my brothers have been having. I picture them seeing the world, and I want to be right there in the thick of the excitement with them."

Rayneh's eyes widened. "So you'd rather be out there somewhere than with me?"

"No, I'd prefer to be out there with you. But someone needed to stay behind to take care of the crops. It's just been hard because Shem doesn't long for adventure like I do."

Emzara put a hand on his shoulder. "Well, if it's any consolation, I think your two favorite women are very happy you're here. Isn't that right, Rayneh?"

"Mmhmm."

They continued on in silence for a while. The world was no longer what it had been, but Emzara understood why the unknown held such excitement for Japheth. *He's so much like his father in that way.*

"Have you thought about afterward?" Rayneh spoke gently as she unrolled a tapestry she had woven.

"What do you mean?" Emzara asked.

"Well, we're building this enormous boat to survive a worldwide flood, which will be an adventure." She looked at Japheth. "And then what about after that? What's the world going to be like when we stand on dry ground again? How much will we get to explore then?"

He paused. "I haven't given that much consideration yet. I've been so caught up in our work that I haven't really pondered what's ahead." He gave one last pound on the peg that he'd already secured. "Well, I think that does it for these."

"Come, Emzara!" Kezia's urgent cry came from outside the door of the ark.

Emzara hurried across the second deck to the large opening and looked out. She spotted Kezia pointing toward the sawmill. In the distance several figures crossed the clearing in the evening shadows. *Noah? Why are there only four?*

As Emzara descended the ramp, she called back to Japheth and Rayneh. "They're home!"

The familiar forms of Noah and her sons grew clearer as she rushed closer. Ham's long curly hair bounced as he leaned on his brother, one arm around Shem's shoulders. *Something must've happened. And who is that woman?* In spite of her labored breathing, she forced herself not to slow her pace.

Noah's group arrived at the tents at the same time as Emzara. Noah wrapped his arms around her and pressed his cheek against her hair. "I've missed you so much."

She stroked his head, holding him to her for a long moment. "What happened?" she asked, finally releasing him and turning to put her hands carefully on her youngest son's shoulders. She scanned the bandages, scrapes, and the amount of dried blood on the cloths, as well as Ham's ashen skin. "Kezia!"

"A pithoct attacked us earlier today," Noah said. "His arm and face have some deep cuts. We'll need to clean them out."

Kezia opened the flap of her tent. "Here, put him in mine so I don't have to move all the supplies I'll need."

"I'm glad you're back." Emzara brushed Noah's arm before moving to the door of the tent so she could hold open the other side of the entryway. Shem carefully moved Ham to Kezia's bed as she feverishly arranged cushions and blankets to create a comfortable spot for him.

The stranger moved to Ham's side and unwrapped the stiff cloths about his arm. "You must be Kezia, the healer. The wound will need to

236

be thoroughly cleansed and sewn up. This was the best I could do with what little we had."

Kezia knelt by Ham and covered her mouth as she studied the damage to his right side. She blinked hard and took a deep breath before looking up. "This wound is deep and could have taken his life. Thank you for stopping the bleeding." She clasped his left hand with a firm grip. "Cleaning this out is going to be extremely painful. I have to see the extent of the damage and whether it reached to your bone."

Ham pulled her hand up and rested it on his chest. "Do whatever you need to."

She stood and lit a lamp, then pointed toward the entrance. "I think it'd be best if the rest of you waited outside. This will be hard to watch."

"I'm going to remain with my brother," Shem said.

"No." Noah leaned close to Shem and spoke softly. "You should be the one to talk to Rayneh. I think it'll be easier on her if it comes from you."

Shem nodded grimly just as Japheth and Rayneh entered the tent.

"What happened?" Japheth asked.

"Where's my father?" Rayneh bit her lower lip.

Shem stepped beside them and said, "Come, I'll tell you outside." He nodded toward the exit. "Please."

Japheth followed Shem but briefly hesitated as he turned to look at his injured brother.

A knot formed in Emzara's stomach. Through pain-filled eyes, she looked at Noah and mouthed, "Elam?"

Noah pulled her close. "Outside. Come on, let Kezia do her work."

"Take care of my baby," Emzara said.

Kezia looked at Ham. "I'll do my best." Turning away, she moved about with quick, efficient motions, collecting the items she would need. From a small clay pot, she drew out a piece of wispy tree bark. "Here, you'll want to chew on this to help with the pain." Her voice turned playful as she said, "You know, this isn't exactly how I envisioned your return."

"Come on, Em." Noah pulled her hand as she continued to watch Ham and Kezia.

"Before you start." Ham took Kezia's hand again. "I promised myself I was going to talk to you when we got home, so I need to ask you something."

Noah pulled Emzara through the exit and closed the flaps behind them. "Let them talk."

Emzara pulled his head toward her and kissed him. "It's so good to have you home." She glanced around the small gathering place in the midst of the tents. Methuselah talked to the newcomer near a small pile of sticks set up in the fire pit. Shem sat with his back to them, facing Japheth and Rayneh. She wept loudly with her head buried in Japheth's shoulder as he tried to console her.

"What happened?" Emzara asked.

"Elam was killed yesterday," Noah said softly. "He gave his life to save us."

Emzara's lip quavered as her eyes moistened. She glanced at Rayneh and then pressed her face against Noah's chest, holding him tightly.

After a few moments, Noah kissed the top of her head and pulled back. "I'll explain more later, but first I need to introduce you to Ar'yel." He led her toward Methuselah and the young woman.

Emzara smiled before sniffling and pushing some hair behind her shoulder. "It's nice to meet you, Ar'yel."

"You must be Emzara. I've heard so much about you that I feel as if this is more of a reunion than an introduction."

Taken by the woman's candor and accent, Emzara embraced her. "Welcome."

Noah gestured with a nod of his head toward Kezia's tent. "Ar'yel not only saved Ham, but she saved the rest of us earlier this week." Noah recounted their harrowing escape from the tree village and Elam's heroic actions to protect them.

A jumble of emotions filled Emzara as he spoke: elation at her husband's return, concern for her son, sorrow over Elam's death, and admiration for Ar'yel's bravery. She watched the beautiful young woman during Noah's retelling and saw how Ar'yel graciously deflected the praise heaped on her.

While Noah spoke of the pithoct attack, Shem walked over and sat a short distance from Ar'yel.

Rayneh appeared to be listening, though she still rested her head on Japheth's shoulder.

"All of that was in the past few days," Methuselah said. "What about the rest of the trip? Did Lamech decide to stay home?"

Noah hesitated and then pulled Emzara close. "Father made it home, but it wasn't as we hoped. Just before we arrived, our boat was attacked and he was struck by a poisoned arrow in his shoulder." Noah's lower lip trembled. "Within two weeks he was gone."

Tears raced down Emzara's cheeks as she watched her husband struggle to describe his father's death. Slowly, she turned to Methuselah, who had slumped down and closed his eyes.

Noah took a deep breath and sat up straight. "The tragedy gave him an opportunity to speak to most of my brothers and sisters. In his final words, he urged all of us to follow the Creator. And when he passed. . . ." Noah shook his head. "It was peaceful. He said that he could finally rest."

After a long silence, Japheth cleared his throat. "Are Garun and Laleel safe?"

Using a small stick, Shem drew in the dirt. "We don't know. They left after Grandfather's burial. They wanted to find their own children and grandchildren and plead with them to follow the Most High before the flood comes."

Methuselah shakily rose to his feet and lifted his arms above his head. "Let us pray the Creator will grant them safe travel and opportunities to speak to their loved ones."

Shem spoke quietly to Ar'yel. She nodded and then copied him as he closed his eyes and held up his palms.

Rayneh slipped to her knees and bent forward, putting her ear next to the ground.

Emzara closed her eyes, smiling through her tears at the way her daughter-in-law chose to pay tribute to Elam.

"O Most High, Creator of heaven and earth." Methuselah sniffled. "We've been reminded again of the price of rebelling against You. You warned Greatfather that he would die if he ate from the forbidden tree. Like him, we have all sinned against You, and one day, we'll all return to the ground. But we believe death is not the end for us. We have hope that we'll see Elam again, and that we'll see—" Methuselah hesitated and sniffled. "That I'll see my. . . ."

After a brief pause, Emzara sensed Noah leave her side and heard his footsteps move toward Methuselah.

"And that my grandfather will see his son again, and I'll see my father, who is now at rest. But until that time comes, You've called us to build this ark, and You've promised to protect us from the coming judgment. Please help Ham to heal from his injuries, and watch over us as we strive to follow Your ways."

Methuselah continued the prayer when Noah stopped. He asked the Most High to watch over Garun and Laleel as well as Purlek and Evet. When he talked about the flood and the Creator's promises to Noah, Emzara's heart quickened with hope. He prayed with authority and conviction and she imagined he spoke just as his father, Enoch, had spoken while prophesying so long ago.

A long silence fell over the group. It was eventually broken by Kezia's soft voice from behind. "Ma-Zara, Ham's asking for you."

Quietly, she stood, padded to the tent, and stepped inside. As she allowed the flap to fall behind her, she asked Kezia, "How is he?"

Kezia grinned. "He whined a lot, but I think he's going to be alright. We'll need to closely monitor those wounds for a while to make sure they don't get infected."

Emzara walked to Ham and knelt down beside him. His face bore multiple stitches, and she imagined his arm boasted many more. She bent down and kissed his forehead. "I'm so glad you're home. How are you feeling?"

He gave her a weak smile and raised an eyebrow. "You need to take that needle from Kezia. She wields it as if it were a weapon. My arm is more thread than skin now."

Kezia lowered herself on the opposite side of Ham. "I told you he was whiny." She smiled at Ham. "I'm just glad that the beast didn't get closer to his eye." She rested a light hand against his cheek, and Emzara did a double take when her youngest reached up and held it.

Ham looked at Emzara. "You told me that Father whines a lot to you when he isn't feeling well."

Emzara shrugged. "Yeah, he does sometimes."

"Well, I guess I'm just practicing how to be a good husband then." Ham kissed Kezia's hand and she giggled.

Emzara's heart leapt and her eyes grew wide as she stared at Kezia in disbelief.

Kezia bit her lower lip and nodded slowly. "You don't mind if I marry your baby, do you?"

Suppressing a squeal, Emzara excitedly patted Ham's good arm as she stood before racing around him to embrace Kezia. "Oh, I've been hoping for this since the day you were born." She let go and smiled at Ham. "It's about time you struck up the courage to ask her."

Kezia laughed. "I threatened to give him more stitches if he didn't."

"How's he doing?" Noah's voice made her jump.

Emzara rushed to embrace her husband. "Wonderful."

* * *

"Ham seems to be healing up. He cut some boards for the ark today." Noah lay back and placed his hands under his head, which he always did while looking up at the stars, for as long as Emzara could remember.

She rested her head on his sturdy chest and stretched her feet out. "I'm so thankful. But each time I see that scar on his cheek, I can't help but shudder at what could have happened."

"I think he likes it — makes him look tougher." Noah rubbed her scalp with his fingers. "But even that mark is looking a lot better."

"Kezia really worked wonders on him."

"Do you mean on his injuries or on his new devotion to her?" Noah chuckled lightly, which made her head bounce a little on his chest.

"Yes." She smiled up into the night sky. The darkened shape of the ark cut into some of the glittery host, and as she listened to his heart beating, she delighted in completing another day of work.

"I'm looking for my favorite grandson, foreman on a major undertaking, but instead I find a mere youth with his lovely young wife."

"Grandfather!" Noah jerked, causing Emzara's head to bounce again.

They sat up, and Emzara tucked her legs underneath her wrapped dress and smoothed the fabric over them.

Methuselah slowly lowered himself onto the grass beside them, wheezing with laughter. "Startling you never gets old, no matter how ancient I become. Pretty amazing, isn't it?" He gestured at the structure behind them. "Everything is taking shape just as the Most High said it would."

"Yeah." Noah's tone suddenly took on a somber note. He picked a blade of grass and wiggled it in his fingertips. The broken pieces, barely visible in the low light, fell to the earth in front of him.

Methuselah tilted his head to one side. "Something wrong with that?"

Noah let out a breath and shook his head. "I don't know."

Emzara had not heard him sound so dejected since Purlek and Evet left. "What is it?" She placed a hand on his leg.

"I don't know if I'm ready for what's to come."

"Oh, well that makes two of us," Emzara said.

"You aren't ready for the flood?" Methuselah pointed to the ark. "That's obvious. It isn't finished yet."

"That's not it, Grandfather." Emzara offered him a gentle smile. "Think about what the Creator told him. The ark is for him, me, our sons, and their wives. We always struggled with that. I mean, we wondered about . . . well . . . about whether those would be the only people on board. And look at all that's happened within such a short time."

"You mean because Garun and Laleel left? And because my son and Elam are no longer with us?

"Yes." Emzara's sad tone nearly matched Noah's.

Methuselah leaned back on his hands. "Of course, you need to think about the good things as well. You already have one daughter-in-law and will have another one by this time tomorrow. And Ar'yel spends most of her days learning more about the Creator from Shem. I don't think any of us will be surprised if she soon becomes your third daughter-in-law."

"Yes, those things are terrific," Emzara said. "And I truly hope you're right about Ar'yel."

"But, what about you, Grandfather?" Noah dropped a hand to the ground. "I'm worried about you."

"Pah! Don't spend your time worrying about me. I don't think I'm meant to be on the ark."

Noah sat straight. "What? Why?"

"I've lived a good long life. I saw from an early age what it meant to trust the words of the Creator. You've heard from Him as well, and you know He was clear in giving you the exact dimensions of this contraption, so I think you know He's been just as clear when He told you who was going to be on board."

"But that would mean that—"

"That I won't be on it." Methuselah shrugged. "Listen, Noah, when He first spoke to you, you had no children at all. And when we moved here, do you not think the Most High knew you would have three sons, each of whom would need a wife?"

Noah dropped his gaze. All was quiet except for the chorus of nightly insects around them.

"Don't be sorry for me. The Creator will always do what's right. Look at those who have gone before me. Trusting Him never guarantees personal safety in this life."

"You mean like Father and Elam?"

"Yes, and a host of others."

Emzara folded her hands together. "Like my father. And our friends Aterre, Tubal-Cain, and Adira." Saying their names brought back memories of cherished times with them.

"Exactly."

"And this doesn't bother you?" Noah looked at the elderly man and clasped Emzara's hand.

"Not anymore. The fact that I'll die isn't a shock to me — it's been guaranteed ever since Greatfather sinned. Sure, I'll miss seeing your children grow up and have their own children, but I'm tired of this world, and I want to see your father and my father again." He lifted his index finger toward Noah. "It helps knowing that my grandson and his wife will be the ones on the ark. You need to know how proud I am of both of you. And, Noah, your father, he was, too. He talked about it all the time. He was so thrilled to know how closely you and Emzara walk with the Creator."

Noah placed his other hand on top of Emzara's so that her hand was sandwiched between both of his.

Methuselah gestured to the form behind him. "This ark is a testament to the Creator's mercy in a world that deserves judgment. I find tremendous comfort in that."

CHAPTER 33

Iri Geshem — Noah's 599th year

Peering at her reflection in the oval-shaped gold panel, Naamah took inventory of her face. The horizontal lines on her forehead appeared deeper than yesterday. Creases also jagged their way from her eyes and worn lips. Tugging at her skin, she tried in vain to coax the sagging areas to tighten. A scowl made the creases even more pronounced. She sighed and brushed on a colored powder to cover some of the blotches, then pulled out a container of kohl and applied it heavily, accentuating the almond shape of her eyes. *That's a little better.* Working her way down her face, she used the kohl to create twisted shapes and patterns that met up with some of the serpent markings across her bare shoulders. *I can still flaunt you, my beautiful friends.*

Carefully lining her lips with a deep burgundy color, she hoped it drew enough attention away from the lines. Nothing could be done for the pinkness in her eyes or the dullness in her gaze. She donned her massive crown that angled back nearly a cubit, appreciating it not only for the power it conveyed but also for its effect of drawing attention away from her aging frame.

The embellishments let people see enough to remember her beauty without letting them see the cruel effects of time. While she masked a couple centuries, she never fully escaped the constant fear of growing old and dying. She looked at her weathered hands and instantly thought of the seer's leathery skin before he died. She sighed and shook her head. *But he was 982 and I'm not even 600. Nachash, when will you teach me how to live forever?*

After two thumps on the door, Nivlac's voice sounded from outside her room. "I'm here, my queen."

"Come in."

He entered her room and stared at her. Dressed in his finest ornate wrap instead of his typical armor, he would serve as both guard and consort tonight. He lowered his head. "My queen, as always, you look exquisite."

The people of Iri Geshem had embraced Naamah's decision to move the empire's capital to their city, and during this initial celebration, they needed to see their queen in a more personable light. They feared and respected her, but her advisors insisted the citizens' loyalty would significantly increase if they witnessed her enjoying a gala.

"Is everything ready?"

"Almost. The banquet hall is filling up. The last of the governors just arrived and will be seated soon." He took several steps toward her until she felt his warm breath on her face. "You'll enchant them with your beauty tonight, just as you always do."

She kept silent and turned away from him.

"Is something troubling you?"

"I don't know where to start."

"Is it about this evening?"

"No." She shook her head and faced him.

"Enemies?" He grabbed her hand and bowed slightly. "Tell me and I'll take great pleasure in administering their torture."

The corner of her lips moved upward in a half-smile before turning serious again. "It's me."

"Tell me what you want of me. You know I'll do anything for you."

Naamah pushed him back into a low cushioned bench until he sat. She paced before him. "I've never spoken these words aloud."

Nivlac rubbed his chin and waited.

"I'm still haunted by seeing my mentor's death."

"But he was so old. Why would that trouble you?"

She lifted her arms. "He gained strength for a while after my intercession, but then later that night, he was gone. Why didn't Nachash spare his life like I asked him to?"

"Maybe he had nothing else to teach you. Maybe Nachash didn't want to save him. What if you were depending too much on the old man instead of our god?"

"It shouldn't matter. I've been a faithful servant all these years — he should've honored such a simple request. But it wasn't so much that he died; it was how he died." She shuddered, recalling the terrifying moments as if they occurred yesterday. "With his last breaths, he screamed about flames. Why would a man so devoted to Nachash be in such anguish?" Leaning in close to Nivlac, she kept her voice just above a whisper. "What if—" She looked around, even though no one else was in the room. "What if Nachash lied, and I've been deceived all these years?" She slumped to the floor.

"Those are disturbing thoughts, my queen." He gently stroked her shoulder.

"And?"

"I can only judge what I see before me. The seer was ready to go and that was no one's fault. If he was in pain, likely it was because of his illness, not Nachash's inability to heal or some malevolent behavior. You're assuming information you just don't know and torturing yourself with it."

She glared up at him. "You weren't there. You didn't see and hear his horror."

"I've killed thousands of people. Most of them are terrified."

"I know, but it wasn't like that." She shook her head. "His fear was far beyond anything I've seen before. I don't want to die like that." She looked down and rubbed her forehead. "I don't want to die at all."

"Why worry about that now? You're healthy and have centuries to live."

"It terrifies me every moment of the day and into the night. Nachash promised to give knowledge and understanding to make his people wise and powerful. You know the Sepha tree that is marked on your back? It isn't just a symbol. It's based on an actual tree that Nachash made. Those who eat of its fruit will live forever as gods. I must find that tree." She shook with determination.

Nivlac pushed himself into a more upright position. "And the House of Knowledge doesn't have anything about it?"

"Nothing. My scribes have covered most of the known world — and they have yet to come up with any news."

"Let me help you. We have no more threats to the empire. I'll pour all my energy into helping you achieve this goal."

"Fine, but you must still serve as my chief protector."

"There's nothing I'd rather do."

"Oh, you wouldn't rather spend this evening with some of the younger, more beautiful women that will be here?"

Nivlac looked into her eyes. "My queen, no one in the world is more beautiful than you."

She forced back a smile. "You've always been faithful to me."

He stood and pulled her up, too. "Let your worries rest for tonight. Celebrate your accomplishments as queen of the world. Celebrate this new magnificent palace that was built to honor all that you've done both as ruler and priestess."

Naamah shrugged and rechecked her appearance. A night of revelry would take her mind off her problems and delight her people. She took his arm and they marched out of the room. As they descended the wide, winding staircase, Nivlac guided her into the large throne room and to her chair on the raised dais.

A herald raced over and bowed before her. He stood and turned to face the audience. "People of Iri Geshem, of Havil, and of the world, I present to you the beautiful, the brilliant, the proud, the pious, the mistress of Nachash . . . Naamah of Havil, Queen of the World."

As cheers erupted, Naamah inhaled deeply and raised her hands. Nivlac stood beside her, beckoning the people to exult her. The volume of praise increased as the frenzied crowd lauded their leader.

"Let us dedicate this night to Nachash!" She bowed her head and waited for the crowd to follow her lead. "O mighty Nachash, thank you for the gifts you have bestowed upon us. Help the people enjoy your festival." *And guide me to the tree of immortality, and you'll receive praise like this from the whole world forever.*

Lifting her head, she flashed a smile, and those in attendance broke into renewed cheers. With a flick of her wrist, her bangles clinked against each other, and the musicians, led by Jubal, played a tune to signal the start of the festivities.

Naamah made her way around the room, greeting each person as if they were her oldest friend. She sipped intoxicating beverages from golden goblets, savored the heavy smell of incense, and enjoyed the pulsating music. But none of that compared to the many praises she received about her beauty and accomplishments.

Eventually, longing for a slight reprieve from the gaiety, she sashayed to the tall colonnades, each crowned by half a dozen rows of scalloped carvings ornamenting the tops like a fine lace.

She rested her hands against the column behind her. The sea breeze dusted her cheeks with a light mist, and she held her face out appreciatively. She grinned as she thought about the two homes that had previously occupied this spot. Noah may have escaped her grasp in the arena, but she would wipe his name from the people's memory as easily as she wiped his home from the land. After demolishing the buildings, she deliberately set the palace's cornerstone on the three nearby graves.

Looking to the east, she spied the bustling shipyard and harbor that boasted her finest ships. An image of its previous owner appeared in her mind, and she glared into the distance. *He was so sure that he'd survive the arena. How could he know?* She shook her head and took comfort in the answer she had given herself many times. *He's delusional and was just very lucky.* Her thoughts suddenly turned to the night she became queen. *My father was so sure that he'd live beyond a thousand years, but he was wrong.* She narrowed her eyes and pursed her lips. *He was wrong about so much. Such a fool. So arrogant. To think that he cursed the person who dared to kill him that he'd be avenged seventy-seven-fold. As if he had such power.* A short laugh escaped her lungs. "Empty words, nothing more."

Uninvited, an image of the seer's final moments pushed into her thoughts, causing a chill to run down her spine. *Will I face death in fear like him or with confidence like Noah?* She shook her head. *I won't face it at all after we find that tree.* Being alone made it easy for her thoughts to attack her, so she reentered the great hall to enjoy the merriment. She returned to her throne and sat down, stroking the armrests and watching the barely clad dancers before her.

In a brief break between songs, Tsek approached her. "Pardon the interruption, my queen."

"What is it?"

"I bring important news and a gift." With a hand signal, he ordered a pair of guards to lead two bound prisoners toward them. The captives' heads were covered with black cloth.

Naamah glanced about the giant hall. Most of the people continued in their revelry, although a handful stared at the prisoners. She tipped her head toward Tsek. "Speak."

"The rumors about your half-brother Jabal and his mother, Adah, were true. We found them living among a group of people in the western frontier."

Naamah sat up and looked closely at the prisoners. "And you've brought them here?"

"We followed your orders." Tsek pointed toward the musicians. "Jubal is all that remains of your immediate family."

A smile tugged at her lips. "Did they suffer?"

He shrugged. "Based on their screams, my guess is that they didn't enjoy being burned alive in their tents."

"Excellent." She pointed toward the captives. "And my gift?"

"Before we torched the village, one of my men overhead these two discussing something you need to hear."

She raised an eyebrow. "Now I'm curious."

Prodded by the guards, the prisoners shuffled forward and knelt in front of her.

Tsek lifted the veil from the female first.

The woman's disheveled black hair hung over her dark face. She breathed in shallow gasps as she glanced around with her wide eyes peering through her hair.

Naamah leaned back, enjoying the opportunity to watch the frightened woman. She turned her attention to the other prisoner, a broad-shouldered man with strong arms.

Tsek gripped the veil on the man's head and yanked it off.

The abductee slowly lifted his head and looked directly at the queen.

Naamah's hand flew to her mouth to cover her gasp. *Could it be? Tu come back to life?* She blinked rapidly, trying to understand the sight before her.

Tsek lifted his sword toward the captives. "State your name and lineage before Queen Naamah."

The woman lowered her gaze to the floor. "I'm Evet, daughter of Bekel, son of Toman."

The man dropped his eyes momentarily but then studied Naamah and spoke calmly. "And I'm Purlek, son of Tubal-Cain, son of Lamech."

Naamah leaned forward. "You're my brother's son?" She kept her tone calm, but her hands gripped the chair tightly. "You bear a strong resemblance to him."

"Thank you."

"And is Evet your wife?" Naamah asked.

He hesitated before nodding. "She is."

"Oh, what a delightful surprise! Commander Tsek, unbind them. After all, this man is my nephew." She smiled at the couple before beckoning a servant with a snap of her fingers. "Fetch them some food and drink. They've come a long way. And bring them some cushions. When you return, I want you to clean them up a little so they can be in my presence."

Before long, Purlek and Evet sat on the pillows. As they nibbled on the choice food, Naamah opened with small talk, telling them about the new palace and the extent of her empire. She asked Purlek about his career and was pleasantly surprised to learn that he was also a blacksmith. Thinking about Tubal-Cain sparked a tinge of nostalgia within her, but as the conversation extended, she decided to get to the true reason her nephew's life had been spared.

Naamah handed her drink to a servant and stared at Purlek. "So Commander Tsek said that you spoke of something I need to hear."

Purlek chewed a few times and swallowed before shrugging. "I'm not sure what he means."

"My dear nephew, do not hide things from me. Not that I'd do this since we're family, but you know that with a snap of my fingers, I could have your wife killed, right? Slowly, painfully, and I could make you watch all of it." She chuckled but included enough of an edge to make it sound sinister.

He put a hand on Evet and narrowed his gaze at Naamah. "I'm sure you could, but I really don't know what the commander is talking about."

"Commander, perhaps you can remind him what your men overheard."

Tsek nodded and nudged Purlek with his sword. "Before you were detained, you told your wife not to speak about a certain place."

"What place would that be, Nephew?"

Purlek bit his lip and glanced at Evet, who shook her head in return. "I don't remember."

"Very well." Naamah yawned and feigned disinterest. "Tsek, bite off one of her fingers, and then take her to Cele-Nach the priest. She can live out her remaining days serving Nachash as a temple prostitute."

"No!" Purlek jumped up and positioned himself between Tsek and Evet. "I'll tell you."

"Then let's hear it," Naamah said. "And your wife can keep her finger and remain by your side."

Purlek breathed deeply a couple of times with his head down. "I told her to make sure she doesn't mention anything about the garden."

Naamah rose to her feet and lifted Purlek's chin. "And what garden would that be?"

"I don't know its name."

"Well, where is it?"

He pulled away from her and faced Evet. "It's in the land of Eden."

Naamah stared at Nivlac, stroking her chin. "Eden? The haunted land?"

"Yes."

"And what's so important about this garden that you didn't want my soldiers to know?"

"I'm not sure. I—" Purlek rubbed the back of his neck. "I've never even gone to it."

"And yet you know where it is. How?"

"We lived very close to it for a while."

She returned to her throne. "But you never went there. Why?"

Purlek held her gaze. "Because it's forbidden and guarded by . . . by—" He shrugged. "By creatures or beings that aren't human."

She cast a sideways glance at him. "And how would you know that if you never went there?"

"Because someone from our group did go there, and he warned us about it."

Naamah drummed her fingers on the throne's armrest. "Commander, were you in Eden when you found him?"

"No, my queen. We did not enter that land."

She pounded her fist on the armrest. "You told me that you lived in Eden. No more lies, or else."

Purlek shook his head. "We did. That wasn't a lie. We lived there for a while, and about a decade ago, we moved to the plains where your men captured us."

She narrowed her gaze at him. "And how far is Eden from where my men found you?"

"A few weeks journey to the west." He dropped to his knees. "Please, I answered your questions. Please let us go."

Naamah smiled at him. "Of course. Just a couple more. What were you doing in Eden?"

"Working."

"Working? As a blacksmith? Who would need a blacksmith in that land? Does anyone even live there?"

"It was just a small group of people — not even a tiny village. We went there to help the leader build a boat. But we grew tired of the work and moved away."

Naamah sat upright and her eyes drifted in the direction of the shipyard. "Last question. When exactly did you move there?"

Purlek scrunched his brow for a moment before his eyes shot open. "It was the year we were married — 99 years ago."

Naamah leaned close to Nivlac and spoke softly. "Is that when we took control of this city?"

Her guard looked toward the ceiling as he seemed to be running the calculations in his head. "Yes, my queen."

A smile spread wide on Naamah's face. "Commander Tsek. Take these two to a guest room. Give them the best accommodations available, but post some guards to monitor them at all times. Then call every available soldier in the region to be ready to march by the end of the week."

Tsek nodded. "Yes, my queen." He ordered Purlek and Evet to stand and directed them toward the exit.

Naamah's heartbeat quickened as she stood and took Nivlac's arm, flashing him a seductive grin. "Would you escort me to my room?"

Nivlac's face lit up. "Of course, my beautiful queen." As they walked away from the throne, Nivlac asked, "Why are you gathering the army?"

"As soon as they are ready, we are marching on that garden, and I will eat from the tree of immortality."

Nivlac's smile faded and he scratched his head. "But what was all that about a man building a boat and the time when we took over Iri Geshem?"

252

Naamah rolled her eyes. "Sometimes you're so foolish. After I eat from the tree, I'll finally kill that shipbuilder."

"Shipbuilder." He spoke the word quietly to himself as he tried to put the pieces together. Suddenly, he stopped and his eyes danced as he beheld her. "Noah."

"Noah couldn't even enter the garden." She lifted her chin. "But I will."

CHAPTER 34

Land of Eden — Noah's 600th year

"Finished already?" Ar'yel asked.

"I wish." Using his arm, Shem wiped sweat from his forehead.

"How long do you think it'll take?" Emzara asked.

Ham's arm muscles rippled as he picked up two steaming buckets of pitch. "Well, the interior only took a few weeks."

With Ar'yel's assistance, Emzara slowly stirred the large tub of tree resin as it simmered over hot coals. "But your father said the outside will take a lot longer."

"It will. It's a larger surface, and we don't have three decks to stand on like we did inside, so we'll have to spend time moving the platforms around." Ham directed his thumb over his shoulder at Noah. "He thinks it'll take six weeks, but I say we can do it in four if the weather stays nice."

"And if you'd start working instead of talking." Noah chuckled as he set four empty pails on the ground near Emzara.

"Well, maybe I'm just being optimistic," Ar'yel said, "but I think Ham's guess is probably closer to—" She squealed as Shem, from behind, spread some of the sticky substance on her cheek. She quickly slid her hand down the large stir stick, allowing it to collect some warm resin, and then spun and wiped it on his neck and beard.

He feigned outrage. "Do you know how long it'll take to wash that out?"

She laughed and fell into his arms.

Ham rolled his eyes. "Probably six weeks if we have to depend on these two."

"Aah!" Ar'yel giggled as Shem stuck more goo on her forehead while they kissed. "You sneak." After grabbing a stirrer, she pointed it at him. She jabbed and he dodged, and then she gave chase.

Noah snorted while dipping the fill bucket into the tub before dumping it into a pail on the ground. "Why do you think I said six weeks in the first place?" He repeated the process to top off his first bucket. "Have you seen Grandfather yet?"

"No," Emzara said. "Do you want me to wake him?"

Noah shook his head. "We stayed up pretty late around the fire last night. Let him sleep."

Tapping his foot as he waited for Shem to fill his buckets instead of goofing around with his bride, Noah marveled at the size of the nearly completed ark looming above them. A sense of satisfaction filled him as he considered the massive labor of love. After finishing the multi-layered hull during the last whole moon, they decided to cover the inside with pitch first to allow it time to air out while they coated the outside.

Gopherwood trees made the perfect timbers for shipbuilding. Straight and strong, yet relatively easy to cut, the trees had also provided them with vast amounts of the resin used to make the pitch. Many years of chopping down trees and preparing the lumber yielded a mound of the viscous substance roughly the size of one of the tents. Heating the resin allowed them to separate impurities and to apply it. Based on how much they had used on the ark's interior, Noah estimated they had more than enough remaining to waterproof the exterior.

Tired of waiting for his brother, Ham filled Shem's buckets and set them at his feet with an exaggerated grunt. "We have work to do."

Shem laughed and whispered something to Ar'yel before backing away. "I'm ready. I was just waiting for you two."

The men walked a short distance to the lift and set their loads on the platform. Through an ingenious system of pulleys and ropes attached to the top of the ark, the mechanism allowed them to move the platform to any point along the side of the ship. A small clay stove loaded with hot coals in its lower half rested on the lift to keep individual buckets of pitch warm enough for application.

"You boys go ahead," Noah said. "I just thought of something at the door I need to check."

Ham shook his head with a half-smile. "You really are determined to make this last six weeks, aren't you?"

Noah chuckled. "I should be ready to help on the next load."

Shem grabbed the rope to lift them off the ground. "At least this will be lighter." Winking, he tugged on the line and the platform slowly rose.

The ark's door posed a slight problem. The door itself could be coated with pitch, but once it closed with everyone inside, the small gaps between it and the rest of the hull would remain uncoated. Making sure the door fit snugly reduced the problem, and they could waterproof the interior. *That might be enough. At least it'll be above the waterline.*

"Father!"

Noah turned to see Japheth running under the ark toward him.

"Where's Mother?"

"She should be at the pitch pot. What's the matter?"

"Nothing, but she needs to see something. Come with me."

Noah and Japheth strode back to where Emzara and Ar'yel transferred hardened clumps of resin from a cart into the smoldering pot.

"Mother, you need to come with me."

Emzara glanced up from her work. "Why?"

"It's a surprise. Can you leave for a little while?"

"Go. I'll take care of it," Ar'yel said.

Emzara briefly stretched her back and then walked with Noah as they followed Japheth back toward the fields. "Where are we going?"

"To the root bulb field. We were harvesting them when something amazing happened."

"What is it?" Emzara asked.

Japheth smiled. "I told you, it's a surprise."

They walked down a narrow trail separating various crops. As they moved beyond the last row of tall pebble fruit plants, Noah spotted Rayneh holding a furry gray animal while kneeling beside another one.

Emzara grabbed Noah's arm and looked at him with wide eyes. "I've never—" She glanced at Japheth. "Where did they come from?"

"They just crawled out of the forest and came right up to us."

Rayneh glanced up, a broad smile across her face. "I don't remember seeing these in your drawings. They're really furry."

"And adorable," Emzara said as she walked quickly toward Rayneh.

Noah followed and looked closely at the creatures. Roughly the size of a chubby toddler, they sported large fuzzy ears, a wide face with a black nose, and relatively long arms. A gray coat covered much of their bodies, with the exception of white fur around their mouths, inside their ears, and over their bellies.

Emzara cooed as she bent down near Rayneh. "Can I hold him?"

"This one is the female." Rayneh carefully lifted the animal toward Emzara. "Look at her stomach. It has a pouch, like the leapers you told me about."

"It does." Emzara grinned at Noah and the tone of her voice went up along with her excitement. "Look at this. I'm sure she carries her babies in there." She took the creature from her daughter-in-law and it soon wrapped its arms around hers, clinging to her much the same way a small child would. Emzara stroked the animal's back. "It's so soft."

Noah cracked a smile. He loved seeing his wife's happiness, but something else stirred his own delight. He had to admit it, these creatures were rather adorable.

"So you've never seen these before?" Rayneh asked.

"Not that I recall." She gently scratched the back of its neck and spoke to it like she had spoken to their sons when they were babies. "And I'm sure I would've remembered something so cute."

Rayneh nodded. "I was sure you would've had drawings of them, so I wonder if these are the first two animals the Creator is sending to the ark. Maybe since you haven't studied them before, He's giving us time to observe them now to figure out what they eat and how to care for them."

Noah raised an eyebrow as he watched his wife. "Interesting. If that's the case, then you'd better start studying them — He may send other animals you haven't seen before."

"Noah!"

He turned at the sound of Kezia's voice and saw her running toward them. "What is it?"

As she approached them, she wiped tears from her cheeks. She glanced at each of them and then focused on Noah. She shook her head slowly. "I brought your grandfather some bean brew, but—" She looked away and blinked back a tear. "He's gone."

"Did you look for him?" Japheth asked.

Emzara stepped to Noah's side and gently brushed his arm.

Noah had anticipated hearing this news before the onset of the flood, but the expectation did nothing to relieve the pit that instantly formed in his stomach. Putting a hand on Japheth's shoulder, Noah took a deep breath to steady his thoughts and voice. "Son, she means that Grandfather is now resting forever."

* * *

"I hope I never have to look at these again. Five weeks of being covered with pitch." Shem stowed the cleaned-out buckets in their designated space on the ark's first deck.

"That was just the outside." Ham waited until his brother's arm cleared the edge of the shelf before he lowered the wooden door and latched it. "How about we forget where we put these?"

"Put what?" Shem asked.

"The pitch buck — oh, right, what were we talking about?" Ham chuckled and scraped at some hardened pitch on the back of his hand with a fingernail.

"Watch out." Noah pushed the low cart bearing the large pitch pot beneath the recently closed cabinet. "I'm going to put this big . . . I-don't-remember-what-this-is . . . under whatever those things were that you just stored." He winked at Shem as he secured the cart with a rope. *Maybe I should wait to tell them that we'll need to pitch the door once it's shut.*

Shem grabbed the oil lamp from the shelf behind them. "What's next?"

"That's just about everything," Noah said. "Not counting the animals and some of the food."

Ham leaned against one of the massive vertical timbers in the middle of the ark. "How about a break to enjoy some bean brew?"

"Oh, I like that idea." Shem looked up the center gap that allowed light from the cubit-high opening along the ark's roof to spill into the lower decks. Even with the illumination from above, the lowest deck remained fairly dark, necessitating the use of oil lamps. "Looks pretty bright out now."

Noah yawned. "Yeah, I could use some. Let's go."

They walked the nearest route to the second deck. A sturdy ramp stood on each end of the ark between the first and second decks and another pair of inclines led from the second to the third deck. Footholds made of long wooden strips stretched horizontally across the ramps. Upon reaching the second floor, they headed for the large door.

A wide array of animal noises filled the air as they neared the opening. Noah paused at the top of the long exterior ramp and shook his head. The Creator's faithfulness never ceased to amaze him. Shortly after the two furry gray animals had arrived, approximately two dozen pairs of beasts showed up. As Rayneh had guessed, they were all new to Emzara, and the two women spent plenty of time recording their habits and diets.

Now Noah looked out over a vista of wildlife. In the past few days, thousands of animals had moved into the clearing, and more seemed to have arrived every time Noah looked at them. He scanned the gathering for Emzara. Consumed by wonder, she had barely slept, and her happy chatter about her new findings kept him up late as well. She wanted the sun to rise early so she might have more time to spend with each of the animals. Off to one side of the field, he saw several pairs of young keluks with Emzara standing among them.

"I can't believe how many there are," Ham said.

"It's amazing. Mother said there are already more than a thousand different kinds here. I wonder how many more will come," Shem said. "I think she is going to enjoy our time in the ark more than anyone. She'll be around them all the time."

Noah headed down the ramp. "Yeah, I might not get to see her until it's all over. Let's go get that bean brew."

"I'll try to find Kezia," Ham said. "She may have already made some."

"And I'll check to see if your mother needs any help before I join you."

"And I'm going to see what Ar'yel is doing," Shem said.

Noah and his sons reached the ground and moved in separate directions. Row after row of cages, each filled with flying creatures of a variety of sizes and brilliant colors, lined the base of the ramp. Rayneh dumped seeds from a bag into the feeding bowl in one of the cages. A short distance beyond her, Japheth led a group of tarocs toward their enclosure.

Noah lifted his eyes toward the sky as he pondered the Creator's ability to bring so many creatures together in an orderly and peaceful fashion. The beasts that had become carnivorous during Noah's lifetime never bothered those that would normally be their prey, and like the tarocs, they cooperated as they were separated according to their kinds.

259

The vast majority of the creatures were rather small and light. Emzara said that only about 15 percent of them weighed more than a large sack of grain. At Ham's suggestion, they had brought out the cages and enclosures for the smaller animals. Housing them now would keep them safe from all the commotion and make it possible to easily carry them onto the ark by the wagonload. Later, the larger beasts would be led directly to their pens inside.

Feathers, fur, and scales filled Noah's view as he made his way toward Emzara. The smells and sounds produced a picture in his mind of what their time on the ark would be like.

"There you go," Ar'yel said as she set two palm-sized furry creatures in a little cage. She glanced at Noah as he passed by. "This is amazing."

"Indeed." Noah shot her a smile as he thought about her past, living among people obsessed with death. Raised to slaughter God's creatures for their bones, Ar'yel now took great delight in caring for the animals.

She pointed behind her. "Emzara is over there by the keluks."

"No surprise there. Oh, Shem is looking for you." Noah stopped as something whizzed past him. A heartbeat later, a striking blue and green buzzbird zipped in front of him and hovered about a cubit away from his face. It watched him as its tiny wings fluttered so fast he could not even see them. In an instant, the miniature bird sped away. *Incredible.* Noah grinned and tried to track the creature, but it soon vanished from his sight.

Spotting the keluks, with their telltale long necks and hairy tufts on their heads, Noah dodged an array of scaly and furry creatures as he walked toward his wife's favorite animals. He found her stroking the neck of one of the brown and white beasts. "Em."

She smiled at him. "This is so exciting."

"How's your counting coming along?"

"It was going well." She patted the animal before taking a few steps and hugging Noah. "I'm sorry. I got a little distracted."

He looked into her eyes. "I can see why. This must feel like a dream for you."

"It does." She spread her arms out wide. "Seeing all of these at one time. Oh Noah, the Creator is so good to us."

Noah snorted. "Just remember that when we're stuck inside the ark and cleaning up their waste day after day."

"I won't mind it at all." She kissed his cheek and stepped aside to pet a different keluk, but it quickly moved away from her, and the others followed. Emzara turned to Noah. "I think they're afraid of you."

Noah opened his mouth to defend himself but froze when he saw two man-sized scaly beasts marching directly toward him. Heart racing, he pointed. "I think they're afraid of those."

Emzara looked where Noah pointed. "What are they?"

One of the creatures opened its mouth, exhibiting a full set of sharp teeth, and let out a mild, high-pitched bellow. Sporting large three-toed feet, tiny arms, and a long tail that swayed and seemed to balance the weight of the body and head, each of the creatures passed Emzara without looking at her.

Noah's eyes grew wide and his feet refused to move. "They're little grendecs. I hope they aren't hungry."

The one on the left tilted its head and watched Noah carefully, while the other one stomped straight to him and sniffed at his waist.

Warily eyeing the beast, Noah raised his arms to keep his hands out of reach of its mouth. He glanced at Emzara but refrained from speaking so as not to startle it.

The grendec nudged Noah with its snout and stared up at him for a moment before turning and snorting toward its companion. The other creature clomped to Noah's side and nuzzled him with the side of its face, while the first one slowly stepped forward, brushing against him as it moved.

Noah let out a nervous laugh before slowly lowering his hand and cautiously resting it on top of the nuzzling grendec's head.

A low rumbling sound, almost like the purring of a pithoct, emanated from the creature as it pushed its face into Noah.

A sense of peace washed over him, and he chuckled as he gingerly stroked the grendec's scaly head. With his free hand, he beckoned Emzara to join him.

She tiptoed to him and carefully placed her hand on the side of the grendec.

Without warning, the beast straightened and stamped away with its mate.

Emzara giggled as she watched them move toward the ark. "Were you scared?"

"Definitely." Noah kept his eyes on the grendecs. "At first, at least. What a great reminder that the Most High is guiding them and will protect us through it all."

"Noah."

Noah scanned his surroundings, looking for one of his sons before glancing at Emzara. "Did you hear that?" As he asked the question, he realized the voice had not come from one of his sons.

Emzara shook her head.

"Noah."

Noah knelt down as he searched for the source. "I am here."

Emzara leaned down and asked him something. He saw her mouth moving, but he failed to hear her words. With his mind and heart focused, all he heard was silence.

"Noah. Enter the ark, you and all your family."

Noah bowed his head as he listened to the thunderous yet soothing voice. "Yes, Most High."

"I have seen that you are righteous before Me in this generation. Take with you seven pairs of all the clean animals, male and female, along with a pair of animals that are not clean, a male and his female, and take seven pairs of the flying creatures of the heavens, male and female, to preserve their offspring alive across the face of the earth. In seven days, I will send rain on the earth for 40 days and 40 nights, and I will wipe from the face of the ground every living thing that I have made."

Gradually, the grunts, squeaks, honks, and other animal noises, along with Emzara's voice, filled his ears.

"Are you well?" Emzara asked.

Noah reached up and she helped him stand. He closed his eyes and breathed deeply before looking at her and stretching out his arms. "We need to load the animals. The Most High says that it's time."

Chapter 35

Naamah slammed a fist on the armrest of her portable throne as she stared at a narrow, three-tiered waterfall ahead. Sparse vegetation dotted both sides of the towering cliffs.

Nivlac glanced up at her. "What is it, my queen?"

"Bring my nephew."

He directed a hand signal to someone behind her palanquin, which sat atop the shoulders of eight brawny servants.

Naamah turned around as two soldiers stepped out of formation with Purlek between them. They led the ragged frame of a man. Behind them, the army stretched far beyond a bend in the river. Moving a force of 70,000 troops caused certain delays, but it had its advantages. They quickly cut through dense sections of the forest alongside the Hiddekel, and no city — no matter how troublesome or rebellious — dared oppose their march along the way.

Turning her attention from the army, Naamah looked down at the two soldiers and her captive as they stopped beside her. The warriors lowered their gaze while Purlek turned his head to the side, refusing to look at her.

"My dear nephew, did you not tell me that we only needed to follow this river all the way to its source? Where is the garden?"

After a long pause, he slowly turned and glared at her.

Naamah chuckled and shot him a mocking smile. "What's wrong? You don't want to talk to your aunt?" She fully intended to keep her promise not to kill him or his wife, but she never told him about the countless abuses they might face from her warriors along the way.

Defiance burned in his eyes, but she held no concerns that he might break free and attack her. In his weakened state, he struggled to even walk.

His eyes gestured toward the waterfall. "You think this is the source? I told you it was atop the highest hill in the region. We must be getting close."

"If you're lying to me. . . ." She allowed the threat to remain unspoken. At some point — and he may have already reached it — he would long for her troops to kill him and his wife rather than suffer the ongoing cruelties.

She snapped her fingers. "Nivlac! Find a way to the top of that thing."

Nivlac broke off his conversation with a soldier. "My queen, the scouts have just returned. There's a fairly simple way to get above the falls on this side of the river. Shall we proceed?"

"Immediately." She snarled at Purlek. "You'd better hope we're close, or you and your wife will learn true suffering."

Throughout the remainder of the morning and into the early afternoon, Naamah's army climbed the rocky path near the waterfall and then continued marching alongside the racing river. Dark gray clouds rolled in as her troops hastily cut through thick vegetation, leaving a wide swath through the undergrowth in their wake. A gradual ascent continued until they reached a plateau later in the day.

Pushing back several of the tight braids that swished in front of her right shoulder, and massaging the shaved left side of her head to calm herself, Naamah glanced around. There were no higher hills in the area, as far as she could see, although trees obscured much of her view. She ordered a company of soldiers to split up, study the region, and report back before dusk. Her servants lowered her litter to the ground and soon provided a light meal, but before she finished eating, a scout raced to bow before her.

"My queen, I believe we've found it."

Energy pulsed through her. "Where?"

"Not far." He pointed past her. "Just through that patch of trees."

"Was it guarded?"

"We didn't get too close. The forest abruptly ended, giving way to row after row of different types of trees, but none of them bore fruit. Then, in the center of the others, we saw one filled with colorful fruit."

"Show me." She turned to look where the man indicated. "Nivlac. My chariot. Prepare the men to move out."

Nivlac nodded before hurrying to his captains. In the meantime, two servants delivered her war chariot and armor. As they assisted her with the breastplate, Naamah pictured herself leading a victorious army through the garden. A smile formed as she imagined plucking the fruit and plunging her teeth into it. *Eternal life. No more fear of death. Nachash will finally break the Creator's curse.*

Nivlac returned with Commander Tsek and three captains. They each bowed and then Nivlac spoke. "The men are ready, my queen."

"Commander Tsek, go quickly and follow this scout. Start planning the attack. I'll arrive with the rest of the army. Remember, no one goes in without me."

Tsek nodded and ran ahead with the scout.

She glanced at her faithful captain and stepped into her chariot. "Nivlac, lead the way. Tonight, we become gods."

He failed to suppress a smile as he said, "Yes, my queen." Nivlac raised his sword and gestured for the troops to follow.

Naamah followed her right-hand man through the small wooded area, and before long they arrived at a large clearing. Just as the scout revealed, a clear break could be seen between the forest and many rows of various trees. She found Tsek in the middle of the open area, gesturing for her to join him.

"Mighty Queen," he said, "I'm not sure how to plan for an assault. It appears the tree is unguarded."

She stepped out of her chariot and strode toward him. "What do you mean?"

"Look there. Could that be it?"

Naamah stared down the rows of fruitless trees until her eyes locked on to one standing in the middle. Large and inviting, it bore oblong fruit that were almost a deep purple on top and changed to a golden red hue at their base. Her mouth watered, and she wondered about the consistency of the flesh — soft and juicy, or firm and crisp like a malid? Large flowers hung like graceful dancers from the branches as well. Mesmerized, she finally pulled her gaze away. "And you're sure it isn't guarded?"

Tsek shrugged. "I see no one."

Nivlac folded his arms. "Rumors tell of mighty protectors who will kill anyone trying to enter. I don't see anything like that."

Naamah narrowed her gaze and studied the area for a long while. Finally satisfied that the tree was unguarded, she carefully considered her next move. She had waited too long for this moment to make a mistake now. If anyone else reached the fruit before her, he could become an invincible adversary and she would likely lose her position. And if two people ate the fruit, then what? Could she bear sharing her rule with another? She trusted only Tsek and Nivlac to obey her in the face of such temptation.

The scout faced Tsek. "Commander, do you want me to run in there?"

Tsek frowned at the man. "That's the queen's decision." He faced Naamah. "My queen?"

Naamah searched both directions but saw no sign of any guardians. Still, she did not want to underestimate the Creator. Somehow, He had kept Noah safe in the arena. Could this be another one of His tricks, or were the rumors about protectors simply that — rumors? She gazed at the fruit in the distance, and a strong desire for it filled her. "Commander Tsek, go get me some of that fruit."

"Yes, my queen." Tsek's eyes gleamed as the sides of his mouth turned upward. He whirled and strode toward the entrance to the garden. He paused for a moment and looked side to side. He took several more steps before glancing over his shoulder. "I don't see—"

A flash of light appeared at Tsek's side. Before the commander could react, a giant being swung his sword through Tsek's midsection, and the master war strategist's upper body separated from his lower half as he collapsed on the ground. A few gasps sounded forth before a hush fell over Naamah's troops.

Another flash of light brought a second enormous being. They looked like humans, except their bodies glowed faintly and they sprouted four large wings from their backs. Roughly ten cubits tall, the two musclebound creatures made her giant soldiers look rather small.

Naamah's face burned with anger as she glared at the entities. *They're real! I knew the Creator would trick us.*

The first sentry sheathed his sword and stood with his arms crossed. "Naamah, daughter of Lamech."

She stood tall, glancing at her troops before returning his gaze. "I am Naamah, Queen of Havil and ruler of all lands. Stand aside or I will kill you."

The second guardian slowly shook his head. "Naamah, sister of my fellow servant, Tubal-Cain, the Creator has stationed us here to prevent anyone from entering the garden."

She spat in their direction. "The Creator is a liar and a coward. Nachash rules this world now, and he has chosen me to lead it. Stand aside or die."

The guardians narrowed their gaze at her and their bodies became brighter. "The Creator is the Most High God, and He will not always tolerate the rebellious ways of Nachash. Like your Greatmother Eve, you have fallen for the lies of the Great Deceiver."

Clenching her fists, she looked back at her army as it continued to assemble inside the clearing. Her confidence grew along with the sheer number of soldiers. She closed her eyes. *O great Nachash, now is your moment. Show your strength and help us defeat your enemies.* Turning her gaze back to the powerful beings, she pointed directly at one of them. "This is your final warning. Stand aside."

"You will regret any attempt to enter the garden," the second sentry said.

"You're trying to deceive me. It won't work. I know you can kill dozens or perhaps hundreds of my men. But tens of thousands will overwhelm you." She turned and focused on the two captains near Nivlac. "On my command, send four companies at each guardian. Let the giants lead them and overwhelm them with numbers. Also, deploy companies around the entire garden. They cannot fight everywhere at once. Nivlac, take a dozen men around the left side. When the fighting begins, see if you can sneak in and grab the fruit. No one touches the fruit except for Nivlac or me. Go."

The commanders quickly dispersed and worked to carry out their orders.

Naamah faced the garden again. "O boastful guardians, I'm afraid it's you who will regret your decision today."

"Hear me, Sister of Tubal-Cain," the second guardian said, and all at once the rumbling of his voice was like that of thunder. "Fear the Most

High and give Him glory, for the time of judgment has come. Worship Him who made heaven and earth, the sea, and all that is in them."

Naamah raised her fist and took a step forward. "No, you hear me. Today, you will be offered as a sacrifice to the most powerful god, Nachash, the Splendor of the World."

The giant sentries spread their wings — two of them out to the sides and a pair far above their heads — and they slowly drew their swords. It seemed as if they deliberately allowed the metallic blades to scrape against the opening of the sheath. The screeching sound of metal on metal may have been intended to intimidate the army, but it did nothing to shake Naamah's confidence.

She walked toward her chariot to wait for her men to move into position and spotted her nephew several rows back. *Interesting*. She pointed to the man guarding Purlek. "Bring him and his wife to me."

A pair of guards led the battered couple toward her. As pitiful as Purlek appeared, Evet seemed even worse, her gaunt frame scarred and bruised from the abuse rendered by Naamah's soldiers. They barely resembled the people she had met in her throne room.

Naamah ordered them to stand before her and face the garden. She lifted her voice. "Mighty guardians, you underestimate me. Behold the son of Tubal-Cain, and his wife."

The taller guardian narrowed his gaze. "Greetings, son of Tubal-Cain. Know that you and your wife are loved."

"How delightful. Let's see just how loved they are." Naamah sneered and then made a hand gesture to the guards, who instantly drew their swords and held them against the necks of their captives. "Hear me, guardians. If you don't let my men pass, then these people will die."

"No one is permitted in the garden."

"Then they die." Naamah drew her own blade and directed it toward Purlek. "Apparently you don't love them."

The shorter protector slowly twirled his sword. "Foolish woman. If you kill them, it does not lessen the Creator's love for them."

His companion smiled. "Son of Tubal-Cain, you and your wife have no cause to fear death." He looked at Naamah. "Sister of Tubal-Cain, you have many reasons to fear it, just as your mentor did."

Rage swept over her. How did they know of the seer's terror?

She turned her glare on the two captives. "Kill them."

Quick movements from the guards, and her nephew and his wife crumpled to the ground. As he fell, Purlek spun to one side.

She saw his face.

Peace.

Gritting her teeth, Naamah climbed into her chariot. *No matter their size, these beings will not stop me. This so-called Creator will not win!* Looking up to the sky, she rolled her eyes back and chanted a curse upon her two enemies. The wind picked up and energy coursed through her. As she repeated the spell over and over, one word filled her mind. *Immortality.* Her eyes refocused on the darkening skies and she slowly shifted her gaze back to the guardians. Burning with intense hatred, Naamah screamed a war cry at the top of her lungs.

A great yell rose from the tens of thousands of soldiers preparing to charge. Led by their queen, they repeated the shout five more times.

Unable to restrain herself any longer, Naamah pointed her spear toward the garden and ordered her army to charge.

The thunder of thousands of footsteps mixed with battle cries rushed past her. Dozens of giants wielding jagged blades led the assault.

Naamah gripped the edge of the chariot, anticipating her moment of glory as the two massive beings raised their swords and steadied themselves for battle.

With their longer strides and freakish strength, the giants arrived first. Sparks flew as blades clashed with blinding speed. Three giants flew backward into the rushing crowd, knocking down dozens of her men.

The guardians' blades danced through the air and through their enemies with unmatched agility and grace. Cutting down attacker after attacker, the glowing beings dashed side to side as they faced the onslaught. One of them ducked low as he quickly spun, and his wings swept several warriors through the air.

Naamah anticipated heavy casualties, but eventually the guardians would grow weary or make a mistake. A smile crossed her lips as she realized the two beings remained engaged at the garden's entrance, leaving no one to guard against her flanking soldiers. A flash of light caught her eye from the right side of the garden. But this light was different. Instead of the glowing brightness of the guardians, this looked more like fire. She spotted it again, but only for the briefest of instants. Looking back to the left side, she noticed the same thing. A moving flame appeared, and in the blink of an eye it was gone, reappearing on the other side of the garden. Setting aside her confusion about the intermittent flame, she refocused on the battle before her.

Screams of aggression mixed with shouts of anguish as the giant sentries dispatched every soldier they faced. Another spin from a guardian launched ten more soldiers away from the garden. The ground quickly filled up with dead and wounded soldiers, and her army slowed their advance as they stepped over and around and on their fallen companions.

Undeterred, Naamah reissued the command to attack, and her eyes lit up when she caught a glimpse of a giant jumping onto the back of one of the guardians. Her warrior wrapped his arm around the being's neck. As they jostled for position, the giant seemed to gain a better hold and fought to hang on. Suddenly, the guardian jumped into the air and performed a forward flip, landing on his back, crushing the giant and a few more soldiers. In a heartbeat, he returned to his position and continued to fight.

The guardians showed no signs of tiring, and Naamah wondered if a break to develop other strategies might be necessary, but would that give the sentries time to recuperate? *They must be growing tired. We should continue attacking.*

She called out for Nachash to strike his enemies while they were distracted. Part of her admired the guardians' matchless skills, although it may have been her sadistic lust for bloodshed that drew most of the appreciation. But every other part of her being flooded with revulsion for them as her initial confidence ebbed.

"My queen!"

Naamah searched for Nivlac's familiar form. *Did he make it to the tree?*

He soon appeared at her side. "They're all gone. All of our companies on the south side of the garden."

She stomped her foot. "What happened?"

"A flaming sword appeared and sliced through our men as soon as they attempted to enter the garden. It kept appearing and then raced away to kill others."

"Ahh! We're so close."

"I know. I have another plan."

She leaned toward him to hear his words over the sounds of the battle. "Tell me."

Nivlac pointed to her left. "Look way over there in the distance, above the trees."

"What am I looking—" She stopped as she noticed a large ship-like structure in the distance. "Is that what Purlek mentioned? That giant ship Noah was building?"

"Yes."

"What does that have to do with this battle?"

"Noah told you the Creator will protect him during a flood, right?" Nivlac rushed his words.

She nodded.

"If we capture Noah and bring him back here, we can exchange his life for access to the garden."

She pointed at Purlek's body. "It didn't work with them."

"But they were never told that they would survive the flood. If the guardians refuse to deal for Noah, then we kill him and turn their God into a liar. But if they agree, then we get what we want."

Naamah turned back to the battle for a moment. As before, Havilite soldiers rushed in only to meet a swift death at the end of a guardian's sword. She nodded. "I like it." Raising her voice, Naamah called out to her captains. "Order the men to fall back! We have a new plan."

Moments later, the fighting stopped. The noisy battle sounds yielded to the anguished cries of the wounded as men hurried away from the garden, abandoning their injured comrades.

Naamah gathered her remaining captains. She pointed to the ark in the distance. "Change of plans. We're going to march through the night to capture the man who is building that."

CHAPTER 36

Standing at the top of the outer ramp, Noah surveyed the bare landscape before him, where majestic gopherwood trees once rose high into the sky. Most of them now made up part of the ark and only some of the stumps remained, littering the terrain beyond the harvested fields, now barren of animals. A dense forest still encircled them, but its borders no longer stretched so close to the expanded clearing that had served as Noah's home for the past century.

The ground rumbled again, just as it had done multiple times throughout the week. Noah stared at the hill in the north, where he had encountered the guardians many years earlier. The evening before, as the family gathered outside the ark, Kezia had noticed flickering lights emanating from the area of the garden. Everyone discussed what might have caused the lights, and they eventually settled on the idea that the Creator had spoken to the guardians to inform them that, with the onset of the flood, their long appointment at the garden would draw to a close. The thought that nothing would ever look the same following the flood saddened Noah.

Stretching his arms, he descended the ramp, but stopped as Emzara drew near, guiding a pair of young keluks toward the door.

"I'm saving the best for last." She smiled at him. "I didn't want to put them in their cages any longer than necessary."

"I'm sure they'll appreciate that." Noah quickly kissed her cheek. "After you lock their enclosure, send Japheth and Ham to the wagon. Looks like we still have room for more firewood."

"Be quick. We don't know when the flood will start. I'll double check the cages to make sure we have all the animals."

Noah passed Shem driving seven pairs of bleaters up the ramp. "Meet me—"

"—at the wagon." Shem slapped him on the shoulder. "I heard you tell Mother. I'll be there as soon as I can."

Noah reached the ground and strode toward a woodpile near the north end of the clearing. The earth trembled again, and he instinctively glanced over his shoulder to verify that the ark remained steady. As the sun disappeared behind thick, dark clouds, he reached the wagon hitched to the pair of tuskers that had arrived in the glade a week ago. Patting one of them on the head, he said, "Looks like you two will be the last to board." The tusker raised its short trunk and let out a whistle.

He led the pair to the woodpile and moved to the back of the wagon. As he tossed split logs into the cart, a light rain began to fall. Glancing up, Noah spotted his sons running toward him as immense, almost black clouds tumbled in from the west.

"Looks like it's ready to start," Japheth said as he grabbed two pieces of wood and threw them into the wagon.

"Mother wants you to hurry," Ham said. "She's checking all the animal stalls to make sure we didn't leave any out here."

"Yeah, she said that she found two open stalls already. One for the tuskers, but she was checking her list for the other kind."

A gust of cold air blasted them, chilling the rain and driving it sideways for a moment. Noah rubbed his arms quickly before continuing to load the wagon. The anticipation of the coming judgment filled him with adrenaline, allowing him to work faster and harder. A sense of dread repeatedly attempted to invade his mind, but he pushed it back by focusing on his work.

"What's that noise?" Shem asked.

"The wind," Ham said.

"No, not that. Listen." He pointed north. "Over there."

As the gust died down, Noah heard cracking twigs and a snort.

"Maybe that missing pair of animals," Japheth said.

Noah's eyes grew wide as dozens of soldiers stepped out of the forest a few hundred cubits away. In the middle, two beasts similar to Captain Iradel's towed a chariot with a female occupant. Despite the distance,

Noah had very little doubt about her identity. *Naamah!* Another chariot pulled alongside her. "Get to the ark. Now!"

As he shouted, Naamah pointed a staff in their direction and yelled to her soldiers, who immediately broke into a sprint.

Ham jumped into the driver's seat of the wagon and Shem encouraged Noah to take the other spot.

"No, you take it," Noah said. "I'll be right behind."

"Come on," Ham said.

Noah and Shem ran toward the ark, while Japheth took the seat near Ham. Glancing back, Noah spotted hundreds, if not thousands of soldiers pouring into the clearing to give chase. The tuskers clomped past him and Japheth and Ham urged him to hurry. Shem's younger legs kept him slightly ahead of Noah.

The earth quaked again. Noah lost his balance and tumbled to the ground. As he clambered to his feet, he glimpsed the army and two chariots out in front, rapidly closing the distance. They would catch him soon.

Shem sped onto the ramp behind the tuskers and his brothers before he turned around. "Father!"

"Keep going. I'll be right there!"

With a hundred cubits or more to cover, another shaking of the earth caused Noah to fall again. This time he heard a high-pitched scream behind him. The quake had knocked Naamah out of her vehicle, and her beasts sped toward him, as did the other chariot. Its rider lifted a spear and directed it at Noah. Noah knew the face that snarled at him. *Nivlac!*

"We need him alive!" Naamah staggered to her feet.

Nivlac spun the spear around to swing the blunt end at his target. "You won't escape this time, Noah! And your whole family will be tortured before your eyes. I have another tree I'm going to sacrifice you in front of." Nivlac steadied himself and reared back.

As Noah prepared to dart to the side, a deafening crack rang out. A fissure split the ground between Noah and Nivlac, with Naamah's riderless chariot safely on Noah's side. Unable to stop in time, the two beasts pulling Nivlac's chariot attempted to leap over the gap. They barely cleared the opening, but the cart fell short. Nivlac leapt for Noah's side of the fissure as the weight of the chariot dragged the poor beasts backward off the edge. Nivlac's arms and shoulders landed above the newly formed cliff. Clambering for a handhold, he found only grass. He called for Naamah's help just before his hands slipped. He shouted a curse at Noah as he fell into the darkness.

Naamah screamed and glared at Noah. They stood only 30 cubits apart, separated by the gaping crevasse. "Your God can't protect you forever, Noah!"

"Naamah, the Creator is all-powerful and can do what He pleases. He told me before that I'll survive this flood, so I know He'll protect me until that happens. Turn from your evil before it's too late."

She turned and shouted for her army to hurry.

The ground shook violently and water rocketed into the sky from the far end of the crack between them. At the same time, the hill with the garden on it exploded and spewed ash and lava into the air.

Naamah staggered. "No! The tree!" She raised her fist to the heavens and screamed, with tears filling her eyes. "Nachash! Hear me. Don't let the Creator win. Prove that you're the highest of all gods!"

Noah pitied her. The most powerful person in the world stood powerless before him. "Nachash cannot defeat the Most High. Naamah, forsake your false god and cry out to the Creator while you still have time!"

Enraged, she balled her fists and faced him, her eyes burning with the most intense hatred he had ever seen. "Never! Nachash is the rightful ruler of this world, and I'm his goddess. You will bow to me before I kill you."

Noah's heart sank. How could anyone reject the Creator after seeing all that Naamah had witnessed? A jolt of energy ripped through him when he spotted her army drawing nearer. "You're deceived. Call on the Most High before it's too late." He spun toward the ramp and stopped after a few steps because Naamah's chariot, still hitched to the two creatures, stood in his way. *I don't remember seeing this kind of animal in the ark.* He jumped into the cart and the beasts bolted for the ramp.

"No!" Naamah screamed as the first group of soldiers arrived at her side. "Make a way across this gap now! And get archers up here immediately."

As Noah successfully turned onto the ramp, he looked back. Lightning flashed about the blackened sky, sending deafening thunder through the clearing. Two giants stood near the edge of the fissure, and each picked up a soldier and threw him across the chasm. The men landed hard, but they cleared it. Two more soldiers followed. Naamah ordered the huge men to throw her next and the other men to catch her. Meanwhile, groups of soldiers attempted to fashion a bridge with rope and wood. Moments later, Naamah stood on the opposite side and commanded several soldiers to pursue Noah.

Huge drops of rain pummeled Noah as he approached the top of the ramp.

Emzara raced out the door and stopped when she saw him. "Hurry up!" Her eyes grew wide as she saw the carnage below.

"Em, get inside."

She nodded and then tilted her head to the side when she noticed the animals pulling the chariot. "Looks like we have a pair of those now. They were the only ones missing from my list."

"I thought they might be." Noah followed her into the ark and jumped off the cart. "Sons, quickly, the door."

Emzara worked to unharness the beast closest to her. "Rayneh, get the other one."

Moments later, Emzara and Rayneh led the two beasts out of the way as Japheth and Ham ran to Noah's side.

Noah pushed the chariot toward the ramp. "Help me get this out of the way." Japheth and Ham joined him, and they successfully maneuvered it up against the ramp's railing and clear of the door's path as Naamah and several soldiers appeared at the base of the incline.

Pointing to the rope keeping the door open, Ham said, "We have to untie it before we can close the door."

"I'll get it," Japheth said as he headed toward the knot.

Another quake caused the entire ramp to vibrate and shift. Ear-splitting cracks of timber rang out beneath them and another blast of water shot into the sky from the middle of the clearing, launching hundreds of Naamah's soldiers to their deaths. Many of the soldiers fled toward the woods.

Noah realized the ramp would not hold. "Inside!"

Ham shoved Japheth into the ark, and Noah leapt for the doorway just as the platform gave way and crumpled to the ground.

Noah looked at his sons.

"That was too close," Japheth said.

"How are we going to close the door now?" Ham asked. "We can't get to the knot."

Noah poked his head out of the opening. With the rain splatting against his face and soaking his hair, he glanced first at what used to be the base of the ramp. Naamah shouted something at her soldiers, but the wind and thunder drowned out any hope of hearing it. One of them produced a torch and tried to light it. *They're planning to burn the ark.* Looking back toward the door, Noah studied the top of it. "If I could. . . ."

"Father," Ham said, water dripping off the sides of his beard. "I can climb out there and untie it. Then I can push it away from the wall and ride it back in here."

"No, I'll do it," Noah said.

"I will. I'm younger and stronger."

"Wait." Noah scanned the room. "Kezia, bring that rope. We'll tie it around Ham."

Ham nodded. "Good idea. I'll need a bit of a boost to grab the top."

Kezia slipped the rope around her husband and several of them grabbed onto it.

They walked toward the edge of the opening as Ham searched for the best place to hold on to.

Noah pointed to the knot that held the door. "Wait. Look at that!"

"It's coming loose," Emzara said.

"How can that be?" Kezia said.

The knot unfastened and the door slowly moved away from the outside wall of the ark.

Shem held his arms out and gestured for the others to step away from the entrance. "Get back."

"The Creator is closing the door," Ar'yel said.

As the door swung toward him, Noah stared down at Naamah and her soldiers and shook his head as a sense of sorrow mixed with relief struck him.

She screamed something at him just before the door slammed shut with a thud that instantly dampened the sounds from outside. An array of animal sounds within the ark overpowered the muffled screams, wind, torrential rain, and thunder.

Noah quickly latched the door. He turned and stared in amazement at his family. Emzara leaned against him and he held her tight. Shem hugged Ar'yel while she let out a deep sigh. Kezia put her hand on Ham's back as he loosened the rope around his waist and let it fall to the ground. Japheth watched Rayneh as she moved silently to the door, her face emotionless, as if she were in shock. She put her hand on it and fell to her knees, sobbing. Japheth hurried to kneel down beside her. She collapsed in his arms and wept.

No one spoke for several moments — the magnitude of everything that had just happened and what must have been occurring outside rendered Noah speechless. Another muffled blast of thunder along with barely audible screams registered in his ears. He imagined Naamah and her army trying desperately to escape the devastation. An image of Garun and Laleel popped into his mind. Had they survived until now? And what about Purlek and Evet? Jerah and Pivi? Misha and the rest of his siblings? Noah pulled Emzara closer as his eyes welled up.

An animal's snort beside them grabbed his attention. One of the chariot beasts sniffed at Emzara's feet and then gently brushed its long brown snout against her leg.

Emzara glanced up at Noah. "I'd better go and put these two in their enclosure."

With a tip of his head, he gestured to the wagon full of firewood in the corner and spoke softly. "Those tuskers need to be put away, too. Shem, would you do that? Then we'll all meet in the sitting room. We need to pray and thank the Most High for His provision and protection."

Emzara lightly kissed his cheek and then gestured toward the rest of their family. "Look, it's just as the Creator told you so long ago. The ark will be for you, your wife, your sons, and your sons' wives."

Still hurting from the heightened awareness that everyone outside the ark would soon be gone, but thankful for God's mercy to him and his family, Noah nodded and pulled Emzara close again. "Another reminder that we can always trust the Creator."

And Noah did according to all that the LORD commanded him (Genesis 7:5).

Epilogue

Genesis 7 Then the Lord said to Noah, "Go into the ark, you and all your household, for I have seen that you are righteous before me in this generation. ² Take with you seven pairs of all clean animals, the male and his mate, and a pair of the animals that are not clean, the male and his mate, ³ and seven pairs of the birds of the heavens also, male and female, to keep their offspring alive on the face of all the earth. ⁴ For in seven days I will send rain on the earth forty days and forty nights, and every living thing that I have made I will blot out from the face of the ground." ⁵ And Noah did all that the Lord had commanded him.

⁶ Noah was six hundred years old when the flood of waters came upon the earth. ⁷ And Noah and his sons and his wife and his sons' wives with him went into the ark to escape the waters of the flood. ⁸ Of clean animals, and of animals that are not clean, and of birds, and of everything that creeps on the ground, ⁹ two and two, male and female, went into the ark with Noah, as God had commanded Noah. ¹⁰ And after seven days the waters of the flood came upon the earth.

¹¹ In the six hundredth year of Noah's life, in the second month, on the seventeenth day of the month, on that day all the fountains of the great deep burst forth, and the windows of the heavens were opened. ¹² And rain fell upon the earth forty days and forty nights. ¹³ On the very same day Noah and his sons, Shem and Ham and Japheth, and Noah's wife and the three wives of his sons with them entered the ark, ¹⁴ they and every beast, according to its kind, and all the livestock according to their

kinds, and every creeping thing that creeps on the earth, according to its kind, and every bird, according to its kind, every winged creature. ¹⁵ They went into the ark with Noah, two and two of all flesh in which there was the breath of life. ¹⁶ And those that entered, male and female of all flesh, went in as God had commanded him. And the LORD shut him in.

¹⁷ The flood continued forty days on the earth. The waters increased and bore up the ark, and it rose high above the earth. ¹⁸ The waters prevailed and increased greatly on the earth, and the ark floated on the face of the waters. ¹⁹ And the waters prevailed so mightily on the earth that all the high mountains under the whole heaven were covered. ²⁰ The waters prevailed above the mountains, covering them fifteen cubits deep. ²¹ And all flesh died that moved on the earth, birds, livestock, beasts, all swarming creatures that swarm on the earth, and all mankind. ²² Everything on the dry land in whose nostrils was the breath of life died. ²³ He blotted out every living thing that was on the face of the ground, man and animals and creeping things and birds of the heavens. They were blotted out from the earth. Only Noah was left, and those who were with him in the ark. ²⁴ And the waters prevailed on the earth 150 days.

8 But God remembered Noah and all the beasts and all the livestock that were with him in the ark. And God made a wind blow over the earth, and the waters subsided. ² The fountains of the deep and the windows of the heavens were closed, the rain from the heavens was restrained, ³ and the waters receded from the earth continually. At the end of 150 days the waters had abated, ⁴ and in the seventh month, on the seventeenth day of the month, the ark came to rest on the mountains of Ararat. ⁵ And the waters continued to abate until the tenth month; in the tenth month, on the first day of the month, the tops of the mountains were seen.

⁶ At the end of forty days Noah opened the window of the ark that he had made ⁷ and sent forth a raven. It went to and fro until the waters were dried up from the earth. ⁸ Then he sent forth a dove from him, to see if the waters had subsided from the face of the ground. ⁹ But the dove found no place to set her foot, and she returned to him to the ark, for the waters were still on the face of the whole earth. So he put out his hand and took her and brought her into the ark with him. ¹⁰ He waited another seven days, and again he sent forth the dove out of the ark. ¹¹ And the dove came back to him in the evening, and behold, in her mouth was

a freshly plucked olive leaf. So Noah knew that the waters had subsided from the earth. ¹² Then he waited another seven days and sent forth the dove, and she did not return to him anymore.

¹³ In the six hundred and first year, in the first month, the first day of the month, the waters were dried from off the earth. And Noah removed the covering of the ark and looked, and behold, the face of the ground was dry. ¹⁴ In the second month, on the twenty-seventh day of the month, the earth had dried out. ¹⁵ Then God said to Noah, ¹⁶ "Go out from the ark, you and your wife, and your sons and your sons' wives with you. ¹⁷ Bring out with you every living thing that is with you of all flesh — birds and animals and every creeping thing that creeps on the earth —that they may swarm on the earth, and be fruitful and multiply on the earth." ¹⁸ So Noah went out, and his sons and his wife and his sons' wives with him. ¹⁹ Every beast, every creeping thing, and every bird, everything that moves on the earth, went out by families from the ark.

²⁰ Then Noah built an altar to the LORD and took some of every clean animal and some of every clean bird and offered burnt offerings on the altar. ²¹ And when the LORD smelled the pleasing aroma, the LORD said in his heart, "I will never again curse the ground because of man, for the intention of man's heart is evil from his youth. Neither will I ever again strike down every living creature as I have done. ²² While the earth remains, seedtime and harvest, cold and heat, summer and winter, day and night, shall not cease."

9 And God blessed Noah and his sons and said to them, "Be fruitful and multiply and fill the earth. ² The fear of you and the dread of you shall be upon every beast of the earth and upon every bird of the heavens, upon everything that creeps on the ground and all the fish of the sea. Into your hand they are delivered. ³ Every moving thing that lives shall be food for you. And as I gave you the green plants, I give you everything. ⁴ But you shall not eat flesh with its life, that is, its blood. ⁵ And for your lifeblood I will require a reckoning: from every beast I will require it and from man. From his fellow man I will require a reckoning for the life of man.

⁶ "Whoever sheds the blood of man,
   by man shall his blood be shed,
     for God made man in his own image.

⁷ And you, be fruitful and multiply, increase greatly on the earth and multiply in it."

⁸ Then God said to Noah and to his sons with him, ⁹ "Behold, I establish my covenant with you and your offspring after you, ¹⁰ and with every living creature that is with you, the birds, the livestock, and every beast of the earth with you, as many as came out of the ark; it is for every beast of the earth. ¹¹ I establish my covenant with you, that never again shall all flesh be cut off by the waters of the flood, and never again shall there be a flood to destroy the earth." ¹² And God said, "This is the sign of the covenant that I make between me and you and every living creature that is with you, for all future generations: ¹³ I have set my bow in the cloud, and it shall be a sign of the covenant between me and the earth. ¹⁴ When I bring clouds over the earth and the bow is seen in the clouds, ¹⁵ I will remember my covenant that is between me and you and every living creature of all flesh. And the waters shall never again become a flood to destroy all flesh. ¹⁶ When the bow is in the clouds, I will see it and remember the everlasting covenant between God and every living creature of all flesh that is on the earth." ¹⁷ God said to Noah, "This is the sign of the covenant that I have established between me and all flesh that is on the earth" (Genesis 7:1–9:17).

BEHIND THE FICTION

Just like in the first two books in *The Remnant Trilogy*, the initial part of this non-fiction section, Questions and Answers, is designed to address certain questions that readers may think of during the story. Many of these issues will be apologetic in nature. That is, in this portion of the book, we will respond to numerous challenges raised by skeptics and critics. The goal is that these novels will also help you defend the truth of Scripture.

You may have noticed as you read the novel that several things didn't line up with what you may have expected, particularly in this story regarding the Ark and the animals. As we mentioned in the other books, this was done intentionally to break certain stereotypes about Noah and the pre-Flood world that many Christians assume are from the Bible, but are not actually found there. We want you to see clearly what comes directly from the Bible and what comes from traditions people have developed over the years.

The second feature in this non-fiction portion is what we call Borrowed from the Bible. Since the Bible only includes scant details about Noah's life and times, we fleshed out his story using artistic license. We certainly do not wish to be seen as adding to Scripture and want the reader to understand that these are works of fiction, with the exception of the few details that come straight from the Bible. In some places we curbed the amount of artistic license taken by drawing from other biblical accounts instead. In Borrowed from the Bible, we highlight certain events and customs in our story that will be somewhat familiar to those who know their Bibles.

The third special feature is entirely unique to this series. We had the incredible opportunity to work behind the scenes at the Ark Encounter for the past few years. Tim was involved in the planning of nearly every exhibit and was responsible for writing or overseeing all of the content while K. Marie took part in designing various aspects of several spaces on the Ark. We wanted to use our experience to bring this series to life in a creative manner. As such, many of the objects and animals described in the book are on display in the Ark Encounter, so visitors to the theme park can see part of what Noah witnesses in our story. The Encounter This section lets the reader know what these items are and where they can be found.

Finally, we included a fourth section in this book that is not found in the other two. Since we never used modern names to describe the many different kinds of animals encountered throughout the series, we have included a list of those animals with their modern names so that readers can properly identify the beasts described in this series.

We hope you have enjoyed reading about what may have been, while learning to better discern between fact and fiction.

ANSWERING QUESTIONS RAISED BY THE NOVEL

SPOILER ALERT! Many of the answers to questions in this section reveal key points in the storyline of the novel. If you have not read the story first, some of these details will spoil important events in the book.

Would animals fear man in the pre-Flood world?

In Chapter 13, Noah finally takes Emzara to see some of her favorite animals, members of the giraffe kind, which are called keluks in this series. She gets the opportunity to get close to them for a while. In our day, wild animals seldom allow people to get so close, but would things be different prior to the Flood?

After the Flood, God told Noah that "the fear of you and the dread of you shall be on every beast of the earth and upon every bird of the heavens, upon everything that creeps on the ground and on all the fish of the sea" (Genesis 9:2). The straightforward meaning of this verse is that following the Flood, animals would have a fear of man, which is something we see among most wild animals today. It seems natural to infer that they did not possess such a fear prior to the Flood, and the next verse appears to confirm this notion. Genesis 9:3 states that God originally had given plants to man for food, but now man would be permitted to eat every living thing that moves (this concept is addressed in more detail in the question and answer section of *Noah: Man of Destiny*). Since mankind was not permitted to eat animals until after the Flood, the animals did not need the instinct to be afraid of people. But once permission to eat meat was given, the fear of man became important for creatures to survive.

So it is quite plausible that someone like Emzara could approach a group of wild animals without causing them to run away.

Were Noah's sons triplets?

Genesis 5:32 states that when Noah was 500 years old, he begot Shem, Ham, and Japheth. At first glance, this verse seems to indicate that the sons were triplets, or possibly a set of twins with the other son also being born within Noah's 500th year. While some Christians interpret this verse as teaching that Noah's sons were triplets, the Bible provides further details that make such an interpretation unlikely, if not impossible. Instead, it makes much more sense to understand the verse as stating that the oldest son was born in Noah's 500th year.

This verse appears at the end of a genealogy describing the people in the line from Adam to Noah. Genesis 11 includes a similar genealogy, but this time it moves from Shem down to Terah and his sons. Of particular relevance here is the fact that Genesis 11:26 states, "When Terah had lived 70 years, he fathered Abram, Nahor, and Haran." While the names and number of years are different, the pattern is the same as Genesis 5:32. When we look at other passages in Scripture, such as Acts 7:4 and Genesis 12:4, we learn that Terah's sons were not triplets because Abram was born when Terah was 130 years old. So it seems that this type of statement in a genealogy merely conveys how old the father was when the oldest of the named sons was born. Also, notice that Abram was not the oldest. Instead, the son most relevant to the book's subject matter is often listed first in these genealogies.

Other clues in Genesis reveal that Noah's sons were not triplets. The oldest was born in Noah's 500th year and the Flood was in his 600th year. In Genesis 11:10, we read that Shem had a son when he was 100 years old, and that this took place two years after the Flood. So Shem must have been about two years younger than his older brother, Japheth. Japheth would have been 100 at the time of the Flood, and Shem would have been 100 years old two years later, or possibly three years later if "after the Flood" in Genesis 11:10 is meant to refer to the time after the family exited the Ark. Either way, the boys were not the same age. We cannot be sure of Ham's age, but we do know that he was the youngest of Noah's sons (Genesis 9:24). In our story, we made him about ten years younger than Japheth.

There is some debate about whether Japheth was older than Shem due to plausible interpretations of Genesis 10:21. In this verse, some Bible translations identify Shem as "the brother of Japheth the elder" (KJV, NKJV, NIV) while several others describe Shem as the older brother of Japheth (NASB, NET, ESV, CSB). Based on the way the same Hebrew construction is translated elsewhere in the Old Testament, it seems that the latter option is a more natural way to render this verse. However, if Shem were the oldest and born when Noah was 502 or 503, how could Genesis 5:32 state that Noah was 500 when the first of his sons was born? Those who favor Shem as the oldest generally see Noah's age as being a round number. But this would be inconsistent with the precision used throughout the rest of Genesis 5 when describing the age of each father at the birth of his son of record.

There is some legitimate debate over this issue, so Christians should hold their own view tentatively. For the story, we decided to make Japheth the oldest. While this is a questionable way to interpret Genesis 10:21 it makes better sense of other factors. Noah's age at the birth of his first son is not simply a round number; thus, this position understands the ages in Genesis 5 consistently. Also, it fits with a common theme found throughout Genesis: the younger son often takes precedent over the oldest. Consider the following sets of brothers and think about which one becomes more important in the text: Cain or Seth, Haran or Abram, Ishmael or Isaac, Esau or Jacob, Reuben or Judah (or Joseph). Finally, if Shem is not the oldest, then Genesis 5:32 is consistent with Genesis 11:26 in listing first the most relevant son instead of the oldest.

How old was Cain when he murdered Abel and who was he afraid of?

In Chapter 19, Methuselah spoke about Cain and Abel, filling in some of the biblical backstory for Noah and his group. Most people tend to think of Cain and Abel as teenagers or twentysomethings when the murder occurred, but the Bible gives several clues indicating that they were likely much older than that, perhaps even 100 years older.

Genesis 4:25 explains that Eve gave birth to another son, Seth, and it is pretty clear that she viewed him as a replacement for Abel. She said, "God has appointed for me another offspring instead of Abel, for Cain killed him." In Genesis 5:3, we learn that this happened when Adam was 130 years old, and that Seth was just one of many other children that Adam and Eve had. Since Seth was viewed as Abel's replacement, then he was almost certainly the next son born to them after Abel's death. This means that Abel would have been murdered nearly 130 years after Adam was created. And if Cain was born within the first few years of Adam and Eve being banished from the garden, then Cain could have been over 120 years old at the murder of Abel. We have no reason to think that it would have taken very long for Eve to conceive since God created Adam and Eve with perfectly functioning bodies, and He instructed them to be fruitful and multiply. Genesis 4 and 5 show us that they certainly did that.

If Cain and Abel were over 100 years old at the time of Abel's murder, then we can solve another question that has puzzled Bible readers: why was Cain worried that someone might find and kill him? As we explained in the non-fiction section of the first book of this trilogy, *Noah: Man of Destiny*, brother would have originally married sister in the first generation after Adam. If Cain and Abel were as young as many people assume, then there would not have been any other people in the world for him to fear. But if he were nearly 130 years old, there could have been plenty of people who might have sought to avenge Abel's death. Abel may have already been married with many adult children and possibly even grandchildren and great grandchildren. This scenario is portrayed in the novel, as one of the Ark's passengers happens to be a descendant of Abel. Also, if Cain and Abel had other siblings at this time, those siblings may have also been tempted to go after Cain.

You may recall from the non-fiction section of *Noah: Man of Destiny* that some Christians have proposed that God created other people apart from Adam and Eve, but this contradicts the clear teaching of the Bible that Eve was the mother of all living (Genesis 3:20). They think this solves the issue of Cain's wife and explains who he would have been afraid of, but it does nothing of the sort. Cain's fear is based on the possibility of retaliation, and the people who might want to retaliate would be those who knew the victim. If God created other people somewhere in the world unrelated to Adam and Eve, as is supposed by some, then why would these individuals be upset with Cain for killing someone that they had probably never heard of?

Why did you depict the cherubim at the Garden of Eden the way you did?

Dealing with the cherubim at the Garden of Eden required us to make numerous important decisions. What should we call them? What did they look like? How should they behave? How should they speak? How much do they know and how much could they tell Noah? This section will explain our rationale behind why we portrayed the cherubim the way we did.

Genesis 3:24 states that God drove Adam out "and He placed cherubim at the east of the garden of Eden, and a flaming sword which turned every way, to guard the way to the tree of life" (NKJV). The Bible mentions cherubim being placed at the east side of the garden along with a flaming sword. Notice that the text does not say that the cherubim wielded the sword. Instead, it states the flaming sword turned every way to guard the tree of life. Also, *cherubim* is the masculine plural form of cherub, so there were at least two of these entities. In our story, we stationed two cherubim at the east side of the garden, and we had the sword protect the rest of it.

Readers may have noticed that we never referred to them as cherubim or angels in the book. The reason for this is that we wanted to think of what someone without the text of Genesis might have called them. How much did Noah know about angels? Was he aware of the many different types of heavenly beings described in Scripture? In the second book, *Noah: Man of Resolve*, Noah and Tubal-Cain discussed their thoughts about the existence of spiritual beings, but they had only a very limited understanding of them. Since we gave Noah a very restricted knowledge of angelic beings, we decided that he would not even know what they were actually called. So in the book, the cherubim are most often referred to as guardians since that describes their function at the garden.

For their appearance, we had several options in Scripture to choose from. When Solomon built the temple, the inner sanctuary boasted cherubim made of olive wood. They are described in 1 Kings 6:26 as being ten cubits tall. We know this passage is merely describing the height of the cherubim depicted in the temple, but we decided to make the living beings at the garden the same height. Also, such height would certainly make them extremely intimidating to Naamah's army.

The Book of Ezekiel includes a few descriptions of cherubim that make them seem rather bizarre. The term *cherub* does not appear in the first chapter, but by comparing the description and role of the creatures in the first chapter with those called cherubim in chapter 10, we can be quite certain they are the same types of beings. Chapter 1 describes them as having feet like those of a calf (v. 7) and four wings, each with human-like hands under them (v. 8). Verse 10 also explains that each of them had four faces: the face of a man, the face of a lion, the face of an ox, and the face of an eagle. Incidentally, the line about the feet of a calf is the main reason many portrayals of Satan show him with hooves (many Christians believe he is referred to as the "anointed cherub" in Ezekiel 28:13–14).

There are other places in the Bible that discuss cherubim while making no mention of them having four faces or calves' feet. For example, Ezekiel 41:18 mentions cherubim with two faces (man and lion). In the story, we gave the cherubim four wings, but we chose not to give them four faces or calves' feet. Part of the reason for this is that we wanted the guardians to focus straight ahead, so Noah would not have been able to see each of the four faces. And we did not want to introduce this idea during the battle at the garden because it would have been confusing for the reader.

For their behavior and speech, we used other angels in Scripture as our model. One of the angels mentioned that they were fellow servants of God with Noah. These words echo what John was told by an angel in both Revelation 19:10 and 22:9. The Bible also indicates that angels are limited in knowledge, so in our story they could not answer all of Noah's questions. They only knew what God had permitted them to know, and encouraged Noah to believe that the Most High would do what is right. We wanted them to be firm yet compassionate toward Noah, but unyielding and intimidating toward the Havilite army. At the same time, they urged Naamah to turn to the Creator, borrowing words from an angel in Revelation 14:7, and appealed to the one tender spot we have seen from her: Tubal-Cain.

How did you decide when certain characters would die?

One of the challenges in writing this series has been to keep it exciting and suspenseful even though most readers would know that only eight people would be alive at the end. This means that some of the characters we enjoy will not survive. Readers had to say goodbye to Ara, Aterre, Tubal-Cain, and others in the second novel. In this book, everyone except for Noah and his family perished. Readers who have been through the Ark Encounter and remember the names given to the women there may have immediately recognized Noah's daughters-in-law in the story as soon as they were first mentioned.

Since many of the characters were fictitious, we had freedom regarding their deaths. However, two of the characters had to die at appointed times because Scripture tells us how long they lived. Noah's father

290

Lamech died five years before the Flood, and Methuselah passed away in the same year as the Flood. It is possible that he died in the Flood, but most Christians do not like that idea. So to avoid frustrating readers, we had Methuselah die about a month before the Flood.

This brings up an important issue to address. Many Christians have been taught that Methuselah's name means something like "when he dies, judgment." This is how Henry Morris defined it in *The Genesis Record*, although he was a bit tentative. People who follow this line of thinking believe Enoch, being a prophet, essentially uttered a prophecy about the Flood when he named his son. Some people have even claimed that when one combines the meanings of the ten names from Adam to Noah they spell out a message of redemption. However, this idea is full of problems in that the names often do not mean what has been claimed. For example, I could not find a single Hebrew lexicon that gives a meaning to Methuselah's name that has something to do with judgment. It seems that his name might be related to a dart or javelin, which is why the Brown-Driver-Briggs lexicon gives a plausible definition as "man of the dart." We knew Methuselah needed to die in the same year as the Flood, but we also did not want to give credence to the idea that his name was prophetic, so we had him die about a month before the onset of the Flood.

Why did you describe the pitch as coming from trees instead of bitumen?

The early chapters of Genesis mention tar or bitumen on two occasions. The builders of the city and Tower of Babel used bitumen for mortar between their bricks (Genesis 11:3). And Genesis 14:10 describes the Valley of Siddim as being full of bitumen pits. Many people have assumed that Noah would have used something like this to coat the interior and exterior of the Ark per God's command in Genesis 6:14. A petroleum-based substance like bitumen might work for preserving and sealing a wooden ship. However, it is unlikely that Noah would have used such a material because much of the petroleum-based substances we know today are likely a result of the huge amount of biotic material buried during the Flood.

Pine-derived tar was often used to preserve the wood that made sailing ships prior to the advent of iron and steel ships. Since Noah used an extraordinary amount of wood to construct the Ark, it makes sense that he would have used a tree-based tar or resin for pitch, especially if gopherwood produced the sticky substance.

Why didn't you show more of the Ark being built?

It might seem strange to some readers that in a book about Noah we only spent a few chapters showing the family working on the Ark. This was not an oversight on our part; it was a conscious decision to keep such descriptions to a minimum. While it is true that the Ark's construction was extremely important and undoubtedly took up many years in Noah's life, reading a story about the Ark's construction would likely be quite boring. This novel needed to span 100 years in Noah's life, from the time when he and his wife were expecting their first son to the onset of the Flood. Since we needed to make significant leaps in the timeline, the natural places for those were during the Ark's construction. Still, we included some planning and details throughout those chapters to keep the Ark in constant focus and to connect with ideas displayed at the Ark Encounter, from animal enclosures to systems for collecting fresh water and much more.

How many people worked on the Ark?

The Bible does not necessarily tell us how many people built the Ark. Hebrews 11:7 says that Noah built the Ark for the saving of his household, and we know that only eight people were on it during the Flood. Did Noah build it by himself or did only eight people work on the Ark? We cannot know the answer with any certainty, or as I like to say, "We just don't Noah." Sorry, bad pun.

Given that Noah apparently had a maximum of 50–75 years to work on the project, it is certainly plausible that his small group could have built the Ark (see non-fiction section of *Noah: Man of Resolve* for details on how long it took Noah to build the Ark). However, it is also possible that many others were involved in the work. As we have seen, Noah's father died five years before the Flood and his grandfather died in the same year the Flood started. If they lived near Noah, then they might have helped him build it. Noah could have also had many other family members and friends helping, and he might have even hired construction workers. The Bible does not preclude any of those possibilities.

In our story, we kept the number of people to a relatively small group of 15: Noah, Emzara, Japheth, Rayneh, Shem, Ar'yel, Ham, Kezia,

Lamech, Methuselah, Purlek, Evet, Elam, Garun, and Laleel. We also had Noah purchase supplies and goods from Jabal's group, so technically there were others involved in the work.

Does the Ark in the book match the design of the Ark at the Ark Encounter?

The way we described the exterior of the Ark in the novel matches the design seen at the Ark Encounter. However, the Ark's interior is laid out differently than what guests experience when they visit the theme park. Keep in mind that the massive Ark in Williamstown, Kentucky, built to the biblical dimensions, was made to accommodate thousands of visitors every day, so it has wide walkways, a huge ramp system with a gentle slope for wheelchairs and powered carts, emergency exit stairwells, restrooms on each deck, and dozens of world-class exhibits.

The Ark described in the book follows the design of the Half-Ark Model seen on the first deck of the Ark Encounter. This model was made to show what Noah's Ark might have looked like on the inside, taking into account all of the animals, food, water, and storage needed. Narrower hallways along with smaller and steeper ramps could have been used on each deck. The family's living quarters may have been on the second floor, which would rock less in the water compared to the third deck, and it would put the family in closer proximity to most of the animals.

Besides the design of the Ark, how well do the novels line up with what visitors see at the Ark Encounter?

For the most part, the details about Noah and his family described at the Ark Encounter are consistent with the novels. Of course, the novels go into far more detail than the signage in the themed exhibits and serve as sort of the semi-official story for the characters on the Ark. For example, the *Who Was Noah?* exhibit on Deck Two of the Ark Encounter is essentially an abbreviated form of these novels, from Noah's boyhood longing to build boats to the construction of the Ark. Many of the answers given by the animatronic Noah in *Noah's Study* are derived from this story. Also, the information on the signs that give a bit of backstory for each of Noah's family members in the *Living Quarters* are drawn from the story told in these novels.

Some very minor differences can be found, such as the fact that the novels never have Noah wearing the hat that can he can be seen wearing at the Ark. Future exhibits at the theme park may not line up perfectly with the novels. For example, one of the future phases at the park is the Walled City, and there has been talk of placing Noah's house within the city walls. This leads us to the next question.

Why did you have Noah move far away to build the Ark? Doesn't the Bible teach that people mocked him while he worked?

Movies and books often depict Noah building the Ark just outside of a city. This gives him the benefit of hiring laborers and obtaining needed supplies, but it also provides the opportunity to include a healthy amount of scoffers who made fun of Noah for building the Ark.

As we have done throughout this series, we sought to go against many of the popular ideas about Noah and the Ark that are not found directly in Scripture. The reason for this is to challenge people to look closely at the Bible and base their ideas on it rather than on popular re-tellings of Noah. This is one reason we chose to move Noah away from a city for the Ark's construction. While there may have been advantages for building near a city, the disadvantages might have outweighed them. For example, since the people were so violent and immoral prior to the Flood, would they have even let Noah finish building the Ark? Of course, ultimately, they could not really stop him, since God commanded him to do it, but it seems likely that some of these wicked people would have sought to destroy the Ark if they lived near it. So, by moving Noah away from populated areas in our story, he was able to build the Ark and raise his sons in a relatively safe environment. Interestingly enough, the Jewish historian Josephus stated that Noah moved away from the populace to build the Ark, but there is no way he could have known this with certainty. Since Scripture is silent on this issue, we really cannot be certain where he built it.

If you are wondering why we did not include mockers during the Ark's construction, it is because the Bible never mentions them. People are often quite surprised, and sometimes upset, when I point this out, but it is true. The Bible never states that people made fun of Noah while he worked on the Ark. We stated this in the "Dear Reader" section at the beginning of the first book, *Noah: Man of Destiny*. However, it may very well have happened. Noah was a godly man living in an exceedingly ungodly world, and based on how skeptics often mock believers today, it is easy to believe that Noah would have been mocked if others were around. To account for this, we included plenty of people mocking Noah in the final chapters of the second book before he escaped Iri Geshem.

In the scene where the animals gather outside the Ark, why did you include more than two keluks (giraffe kind)?

At the Ark Encounter, we needed to answer some tough questions about the animals. One of the reasons this task was difficult is that we do not possess enough information about every type of land-dependent animal that has ever lived. With that limited information, we needed to ascertain what the animal kinds were and whether there would be a single pair of them on the Ark (unclean and non-flying animals) or if there would be seven pairs (clean animals and flying creatures). We cannot be sure that Noah's system of clean and unclean creatures matched the specifications described as part of the Mosaic Covenant in Leviticus 11, but since we had nothing else to go on, this is the system we used both at the Ark and for this story.

The animals that the Israelites were permitted to eat included those that had cloven hooves and chewed the cud. Popular animals like cows and sheep fit this description, but it also includes an animal that most of us would never consider as belonging in that category: the giraffe. If the giraffes are clean animals, then there would have been seven pairs of this kind on the Ark instead of just two, as is commonly depicted (see the question below about how Noah fit the animals on the Ark for the answer to why the Ark Encounter used seven pairs instead of just seven for the clean and flying creatures). Interestingly enough, in 2008, Jewish rabbis and vets determined that giraffes are considered clean animals and can be eaten as kosher, although they did not anticipate anyone doing it since they are endangered.

How did Noah find all the animals?

If you have already read the story, you know that Noah did not travel the world to find and catch all the animals. However, this is the impression many people have about the Ark's animals, and skeptics frequently pose this question. The simple answer is that Noah did not need to find the creatures. God told him that the animals would come to him (Genesis 6:20).

This fact also relates to the previous question. Noah did not really need to know the difference between all the clean and unclean animals, at least initially, because God sent the correct number of creatures to him. However, he probably did possess such knowledge, given that he offered a sacrifice of each kind of clean animal and flying creature after the Flood.

How did Noah's family know how to care for so many different animals?

Feeding and caring for over 1,000 kinds of animals would not be an easy task when one considers all their different needs. In his thorough study on the Ark, John Woodmorappe proposed the possibility of Noah having a menagerie prior to the Flood so that he could learn all about the animals. This would require God to bring the animals several months or years earlier so that Noah and his family could observe them and then grow or purchase the proper supplies and food for each creature.

While such a scenario is plausible, it seems unlikely. Noah surely had enough work to do in building the Ark and procuring enough food. If thousands of animals arrived months in advance, it would drastically increase the workload for Noah and his family and would require them to have even more food on hand to care for so many animals for an even longer period of time.

In our story, we answered this question in a different way. Rather than assuming that Noah needed to be the expert in every area, we made Emzara the animal expert by giving her a love for animals from an early age. Throughout the series she learns about various creatures and keeps records of them. Just as we had God prepare Noah to build the Ark, we had Him prepare Noah's wife with the knowledge and ability to care for thousands of animals. We hinted at the menagerie idea when we described about two dozen animals arriving several weeks earlier than the rest. These were the ones that Emzara had never studied before, so this gave her time to complete that task before the Flood began.

How did Noah fit all the animals on the Ark?

To answer this question, we need to know two major details: the size of the Ark and the number/size of the animals. The first issue is easier to deal with since the Bible gives us the Ark's dimensions. However, it uses cubits as the unit of measurement, so unless we know the length of the cubit

Noah used, we cannot be completely certain of the Ark's size. A cubit is the distance between one's elbow and longest finger. Since many ancient structures were based on a royal cubit (a cubit plus a handbreadth), it is possible that the Ark was as well. The Ark Encounter used a royal cubit of 20.4 inches (one of the shortest of the royal cubits from ancient cultures). If this was the proper length of the cubit Noah used, then the Ark would have been 510 feet long by 85 feet wide by 51 feet tall.

Determining the number of animals to put in the Ark is more difficult since we do not have enough knowledge of every kind of land-dependent animal that has ever lived. We cannot always be sure which animals are members of the same kind. For example, we know that lions, tigers, leopards, bobcats, and the common house cat all belong to the same kind. So, Noah did not need to bring two of each of these types of cats on the Ark, he just needed two members of the cat kind that would become the ancestors of all the cats in the world today. But there are scores of animals for which we do not have information about whether they can interbreed (which means they would be the same kind). So researchers conducted an extensive study to reach a conservative estimate of the number of kinds that would be on the Ark. Whenever they lacked data about whether certain animals belonged to the same kind, the animals would be separated into different kinds, even if it seemed likely that they were the same. As a result of this study, it was determined that nearly 1,400 land-dependent animal kinds needed to be represented on the Ark, and it is very possible that this number is much too high.

Next, we needed to determine how many of each kind were needed. We know there were two of every unclean, non-flying, land-dependent animal. Obviously, Noah did not need to worry about bringing fish, whales, lobsters, etc. Some Bibles mention that Noah brought seven of each clean animal and flying creature, while other Bibles state that he brought seven pairs. The Hebrew text states that he was to bring "seven seven, a male and his female." It seems that a stronger case can be made for the "seven pairs" position. However, even if one favors the other view, the Ark Encounter always went with the higher number whenever there was uncertainty. So it included seven pairs of all flying creatures and all clean animals.

Using this approach, the total number of animals would have been fewer than 6,800 with 85 percent of them being smaller than 10 kilograms (22 pounds). Taking into account all of the food and water requirements for the animals and eight people, the Ark Encounter team demonstrated that all of the animals and supplies would fit nicely in the Ark. Skeptics often think the Ark was too small, but what is often left unspoken is that they typically include every *species* of land animal (not every kind, which is often more like the family level in our modern taxonomy), along with marine creatures, insects, bacteria, and plants in their estimates. Some Christians think the Ark was way bigger than it needed to be, presumably so that other people could go on board if they decided to. However, the Ark researchers discovered this was not the case. Everything fit rather well, without much space left over. If you think about it, this makes perfect sense. God knew how big the Ark needed to be. Why would He tell Noah to waste time making something that was too small or much bigger than it needed to be?

The Ark Encounter goes into these points in much more detail, and the team has also produced a number of resources that explain this issue, such as *How Many Animals Were on the Ark?* and *Inside Noah's Ark: Why it Worked*, both available at www.answersingenesis.org.

Didn't Noah's family board the Ark and wait for seven days before the Flood started?

This idea is somewhat common among Christians, but it is based on a misunderstanding of Genesis 7. In verses 1–4, God told Noah to enter the Ark along with his family and the animals because in seven days the Flood would begin. Since verse 5 states that Noah did everything God commanded, those who hold this view assume that they boarded the Ark on the day God spoke to Noah and then waited seven more days for the Flood to start.

The problem with the above scenario is that it forces a contradiction into the text because it does not take into account the rest of the passage. In verses 7–9 we read about Noah and the animals going into the Ark, and in verses 10–12 we read about that seven-day period and then the start of the Flood. Up until this point, it might seem reasonable to interpret the passage as described in the question; however, verse 13 rules out such a view. Referring back to the day that the Flood started when the fountains of the great deep broke open (v. 11), verse 13 states, "On the very same day Noah and his sons, Shem and Ham and Japheth, and Noah's wife and the three wives of his sons with them entered the ark."

So Noah and his family entered the Ark on the very same day that the Flood started? How is this possible since previous verses in Genesis 7 seem to indicate that they entered the Ark seven days earlier? The solution is that it took Noah and his family seven days to board the animals and whatever other supplies they may have needed to load. Yes, they did enter on the day God commanded, but they also entered seven days later. Verse 7 states that they entered "to escape the waters of the flood." The phrase in Hebrew seems to indicate that Noah could see the waters as he entered the Ark, so this would not have occurred on the day God told him to enter. It is only after they spent seven days loading the Ark that God shut the door (v. 16).

Why did you have God tell Noah to "enter" the Ark instead of to "come into" the Ark?

In Genesis 7:1, the New King James Version states that God told Noah to "come into the ark," and some other Bibles have similar wording. Based on this reading, some people have claimed that God was in the Ark with Noah and his family during the Flood. After all, how could He tell Noah to "come into" a place if He were not in it?

The ESV does the opposite. It has God telling Noah to "go into" the Ark. Does this mean that God was outside of the Ark when this command was spoken?

The solution to this problem is rather quite simple, but it occasionally upsets people who have grown attached to the idea that God's presence was in the Ark with Noah and his family. The Hebrew word translated as "come" or "go" actually gives no indication about the location of the speaker. Perhaps the best way to translate the word in Genesis 7:1 is to have God tell them to "enter" the Ark, as is found in the NASB and HCSB. This rendering does not tell us whether God was inside or outside the Ark at the time.

In one sense, since God is omnipresent, He was in the Ark with Noah. But the idea that God's special presence was in the Ark is not supported by the Hebrew language of Genesis 7:1, and such an idea is very difficult to support in light of Genesis 8:1. In that verse, some 150 days after the Flood started, we are told that "God remembered Noah" and all the animals. This does not mean that God had forgotten about Noah, but it means that He turned His attention back to Noah with an eye of fulfilling His promise to preserve him and his family through the Flood.

Where did you come up with the names of the women on the Ark?

The Bible does not mention the name of Noah's wife or of his daughters-in-law. At the Ark Encounter, we decided to name them to enhance the guest experience at the themed attraction. They were real people who had real names. We just do not know what they were. By giving them names we were able to make them seem more like real people. We included multiple signs throughout the Ark to inform visitors that we used artistic license in naming the women.

As content manager for the Ark Encounter, I (Tim) had the opportunity to decide what names we would use, although I asked our team members to submit their choices for a couple of the names (Rayneh and Ar'yel). Kezia was taken from Job 42:14. After his trials, Job named one of his daughters Keziah. We dropped the last letter and assigned this name to Ham's wife. As mentioned in the non-fiction section of *Noah: Man of Resolve*, Emzara's name comes from the Book of Jubilees, an extra-biblical, Jewish writing popular during New Testament times.

Encounter This

Since we worked on the Ark Encounter project, we had the unique opportunity to include details in our story that can be seen in various exhibits. We were also able to influence the design of certain elements so that they connected with our story. If you visit the Ark Encounter in Williamstown, Kentucky, you will be able to see the following items that were included in the story.

Chapter 14: As Noah's group traveled across the Western lands toward their eventual destination, they started using a different type of beast to pull their wagons. The large-eared tuskers are palaeomastodons, an extinct creature belonging to the same order as modern elephants, although they were quite a bit smaller than elephants, standing seven feet tall at the shoulders. In a piece of art in the Ancient Man exhibit on Deck Two, a palaeomastodon can be seen pulling a loaded wagon toward a waiting ship.

Chapter 17: A highlight of this chapter and the next are the small paintings on the walls of Greatfather's house. The use of small images to tell the story of the world before the Flood can be seen on the large monument stones in the East Village (outside the Ark) and on a tapestry in the *Library* on Deck Two.

Chapter 18: After centuries of waiting, Noah and Emzara finally had children. This chapter tells about the birth of Japheth and ends with Noah carrying Japheth out to show him to their friends. In the *Who Was Noah?* exhibit on Deck Two, guests can see a similar scene, although in this one Emzara, along with Japheth and Shem as young boys, are standing nearby as Noah holds Ham in the air.

Chapter 22: The cherubim at the edge of the garden play a significant role in our story (also appearing in chapter 35). To get a glimpse of these beings and the flaming sword, be sure to visit the Pre-Flood World exhibit on Deck Two. There is an illustration of Adam and Eve being banished from the garden. Standing at the entrance of the garden are two giant cherubim.

Chapter 24: Noah enters his tent to find Emzara working on her scrolls filled with information about the animals. Visitors to the *Library* on Deck Two can see two of her studies, complete with illustrations, of two animals that appear in this series. In the first book, a large strange-looking animal called an anisodon crossed the path in front of Noah and Aterre. The other creature, a thylacosmilus (called a pithoct in the series) made an appearance in the arena in the second book and another one attacked Ham in this book. In fact, Ham wrote a warning about this animal for his family members in the Ark's "Noah language," and if you look closely at his face, you can see a scar on his cheek.

Chapter 25: Emzara and Kezia discuss the small animal cages that Ham designed. Numerous racks full of these cages can be seen in the *First Floor Show*. Later in that chapter, Ham demonstrates how a portion of the Ark's water collection system will work. In the next chapter, Noah mentions that Ham is likely working with Garun on the Ark's waste-removal system. Both of these systems are shown in the *Animal Care* exhibit on Deck Two of the Ark.

Chapter 25: When Purlek announces that he and Evet are going to leave Noah's group, there is discussion about the small forge that had been installed in the Ark. He mentions that Noah and Ham know how to use it. On Deck Two of the Ark, visitors can see Ham working in the forge.

Chapter 28: The scene where Noah and company come across a herd of slaughtered "horn faces" (ceratopsian dinosaurs) is portrayed in the Pre-Flood World exhibit on Deck Two. To demonstrate an aspect of man's wickedness prior to the Flood, a vivid illustration in this space shows a group of poachers killing these creatures for their large horns. In the novel we learn that these are Ar'yel's people and that her first husband was killed during this hunt.

Chapter 32: This chapter opens with Emzara, Japheth, and Rayneh working on the Ark's living spaces. On the third deck of the Ark Encounter, guests can walk through the family's *Living Quarters* and see plenty of items that interact with our story. Each family member has a sign telling of their background and interests. When not taken straight from Scripture, these details come from this series.

Chapter 34: There are a couple of references in this chapter to Kezia making bean brew. At the Ark Encounter, the coffee shop is called Kezia's Coffee, so visitors can enjoy some of her caffeinated beverages.

Chapter 34: As Noah walks among the thousands of animals that God sent to him, he pauses and watches a tiny buzzbird hover in front of him for a few seconds. In *Noah's Study* on Deck Two, guests can ask Noah what his favorite animal is and he describes the tiny buzzbird, stating that it can hover and fly in all directions, even backward. Obviously, the buzzbird is a hummingbird. He also describes Emzara's favorite animal, and readers of this series need no explanation about what those are.

Chapter 36: At the opening of this chapter, Noah stands at the top of the ramp and looks toward the hill in the distance. He thinks back to the previous evening when the family gathered outside the Ark. In the *Who Was Noah?* exhibit on Deck Two, guests can see a picture titled "The Calm Before the Storm," where Noah and his family are looking at the Ark on the evening before the Flood starts.

Chapter 36: The animals that pull the chariots and end up being the last pair of creatures in the Ark are called entelodonts, which are now extinct. They have been given the nickname "terminator pigs," because they look like a cross between a wolf and a pig. You can see a pair of these interesting creatures on Deck Two of the Ark, although these two represent juveniles, whereas those in the book would have been adults, standing about six feet tall at the shoulders.

Chapter 36: Once the door shut, Rayneh walked to it and wept because she realized that the fate of everyone outside had been sealed. On Deck Two of the Ark, visitors can see Rayneh pondering some difficult questions about judgment and God's character. When the Ark first opened, guests could hear an audio that revealed Rayneh's inner thoughts about lost loved ones outside the door, especially Evet. Now instead of hearing an audio track, guests can read some of the issues she struggled with on signage behind her.

Chapter 36: Near the very end of the story, Noah asks Shem to put a pair of animals in their pen and then join the family in the sitting room for a time of prayer. This prayer scene is shown at the end of the *First Floor Show* at the Ark Encounter.

BORROWED FROM THE BIBLE

Since the Bible does not give us many details about Noah's life, we needed to use artistic license. To keep the story more closely tied to the Bible, we decided to borrow and slightly adapt some concepts found elsewhere in Scripture and work them into Noah's story. This book includes several obvious events taken right from Scripture, such as anything having to do with the building of the Ark. We will limit this section to discussing those items that are not so obvious.

Major spoiler alert! Do not read this section unless you have first read the novel.

Chapter 7: Naamah's ritual of harming herself in worship of her false god has similarities to other pagan practices, including one well-known biblical account. In 1 Kings 18, Elijah challenged the prophets of Baal and Asherah on Mt. Carmel to see which god (or God) would respond by sending fire to light a sacrifice on an altar. After pleading all morning to Baal, the false prophets cut themselves with swords and lances until "blood gushed out" (1 Kings 18:28). Since Naamah worshiped the serpent god, we decided that her self-inflicted injury would be consistent with a snake bite. However, unlike the Apostle Paul who was bitten by a venomous snake and suffered no ill effects (Acts 28:3–6), Naamah suffered great pain for a time.

Chapter 8: Captain Iradel repeatedly insulted King Lamech, Naamah, and their army as his Nodite forces assembled outside the gates of Iri Geshem. This practice of attempting to instill fear in one's enemies has been practiced throughout much of history, and it is also found in the Bible. In 2 Kings 18, King Sennacherib of Assyria sent his forces to Jerusalem and they surrounded the city. His spokesman, known as the Rabshakeh, boasted about all of Sennacherib's victories against the surrounding peoples and how their gods could not rescue them from the Assyrian army. A Jewish man named Eliakim asked the Rabshakeh to speak to them in Aramaic because they could understand it, but the Rabshakeh refused. Instead, he raised his voice and continued speaking in Hebrew, attempting to frighten the people by telling them that their God could not protect them. Read 2 Kings 19:35 to see how God responded to this man's taunts. Our story borrowed the idea of a military man mocking the opposition before his defeat.

Chapter 21: In the second book, King Lamech boasted about his greatness at a ceremony and was immediately humbled when his city was leveled by an earthquake and volcano. In this book, he took his boasts to greater heights, claiming to be the highest of all gods, and it did not work out well for him. This is similar to what happened in Acts 12:22–23 to Herod Agrippa after the people proclaimed him to be a god.

The means of King Lamech's demise was borrowed from one of the Bible's most famous scenes. In Exodus 7:10–12, Moses' brother, Aaron, threw down his rod and it became a serpent. The Bible states that Pharaoh's magicians *did the same thing* by their secret arts, "for every man threw down his rod, and they became serpents" (v. 12). Some Christians believe that Pharaoh's magicians faked this miracle by using serpents that had been in a rigid position and then writhed about when they hit the floor. But the biblical text does not give any indication that this miracle was faked. It says that they did the same thing as Aaron, and it states that their rods became serpents. Of course, this gets into a theological debate about whether evil spirits have the capacity to perform such a feat. It seems that in this case, God permitted them to do it so that He could show His power over them, which He demonstrated when Aaron's rod-turned-serpent swallowed up the others. In our story, we decided that God might permit Nachash to achieve a similar act to execute judgment upon a wicked tyrant. Eventually, Nachash would be shown to be powerless to help Naamah when the Creator sent His judgment.

Chapter 35: Naamah's arrogant boasting seemed to know no boundaries. She repeatedly threatened the cherubim at the entrance to the garden that she would kill them. The response from one of the cherubim was nearly identical to the words of an angel in Revelation 14:7 who will urge the people of the world to fear and glorify God.

306

ANIMALS IN THE SERIES

Since we did not use modern names for the animals, here is a guide to some of the creatures described in the series. If the name of the type of animal is given in the series, then that name is in parentheses. Asterisks indicate the animals that can be seen at the Ark Encounter in either artwork or sculpted form.

Beasts of burden:

> Prolibytherium — Taht pulled Noah's cart in book 1
>
> Entelodont* — pulled the chariots in book 3
>
> Macrauchenia — (lunker) Meru pulled Lamech's wagon in book 1
>
> Theosodon* — pulled Lakh's wagon in book 3 (small representative in macrauchenia kind)
>
> Palaeomastodon* — (large-eared tuskers) pulled Noah's wagon in book 3

Flying Creatures:

> Pterodactyl* — (supergliders) featured in book 1
>
> Hummingbird — (buzzbirds) mentioned in each novel
>
> Vulture/Eagle — (tarocs) mentioned in each novel

Dinosaurs:

> Pachycephalosaurus* — sparring animals in book 2
>
> Tyrannosaurus rex* — (grendec) mentioned in each novel
>
> Carnotaurus* — (horned grendec) featured in books 2 and 3
>
> Ceratopsians* — (horn face) featured in book 3

Sauropods* — (earth shaker) featured in book 1

Others

Giraffe* — (keluk) mentioned in each book

Goat/Sheep* — (bleater) used for sacrifice in each book

Cattle* — (bovar) used for sacrifice in book 1

Thylacosmilus* — (pithoct) featured in books 2 and 3

Snakes — (serpents) featured in book 2 and 3

Rabbit — (bounder) mentioned in books 1 and 3

Kangaroo — (leaper) mentioned in book 3

Dog* — (calic) mentioned in book 1

Anisodon* — large furry beast seen by Noah and Aterre in book 1

Koala* — furry gray animals first to arrive at Ark site in book 3

Chameleon — Noah and Aterre watched this creature in book 1

Mosasaur — sea monster that nearly swamps the boat in book 1

Dear Reader,

Thank you for sticking with us through all three books of *The Remnant Trilogy*. When we started the series, we were highly aware that there would only be a remnant — eight people — who would survive the Flood. That meant that all the other characters we grew to love would have to face some kind of death, which in several cases, was hard to write.

Even though they survived the Flood, Noah and his family only lived a certain number of years before they too faced the inevitable consequence brought on by Greatfather Adam's sin. But death is not the focal point of our story. The Creator is. He's the Author of life. He is the one who at the beginning breathed life into man so that he became a living being.

Colossians 1:15–16 and Hebrews 1:3 teach that Jesus Christ was actively involved in the creation of the world. As the Creator warned the newly alive Adam that death was the punishment for disobedience, He knew that one day He would endure the punishment He had set.

The Bible describes Jesus as the Lamb slain before the foundation of the world. So as He brought about life, He knew there'd be death for all mankind and also for Himself. He took on human life so that He could die on the Cross and pay the penalty of our sins. But death was not the end — if that were the case, we of all people would be miserable. Instead, Jesus rose in triumph over death and the grave.

Death and life. Just as we knew who would live and die in this series, all of us know that we, too, will one day die. However, those who believe on the Lord Jesus will be saved and will live forever with Him. If you haven't considered this before, we pray that you may come to know Jesus as your Savior.

Someday we will all pass from this life into the next. If you are a fellow believer, we look forward to gathering with you and with Noah and his family at the feet of our Lord Jesus Christ as we spend eternity growing in our understanding of the depths of His greatness and glory.

Sincerely,

Tim Chaffey and K. Marie Adams

ABOUT THE AUTHORS

Tim Chaffey is the Content Manager for the Ark Encounter and Creation Museum. A former pastor and teacher, Tim is also a leukemia survivor and competes in half-marathons with his wife and son while his daughter cheers them on. He has earned advanced degrees specializing in apologetics, theology, and church history. Tim maintains a popular blog (www.midwestapologetics.org/blog), contributes regularly to *Answers* magazine and the Answers in Genesis website, and has authored over a dozen books, including *The Truth Chronicles* series and *In Defense of Easter: Answering Critical Challenges to the Resurrection of Jesus*.

K. Marie Adams has an obsession with words that once resulted in her being grounded for reading too much. Later, it served her well as she worked for many years at a bookstore and as a literature and grammar instructor. Now, as a graphic designer, her love of language goes by the fancy name of typography. K. Marie also volunteers for several ministries dedicated to rescuing young girls from modern-day slavery.

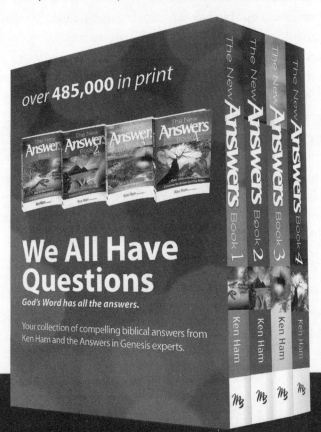

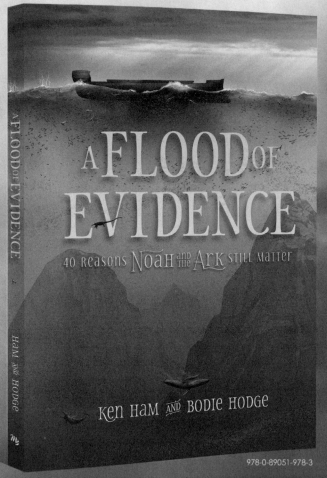

THE REMNANT TRILOGY

NOAH: MAN OF GOD
978-1-68344-105-2

NOAH: MAN OF RESOLVE
978-1-68344-074-1

NOAH: MAN OF DESTINY
978-089051-972-1